The  Ropewalk

The Ropewalk

JOHN KNAUF

iUniverse, Inc.
Bloomington

THE ROPEWALK

iUniverse books may be ordered through booksellers or by contacting:

iUniverse
1663 Liberty Drive
Bloomington, IN 47403
www.iuniverse.com
1-800-Authors (1-800-288-4677)

ISBN: 978-1-4620-5273-8 (sc)
ISBN: 978-1-4620-5272-1 (ebk)

Printed in the United States of America

iUniverse rev. date: 10/26/2011

♦ ♦ ♦

To all the people who, over time, have played the various main characters in the "story" that became my life, but especially the following:

My parents

who provided the uncompromising security a child needs in order to dream;

My wife, Rhonda

whose encouragement and unshakable belief in me kept the path open

Dr. Wolfgang Claus

my lifelong friend, with whom I've shared many adventures, and who is the only other person on this planet who knows where and what the original "Ropewalk" really was.

◆ ◆ ◆

Acknowledgments

Special thanks are due to several people whose input was essential in keeping me on the right path. These are

Karen Emerick

whose tireless review of the manuscript and amazing attention to detail were essential in catching errors in the text,

Rob Carr

who shared his professional experience with writing and editing without the slightest hesitation and whose initial review of the story was so encouraging.

5-12-12

To Caroline,

So glad you enjoyed it.
The German version won't
be out for a while.

All the best.

[signature]

◆ ◆ ◆

Anyone who understands at all what is meant by saying that the soul is the idea of an existence, will also divine a near relationship between it and a sure sense of *destiny*, and must regard life itself . . . as directed, irrevocable in every line, and fate-laden.

The only space that remains open to us is *visual* space, and in it places have been found for the relics of the other senses as properties and effects of *things seen in the light* . . . salvation is emancipation from the spell of that light-world and its facts.

Oswald Spengler, *Decline of the West*

◆ ◆ ◆

Chapter 1

The first thing I should explain is how I came to find myself sharing a rather large apartment building with only one other person. Actually, I should correct that to say "a person and a half" because the person in question was a woman who had a young daughter about five or six years of age. So in reality there were three of us residing in the building, of whom only two were capable of what I would consider rational thought. All the other occupants had already left for parts unknown for the upcoming holidays. She lived in the hall below mine, in an apartment approximately in the center of the building.

The building itself was curious in that it was long and narrow and only had the two floors, but sprawled for a considerable distance because it was a renovated rope factory originally built in the latter part of the eighteenth century. Back then they made long ropes for sailing ships in there, and in order to get a continuous braid, the "rope walk" had to go on for however long the ropes themselves had to be. Historically, some of these buildings went on for nearly a quarter mile, but the one I lived in was considerably shorter, being just a little over five hundred feet in length. Rumor mill sources claimed it had originally been much longer.

It had bustled with activity for nearly a century, but eventually steam power began to replace the sails, and its days were numbered. Then it gradually slowed down until finally, down to its last few employees, it closed its doors sometime in the late eighteen hundreds.

After that it sat for decades, remarkably undisturbed by the elements and preserved, so said the local legends, by the sheer quantity of pitch, tallow, tar, and whatever else was used on the ropes back then as a preservative. In the latter years of the nineteenth century, an enterprising development firm bought it and turned it into an apartment building in anticipation of a college being founded somewhere on the adjacent peninsula. Once the college opened, it was reasoned, both students and faculty would need a place to live. It was an insider's deal, but the sagacity of the political informants who championed it quickly fell into disrepute when the college never materialized. The way I heard it, the entire speculative process boiled down to a visit by Joshua Lawrence Chamberlain, the President of Bowdoin College and hero of Little Round Top in the Civil War, who, over dinner in the nearby town of Bowford, once casually commented on how nice it would be to have a branch of Bowdoin College situated in such a beautiful area. By the time that idle thought reached the speculators, it was a done deal, and it was assumed that Chamberlain's reputation alone would make it happen. So the old ropewalk was purchased and quickly turned into a rooming house. Then, when Chamberlain showed no signs of expanding the college, funding dried up, the speculators slipped away, and the building was once again left to the elements.

Even the spelling of the town was changed to accommodate the arrival of the college. Originally, it was a French name, which was not surprising since the town was so near the border with Canada. It was spelled "Beaufort" then, and only became "Bowford" after Chamberlain's visit, the "B-o-w" part intended to mimic the beginning of "Bowdoin" and flatter the future patron. The "fort" became "ford" probably through a simple language ambiguity. When I once pointed out to a local that the "ford" part made no sense since "ford" usually meant a river crossing and there was no river to cross, that person rather indignantly replied, "Well, maybe there was a river here back then," as if rivers came and went geologically in the span of a few human lifetimes.

One of the consequences of the renovated building never having been used for its intended purpose was the fact that the plumbing, though primitive by today's standards, remained functional through its idle period. This, coupled with the appearance not of a college but of a boarding school in the nineteen-fifties, saved it from eventual extinction. A new group of speculators bought it, cleaned it up, and sold it to the school as a dormitory. Since it was intended to address the housing needs of a school located rather far from the nearest town, the designers' original plan included rooms for students and apartments for teachers, a curious anomaly first seen as objectionable but later appreciated by the administration when they came to realize that having teachers living in the same building ensured a staff of hall monitors at no additional charge.

Because the plumbing was of an antiquated design, though, the building had a curious anomaly—the only water service the rooms had was a simple sink and a cold-water spigot. Hot water could be had by filling a small water heater over the sink and heating it electrically, but none of the rooms had bathrooms or toilets. To deal with this, the new developers had converted the old latrine-like water closet on each floor to modern showers and toilet stalls. The arrangement worked fine and even added a certain Victorian panache to the building, but I doubt that anyone could ever have imagined the unexpected role this layout would play in what happened there.

The upper floor, the one I lived on, was dominated by individual rooms, some too small for more than one occupant and others large enough for two beds and the meager amenities called desks and bookshelves. Actual "apartments" of more than one room were to be found mixed in with the rooms on the first floor. Rumor had it that some of the apartments even had bathrooms, but since I had never been in one, I could not substantiate the report. All of these multi-room apartments were occupied by teachers at the school who were married and/or had children of their own. Since I was single, I was shunted off to one of the one-room enclaves on the upper floor. Also, since I was single, I was evidently deemed not worthy of the extra space of a double room and thus ended up in one of the smaller, single-bed rooms, which, "status" considerations aside, didn't bother me at all.

I had come to the Ropewalk—the building had retained the name of its original function—the year before, 1977, because I was a teacher who had been looking for a job that would take me away from the overdevelopment of southern New England. That euphemistic word "development" had become synonymous with "special interests pandering" for me, and I realized I had to either get away from it or do something desperate. So when I found out about the job opening in northern Maine, I figured, "Well, here's a place that will escape the ravages of insider corruption for a while. Why don't I take it?" What worked in my favor was the fact that there were not a lot of people anxious to move to the edge of the earth. I suspected that mine may have been the only résumé they received.

I was a history teacher, one of those dodo birds who were obsessed with knowing the truth behind history's constantly moving tides. Being single allowed me the latitude to go where I wanted and do what I wanted, but denied me the comfort—which on some level I equated with complacency—of actually bonding with another human being. I had had two marriages, the first failing because we were simply too young and too suffused with the residual efflorescence of the sixties, the second because, despite moving into the seventies, I was not able to shake that sixties glow from my overweaned sense of soul-mate idealism. It was doomed from the start. Her father, an extremely pragmatic and highly successful businessman, had never really liked me, thought I was too impractical.

"Drummond," he'd once said—he never called me by my first name, Egan—"You're like the alchemists of the Middle Ages. You'll spend your entire life looking for some sort of elixir to turn lead into gold while your family slowly starves." He was probably right. But history, and its sister, archeology, were full of characters much more interesting than anyone I actually knew. The mundane had opened its umbrella of mediocrity over all of us, leveled the playing field of the passions, given us security, and made us all uninteresting.

The reason the building was empty just then was because the Christmas vacation had started, and all the students had returned to their homes and would not be back until after the new year. The teachers had also left to spend the holidays with family or other relatives. The reason I was still in the building was because I wanted to take advantage of the peace and quiet that would prevail when everyone else was gone. I had set personal goals for myself, things I wanted to accomplish—as a history teacher I had decided to enhance my professional reputation by writing a history of the region—but had become negligent because I had allowed myself to be interrupted and sidetracked by my many "acquaintances" among the students. They visited me constantly. This came about because I was the coach for the baseball team. No one else had wanted that sidebar activity, and the program was threatened with shutdown until I, literally, stepped up to the plate. I instantly became the athletic wunderkind. It didn't even matter how well we played; it only mattered *that* we played.

I had also started a martial arts club, resurrecting my long-dormant abilities in that arena under the guise of instilling a sense of personal discipline in the students. I had gotten my black belt in Tae Kwon Do about ten years before, the culmination of an interest developed in my adolescence. My instructor, a Korean master, had told me I was "ideally suited" for the fighting arts, both because my six-foot height was not so tall that I had too much body area to cover, and because my long, lean legs—I'd been a runner in college—allowed me to kick to an opponent's head with no special effort.

He'd also encouraged me to develop what he called "the look." I had had a thin, black mustache in those earlier years, and this, along with my dark hair, pronounced cheekbones, and deep-set, dark eyes, could, with a carefully practiced sneer, make me look quite threatening, an ability that went a long way toward unnerving an opponent. "To fight is about unbalance opponent," he'd said in his broken English. "Psych him out," was what he had been trying to say, and it worked well, both in and out of the practice ring. It sometimes backfired with women, though, so to soften my look, I got rid of the mustache.

Nevertheless, I hadn't practiced the art in so long that I was seriously rusty and knew that I had become stiff, slow, and badly timed. In spite of this, some of the students took to it like a fish to water, warrior ethic and all. It was good exercise in any case, and I had no illusions about aspiring to be some kind of champion. And it was safe; there were so few people in that part of New England who had ever studied the fighting arts that the chances that I would be challenged were extremely remote. And the mystique of the art itself kept the undecided challengers at bay.

The one thing I was not qualified to coach the students on was relationships, so I stayed away from that subject on the pretense that their adolescent love and lust affairs were too far beneath me to notice. The reality was I had absolutely nothing to tell them about how to make a relationship work. How could I with my track record? In spite of that shortcoming, I seemed to be inordinately popular through no conscious effort of my own. But the upshot was, I never seemed to have a moment's rest. I would no sooner sit down and begin to work, when the floorboards in the hall would creak and announce the approach of one of my many "friends." A moment more and there would be a knock on the door. Once interrupted, I knew there was no hope of returning to what I had been doing; my caller would invite himself in and remain sometimes for hours either unloading his problems on my attentive ears, updating the rumor-mill file with the latest suspicions, or simply bending those ears with his talk. I was a good listener and because of that had become a sort of unofficial father confessor, a decidedly one-sided virtue.

Thus conditioned to expect the worst whenever I had an unoccupied moment, I soon abandoned all hope of ever accomplishing anything as long as the building was full of people. I therefore had been looking forward to the approaching holiday with a sense of relief, not because it was Christmas but because I would finally have some time to myself. Once everyone was gone, however, I found to my amazement that the stillness was almost maddening. The vastness of the building only then became apparent, and at one point I had this unsettling feeling that the whole world had either sunk beneath me, or I was the only one who hadn't gotten the message to move out. I resisted the temptation to do the Robinson Crusoe thing and shout into the empty hall just to hear if my voice would echo. I took the whole first day getting accustomed to what I could only describe as the voluminous silence.

It was during that period that I discovered I was not alone in the building after all. It happened on the second evening while I was preparing my supper. The building had a communal kitchen on the first floor, about halfway down the length of the hall. This kitchen, like the communal bathrooms, was an afterthought added by the developers to cover the possibility that there might be people who wanted to prepare their own meals rather than eat in the school cafeteria. So one of the rooms was turned into a no-frills kitchen. It had a stove, cold-water sink with its electric water heater, refrigerator, cabinets, and two small restaurant-like bench booths. Not exactly a class act but enough to get the job done. I was down there concocting one of my no-frills meals when I was suddenly confronted with Margaret Gillespie, one of the English composition teachers, who also, oddly enough, doubled as a phys ed teacher. Her little daughter, Sonya, was with her.

I was caught completely off guard by her sudden appearance. For some reason, I felt that she, of all the people there, would be one of those most anxious to leave the Ropewalk because of stories I'd heard from my many student visitors about how unhappy she was. She was young, married, and evidently bored to tears by the lack of social life in nearby Bowford. Yet there she was, with Sonya in tow, still in the building when everyone else was gone.

This was an interesting development. Margaret was, by general consensus, a real "looker," and most of the men at the school, whether they articulated it or not, whether married or single, yearned for some sort of contact with her—a touch, a moment of discourse, a one-night stand, or, in some cases, an outright affair. She had dark brown, shoulder-length hair and, although only of average height, moved with an athletic suppleness that made her seem taller, or at least more commanding, than she actually was. I surmised that this suppleness was a product of her physical education activities, but since I knew nothing about her, I couldn't be sure.

What I *was* sure about was that there was something else about her that was so startlingly different that I couldn't help but notice her. It was her eyes; when I first met her at the school, I'd noticed that her brown eyes had a slightly elliptical aspect to them, oddly out of sync for a Caucasian, that had led me to believe that maybe there was some oriental or possibly South American ancestor somewhere in the family tree. It was none of my business, of course, and whether that was true or not was completely irrelevant in view of how well it all went together. Her projected persona, out of reach but not lost on me, was one of quiet self-assurance built on a subtle sensuality.

All of this resonated on an instinctive level the moment I saw her, of course, causing a reaction that I was sure registered on my face for at least a passing moment. I recovered quickly, though, assumed my usual "social neutrality" attitude, and smiled as she and Sonya stepped into the kitchen.

If Margaret had an arresting aspect to her, it was nothing in comparison to her daughter, but for a completely different reason. Sonya had always seemed strange to me, not because she was in any way unattractive but because she was so different from both of her parents. She had Margaret's eye shape and color, but her mother's chestnut-colored hair and her father's curly, blond locks were not conducive to the straight, black hair that Sonya had and that seemed to grow unusually low on her forehead. That could've been just the way it was combed, of course, but when combined with facial features that I could only describe as somehow unsettled, changeable, and amorphous, she had such an aspect of the rare and exotic about her that she actually made me a bit uncomfortable.

Even stranger was her apparent ability to actually use this unsettledness; she would look at me one way, then change her position and expression and seem to be a completely different person. "Rubbery" was the only word that came to mind whenever I saw her features going through their odd metamorphosis. The first time I saw it I was totally transfixed, standing there watching the child become some other child right before my eyes, then reverting back to the original. But even while she was doing that, there was no point when her features seemed to resemble those of her parents, and all I could think of was that some sort of genetic "back-tick" was at work, one of those rare events that cause a child to look more like an earlier ancestor than her actual parents.

What I found most remarkable about this was that Margaret's features didn't reveal any of this ability. She was, by all accounts, unselfconsciously attractive—really quite stunning when dressed up for some school event—and her husband, tall, blond, and blue-eyed, but with a slight propensity to put on a little weight, was still able to turn a few female heads. How their offspring inherited this unusual characteristic was, to me, the consummate genetic mystery. But there was no point in denying what was true. I found the child oddly—and, admittedly, maybe reluctantly—"different." Naturally, I never uttered a word of this to anyone, not even casually. Some things were better left unsaid.

"Margaret," I said. "You startled me. I thought I was the only one in the building." I was taking some liberties with my familiar tone. In actual fact, she and I tended to move in different social strata, and although I'd seen her almost every day at the school, I had only ever spoken with her a few times at various faculty functions, and even then only briefly. The truth was, I hardly knew her at all.

Her response surprised me. There wasn't one. She simply stood there staring at me as if she hadn't heard me.

"I didn't realize you could cook," she finally said.

I took that at face value, which is to say I assumed it was some sort of caulk to plug up the hole in the conversation.

"I wouldn't exactly call this 'cooking,'" I said with a smile. "All I'm really doing is satisfying a biological need. 'Cooking,' on the other hand . . . ."

"Are you staying here right through Christmas?" she interrupted. Little Sonya looked up at me with her coal-black eyes. Her face was a rubber mask slowly crinkling into a smile.

"Ah, well, I don't know if I'll actually be here on Christmas day, but I do plan on being here at least up to the day before Christmas Eve. Would that be Christmas Fore-eve?" I smiled at my own little joke but she didn't pick up on it.

She seemed tense about something. She smiled, but I noticed, or maybe sensed, that it was a forced smile. Maybe it was because even while smiling her eyebrows remained taut, as if she were shielding her eyes from the glare of the overhead light. But the fluorescent overhead was not harsh; indeed, as the gloom thickened outside, it was obvious that the one light alone was barely enough for a room that size. Like virtually everything else in the building, it was probably one more aspect of its checkered construction legacy.

"Could probably use more light in here," I said.

She nodded and looked past me through the window to the rapidly falling curtain of darkness outside. "It gets dark early this time of year."

I nodded.

"There's a storm coming in," she went on. "Sleet, hail, snow, high winds. Coming right in off the ocean. I hope we don't lose power." She stepped over to the window and peered out. "It's already started."

In truth, it had. I could hear the first faint hits of the sleet on the glass. I had been so intent on eating that I hadn't noticed. Beyond the sound of the sleet, I could hear the pounding of the surf on the rocky coastline, a scant hundred yards away. The Ropewalk was located very near the ocean precisely because back then they were making ropes for sailing ships. It would not have made sense to make the ropes in town, five miles away as the crow flies but three times that by road, and then have to pay some mule teamster to bring them to the harbor.

She hugged herself as if suddenly cold. "So, how long are you staying?"

"At least until the day before Christmas Eve."

"Oh, yes, right. You just told me that." She stuck her hands in her pockets and hunched her shoulders. "Ah, Egan, you realize that you, Sonya, and I are the only people in the building, right?"

"Actually," I replied, "I thought I was the only person in the building. I didn't realize that you were still here until now. So I guess I can't say for certain that there might not be someone else hanging around for a few days. And to be honest," and here I looked out at the gloom, "this storm might make it difficult for anyone to leave for the next day or two. So if you or anyone else plan to leave, you better do it now." I realized the moment I said it that it could be mistaken for an antisocial comment on my part, so I added, "Not that I wouldn't want the company. The emptiness is so huge it may take me a day or two to get used to it."

Once again, she didn't react to my comment. Instead, glancing from the window to me and then back to the window, she said, "So you'll be here for at least the next four days? You wouldn't, ah, leave early or anything, would you?"

By this time, I had brought my dinner over to one of the booths and sat down to eat. Sonya climbed up on the opposite bench and stared at my plate. "No, I won't be leaving early. I plan on using this time to catch up on some research and writing that I've been trying to do."

"What are you writing?"

"A history of this region, including, eventually, the building of this establishment," and here I waved my hand in an arc towards the ceiling to indicate I meant the Ropewalk. "I haven't gotten too far," I added.

"You should talk to Sil," she said. "He grew up here, knows all the stories."

She was referring to Silio Muraceau, the maintenance man. In fact, I had already considered approaching him for that very reason but as yet had not had the chance. Or, for that matter, summoned up the nerve. Sil was a large-boned swarthy man with jet-black hair and something of an attitude. While only of average height, he had massive shoulders and arms, and his constant scowl did not invite overtures of friendship. "He doesn't seem to be very friendly," I said.

"He's alright once you get to know him. He's an Indian, you know. A Native American."

I nodded. "So I hear. People tell me he knows all the legends going back through the memory of his people." I hoped I didn't sound too patronizing. The fact was, I had my doubts about how thick the strain of Indian blood in his veins really was. Someone had told me he was an Algonquin, and someone else had told me, no, he was an Abenaki, the very group attacked and decimated by Rogers' Rangers in the French and Indian War. I, in my infinite patience, did not bother to inform the speaker that the Abenakis were, in fact, members of the Algonquin group. I had long since accepted that most people did not appreciate historical accuracy the way I did.

"What is his obsession with keeping the grass mowed?" I asked. "I watched him several times during the summer almost frantically attacking the lawn with the mower. It was like he was locked in mortal combat with the weeds and brush. What's up with that?" It was a feeble effort on my part to add some levity to the conversation.

She smiled briefly and shrugged, glanced out the window again at the gathering storm, then said, "So you're not aware of anyone else having stayed in the building?"

Something in her tone caused me to stop eating. I studied her expression for a moment and realized there was some meaning—a second question—behind the question. "No. Like I said, as far as I knew I was the only one here. If you don't mind my asking—why are you and Sonya still here? Where's Ben?"

Ben was her husband. His full name was actually Benton, not Benjamin, and I knew from my student visitors that it annoyed him whenever he received mail addressed to "Benjamin Gillespie."

"He had to attend a conference. Can you believe that someone would actually organize and hold a conference right before the Christmas vacation?"

"He couldn't take the two of you with him?"

"Well, not really. At least he said he couldn't. He's coming by to pick us up on Christmas Eve. Then we'll be heading south to Connecticut. My parents live there. Benton's, too, for that matter. It's about an eight hour drive, maybe longer if the weather doesn't improve by then." She paused to pull Sonya away from the table. The little girl had reached out for the food on my plate. "Is there any chance that you might stay until Christmas Eve?"

"Sure, that might happen. If I get on a roll with the project, I probably won't want to stop. The Christmas Fore-eve plan is not carved in stone." I smiled again at my little joke, and this time a faint flicker of a return smile crossed her lips. "Why do you keep asking if I know if anyone else is in the building?"

She drew Sonya to her. The little girl wrapped her arms around her mother's leg and stared at me. Margaret stroked the child's hair for a moment before turning her attention back to me. "Because," she said in almost a whisper, "someone else is. I can hear his footsteps out in the hall when I'm trying to sleep."

♦ ♦ ♦

Chapter 2

The northern, rock-strewn coast of New England has a certain haunting beauty that has always been appreciated by generations of both artists and vacationers. But this far north on that rocky coast caused the sun to set early at that time of year and created not so much a haunting beauty as simply a haunting impression. It was already dark by four-thirty. The trees, except for the evergreens, were stark and skeletonized by the arrival of winter. Scudding clouds in the ice-blue sky heralded the onset of the merciless cold that characterized the region at that time of year. A certain frozen lifelessness was the norm, and people took to their firesides—and often to their moonshine—to wait it out. No matter how certain the arrival of spring was, it did not make the wait any more endurable. It seemed like every year, in some hidden corner of the landscape, someone would give up the race and end it all.

On top of that, the hammering of the surf and the shrieking of the wind as it drove the sleet inland told me that the storm would last through the night, which was fine with me because I had no plans to go out, and like everyone who lived in a remote place, had enough food squirreled away for several weeks. Besides, the tinkling of the sleet on the windows was the perfect white noise for research—soothing and rhythmic, it reminded me of childhood and the simple security of a warm blanket and a cup of hot chocolate.

So when Margaret told me there was someone else in the building, it had a kind of cascading effect on me. The first part was disappointment, because if anyone had intended to stay, I imagined I would've heard about it from one of my student visitors. Finding out about the various undercurrents, plans, and intentions—to the extent that they were aware of them—was one of the advantages to having so many visitors. It was how I knew that Margaret was unhappy.

Beyond the question of the reliability of my "informant" network, the second part was suspicion about the story itself, precisely because of the effect the weather and the lonely environment could have on someone accustomed to a lot of social interaction. The third part was annoyance, because my whole purpose for staying was to not be bothered with mundane affairs; the last thing I wanted to do now was lose precious time looking for a prowler or burglar. But the forth part was resignation. I could see that she was agitated, and I was the only person she could turn to. So, like it or not, I was forced into the role of father confessor once again.

"You heard someone walking out in the hallway last night?" I asked.

Margaret nodded. "And the night before."

I shrugged and smiled in a gesture that I hoped would convey the impression that her concern was unwarranted. "Are you sure you weren't just hearing me going down the hall to use the bathroom? I was up pretty late last night and took one more 'trip' before I went to bed."

She shook her head. "No. I mean, yes, I'm sure it wasn't you."

"But how can you be sure? You didn't even know that I was still in the building until just now, right?"

She nodded, but was insistent. "It wasn't you."

"Because, you know," I persisted, "sounds telegraph pretty easily through the walls when there's no background noise."

She studied me for a moment, and the expression on her face—mouth partly open, eyebrows pinched—was a pretty clear signal that she thought I wasn't taking her seriously. "Let me put it this way," she explained, "If it was you, you either have insomnia or a bladder problem."

Since I had neither, and since the nervous lilt in her voice told me that that "explanation" was a closed issue, I opted for the next most likely possibility. "Well, okay, maybe it was Sil checking to see if everything was buttoned up for the holiday. He's a pretty thorough guy."

"That's what I thought at first, but then I asked myself why he would be walking around all night. The guy has a family and lives in town. I could see him stopping by just to make sure that no unneeded lights were on and all the windows were closed and outside doors locked, but all night? For two nights? No, it wasn't Sil."

There was an unspoken certitude in her conclusion that led me to believe there was some other aspect of all this that she had not yet revealed. What was she not telling me? "Okay," I said, "how about this: maybe one of the parents is doing the Ebenezer Scrooge thing with his kid and not allowing him to come home for Christmas. So somewhere in the building is a school kid with nothing to do but walk around all night and sleep all day. You know how kids are—the moment he has the chance to do something he shouldn't be doing, he'll do it."

It seemed perfectly plausible to me, and I could tell by the way her eyes shifted away that she was thinking about it. I harbored a momentary hope that I might actually escape the need to play Sherlock Holmes. But, no, she brushed it off. "I doubt it," she said.

"Why?"

"Because the school itself is also closed. Where would he eat? What would he eat?" She stepped over and opened the refrigerator door. "Is all of this your food?"

"Yes."

She shrugged. "What would he eat?"

I didn't know. "Well, he's a kid. Maybe he's living off crackers and cold soup. You know, canned stuff. Anything's possible with kids." I involuntarily glanced at Sonya, who apparently was not reacting to any of this. "Look, why don't we do this: I'll finish up my supper and wash my dishes, then the three of us will do our own prowling and try to find this stowaway. I'll bet money on it that it's a kid who's been running around the halls all night and is probably getting himself primed to do the same thing tonight."

That idea seemed to encourage her somewhat. "What about, you know, if we actually find somebody?" she asked.

"What about it?"

"What do we do?"

15

I gathered up my things and brought them over to the sink. "Invite him to dinner. The poor s-o-b must be starving." I filled the water heater and turned it on, glancing back to see how she was reacting. She was smiling. Faintly, but smiling. And this time even her eyes seemed to smile. "Do you have a flashlight?" I asked.

"Yes."

"Why don't you go get it while I wash the dishes. By the time you get back, I'll be done and we can begin the search." So she picked Sonya up and went down the hall to her apartment. I was finished before she got back.

"We need to do this methodically," I said. I walked out into the hall and glanced in both directions. The hall was dark, illuminated only faintly by small nightlights mounted in the walls to suggest antique gaslights. There was enough light to find one's way down the hall, but one had to use each light as a beacon the way ships used lighthouses. Between each one was a pocket of shadow. "Good old Sil," I said. "He probably disabled the circuit breakers for the main hall lights, knowing only a couple of people would be here." I shined the flashlight in both directions and decided that the first thing we needed to do was check to see if the front door was locked. "Okay, let's head for the door. As we pass each room, you check those on the left and I'll do the right. Every door should be locked. We'll check out any one that isn't." The flashlight beam played briefly over her hand, and I saw that she had returned with something other than just the flashlight. It was a knife. "What's that for?"

"Just in case."

Once again, I sensed that there was something she wasn't telling me. "In case of what? If there is another person in the building, it'll more than likely be a student. You'll scare the crap out of him if we surprise him and you have a knife."

"Even so. Just in case."

I let it go. I needed to get this over with. "Okay, you on the left, me on the right. Let's go." She took Sonya by the hand and we began.

I was anxious to get it behind me and put her at ease, so I quickened my pace as I went from door to door trying each to see if I could open it. The result was I got ahead of Margaret and did not notice that she had stopped.

"Egan," she called.

I turned to look at her. She was standing before a door with her hand on the knob. As I watched, she turned it and gave a little push. The door opened about a foot and stopped. She stepped away, inviting me to take the lead.

I went over to her, pushed the door fully open, and shined the light into the room. It was a double room, one of those that housed a pair of students. The overhead light switch was near the door, so I flicked it on and quickly studied the unmade beds first, fully expecting to find our hallwalker just then shaking off the effects of his all-night escapade. But there was no one there. I motioned for Margaret to stay in the hallway while I entered the room. "I'm just going to take a quick look around," I said. "Might as well be thorough about it."

The first thing I did was check the lock on the door to see if it was working. It was the same type of lock I had on my door, one of those push buttons in the center of the knob. The button was there and it seemed to be fine when I pushed it. But when I checked to see if the door was actually locked, I noticed that my jiggling of the outside knob caused the button to pop out and allow the knob to turn. So that explained the mystery. The students who lived there had no doubt thought that the room had been locked, and their own handling of the doorknob on the way out had probably caused the defective lock to release.

I checked behind the bookcases and under the beds and then rummaged in the one closet. "Nobody," I said to her. Just to be sure, I checked to see if the window was locked. The rattling of the sleet on the glass had become louder and more constant. The storm was getting worse.

"The door probably won't stay locked," I said. "The button isn't working right but I'll try it." So saying, I pushed the button in, stepped out into the hallway, and pulled the door closed behind me. Then I turned the knob to try to open it. It resisted the first couple of twists, then suddenly let go and opened. "Might as well leave it unlocked," I said. "For all we know, the creaking of the building might be enough to cause the button to pop. If we lock it and then find it unlocked, it will just cause confusion about how it got unlocked if neither of us touched it. But it can't possibly lock itself if we leave it unlocked."

She nodded in agreement. "It's room number eleven," she said. "Make a mental note so that we won't get it mixed up with some other room."

17

We continued down the hall until we reached the lobby for the main entrance and did not find any other rooms unlocked. I did not mention, of course, that simply because we did not find any did not mean that all the rooms were empty. Someone could still have been in one of those that were locked. But I wasn't going to raise this point because I didn't want to complicate things. Besides, I had been scanning the bottoms of the doors for telltale slivers of light in the hopes that our phantom might reveal himself through that oversight. But everything was dark.

The hallway ended in an enlarged space, complete with sofas and potted plants—artificial, of course—and the large double front door. I pushed on the door just to see if it was ajar or not securing properly, but it was fine. "I'm going to step out and just check to make sure the door locks behind me. I'll give it a quick pull to see if it opens, and if it doesn't, you can let me in, okay?"

She hesitated. "So we'll be alone in here?"

"Yes, but only for a moment. Right after I try to open the door, you can let me back in. Besides, I don't want to be out there for more than a few seconds in this weather." Instinctively, I felt in my pocket for my key ring, which held a copy of the front door key. My own version of "just in case."

She glanced around at the darkened lobby. The moon was hidden by the storm clouds, so despite the narrow window above the door, the only illumination consisted of two small nightlights mounted on opposite walls. "Can we check around in here first?"

I thought it was a little melodramatic but concealed my reaction. Only when she turned momentarily to point out the deep shadows behind the large plants in the corners did I allow myself to roll my eyes in disbelief, which I immediately regretted because I was sure Sonya saw the gesture. "Okay. We'll take a quick look and then check the door." So I went from corner to corner shining the light into every darkened pocket and checking behind the plants and the sofa. That done, I turned back to the door. "All clear. I'm going to go out and let the door close behind me, then try to open it. I'll knock to let you know I'm ready to come back in. It should only take a few seconds."

I pushed the door open and was immediately hit in the face by a blast of wind and sleet. "This is going to be fun," I said sarcastically as I steeled myself for the onslaught. "Here goes." I pushed it open and jumped out. It was freezing out there. The sleet lacerated my neck and cheeks like hundreds of tiny needles as I tried to keep the wind at my back while I released the door. It slammed shut, and I immediately grabbed the large iron handle and depressed the latch to let myself in. It wouldn't open. Good, I thought. The lock was working. No one was getting into the Ropewalk without a key. I pounded on the door with my fist so that Margaret would let me back in.

But it didn't open. "What the hell?" I said aloud. I pounded again and could already feel my hands getting numb from the cold. Still the door didn't open. "Hey," I yelled as I pounded some more. "Let me in. It's freezing out here." I began to dance around to try to warm up and instinctively hunched up my shoulders to keep the lancing sleet off my neck. But still the door didn't open.

I had been out there only a few seconds but realized I had to get back inside quickly. I didn't know what the temperature was, but with the sleet and wind chill, I knew that hypothermia was a very real danger. I also knew that my fingers were starting to freeze and would soon lose their nimbleness, so I dug into my pocket for my key ring and began sorting through the bundle for the front door key. But I had to hold the flashlight in one hand while I did that, and my fingers were already so stiff that when I found it I dropped the ring and it skittered over the layer of ice on the walkway and slid a few feet away. Frantic now, I went after it but slipped and landed flat on my back, almost knocking the wind out of myself. I grabbed the ring and tried to stand, slipped again but caught myself with one of my now freezing hands, then worked my way back to the door.

I slipped two more times before I got there, but when I did, I grabbed the handle and used it as an anchor while I bent down to find the keyhole. I was shivering, my hands were hardly working, and I knew that I was getting close to the limit. I stuck the butt of the flashlight in my mouth, aimed it at the keyhole, and brought the key up. That was when I saw that the keyhole was iced over. In desperation I clawed at it with my frozen fingers, then, coming back to my senses, stuck the hand holding the keys into my armpit to warm it up, held the flashlight between my knees, and began frantically breathing on the keyhole to try to de-ice it. My other hand felt like it was freezing to the door handle. I was about to try the key once again, when I felt a movement in the handle. The door cracked open a few inches and I could see Margaret's face. In desperation I grabbed the edge and virtually threw it open. I had scarcely pulled myself into the lobby than it slammed shut behind me. I looked at her, scarcely able to conceal my anger.

"What the hell happened? Why didn't you let me in when I knocked?" I was still shivering and had stuck both hands under the opposite armpits to thaw them out.

"I'm so sorry," she said, her face showing how real her apology was. "The moment you stepped outside, Sonya broke away from my hand and began running down the hall. I had to go after her. I heard you pounding and felt awful, but what could I do?" She had stepped behind me and was brushing the still frozen granules of sleet from my shoulders and hair.

Indeed, I thought somewhat sarcastically, what could she do? Her instinct-buttons seemed to be working fine. She'd rather leave me outside to freeze than allow her daughter to run down a darkened hallway, which ended in a cul-de-sac and allowed no escape. If she had been *thinking* rather than *instincting*, she would have realized she could have let the child run, opened the door, then caught up to her before she got halfway down the hall. I couldn't help but wonder how long she would have let me stay out there if she had not been able to catch Sonya right away.

I looked down at the child and her features crinkled into a smile when she saw me looking at her. How coincidental that she would decide to play hide-and-seek with her mother the very moment I needed Margaret to open the door. I couldn't help but think that there was something deliberate behind it. As if reading my mind, her smile broadened but somehow, through that amorphous aspect of her face, seemed to be less convincing. Then she broke away from her mother's grasp again and began jumping up and down, playing some sort of hop-scotch game with the floor boards.

"Does she ever talk?" I asked.

"She can't. She's mute."

Now that I didn't know. Looking at the child, I had already begun to think that there was something psychological wrong with her, and now, learning this new piece of information, I was sure of it. There was some genetic disorder at work there. I was suddenly ashamed at what I had thought about her earlier as I came to understand the burden under which Margaret and Ben were struggling. Their daughter was not normal. Some genetic microswitch had not turned on the way it did for normal people. The one-in-a-million probability had happened to them. The odds were probably the same as flipping a coin and expecting to get twenty heads in a row. Impossible, yet there it was. No wonder the child didn't seem at all disturbed by her mother's agitation.

Learning this about her helped me to get over how pissed off I was about being left out to freeze. Perhaps a mother would have let a normal child run down the hall while she waited for me to pound on the door, but I could see how she would not want someone like Sonya to just run wild. It occurred to me that my dishes and eating utensils—including a knife—were still in the kitchen. Who knew what Sonya would do if she got it?

"I'm sorry. I didn't realize that about her," I said.

She waved it off. "We're used to it. She's going to need special schooling." She looked down at her daughter, and her face was an impassive mask of either resignation or simple, unadorned love for her child, defects and all. I could not tell which.

"In any case," I said, "the outer door works fine. As long as we keep it locked, no one can get in without a key, so that's our control on that part of it. Let's check the rooms down past the kitchen now so that you can get some sleep tonight."

She nodded and took Sonya's hand, interrupting her game of hop-scotch. As before, the child did not appear to react with either happiness or annoyance, which surprised me because I would've expected that a typical child would protest its mother's interference. Sonya, however, simply stopped the game and went with her mother as if the game had never taken place.

As we went by room eleven, I tried the knob just to make sure I had left it unlocked. It turned, of course, and when the door opened, I flipped the light on, still harboring some irrational hope that our nightwalker might have taken up residence in the short time I was outside. But the room was empty. I turned the light off, pulled the door closed, and we went on.

None of the other rooms were unlocked, and although this reassured me, it did not seem to have that effect on Margaret. She had finally realized that there was no connection between finding a locked door and assuming there was no one in the room. Or maybe she had known that all along and was only going along with my plan so that she would

21

not alienate the only other person she could turn to. In any case, she voiced her suspicion.

"All we've established here," she said, "is to prove that all the rooms are locked. That doesn't mean they're all empty. Also," and here she paused and stared into me with a fleeting trace of that lecturing schoolmarm that every kid hates, "we haven't checked your floor yet."

For some odd reason, I hadn't even thought that, whoever the alleged intruder might be, he might be operating out of the upper floor. She was right, of course and, with a sigh of resignation, I led her and Sonya back down the hall toward the stairway that went up to the second floor. When we got to the kitchen, I went in and retrieved my eating utensils. Everything went into a small cloth bag that I used for carrying those items back and forth for cooking. I was about to turn off the light when Margaret stepped in and stopped me.

"Leave it on," she said. "I'll turn it off when we're done."

So I left it on. Before we continued our search, I stood there for a moment listening to the sleet hitting the window. It had escalated from a faint but persistent hissing to a cacophony of sharp pings against the glass. The wind had picked up. "Listen to that sleet," I said. "It's getting worse."

She nodded, stepped up to the window, and cupped her hands against the glass to look out. Sonya stared at my bag of eating utensils.

"Everything will be iced over by morning," I went on. "It won't even be possible to drive because they won't get around to sanding the road until all the other roads have been taken care of. We'll be dead last."

Margaret ignored my comment. "There's someone up there," she said.

"What? Someone up where?" I moved forward to look out the window, thinking she was referring to the outside.

But she moved away from the window, took Sonya by the hand, and stood in the doorway to the hall. "Up on your floor."

"Yes there is," I replied, trying to be lighthearted about it. "Me."

She did not return the levity. "No, that's not what I meant. I mean there's someone up there now. I just heard him move."

♦ ♦ ♦

Chapter 3

Margaret's touch was cold as ice as she held onto my arm while we ascended the stairs up to the second floor. That floor, like the lower one, was illuminated only by a series of nightlights that left the hallway as deeply shadowed as the first. Also like the first floor, its only sources of natural light were the windows at either end of the hall, neither of which would have been of much use with the overcast obscuring the moon.

About halfway up, the staircase turned ninety degrees, and as I took that corner, I shined the flashlight up to the next floor, then quickly right and left, hoping to catch a glimpse of our stowaway.

At the top, directly ahead, was a landing in which two rooms were located. One of them, the one on the right, was mine. The hallway then turned left and disappeared behind the overhead wall that defined where the rooms on that side began. I went to my room and opened the door, intending to drop off my eating utensils before we began. I had left my light on, and a brilliant rectangle of light suddenly flooded across the floor. I looked down at it, and both Margaret and I had the same thought simultaneously. "Maybe I should leave the door open for extra light while we check the rooms," I said.

"Yes." She pulled Sonya closer to herself. "But don't leave the knife there."

I had to agree that, logistically, it was a sound idea, but still felt that it would scare the pants off whatever student was still in the building. Overall, not a good idea. I gave her a look that I hoped would convey that opinion, but retrieved the knife anyway. At the very least, I had to completely remove the possibility that Sonya might get it.

"Okay," I said, "Just like downstairs, you go left and I'll take the doors on the right." We started down the hall. "Oh, by the way, as you're checking, see if you can see any light coming out from under any of them. Maybe you can have Sonya check that for you. You know, make it a game." I started down the hall checking the doors on my side. I glanced back and saw that Margaret had squatted down and was talking to Sonya, who immediately clapped her tiny hands and tried to peer under the nearest door.

We worked our way down the hallway. Every door I tried was locked, and whenever I looked back at Margaret, I saw that she was finding the same thing. Sonya, thinking it some kind of game, scrambled ahead of her mother on all fours, looking under each door. I was amazed at how fast the child could move that way. It almost seemed a more natural motion for her than walking upright, and it occurred to me that, whatever the missing genetic element was, it seemed to have allowed some ancient somatic memory to emerge, hearkening back to a time before mind itself when what was to become humanity actually walked on all fours. The child saw me watching her and apparently decided to show off for me, as children often did when they realized they were the center of attention. She quickened her pace. I watched in silent stupefaction as she went skittering by me with the speed and agility of a chimp. When she was about twenty feet ahead of me, she stopped in one of the pockets of darkness between the nightlights and looked back at me. I didn't know if I was supposed to show some overt sign of being impressed, so I did nothing, whereupon Sonya moved forward into the faint glow of the next light and looked back again.

Obviously, what happened next was some trick of light and shadow. When she turned and looked at me, what I saw was not the face of the child, even with its amorphous aspect, but that of an animal staring out of the semi-darkness, a snouted thing with shadowed eyes and hunched shoulders. I was so stunned at the effect that it took me a moment before I remembered that I had the flashlight. But before I could bring it up, Margaret called from behind. "Sonya, don't get too far ahead. Wait for

Mommy." I looked from her to Sonya, then shined the light on the girl. She hadn't moved, but when the light fell on her, she was normal. I was amazed at how the darkness had distorted my vision.

"Everything okay?" asked Margaret as she came up parallel to me.

I was still staring at Sonya. "What?"

"I asked if everything was okay. You seem startled by something."

"Oh, no, everything's fine. I was just surprised by the effect that the shadows had on your daughter. For a moment there I thought, ah, it looked like she, ah . . ." The little girl was staring straight into the flashlight beam unblinking. She wasn't even squinting.

"She what?"

I waved the whole idea away. "Nothing. The shadows made her look different, that's all. It's amazing how fast she can move on all fours. Has she always been like that?"

"Pretty much. When she was very young, she used to waddle across the floor on her butt. We had to tape extra rubber on her shoe heels for traction and so that she wouldn't wear the shoes out too fast. I know it's hard to imagine, but she could move so fast you almost had to run to keep up with her."

I smiled at the nostalgia she was obviously experiencing but did not want to imply in any way that I was interested in hearing about Sonya's babyhood. So I hurriedly brought her back to the matter at hand. "Find any unlocked doors?"

"Nothing yet. You?"

"Nothing. Let's finish this up so that you can relax."

She nodded, but her smile was tense again, like it was when I first ran into her earlier in the evening. We continued our search. She caught up to Sonya, who scrambled away up the hall once again. This time I ignored her. We got to the end of the hall without finding any doors unlocked or any slivers of light coming out from under any of them.

"So," I said, "what exactly did you hear when we were down in the kitchen?" We began walking back up the hall towards my room. The rectangle of light was visible only as a yellow splash on the floor.

"It was just a noise, that's all. Something that sounded like movement."

"Footsteps?"

"No, just, you know, movement. A thump. Like someone bumped into a desk or something."

Now that, to me, put things in an entirely different light. The building was constantly creaking and moaning under the weight of its age. What she had probably heard was the timbers contracting from the increasing cold, or possibly from the weight of the accumulating ice outside. I was annoyed with myself that I hadn't asked that question first, before we went to the trouble of checking every door. I had just assumed that what she had heard were footsteps.

When we got back to the head of the stairs, I wished her and Sonya good night but could see from her expression that she was still tense, so I offered to walk her and her daughter back to their apartment. She accepted with obvious relief. As we headed down the stairs, I stopped and looked back at my room.

"You know," I said, "I can see anyone going up or down the stairs from the peephole in my door. If I hear anything suspicious in the hall, I'll check to see if anyone is out there. How's that sound?"

"That—would be helpful," she said, sounding only half convinced. "But you know what would make more sense? Tape some fishing line across the opening to the stairs at about thigh level. It will be invisible in the dark, and anyone passing through will dislodge it. It'll be so faint that, even if the person senses what he's done, he won't be able to find it in the dark to replace it. Then you'll know that someone passed through."

I was surprised at how cunning she was. Obviously, she had thought about this before. "Good idea, but I don't have any fishing line."

"Sil has some out in the shed."

I was startled again. This was no spur-of-the-moment scheme. She had not only considered it herself but had even gone to the trouble to locate a source for the line. "Ah, well, I have no desire at all to go out into that storm again. By now it must be so slippery that I probably won't be able to get to the shed without falling and killing myself. Besides, how do I know the shed isn't locked?"

"It's not locked. I was out there earlier today. And he has crampons out there, so you'll only be slipping on the way out."

"You were out there today? What were you looking for?"

She turned away and started down the stairs. "Just stuff."

I was supposed to accept that? The woman was obviously on edge about this alleged nightwalker and she went out to the shed to look for "stuff"? "What kind of stuff?"

She waved the question off and continued down the stairs. About halfway down, she stopped and looked back at me. "Are you coming?"

So I started down the stairs, having to content myself with the realization that there were some things she was not going to tell me. Maybe I didn't want to know about whatever the "stuff" was anyway. Why sink deeper into this than I already was? But I did have one question: "If you were already out there, why didn't you bring the fish line back with you?"

"Because," she said, pulling Sonya closer to her and turning toward the long hallway, "it didn't occur to me until just now that there would have been a use for it. I didn't go out there looking for fish line."

"Oh, yeah, right," I said. "You went there looking for 'stuff.'" I could tell by the look she gave me that she caught the undercurrent of sarcasm in my voice.

"That's right," she said. "Are you going to walk us back or not?"

Feeling rebuffed, I came down and walked beside her while we made our way down to her apartment. The bright splash of light coming from the kitchen was like an unmoving searchlight compared to the anemic nightlights on the walls. I didn't realize it, but Margaret's apartment was right next to the kitchen. When I commented on this by way of small talk, she replied, "That's how I knew someone was in there. I could hear the activity through the wall. And I knew by the clanging of the pans that it was not someone trying to be quiet." We had reached her door by then, and she took out her key ring and unlocked it. She saw the questioning look in my eyes and said, "Just a precaution. Keeping it locked while we're gone is just a common sense way to rule out uninvited visitors. What did you call it? A 'control'?" She swung the door open and flipped on the overhead light. "Actually, in spite of what I said earlier in the kitchen, I at first really *did* think that you were the person walking around during the night. But as I listened to the noise you were making, I thought, *If this is the person, then there's nothing to worry about.* Then, when we were talking about it and I mentioned the incident, I knew it could not have been you because your one-time-only 'trip down the hall' story would've been more like 'I get restless and pace the halls at night.'"

So she had been testing me, letting me go on with my story to see if it squared with what she'd heard. This unexpected role reversal left me mildly stunned; in spite of the bathroom story, it had an oddly accusatory effect on me to think that she had believed, however briefly, that I was the nighttime visitor. I took it in stride. "I'll turn off the kitchen light for you," I said.

"Would you like some coffee?" she asked. "It's the least I can do for you considering the trouble I've put you through."

I didn't usually drink coffee in the evening because the caffeine tended to keep me awake, but since it was still early and I intended to be up until at least midnight, I reconsidered. Besides, it would not be an unpleasant experience to share some time with a beautiful lady, my own track record with women notwithstanding. At the very least, considering the music of the sleet on the window and the season of the year, coffee was as close to hot chocolate security as I expected to get. "Okay," I said. "I'd like that. I'll turn off the kitchen light and join you."

It was my first opportunity to see what one of the apartments in the Ropewalk looked like. It had a living room and two bedrooms, one smaller than the other, and a small kitchenette or "efficiency kitchen" with enough room for a small table. "So the rumors are true," I said. "The apartments really do have their own kitchens."

"Right. Toilets, too, but no showers. We still have to use the facilities down the hall for that. It adds a certain rustic flavor to the living experience. How do you take your coffee?"

"Extra cream. One sugar."

"Would you like some Kahlua?"

"Oh, wow, one of my favorite combinations. In that case, I'll take just cream and Kahlua."

Sonya sat on the floor in the living room with a large picture book open on her lap. She appeared to be reading, something that surprised me, both because of her age and because of her mental state. "Can she read?" I asked.

Margaret continued with the preparations for the coffee. "No, she just pretends to be able to. She's mimicking what she sees me doing, kind of the way children who can't talk yet babble on and on in imitation of the sounds they hear around them."

The child was remarkably focused. "It sure looks like she can read," I said. "It even looks like her eyes are following the words in the sentences."

Margaret stopped what she was doing and leaned to her left to look out the kitchen door into the living room. "It does, doesn't it? Sometimes I think that she really can recognize certain letters, or even whole words, but there's no way she can actually read a sentence." She went back to making the coffee.

I sat there and listened to the storm outside. The clicking and tapping of the sleet on the windows was lulling me into a state of that warm coziness that I remembered as a kid in my parents' house. No matter how cold I got playing outside, I knew that there would always be this warm, secure place to return to. Kitchen smells on wintry nights brought it back to me, as if the mood were opening an old photo album in my mind. I have never felt that secure since.

"So, what do you think about the idea of using the fish line across the stairwell?" she asked, looking over her shoulder at me.

That blew my warm security motif. "I think it sounds like some kind of James Bond thing. I mean, not that it's a bad idea or anything, it's just that I think it's kind of pointless. What I mean is, you claim to have heard the intruder on your floor, but I didn't hear a thing on mine, and I'm a light sleeper. If anyone had been up there, I guarantee I would've heard him, what with all the creaking floorboards in the hallway." The smell of brewing coffee began to fill the air. Enough of this midnight intrigue, I thought. Bring on the Kahlua.

"So you don't want to do it?" The question had an obvious undercurrent of impatience.

"Well, if it will make you feel better, I'll do it. But I am worried about someone, if there is another person in the building, tripping over it and falling down the stairs. I'd feel awful if that happened. Not to mention the legal problems." She handed me a cup of coffee and slid the cream and Kahlua toward me.

"You don't *tie* it across the stairs," she said. "You *tape* it. If you tie it, someone *will* trip over it and fall down the stairs. If you tape it, anyone going by will simply dislodge it. They may not even feel it happen. Then, the next morning, we check to see if the line is gone.

It'll be another one of your 'controls.'" She sat down, glanced once over her shoulder at Sonya, and turned her attention to her coffee. "So you'll do it?"

I knew when I was beaten. "Yeah, okay. But not tonight. I'm not going out in this storm to try to find some fish line. I'll get it in the morning and set it up tomorrow night."

I could tell she did not agree with my decision but seemed resigned to make some kind of accommodation. "Okay," she finally said. "And what if I hear the footsteps again tonight? What do I do?"

I was already getting tired of hearing about it and hoped that my impatience was not obvious. But there was a certain social expectancy at work, and in spite of the inconvenience, I knew I would have to come up with a plan. There was only one option open to me. "Do you know about what time it was when you heard the footsteps?"

"I heard them several times, but only thought to check the time once. The clock said it was about quarter to three."

"So it was between two and three in the morning."

"Yes."

"Okay. I'll tell you what," I said. "I'll set my alarm clock for two o'clock. As odious as I imagine it will be, I'll drag my butt out of bed and inspect the entire building, including both floors, the front door, even behind the big plastic plants in the lobby. Let's face it—there's no place to hide out there in the hallway, so if anyone is out parading around, I won't be able to miss him." That idea seemed to have a calming effect on Margaret and she smiled in gratitude, then immediately seemed troubled by something.

"The only thing is," she said, "How will I know that the footsteps I hear in the hallway will be yours?"

Good point, I thought. The last thing I needed was for her to come charging out of her room with some kind of weapon and nailing my ass before the adrenalin wore off. "Ah, you don't have any kind of weapon in here, do you? A gun or anything?"

"No. Well, that is, Ben does have a shotgun in the bedroom closet, but I have no idea how to use it. I don't even know if he has ammunition for it. Why, are you worried I'll shoot you?"

"It has crossed my mind, yes."

For some reason she found that comical. "Don't worry. By the time I figure it out, you will have had time to run all the way into Bowford."

"Okay, then. We need to have some sort of signal. Something simple. How about if I knock on your door to let you know that it's me out there? Oh, wait a minute, that's no good. I'll wake you up."

"No you won't. Believe me, the moment the first floorboard creaks, I'll be awake. So that will work fine as a signal. How about if you give two quick raps on the door?"

"Okay, two quick raps it is. Expect me sometime between two and three."

She smiled and nodded. "Okay. Fair enough."

I took a sip of my coffee-Kahlua combination and sighed in contentment. "I love this stuff," I said. "I remember the first time I tasted it. Suddenly the meaning of life became clear."

She laughed at the joke and I realized that she was starting to relax. Apparently, all it took was some sort of plan to deal with, or at least get to the bottom of, what she thought she'd heard in the hallway.

But I was hurting for small talk. It had never been one of my strong points, and I often imagined that there might be a market for "interaction index cards," a series of flashcards broken down by subject and temperament type and carried in one's wallet or shirt pocket to ward off the bugbear of embarrassing silences. The idea was that, if you felt one coming on, you could excuse yourself for a minute, pull out a card, read off a subject for discussion, then return with renewed confidence in your dialectical ability. I could have used one right about then. I could feel the bugbear tugging at my sleeve. "So, ah, what kind of 'stuff' were you looking for when you went out to the shed earlier today?"

"Funny you should ask," she replied, putting down her cup and pushing herself away from the table. She went to a desk in the living room, took two objects wrapped in newspaper out of a drawer, and brought them over to me. "I need help with these."

I picked up one of the packages. It was heavy. I unwrapped it and discovered an old deadbolt, a massive thing of hand-wrought iron that looked like it could have come from a colonial prison. The second package yielded another one just like it. "Deadbolts?"

"I found them in the shed. I went out looking for anything that I could use to secure the door and found these on one of the benches. I need to get them mounted on the door." Her look told me that would be my next activity.

I hefted them. They must have weighed a full pound each. "They look like originals from the days when they made ropes in here. Do you have a drill and some screws?"

"Ben has some tools in a box in the bedroom." She glanced over at me as she took another sip of coffee. Drilling the point home.

"Okay. Let's check it out."

She led me into the bedroom and over to the closet. There was a small rollaway toolbox in there, the type mechanics and toolmakers used. I grabbed the handle and rolled it out into the room, noting that it had a keyhole at the top. "Is it locked?"

"Should be. We usually have to keep things like this locked because of Sonya. He keeps the key on a nail in the wall." She stepped beyond me and into the closet, emerging with the little silver key. In a moment she had it unlocked and had grabbed one of the drawers and pulled it open. It was full of screwdrivers and pliers.

I opened the large panel at the bottom hoping to find an electric drill. Sure enough, he had one. A brief search in the other drawers turned up a drill index and a long, flat plastic container filled with miscellaneous screws. "Okay, it looks like everything we need is here. Might as well do it now."

We went out to the door and she showed me where she wanted them, one at the top and the other at the bottom. "You want both bolts on the same door?" I asked.

"Yes. What did you think I wanted?"

I looked at the massive things and couldn't help but think it was overkill. "I just thought maybe you might like to have one on a closet or something. You know, to make sure Sonya can't get into it."

"No. I want them both on the door."

So I put them where she wanted them, top and bottom. I slid them back and forth to make sure they operated smoothly. Each time it sounded like the bolt of a heavy rifle opening and closing. "These look like they can keep out a goon squad with a battering ram," I said.

She stared at them for a few seconds, as if undecided about whether they would do the job, then stepped up to the door and tested them to see how freely they moved. "Genuine antiques," she said. "Sil will notice that they're gone when he comes back after the vacation. I'll make sure he knows I have them. I'll either pay him for them or replace them with new deadbolts and give his back."

I brought the drill back to the bedroom and replaced it in the rollaway. As I was pushing the toolbox back into the closet, I noticed the shotgun she had mentioned earlier, standing up in the corner. A pump-action twelve gauge. I did not see any boxes of shells near it. She had come in behind me and stood there while I scrutinized the gun. "Do you shoot?" she asked.

"I used to. Not too much any more. And it was mostly rifles and handguns, not too much with shotguns. May I?" I extended my hand toward the gun.

She nodded. I picked it up, brought it to my shoulder, and sighted along the ridge. "I don't hunt," I said. "All I ever did was target shoot, so I never really got into shotguns, although I did do some skeet shooting. Is Ben a bird hunter?"

"Used to be, before Sonya was born. I don't think he's used it even one time since then."

"Ah, the pressures of parenthood." I smiled and returned it to its position in the corner. "I don't see any shells for it. If there are any I can show you how to use it, if you'd like."

She raised both hands, palms outward, in a gesture of refusal. "No interest. Guns scare me. And I think he got rid of the ammunition as Sonya got older and began to walk and explore."

We went back to the table and finished our coffee, I, for my part, straining to keep the conversation going at that point. She tried to press a second cup onto me but I had to refuse. "I'll get the jitters for sure," I said. "Besides, I have to be going. I intended to spend most of this evening working on my writing project, remember?"

"Yes, of course." She got up when I stepped away from the table. "Thank you for attaching the deadbolts."

"No problem."

"And I can expect two knocks on the door tonight?"

"Right. Between two and three o'clock."

"Okay." She began nervously rubbing her hands together, saw that I noticed the gesture, then pretended to be cold. "This storm. I don't know—it looks like it's going to last a while."

"It sure does. Do you have enough food?" She nodded as I moved to the door and opened it. The hallway, even with the nightlights, was so dark I realized my eyes would have to adjust or I could walk right into a Sumo wrestler and not know he was there. "Well, good night."

"Yes, good night. And thank you again."

"You're welcome." I was about to step out, then hesitated. "You know, all this time I've had the feeling that there is something about the incident that you haven't told me. It's just something I've been sensing, so feel free to straighten me out if it isn't true. But is there some other aspect to this that I haven't heard yet?"

She offered a tense and unconvincing smile in reply, then rested her right hand on the thick shaft of the newly installed upper deadbolt. "How astute, Sherlock Holmes. In fact, there is one other thing I haven't told you." She slid the bolt back and forth one time. "The reason I'm so convinced that there really is someone walking the hallway is because he tried to get in here. I laid there absolutely frozen with terror, wondering if I had remembered to lock the door."

◆ ◆ ◆

Chapter 4

"Christ," I mumbled as I headed up the stairs to my room, "If anybody's looking for me, I'll be meditating under a waterfall."

I really didn't need this kind of diversion. There she was, claiming that the nightwalker had actually tried to get into her apartment. How could that be unless the person specifically knew that she had stayed in the building? Even if an intruder were hiding somewhere and had seen her, how could he know which room was hers? The *only* people who would know that would be those actually living in the Ropewalk. Which brought me back to my original suspicion that there was an errant student wandering around the halls at night.

"Did you actually see the doorknob turn?" I had asked.

"No," she had replied. "I heard it move. Or thought I heard it. I can't see the door from my bed, so there's no way I could've actually seen it without getting up, and I was too petrified to even move."

It was the instinctive fright mechanism at work. When confronted with mortal danger, stay as still as possible, a reaction reaching all the way back through time to when we were four-legged foragers trying to avoid the big carnivores. It brought with it heightened sensory ability but simultaneously clouded the rational mind. You can run or fight, but you can't make a sound judgment until it passes. I could not rule out that mental state playing a role in what she imagined she had heard.

The other possibility, of course, was that it was simply a thief trying every door to find one that was unlocked. That seemed the likelier explanation to me at first, since I was sure that there were local "townies" who would know that the building was empty at this time of year, and who might be inclined to take advantage of that. But then I thought about room number eleven. It was unlocked, yet had not shown any sign of having been rifled or searched, ruling out a thief. But the obvious counterpoint to that, of course, was that the room *was* locked when he tried it, and it was his fidgeting with the knob that caused the defective lock to release, in which case he would not have known that it was accessible.

I knew I had to settle down and get to work, but it was becoming clear to me that I was more affected by Margaret's story than I wanted to admit. Because of that, my attention was divided. I knew it would take me at least an hour to review where I was in my project, and probably another hour to get my head into the proper mode for continuing. It was already nearly nine o'clock. That meant that I wouldn't really start working until eleven. By then I would be tired. I also knew that I had to get up at two o'clock to check out the building, which meant that I either had to go to bed right then or risk possibly sleeping right through the alarm. That thought reminded me that I had not yet changed the alarm, so I got up from my desk and set the clock radio for two o'clock.

I regretted having agreed to search the building in the middle of the night and played with the thought of not bothering. The problem with that was twofold, however: one, I was a lousy liar and she would see right through my efforts to persuade her that I had actually done it, and, two, she was expecting the two rapid knocks on the door as confirmation. There was no way to fake that. So I was resigned to it, and that was that. I went back to the desk, opened the loose-leaf notebook that contained my notes and research topics, and tried to read. The sleet drummed and hissed on my window in alternating rhythms of loud and soft strokes, as of a whiskbroom on a rough surface. But it did not soothe me the way it usually did.

The fact was, Margaret's story had begun to grow on me. I could not concentrate on the notes as long as part of my attention was directed at what might be happening in the hallway. I finally relented and went back downstairs to the lobby to satisfy myself that the front door really was locked. I had no intention of going *out* into the storm again, but simply wanted to see if the door was securely latched. I also wanted to check out the possibility that there might be a way to secure the door from the inside. A chain through the handles, for instance, or some sort of crossbar.

From the inside, the door was always unlocked, of course, so a test on the mechanism from that side was meaningless. So I pushed on the panels to see if they would open. Neither moved, but I still could not know whether the door was actually locked without going outside again and trying it. Or maybe I could. Maybe I could get a sense of whether it was locked by simply holding the door open and checking to see if activating the outer handle caused the catch to move.

I opened it a crack, and instantly a blast of frigid air sliced through the opening and into my face, carrying the sting of sleet with it. I reached out and around, grabbed the handle, and depressed the latch with my thumb. It moved, but the internal catch did not, indicating that the door was indeed locked. I pulled my rapidly freezing hand in and let the door close.

I was convinced now that it was locked, but like Margaret with her deadbolts, I had to acknowledge that I would have felt a lot better if I could actually see a crossmember securing it. Even a two-by-four stuck through both handles would have done it. I resolved to search the shed in the morning for something that would work. I had to go out there anyway for the fish line I agreed to tape across the stairwell.

But for now there was nothing to be done except go back to my room and get to work. But it was nine-thirty, I was feeling distracted, and I knew I was going to have to get up at two o'clock to check the building. It seemed pointless to even start. "Alright," I said to myself, "I know you're making excuses to not sit down and do this thing, but for tonight we may have to accept that. So, what can I read that will contribute something to the project so that I don't feel so guilty about it?"

True historical perspective was *the* essential ingredient in what I was trying to do. Make sense of the senseless, find a rational path, some kind of logic, in a playing field marked with the ruts of randomly moving events, like the projectile logic of a pinball machine. Destroy the scene in the moment of trying to capture and explain it. It was what we all did, large or small, on one level or another. But the historian had to put it in order and *explain* it, a doom writ large on his usually

37

eggheaded brow. We were all the same; we would cling to theories in the face of withering opposition, ending up like battered ragdolls sleeping off the bender in a cardboard box somewhere off campus.

Academia was the Nifelheim of the modern world, a fog-world of shady characters like the Norseman's Hades, unallied in any way to reality. That was what I loved about it, its non-reality. With that in mind, and to assuage my guilt, I decided to begin my long-delayed second attempt to read Spengler's "Decline of the West." It was the perfect evening for it—cold, dark, and stormy. When I got back to my room, I pulled it off the bookshelf and blew the dust off the top. Then I found an index card to use as a bookmark and lay down on the bed to read with the book propped up on my chest. I flicked on the reading light fixed to the wall right above the bed and settled in to slug my way through the two-volume tome.

"Is there a logic to history?" it asked on the first page. Was there some mechanism behind it, like a giant windup clock whose time runs as long as it runs, uninfluenced by anything that happens on the face of the dial? Were human events nothing more than the sum total of the bleeder lines needed to drain the energy from that clock so that, in spite of ourselves, the "End of Days" became the inevitable outcome of simply getting up each morning?

I didn't know at what point I dozed off, but I woke up to the sound of voices outside my door. I was so startled and confused that it took me a moment to realize what was happening. The reading light was still on, "Decline of the West" was lying face down, pages folded, on the floor, and the voices I was hearing were actually only one voice, and it was the announcer on the radio. It was two a.m. and my clock radio had woken me up. I lay there listening to his inane babble, the ceiling appearing to waver before my exhausted gaze, thinking: What kind of Cyclops takes a job that requires him to blather away all night to an audience that wasn't even awake?

I sat up and realized that I was still dressed. I had fallen asleep while reading, yet somehow still had the presence of mind to pull the blanket over myself. That was probably how the book ended up on the floor. I reached down to retrieve it and was dismayed to discover that several pages had folded back on themselves and would forever have a crease in them. The bookmark was lost, probably under the bed somewhere, so I used the folded-over end of the jacket to hold my place and got up to put it back on the shelf. I was so tired I was having trouble keeping my eyes open.

It was chilly in the room. It sounded like the storm had stopped, so I went over to the window to check. It had subsided but not stopped, and I could still hear the faint tinkle of sleet pellets against the windowpanes. But the moon was nearly full, and with the overcast thinning out, it was possible to see all the way to the school itself, about two hundred yards away. It was an absurd anachronism of a building, surrounded by the carefully contrived artificial ruins of a long-vanished Greek civilization, as if such a thing had ever actually existed in New England. Fluted columns held the upper veranda aloft in a poorly executed parody of the Parthenon. Yet there it was. Rumor had it one of the first teachers there actually ran around in a toga and sandals. I fleetingly wondered if he wore underwear with it.

The whole idea of the artificial ruins was a carryover from some imagined golden age of higher learning. Wealthy poets of the nineteenth century, patrons of the passions, who had the monetary wherewithal, would build artificial ruins on their estates just so they could brood over them. The founders of the school, who apparently imagined themselves the last escapees from some hypothetical Age of Passion, had followed that example. The result was the school sitting in the middle of a large field strewn with ruins—not whole buildings like the Roman Forum but stone enclosures a few feet high or, in some cases, at ground level. Random bits of unconnected stone debris also lay about like shards of giant pottery dashed to the earth and kicked across the field. Some of them seemed to have been statuary.

And none of it was authentic. It was all a reproduction ruin, a drawing-board delusion deliberately planted the way a gardener might lay out his future harvest. It could even have been made of Styrofoam, for all I knew. I grinned as I imagined the "stone" underlayments wobbling in the wind like giant masses of pudding. That the whole thing was created to illustrate the school's connectedness to the classic past was what I found most amusing. Maybe in a simpler age, with television in its infancy and whole generations not yet programmed by mass media, it might have seemed impressive, even awe-inspiring. But now it seemed ridiculous, inappropriate, the way the live circus had been eclipsed by special effects in the movies.

39

"Okay," I said to myself, "Time to get this over with." So I grabbed my flashlight and headed for the door. Just before I opened it, however, the thought struck me that I should follow up on what I had said to Margaret earlier about being able to see part of the hallway and staircase from the peephole in my door. So I switched off the reading light and looked through the hole. But the feeble nightlights did not help, and it was so dark out there that all I could see was the misshapen points of light that were those nightlights. Everything else was indistinct. There could have been someone standing at the head of the stairs and, unless he moved and I happened to notice it against the weak backlight, I would not have seen him. "Pretty useless," I muttered as I turned the light back on and opened my door. The head of the staircase was suddenly illuminated as I stepped out into the hall. I very quietly closed the door behind me, an instinctive—or rather, conditioned—response that I had acquired so that I would not disturb sleeping students.

I stood there with the flashlight off for several minutes, not moving. The idea was that, if there were someone in the building, I might be able to hear him. I listened. The building groaned under the weight of the still accumulating ice and produced random bumping sounds, but nothing was rhythmic enough to suggest someone walking. I decided to start my search on the top floor.

I had taken my shoes off when I laid down to read and, rather than put them back on, I had simply stepped into my slippers, so my tread was virtually noiseless as I moved down the hall. Noiseless, that is, unless I stepped onto one of the many partially loose floorboards, which would then creak in tones that, I was sure, were loud enough to alert anyone to my presence. But it could not be helped; unless I wanted to map out where the creaking boards were, it would simply be one of the hazards of the job.

The nightlights provided enough illumination to allow me to walk the length of the hall without the flashlight being turned on. I wanted to do it this way so that I, too, would remain as "invisible" as possible, just in case there really was someone in the building. It also would make it easier for me to spot any light coming out from any of the doors, which was what I fully expected to discover. I tiptoed down the hall, staying close to the right wall in order to avoid as many of the creaking boards as possible, which tended to be in the middle of the hall. All the way to the end I slithered, listening for sounds of movement at every room and looking for telltale slivers of light. But there was nothing. I crossed to the left side at the end and repeated the same procedure as I came back. Once again, I heard and saw nothing. The whole affair had taken about twenty minutes.

I paused at the head of the stairs before heading down to the first floor. That floor seemed darker than the one I was on, and I suspected that maybe some of the nightlights had blown out. I had no idea where to find any replacements if that were the case, except maybe in the shed when I went out there in the morning.

I needed the flashlight just to be able to see the steps. Nevertheless, I cloaked the beam with my hand, allowing just enough light to escape to make it possible to see where the landing was at the halfway point, where the stair turned and descended to the floor. When I got to the lobby, I saw immediately why it seemed darker than the floor above: it wasn't that some of the nightlights were out—they were all out. The only ones still functioning were the ones in the lobby itself. The narrow window above the front door allowed diffuse moonlight to filter into the lobby, but the hallway leading down towards Margaret's apartment was an absolutely black, featureless tunnel that could have been the inside of a cave. There was no light whatsoever.

"What the hell?" I mumbled, and was about to shine the light down there when an enormous "boom" exploded from the front door, as if a gigantic fist had been slammed against it. I nearly jumped out of my skin, whirling around with my nape hairs prickling and instinctively landing in a defensive position. I shined the light at the door, saw nothing, quickly shined it left and right, saw nothing, then whirled again and checked behind me. There was nothing. I stepped up to the door very slowly, the light out in front, holding it ready to temporarily blind anyone who might be trying to get in. And listened. I could hear the wind, which apparently had not died down. Other than that, I heard nothing. I was about to push the door open a crack when the sound came again. This time it was not so loud, more like a muffled thump, as if someone outside had banged his fist against the outer wall rather than the door. I pulled my hand away from the latch and listened.

"Some kind of animal?" I wondered. "A bear, maybe? Coming around to see what he can find with the humans gone?" My mind, which had been racing under the adrenalin rush, was starting to calm down. Whatever it was, it was not able to get in. I pressed my ear to the door to listen for anything going on outside. The sounds of the storm were instantly magnified, but other than that, I did not hear anything. If it had been a bear, I would have expected to hear him sniffing the door, or would hear the scratching sounds of his claws on the ice.

I decided to chance it. Surprise, after all, was a two-edged sword. The animal would be so startled that its first instinct would be to run, allowing me enough time to close the door again, at the same time alerting it to the fact that the building was not empty.

I reached for the handle, my thumb hovering over the release. "On three," I said to myself. "One, two, three." I pushed down on the latch and leaned into the door, intending to add some momentum to the suddenness of the move.

But it didn't open. I bounced back as if I had thrown myself against the wall.

It would be hard to describe the sensation that went through me at that moment. I could feel the adrenalin coming again, my heart rate increasing, my breathing deepening. Something was holding the door closed from the outside. Something wouldn't let me leave. But before my reasoning mind submerged into the animal-mind of pure reaction, that reasoning mind, now just an appendage to the million-year-old fright instinct, said, "Try it again."

So I did. I pressed the latch down with my thumb and pushed against the door. Once again, it didn't move. A bear, I reasoned, would not play some sort of "knock-knock, who's there" game with me; this had to be something else. I pushed harder and felt the door give a little. Harder still and it opened a crack, just enough to let in the arctic air before whatever was out there forced it closed again. I stopped and listened again. Nothing. So I pressed the latch again and, rearing back to gain as much momentum as possible, threw myself against it.

With a suddenness that was startling, it flew open, and I had to hang onto the door handle to stop myself from slipping and falling on the icy landing, fully aware now that all efforts at surprise were gone. Frantic now, slipping and flailing my legs like a drunk in a soccer game, I fought to stay on my feet while looking everywhere for the thing that had held the door, fully expecting to be set upon by *something*. When I finally regained control and was able to steady the flashlight, I found myself face to face with the thing.

It was a tree branch. An ice-laden tree branch. A huge elm, probably as old as the Ropewalk itself, overhung the building and had lost one of its limbs in the storm. It was easy to see that the limb had let go, swung down like a pendulum, and hit the door before it broke free and fell, preventing the door from opening. The thunderous boom that I heard had been its impact. The second thump had no doubt happened when it broke free. I stood there staring at it, being pelted by the sleet, shivering in the cold, and laughing at myself for the scare I had just experienced.

My efforts had moved the limb far enough out of the way to open the door, and for now, that was enough. I would get it fully out of the way in the morning. I stepped back inside, checked the outside door handle to make sure it was locked, and pulled the door closed after me. I stood there a moment shaking my head in disbelief that I had reacted in such a way. What if the building had still been full of people and the limb had fallen against the door? Would I still have had an adrenalin rush? I doubted it. It was amazing what kind of transformation one's head went through when one was alone. When you're in a group, you share in the security of that *tribal* strength, even if it's an illusion. When you're alone, the bugbears of the night can have their way with you. And all this time I thought I was at an age when I was no longer susceptible to that.

"Alright," I said to myself, "tomorrow I'll have to find a ratchet, come-along, or something to move that limb. But for now I have to finish this and get some sleep." I turned and shined the light down into the hallway. The end was so far away that the light was too weak to reach it, creating the illusion that it went on forever.

I knew that the only thing that could cause all the lights to go out would be a tripped circuit breaker, and I also knew that the electrical box was in a closet down at the far end of the hall. What I didn't know was whether that closet was locked. If it was, I would have to break into it.

It was obvious at that stage that anyone walking the hallway would long since have become aware of my presence, making a stealthy search of the rest of the building somewhat moot. Nevertheless, I kept to the wall on the right side as I made my way down towards the box in order to avoid the ubiquitous creaking floorboards. The flashlight was indispensable; the hall was so dark that, without it, I would have had to feel my way along the wall. As I walked, I scanned the bottoms of the doors for telltale slivers of light.

When I got to Margaret's door, I knocked twice in rapid succession, but before I could move on I heard a voice from the other side say, "Egan?"

"It's me," I said, louder than a whisper but not so loud that I might wake Sonya.

I heard her sliding the deadbolts, and a moment later her door opened and she appeared silhouetted in the frame. She was wearing a bathrobe so thick it looked like a parka. "Sorry," I said. "I didn't mean to wake you."

"What was that awful noise?" she asked.

"Oh, a limb fell from the big elm and hit the door. I'll pull it away in the morning."

"A tree limb?"

"Yes."

She shook her head and smiled, her shoulders visibly sagging in relief. Then she reached out with one hand and lightly touched my chest, running her hand down and letting it fall to her side. "Thank God you're here. I don't know what I would've done if I were here alone and that happened. I would've lain awake all night waiting for someone or something to batter my door down." She smiled, and the light from inside illuminated half of her face, making her look strangely exotic, the way the publicity people used to pose movie stars in the thirties. It highlighted how delicately beautiful she really was.

I reveled in her touch but had to quickly mask my reaction lest it became awkwardly obvious how great my sensory deprivation had been since coming to the school the year before. She seemed to somehow sense this and backed up just the slightest bit, as if adding distance between us, as if reinforcing that the touch was nothing more than a gesture of thankfulness.

"It was pretty loud," I said. "Did it wake Sonya?"

She looked over at the closed door that was obviously Sonya's room. "I don't think so. At least I didn't hear anything. She tends to be a very sound sleeper." Then she stepped forward and looked out into the hall. "Why is it so dark out here? What happened to the nightlights?"

"The circuit breaker must've been tripped by something. Maybe ice got in somewhere, melted, and shorted out the line at some point.

I'm going down to check the box now, assuming the closet that hides it isn't locked."

"Oh, okay. I'll let you go then."

I nodded, wished her a good night, and turned to continue my journey down the hall.

"Egan," she said.

I turned back to her.

"I, ah—thank you so much for doing this. Really, I don't know what I would've done. I mean, you can't imagine . . . ."

I smiled and indicated with a wave that she need not go on.

"Would you like to have breakfast with us in the morning? I mean, that's the least I can do after putting you through all this."

"I'd love to. What time?"

"What time is good for you?"

"Well, considering it's almost three in the morning now and I only have a few hours sleep behind me, how about nine o'clock? Is that too late for you?"

She smiled and shook her head. "Nine o'clock is fine."

"Okay. It's a date."

She nodded. "Thank you again."

"Okay. You might as well go get some sleep. I'll see what I can do with the box and then I'm heading back to bed myself."

She raised her hand and offered a tiny wave in reply, then stepped back and closed the door. I could hear the deadbolts sliding into place.

I chuckled to myself. There she was, praising and thanking me, and there I stood, the hollow hero, not wanting to taint the mood by admitting I was out there soiling my undies while the whole thing was happening. Apparently, I still felt at some level that I had an image to maintain.

The utility closet that held the electrical boxes was at the end of the hallway, the last door on the right. I reached for the knob somewhat tentatively, expecting to find it secured, but it opened even before I had fully turned it. How odd, I thought, and how unlike Sil to leave one of the portals to his domain openly accessible. I stepped in and shined the light on the wall. A series of three gray boxes was mounted there, each with one or more large electrical conduits emerging from the top and disappearing into the ceiling above. Since I had no idea what went to what, I figured I might as well start with the box on the left.

It was cold in there. I could see my breath as I examined the first box. Everything was properly labeled on the inside panel of the door, but there were so many entries that I realized the sensible thing to do was simply to scan the breakers themselves and see if any were switched off. I went from box to box doing this and found some that were turned off, but for a good reason. One marked "compressor," for instance, was obviously of no use to me, although I did fleetingly wonder where the compressor was and what it was used for.

In the third box, I found the one that controlled the main lights in the hall. It was switched off, of course, but I noted its position in the event that I ever needed to turn them on. Right below that breaker was the one for the lights on the upper floor, also off. And just below that was another whose corresponding legend on the door panel told me it was the one I was looking for. The hall nightlights. I switched it on and stuck my head out of the door to see if it worked. Instantly the hall had gone from total blackness to shadowed half-light. Okay, I thought, that was it. I closed the panel door and left the closet, pulling the door closed behind me. It didn't quite catch and popped open an inch or so, so I pulled it more firmly to make sure it stayed closed.

As I walked up the hallway, I fully expected the lights to go out again, since whatever had caused them to switch off was obviously still a problem. I was convinced that ice was getting into the building and melting onto a line or junction somewhere. But there was no way in hell I was going to go looking for that.

It was nearly three-thirty when I finally got undressed and crawled under the covers. I was so tired I didn't bother resetting my clock radio to get me up in time for breakfast with Margaret. I figured I would let nature take care of that. My body clock usually woke me at six-thirty, and I expected that that would happen this time as well, except that I would have the sublime pleasure of ignoring it and sleeping for several more hours. I was too tired to go back to reading; "Decline of the West" would have to wait. Tomorrow I would go over to the school and retrieve some books from the library to continue my research. I would also go over to the shed and get the fish line, come-along and, yes, something to use as a crossbar for the front door. I might even see if I could chisel my car out of the casement of ice in which I was sure it was embedded.

I fell asleep and dreamed I was looking out over a green field somewhere in New England. I knew it was New England because the field was sloped on a hill and parts of it were worn to bedrock, as was common when the area consisted of mostly farmers whose animals wore the land down to its bones. As I watched, an eruption stirred the soil in front of me, and while I stood there, the sod burst open and a huge rock, the size of a Volkswagen, squeezed out of the hole, skittered like a drop of water on a hot plate, and rumbled to a stop in front of me. It was oddly shaped, unnaturally rectangular, and on its side was carved a single word: halfway. I stared at it and read the word over and over in the hopes that some meaning would emerge, until at last the total exhaustion of deep sleep made even that vanish. I slipped into timelessness and rode out the rest of the wintry night in the secure folds of my quilt, the last thing that connected me to my long-gone second wife.

$\blacklozenge\ \blacklozenge\ \blacklozenge$

Chapter 5

Right on the outer edges of the reasoning mind there is a gateway, an archaic synapse perhaps, that leads directly from the world of logic to the glowing chaos of the instinctive mind. It is a gateway humming with the collective memory of what we, as a species, were a million years ago, of what we went through, saw, and felt, imbedded in the very cells of the brain. Pass through that gateway and the world of reason disappears.

I knew a guy once who, as a teenager, had tried to cross Long Island Sound on a small Sunfish sailboat. He set out and made good time until he came to a derelict buoy floating in the water. He sailed up to it and saw that it was secured by a rusty chain. For no particularly good reason, he decided to see what was on the other end of the chain, so he grabbed it and began hauling to the surface whatever was holding it in place. He saw a large, whitish object begin to come into focus below him, and a few more pulls revealed that it was nothing more than a cinderblock. Curiosity satisfied, he let it go and it sank back to the bottom. He was about to resume his journey when something else caught his eye. There, slithering through the water a mere five or six feet below him, was a gigantic snake-like sea creature, at least three feet in diameter. The mere sight of it caused that peripheral gateway in the mind to open. He freaked.

"Whatever it was," he told me, "it was a lot bigger than me and I was on its turf." He became so irrational that he almost tried to climb the mast of the Sunfish. "The mast," he said. "Imagine. The mast on a Sunfish is like a broomstick. The thing would've turned over the moment I tried it. But you don't care because all you can think about is getting away from this thing." But he was saved from disaster when he finally realized that the giant "snake" that he had disturbed was nothing more than a large growth of seaweed attached to the cinderblock that he had just hauled up from the bottom. So he had indeed disturbed the lair of the creature, but only its form was in the water; its image was in his mind. On the other side of that gateway.

That's where this gateway leads to. That was where Margaret was going to take me if I let her. Somewhere in the collective experience of humanity, some proto-human really *did* run into a three-foot wide sea serpent while floating on a log looking for shellfish. And the guy on the Sunfish was seeing it again. When you pass through that gateway, you enter the collective memory of the species. I realized I could not let that happen to me.

I was up, shaved, and ready for breakfast with Margaret and Sonya by eight-thirty. The storm had stopped, the sun was out, and the world beyond the window was a dazzling mix of blinding white, startling blue, and the opalescent sheen of ice-laden trees. If I crammed my face against the glass and looked down and to the left, I could see the tree branch that had fallen against the door. Two hundred yards away was the school, now an ice palace, sitting in the middle of its absurd field of ruins. In the light of day, I felt utterly foolish for the way I had reacted to the events during the night.

And that was where the problem lay. I wondered, fleetingly, if Margaret were prone to some kind of hysteria, an exaggerated misapprehension of the events around her, perhaps brought on by the endless strain of having to deal with a handicapped daughter. If that were true, then it was imperative that I distance myself from her as much as possible. For the first time in months, I had some free time to pursue a long-cherished goal; if I were to let myself be sucked into her world of bumps and shadows, that small advantage would disappear in short order.

So I resolved to back away from all of it. After all, it was not like there was any possibility of developing any kind of relationship with her—she was married and had a child. And even if that did develop—and I had to admit it was a pleasant fantasy—there was no way it could end well. Ben would return, things would get ugly, one or both of us would lose his job, and Sonya would end up a yo-yo among the three of us. And all because of some things going bump in the night.

I knocked on her door at exactly nine o'clock. I could hear her approach from the inside and, just to make sure she was at ease, I announced my arrival. "It's me." The deadbolts slid back and the door opened. She stood there holding Sonya by the hand.

"Welcome to the breakfast club," she said, then leaned down and whispered something to Sonya. The little girl's face crinkled into a rubbery smile that somehow seemed too big for her face. She raised her free hand in an awkward wave and moved her lips as if trying to speak. "That's her way of saying 'hi'," said Margaret.

"Hello," I replied, reaching down and offering my hand. Sonya looked at it, glanced up at her mother, then reached out, grabbed just my forefinger, and gave it a shake. "And how are you today?" I asked her. She pulled her hand away and brought it to her face, fingers spread, looking out at me from between them.

"She thinks she's hiding from you," Margaret explained. "That means she's playing hard to get. She must like you. Come on in." She stepped aside and I entered, closing the door behind me.

"You know," I said, glancing at the deadbolts, "I've been thinking about this. I really feel you should take the bottom deadbolt off."

"Oh? And why is that?" She led Sonya away toward the kitchen.

"Because Sonya can reach it. What if you have to step out of the apartment during the night or something, and she goes and bolts the door? You'll be locked out of your own apartment. And there won't be any way, other than brute force, to get in."

She glanced back at me, then over to the door. "Maybe you're right. I'll think about it. Right now I prefer the security of the two bolts."

"Seriously, Margaret, just one of those things could resist everything short of a battering ram."

"I'm sure you're right," she said, but I could tell from her tone that the subject was better left alone.

Breakfast was already set to go. I no sooner sat down than she had a plate of scrambled eggs and bacon in front of me. It was an incredible treat for me because my usual breakfast, typically thrown together while

50

on the run to get to the school, consisted of little more than juice and toast. On weekends, I would usually treat myself to something more substantial at one of the diners in Bowford, but it had been ages since I'd had a real breakfast with a personal touch behind it. I had to restrain myself until Margaret and Sonya were ready. I didn't want to swoop down on it like the proverbial hobo on a ham sandwich.

"So," I said, once again finding myself stretching for small talk, "did you sleep okay last night? Other than the tree limb incident, I mean."

She helped Sonya get a forkful of eggs into her mouth. "Not really. I haven't slept soundly since Ben left. Knowing that you were going to check the building helped, of course, but I still had trouble getting to sleep. I react to every thump and creak. I eventually do fall asleep, but last night that tree limb hitting the door almost gave me a heart attack. I looked at the clock and realized—hoped—that you were up checking it out. When I heard the footsteps coming down the hall, I waited at the door for your signal." Sonya had in the meantime eaten some of her breakfast and lost interest in the rest. She stood up on her chair, turned, then swung herself over the side rails and climbed down with the nimbleness of a gymnast. Margaret let her go. "I have to tell you—if those two knocks hadn't come, I don't know what I would've done."

I heard what she said but was astounded at the little girl's display of agility. Margaret must have picked up on it. "Doctors have told us that children like Sonya sometimes have a special gift that can be developed," she said. "She seems to be a natural athlete. We've been working with some of the therapists to develop this talent so that maybe she can lead something close to a normal life."

I looked over at her, saw the worry in her eyes—a distance, unfocused and opaque, and unseeing of anything but the unfair fate handed to the two of them, or maybe behind it the stern serenity of resignation. Or of some secret knowledge that was strictly a woman thing. I had a book on women's mysteries, which I had marginally tabulated a decade before, that I suddenly wished I had read more thoroughly. She caught my gaze in her own and I felt impinged upon to say something.

"You being a phys ed teacher no doubt makes it easy to get at the equipment in the school," I said.

She smiled and nodded, put her fork on her plate and hugged herself as if cold while she chewed. I stuffed my mouth with food just so that I would have a few seconds to think of something else to say. I could have used one of those dialog flash cards right about then. "So," I finally said, "Where did you and Ben meet?"

"At a sword fight."

"You met at a sword fight?"

"I've been a fencer for almost ten years, foil and epee. I was an assistant instructor in a class, and Ben showed up one day wanting to take lessons. It was love at first strike."

I grinned at the joke. "So I guess when the two of you fight, it can get pretty dramatic, like something out of an old Errol Flynn movie."

"We have an agreement—no swords during an argument."

"Good policy." I stuffed my mouth with food again because I was running out of dialog. "Who won?'

"I did. As soon as I skewered him, he knew I was the girl for him. How about you?"

"Never touched a sword," I replied. "I'm not bad with a broom handle, though, especially when forced into a corner."

She laughed and shook her head. "No, what I meant was, how about your, you know, personal life? Were you ever married?"

"Twice. The first time for love, and the second because I had lost my mind."

"Do you ever have contact with either one of them?"

"Not any more. My first divorce was a long, winding downslope firmly anchored in denial, almost like a type of withdrawal. I loved her, but reality got the better of us. I stayed the same but she changed. Of course, according to her, she stayed the same and I was the one who changed." I stopped to take a sip of coffee.

"And the second?" she asked.

"Ah, the second. She was a would-be model with a wealthy daddy who had taught her that reality could be forced to conform to her view of how things worked, which was probably true for him. For her it was a little different. We only lasted a little over a year."

"And you're divorced now?"

"For the second time. The first time I lost all the furniture, and the second time I lost the furniture *and* the house." I grinned at her look of consternation. "It's not a big deal for me. I seem to be afflicted with an incurable wanderlust, and domestic 'rootedness' felt more like a millstone to me. So I'm glad it's officially over, even if it meant loading up the duffel bag and moving on."

"Do you miss her at all?"

I thought about this before answering. "I miss her beauty and sensuality, but not her volcanic temper and propensity to overwrought melodrama. She was like some kind of Valkyrie trapped in the skin of a mortal female, except instead of selecting which dead would enter Valhalla, she wanted to kill them herself. It usually focused on me. I had my revenge, though. She found a new boyfriend almost immediately, a guy who had lost an eye in 'Nam and was as unstable as she was. Her father must have had a coronary when he met him. The way I look at it, my purpose for that part of her life had evidently been fulfilled. And she, in turn, taught me a lot."

"And how about the first one? Do you still miss her?"

It was an odd question for me. She—her name was Mae—seemed very far removed in time. "I try not to dwell on that. As far as I know, she's entrenched in her new adopted life. It really didn't suit her, hearth, home, and PTA meetings, but there was something about what she called the 'nervous instability' of my life that had begun to bother her. We had to cut each other loose and try something else. Actually, I had noticed that she had begun showing signs of that quiet desperation most of us live under—the fight all of us wage to hold onto a piece of planet, like grabbing a flagpole in a windstorm. I just wasn't interested in doing that."

Margaret seemed to be internalizing all this, staring at her plate as if analyzing the information in her head. An awkward silence had fallen, and I began looking around for something—anything—that would bridge the chasm that was widening between us. I spotted a picture, hand drawn, of her and Sonya on the wall. It was very well done. "Who drew the picture of the two of you?" I asked.

She looked up at me and then over to the picture. "Oh, that was done by Nick, the art teacher. Nick Cephalos—you know him?"

"Yes, we've run into each other in the bars in Bowford. I didn't realize he was so good."

"Oh, he is. He's a great portrait painter, too. Wanted to do that for a living but was forced to take a job teaching so he could make ends meet."

Nick Cephalos was the resident Bohemian, a renegade art teacher with a flair for the dramatic, running around like a leftover hippie from the sixties, with long, thinning hair, frumpy clothes, sandals, and a vocabulary frozen in time. He was immensely likable, but had no sense of personal accountability; if anything went wrong in a relationship, it was always because the other person was looking at things the wrong way.

"What did he charge you?"

She waved it off. "Nothing. It was just something he said he wanted to do."

"You know him well?"

She had raised her coffee to her lips, looked over the brim at me, said, "Hmm," then took a sip. "I take it you never had much contact with him?"

"No. I'm not an artist, so we don't have much in common. I did run into him in one of the pubs in town last summer. He had come home and discovered that his newest wife, number four I believe he said, had left him, taking his van with her. He said he had been teaching at some private Catholic school before this and noted that there seemed to be some sort of inverse relationship between his personal and professional lives. He said he wasn't making as much money then as he is now, but for some reason his personal life was better. Now he's making more money, but the other part is on the downslide. He figured it had to be some kind of cosmic compensation thing."

She smiled, but I sensed she was disinclined to go any further into that subject. She abruptly excused herself and got up to check on Sonya, though I could see the child from where I was sitting and could have told her everything was alright. But it was a timely move because I was running out of topics.

"So," I said when she returned, using the last idea I had for conversation, "What kind of conference did Ben have to go to so close to the holiday?"

"There's no conference," she said almost apologetically. "He's having an affair. He thinks I don't know about it, or that I haven't figured it out yet." She paused for a moment, staring at her coffee, then looked up at me. "The only 'conference' he's at right now is sexual congress with his newest acquisition. I think I might even know who she is."

That caught me off guard. As someone who did not have a long, florid history of being able to say the right thing at the right time, I thought the best thing to do would be to keep my mouth shut.

"This isn't the first time. He had a brief fling with a married woman in Alaska last year," she went on, "and afterwards she was cool and remote to him."

"Alaska?"

"Yes. A long-range affair thinly disguised as a high-adventure fishing trip. He told me, after I found out about it, that the lady had only wanted to 'use' him, but he must've known that in view of her marital status. Afterwards she was reputed to have run off with an escaped convict. Real smart, huh?"

"How did you find out about it?" I asked.

She stood up and leaned over to check on Sonya. The little girl was sitting motionlessly on the floor, staring at the door. "Sonya, honey, come back and finish your breakfast." The girl did exactly that—she came over, grabbed a handful of scrambled eggs, and stuffed them into her mouth. She looked up at her mother and smiled, her face smeared with yellow flecks of egg. Margaret cleaned her up and sent her back to playing.

"He got careless. I was looking for something on his dresser and found a note he had written on the back of an envelope, as if as a reminder to himself. Something he evidently wanted to say to someone. Whoever she was, he wanted to get her naked in the forest and weave wildflowers into her hair, which would have been a great idea if it had been intended for me, but it obviously wasn't."

"How could you have known that it wasn't for you?"

"Because the note went on to mention his doubts about his marriage, about the burden Sonya has added to his life, about the 'rapturous innocence' of embracing other men's wives. It was clear he was jotting down things he wanted to say to someone in a letter. He just wasn't careful enough." She paused to take another sip of coffee. "I couldn't sleep that night and finally ended up waking him at four o'clock in the morning to ask him if he were having an affair. He was so stunned he couldn't say anything, but I knew just by his look that it was true. He finally admitted it."

I was at a loss for words. "And now you think he's doing it again?"

She nodded, looked at me, looked away, and got up to take a plate to the sink. "When will we ever face the fact that it *is* possible to get tired of one another?" she said matter-of-factly. "It was after that when Nick did the drawing of me and Sonya. That's why Ben's not in it." She sprayed the plate off. "I read an article that said that perhaps it was natural that men and women wandered from mate to mate every three to four years. Something about the probability of finding a successful match that would survive long enough to continue the race."

"Ah ha, a genetic crap shoot. The dichotomy of biological probabilities versus emotional commitments."

She glanced over at me, her eyes conveying the question.

"It's one of the themes—or rather sub-themes—that I plan on including in the book I'm trying to write. The role of instinctive drives in the founding and development of a culture. Look at the Medicis and Borgias in Renaissance Europe, profligate scoundrels from an 'ethical' standpoint, but powerful agents for shaping the culture. If the probability of species survival is tied up with that 'natural need' to change mates every few years, then no amount of religious strictures or psychotherapy is going to do us any good. It will happen in a predictable percentage of the population as long as the means are available, women as well as men. What we would need to know is where the limit is. When does the percentage shift from 'natural and expected' to 'too much'?"

The way she was looking at me, I realized there was no place to go but down at that point, and I had to remind myself of my commitment to distance myself from her so that my time would be my own. I could not fix her failing marriage, and any attempt to do so would only backfire on me. I began searching for a way to excuse myself and leave, but she was preparing more coffee with what looked like a pretty clear expectation that I would be there a while. "I can't stay too long," I finally said.

"Why? Is there some social event that I don't know anything about?"

I smiled. "Social event? Here? No. But I do have to get over to the school to get some books out of the library. I also have to move the limb away from the door, chisel my car out of the ice, and find that fish line out in the shed. I'm swamped."

"Can you stay for one more cup?"

I relented. "Sure." Transfixed now for a conversation piece, and deeming it unwise to delve further into Ben's infidelities, I turned my attention to the drawing of her and Sonya again.

"When I saw Nick in the pub last summer, he told me all about how the newest wife had run off with the van. The guy is a master of existential understatement. He comes home, finds the place cleaned out, the van gone, the kids gone, and all he can say is 'Oh, wow, what a head trip.'"

She laughed. "That sounds like him."

"I wasn't much more than a stranger to him, but he unloaded the whole story on me anyway. I remember it almost verbatim." I tried to mimic his far-out, go-with-the-flow, hippie-like drawl. "'She's been going through a lot of changes, man. You know, like having to deal with four kids and stuff. Lots of stress. I guess she couldn't handle it. There were things like money problems, too, you know. She bitched about 'Why does God do these things to me?' and I said that maybe it was a systems check to see if her adrenal glands were still working. I mean, come on, man, how would I know?'"

She laughed again.

"All I could think of was 'Good job, Cyrano. The lady wasn't looking for a sonnet. All she wanted was some sympathy, and the best you can do is talk about adrenal glands?'"

She burst out laughing and had to put her coffee down to keep from spilling it. I was on a roll.

I continued the mimic. "'Lot's of times I couldn't tell where her head was at, man. So I came home one day and found the place cleaned out. She even took my van. I thought, *Oh, wow, man. This is heavy.*'" We were both laughing at that point. "She eventually came back to him," I said, abandoning the hippie drawl, "but not before he had time to have an affair with someone. He told me all about that, too, but wouldn't tell me who it was with. I pressed him for details, but all he said was 'That would, like, you know, kind of blow her cover and put her under a lot of stress. She lets stress get to her.' It's typical of him to not acknowledge his role in having created that stress. He's a nice guy but sort of goes out of phase every time personal accountability becomes an issue."

I took a sip of coffee, glanced up at her, and saw that her look of amusement had momentarily frozen and her eyes had widened, as if fruitlessly searching for an outlet. She looked away from me and focused on Sonya, and in that moment, it hit me with absolute certainty that the lady with whom Nick had had his inter-marriage affair was Margaret. I knew it with such unshakable conviction that it was like a direct intervention from Mount Olympus itself. A gift of the prescient gods. I had stumbled, like the social buffoon I half suspected myself to be, into the one place where I dare not tread. I backpedaled like a clown on a unicycle, hoping to put as much distance between myself and the abyss as possible. "I really think I should get going," I finally said.

She smiled in response, then got up and took my nearly empty coffee cup to the sink.

"Thanks for the coffee," I said, trying desperately to induce the casual atmosphere we'd been enjoying just moments before.

"You're welcome. Dinner?"

"Excuse me?"

"Well, I assume you'll be running around all day and will be hungry by this evening. Would you like to have dinner with us?"

I was grateful and dismayed at the same time, grateful because she was beautiful and gracious, and dismayed because I had to distance myself from her in spite of that. But there was a million years of evolution bearing down on me like a glacier, absolutely unstoppable and irresistible, grinding to powder everything that didn't get out of its way. So I relented. "Sure," I said. "I'll bring the wine."

◆ ◆ ◆

Chapter 6

I balked at the thought of Nick and Margaret together as I made my way gingerly across the iced-over ground to the shed. I didn't want to believe it. I mean, the guy didn't even bathe that often, so how could someone like her be drawn to him? Was it the Bohemian lifestyle? The counter-culture veneer? The whimsical wanderlust? What was it?

I wasn't naïve. I knew, of course, that there were no limits to passion's playing field. The rational mind takes a bleacher seat to the game that unfolds once that door is opened. I should have known and accepted that by now, and I knew I was just being a jerk about it; I even had to admit that I felt a tinge of jealousy.

But she had missed the point also. What the woman in Alaska had done by running off with an escaped con was commit one of those visceral heresies that, at some point, happen to all of us but are not acted upon by most. There comes a time when even the price of security and reputation is more than the body can bear to pay. So the body, with its million-year memory, sloughs it off and does what it must. The earth-memory demands it. Ben had done it with the Alaskan woman, and she had done it with Nick. I had no way of knowing which came first or even if it mattered.

◆ ◆ ◆

The shed was unlocked, something I found oddly out of character for Sil. Even knowing him as superficially as I did, I could not imagine him going off for several weeks without securing all possible inroads into his personal turf. It was usually padlocked. He was so possessive of the place that he normally took extra precautions to make sure none of the students could get in—like installing bars across the lower windows. You could not even see into it—the lower windows were typically covered with old shades or sometimes pieces of newspaper. Yet here it was, unlocked. The only explanation I could think of was that he knew a couple of people would still be in the Ropewalk and might need access to it, so he had left it open.

Odd that we all called it a shed, when in fact it was actually a barn. The hayloft was still operational from what I could see from the outside; the arm with its block and tackle was still there and looked functional. An exterior staircase had been added to the back of the structure, leading up to an enclosed landing that was easily big enough to serve as a storage area, but that had nothing in it. I had gone up there once, the previous summer, intending to try to get into the shed, and discovered that, oddly enough, that exterior enclosure did not have a door into the shed itself. It didn't even have a window that would allow me to look in. It was simply a separate room attached to the back of the original structure. Baffled by the intent behind its design, I had come back down and discovered Sil waiting at the bottom, his arms stretched across the staircase, his look one of barely controlled fury.

"What the hell are you doing up there?" he grumbled.

I had been caught red-handed. Doing what, I had no idea, but whatever it was, Sil evidently thought it was serious. "I was trying to find a way into the shed," I said. I had decided that up-front honesty was the only route open to me given the circumstances.

"There's no way into the shed from there."

"I know. I just discovered that." He was blocking my exit, so I was several steps above him on the stairs, a perfect defensive position. He must have seen this as well, and there was a moment of undecided tension as we stared at each other. He looked angry enough to come at me, and I knew that if he did, I would front kick him right in the face, let the consequences be what they may. I was thirty-six years old, had tolerated all the bullies I intended to tolerate, and had finally learned that I didn't have to be polite to social warthogs. The guy was, to me, a nasty-ass windbag, and if he thought he was going to have some down-east redneck fun with one of the school eggheads, I was going to make him pay the dues.

"Mind if I get off the stairs?" I snapped, adding a nasty edge to my own voice.

His look then changed, vacillated, as if he were confused. But he complied, backing away and allowing me room to pass. "What the hell were you trying to get into the shed for?"

I was moving past him by then, half expecting him to jump me, awaiting the worst, but I turned to him anyway and said, as defiantly as I could, "Just wanted to see what the big fucking secret was, that's all." Then I turned my back on him and headed back to the Ropewalk.

"No secret," he called after me. "Just don't want people getting in there stealing things. Kids and all. Lost a lot of stuff over the years. No money in the budget to replace most of it."

All of which made sense to me, but which I surreptitiously dismissed with a flippant hand gesture, not even turning to look at him.

And that was the event that had shaped my relationship to Sil. Hence my reluctance to consult him about the Native American stories associated with the region. Hence also my surprise at finding his private domain suddenly accessible. I grabbed one of the handles and gave it a tug. It opened a couple of inches, but the snow and ice in front of it prevented it from going any further, and it took me a good ten minutes of kicking enough of it aside so that I could get in.

It was dark in there. After a few seconds, my eyes adjusted and I spotted a light switch. I flicked it on and instantly the overhead fluorescent lights blinked and came to life. The place seemed somehow bigger than the outside suggested, an effect, no doubt, of the open beam construction. In the middle of the floor was the riding lawnmower he used in summer, the one that he rode like a gladiator in a chariot, attacking the brush at the edge of the lawn in ever widening arcs. Next to it was a large snow blower with a shielded compartment for the operator, and next to that a tractor fitted with a snowplow. Bags of salt and traction sand were stacked up against the wall on the right.

Being a barn, I could see that it had originally had stalls or partitions for either animals or grain storage, most of which had been removed to make space. Towards the back, however, it looked like the stalls on either side had been lengthened and heightened so that they formed a partition that extended to the ceiling which, surprisingly, was only the usual height above my head, and which clearly meant that there was a functional second floor. The partition had a windowless door that I was sure was locked.

In front of it, on its left side and extending in an "L" shape along the wall on the left, was a long workbench piled high with all sorts of things—car and truck parts, hose attachments, jars of screws and nails, coils of rope, an occasional bottle of some kind of fluid, and so on. It was chaotic as hell. My kind of place. I headed over to the workbench to begin my search for the fish line and something to move the tree limb.

I should have asked Margaret where she had seen the line. The bench ran the whole length of the wall, and in addition to being overrun with junk, it had drawers underneath and shelves above it. I figured I could be out there an hour or more just trying to find it.

As luck would have it, I found a large pinch bar that I could use to move the limb. I figured it was better than nothing, so I propped it up near the door and went back to searching for the fish line. I pulled open one of the drawers and discovered a box of shotgun shells—twelve gauge, birdshot. That was the gauge of the gun Margaret had in her closet. I thought about it for a moment, then reached in and took half a dozen. Sil probably inventoried them before he left, but what the hell. He would know it could only have been me who took them, but I figured our relationship could not have gotten any worse.

I didn't find the line until I had worked my way down the entire length of the workbench to where it bent in the "L" shape and was affixed to the front of the partition. There it was, a spool of it hanging on a nail above the bench. Just my luck—I should've started my search at that end. I took it down and stared at it, shaking my head in disbelief that I was actually going to tape it across the stairway to detect intruders. I stuffed it into my pocket and headed for the door, but stopped when I remembered that I also wanted to find something to secure the front door of the Ropewalk from the inside. I looked around for something that might work and, finding nothing, headed for the door in the partition to see if it was unlocked.

Against all expectations, it was. I opened it, flipped on the light, and looked around. The walls were hung with v-belts, lengths of wire, spools of cable, and pieces of chain. Tires were stacked up in every corner. I went over to where the chains were hanging, found a suitable candidate, and began untangling it. As I took it down, another piece—a good six-foot length whose massive links looked like each one weighed half a pound—went crashing to the floor with a thud like a huge fist on an empty crate. The hollowness of the sound startled me, and as I hung the piece back up, I realized for the first time that the shed had a basement of some kind. It was only when I saw a square trapdoor in the floor that I made the connection: the partitioned room was actually the old granary, and the trapdoor was how the feed was shoveled down to the animals housed below. So there had to be an outside door big enough for the animals to get through. I had never noticed but, then again, had never bothered to look, either.

I threw my piece of chain over my shoulder and headed for the door, where I grabbed the pinch bar, turned off the lights, and headed back towards the Ropewalk. I had only taken a couple of steps when I remembered that Margaret had said there were crampons in there. I figured I would need them if I was going to move the limb and get my car out of the ice, so I went back to try to find them. I left the pinch bar and chain outside, the former leaning against the wall.

I scanned the workbench but didn't see them, so I went back to the granary and looked around in there again. They weren't there either. I pulled open the trapdoor in the floor to see what was below, but nixed any thought of going down there because it was too dark to see anything, and I didn't have a flashlight with me. Maybe over near the traction sand? I wondered.

So I went over to look and, sure enough, there they were, hung on a nail next to a pair of snowshoes above the sand. As I lifted them down, I glanced to my left and saw that the granary partition did not extend all the way to the outer wall on that side, that it stopped just short by a few feet, and in that space were the stairs to the next floor. Well, I thought, how could I leave the building without first seeing what was up on the second floor? So I left the crampons there and went up the steps.

Windows had been cut into the walls on that floor, looking to me as if they were afterthoughts, as indeed they probably were. The second floor had clearly been added some time after the original structure had been built. I knew this because the original frame, with its massive hand-hewn beams, was held together with wooden pegs, but the secondary uprights that I saw around me on that floor were anchored with wrought-iron nails. The nails were a luxury item beyond the reach of the early New Englanders, who had to bore holes in their house frames and secure the joints with whittled pegs.

Those windows were not covered, and as a result, the entire floor was flooded with natural light. I could see that the whole area was a single, unbroken span of floor marked only by more stall-like partitions, as if animals had been housed on this floor as well. But I could not see how that would have been possible unless some sort of exterior ramp had at one time existed. The stalls were full of items apparently belonging to the school: one held the small, Spartan chairs found in the classrooms, while another had bits and pieces of old desks that Sil obviously cannibalized to repair those in use. Still another held boxes of different types of paper, some of them so old that the boxes had burst or been eaten by mice and the paper oozing out had the appearance of fragile parchment. As I walked along the wall, I also noticed that some of the stalls had names on them and were being used to store the personal belongings of some of the teachers. "So this is where they stashed all their stuff," I said aloud. I had been wondering what happened to the possessions of those teachers who lived at the Ropewalk and who, thus, did not need all of their furniture.

The mystery of how the larger furniture got up there was answered for me when I saw that there was a large trapdoor cut into the ceiling adjacent to the front wall. There was yet another level, and on that level was the block and tackle that hung on the outside beam. This was obviously used to lift the stuff to that level, then pull it in and lower it to the second floor. Very clever. The trapdoor was closed, so I could not see what might be on the next floor. Nor did I see a way of getting there from the second floor; the staircase that I had just ascended ended there.

As I walked around, I noted the names on the stalls but stopped when I saw the name "Gillespie." These were Margaret's and Ben's belongings, either the residue or detritus of what they had been before the Ropewalk, depending on point of view. An old chest of drawers was there, the frame from what looked like an antique bed, an old wooden-slat, leather-bound sea chest, assorted luggage, and numerous other odds and ends.

Toward the back wall, I found several stalls full of old books. Most of them looked like the original textbooks from when the school first opened, but in one corner stood a huge pile of what appeared to be older volumes donated or bequeathed to the school years before. There was a three-volume set of history books dating from the 1880s and, near it, a curious "Household Encyclopedia and Treasury of Knowledge" dated "MDCCCLXXIX," which I haltingly translated into 1879. God, how I hated Roman numerals. Obviously, these antique tomes had been purged from the school library and mothballed, quite literally from the scent that permeated the area, there in the shed. There was an old helmet there as well—actually, a pair of them—such as were worn in World War One, while nearby, on an old table, sat the moth-eaten remains of one of those old top-hats that were de rigueur in the nineteenth century.

It suddenly dawned on me that I had stumbled onto what might have been a treasure. Old reference books, old histories—it was exactly what I needed for my project. Without giving it another thought, I moved several boxes of newer books aside so that I could get into the corner. Most of the titles on the spines were difficult to read, even with the strong light, but there was no doubt that I would want to take some of them back to my room. For starters, I checked the index of the three-volume history set and found references to Maine. I put the set out on the floor.

The rest turned out to be of no particular interest to me. There was the usual "History of Freemasonry," such as seemed to show up in every antiquarian bookstore I'd ever been in. There was also a two-volume set of "The Intimate Papers of Colonel House," that shadowy figure from the Wilson presidency who was considered by some conspiratoralists to have been the prime mover in getting America into the First World War. But these were "newer" volumes, dating from the 1920s. None of them interested me.

Next to this pile was something covered with a shroud. I pulled it off and discovered an enormous pile of old newspapers—The New York Times—aging and yellowed, some of them crumbling at the corners. On top of these was a very old book whose spine had either fallen apart or been eaten away, or that maybe had never been there at all, and whose ragged pages were fan-folded beyond the edges of the cover like a poorly shuffled deck of cards. There was no title that I could see, so I very carefully turned the cover, which felt and looked like desiccated rawhide. It turned out to be an old accounts ledger of some sort. The date on the page I opened to caught my eye—September 30, 1676. I was astounded. The writing was quite legible despite the archaic language. "Whereas daniel olmstead," it began, ignoring capitalization for the name, "with his family were upon the remove to massachuset, and on that juncture of time, the divine providence of god hath removed the sayd daniel out of the Land of the Liveing. Out of compassion to his relict left behinde him, we do grant the sayd Relict shall hould her allotments firme and good to her selfe, only advising her selfe that a dweling House be errected there with all possible speed, and that she in habit there." Despite the mistakes—it was, after all, from an era that had no standards for spelling—it was easy to read. I assumed that "relict" meant "relic" and referred to either the surviving family members or perhaps some aspect of their worldly goods.

I randomly flipped through a few more pages. Land grants, records of deeds to certain holdings, the sale and purchase of property, notations of landmarks defining ownership boundaries—it was some sort of town council registry, complete with references to deceased persons. I realized that what I had in my hand was an indispensable key to outlining the earliest history of the area. It was an historian's gold mine. I knew that, unless that book had been typeset and published sometime in the three centuries since it was written, which was doubtful, I would be the first person to write a history of the region containing this information. What a coup. I very carefully straightened the pages I had looked at, closed the book, and put it on top of the history books.

I turned my attention to the newspapers and looked at the headline of the one on top: "Andrea Doria and Stockholm Collide." The date was July 26, 1956. Reaching deeper through time, I pulled one out dated Friday, July 7, 1876. The headline was "The Little Horn Massacre," and the article went on to describe "the slaughter of General Custer's command." And there were others below those. It was another treasure for an historian, but one that would take countless hours to research for anything useful. I made a mental note for myself and went back to the books.

Other than the history books and ledger, the only thing I decided to take was a crumbling volume of "Concise History of the Northeast Aboriginals," a tedious tome from 1837 that I felt might have some useful information in it regarding the folklore of the New England Indians. I noted there was a section in it that covered the Wampanoag

War waged by King Philip—Metacomet—in one of the earliest efforts to drive the whites out of America. It was something I was going to need to include in my project.

I started to cover the newspapers when it suddenly occurred to me that I was having dinner that evening with Margaret and her daughter and would need something to keep the conversation going—the dialog cue cards, or whatever I had dubbed them. And here they were, being handed to me in the form of old newspapers. I pulled out the one with Custer's last stand as the headline. That would be perfect. We could scan the article for names and see where the men had come from. I pulled out another one, December 6, 1933, with a headline announcing that prohibition had been repealed. "I'll prop this one up next to the wine and Kahlua," I said aloud.

That was enough. I re-covered the rest with their dusty shroud, picked up my treasures, and headed for the stairs. I hesitated for a moment before going down, scanning the ceiling and wondering how anyone got to the third level. There had to be a ladder or something. But I didn't want to waste any more time; it was already nearly noon, and I still had to move the tree limb and try to chisel my car out. With the books I'd found, I realized there was no reason to go to the school library to find research material, so at least there I had a break.

I picked up the crampons and headed for the door, then thought the better of it and went back for the snowshoes. One never knew. If I did end up going over to the school, they could come in handy.

I now had so much stuff—the pinch bar, chain, snowshoes, crampons, books, and newspapers—that I knew I was going to have to make two trips to get everything back to the Ropewalk. I strapped on the crampons and reached for the pinch bar, but it fell over and punched a line through the ice-covered snow, clanging against a rock or something as it buried itself. I got it out, then took it, the books, and the newspapers back first, left them in the lobby, then went back for the chain and snowshoes. At the door, I stopped and looked up at the giant elm that had lost the limb. How lucky we had been. If it had been even a few feet closer to the building, the limb would have come down right on the roof. I had no doubt that the building would have been able to withstand the blow, but not without some damage, maybe even a serious hole.

With the pinch bar, I was able to move the heavy end of the limb far enough from the door so that it was no longer an obstruction. I thought about finding a saw and cutting it up, but realized I would have to be out of my mind to even attempt it. The limb was frozen; it would be like trying to cut a block of ice with a nail file. Besides, I thought with some rancor, that was Sil's job.

Then I went up to check on my car. The ice coating the top and hood looked to be nearly an inch thick, and I realized that chopping it free would not be enough. I would need something that would allow me to break the ice off it so that I could get into it, but without damaging it. The pinch bar wouldn't do—it could easily dent the vehicle. Not that it was any prize; I was driving a ten-year-old Volkswagen beetle whose heating ducts were half rotted away, which had forced me to install a separate gas heater just so that I could defrost the windshield. Even so, it wouldn't do to be seen driving around in a car that looked like it had gone through a meteor shower. I would have to go back to the shed and find an axe handle or something. Margaret's car, a brand new '78 Oldsmobile Cutlass, was no better off. With the flattened end of the bar, I began chipping away the ice around the tires.

It seemed futile. I was able to get the tires free, but even assuming I could break my way into the car, I would need traction sand to get out. Even a Volkswagen, with its legendary rear-engine traction, could not make any headway on sheer ice. On top of that, the parking lot was pitched upward at a slight angle from the cars, only a degree or two, but enough so that the vehicle could not be pushed to some other spot. I walked over the slight crest of the little rise to survey the macadam road that led out to the coast road about a mile away. It was covered with iced-over snow, in some places drifted to a depth of several feet.

I pondered my dilemma. There was no point in digging the car out if the road was so drifted over that I would not be able to get out anyway. On the other hand, the snowplows would have to clear the road sooner or later, if only so that Margaret and I could get out for the holidays. I had to be ready to leave in case it was later rather than sooner. So I went back down to the shed to try to find an axe handle or some kind of club. On the way down, I ran into Margaret and Sonya coming out of the Ropewalk, all bundled up, scarves across their faces and ice skates slung over their shoulders.

"Well," I said, "the two of you look like you're expecting another ice age."

"Care to join us? The wind kept the snow off the millpond and it's nice and clear. We're going to have hot chocolate afterward."

There it was again, the complacency trap. "Ah, thanks, but no. I have to find a way to get my car moving. I'll clean yours off, too, and get it out of the ice, if you want. Are you going to need it before Ben picks you up?"

Her eyes darted away from me for a moment, seemed to search for something to light on, then returned. "Probably," she said. "So, yes, if you could do that for me, I'd greatly appreciate it." I couldn't tell if she was smiling behind the scarf.

"Okay," I said, and turned toward the shed to resume my quest for a club or axe handle.

"You're sure you won't join us?" she said.

"No, I can't. I really need to get my head together for my project. I found some stuff in the shed that might be useful and am kind of anxious to check it out."

"I know. I saw your 'treasures' in the lobby." Despite the scarf, this time I could see that her eyes were smiling.

"Interesting stuff. I hope you didn't sneak a look at any of it."

She laughed and shook her head. "No."

"By the way," I went on, "Stay off the walkway. It's very slippery. You'll be much safer crunching through the iced-over snow, even if it is a little more effort."

"Okay. Thanks."

I nodded, offered a small wave to both her and Sonya, then headed for the shed. She returned the wave and the two of them headed through the snow for the frozen pond behind the Ropewalk. It was a small, manmade thing such as were found all over New England, a massive wall of stones forming a rampart that held back a small stream and created a source of water power. Its now defunct waterwheel had once powered the winding and tensioning apparatus that made the ropes. In the hot weather, some of the students would swim in it. To me it looked too spooky for that.

In the shed, I found a sledgehammer whose handle was loose and, with the help of a smaller hammer and using a large bolt as a set, I knocked it free and brought it back to my car. It took some vigorous whacking, but I was able to break the ice away from the door. I got in, started it up, and let it warm up while I did the same on Margaret's car. By the time I had broken enough ice away from her doors, the VW was about as warm as it ever got. I got in, put it in reverse, and engaged the clutch. The tires spun, the car rocked, but it appeared there was no way it was going anywhere without sand. I tried the rocking back and forth technique that had worked for me in the past and actually succeeded in getting out of the ice ruts, but the car then slid and spun like one of those articulated toys that change direction every time they hit an obstruction. It just wasn't going to happen.

"Damn it," I said aloud. Now I needed to haul traction sand up there and spread it all the way across the parking lot. I checked my watch. It was already quarter to two and I hadn't spent even a single moment doing the research I had intended for that day. Here it was, fate snagging me once again and pulling me away from my goal like one of those cartoon characters caught on a conveyor belt. Well, I thought, the hell with it. I couldn't get anywhere even if I got out of the parking lot, so what was the point? I shut the car off and got out.

I picked up the pinch bar and headed over toward the path that led to the Ropewalk, leaving my car where it was, jammed against the curb at a forty-five degree angle. Since the parking lot was on a slight elevation, I could see Margaret and Sonya on the pond. Ice skating—it was something I hadn't done since I was a kid when, with my best friend Rick, we would skate on a stream in the nearby woods, a long, sinuous, frozen ribbon that went for more than a mile before a small waterfall would stop us. Then we went home to hot chocolate.

I could see Sonya standing and looking down, staring at something under the ice, then rousing herself and sprinting away with that unexpected agility I'd seen at breakfast. She really was a natural athlete.

For a moment, the simple happiness of the scene filled me with longing for a piece of that life—hearth, home, and family. The windswept pond framed by the glistening trees even looked like something out of a Currier and Ives painting. It was a rare moment of perfection—the sky, the pond, the mother and daughter skating, the silver ring of Margaret's laughter in the still, cold air. And in that moment I thought of how nice it might be to have a family like that, and maybe, just maybe, even a place I could actually call home.

♦ ♦ ♦

Chapter 7

Maine was "discovered" in 1605 near the mouth of the Penobscot by Martin Pring, a friend of Sir Walter Raleigh. In 1652, the settlements came under the jurisdiction of Massachusetts, which was then assumed to be "the perfect republic." It became a state in March 1820. Question: How do you "discover" a piece of ground connected to, and indistinguishable from, the one you're already on? Was it a different color? "Oh, look, this ground is a shade darker. It must be Maine."

The set of history books from the 1880s was a trip. The one thing that came through the loudest for me, apart from the somewhat stilted style they used back then, was the arrogance that was barely assuaged by the wording. The first volume gave a brief overview of the races of men such as those races were perceived at that time. At the head of the list, of course, were the Caucasians, a race "destined for mastery, characterized by symmetry of limb and beauty of face."

"Symmetry of limb and beauty of face?" I mumbled. "Evidently these guys had never been in the New York subway system. That'll curdle your romantic notions of Caucasian symmetry." Still, the long-festering misapprehensions that passed for truth back then gave evidence to the depth of the blindness that swallowed humanity for nearly a century after those words were written. It was ideas like these, uttered in the baneful "innocence" of an age that didn't know any better, that ushered in the dirge that became the twentieth century. A mere notion gone rancid. The failure to see that an accident of fate and circumstance did not mean that God had burdened a particular race with a special task. We just happened to be there when the sun came up.

I got up from the desk and paced. I had taken all my notes, index cards, drafts, and assorted jottings out of the box that held them and spread them out across the bed. It was daunting. I was coming up short on ideas about how to approach the project. I had all these piles but no outline, no plan. Living at the Ropewalk had made it almost impossible to count on having a set time every evening that I could devote to getting it done. There were simply too many interruptions. And now, with that burden suddenly lifted, I found myself staring into a jungle of papers with no map to guide me. And burrowing into the back of my brain was the realization that I would be constantly disturbed again in the future, making the present opportunity seem futile.

I had to face the fact that I had no real idea how to manage the enormity of the task. I had a pile of papers and not much else. How should I start? Should I use a simple dating chronology or some sort of simultaneous-theme technique that combined political, military, economic, and indigenous culture themes against the larger backdrop of "historical inevitability"?

I pondered my dilemma. The cold, hard fact was, my head had been in dry dock over this project for so long that even the barnacles had begun to migrate. I was simply out of ideas. And now I had this accounts ledger that was a concise history of all the property transactions that had happened in the area since the mid-1600s. Obviously, for that to have any meaning, I would have to tie property divisions and transactions into what ultimately became zoning laws. And it would have to *mean* something. I wondered if maybe I could trace the ancestry of one of the patrician families of the area and graft that onto the interplay of historical events. I picked up the ancient volume from the bed and sat back down at the desk to leaf through it.

The oldest entry, the one on the first page, dated from 1647 and was mostly land grants with streams as boundary markers. I flipped through the years, scanning the writing, which in some cases was very difficult to read. I found the 1676 entry concerning the "relict" of Daniel Olmstead again and looked the word up in my dictionary. It was archaic and meant "widow." Ah ha, I thought, so Olmstead had died and left the widow with no place to live. The entries went on but ended abruptly in

1740, at which point there seemed to be an increased frenzy of selling for some unknown reason. The next few pages were blank, and then suddenly the writing resumed, but in a different hand. I read the first few lines expecting to find the same dull commercial information but realized immediately that this second part was something else.

It appeared to be a diary or journal. The first entry dated from the same year that the commercial records ended—1740. From the tone, I assumed it was written by a girl or young woman, which surprised me since girls back then were generally only schooled in the domestic arts.

I read the first page. It was an account of the family's preparations for the visit of a Mr. Michaels, who apparently was coming some distance to visit and stay with them for a while. I had not seen that name as I leafed through the accounts ledger, so I assumed he was either not from the area or had no deep roots. Since there was nothing of any substance in the account, I skipped several pages and tried again. Still nothing, except her exasperation at her mother's "philosophy" of recognizing Saturday as the true Sabbath rather than Sunday and thereby causing her some social inconvenience. Further on, there was a reference to her concern over the fact that this Mr. Michaels did not come calling after all, and that she feared it was perhaps because he had sensed she was leading him on. She was obviously fixated on him—there followed a long, emotionally-charged paragraph in which she unveiled the secrets of her heart, now nothing more than a dead echo trapped in the pages of a discarded ledger.

From an historical standpoint, it was interesting in that it provided a window into the daily life of a young woman living in that era. The United States, as a country, did not yet exist. England and France were still building the foundations upon which each hoped to dominate the continent. The French and Indian War, which would decide that contest, had not yet started. Daniel Boone was only six years old and the "Wilderness Road" was not yet even imagined. The "Northwest Territories" began at the Hudson River. Daily life was a coin-toss—so many were taken by what we would consider "casual disorders" today that it was no surprise they placed such importance on the rituals designed, or imagined, to keep God either happy or preoccupied with other matters so that He would not send yet another affliction their way.

I scanned a few more pages and noted that references to Mr. Michaels had stopped. The young lady's reaction to his failure to arrive was evidently not recorded. Several weeks later, she went into some detail recording a visit by her grandmother.

"Grandmother recounted her Story once again of the time when she was but a Young girl and the savages came to take them. I love her dearly but the story now with so much repetition has become tiresome. Indeed Timothy could not bear it yet one more time and made hence to one of his places of Concealment. I was thus alone with her and perforce must hear it once again. I bore up rather well under the torturous Recounting of the most miserable death of her uncle, tied to a tree and the flesh flayed from his bones by the savages. Some of the savages cast their lot with the wampanoag King and thus paid the price when cap'tn Lewis gave them chase. Those he caught in a wooded hollow and forthwith harried into a Declivity in the ground. He sought to burn them out and indeed several attempted to flee and were dispatched with gun and sword. Two were slain as they made haste to conceal themselves in holes in the Barrow and were left where they lay, half into the earth. The cap'tn ordered they be left there to waste as a warning to others."

The Wampanoag King. She meant Metacomet, known to the whites as King Phillip. So the grandmother must have been a young girl at the time of King Phillip's War, which began in 1675. That war began in eastern Massachusetts, spread to the Connecticut River valley, and then north to Vermont. But what startled me was the sudden realization that it had even reached here, this far north in Maine. Now *this* was news. No one in the historical community knew this. We all knew that Metacomet had sought and received help from the Nipmucs and Narragansetts, but could never have imagined that he actually approached—and apparently got—the Abenakis as well.

This was a find, a discovery, a Balboa-like flag-planting that could change the historical face of early New England. I could scarcely believe my luck. Fate was handing me a way out of my dilemma, leading me toward the door with the prize. All I needed to do was step through it.

I realized that the first thing to do was read the journal in its entirety to see what else might surface. This would take a while; the whole thing looked to be no more than maybe fifty pages long, but the handwriting was small and tightly packed so that each page was probably equivalent to two or two and a half pages of modern text. Not to mention the fact that this was cursive, longhand, complete with blotted letters and archaic spelling. I figured it was a good thing I didn't have any kind of social life.

It was four-thirty by this time. Dinner with Margaret was at six. I set aside the old newspapers so that I wouldn't forget them. To this little pile I added a bottle of wine—a Riesling—from my extremely meager reserve. It occurred to me that I had no idea what we were having and whether that type of wine was "appropriate," but I figured an abandoned school dormitory on the frozen edge of the known world was not the place to start worrying about social fine points. I didn't give it another thought as I sat back down to read more of the journal.

The story told by the grandmother continued. "Grandmother has at last told the Story of how it was that she alone was not taken by the savages. She was walking alone through a field. It was grown high with Grasses. Then she said she did enter a dense tangle of growth with branches twined together as if from a Weaver's loom. Nevertheless there was a faint path. She heard a horse nearing with Great Speed and stepped to the side to conceal herself. The animal went by to which several ragged and frightened people were clinging, some on top one under the Neck and one holding fast to the tail while the staggering beast summoned its Greatest speed, pursued by who knew what foe. But scarcely had it passed her than the savages were upon them with terrible swiftness. They set upon the luckless group with Club and mace. She did see all this happen and much affrighted sought to burrow yet further into the Tangle and thus escape discovery. One she said, a wretched man whom Providence had abandoned, attempted to steal away from the savages through the grass and he came toward her and she was much fearful of being found out. But one of the savages did sight him and set upon him with his stone hatchet. The man saw her yet he did not entreat her for help, seeing no doubt that she was but a Child and thusly did the savage not espy her. The man expired under the blows yet in his passing seemed lightened as if it were with some relief that the end, Foretold years before, had finally come."

I set the book down on my lap. So the grandmother witnessed this horrific massacre as a child, even at some point seeing her uncle being flayed alive. But she herself was never taken, an apparent accident that had left her hidden in the brush while all this was going on. I wondered how anyone could possibly be normal after seeing something like that. I also wondered about how to effectively use the information in my own work and began to ponder the idea of using historical narrative for the first part, derived from both the ledger and the subsequent journal. I jotted some notes for myself on an index card and continued reading.

The next part made no sense to me. Some of the words had been smeared, as if water had gotten on the page, while others were simply indecipherable. It appeared that the grandmother was talking about hiding in the brush for a long time and noted that "presently the Birds appeared," speaking of these birds as if they were a natural and expected follow up to an event of that sort. Her only description was that they were large, had long beaks, and snapped at other, smaller birds that flew by. And then she apparently heard the bleating of a sheep and "was much affrighted" because she had been told that was the sound used to draw out the unwary and incautious. Used by whom was not clear, but it evidently meant that "they" suspected she was hiding in the area and were trying to fool her into revealing herself. I assumed that "they" were the Indians who had just perpetrated the massacre. She apparently didn't fall for it and stayed where she was, scarcely moving a muscle for the rest of the day and right through the following night. The next day she noted that the birds were gone and all seemed quiet. She could see what was left of the massacre victims from where she was and got up to run away, but then saw the head of a large animal protrude from the brush near the site of the killing. At first she thought it was a bear, but then saw that it had curved horns and had no idea what it was. So she stayed hidden for most of that day. Finally, driven to desperation by thirst and hunger, she ran, tearing through the brush half barelegged and being scratched to ribbons by the wild thorns.

"A large animal with curved horns?" I wondered. "A buffalo?" I knew there had been buffalo in the eastern forests when the first settlers arrived—Daniel Boone had hunted them in Kentucky—but I never would have guessed that they had actually been on the eastern seaboard as well. This would be another revelation.

It was quarter to six by that time, and I had to get going. I collected the newspapers and bottle of wine and was about to leave, when I suddenly jolted to a halt and looked back at the journal. It had finally registered—what had the writer meant when she said the end had been foretold years before? Was that some kind of biblical screed? I had no time to ponder it just then, so I wrote myself another note on an index card and headed down to Margaret's apartment.

◆ ◆ ◆

Chapter 8

We were having chicken. Good thing, too, because otherwise the Riesling would have been so out of place, so gauche, so déclassé, that I would have gone through all my dialog flash cards just trying to keep Margaret's attention off my culinary ineptitude. Well, not really. She didn't care what kind of wine it was any more than I did. A much more immediate concern was trying to find a corkscrew to get it open.

"I'll give you thirty more seconds of searching," I said, "and then I'm going up to get mine."

As fate would have it, she found it at the nineteen-second mark. "Do you have any wine glasses?" I asked. "Or should we go all out and use paper cups?"

She laughed. "Paper cups are always nice because you can get seasonal designs. Also, when the bottle's empty, you can wring them out for a few more drops."

I chuckled. "Well, when this one's empty, I have another one upstairs."

She glanced over at me, and I could tell by her look that I had just uttered one of those unintentional double entendres that get a social splayfoot like me in trouble all the time. Unformed, unuttered, it flashed through my mind: now, how do I signal that I did not mean I was intending to get her drunk?

"Sounds like you're trying to get me drunk and take advantage of me," she said, as if reading my mind, which at that point was probably as transparent as a bell jar.

I stood there like a totem pole, my mind groping for flash cards.

She reached out with a smile and touched my arm. "Relax. It was just a joke. I know you wouldn't do that. And, yes, I do have wine glasses. Here." She reached up to the top shelf of one of the cabinets and handed me one, then a second.

"I didn't realize you were so, well, so reserved," she went on, still chiding me.

I was fidgeting with the wine bottle by then. "Not so much reserved as inept," I corrected, relieved that I hadn't derailed the evening after all. The cork squeezed out of the bottle with a pop and I poured us each a glass. "A product of my personal history, like everyone else." I handed her one of the glasses and raised mine in salute. "Season's greetings."

She raised hers and we clinked the glasses together. "Thanks for all your help," she said before taking a sip. "Really, you can't even imagine what I'd be going through right now if you weren't here." I looked toward the door to the living room and saw that Sonya had come into the kitchen and was looking up at her mother. "Sonya, honey, would you like some eggnog?" The little girl nodded, and Margaret filled a small plastic cup from the half gallon that she had in the refrigerator. "There you go, sweetheart. Merry Christmas." She had squatted down so that she was at Sonya's level. I followed her example, and the three of us raised our glasses to the season. Sonya watched her mother take a sip, uncertain, then looked over at me. I did the same and then nodded my encouragement to her. She brought the little cup to her lips, took a sip, then raised it again. So we all clinked a second time.

"It doesn't take her long to catch on to rituals, does it?" I observed.

Margaret rose to her feet. "Imitation has always been one of her strong points. Since she's so good athletically, I try to bring her to as many gymnastic events as I can so that she can watch."

I was still at Sonya's level when she said this, and I saw the little girl momentarily pause in her drinking and freeze her look, as if she were focusing on what her mother was saying. Then she looked at me, gave me that overly large smile, handed me the cup, and turned to run back into the living room. I stood up. "She does understand what we say, right?"

"To some degree, apparently. But none of us are really sure if she actually understands the whole sentence, or is only reacting to individual words that she's heard before."

"Like a well trained dog," I blurted. It was out before I even realized it. "I'm so sorry. I didn't mean . . . I mean, I didn't intend to imply . . ."

She was gracious about it. "No offense taken. I knew what you meant. And the fact is, we're not sure if she responds simply by highly developed rote, or if actual understanding has taken root on some level."

I winced and shook my head at my stupidity. "Told you I was inept," I said.

"I suppose you're right," she said with a sigh, turning to add a little more wine to her glass. "I mean, it's a wonder you ever got married at all, let alone twice."

I was so stunned at her reply that I didn't know what to say. But then she couldn't hold it in any longer and broke out laughing, turning toward me with the bottle to top off my glass. She was joking to make a point. "Okay," I said. "You win."

She put the bottle down and, still laughing, put her hand on my shoulder. "Stop being so hard on yourself," she said. "And maybe you should go up and get that second bottle after all. We haven't even started eating yet, and this one's half empty."

I held my hands up in surrender. "Okay, but I hold myself blameless for the outcome."

She laughed and waved me off on my errand. "When you come back, everything will be ready. Now don't get lost or bury your nose in a book or something." She shooed me away.

It was pitch dark in the hall, of course, since the sun had gone down almost two hours before. The nightlights were on but seemed so feeble after I had been in Margaret's apartment that I still had to feel my way along the wall. My eyes had adjusted by the time I got to the lobby and started up the stairs. When I opened the door, my room was an absolutely impenetrable black hole until I reached around and flicked on the light. I hadn't locked it and it occurred to me that maybe

I should, since if there really was someone else in the Ropewalk, it would be a good idea to prevent a nasty surprise for either party.

I kept my wine stash in a box under the bed. I had six bottles left, four of them white and two red. I grabbed another white, slid the box back under the bed, and went over to my sink to rinse and dry it. I stared absently out the window while I did that.

The moon was just rising, not quite full but close, and the shadows thrown by the skeletal trees were like the broken strands of a giant ephemeral web reaching out to ensnare the school. The field of artificial ruins was starkly outlined against the snow, clear enough even at that distance that I could almost make out the different shapes. As I stood there looking out, I saw a form detach itself from one of those amorphous mounds. From that distance I could not tell if it was two-legged or four-legged, but with the light on, I was sure I was silhouetted in the window, and when the thing—whatever it was—appeared to turn toward me, I got the distinct impression it was looking at *me*, not at the building, and a moment later my suspicion turned to shock when the thing abruptly began sprinting in my direction.

"What the hell?" I said aloud, then, thinking it was either going to crash itself against the door or was chasing someone or something I couldn't see, I dropped the wine on the bed, ran down the stairs, and lunged for the double doors, throwing my weight against them. But no impact came. Nor could I hear any activity when I pressed my ear to the door. So I very cautiously opened one of the panels, just enough to allow me to look out. It was bitterly cold, so cold that it almost hurt to breathe. But nothing—and no one—was out there.

"What the hell was that?" I asked aloud. "A bear maybe?" That must have been it, I thought. It was either drawn to the Ropewalk by the light in my room, or maybe saw something in front of the building and went after it, creating the impression that it was going for the building itself. Nevertheless, it left me feeling slightly uneasy, so I went over to the corner where I'd left the chain I'd gotten from the shed and wrapped it like a rope around and through the two handles of the double door, then simply tied it. It would be impossible to unravel from the outside, but could be quickly removed from the inside if necessary. Then I went back upstairs, retrieved the wine, locked my door, and headed back to Margaret's apartment. I left my reading light on so that I would not return to a black hole a second time.

I gave the two-quick-knocks signal before attempting to enter, then discovered that she had locked the door behind me. "It's me," I said.

The door opened. She stood there with one hand on her hip and her eyebrows arched. "Did you get lost after all?" she asked, her tone one of lighthearted accusation.

"Not exactly," I said, closing the door behind me. "I saw something outside and just wanted to make sure the door was secured."

Her look instantly hardened. "What was it?"

I shrugged. "Don't know. It was too far away to identify. A bear, I think."

She relaxed. "Oh. It was probably drawn to the odors from the kitchen."

Of course, I thought. That was why it sprinted toward the building. The wind must have shifted and carried the scent of the meal over in its direction, and it was simply reacting to the food stimulus. Of course.

She led me back to the kitchen where the table was set and Sonya already had a fistful of peas in her hand. "Sonya, honey, use the spoon like Mommy showed you." The little girl gave her mother a blank look and continued to squeeze the peas into a pallid green pulp. Margaret wiped her hand off, showed her how to hold the spoon, and then went through the motions with her. Once she saw the pattern, she seemed fine.

"Well," she said, "have a seat. It's nothing fancy but it is warm and home cooked."

"Believe me, that's fancy enough for me." I helped myself to the potatoes and meat. "So, how was the skating?"

"Great. You should've come with us. The ice was like glass. Do you skate?"

"I used to, as a kid. My best friend Rick and I used to skate on a brook that wound through the woods near where we lived. It was a multi-purpose brook—in summer we would catch frogs and turtles there, and in winter we could skate on it. It was better than a pond—we could go for over a mile, starting at the cannibal bowl and ending at a small waterfall."

"Starting where?"

"We would start at what we called the 'cannibal bowl.' The stream went past what, at one time, had been a farm. It had reverted to woods by then, but part of the house was still there when we first found it.

The cannibal bowl was really a large scalding pot mounted in a stone framework and used, as I now know, as part of the slaughtering process. But we were kids and didn't know any better, so we thought that a bowl that large could only have been used by a tribe of cannibals to cook people. Hence the name. How the cannibals got into the woods of Connecticut was never explained, of course."

She laughed, setting her coffee down so that it wouldn't spill.

I grinned. "It was a perfectly logical conclusion for a kid that age. The universe only extended as far as the horizon. I mean, there was a defunct factory a few miles from my house that had a façade that looked like the front of the Alamo. I was sure I would find Davy Crockett's rifle there if my father would just let me out of the car so I could look." She laughed again. "A Texas Tennesseen fighting Mexicans in Connecticut. Think of the logistics problems behind that combination." I took a sip of my coffee. "On the other hand, if we had never encountered Mexicans, we might not have Kahlua today. Think where that would leave us."

She smiled. "I guess I already know what you're going to want after dinner." She helped Sonya with another spoonful of peas. "So, tell me about the treasures you found in the shed today."

"Well, I found the fish line, so I'll tape a strand of it across the stairwell. I also found a piece of chain to secure the front door. It's there now, in fact. I put it on after I saw the bear, or whatever it was."

She nodded her approval and turned her attention back to Sonya.

"I also found these," I said, getting up to retrieve the newspapers that I'd left on a chair in the living room. "Check this out—Custer's last stand made the front page of the New York Times."

She reached over and took the newspaper from me. "Oh my God," she said. "Where did you find this?"

"There's a whole stack of them in the shed, on the second floor. They're up there with all the stored furniture."

She began reading the article while still leaning toward Sonya after helping her with her spoon again. "Hey," she said, "Look at this. There was someone from Connecticut in the regiment. Someone named J. E . . . ." she paused, "Tourtellotte, I think, appointed captain in the Twenty-eighth Infantry. It's kind of hard to read. There was somebody from Maine there, too. And, look, even Massachusetts sent a representative to the massacre."

"What a dubious honor," I said. "It's funny, though, to think that people in Custer's command came from places this far east. You tend to think of them as having come from the Midwest or rural South."

She nodded and returned the paper to me. Sonya seemed to be successfully navigating the intricacies of eating with a spoon.

"I found this one, too," I continued, "just by way of making you feel better about the wine and Kahlua." I held up the paper with the "Prohibition Repealed" headline. She took that one from me as well, glanced at it, and chuckled a few subdued notes.

"'New York celebrates with quiet restraint,'" she quoted. "Yeah, right. New York doesn't do anything with quiet restraint. 'Crowds swamp licensed resorts.' I'll bet. 'Celebration in Streets. Marked by absence of undue hilarity and only normal number of arrests.' What the hell does that mean—absence of undue hilarity?"

"No idea. I guess the scene was dominated by a certain sober propriety in spite of the elevated alcohol content."

"'Only normal number of arrests,'" she went on, adding a satirical edge to her voice. "Well, that's a relief. I'd hate to think repealing prohibition caused an unnecessary strain on the penal system." She handed it back to me and helped Sonya with another mouthful.

And that exhausted my dialog flash cards. For some reason, I expected that they would sustain me for some time, but there was an air of finality in the way she returned that second one. I suspected I was boring her. "Undue hilarity" gave way to "only normal number of doubts" about my ability to keep the conversation going. From that point forward, I was on my own. "I also borrowed some old reference books being stored up there," I said. "I found an accounts ledger from the sixteen hundreds also, with some sort of diary in the back of it."

She smiled and nodded. "Did you get the cars out of the ice?"

There it was, proof positive. She had ignored my comment. I was loosing her. I had a momentary vision of the robot from the old "Lost in Space" series waving its stubby arms around, its globular head whirling and crackling, yelling over and over, "Warning, warning." I took a moment to gather myself. "Well, ah, yes and no. I did break them free, but I couldn't get mine to move up the slight incline in the parking lot. I'm afraid I'm going to have to spread traction sand over the whole lot."

"You know the phones are out, right?"

"They are?"

"Yes. Apparently that limb tore down the lines when it fell."

Well, I thought, that's just perfect.

"It must have done something to the antenna as well because TV reception is terrible. Either that or the storm did something to it. So we're effectively cut off from the rest of the world."

For a moment, just a moment, I saw her look waiver when she said that. A fleeting change passed over her face, a quick glance from her eyes, a momentary tautness in her lips. She was worried. "Suppose the road crews don't even know we're here?"

"Well," I said, trying to be lighthearted about it, "We're only about a mile from the coast highway, and I'm sure that's been plowed and sanded by now. If necessary, we could walk out and flag down a passing car. We might even be able to get the tractor started and be able to plow the road ourselves. We only need one lane anyway. So if they don't clear us out by the time Ben is supposed to pick you up, we have an alternate plan B." Even knowing it was impossible, I didn't dare suggest she somehow try to call Ben to advise him of all this; to do so would resurrect the specter of his infidelity.

She smiled and nodded but quickly looked away. "How's all this going to affect your research project?"

I shook my head. "It won't have much impact. It's gotten off to a pretty slow start anyway. Actually, since school doesn't start until the second week of January, I was intending to return right after Christmas and pick up where I left off, which should be pretty easy to do since I left off at the beginning."

Dinner was over by then and Sonya, apparently anxious to get to whatever amused a mind like hers, stood up on her chair and demonstrated once again the vaulting nimbleness I had seen at breakfast. She was down from the chair and sprinting for the living room in the blink of an eye. I couldn't help but stare.

"Sorry," I said, catching Margaret watching me. "It's just that I'm completely amazed at her agility."

She smiled. "Coffee? With Kahlua, of course."

"Absolutely. Can I help?"

"Sure. Open the second bottle of wine. Looks like we're going to need it." She got up and removed our plates, then busied herself with the coffeemaker.

I wasn't quite sure what she meant by "needing it" but figured the meaning would come through for me at some point. I got the cork out and let the bottle sit so that it could breathe. The smell of fresh coffee began to fill the room, and once again, I was suffused with that sense of coziness and security I knew as a kid. Instinctively, I looked out the window, as if gauging for myself the harshness against which a warm kitchen stood sentinel. I noticed movement in the air outside and got up to look. It was flurrying, with fine, dry, mist-like crystals filling the air in swirling eddies. It wouldn't amount to much, that type of snow; in the morning it would be little more than a cold sugarcoating on the already existing frosting.

She poured us both a cup, brought the Kahlua to the table, and sat down. "So," she said, warming her hands on the coffee mug, "What was in the old diary? Anything interesting?" She stood up and leaned over the table as she said this, checking up on Sonya in the living room.

The question caught me off guard since I had already resigned myself to cue-card social obscurity, fending off the bugbear of awkward silence with improvised banalities that normally held no interest for me whatsoever. I was delighted that she was actually interested. "Well, yes, as a matter of fact. It describes a story told by the writer's grandmother, who apparently was the accidental survivor of an Indian attack during the Wampanoag War."

By her look, I could tell that she did not know what that was, so I explained. "In 1675 Metacomet, the Chief of the Wampanoags, who has the Metacomet Trail named after him, staged an uprising against the whites in the New England colonies. He got help from the Nipmucs and Narragansetts, and later on some of the other tribes in the area got drawn into it, including some affiliated with the southern New England Abenakis. He had some initial successes but was finally defeated by the colonists and captured. They executed him, of course, as self-righteous, God-fearing folk are prone to do."

I glanced over toward the living room while I spoke. The little girl was sitting on the floor with her back against the couch, a picture book open on her lap. As before, I noticed her lips were moving, as if she could actually read the words.

"What I didn't know, and what nobody in the 'historical community' suspected, was that the northeastern Abenakis were also drawn into the fight. According to the diary, the massacre that the grandmother witnessed was done by the local 'savages' who had joined the 'Wampanoag King.' That was Metacomet. Up till this time, the general consensus has been that the Abenakis in this area were not part of all that. It's an incredible coup for an historian, and may even have set a new tone for my writing project." I brought my coffee to my lips in what I imagined was a sweeping gesture of self-congratulation, an unknown convinced he was on the verge of making a name for himself.

She nodded and sipped her coffee, glancing up at me over the rim. "How do you know the diary is describing events that took place in this area? Just because you found it here doesn't mean it took place here. Maybe it was written in southern New England and somehow ended up here. Is that possible?"

A nauseating surge of panic lanced me in the gut and bulged upward into my disbelieving brain. I hadn't thought of that. I suddenly felt like a complete idiot for having leaped to a conclusion without first considering all the possible alternatives. Of course. Of course it could have taken place somewhere else. Why hadn't that occurred to me?

All that came to mind was "Duh."

She evidently saw my distress. "Was there anything in the diary that could tie the events to this area?"

"Well, ah, there's the first part, the transaction records. They're definitely about this area. And the last entry has the same year as the first entry of the diary."

"Not conclusive," she said. "Paper was a rare commodity in those days. That's why they wrote so small and so close together. She could've found the ledger in someone's discarded belongings and decided to use the remaining pages just because that was all she had."

I knew she was right. I slumped there like a toad, scarcely animated. In an instant, I had become the lowest point on the academic food chain. I watched my claim to fame, my big opportunity, my way out, vanish as my swollen euphoria popped and began deflating like a runaway balloon, farting its way around the room in random arcs.

"Maybe there's some other way to tell," she went on. "Did the diary mention any landmarks or town names, or make reference to shipping activity—like rope making—that could be related to this area?"

I was seriously bummed. "I don't think so. The grandmother described the attack and the subsequent retaliation by the colonials under a Captain Lewis."

"Now there's something," she said. "Any way to track down the name and see if he was from this area, or commanded militia in this area?"

"Maybe. It's a thought, but there's definitely no way any of the resources here at the school can be used to do that kind of research. I'll have to postpone that part of it until I can get to a regular library." I shook my head at my own stupidity. On the other hand, I was glad she had pointed this out before I blithely proceeded with a presumption that would have gotten me ridiculed in the academic world.

"So, what did this Captain Lewis do?"

"Hunted down the perpetrators and trapped them somewhere in the forest. His men apparently killed two of them who were trying to hide 'in holes in the barrow,' and he ordered that they be left there to rot as a warning, sort of half in and half out of the ground. Exactly what the 'barrow' was I don't know, but I believe the word was commonly used back then to refer to a low hill. That sort of barbarity was typical of how war was waged back then. Not to imply that today's version is much of an improvement."

She had just taken a sip of coffee and was lowering the cup when her hand froze in the air. "The bone barrow," she said.

"What?"

"The bone barrow. That has to be what it's referring to."

"And what exactly is that?"

"It's a place not far from here. I went there on a hike this past summer with some people, one of those rare occasions when Ben agreed to watch Sonya. That's what the locals call it—the bone barrow—but no one seems to know why. That must be how it got its name. It makes perfect sense." She paused and thought about it for a moment. "Of course. The name goes all the way back to that event. I'll bet some of the oldest residents know the origin of the name. I'll bet Sil knows, too. In any case, there it is—your proof. The grandmother knew of the two Indians who were killed while trying to hide in holes in the barrow, and the local culture still remembers it."

I was stunned, elated, cautiously optimistic as I envisioned the door to success opening again. My hand was actually shaking as I put my coffee down. "And where is this bone barrow?"

"Not far from here. No more than a few miles. When we went there, we drove from here to the head of the trail, which is actually an old and mostly impassable cart track that led up to where the old village used to be. We parked there and walked the rest of the way, probably another two miles or so. A total of about five miles from here."

I scarcely heard her. "Old village? What old village?"

It was nearly eight o'clock by then, and Sonya had fallen asleep on the couch. Margaret went over and covered her with a blanket, kissed her lightly on the forehead, and returned. "There are the ruins of what was evidently a village of some sort in the vicinity of the bone barrow. Some of the houses are still fairly intact. Some of the locals think the place is haunted or something."

"Houses?" I was having heart palpitations. There I was, an historian writing a book about the area, and I had no idea that a village had ever existed there. "There are houses there? What kind of houses?"

She shrugged. "I don't know. Typical New England houses. You know, the old type with the big central hearth that took up the whole center of the house, fireplaces in every room. That kind of thing."

"Central hearth?" Only the oldest houses in New England had a central hearth. Occasionally, I would find the cellar holes of such places in the woods in Connecticut, easy to identify because the base of the hearth was still there in the center. Once I even found the penny—or whatever it was—that the builders would typically imbed somewhere in the house as good luck. It was dated 1749, the date still clearly visible because the coin had never circulated. Any house built with a central hearth predated the introduction of heating by wood stove, which began in New England in the very early eighteen hundreds.

"Yes, you know, the type of house heated by fireplaces."

"Yes, I know. I'm just a little stunned. I didn't know anything about some sort of village in this area."

She grinned and wagged a finger at me in mock scolding. "Well, you better do your homework if you expect to write this book. It sounds like the first thing you need to do is get out of your shell and start talking to the locals about the area."

I smiled in agreement. "Actually, it sounds like the first thing I need to do is visit this bone barrow for myself and see what it's like."

"Well, spring is a long way off, so you're going to have to sit tight for a while."

"Who said anything about waiting for spring?"

She got up to remove the coffee cups and replace them with the wine glasses, newly filled from the second bottle. I was on my way to a serious buzz. "You don't mean you're going to go there before then, do you? Everything's covered with snow."

"I found snowshoes out in the shed. I know I can do two miles an hour on a trail with a full pack, and a daypack on snowshoes won't be any slower."

She raised her glass and we clinked them together again. "What are you saying?"

"I'm saying there's no time like the present. I'll go tomorrow."

I could tell she doubted my conviction. "You're serious?"

"Of course. I've done a lot of snowshoeing. Like I said, I can do two miles an hour with a full pack, and snowshoeing is easier than hiking with a heavy pack. If I leave by eight o'clock, I'll be there by ten-thirty, assuming I don't get lost. All I need is some indication where this cart track is." I took a hefty swallow of wine and felt myself getting happier.

She followed my example, then got up to bring the bottle to the table. "It's easy to find. Once you reach the coast highway, turn right for about a half mile and watch for an old fieldstone wall on the other side of the road, the north side. The trailhead, or cart track, is right where the wall ends. Head inland from there and go for about two miles—an hour for you—until you come to a stream. That stream was the water source for the village and its livestock. The cart track pretty much ends there, although there is some sort of trail that continues, but you need to leave it at that point and follow the stream. It'll take you to a ledge, where it forms a very beautiful waterfall. Below the ledge is the village, in the little valley. Beyond that, near a swamp formed by part of the stream, is the bone barrow. You'll know it because it's almost perfectly dome shaped."

Perfectly dome shaped. How odd. Was it artificial? Had anyone checked out that possibility? A barrow, I knew, was now used to indicate a burial mound, although traditionally it may have been used to describe a hill in general. My excitement grew.

She looked out the window and saw the swirling granules of snow whipping against the glass. "You're really going to go there tomorrow?"

I stood up on unsteady legs and raised my glass in salute. "Ladies and gentlemen," I propounded, imagining myself addressing an audience, "how could I, knowing myself as I do, possibly resist something called the 'bone barrow'?"

♦ ♦ ♦

Chapter 9

"There are no bears in Connecticut," my father had once insisted when I was a kid. But there were. I knew because I had seen the tracks left by one during one of my frequent hikes into the state forest north of my house. A small mud flat held the evidence. Deep, with a smudge of water at the bottom, that curious full- and half-step trail that they left. I'd seen it often enough in the outdoor books I had, but the real thing was a thrill I never thought I would experience.

I was no one's idea of a tracker, but I knew—couldn't resist the idea—that in the morning I would have to try to find the tracks left by whatever I had seen in the moonlight from my window. So I wrote myself a note and left it on my desk, right under my canteen. Before I headed down the macadam road toward the coast highway, I would check it out. If it was a bear, I would be able to recognize the tracks.

My daypack was a hastily constructed affair—extra socks, matches and emergency fire-starting implements, extra mittens, sunglasses, the crampons wrapped in a towel, my ever-present space blanket, and a fold-up camp saw, just in case. I would be traveling as fast as possible, so I prepared what I called a "walking lunch": cereal bars, jerky, and a banana. But these items, like the canteen, I would have to carry inside my parka or they would be frozen solid by the time I was ready to eat them. Other "internal" items included my compass, small field binoculars, and my trusty but hardly ever fired .380 automatic.

I never hiked without a weapon, a practice that I knew might have stemmed from seeing the movie "Deliverance" too many times. At the last moment, I included a flashlight in case it was dark by the time I was heading home.

Before going to bed, I ran a piece of fish line across the stairwell at the top. Since this was supposed to be in lieu of getting up at two o'clock to inspect the building, I decided to go one step further and run a second line across the hallway on Margaret's floor. I secured it just a few inches above the floor, right at the start of the hall. She was right—they were completely invisible unless you shined a light on them and caught the faint reflection. Then I went back to my room and wrote another note to remind myself that they were there so that I wouldn't blunder through my own detection device in the morning.

◆ ◆ ◆

I had stayed at Margaret's until nearly ten o'clock. She carried Sonya to her room and put her to bed sometime around nine, and then the two of us polished off the second bottle. Two bottles of wine and a couple of coffees with Kahlua—we were pretty sauced by the time it ended.

"Good thing I'm not driving," I'd said. "As it is, I'll probably get halfway down the hall and end up sleeping right there on the floor. I'll be in a perfect position to observe our nightwalker, assuming I could wake up."

She laughed at the joke, and for the first time since we had discovered each other in the Ropewalk, she seemed actually relaxed. "So," she said, "What time are you leaving in the morning?"

"Between seven and eight."

She nodded, took another sip of wine. "Quickie breakfast?"

"Yeah, a couple of eggs, some toast, and I'm on my way."

"Want to do dinner again tomorrow? I mean, it's not like we won't run into each other in the crowded hallway."

For some reason, fueled by the wine no doubt, I found that amazingly funny and began to envision myself body-surfing over a sea of curious faces, nimble hands passing me along as if I were a log in a military training film. "Yeah, okay. I'll probably be pretty hungry by the time I get back. What should I bring this time?"

91

She stared at her glass. "Well, no more wine, that's for sure. This stuff went right to my head. One more glass and you'll have to put me to bed the way I did Sonya."

Buzzed or not, I had enough presence of mind to not run with that comment. The last thing I needed was sexual innuendo probing at the edges of the conversation like the ghost of Pan haunting a garden party. I smiled and nodded but deliberately said nothing.

"I didn't mean . . ." she began.

I waved it off. "I know. And I didn't take it that way."

"I'm lucky it's you I ran into and not Moss Breitlinger. That lunatic thinks everything has a sexual meaning."

Moss Breitlinger was the Sociology guru. He was married and lived in one of the apartments of a duplex over in Bowford. He taught Social Studies but was, in fact, a Psychology major, a background he was always honing on the unsuspecting minds of whomever he was interacting with. It was a tiresome game, an academic gladiatorial contest thinly disguised as some sort of science. I despised him. "He's a certified lunatic as far as I'm concerned," I said. "Good guy to stay away from. Imagines himself an alpha male but gets blisters on his hands just from using a lawn spreader. Completely hung up on onion soup. Heavily into porno." I glanced up at her. "End of message."

She laughed, reeled back in her seat as if exhausted, and gave me the thumbs-up signal. "You pegged him," she said. "How did you meet him?"

"He was one of the first people to introduce himself to me when I got here. Came across as an extremely friendly, open-handed type of guy who'd give you the shirt off his back. He invited me to dinner one day at his place, ostensibly to 'break the ice' socially. It was one of the strangest meals I'd ever had. He was so tight with the salad that I ended up eating what looked like a shredded paper bag doused with oil and vinegar. At least I think it was a paper bag. Either that or he got a special deal on brown lettuce." She was laughing so hard by then that she had to put the wine down. "I didn't put it together until later that the meal was just a test to see how much trouble it would be to manipulate and control me, based on how I reacted to what he was serving. He was testing to see how far he could push me before I would react or say something. A measure of my pliability, or of my willingness to 'look the other way.' A royal flamer."

She was still laughing, that giddy silliness that only alcohol can induce. "And that car he drives is so not him," she said. "A guy with his swagger should be driving a sports car, not an Oldsmobile Bitty Bight."

I almost blew wine through my nose when she said that. "An Oldsmobile what?"

"Bitty Bight. I've seen the name on the back of his car, one of those chrome attachments."

"No, no," I said, the laughter rumbling up inside me. "It doesn't say 'Bitty Bight.' It says 'Eighty Eight.'" My whole viscera was turning into jelly as the hysteria took hold. "Oldsmobile Eighty Eight. Olds doesn't make a Bitty Bight. I think that's made by Ford." I lost it at that point and nearly slid off the chair, I was laughing so hard.

"Well," she said, caught in the contagion of her own unintended joke, "that explains a few things. I never did understand why anyone would call a big car like that a Bitty Bight. I thought, *What idiot thought that was a good idea?* I guess the idiot was me."

I was doubled over by then, scarcely able to breathe from laughing so hard. She lost it at that point as well, and the two of us alternately lolled back in our chairs or draped ourselves across the table. I was nearly crying.

"Then," I gasped in between bursts of laughter, "Then he tries laying one of those obscure psychological befuddlements on me. It was this ridiculous rap about the perspective problem that humanity had before mirrors were invented. And he was serious—his point was that, not only would you not know what you looked like and, hence, couldn't know why people were reacting to you the way they were, but you couldn't even know for sure that you actually had a head, since you'd never seen it. He thinks that's the source of all modern social ills—we're all still looking for our heads. I said to him, 'In that case I guess I don't have an ass, since I haven't seen that either.'"

She roared. We were out of control. "You have an ass," she finally managed to gasp. "Trust me. It's there."

"Well," I said, "That's a relief. I'd hate to think it was just a pink smudge like some simian in a zoo."

And that had pretty much capped the evening. We had started out with Custer's last stand, moved through the old diary, touched upon the

Wampanoag War, unveiled the bone barrow, vilified Moss Breitlinger, and ended up talking about my ass.

I gathered up my newspapers and she saw me to the door. When I opened it, I saw to my relief that the nightlights had not gone out as they had the night before. "Alright," I said, still giddy from the laughter, "I'll see you tomorrow evening. I'll bring some frozen vegetables and help you cook them. I expect to be out of the woods by four o'clock, which will get me back here sometime around five at the latest."

"Okay." She nodded, smiled, brushed an errant strand of hair from her face, then reached out and embraced me.

◆ ◆ ◆

I sat down on my bed, turned on the reading light, and began to tackle "Decline of the West" again. Before I got going, though, I decided to get myself ready to go to bed so that all I had to do was turn off the light and pull up the covers when I was too tired to go on. I brushed my teeth at my sink but had to go down the hall to the communal bathroom to use the facilities one last time. As I stepped away and headed down the hall, I halted for a moment and wrestled with the idea that, as ridiculous as it sounded, maybe I should lock my door, just in case. But I dismissed the thought as nonsense, then berated myself for even considering it. I was identifying with Margaret's nervousness again.

The door to the bathroom had a tendency to rub on the floor tiles and stay open if pushed too far, and that was exactly what happened when I entered. Since I was only going to be there for a few minutes, I didn't bother pulling it free to close it. Instead, I reached around for the light switch and turned it on. The overhead fluorescents blazed like a bank of searchlights, flooding the hallway with a large rectangle of light. The urinals were against the wall on the right, and when I finished, I turned to go to the opposite wall where the sinks were located. But as I did that, I froze. Out of the corner of my eye, I thought I saw something move in the frame of light cast by the doorway. It was impossible to tell what it might have been, or even if it had actually been real. I stood there motionless for several seconds watching the doorframe.

But nothing happened. I knew I could not let myself get nerved up over what was probably a phantasm, so I cautiously worked my way towards the door. I had the advantage of being on a tiled floor that would not betray my movements; by contrast, if someone were actually out in the hallway, it would be nearly impossible to move to one side or the other without encountering a creaking floorboard. As I moved towards the door, though, I realized that the overhead light began to lengthen my shadow and that it would get through the doorway before I could. Since I had not heard any creaking boards, I realized that, if there were indeed someone out there, that person had to be still just outside the door. So the only way for me to use surprise was to lunge for the door and sprint to the opposite wall. I took a deep breath and bounded through.

I overcompensated and slapped the opposite wall pretty hard but still turned with enough speed to be able to face anyone coming toward me with sufficient time for defense, if necessary. I was already in a fighting stance even before I stopped moving. But there was nothing there. I looked right and left down the hallway and berated myself for not bringing a flashlight. As was the case downstairs, it was too dark to be able to see anything that may have been at the end of the hall. But I doubted there was anything down there because I had not heard any boards creak.

All wired up because of the incident, I nonetheless felt like an idiot. "Good thing Margaret didn't see that," I mumbled. I shook my head at my own foolishness, went back and washed my hands, then switched off the light, pulled the door free, and headed back to my room. The utter darkness of the hallway after being in the bathroom made me realize just how vulnerable a person would be to someone concealed in one of the dark pockets between the nightlights. I resolved to bring my flashlight from that point forward.

When I got back to my room, I went in, grabbed the flashlight, and shined it at the staircase to see if I could spot the fish line. It was still there. Obviously, no one had come that way since I taped it over the passageway. I then stepped into the hallway and shined the light down to the other end, which was so far away that the beam barely reached it. There was nothing there. Whatever I had "seen" was evidently in my mind and nowhere else.

I had resolved to get to bed relatively early so that I could get an early start in the morning, but it was already nearly ten-thirty, and my mind was in such turmoil that I knew sleep would be difficult. I lay down and propped "Decline of the West" on my chest and tried to read and concentrate. I played mind games with myself—fully conscious that that was what they were—wherein I tried to grid out the content of "Decline" and match the core concepts to my own project. "Still no way to account for the sudden appearance of civilization," I lectured to myself. "All at once, there it was. Not even a warm up. How? And why not everywhere?" That would be relevant, I sermonized, because civilization as we understand it did not take root in North America, even as it flourished elsewhere. On an analog meter, which condition dictates inevitable decline, the one that stepped forward and built cities, or the one that looked inward and built an unfathomable bond to the natural world? How can the two conditions even be compared or measured? Was it the energy level required for civilization that inexorably carried within itself the need to move toward a less complex state, just as order naturally moves towards disorder? Would that be why the entropy-state of the static hunter-gatherer culture can endure for so long?

I lowered the book onto my chest and stared at the ceiling. Who was I trying to kid? When I stood at the door with Margaret, she had embraced me and I held her for a moment, fully expecting her to give me a friendly pat on the shoulder and pull away. But that didn't happen. Instead, she had held on, her arms encircling me and her face nestled into my shoulder. Then I felt that strange tension grow between us, a sort of exaggerated nonchalance that spoke louder than any words. I held her and began stroking her hair, and she lifted her face to mine as I stood there like an idiot, sensing the beginning of an emotional bond that I hadn't felt in years, wanting to take the next step, yet not daring to.

"It's the wine," I had explained to myself. "That and the circumstances. Alone and mutually dependent." And maybe it was, but that didn't matter as our lips touched in what at first was just a casual kiss, a kiss of friendship alone and nothing more. But then her lips parted and I felt the flame ignite itself, a volcanic passion as unstoppable as it was irrational, an outburst against all reason.

She had smiled, pushed away gently, using it as an excuse to touch me, the same sudden happiness and confusion on her face that I knew was on mine. Only a moment, though, and then she came back to me and pulled herself to me again, and I held her for what seemed a long time. Silence passed between us, more meaningful than all the world's wasted words.

It was a scene reminiscent of others from my past, the unattainable love-object and the endless yearning to feel complete, reunited once again with the world made flesh in the person of the beloved. An almost-agony of enforced denial, the masking of the realization of the nearness of the sought-for ideal and the suppressed understanding of one's own incompleteness. For a moment, all other resolutions failed. I was spellbound.

"It was the wine," I said to myself. But I knew I was committing one of those visceral heresies that had caused Ben's Alaskan lover to run off with an escaped con, pining away for the only ecstatic experience left open to me.

I lifted the book off my chest and opened it again, flipped to some random page, noted the comment that morality plays no part in the formation of a state—oddly appropriate for what I was feeling just then—then gave up, closed it, and put it aside.

What was I thinking? All this time, I had imagined that I was walking proof of the effects of living your life like you had nothing to lose. And my life's circumstances had supported that belief. Yet here I was, back in the fight for reality all over again.

I knew I needed to get to sleep. My current status was terminal. In just a couple of days, Ben would come for Margaret and Sonya, and whatever had passed between us would fade away. I needed to fight the illusion that there was something real and lasting there for me, when I knew there wasn't. It was nothing more than a commentary, a note on the cyclic nature of happiness, of sometimes yes and sometimes no. Reality, if not a wave function, was an oscillating function. Of that I had long since become convinced. And I didn't mean that in the context of simple mood swings.

What I had to do was concentrate on the bone barrow and not let myself become confused or misled by the feelings of the moment. I had set a task for myself, and the only way I was going to achieve it was to stay focused on the goal and ignore the peripheral events that wound their way through my life. I had to untangle all the fibers weaving into and out of a single strand that was the Moebius strip of history, twisting and rejoining itself for another look at the same madness in different garb. That was what historians did, and if I were going to make a name for myself, I had to do the same. And I wouldn't be able to do that by allowing myself to be distracted.

I reached up and turned the light off, still feeling unconvinced. Nevertheless, fatigue came quickly, and I nodded off and almost immediately had one of those odd, half-waking dreams. It was a voice, some goddess perhaps, or maybe my first wife, Mae, a dream-wraith always at the edge of my mind reaching out to ensnare me. And she said to me, "You can't love until you know the owner."

My eyes flew open. The owner of what? The passion? I saw that the rising moon had cast a long shadow across my window, the fingers of the muse, and I remembered that Mae had known of one of my hidden convictions: I needed no philosophical essay or anthropological research to know that, if there was a God, it was a woman. Once that was understood, everything else became clear.

Just before falling asleep, in that twilight between the waking and unconscious minds, I was sure that I heard, off in the distance like a faint echo, a barely audible click. And I knew, even as I drifted away, that the nightlights in the lower hall had gone out again.

♦ ♦ ♦

Chapter 10

I had set my alarm for seven o'clock but was fully awake at six-thirty. I got up, shaved, threw on my clothes, and grabbed my eating utensils. I saw my note about the fish line and made a mental note to check for it, then took my flashlight and headed out for the kitchen. The line across the stairwell was still there. I stepped over it, went down to the lobby, and swung the light beam over to the door to check the chain. It was undisturbed. When I turned it toward the hallway, I saw that, yes, as I had either heard or sensed the night before, the nightlights were out once again, and the hall was as dark as a cave. I would need the flashlight just to be able to find my way to the kitchen. Only after I had taken several steps into the hall itself did I remember the line I had strung across the entrance and realized I had just blown right through it. So much for my cunning.

I hugged the wall on the side opposite Margaret's apartment so that I wouldn't step on any loose floorboards and alarm her. When I reached room eleven, I grabbed the doorknob and turned. It was still unlocked, which was no big surprise. I pushed it open a few inches and shined the light inside. Nothing. Also no big surprise.

As I drew opposite her door, I wrestled with the thought of stepping over and giving the two-quick-knocks signal, just in case she was awake. But I decided not to, in part because I was still conflicted and confused about what had happened the night before, and in part because I didn't want to get drawn into a delay of some kind, even if it was just sharing a cup of coffee. I had reckoned on two and a half hours to get to the bone barrow, but that depended on several things, any number of which can typically go wrong in the woods. I could lose the trail and get lost. I could encounter rough or obstructed terrain. I could find a beaver pond that wasn't there the year before. Or any combination thereof. So I realistically had to figure on three hours to get there, or maybe even longer. I needed to leave as quickly as possible.

The kitchen light blazed alike a supernova in the utter blackness of the hall, and for a moment, I had this weirdling idea that its intensity alone would alert Margaret to my presence. The first thing I needed to do, I realized, was go down to the closet at the end of the hall and turn the nightlights back on so that when she did come out she wouldn't be alarmed. So I left my utensils and headed down to the end with my flashlight, taking care to stay near the far wall to avoid loose floorboards.

The door to the utility closet popped open even before I had fully turned the knob, just as it had the last time. And, like last time, it was cold in there, which had to be because of the meager insulation in the outside wall. This time I went straight to the third box, opened it, and found the breaker for the nightlights. I switched it on, stuck my head out to make sure they were working, then stepped out and pulled the door shut, making sure that it latched. The hall was now bathed in the murky half-light that Margaret was accustomed to, so I went back to preparing my breakfast. I tried to be as quiet as possible so that I wouldn't wake her. Her apartment was right next door.

I had the juice poured, the toast done, and the eggs just about ready when a hand touched my shoulder and nearly launched me through the ceiling. I spun around, spatula out front and ready to wag at my assailant, who, of course, turned out to be Margaret. She stepped back and held her hands up in mock surrender. "Hi," she said softly. "Just wanted to see you off on your adventure." She looked over my shoulder toward the counter. "No coffee?"

I looked at her, all warm and soft and fluffed up in her parka-like bathrobe, and my Spartan resolve melted away. "I, ah, haven't gotten that far yet."

She nodded toward the frying pan. "Get your eggs out and sit down. I'll make some. You don't mind if I join you in a cup, do you?" Her eyes were smiling—I mean, really smiling—as she said that, knowing full well that I would never have said no. "It'll be ready by the time you finish your breakfast."

"Okay, yeah, good," I blathered, suddenly up against both the doubts and the taboos, not to mention my own rapidly withering convictions about leaving on time. "I, ah, don't have a lot of time, though. I figure it could take me three hours to reach the bone barrow, so I need to get started as soon as possible. You know, just a precaution. Or maybe not so much a precaution as an expedient—or something." Stop blubbering, I thought. I could feel myself devolving before my own eyes into one of those lipless adolescents that I "counseled" all year long.

"You said you wanted to leave between seven and eight o'clock, didn't you?" she asked.

"Well, yes."

"What time is it now?"

I glanced at my watch. "Five after seven."

She sat down opposite me and stuck her hands into the opposing sleeves of the bathrobe to keep them warm. "So you've got plenty of time for a cup of coffee. Besides, it'll make a difference for you in the long run."

I smiled and nodded. "You're right. It will. What's the rush, right? The bone barrow has been there for at least three centuries, so another half hour won't matter." I could hardly make eye contact with her and kept turning away from her gaze. "How did you know I was in the kitchen? I tried to be quiet."

"Not quiet enough, especially when you turn the water on. From my bed it sounds like a train in the wall."

"Ah. I'll have to remember that."

I sat there mopping up the last of my fried eggs and wondering how I was going to get through this when Margaret said, "It looks a lot different now that we're sober, doesn't it?"

The smell of coffee began to fill the air as I looked over at her. "Yes, it does. Listen, about last night, I mean our little . . . tryst, or whatever it was, I don't want you to think that I would, you know, take advantage of the fact that Ben isn't around and that you have no one else to turn to. I mean, that's not me, and I'm not a home wrecker or anything, so, you know, I think maybe I just got a little carried away or something. Too much wine maybe, like you implied."

"Then we both got carried away." There was no apology in her voice or manner, no hint of regret or embarrassment. She got up and got the coffee, found herself an errant, unclaimed cup in one of the cupboards, washed it, and poured us both a cup. "I'd offer you some Kahlua, but it's a bit early for that sort of thing," she said as she sat back down.

We looked at each other in silence for some time, and I knew she was wrestling with the same thoughts I was trying to articulate: What did it mean? Where do we go from here? Do we go *anywhere* from here? The difference between us, though, was that I was tormented by the implications of where it was going, and she seemed not only relaxed but genuinely happy.

My rational mind told me it was a dead end. I pictured Ben coming in on the two of us and drawing a sword to settle the account the old fashioned way while I did a frantic Keystone Cops defense with my spatula. Then Margaret swoops in for the ultimate reversal of who's rescuing whom as, with her flashing epee, she drives him back, right out of the fantasy. I pictured her dressed like Zorro, long black cape and all, but had to rein in my imagination when, in my mind, I zeroed in on the thigh-high black boots. I grinned in spite of myself.

"What's so funny?" she asked.

At first I waved it off, then told her. "I was just picturing you dressed up like Zorro and jumping in to defend me from Ben and his foil." I didn't mention the boots.

She winked at me and brought her coffee to her lips. "I can still beat him," she said, "so don't worry about a thing."

Her easy manner was starting to make me feel more relaxed. "Listen, Margaret, I know the circumstances here have sort of brought us together, maybe even created a bond, but . . . ."

"But?" Her eyebrows arched as she formed the question.

"But it's a temporary thing, don't you think? I mean, in two days Ben will be here, and we won't see each other for three weeks, and by then you won't remember me as anything other than the guy with the old newspapers. You'll go back to family life, and I'll go back to being an academic vagabond, and occasionally we'll see each other at the school and maybe nod to each other over the punch bowl at the next faculty party. There just doesn't seem to be, ah, any other way this can end, don't you think?"

She looked away for a moment as if searching for an answer somewhere on the table, then smiled and locked on my eyes again. "Maybe. Maybe not. The fact is . . . ." She broke off as if reconsidering what she was going to say. "Well, anyway, what I'd like to do right now, but I know it's impossible, is go with you today. I'd love to be there when you see this place."

I had been disarmed and derailed. I didn't know what to think at that point, other than that I was on the upturn side of the cyclic happiness roller coaster. "You want to come with me?"

"I can't, of course, because I don't have a sitter for Sonya. But otherwise I'd love to." She paused and took another sip. "Maybe, when the spring comes, we can find time to hike together. What do you think?"

When the spring comes. That was months away. This was a long-term plan she was talking about, not some extended one-night stand. "Sure, I'd like that. Where should we go, any ideas?"

"How about the bone barrow? The area is very beautiful—waterfalls and pools and shadowed glades—a great place for a picnic and clandestine swim. You'll see. A perfect place to take a lady."

She said this with such insouciance, such total detachment from the reality of her married life, that at first I thought it was a joke, a simple exaggeration intended to caricature the obvious unlikelihood of it ever happening. But she didn't appear to be joking. She really wanted to do this.

"But . . . how?" I asked. "I mean, you have a family. How are you going to explain to Ben that you've decided to take the day off from him and go on a hike with me?"

She lowered the cup to the table. "Why don't we talk about that tonight, okay?"

"Okay, sure." There it was, a reprieve, a delay, something that would postpone my rendezvous with destiny for half the day. Who knew what could happen in that time? The world might end, aliens might attack, Nazis escaping from a time-bubble might invade Bangor. Almost anything might intervene that would enable me to escape the need to actually make a decision on where I thought this was going.

I was more confused than ever, so I got up the moment the last piece of egg disappeared into my mouth and brought the eating utensils to the sink. When everything was washed, I turned intending to make a feeble gesture of farewell but realized that I hadn't finished my coffee, so I sat back down and fidgeted with the cup.

"In a hurry?" she asked. "It's still early. It can't be later than seven-thirty. What time is it?"

I glanced at my watch. "Twenty after seven." Then, thinking about later in the day, I asked, "When's dinner?"

"A little later than usual, since you'll need some time after you get back. I figure seven o'clock is good. Don't be late, especially if you're bringing the vegetables."

I nodded and gulped a mouthful of coffee, looked up at her, tried to guess what she was thinking, tried to pierce the veil of Isis, as it were, knowing full well the historical warning to mortal men who might attempt that. "No man hath ever me unveiled," it said, and looking at Margaret, I had an inkling why. What was behind those eyes was something as old as life on earth.

"I still wish I could go with you today," she said. "When I went there last summer, we ended up swimming in one of the pools formed by the stream. It was wonderful. Cold, but wonderful."

"Who did you go with?" It was a casual question, but the moment it was out I realized she had probably gone with Nick, the eternal Bohemian. It would be just like him to take her someplace like that, pontificating on the beauties of nature while scheming of nothing more poetic than getting into her pants.

"Oh, it was a group of us. Even Moss was there, as unlikely as that seems. Sil was the one who led us there. If it hadn't been for him, we would never have found it."

So I was wrong. "Sil led you there?"

"Yes. I told you—he knows all the local legends and Native American stories. You really should talk to him for your project." She raised a hand for silence. "I think Sonya's awake. I've got to get back or she might be frightened if she doesn't see me there." She got up, stood by the table for a moment, then stepped toward me.

Isis and her secrets be damned, I thought, as I rose to meet her halfway and she wrapped herself around me just as she had the night before. And I held her as if she had been mine all along, as if it were only some karmic accident that had held us apart all this time, as if we had been waiting for the turning of the earth to catch up with that dot in space-time that would bring us together.

Was any of this real? I wondered, then made a conscious decision to do the Zen thing, to live now and make every moment for the next two days seem like eternity. You never knew when it was going to get up and leave you.

She kissed me and gently pushed herself away. Even I could hear the stirring in her apartment next door and knew that Sonya was awake. "Bye," she said. "Be careful. See you tonight."

And with that, she was gone. I waited a moment, and then could hear a muffled voice from the other side of the wall as she reassured Sonya. Then I collected my things and went back up to my room.

◆ ◆ ◆

The pack felt heavier than I'd imagined it would as I hefted it, but I figured that was because I'd been sedentary for months now that the weather had turned cold. When I pulled it on, it felt fine. I had only one topographical map of the area, relatively large scale—a half inch to a mile—and at the last minute I located my map holder, which I hung around my neck with the transparent window showing the map facing outward. One last inventory pat down and I was out the door and down the steps. It didn't occur to me until I had crossed the lobby that I had just blown through the fish line at the top of the stairs and hadn't felt a thing, just as had happened at the hallway entrance. So the idea would probably work fine as a detection device that did not signal the unwary that they had just been noticed.

I had to get the chain off the door, of course, so I began to untie it, and then suddenly stopped. Something about it looked different, as if the knot had been reversed. I stood there trying to absorb what I was seeing. Had I inadvertently reversed the way I normally do it? I couldn't rule that out, of course, and it seemed the only possible explanation. Margaret would have had no reason to come down a darkened hall and untie the chain. Or maybe I wasn't even seeing it correctly. I looked at it again, untied it, retied it, took a closer look, then did it again.

"Okay," I said aloud, as if explaining myself to some other part of myself. "I had just had a glass of wine on an empty stomach and seen something outside come racing toward the building. Who knows what I did in the dark after that?" So I shrugged it off, untied the chain, and coiled it on the floor in the corner.

105

It was savagely cold outside, so cold that my resolution wavered for a moment, and I momentarily doubted the wisdom of the idea. But I knew that would pass, especially once I was moving. The sun was barely above the treetops, and its lancing rays lit up the entire ice-coated forest around me in a blaze of sparkling white punctuated by the occasional glimpse of a prismatic rainbow. It was spectacular, the ice mantle adding to the haunting beauty for which the area was legendary.

Nevertheless, the doubt remained, and I stood in front of the building for several minutes, one foot propped on the tree limb, while evaluating such unpleasantries as freezing to death somewhere in the ten-plus miles to the bone barrow and back. "Let's see," I mumbled, "Ten miles in the bitter cold or a cup of coffee and a warm sweater? Hmm. Tough choice." Or maybe, I wondered, maybe I was just fighting the notion that I would simply rather be with Margaret. I began to think that I should have gone skating with her and Sonya after all and fleetingly wondered if that was what she was going to do that day.

But it was useless to speculate. I steeled my resolve, strapped on the snowshoes, and headed toward the school. On the way, I glanced at the shed and berated myself for not thinking of trying to start the tractor. If I could get it going, I would be able to drive it probably all the way to the start of the cart track and save myself about two miles of legwork. It was too late for that now, but I decided to try it either later that day or the next.

I went past the parking lot and headed for the spot where I'd seen the bear—or whatever—the night before. The thing had come out from behind the remains of a Greek open-air theater, the largest of the phony "ruins" on the school property. Forlorn looking columns stood there supporting nothing, and off to the right was a row of statues, male and female, mostly nude, mostly beheaded. The remains of a stone wall wrapped around behind them, and it was apparently from there that the thing had emerged. I went over to look.

The tracks were plainly visible as round, dark holes punched through the icy crust on the snow. But they were amorphous, shapeless, partially filled in or eroded away by the granular flurries from the night before. I bent over to take a closer look, but there was simply no way to tell if it had been a bear. They were too obscure. I noted that they led in the direction of the Ropewalk and made a mental note to follow them after I returned from the bone barrow. I was curious to see where they ended up.

I headed up the macadam road that ran like a spur line from the main highway to the school. It wound through a forest hung with vines and creepers, now suspended like frozen threads in the still air. Where it turned to the left, I saw what was supposed to have been the science and engineering building higher up, on a wooded hill among the trees. Funding to develop that part of the project had dried up shortly after the school opened in the fifties, so it had never been completed. Its massive entrance portal and stairway were heavily littered with brush and branches, and it was obvious that even Sil had not been in there for some time. The concrete of the structure had been stained brown, the lower windows long since bricked over. The portal was angular and cyclopean in size, without even the suggestion of a decorative façade. All it said, embossed in the stone lintel, was "Engineering."

I walked on. Soon the embankments defining the road ended, and I found myself walking through a field following the barely noticeable parallel ruts that indicated where the road lay under the snow, which ranged in depth from barely an inch to drifts almost two feet high. Over humps and through ravines I went, until finally I saw a telephone pole and knew I had reached the coast highway. The stone wall that Margaret had mentioned was already visible on the other side. I wondered if I could thumb a ride for the half mile to the start of the trail.

But the coast road had only been plowed once, with only one lane cleared, the southbound side, which meant that even if we got our cars as far as the road, we would not be able to cross the unplowed section to get to the open lane without first clearing a path to it. How odd. Even the plowed lane looked glazed and unused, as if nothing had passed over it since the plow went by. I could not imagine what was taking them so long, but harbored no hope of hitching a ride as I turned right and resumed my hike.

I reached the end of the stone wall about ten minutes later and noted the gap in the trees beyond it that showed where the cart track led. I had taken the snowshoes off in order to walk on the road and had to take a few minutes to strap them back on, which was no small task given how cold my fingers were and how stiff the leather had become. No cars had come by in the time it took me to get there, and none appeared while I was re-securing the snowshoes. I was beginning to feel as if the entire world, not just the school, had left to go somewhere else for the holiday.

The cart track led me across a landscape that was somehow vaguely reminiscent of a college campus I had seen somewhere, and I had this bizarre idea that I had crossed it once before, at some other time, yet when that time was, I could not even guess. Beyond it, the cart track continued through a forest that had grown into a chaotic wild tangle, a stark contrast to the manicure of the campus-like scene that bordered it. Several strands of very old, rusted barbed wire, almost concealed behind the brush and snow, paralleled the track on the left side, the side where the stone wall had been. Evidently, this had been someone's property boundary at some time.

A little further along, the wire formed a border on both sides of the track and rose to a height of almost five feet, effectively prohibiting me from leaving the track even if I wanted to. Still further, the age of the track became apparent as it recessed deeper and deeper into the ground until the dirt walls on each side were themselves nearly five feet high. I'd seen this feature before in other New England dirt roads—worn down from the sheer number of feet and wheels passing over them through the centuries, the surface of the road eventually sat well below the level of the surrounding ground. In this case, a five-foot embankment topped with five feet of barbed wire left me feeling like I was on a controlled-access causeway into a restricted area.

By nine forty-five I had been walking for just short of two hours and figured I had covered at least three miles, which put me about halfway to the stream that Margaret had mentioned as the place where I had to leave the cart track. The track itself had begun to lose its deeply rutted aspect and had risen again to the level of the ground around it. The barbed wire was also gone, or at least hidden under the snow.

At that point, I found myself in deeper snow, the result, no doubt, of the gradual incline I had been ascending since I entered the woods. The snowshoes had become absolutely essential, but as I continued, I noticed that sticks and bits of brush began poking through the surface of the snow with increasing frequency, sometimes snagging the webbing. The track was thinning out, gradually disappearing, just as Margaret had said it would.

At ten-fifteen, I reached the stream. At my usual walking rate, I would have covered about four and a half miles at that point, but I was sure the actual distance was closer to four because of the delays with the snowshoes and obstructions. Margaret was right about the track—it virtually disappeared into the landscape, although there did appear to be some sort of trail that one could follow from that point. I scanned it using a trick I had learned as a kid from one of my "Indian How-To" books: I squinted as I looked at it. The eyelashes would filter out the smaller brush and trivial obstructions and allow you to see if a trail or clearing was present. I had used it many times to find the best way out of dense foliage, which was plentiful in New England. This time I could see that, yes, there was a trail that continued north by northwest and that, unless it changed its bearing, would eventually bring one to the inland highway which, from that point, was only about four miles away.

It was not possible to follow the stream too closely while wearing the snowshoes, so I stayed about twenty feet away while I worked my way through the trees. I was now heading uphill at a steeper rate than before. What I couldn't reconcile with the instructions that Margaret had given me was the fact that the stream appeared to be flowing in the wrong direction. She had said that it was the water source for the village, and that the village was in a valley. But this stream was flowing downhill from an elevation that, from my topographic map, did not hold a valley or depression, and that thus could not possibly be the water source—unless the village lay in the other direction.

I stopped. Was I going the right way? I had foolishly not written down the instructions she had given me because they seemed so simple, but now I had a dilemma: in my mind I had envisioned a right turn at the stream, but had she actually said that, or had I simply interpreted it that way? Maybe she had meant a left turn? I tried to call up the memory of the conversation, but it was too vague; for all I knew, she may simply have said "follow the stream," without indicating which way I should follow it.

I studied the map. It showed the stream flowing out onto a broad, low-lying area that was part swamp. It was unlikely that a village would have been built near a swamp unless, of course, it had not been swampy at that time. On the other hand, Margaret had also said something about the stream flowing over a ledge and forming a waterfall, and that clearly was not shown on the downstream side of the map. But the upstream side didn't show it either; it indicated that the stream joined with another stream somewhere on the slope, but did not show a ledge. But then, the contour intervals on the map were thirty feet, which meant that unless the ledge was especially high, it would only show up as a single line on the map. Or would not show up at all if the waterfall was less than thirty feet high.

But the land was too flat on the downstream side for any kind of ledge, so it had to be upstream. Also, I noted with some conviction, there would be a natural inclination for anyone following the stream to go downstream into the lowland where the foliage was much less dense and the walking would be a lot easier. This would explain why the village remained largely unknown, and why Sil would have had to lead them there. I could see that the trees became closer and denser as the slope got higher, adding a forbidding aspect to a hike in that direction. I pushed on upstream.

After about half a mile, I came to the intersection with the other stream. Margaret had made no mention of this second stream, but such omissions were not unusual for someone unfamiliar with an area, especially since she'd only been there once. She probably remembered it simply as following a stream that led to the village. This, however, was bigger than the one I had followed, and I now saw that the first stream was only a branch of this larger body.

There was no point in going any further uphill—this stream raced downhill into a dense wall of fir trees, and even from where I was standing, I could hear the faint roar of a waterfall. That had to be it. I crossed over a frozen section of the stream I had been following and began slugging my way through the brush.

This was New England jungle at its worst. The forest was so thick that in places I could not even move through it and had to find detours. Several times I had to remove my snowshoes to "cannonball" through. Although it was not of Indian origin, this, like the squinting, was a technique I had also learned as a kid. The idea was to leap at the foliage with all your weight, at the last second turning around in the air so that you blew through it ass first. It didn't always work; sometimes you'd end up caught in the brush like an insect in a spider web. And sometimes, when it did work, you would end up on your ass anyway from your own momentum.

When I came to another blockage, I took the snowshoes off, stepped back a few steps, and launched myself at the obstruction. I blew through it and tumbled backwards out of control, finding myself speeding along on my back in a deep rut in the forest, like a small chasm or a bobsled track for skiers. Landscapes flitted past like the uncoordinated attempts at primitive movies, stiff and unsynchronized.

When it bottomed out, I slammed against a mound and lost my grip on a snowshoe, watching it shoot over the crusted snow and into the trees like an arrow. I wasn't hurt, which was fortunate given the circumstances. I got up, did an inventory pat down, found the errant snowshoe and put them back on, then continued. In my efforts to get through the brush, I realized I had wandered some distance from the stream, but the thunder of the waterfall, which I could not yet see, left no doubt that I was in the right place. Eventually I spotted an opening in the trees and came to what resembled a long, broad staircase of stone partially covered with frozen mud and ice. I'd seen these formations before—the land had been ripped open by the glaciers during the Ice Age, and these wounds bore mute witness to the violence of that event. I opted not to try to snowshoe down it.

The only way around it appeared to be through a stand of very large fir trees that had completely choked a small valley or depression in the land. It would be slow going, I knew, but I had to follow the sound of the waterfall to get to the village. I stood in front of the impenetrable wall of trees and squinted, looking for an opening. And I saw one. There, between two enormous cedars, was a cave-like path that I could use. I approached and saw that, due to the closeness of the trees, the snow was not very deep, so I removed the snowshoes and headed into the gloom. It was so tight I had to duck my head to enter.

But I only took a few steps and stopped dead, scarcely believing what was before me. For the forest had suddenly vanished, and I found myself standing in somebody's living room, the lady of the house frozen in mute surprise as I fumbled for an excuse.

♦ ♦ ♦

Chapter 11

Even knowing that the village had to be someplace nearby did not prepare me for this. I looked over at the lady of the house standing in the far corner near a doorway and was so stunned, so caught off guard, that my first instinct was to excuse myself and back out. I started to apologize when, with a closer look, it all came together. It was a derelict house, completely hidden by the forest that had grown up around it, its door oddly framed and totally hidden by the two enormous cedar trees that, for all I knew, might have been planted there by the original owners. The "lady" standing in the corner was nothing more than one of those dressmaker forms, still hung with the tattered remnants of the last piece being fitted. Decaying or broken furniture, some of it quite ornate, still stood where the last owners had left it. To my left, near the large fireplace, stood a display case that still had its glass intact. Inside, I could see that the family china was still in there.

I stood there unable to assimilate the sudden new surroundings, unable to make the leap from impenetrable forest to domestic enclosure. It was like something out of the "Twilight Zone," and I had a creepy feeling that Rod Serling would appear from some hidden panel and solemnly explain my pending fate to an unseen audience. When that didn't happen, I cautiously stepped forward into the room.

It was gloomy in there, which I realized was part of the reason the dressmaker's model seemed so real to me when I saw it. There were windows, of course, some of them still shuttered against the winter winds, although the shutters themselves were half rotted away. What really surprised me was that the old glass was still intact. I saw only one broken pane and a small drift of snow on the floor below it. Evidently, the dense forest around it had protected it, had held it in the palm of its hand, as it were, and had gradually closed it off from both the bleaching effects of sunlight and the withering effects of wintry blasts. The floor appeared to be rotting in places, and I realized that trying to cross to the other side could have dire consequences even if I avoided the obvious weak spots. Yet I couldn't resist. There was a door to my left that looked like some kind of closet, so I moved back to the wall, where the floorboards would be the strongest, and stepped over to it.

It had a latch rather than a knob. Lift latches preceded knobs, so this was significant because it meant the house was probably older than the nineteenth century. It was of hand wrought iron, rusty but complete. I gave it a tug but it didn't move. I hadn't thought to bring any kind of hammering instrument with me, like a hatchet, so the only thing I could do was tap it with the butt of my .380. After a couple of raps, it broke free. The door itself was partly frozen in place—either literally frozen from the cold or figuratively from long disuse. In any case, I was afraid I was going to break it and was suddenly overcome with a feeling of violation—this place had obviously not been disturbed for nearly two centuries, then along comes a clod like me who proceeds to break down the first door he can reach. I found myself fighting the feeling that I shouldn't even be there.

As luck would have it, the door opened. The hinges snapped and squeaked, protesting every inch of entry that I forced upon them, but they yielded. It was indeed a closet, and full of clothes—moth-eaten, decaying, threadbare, but still recognizable as clothes. I saw the arm of a coat rustle, then move, as if animated from within. A moment later the head of a squirrel appeared and, seeing me, the animal shot out like an arrow and disappeared into the ceiling. It was too dark to see anything, so I got out my flashlight. In the ceiling above a shelf was a small square opening, like the access to an attic. It had obviously been paneled at one time, but the cover was partly rotted or eaten away. The squirrel had gone through there. It seemed like an odd feature to include in a house, this access to what I supposed was the floor above. What was the point of getting there through a closet?

I stepped back and closed the door. Look at this place, I thought. It was an historian's nirvana. It was an impossibility, yet here it was, an untouched un-museum, a postcard frozen in time in a way that none of us had ever hoped to find. I could not—could *not*—simply walk out without seeing what else was in there.

I glanced at my watch. It was noon. Estimating the time I'd spent finding a way through the brush and now in the house, I figured I arrived at the junction of the two streams around eleven-thirty. That meant it had taken me roughly three and three-quarter hours, which, under normal walking conditions, translated into just over seven miles. But these conditions were far from normal, and, what with the delays from the brush itself and the constant detouring, I figured that my usual two-miles-per-hour rate had probably dwindled to one and a half. That translated to roughly five and a half miles, which was very close to Margaret's five-mile estimate. But that meant it was three and a half miles to the coast highway from the juncture of the two streams. The sun would begin setting around four o'clock, which meant that I had to be back at the two streams by two or two-thirty if I expected to clear the woods by sundown. That was not a lot of time.

I was not feeling particularly hungry but knew that I had to get food into me for the difference it would make in the long run, so I ate the two cereal bars and started in on the jerky. The banana I would save for dessert. I decided the safest way to cross the floor was on snowshoes—after all, if they could bear me up on snow they could also bridge my weight across floor joists. So I put them on and, as absurd as it looked, headed across the floor staying as close to the outer wall as I could. My destination was the door where the dressmaker's model stood.

When I got there, I saw that it led into a short hallway. Straight ahead was another room, possibly a second sitting room. To the right it expanded into a formal hallway that ended in another door, which I assumed was the formal front door. An ornate chandelier of what appeared to be brass lay in the middle of the floor, having fallen from the ceiling, still almost entirely untarnished. "Quid aere perennius?" I mused. What is more lasting than brass?

To the left was the staircase to the upper floor. It was dark, but I could see streaks of light at the top. As was the case with most of those old staircases, the steps were narrow and very steep, as if the builders could not get the image of a ladder out of their minds. I would start my "tour" there. I wanted to be out of the house by twelve-thirty so that I could see the rest of the village and find the bone barrow. That was, after all, the reason why I had come.

I had to take the snowshoes off and while I was doing that, I decided that the best way, the safest way, to do this was to plant my feet as close to the walls as possible, thus in effect straddling the staircase. I did this, cautiously advancing one step at a time and testing each one for strength.

The stairs began to arch at the top, becoming more and more vertical as I reached the floor above and making my straddle-climb more difficult. Oddly, the ceiling level was low at that point, necessitating a head ducking as I pulled myself out of the stairwell and onto the floor. It was obviously a design flaw; it almost appeared as if the builders had added the staircase as an afterthought and had miscalculated both the angle of the steps and the placement of the frame. Directly ahead of me, not two steps away, was the central hearth that had heated the house. This layout forced me to turn right the moment I reached the upper landing, and I noted with the surety of foreknowledge that the floor at that point had been worn down to a hollow from the thousands of passing feet that had preceded mine. I strapped the snowshoes back on before I stepped out into the room.

I noticed then that the house was enormous. Before me lay what seemed to be one large room with a balcony of sorts around its perimeter serving as a sort of second floor. The ornate carving on the balcony and the wall paneling itself was evidence of an opulence long since faded from that part of New England. Whoever had built it must have had a rather large family and must have been wealthy. What the intent was behind the balcony, what its function was, I could not even guess. Other than a large wooden box against one of the walls, it had no furniture at all. The windows all appeared to be intact, and the only sign of damage was a break high up on one wall where a tree limb had partially grown through the building. Overall, the house was large, ornate, in remarkably good shape, and totally inexplicable.

I went over and opened the box. Inside were the remnants of what appeared to have been more clothing, or maybe blankets. It was all so decayed it was not possible to actually identify what I was looking at other than as very old cloth. An object at one end caught my eye, and when I attempted to pull it out from under a fold, it simply crumbled to dust in my hand. But part of it remained intact—the head. It had been a doll. I realized then that this had been a child's room or a playroom for children. That explained the lack of furniture, but the sheer size of it made me wonder about the number of children—and the monetary resources—needed to provide a playroom that large. One of the walls seemed to be badly scarred, as if ruffians had played there or were still playing there, escapees from a previous century time-warped into this one.

There was not much more to see in there, so I headed back toward the stairs. The hearth, a huge column of stones and bricks that took up the entire center of the house and provided fireplaces in every room, looked to still be relatively sturdy. The fireplace was enormous, as indeed it would have to have been in order to heat so large a room. Seeing the hearth reminded me of the opening in the closet ceiling on the first floor, and I was curious to see where it emerged on this floor. I figured it would have to come out on the right side of the hearth, maybe through a panel in the wall. But close examination of the wall did not reveal any kind of opening or concealed door, so I was forced to conclude that, wherever it led, it was not to the second floor. Evidently, the only way I was going to satisfy my curiosity on that score would be to climb up there through the closet and see where it ended up. I was consumed with curiosity but not foolish enough to try such a thing while alone. "No good," I mumbled with a shake of my head, fully mindful of the danger of getting caught somewhere or being injured. The freezing-to-death scenario was still a very real possibility.

But I had begun to suspect that the house may have been one of those way stations on the Underground Railroad for runaway slaves prior to the Civil War. Such houses always had hidden rooms cleverly concealed where the authorities would never find a fugitive. Either that or the closet crawlway led to a family hiding place, someplace to run to when danger threatened. With that thought in mind, I looked up at the balcony again. All along its length were what appeared to be small, paneled windows. Looking at them I suddenly understood—they were gun ports. The "playroom" became the vantage point for defending the house when under attack, which would have been a constant threat throughout the seventeen hundreds. The New England colonists fought with the Abenakis right up through the end of the French and Indian War.

These people would have had to defend themselves. The second-story balcony gave them the advantage of being able to see them coming from a long way off.

I headed back to the stairs, removed the snowshoes, and started back down. One thing had become clear: I needed to come back with a camera. This *had* to be preserved on film. It had remained largely untouched by the hand of time for at least two centuries, but who knew how much longer it would hold itself together? The other thing that bothered me was the realization that sooner or later someone else would find this place and plunder it. It was full of things—antique dishes, some furniture still in sellable condition, even wall panels and floorboards of a width no longer possible to obtain, in some places as much as two feet wide. I knew how those parasites worked; once discovered, it would vanish in no time. Two centuries of undisturbed solitude would end up in an antique store or flea market.

The only place left to see was the cellar. Given the layout of the staircase, I assumed that its door would be in the second sitting room, opposite the first. This room, too, still had furniture in it and even a badly decayed rug in front of its fireplace. The mantle held several upright dishes, including drinking noggins. A large desk, partially rotted on one corner, stood against one wall. A door on the far side of the hearth, opposite the closet in the other room, was what I took to be the cellar.

It, like the closet door, took some encouraging to get it open. But it was indeed the cellar. A gaping black hole stared back at me as I stood there fumbling for my flashlight. When I shined it down there, I saw that the steps were only partially intact, and those that were looked very questionable. It was fieldstone with a dirt floor. I figured there were probably several root cellars and storage bins down there as well, but I could not see anything beyond the stairs and part of the wall. It was way too risky to consider attempting to go down there. That, too, would have to wait.

I decided to go out through what I had taken to be the formal front door. It was twelve thirty-five. As I went past the fallen chandelier, I realized I needed to return with a second person before I could consider exploring the hidden passage and the basement. But who would that be? Certainly there was no one at the school whom I could trust with such a find. I could imagine what Moss Breitlinger would do if he knew about it. Then it hit me—according to Margaret, Moss *had* been at the village. So had a number of others, but none of them apparently knew of this house. Certainly Margaret had not said anything about it, yet it was such a novelty that anyone who had been in it would most likely have mentioned it. That meant only one thing—for some reason they hadn't seen it.

The door had a massive cast iron lock that, fortunately, was not locked. It opened surprisingly easily, and as I exited, I imagined spirits long past looking up with a start as the first person in two hundred-plus years walked out into what must have, at one time, been the garden.

It was immediately obvious how the house had remained undetected by the other hikers. The forest on that side was as dense and impenetrable as it was on the other side. So dense, in fact, that I saw no easy way through it, even though I could hear the waterfall somewhere on the other side of the wall of trees. Since they were evergreens, they concealed the house all year round, and a casual visitor following the stream to the waterfall would not notice anything. Nor would that person be inclined to enter the dense wall of trees simply because of the difficulty in walking. So the house, by sheer accident, was both invisible and protected. The fact that I had blundered into it from the other side told me that the infrequent visitors to the village site typically approached from some other point. My deviations and detours must have sent me in a very different direction.

Since I could not detect a path, or even a substantial clearing, I decided that I might as well head for the sound of the waterfall. I had to take the snowshoes off again; the trees were so densely packed that there was virtually no snow at all between them. And it was so dense that I found myself on hands and knees several times trying to clamber between, under, and around the branches. The lack of snow was a good thing, however; I realized that anyone approaching the village from the waterfall side might get curious if he saw tracks emerging from the dense wall of trees and might be tempted to follow them.

When I emerged from the trees I saw two things immediately: a broken mass of bloodstained fur beaten into the muddy snow where some night marauder had snagged its prey, and beyond that an enormous hole. The brush was much thinner at that point and the sound of the waterfall was very loud. I deliberately did a wide detour, hugging the fir trees so that when my tracks appeared in the snow it would not be obvious that I had emerged from the evergreens. Another Indian "How-To" trick. I would never forgive myself if someone found the house because of my carelessness.

The hole turned out to be the village well and was at least five feet across, hand dug and lined with stones. It was still functional—I could see the water at the bottom, some twenty feet down. Oddly, there appeared to be a tube or side tunnel down near the surface of the water. Another hiding place? I wondered. Of course, I could not be sure it was an opening; it may have been nothing more than a patch where the stones had fallen out of the wall.

Within about fifty yards, I saw the ridge. I also saw a line of blank-faced ruins staring down at me, all windows and no doors. It was the village, or part of it. I was surprised to see ruins up on the ridge because I thought Margaret had told me the village was below the ridge in the small valley. Was it possible she had missed these as well, even when they were in such an obvious place, a place where so many had explored so often? Maybe. She had been here in the summer, when the thick foliage would have hidden a lot of things. It was entirely possible that the silhouette of the houses on the ridge was completely invisible. I made tentative plans to go up for a closer look but knew that would not happen that day; there was simply not enough time.

The ruins appeared to extend all the way along the ridge as far as I could see. I was watching them as I walked along and thus was taken by surprise by the sudden appearance of another house before me and off to the left. This one, unlike the one I'd just left, was a total wreck. A huge maple had grown in front of it and the whole structure seemed to be leaning against it, as if the tree were the only thing holding it up. It had a double front door, both of which were open, and none of the vacant windows had so much as a pane of glass left. It was big, like the other house, and this one had two hearths whose chimneys were still intact and poking through the stippled roof like a pair of giant thumbs. But it was obviously ready to collapse. A good place to stay away from. Behind it, also badly leaning and strangely distorted as a result, was a shed or small barn. I could see that it was full of either debris or nameless articles of unknown purpose long since rusted and rotted and being reclaimed by the earth.

Then I went on past the whitewashed stones of an ancient cemetery, noteworthy for its opulence. This had obviously been a place of means.

The stream ran behind it, its banks replaced by man-made stone walls that encased it in granite. And beyond those stones stood a line of large houses, all multi-level, all imposing in stature. Some were in better shape than others, and I fantasized about what it would take to save one, about buying it and moving it, rebuilding it, and living in it. They were garish, huge, pot-bellied money pits that would suck the soul out of whoever had them, yet I still wanted one, well nigh impossible as that was. Further along, one such house stood alone—a bizarre, squarish-looking structure, four stories high, crowned with a cupola. Each story looked like it was only one room, growing progressively smaller as the thing rose. It was dilapidated but not ready to collapse like the other house.

Not far from that unusual house, whose huge windows dominated its sides like open mouths or blank, staring eye sockets, was its carriage house. It was half buried in the hillside but its door gaped open, and inside I saw holes in the walls and glassless windows. I could see that there were things scattered about inside, but it was too dark to make out what they were. I assumed they were artifacts related to horses and carriages, but I didn't stop to investigate.

I went on past. Huge cemetery stones in unusual shapes—eagles with outstretched wings, for instance—loomed to the right. Further along was the burial ground for the poorer folk, marked by small, amorphous stones with scarcely any ornamentation at all.

Margaret had said that the bone barrow was beyond the village and near a swamp that was formed by part of the stream. Unfortunately, she had not mentioned how far beyond the village. It was one o'clock by this time, and I had to be back at the intersection of the two streams by two-thirty at the latest. Since I didn't know how long it would take to get there from the village, I had set myself a two o'clock limit. At two, regardless of how far along I was, I had to leave and get back to the juncture of the streams. I picked up my pace as I followed the stream out to what must inevitably become a pond or low-lying area.

I followed what appeared to be a path that led me over small bridges that were usually nothing more than logs laid across the struts from the original structures. This path led me ever downward between yet more dilapidated buildings, as if the entire place were a maze game and I were the little marble that had to find its way out. I finally arrived at a man-made stone enclosure—very deep, square, with various chambers in it, and open on top. On one wall was a large opening, and since the stream flowed into it, I surmised it was a dam—water running off from the opening was no doubt used to turn a waterwheel and provide motive power. Sure enough, nearby were the remains of a sawmill, its sawing frame and cutting bed still visible despite the collapse of the timbers around it. The waterwheel itself was gone.

Beyond it was a pond bordered by swamp, and on the far side of that, situated on a peninsula, was a low dome-shaped hill. The bone barrow. She was right—it was almost perfectly shaped like a dome. It was also further away than I thought it would be, maybe another quarter mile. That was eight minutes of walking as the crow flies, which meant heading straight out across the frozen pond. Skirting the perimeter would take longer. It was one-twenty. Getting to it across the pond would bring me to one-thirty. But I was also now outside the village and figured I had to add fifteen minutes to the time needed to return to the streams, meaning that I would have to start heading out at one-forty-five. There was no choice—I had to cross the ice to get to it. Following the perimeter wouldn't work; I would get to it and immediately have to turn around and leave.

The ice looked sturdy enough to hold me, especially since I would be crossing on snowshoes. I took a couple of tentative steps, then struck out for the barrow. I had progressed about fifty yards when I heard the first ominous crack that told me all was not well. I froze. I could see bubbles under the ice and, to my right, reeds and grasses frozen fast in the surface. But beyond these, near the shore, I noted the appearance of a wet spot. This was not a good idea. Evidently, part of the ice was rotten, probably from an underground spring. Slowly, taking small steps to keep my weight distributed, I turned and headed for the shore.

A loud report, almost like a gunshot, erupted from the surface and I froze again, frantically searching for signs of the crack. It was like walking on a tightrope, except it was not obvious which was the right way to go, however narrow that right way may have been. I shook my head at the irony of my situation—I had had sense enough to not explore secret passages and dank cellars, only to commit to the foolhardy crossing of what was sure to be a much greater danger. What a prosaic way to end. Hardly a death worthy of an adventurer.

Out. I had to move, to risk taking a step. I thought of lying down to spread my weight out but feared the ice would break just in the effort of applying my weight to a single point like a hand or knee. No, I had to move.

I took one sliding step, then another. Nothing happened. Several more steps and I heard another crack, except this time I could see it as well, a silver line in the ice running from under my feet out into the pond. I was only about twenty yards from the shore—surely, I could run that distance and reach safety before anything let go. I had to chance it.

I had never been a distance runner, but sprinting had always been my thing. Even with winter clothes, a pack, and snowshoes, I figured I had more of a chance than standing out there waiting for fate to deal me the joker. Very slowly, I slid my left leg forward, crouched, inhaled, and took off.

The effect was almost instantaneous. Another loud report burst from the ice and I felt the surface tilt slightly towards the rear. Water began to wash up, and I knew what was happening—that entire part of the surface was separating and becoming an ice floe, except it was not strong enough to support me. My own weight was making it sink. I felt panic seize me and pump new energy into my legs even as the floe began to pitch and water washed over the snowshoes. In one last desperate and awkward jump, I pushed off on one leg, forcing the ice below the surface of the water while I landed on a frozen tangle of sticks with the other leg. I was not yet on the shore, but it was only a few feet away and I was able to walk across the frozen tangle using the snowshoes as temporary bridges. I looked back at the pond in time to see the ice reappear, slough the water off its flanks, and settle into a barely perceptible drift. Then I moved away from the edge of the pond and took a moment to let my heartbeat go back to normal.

I had been fast enough with the jump so that my feet were not wet. But it was now one-forty, five minutes before the turnaround time. I would have been better off following the shoreline, even if it meant turning around the moment I got there. At least I would have gotten there. Now the best I could do was examine it with my binoculars.

There wasn't much to see. It was on a peninsula, which I already knew, and seemed to be accessible only from one point on the land. I assumed that it could be reached by boat or canoe from the pond side, but there was no way to be sure. If this was indeed the barrow mentioned in the old diary, it was easy to see how the militia were able to trap the "savages" in a declivity—if they attacked the Indians from the ridge and the plain, they would have had their backs to the water and no way to retreat. As for hiding in holes in the barrow, I would have to come back to understand what that meant.

It was time to go. Despite the fact that I hadn't reached the barrow, it had still been a phenomenal day. I would need to come back once I returned from the holiday. And I would need to bring someone with me, someone whom I could trust. And, of course, I knew even then that it would be Margaret, could only be Margaret.

It occurred to me when I thought of her that, despite hearing it in the woods, I had not yet seen the waterfall or any of the pools that she had told me about. This was because the wide detours I had taken to get into the village had led me away from the stream. But there had to be a better way in and out than the route I had taken. I had *slid* down the ridge, for Christ's sake. If it hadn't been for that natural shoehorn I fell into and the soft hummock at the bottom, I might be lying there now with a broken back, waiting for the frost giants to claim me. But if Margaret had gone past the stream getting into the village, there had to be a path—or something—paralleling the stream. I had no desire to go back the way I had come, so I followed the stream out of the village and up toward the ridge.

Once I got past the houses in the valley, the scenery changed. I found myself on a steep slope overlooking a wild scene of chasms and pinnacle-like outcroppings with the stream raging and frothing in between. I continued upward and eventually came upon a rocky woodland enclosure hemmed in by heavy fir branches and natural stone walls. In it, the stream had formed a flume-like spout in the face of a granite outcropping—water brimming over the edge of a pool had, through the eons, sculpted a sluice. Below it was a stone basin filling with water from the stream above it. The basin itself was on a ledge, and at its lip the stone had been worn to resemble a pour-spout from which the stream flowed over and down in a spectacular waterfall. Looking down, I saw a round pool, mostly iced over but a natural swimming area, surrounded by sloping ramps of rock that would allow one to enter the water gradually. To one side of the waterfall was a second, smaller fall that was a natural shower and that had probably been used as such by occasional hikers, and maybe even by the original villagers.

I was stunned by the natural beauty of the place. Margaret had been right—it was a perfect place to take a lady. I stood there taking it in and letting the rushing melody of the water reach into a place far inside of me, where my immovable memories dwelled, where Mae, my first wife, the elfmaid of my fantasies, still reached for me the way she had when we first met. It had been a similar setting, but on a lake, not a stream, a place in Vermont that everyone called "the ledges," a hangout for die-hard skinny-dippers and assorted sun worshippers. I had been hiking along the edge of the lake, oblivious to the existence of this enclave of subterraneans, when suddenly an improbable vision stepped out from behind a large rock, a beautiful girl with long, strawberry-blond hair fluttering in the breeze, nude and smiling as if she had been waiting for me, beckoning me with a look that said, yes, it's me, and won't you come for a swim? I could not even remember at that point how it had transpired, but I put my arm around her and she did the same to me as we sauntered off. Next thing I knew, I was swimming with her, and she showed me how she would push off a nearby overhang and onto a smooth ramp of white granite, oddly polished as if by design, and she would land in this sluice and slide down into the water. This she did several times. She loved it. When I tried it, with some reluctance, fearing a landing on the wrong part of my anatomy, she laughed and clapped. When I asked her name she said, "Moonbeam."

The name fit her perfectly, perhaps because she seemed so ethereal. And she had asked my name and I said "Egan," and she replied that that would never do, that my name had to reflect some essential me-ness, so she called me "Roadbeam," having sensed even then the impermanence that was part of me, that need to keep moving. And then we had embraced and kissed—she was a wonderful kisser—and she laughed and changed my name to "Highbeam" when she saw the effect she was having on me.

This fantasy of Mae became so real and intense that for a moment I felt as if I had actually gone back in time, or that she was actually there and I could see her. The icebound world had vanished for a single heartbeat, and in its place I could actually feel the warm breath of a late summer breeze and see her there in the pool, under the "shower," and in my mind I saw her saying again what she had said to me then, that if I didn't swim with her I'd be frustrated all day.

How right she had been.

A cold gust of wind stinging my face with needles of ice brought me back to reality. I looked at my watch—it was already two o'clock and I had no idea how far it was to the juncture of the two streams. The sun was still two hands high—the width of one hand represented about an hour of sunlight, another old Indian trick—so I knew I still had a large safety margin. Regretfully, I let the memory of Mae drift back into that immovable place and headed upstream once again.

I arrived at the juncture of the other stream around two-fifteen, but then had a new dilemma. I was now on the wrong side of the stream. This stream was bigger than the little one I'd followed to get to the village and its current much swifter, meaning that it was not completely frozen over at any one point. I didn't want to risk a crossing on slippery rocks, so I went further upstream and eventually found a tree that had fallen across the water. I guessed that this had probably been the way that Margaret and the others had crossed the previous summer. If I had found this on the way in, I would have entered the village by a completely different route and never discovered the house full of furniture. I would only have needed to go a few yards upstream to have changed the entire course of the day. "Destiny logic," I whispered, borrowing a phrase from "Decline of the West." The unavoidable polarity of circumstance and causality and that primitive, indwelling sense that one's life is somehow directed and not the result of random acts borne of random decisions. If I go back far enough, I mused, I would have to concede that I had learned to cannonball through the brush as a kid so that many years later I could find that house.

It was exactly two-thirty when I headed downstream back to the cart track that would take me out to the coast highway. It was at least an hour's walk to the intersection, but that would still leave me about a half hour of sunlight when I got there. Once I was on the track, I would consider myself "out of the woods" regardless of how dark it got because I could follow it even in the twilight. The main consideration for me was to not be caught in the woods when the sun went down, which could be a very unnerving experience.

Even having a map and compass was no consolation to someone caught in the gloom of the forest, the sun setting and the first deepening strokes of the darkness that would consume everything falling around him. At such times one could feel the ancient mystery of the forest, could sense the underlying reality of the old life that it kept hidden.

One could almost hear its whispers, see its long-dead spirits, and touch a small part of that life-chain immortality of which every tree and shrub was a part. One was suddenly immersed in the old life, the old world, that husk that humanity sloughed off eons ago when we sacrificed instinct to reason and paid the price in eternal estrangement from the earth. But the memory was still in there, and one only needed to be lost in a forest at sundown to know how close at hand that world still is.

The light was pale yellow, the shadows long and interwoven when I arrived at the cart track. The sun was only one finger high, indicating fifteen minutes to sundown. But I was on the track. It was about an hour and a half to the campus-like clearing and only a few minutes more to the coast highway. Maybe I'd get lucky on the way back and get a ride down to the macadam road that went to the Ropewalk.

It started to get very cold when the sun went down, and I realized for the first time how sweaty and tired I had become from my exertions. I had no trouble following the track, but by the time I reached the highway, I could feel that I was getting close to shivering and dared not stop. There was no real danger; if necessary I could wrap myself in my space blanket, but I really didn't want to look like Doctor Zhivago escaping from the partisans in the middle of winter. It was more fashion than survival that was at stake. After all, someone might drive by and take me for something other than human. Next thing you know I'd be the source of another Bigfoot legend.

It was now five-thirty and painfully obvious that no cars had come by in the time I had been in the woods. I knew this because I recognized several shallow drifts across the road that I'd seen on the way in. They were still fully intact. For whatever reason, no vehicles were traveling south on the coast highway that day. That seemed odd but that part of the highway was a long, empty stretch and the tourist season was definitely over, so I suspected that maybe most people had already gotten to wherever they were going, what with the holiday right around the corner. I took the snowshoes off and began the half-mile trek to the macadam road that led to the Ropewalk.

The moon had already risen and, being nearly full, it illuminated the snowfields with an almost daylight glow. Because of this, I was able to see very far ahead, and as I walked along I suddenly saw a large animal with long, gangly legs loping across the road about a hundred yards ahead of me. I stopped when I saw it, and at almost the same moment, it stopped and looked back at me. Even at that distance, I could see the yellow illumination from a pair of eyes in a large, triangular head. It took a moment before I realized what it was—I at first took it to be a large dog but, in fact, it was a wolf. Despite the recent efforts to romanticize them, I knew from stories written by people who had lived in the far north that these creatures, though legendary for their caution and cunning, would indeed stalk a human if hungry enough and the circumstances were right. Fat chance, I thought, but just to hedge my bet I pulled my .380 out of its holster and chambered a round. A .380 was not much of a hitter against a brute like that, but it was still a country mile ahead of one's bare hands. I lowered the hammer to the half-cock safety position but kept the weapon in my hand; if an attack did come, it would be lightening fast and there would be no time to do anything except cock the hammer.

The animal watched me for several seconds and then continued its loping gait across the road and into the woods. This made me a little nervous because it was obviously headed for the same general area of the Ropewalk—the macadam road was only about a hundred yards beyond where it had stopped. If it stayed straight, it would come out somewhere near the school.

Only then did the obvious become apparent. *This* was the thing I had seen the night before, running toward the Ropewalk. *This* was the thing drawn to the odors from Margaret's kitchen, and now that it knew there was a potential food source there, it was planning on coming back. Maybe it lived somewhere in the woods around the school. It had come out from behind that reproduction Greek open-air theater, so maybe it had a lair someplace nearby. The theater was at the farthest limit of the lawn maintained by Sil during the summer; right behind it was the forest. I hadn't thought about following the tracks *away* from the Ropewalk to see where the thing had come from, but now that I had put it together, I figured that should be on the agenda for tomorrow.

The last mile down the road to the Ropewalk seemed to take forever. Not only was I exhausted physically, but now I had to be extra vigilant because of the wolf, which added another drain to my already depleted energy reserves. I had no doubt the thing was watching me, maybe even following me; after all, I was now an intruder in its world. Knowing that they did not typically attack humans was not much of a consolation when walking through a darkened forest in the dead of winter. It was like being lost at sundown, except the secret life of the forest had become all too real—I felt as if I were about to get my own personal introduction into Jack London's "law of club and fang." As I became more tired, the fantastic images became sharper until, when I entered the stretch of road overhung with vines and creepers, I imagined the thing bursting from the brush and coming at me like a torpedo, all fangs, fur, and momentum. I cocked the hammer on the .380, getting it ready for instant use; my hands were so cold that it occurred to me they might not work in an emergency.

"This place gives me the willies," I mumbled with a smile. It was something Rick had said when, as kids, we first found the stream in the woods, the one we used to skate on. We had found it at sundown by following a small, shallow chasm in a rock ledge. On the other side was the stream, as lovely and pristine as anything I'd seen since. But it was dusk. Bats had begun darting through the darkening sky and the rustling of the night creatures in the woods set us on edge. "Let's get out of here," he had said. "This place gives me the willies at night." We were kids—the willies were everywhere.

But they were nothing compared to knowing you were being followed by a wolf.

I knew the vines and creepers meant that I was getting near the school, and it was with no small relief that I saw it silhouetted in its vast yard with the Ropewalk off to the right. There were two lights that illuminated the parking lot, and these two beacons were the only points shining from an otherwise moonlit emptiness framed on two flanks by the forest and on the third by the ocean. I zeroed in on them as I moved forward.

Suddenly the brush to my left exploded and a hulking shape launched itself onto the road in front of me. The .380 came up of its own volition and I saw the hurtling shape slip, then regain its feet and bound forward. I tried to shoot but it happened as if in a dream—my hand was shaking, lifeless, so cold it wouldn't work, so cold I could not get my finger into the trigger guard, so lifeless I could not aim the weapon. I stood there in a defensive half crouch pointing the useless gun while the hurtling shadow snorted and bounded past, cleared the road in a single jump, and crashed into the brush on the other side. A moment later, it had already vanished.

It was a deer. I stood there still pointing the gun, still unable to get my finger into the trigger guard, marveling at my failure to respond to the one thing I had been expecting the moment I stepped onto the macadam road. If that had been the wolf, I would already be the main course. My heart felt like a sledgehammer in my chest as I slowly got hold of myself.

A deer. No doubt spooked by the wolf, then startled into slipping by finding me blocking his escape route. Why had the wolf not followed? I wondered. Was it, in turn, spooked by my presence in the path of its quarry? Or was it just more interested in me than the deer? Or maybe it just wasn't hungry?

I lowered the .380 and looked at it. My hand was still shaking, and I realized for the first time how hard it was to get my semi-frozen finger into the trigger guard. The gun was virtually useless under these conditions unless I threaded my forefinger into the guard and left it there. I lowered the hammer to half-cock again and did exactly that. At least that way I could cock it with the other hand if I had to. I considered firing a warning shot into the brush where I knew the wolf was skulking, but then rejected the idea because there was a chance that Margaret would hear it and become nervous. I picked up my pace and went on.

When I got to the parking lot, I looked over at the Greek theater but saw nothing. Nor did I have the energy to go over there and pick up the trail from the night before to see where the wolf had gone after approaching the Ropewalk. That would have to wait for morning.

When I reached the door to the Ropewalk, I put the .380 away, removed the snowshoes, and fumbled for my keys. My fingers moved in slow motion as I sorted through them for the one I wanted and then let myself in. I pulled the door shut behind me and made sure it was latched, then wrapped the chain through the handles. It took me a moment to realize how warm it was in there. Even knowing that the hall temperature was barely scraping sixty degrees, it felt like I had entered the tropics. I marveled as I felt life returning into my hands, bringing the dull pain of warming flesh with it. I looked at my watch—it was six-fifteen. Just enough time to get thawed out, cleaned up, and bring my donation of frozen vegetables down to Margaret's apartment.

It was twenty of seven when I knocked on her door. I was apprehensive—the world had not ended, and now I would be forced to confront the bond that was growing between us. I had no idea what I was going to say.

But once again, fate intervened. The door opened and flooded the shadowed hall with a rectangle of light. And Margaret was standing there with a strange look in her eye and a hatchet in her hand.

♦ ♦ ♦

Chapter 12

Stepping up in the full expectation of the warmth and relaxation that I
knew I needed, I was caught completely off guard by her appearance.
I glanced from her face to the hatchet and back to her face, then forced
a smile. "Something I said? Or have you decided to take up serial
killing?"

Her look immediately lightened and she smiled. "Neither. Come in."
She took the frozen vegetables from me and handed me the hatchet.

"Am I expecting a problem of some sort?" I asked as I checked the
edge on the thing.

"Can you cut us a Christmas tree?"

"Now? It's kind of late for that, isn't it? Ben will be coming for you
the day after tomorrow."

She stood there saying nothing.

"He *is* coming for you, right?"

She shook her head.

"He's not coming for you?"

"No, and I hate to be the bearer of bad tidings, but you're not
heading south either."

"I'm not?"

"No. The phones are dead and the television's as good as dead, but
I did pick up some news on the radio. The coast highway is closed, all
the way from Cider Mills to Prescott. All traffic is being directed to

the northern, inland route. Apparently, the storm made road conditions extremely hazardous and caused some accidents that damaged a couple of the bridges. And the repairs may take a while because another storm is headed our way."

It took me a moment to digest this information. From Cider Mills to Prescott—that was an enormous stretch, nearly thirty miles. And since virtually nobody lived on it, there would be no urgency about getting it opened before the holiday. "Well," I said, half thinking aloud, "that explains why I saw that only one lane of the highway had been plowed. It also explains why they didn't bother coming back, and why no one passed by while I was in the woods."

"Did you reach the bone barrow?" she asked as she ushered me into the kitchen. Sonya was sitting on the living room floor looking through another picture book.

I put the hatchet in a corner of the counter. "Margaret," I said.

She turned to look at me.

"Do you realize what it means to have the coast highway closed? We're trapped. Even if we got to the highway by car, we could only go north or south, and from what you just told me, both routes will lead to a dead end."

She turned away from me, put the frozen vegetables in a pan, and added some water. "Don't you think I know that?" she said. "I've been sitting here all afternoon trying to think of a way to tell Sonya she won't be seeing her daddy on Christmas, that she won't be seeing anybody on Christmas." She put it on the stove and turned it on, then turned to me. "Don't you think I've been wrestling with my own panic all day? And you were gone . . ." She turned away again. "You have no idea how worried I was about you."

I finally understood. I stepped up and put my arms around her, felt her tremble and knew she was fighting back tears and that I had to just let her do it. She turned around in my arms, wrapped herself around me, and buried her face in my shoulder. Only a moment, though, and then she raised her head and wiped her eyes, looked over my shoulder to check on Sonya, and apologized.

"For what?" I asked.

"For being so childish about it. I was just so scared. I pictured you not coming back and me helpless to do anything about it, trapped here and scared to death of this huge, empty building, while you froze to death somewhere in the woods. You can't imagine what was going through my head."

I raised her chin and lightly kissed her. "But surely Ben will find some way to come for the two of you, even if only by snowmobile."

She shook her head. "He's not coming."

"But how could you possibly know that?"

She pushed herself away gently and turned to check on the vegetables. "He's not coming. I know he's not coming. This circumstance may be a convenient excuse, but he's been planning this for a long time. He's not coming back, either to me or to the school."

I thought it was just her bitterness talking and was about to say so when she reached into her pocket, pulled out a piece of paper, and handed it to me. It was a small note citing a time, date, and number. It meant nothing to me. "What is it?"

"I found it the day he left to go to his 'conference.' At first I thought it was just a note reminding him of the date and time of the 'conference,' but the more I thought about it, the less sense that made. For one thing, the day he left he told me the event was scheduled to start the next day in Boston. He left on Sunday, the seventeenth, which meant that the start date was the eighteenth. What's the date on the note?"

"The twentieth."

"Two days after it was supposed to start. What do you suppose that other number is referring to?"

I looked down at it. A simple four-digit number, 2411. "I have no idea."

"I didn't at first either. Then it hit me—it's a flight number. The 'conference' must have been at Logan Airport, where his newest lady friend must have been waiting."

A whole constellation of reactions and emotions collided inside of me like a pileup on an icy highway. Part of me wanted to console and reassure her that her interpretation of the note was wrong, that its true meaning would come out when Ben returned, and wouldn't she feel foolish then? Another part was concerned for her and Sonya's safety given the circumstances. Still another part was emotionally charged uncertainty, sensing myself as nothing more than a convenient stopgap in the catastrophe she saw opening before her. And another part, the part I latched onto, into which I poured my own feeble hopes for something more lasting than the academic overtures I pretended to believe in, was happiness. Cautious, disbelieving happiness. Not the destructive happiness of someone reveling in another's misfortune but the happiness of fateful deliverance. I happened to be there when she needed someone; I needed to believe that the rest was real.

"I, ah, guess the only way to know for sure if you're right is to wait to see if he shows up," I said. "But if he were intending to leave you, he would have to take something with him, some clothes at least. I mean, he wouldn't just leave empty-handed."

"His luggage is gone. I only found that out today while you were gone. I'm not talking about a day-bag—his large suitcase and folding bag are gone. It didn't occur to me to check his side of the closet until then. His better suits and jackets are gone. He left the older ones in front of the closet to make it look as if it still had everything in it."

"How did you not discover that the luggage was missing until today?"

"Because it's stored in the shed. When I heard the news about the highway, I went out there with Sonya to see if I could find our Christmas ornaments. We have a cubicle, or stall, on the second floor for storing things."

"I know. I saw it."

"I found the ornaments, but as I was pulling them out it struck me that something was missing. Then I saw that my luggage was still there but his was gone." She lifted the lid on the vegetables and checked to see if they were ready. "I don't think I have to tell you that you don't need that kind of luggage for a simple two-day conference. It all came together for me at that point."

And that clinched it. She was right. He had abandoned her and Sonya, committed the ultimate visceral heresy, leaving his own child to the random winds of chance. I didn't know what to say; if I had had my dialogue flash cards, I would have pulled one out to find a suitable deflection. Instead, I stood there like a totem pole.

She must have seen my discomfort because she turned to face me and, gracious as she was, asked me again, "So, did you see the bone barrow?"

◆ ◆ ◆

The meal was delicious—simple, satisfying, and hot. As I ate, I could feel it flowing through me and slowly bringing me back to life, reaching all the way down to my still half-frozen feet. Only as I settled into the comfort and closeness of the scene did I realize how tired I was. At one point, I actually felt myself nodding off and had to rouse myself, take deep breaths, start the coffee early, anything to get up and keep moving so that I didn't drift into a half-conscious torpor. Sonya sat in her chair as self-occupied as ever, sometimes staring out the one window in the kitchen, sometimes playing with her food. She seemed to have already forgotten the lesson in using a spoon that Margaret had given her just the day before.

When she asked me if I had seen the bone barrow, I told her about seeing the village and not having had time to reach the barrow. I did not tell her about how I had entered the village, about cannonballing down the ridge and finding that house still full of furniture. Some part of me was undecided about whether I wanted to keep that artifact hidden from everyone; it occurred to me that she could casually mention it at a social gathering and set in motion a catastrophic series of events that I would forever regret.

"Did you see the waterfall?" she asked.

"Yes, I did."

"What did you think of it?"

"It was spectacular, just as you said. Great place to take a lady. Did you guys go swimming there when you went on that hike?"

"I did. I couldn't resist. It was so hot and the setting so beautiful that I couldn't just walk on by. I wanted to keep my boots on in case there were turtles in there, but I knew I couldn't hike in wet footwear, so off they came."

Of all the things that can trigger the male mind into running away with itself, the notion of a beautiful lady in a sylvan pool on a hot summer day talking about "off they came" has got to be near the top. We become so mechanically irrational that it doesn't even matter what the "they" is referring to. All we hear is that "they" were on and now "they" are off. There's a whole inventory of fill-in-the-blank items that cover the gaps in that information. We know right up front that she's not talking about her reading glasses. My head, hardwired like the head of every male, short-circuited its micro-switches the moment she uttered the words. Even knowing she was only talking about her boots did not redirect the instinct-signal to another pathway. I needed to hear more, hoping against hope that nobody in her hiking group, and Moss Breitlinger in particular, had seen her swimming nude.

"I knew that everything else would dry out in no time but the boots would stay clammy and slippery," she continued. "Sil led the others down the slope to the village while I took a swim. He said he'd make them have lunch and wait for me. I have to tell you,"—and here she glanced at Sonya—"I had heard of this basin before and had tried to find a way to get there earlier in the summer, but it was impossible. So when I heard that Sil was taking a group up there on a day hike, I jumped at the chance. When I saw the pool, I knew I had to go in. I was tempted"—and here she glanced at Sonya again, as if checking for understanding—"to take everything off and swim in the nude. The place is so hauntingly beautiful that I wanted nothing to come between me and the water."

I took a deep breath, trying to appear nonchalant about it. "And did you?"

"No, I left everything on but the boots. Too risky. Even with Sil taking them down into the hollow, there was a chance one of them would come back to check up on me. With my luck it would have been Moss." She rolled her eyes. "Can you imagine? I'd never hear the end of it—or see the end of him."

I nodded and smiled, strangely relieved. I had this fly-by fantasy of her in the role of Audrey Hepburn in "Green Mansions," the innocent bird-girl, the wood nymphet, unaware that her very unawareness of her irresistible sexuality was turning the collective male libido on its head.

And, of course, I knew what it all meant. I was becoming emotionally involved. "I know what you mean," I said. "I'm a skinny-dipper from way back. That was how I met my first wife."

She smiled and reached over to help Sonya with a spoonful of potatoes. "It was almost like it held some memory for me, the place itself," she said. "I can't describe it, but it somehow felt familiar, as if I had been there before, or had some kind of bond with it." She paused and looked inward for a moment, then glanced at Sonya. "Do you think it's possible that a place can have a memory?"

The suggestion stunned me because that was exactly how I had momentarily felt when I saw that campus-like clearing prior to entering the woods. As if I had been there once before. As if the place itself remembered me.

"Don't look at me that way," she said with a laugh. "I'm not crazy."

"Oh, sorry. Didn't mean to in any way suggest that you were. I was just thinking about your comment because I had a similar impression today while heading into the woods."

"Some kind of place memory?"

"Well, I don't know. There was just a very strong sense of having been there before, or maybe of having seen it before. Maybe it was just so much like some other place that I'd seen that my own memory became confused."

"Could be. But for me it just felt too real to be nothing more than a confused memory. Besides, I've never swum in a pool under a waterfall before. I don't even know of any other such place, so I doubt that it was simply reminding me of something. Did you see the door at the top of the hill?"

"Did I see the what?"

"There's a door at the top of the hill, just sort of standing there. If you leave the stream and go left up the hill, following a sandy path—at least it was sandy at that time—you'll find a door at the top. It looks like it leads to a stairway going into an adjoining structure of some kind. I wanted to check it out on the way back, but Sil was pretty insistent that we shouldn't go there. He all but physically 'urged' us to hurry. Said if we didn't, we wouldn't get out of the woods before the sun went down."

There seemed to be no end to the surprises. "No, I didn't see any kind of door. But I did notice that there was a line of ruins on top of the ridge, which I thought was odd because you hadn't mentioned them to me. Was this a door just standing there in a frame of some sort?"

"I guess so. I really didn't get a good look at it, but I assumed it must have been the entrance to something up there. We never saw any ruins on the ridge, but it all makes sense now. The door must have been connected to those ruins at one time. Evidently the building collapsed around it." She leaned over to help Sonya once again and the little girl, either full or frustrated, pushed the spoon away, stood up, and launched herself off the chair and onto the floor. Her amazing agility was no longer such a novelty to me. Margaret watched her scurry into the living room and back to her picture book.

So for a moment, we were alone with each other, and I sensed that the time had finally come. She must have sensed it as well because she got up to get us some coffee, but the gesture seemed somehow expectant, as if it were part of a script. Without turning to look at me she said, "I'll start the divorce proceedings after the holidays."

I knew that was my cue but I had no flash cards. "I'm sorry," was all I could think of.

"Oh, don't be. It's been a long time coming. In a way, it's almost a relief to finally be getting it over with. And I doubt there'll be any custody battle over Sonya." She brought the coffee pot to the table and poured us both a cup without looking at me. "Kahlua?"

"Sure. Sit down. I'll get it."

She nodded and sat, reached out for the milk, spilled a few drops on the table, and mechanically wiped them away. "Are you going back to try to reach the bone barrow?"

I put the Kahlua on the table and sat down. "Yes. I'm going to have to establish some sort of positive connection between the diary and the barrow, and I need to do that as soon as possible so that I can finally decide on a format for the project. I'd also like to see if there's anything in the diary that connects it to the village itself—a family name, for example, that might also be on one of the gravestones. But first I want to try to get the tractor started so that I can save myself a couple of miles of walking. I'll do that tomorrow, then cut you a Christmas tree."

"You're cordially invited to our tree trimming party. Tomorrow afternoon, starting the moment I get the tree set up in its stand."

"How about if I set it up for you, then just sort of hang around for the party?"

She smiled and nodded. "Deal. Doing anything special on Christmas Eve?" There was a tinge of lighthearted satire in her voice.

"Well, ah, my original holiday plans seem to have fallen through, and it's a little too late to send out invitations for a beer bash in my room, so I'm in the market for a spur-of-the-moment alternative. Any ideas?"

She laughed and reached out to touch my hand. "Well, I know there are all kinds of social events going on around here, and how much in demand you must be, but if you can in any way fit it into your schedule, we would love to have you join us."

"Thanks. I accept. I'll even bring the wine again." I paused for a moment to gather my wits. "Do you think Ben realizes that this is the end of his academic career? He just walked off the job, just quit. That will follow him wherever he goes."

"He hated it anyway. He never wanted to come here and he didn't want to do this—he doesn't like the area, or the idea of being a teacher. He's really a city guy, wants to be around traffic and theaters and have a pub on every corner. He only came here because of me, because I thought that getting him away from the constant party-animal scene would strengthen our marriage."

"And how do you like it here?"

"I love it. A bit lonely at times, but so beautiful, so close to nature."

All this time I had been under the impression that Margaret was the social butterfly, the one who didn't want to be there. Now, here I was, learning that she *wasn't* the one who hated the area and wanted to leave. It was Ben. So the student "informants" who had told me about her had, once again, not been as reliable as I assumed they were.

That staticky silence that betokens awkwardness had begun to fall between us. I was sure she felt it as keenly as I did and undoubtedly for the same reason—apprehension. What before had only been a remote possibility, a passing dalliance whose days were numbered, was now a real probability. Ben was out of the picture. For real. The door was swinging open, but much as I wanted to, I could not bring myself to broach the subject of "us" without feeling my own past creeping back like an assassin with a knife between his teeth. How could I possibly think I could make this work given my track record?

"I'd like you to join us on Christmas day, too," she said. "Of course, if you'd rather be alone . . ."

"No," I said. "No, not at all. I just don't want to impose. I mean, I'm not your family and Sonya doesn't know who I am, and I don't want to somehow ruin it for her." I shrugged. "I guess I just need to be sure in my own mind that it's okay."

"It's okay. I'd very much like it if you were with us. And Sonya won't mind." She looked past me at her daughter in the living room, thinking who knew what thoughts. I turned and followed her gaze and saw the little girl moving her mouth once again, as if reading the words. "You can consider yourself an honorary member of the family," she said.

"Oh, wow," I replied, comically exaggerating the significance of the event. "Does that come with some sort of written confirmation?"

"What do you want, a 'Certificate of Induction into the Family'? How about a small note to paste on the back of your social security card?"

"Do I get a decoder ring, too?"

She narrowed her eyes at me. "Smart ass."

We smiled at each other and then, sensing that it was now alright, I went over to her, took her hand, and knelt down beside her. She turned to me, and although I could see her fear and uncertainty, she reached for me and I for her and we kissed and she stroked my hair and whispered, "Just don't ever leave me." And since I knew as much as anyone about being left, I said, no, I wouldn't, and could scarcely believe what fortune had delivered to me, to *me*, the social pinball bouncing from fate to fate and place to place looking for a loophole to escape through. So we kissed again, deeply this time, and I searched for words but nothing came, and I held her until I looked up and saw Sonya watching us. When I suddenly pulled away, Margaret questioned me with a look and I nodded in the girl's direction.

"Sonya, honey," she said, "Would you like some cookies?"

The little girl simply stared at us as if she hadn't heard the question. "Sonya? Mommy asked if you would like some cookies." I casually let my arms slip away from around Margaret and moved away. When I stood up Sonya's eyes followed me, then darted back to her mother. My God, I thought, she understands perfectly that someone other than her father was holding and kissing her mother. She knows something is wrong.

"Sonya?"

I leaned over and whispered to Margaret, "She knows something is wrong."

"Oh, I don't think so. Her comprehension skills . . ."

"She knows," I repeated. "She was watching me as I moved away." Even though her look had lasted for only a moment, I was fully convinced that real comprehension lurked behind those otherwise black, expressionless eyes. Something in the way she had angled them at me, a subtle shift in her mercurial expression perhaps. But she knew. Of that I was convinced.

Margaret had in the meantime gotten up, gone over to her daughter, and knelt down beside her. She said something I could not hear and the little girl smiled and reached out. Margaret picked her up and brought her into the kitchen and over to the counter. "Here you go," she said, handing her a cookie from the clear glass jar in the corner. Sonya immediately took a bite out of it and squirmed to get out of her mother's grasp, which she succeeded in doing as Margaret put her down and watched her scurry back into the living room. She didn't look at me at all; it was as if I had become invisible once she had the cookie.

"I'm sure she was curious about you," she said, "and maybe on some level she was trying to fit you into her world. But I doubt that she was able to take the leap from seeing you to concluding that something had to be wrong. She just can't connect that way. She was probably just registering that things looked different. But I doubt that she was able to make any kind of value judgment."

I shrugged, only half convinced. "Maybe you're right."

"Egan, she's only six. Even a perfectly normal child can't fully rationalize much before twelve." She came over and put her arms around me. "Trust me. I've known her all her life."

I held her for a moment and then the two of us, as if unconsciously doubtful of her explanation, simultaneously broke apart and went back to the table before Sonya could see us again.

"So," she said, "tell me about your hike to the village. Did you have any trouble finding it?"

So I told her about how the stream was actually a branch of another stream, and about how I had not found the tree-bridge until I was on my way back, so that I ended up entering the village from behind. I did not tell her about my reckless cannonballing technique that resulted in an unexpected luge ride down the ridge, or about the wolf I had seen on the way back. But I did mention the "uncertain" ice on the swamp.

"And you tried to cross anyway?" she asked.

"Tried to but had to retreat," I offered in reply. "It started to look much too questionable." I mentioned the cracking sounds and, by omission, implied that a quick one- or two-step probe caused me to retreat; I did not go into the details of the ice breaking and my mad

141

scramble to reach the shore. She didn't need yet one more thing to worry about. "What I need to do is find something there that would tie the old diary with the barrow. I mean, it makes perfect sense that the village would be where this person had lived, but I didn't have enough time to fully explore the possibilities. The obvious place to start would be the cemetery, maybe find some names that then show up in the diary."

She nodded. "The barrow itself is a curious thing, isn't it? I mean, it's so perfectly dome shaped that it almost doesn't appear to be natural."

"Maybe it isn't. Has anyone ever investigated that possibility?"

"I don't know. I don't think so. Why, do you think it's man-made?"

I shrugged. "The only way to know is to take a good, close look. But it's not impossible—there are mounds and earthwork figures all over the country that were made by the Indians centuries ago. There's also the Viking connection—the Spirit Pond Runestones have pretty much proven beyond any doubt that the Norsemen were in Maine centuries before Columbus arrived, as uncomfortable as that makes many academics."

She seemed startled. "I didn't know runestones had been found in Maine."

I nodded. "A few years ago, back in '71. Found by a local who had grown up in the area. He even tried to find an archeologist in Bowdoin College, the very same Bowdoin whose hoped-for sponsorship was the driver that first caused the Ropewalk to be converted to a rooming house."

"What became of the stones?"

"I don't know. I know a storm of controversy erupted around them. Academics whose tenures were supported by the 'no Norsemen in North America' chapter of the U.S. Olympic Denial Team tried everything short of murder to shut him up. But I don't know how it all ended."

She chuckled at the joke but was looking past me into the living room. When I turned around, I saw that Sonya had fallen asleep on the sofa with the picture book still in her lap. "I have to put her to bed," she said. "Give me a few minutes." She touched me lightly on the shoulder as she went by.

I ruminated on what the impact would be on my research project if I were able to ascertain that the bone barrow was, in fact, an artificial mound. That was not such an outlandish notion. The fact was that New England was dotted with odd anomalies and out-of-place geologic knick-knacks that were almost universally attributed to the random acts of glaciers, but that even an untrained eye could see were evidence of the hand of man. On a mountain in Norfolk, Connecticut, there was a configuration that was so obviously a dolman such as the Celts built in Europe that attempts to explain it as an Ice Age remnant were like the feeble guesses at a math problem in grade school. In the Mattatuck Forest in Connecticut, I had once found a cave that held a strange four-sided enclosure made of upright slabs of stone that no glacier could possibly have deposited.

So would it surprise me to learn that the bone barrow was man-made? No, not at all. Would it be accepted? No, not at all. The Denial Team was vigorous, ruthless, focused on self-preservation, and controlled all access routes to the top. Cross them and your fate was sealed. You would end up doing hard time in some university gulag, eventually ending your days cleaning locker room toilets. Such was the nature of the "enlightened" establishment. It always came down to who was in charge. And none of them wanted the boat rocked. I needed to keep that in mind if I uncovered evidence that the barrow might not be natural.

A moment later Margaret returned and put her arms around me from behind. "So, did you have a girlfriend when you were a boy growing up?"

How deftly she had steered me away from the subject. "Not really. Like a lot of kids back then, I just sort of worshipped from a distance. I was in love with Rick's sister Nadine, but of course I couldn't tell her that. She came with us a few times to that stream where we caught turtles in summer, and although I pined away in silence, it never went anywhere. All I remember is warm summer evenings basking in her nearness and punctuated by spasms of hay fever misery. Why do you ask?"

She laughed and sat down. "Just wanted to know what kind of Casanova I was dealing with here."

"Casanova? I've been called a lot of things, but never that."

"I'm just teasing. Whatever happened to Nadine? Did you ever go out with her?"

"No. When Rick and I drifted apart I had no reason to go to his house any more and so, by default, had no reason to see her either, much as I wanted to."

"You didn't need to visit with him just to see her. What held you back?"

I paused to look inward. She was dragging me back through some embarrassing and sometimes painful memories. Nadine was one of those ephemeral losses that stalk the corridors of every person's memory, gone out of reach but for a moment of decisive action on my part, which I failed to do. And now her memory had become so rarified, so frozen in a moment of time, that she had become part myth. I wasn't sure exactly what had held me back, but my youth, inexperience, and fear of rejection were the top contenders. "I don't know. Didn't want to make a scene, I guess."

"Flimsy excuse."

"I know."

"Have you seen or heard from her since?"

"No, not in years, decades even. Someone told me a while ago that she had married young, had a child, and then, for whatever reason, had disappeared, run off with someone maybe, or just gotten tired of the domestic scene and gone looking for herself."

"Or maybe looking for you. Allegorically, of course."

As with many of those failings at decision points in one's life, it had never occurred to me that the route I had chosen for myself might have impacted someone else and sent her in a direction she had never wanted to take. But who could have guessed that she might then backtrack, go searching for the missing piece that would explain why I never showed up, and end up losing herself in the blur of a search without meaning or object? As remote as it was in time, I felt an odd tinge of passing guilt, sitting there accused of running from an unrealized longing.

"In any case," she went on, "I guess it's safe to say I won't lose you to her."

I shook my head and smiled. "No, not likely."

There was a moment of silence between us, and then she said, "So, when are you going back to check out the bone barrow?"

"Depends. I'm pretty tired, so tomorrow will probably be too soon, but the day after that is Christmas Eve. When is this new storm supposed to hit?"

"Sometime tomorrow evening. Sleet, mostly, from what they said."

I nodded. "Then I guess it's going to have to wait until the day after Christmas. But I can check out the tractor in the meantime and maybe get the road plowed. Right now, though," and here I looked at her with the most world-weary smile I could muster, "I need some sleep. That ten-mile jaunt is catching up to me pretty fast."

She smiled. "If it's nice tomorrow, I'm thinking we'll probably go skating again. Want to join us? Coffee and Kahlua afterward."

"Sure, I'd love to. Just don't expect any fancy footwork. Since I grew up skating on a stream, my specialty is going in a straight line. I'm a riot on a hockey rink. How does that fit into the tree trimming party?"

"We'll reschedule the party for tomorrow evening. Plow in the morning, cut and mount the tree, go skating in the afternoon, come back for coffee or hot chocolate, trim the tree. You'll even have some time in there to read more of the old diary. How's that sound?"

I nodded, suddenly feeling utterly spent. It was definitely catching up to me. "Sounds good. Breakfast at eight?" I got up to leave.

"Okay." She got up with me and went to the counter. "Don't forget the hatchet."

"Right." I took it from her, and in so doing noticed that the picture of her and Sonya that Nick had drawn was gone. "What happened to the picture?" I nodded toward where it had been on the wall.

"Oh, I just got tired of it and decided it was time for a change."

I looked at her and fancied that I saw in the flicker of her eyes her own painful and embarrassing memory. "Flimsy excuse," I countered with a grin. "Touché."

She smiled and pulled herself into me. "I know."

I put my arms around her. In spite of what was happening, the reality of the two of us together was an image so fragile to me that I dared not touch it too strongly. I had long since learned not to trust the Fates, but fragile reality or not, I would live for the moment. Exhausted as I was, I raised her chin and kissed her, no Sonya to be confused this time, and she returned it and I thought, no, this could not be the simple measure of someone securing the help of the only male around; this *had* to be something else.

♦ ♦ ♦

It seemed to take forever to get back to my room. I was so weary and the building so long that I could feel every step draining me a little bit more. I eyed the front door to make sure I had wrapped the chain around the handles, then climbed the stairs with my last reserves of energy, promising myself I would stretch the fish line across the stairwell again but doubting I would be able to get up if I sat down. I scarcely had enough left in me to brush my teeth.

But since I had to drag myself down to the bathroom anyway, I took the opportunity to tape the fish line across the stairwell. By the time I got back, I felt as if I were sleepwalking. I looked out the window on a whim and sought out the amorphous shape of the Greek theater, expecting to see my buddy the wolf standing there, but there was nothing but frozen shadows being swallowed by frosty night. Crawling under the covers was the greatest feeling in the world. For a moment I just lay there staring at the ceiling.

Does what I'm looking for even exist? I wondered. Margaret was perfect in both mind and body, and that was precisely what alarmed me. Unity had always escaped me, yet I could sense it with her, but since I did not fully trust what I was sensing, I had trouble accepting what was happening. Life had always come at me in fragments, not totalities, fragments that I found at different times in different women. One would attract me physically, another would have the mind and wit, still another the personality. But unity had always been missing. Beauty alone, I knew, was not enough; although it was bound to the earth whence it sprang and its siren song would bewitch me forever, it was not enough. My own past was proof enough of that.

I had always felt that my life was somehow synchronized with the tail end of the epochs that had preceded me, both large and small, and being so close to Margaret had brought with it the sense of another epoch drawing to a close. It had sharpened the feeling of overwhelming loneliness that I had been denying since my second divorce.

The warmth and comfort of my bed soon overrode any further efforts at trying to sort out what I imagined might be the misgivings probing at the corners of what was happening between Margaret and me. So I let it all go and began to drift off to sleep.

My mind carried me back to the bone barrow. There I saw a cave wall covered with images of bison and mammoths, like the paintings in the Lascaux Caverns in France, and a disembodied voice sounded in my head, saying: "See, it *is* man-made, and how will you ever convince the Grand Inquisitors on the high thrones of Academia? What proof can you offer?"

And then a pointing finger directed me away from the pictures, and next to them I saw, in high charcoal relief, the unmistakable image of a Volkswagen Beetle surrounded by hunters and being speared to death. And the voice said to me: "That ought to put them into a tailspin."

I burst out laughing, relief and happiness flooding through me simultaneously. And I continued to laugh even as I fell into the black hole of utter exhaustion and drifted into the deepest, most profound sleep I'd had in a long time. There was no way I would ever have heard anyone walking the halls; the entire Abenaki Nation could have tramped through the Ropewalk with a marching band, and I would not have heard a thing.

♦ ♦ ♦

Chapter 13

I woke up sometime around four o'clock in the morning, not because I was rested and ready to go or because I habitually woke up at that hour. I woke up because there was something in my room. I knew because I could hear it moving. My eyes nearly bulged out of my head in an effort to see in the dark without revealing that I was awake.

I heard subtle shuffling noises of activity on the desk. Someone or something was going through the papers I'd left out, perhaps through the old diary itself. Had I been snoring before I woke up? I wondered. Would my visitor notice the change in breathing and react? I lay there scarcely breathing at all as I formulated a plan. The shuffling noises continued as I slowly, noiselessly, reached down for the flashlight that I always kept near the bed. Then, just as I grabbed it, the noises stopped. With my heart pounding, and figuring I had nothing to lose, I abruptly sat up and turned the light on, aiming the beam at the desk.

There was nothing there. I flashed the light left and right as if doubtful of the witness of my own senses. Had I dreamed the noises? There was no place to hide in my room, and even if there were, a quick glance at the door assured me that no one had gotten in. I sat for a moment listening. The moon must have been just then setting because a steeply angled rectangle of light splashed over part of my desk and flooded the wall near the window. And in it, just disappearing out of reach of the moonlight, something moved. I snapped the light over to it and saw, to my relief and amusement, a field mouse, startled into motionlessness, jaws bulging with the prize of a crust of bread that it had snitched from a plate on the desk. I laughed aloud and the noise startled the thing into action. With lightning speed it vaulted from the desk to the floor, over to the wall, up the side of the wardrobe, over to a ceiling beam, then vanished into a small hole in the ceiling. It was so fast I could hardly follow it with my flashlight.

I got up to make sure that the mouse had not damaged any part of the old diary. It seemed intact, and to make sure it stayed that way I put it into a plastic container and sealed it. It was, after all, irreplaceable, and it would be with more than simple chagrin that I would greet the loss of critical sections of text. It would be catastrophic, like letting the whole world know of the house in the woods that was still full of furniture.

I had some old steel wool in my catchall drawer, so I ripped a piece off, pulled my chair over to the wall, and stuffed the hole. That done, and the mystery of the shuffling papers solved, I turned back towards the bed but then stopped and examined the route the thing had taken to escape. There were partially exposed beams in the ceiling, and the hole was at the end of the one over the wardrobe. I stared at it for several seconds while the realization dawned over me—the Ropewalk had an attic. An attic. I had been up there once, months before, and only briefly, and had completely forgotten about it. It was full of stuff—old school furniture, bizarre "artwork" done by the students, abandoned luggage, crates of old bottles, even some remnants of the ancient machinery that once made the ropes. It was one long, unbroken room. It could easily house a small army without raising an alarm. Or a single person, permanently ensconced in a rent-free silo. I stared up at the hole as if expecting to see some clue—I conjured up the absurd image of a finger poking the steel wool out of the way—identifying once and for all the hiding place of Margaret's mysterious hall walker.

But that seemed unlikely. For starters, if anyone were actually living in the attic, he would be so cold all the time that he'd probably stay rolled up in his sleeping bag. Or, a little counter-voice echoed in my head, he might come down into the Ropewalk itself at night in an effort to warm up. But that raised the problem of getting down from the attic. I knew where the entrances were—one was sort of half hidden within the wall paneling on my end of the hallway, and the other was the last door on the right at the far end of the hall. But they were padlocked. And as far as I knew, only Sil had the keys.

I stood there undecided, wondering but skeptical, knowing that I would have to examine the padlocks in the morning just to be sure.

Then, since I was up anyway, I thought that maybe I should check my end of the building, even if only superficially. How much of this was subconsciously intended to endear myself still further to Margaret I could not say, but part of it was simple practicality. If there really was someone out there, it was not realistic to assume that habitually checking around the same time would reveal his or her presence. I was no mathematician, but I intuitively knew that only by randomizing my own movements would I be likely to find a culprit who might otherwise time his visits around my habits. I grabbed my keys, stepped into my slippers, threw on my bathrobe, and went to the door.

I listened before I opened it. An occasional creak or groan came to me through the wood, but these were simply the arthritic protests of the building itself. It was windy outside; I could hear it exploding against the Ropewalk and lashing it with pellets of ice. Other than that, there was no sound. I quietly unlocked my door, turned off my flashlight, and went out into the hall.

It was cold out there compared to the snugness of my room. I pulled the bathrobe closed and moved soundlessly toward the entrance to the hallway. The huge emptiness of the building was magnified in the dark, and the feeble nightlights only added to the impression of a tunnel of bottomless darkness. Some instinct in me kept me from turning the flashlight on, as if, on some animal level, I had perceived something of which I had not yet become conscious. I was not nervous or even apprehensive, and was certainly not expecting to run into anyone. Nevertheless, I noted with satisfaction that my bathrobe was dark blue and would not show up in the nightlights.

I stood leaning against the wall for several minutes simply listening. The wind blasted the building with such force that I imagined I could almost feel it swaying. Cold, swirling drafts snaked around my ankles from unknown crevices, and I realized I should've put my socks on. I felt my way back along the wall to where I knew the door to the attic was located. "Might as well check it now, I'm already out here," I mumbled. Half apprehensive that the padlock wouldn't be there, or would be unlocked, I reached out in the dark, letting my fingers slide along the wall. I found the seam, the mismatch in the wall, that I knew was the edge of the door and then slowly slid my hand down until I encountered the hasp. The padlock was there, closed and secure.

Soundlessly, staying close to the wall to avoid the creaking floorboards, I worked my way down the hall to the other end, still with the flashlight off. I *had* to know if the other door was also locked. If I didn't do it then, I knew, I would lie awake in my bed for who knew how long wondering about it.

The last door on the right looked like every other door on that floor, except instead of a doorknob it had a hasp with a padlock. A nightlight directly across from it revealed to me that it was secured even before I got to it. I checked it anyway, just to be sure.

And that was that. If the mouse hadn't reminded me of the attic, I would never have thought to check. The locks were in place and secure and the hasps were solid and had not been tampered with. The attic could therefore be ruled out as any sort of hiding place or, at the very least, as any place that provided access to the main building. I headed back for my room, once again staying as close to the wall as possible. In spite of my self-assurance that there was no one else in the building, I scanned the bottoms of the doors looking for slivers of light. But there was nothing.

I paused at the head of the staircase thinking I should probably check the first floor as well, but I felt my fatigue returning now that the last of the adrenalin spike had worn off. I could not see the fish line that I had taped across the entrance and did not want to turn the flashlight on in order to find it, so I squatted down and ran my fingers along the railing post, from the floor upward, until I encountered the faint resistance that signaled its presence. A moment later I heard a click echo in the lower hall, and in the same instant it was engulfed in impenetrable darkness, as if the shadows had leaped to life. The nightlights had gone out again.

For whatever reason—animal instinct again, perhaps—I remained in a squat after the lights had gone out. On my floor they were still on, of course, and it was possible that my silhouette might have been visible from the lower floor had I been standing, and perhaps it was that unarticulated thought that kept me close to the floor. But it was a very awkward position, and I knew that because of my exertions on the hike, some part of me would start to cramp if I tried to stay that way, so I slowly stretched out across the floor until I was lying flat on my stomach. I was able to look down onto the floor below from between the vertical railing bars.

I didn't know what I was expecting. Somewhere deep inside, despite the skepticism that I had gone to considerable lengths to demonstrate, I knew that some part of me was holding onto a residual doubt about my conviction that there was no one else in the building. Despite the obvious pressure Margaret had been under—a wandering husband and a challenged daughter—she did not seem to be the type prone to hysteria or melodramatic exaggeration. She said someone had tried to get into her apartment and I had doubted her on the grounds that she had not *seen* the doorknob move. But she had *heard* it, which I had discounted or devalued because the sound could have been confused with other sounds. But even as I sloughed it off, I knew it had taken root in me somewhere precisely because she was not an excitable person. What exactly had she heard?

Just then a faint "snicking" sound echoed out of the darkened hall below me. I remained absolutely still and listened while simultaneously trying to "catalog" the sound in my mind. I knew I recognized it, but it took several seconds before I was able to place it. It was a door latch, the sound a door makes when it gently pops open. For several seconds there was absolutely nothing, and then from deep inside the hallway another sound emerged, faint and almost inaudible but absolutely unmistakable—the creaking of a floorboard. I held my breath and waited.

How long I waited, I didn't know. No more sounds emerged from the darkened hall and I began to think that maybe I was wrong, that the sounds were nothing more than the normal creaking sounds that the building made. The cold air that previously had been swirling around my ankles was now swirling around my head, so I turned the collar up on the bathrobe and tried to pull myself into it. I waited for what seemed like an hour but, in fact, could not have been more than a few minutes.

The next thing I knew a pain in the side of my face roused me to full attention. My head shot up and I frantically looked around. My face hurt, my neck hurt, and my hands were so cold they were starting to stiffen up. I had fallen asleep, nodded off like a turtle on a mossy log, my head sucked into the collar of my bathrobe and the grain structure of the floorboards working its way into the left side of my face. How long was I out? A minute? Two? A half hour? "What the hell happened to my watch?" I whispered, as returning consciousness overrode whatever I'd been dreaming. "Oh, yeah, that's right. Back in my room on my desk."

It was useless. I was exhausted, so tired I was fighting to keep my eyes open. I listened for a few more minutes and then slowly pushed myself to a sitting position, listened for another minute or so, then got up and went to my room. I had the presence of mind to not turn on the flashlight and to open and close my door soundlessly. I pushed in the lock button as quietly as I could before I flicked the light on. The moment I did that I heard a faint rustling noise coming from under my bed and, figuring my buddy the mouse had somehow gotten back in, I got down on my knees and shined the light under there to have a look.

What I saw jolted me to full wakefulness. It was not a mouse. It was a huge spider making off with something that looked like a chunk of bread. I leaped to my feet and jumped back so abruptly that I crashed into the wardrobe. "Jesus!" I half shrieked. "What the hell is that?" Then, realizing my feet and ankles were vulnerable, I sprang over to my boots and hurriedly stepped into them, then vaulted back to the bed, grabbed the corner of the frame, and yanked it away from the wall with such force that it, too, crashed against the wardrobe. There, frozen against the wall as if undecided, was the monstrous spider. What it was carrying was not a piece of bread but what looked like the remains of an insect. Beetle skeletons seemed to be everywhere. We stared at each other for several seconds, the monstrous thing no doubt sizing me up as a potential danger while I tried to assimilate its hideously unreal reality into the catalog of things I knew about.

Should I kill it? I wondered. As if sensing that thought, the thing suddenly sprang to life and took off along the wall, its scrabbling gait clearly audible even above the beating of my heart. A moment more and it vanished into a large crack in the floor at the base of the wall. I stood there unmoving, bizarre thoughts rampaging through my head like: Should I boil some water and dump it down there? But I knew that was stupid. All it would do would be to leak into the lobby below me.

Jesus, I thought, how long has this thing been sneaking into my room while I was asleep? Frantic now for some measure of assurance, I got the last of the steel wool out of my catchall drawer, tossed it down over the crack, and pressed it into place with my foot. But I sensed it was not enough; I needed to make sure. So I took a thin board that had been hiding behind the wardrobe ever since I moved in, placed it over the steel wool, then moved the bed back into position and placed one leg of the frame onto it. There, I thought; that should do it. If that thing was strong enough to move the bed with me in it, it was time to get out of Dodge.

My heart was still racing. I looked at the clock. It was nearly five a.m., which meant that this whole mouse episode had lasted nearly an hour. It also meant that, when I fell asleep in the hallway, I must have been out for almost a half hour.

Just for good measure, I checked under the bed one last time before I pulled my boots off. I also checked the wall behind the wardrobe, just in case another portal into my domain was hidden back there. That done, and my heart at last quieting down, I tried to relax. In three hours, I would be having breakfast with Margaret, and I knew I was not yet fully rested from my hike. I needed to get back to sleep.

For nearly a full minute, I stood frozen before the impenetrable barrier that was the wall, placed my hand against it as if expecting to feel the vibrations of something moving, and thought: What the hell is living in the walls of this place?

◆ ◆ ◆

What was left of my sleep was not restful. My nerves were riding a roller coaster, and I found myself drifting between waking and dream states with such frequency that I began to confuse the two. At one point I rolled over to look at the floor and the first thing I saw, sitting there like a hideously disembodied hand, was the huge spider. It had somehow found its way back in, and this time whatever it had was still alive, squirming in abject terror at what was awaiting it. Beetle skeletons, big, brown crunchy things, were everywhere and, hurrying among them, scores of huge, reddish-brown beetles. That sight was frightening enough, but even it did not prepare me to face the thing that had crawled onto my bed while I wasn't looking.

Down at the foot of the bed something like a cross between a huge beetle and an animated skeleton crouched. I struck at it in a panic, then grabbed a baseball bat and started beating it off the bed. The bat was too light to be effective, and in time I was forced off the bed with the thing squaring off with me. Still I beat at it, seeing no other option.

Then, as I watched, it grew fur and looked like a small ape of some sort. It seemed less aggressive, and I discovered it was far easier to be friendly with the thing than to fight it.

And then I woke up. My heart was racing. I glanced at the clock—six-thirty. I grabbed the flashlight, looked down at the floor, and saw that there was nothing there except that one of my boots had fallen over after I pulled it off a scant hour and a half before. And, of course, there was nothing on the bed. I knew I could squeeze out another hour's sleep before having to get ready for breakfast with Margaret, but I was too wired. I sat up and turned on the light over the bed. I was better off spending the next hour reading more of the old diary.

I threw the covers off and was about to swing my feet over and onto the floor when I had second thoughts. I pictured that huge spider waiting at the rim of the bed, just out of sight, crouched like a jack-in-the-box and ready to tackle my ankles the moment my feet appeared. So I figured I had to get out of bed by leaping to clear the reach of anything living under it, like I did as a kid when I was sure there were monsters under there just waiting to grab me. I felt like an idiot, but the night's events had injected a retrogressive, irrational tenor into my behavior, so I stood up on the bed and took a long, half-leaping stride onto the floor. Then I quickly knelt down and shined the light under the bed. The board was still firmly in place under the bed frame and, apart from the bug skeletons, there was nothing to see.

The fallen boot then looked suspicious—I remembered admonishments from my various survival books saying that, if you found yourself in scorpion country, store your boots upside down to avoid a nasty surprise. I shined the light into it and saw nothing, so I picked it up and shook it. When nothing came out, I loosened the laces and pulled it open for a closer inspection but knew even then that the thing was so big I would have seen part of it by that point. I checked the other one as well, just to be sure.

I looked out the window, cupping my hands around my face to keep out the light. It was still dark and the moon was almost gone, making it appear even darker than usual. Still, because of the snow it was possible to see shadows and shapes in the field between the Ropewalk and the school. Half wistfully I expected to see the wolf, or maybe a bear this time—on some primitive level it was a rare privilege for a fully domesticated human to have even fleeting contact with the instinct world—but there was nothing there. It was very still; even the wind had stopped.

It was Christmas Fore-Eve, the day I originally planned to leave, and I was feeling that odd mixture of joy and sadness that haunted me every year around that time. Even a self-made pariah like myself couldn't help but feel a tinge of regret over the loss of the magic circle in which I had lived as a child. "It's the lack of light that does it," I mumbled to myself. "Induces depression and detachment, a sort of emotional cave-in." I remembered a line from one of the Icelandic sagas, where the author described daylight in winter as nothing more than "a glimmer between two gaping darknesses." Had anyone ever factored that into the root cause behind the Viking invasions? I wondered.

I stepped over to the wardrobe, opened it, and pulled open one of the drawers. Inside were a number of neatly wrapped gifts. Should I give Margaret the presents I had bought for my sisters? How odd it would seem, this default giving. But then, we were trapped there, it was Christmas, and each of us only had the other.

◆ ◆ ◆

I didn't have a chance to read any more of the old diary before I left for breakfast. By the time I had checked out every inch of my room for other potential points of entry, shaved, dressed, cleaned away the bug skeletons, removed the fish line from the stairwell, and checked the room again, it was nearly twenty of eight.

Before I knocked on Margaret's door I went once again down to the end of the hall to turn on the nightlights. There was a small, narrow window in the end wall, mounted up near the ceiling, that allowed enough light into the hall so that I could see, even before I got to it, that the door to the utility closet was open. I pondered this for a second before I went in, thinking it unusual but not unexpected since the latch was so questionable. I knew by then exactly which box and switch to go to, of course. Before I left to go to Margaret's apartment I pushed the door shut very slowly, heard it catch, then released it. It popped open with that same "snicking" sound I had heard a few hours before when I was in the upper hallway.

"Ah ha," I mumbled. "It was the utility closet. Probably popped open from the cold draft or the movement of the building itself. Mystery solved." I pushed it closed again and held it firmly for a moment to make sure that it would stay closed, then headed back.

It was slightly before eight o'clock when I got to her door. I knocked twice quickly so that she would know it was me—not that it was likely to be anyone else—and a moment later, I heard the deadbolts sliding back and the door opened. She was wearing a bright red turtleneck covered with Christmas icons, everything from fir tree branches to reindeer.

"Well," I said, "You look seasonal."

She glanced at her watch. "You must have some German blood in you," she said. "When you say 'eight o'clock' you mean 'eight o'clock' and not a minute later."

I grinned. "I'm not aware of any, but I've always admired their sense of punctuality. People who have been to Germany have told me that, if the train is scheduled to leave at eight, you better have both feet in the door at seven-fifty-nine. Don't know if that's true. It could be just one of those pop culture rumors. Can I come in?"

She stepped aside and ushered me in with a sweep of her arm. "Well, my married name is Irish and my maiden name is Welsh, so I can't be expected to be on time. Breakfast will be a few minutes late."

"Ah, a genetically encoded excuse. They're the best kind. I use them pretty often myself. As for being late . . . ," I glanced at my watch, "I hope this doesn't make me miss the next train out of here." I stepped into the room and closed the door behind me. "Can I help with any . . . ?" She stepped up and folded into me at once, cutting me off in mid-sentence with a kiss so passionate I staggered a step. Like Mae, she was a great kisser.

"I used to watch you when you held your martial arts class," she said, stroking my arm. "I'll bet you never knew you had a secret admirer."

"No, I never did. But if I had, I would've gone to enormous lengths to show off." I kissed her, but only lightly—an angel kiss—and glanced past her into the room. "Where's Sonya?"

She nodded toward the door to the girl's room, which was closed. "Still sleeping. Don't worry—she won't see us. We're safe."

157

I nodded and we kissed again, deeply this time, she in the happy abandon of new-found love, and I feeling myself coming back from a loneliness more profound than mere isolation, a loneliness of more depth and duration than simply not having someone to talk to. The dream-words of Mae, my first wife, came back to me—"You can't love until you know the owner"—and I suddenly realized what they meant. The owner was me. I could not love again until I understood what I had become—I was a sentinel on the outskirts of reason, holding at bay what I imagined was the frivolous everyday, but with my back to an emptiness that I had refused to acknowledge.

And Margaret was teaching me the way back.

We broke apart momentarily, holding each other at arm's length, she smiling and thinking her hidden thoughts while I smiled back, fully aware that I was regressing to the state of a captive adolescent. And like a captive adolescent, there was an aspect of what was happening between us that was not being addressed: at some point, we would have to come to terms with sex. I could see the same question in her eyes, but just then a sound emerged from behind Sonya's door and it was obvious the little girl was awake. She raised a finger for silence, then slipped away and went to her room.

I went into the kitchen. The coffee had already been brewed, so I poured a cup for each of us. I knew by then how she took it, so I had it ready when she came in with Sonya in her arms, all bundled up in her blanket. "It got chilly in her room," she said. "Almost as if the heat weren't working. Fortunately, she had extra blankets. Can you check the radiator for me?"

"Sure. Here's your coffee." I put the cup down on the counter beside her and went to Sonya's room. Her statement about the heating in the girl's room had sounded a dark note in my stomach, one that I had been avoiding more or less by default for the last week—specifically, how much heating oil did we have, and should we turn down the thermostats in the hallway to conserve fuel? I hoped—prayed, actually—that this incident was not some portent of a much bigger problem heading our way.

But when I got to her room, I did not find it unusually cold and the radiator was, in fact, emitting heat. Since the thermostat was in the living room and Margaret slept with her door open, equalizing the temperature, I surmised that there had been no signal calling for heat.

Since Sonya's door had been closed, her room naturally got colder. The moment Margaret opened it, the cold air must have signaled the thermostat to turn on the heat. I checked the radiator valve just to be sure, but it was full open. I also checked the window to make sure it was securely closed and locked. Then I made a mental note to find out how much heating oil we actually had.

I was about to leave when I felt a cold draft on my ankles. My first thought was to look at the window again, but I realized it seemed to be coming from the closet, which was built against the outside wall and whose door was partially open. "There's the culprit," I said to myself, imagining a loose wallboard flapping away in the wintry wind like an errant coattail and letting icy gusts puff into the room. "Probably lost whatever insulation it once had." I pulled the door open and turned on the inside light but could scarcely see the outer wall because of the pile of shoes, boxes, toys, and unknown sundries in front of it. By moving some things I was able to run my hand along the panels, checking for drafts. I didn't notice anything until I felt along the side wall, the one at ninety degrees to the outer wall and that paralleled the inside wall. A very strong draft was coming out from between the panels. "No insulation," I muttered. I remembered seeing some out in the shed and knew that the only way to fix this problem was to take down a few panels, stuff the opening, and remount the panels, which was something I could take care of right after I got the Christmas tree.

And then I remembered the monstrous spider living in the walls. I had this horrific vision of peeling away a panel and finding a colony of the hideous things hanging there in their webs like obscene Christmas ornaments. I imagined a pulsating swarm cascading out, hitting the floor, and bounding away in all directions while I kicked them around like ping-pong balls. The very thought made my arm hairs stand on end.

But, I reasoned, it—or they—had to travel on or near the heating pipes; how else could it stay alive at that time of year? That would limit its range to areas near the radiators. I went over and examined the holes in the floor through which the radiator pipes emerged. There did not seem to be room enough for anything bigger than a gnat to get through.

Should I tell Margaret? I wondered. What was I going to say? "Oh, here's something new to worry about—there's a spider the size of a bullfrog living in the walls. Make sure all your vents are screened." No, as with the wolf and the house in the woods, I could not tell her about that. She would never sleep again.

"What did you find out?" she asked after I had returned to the kitchen.

I sat down as she began serving breakfast. "The radiator's fine. It looks like her room gets cold because you keep the door closed. The ambient temperature in the living room is higher and doesn't call for heat, and because she's cut off, her room cools down."

She had put Sonya in her chair and was preparing pancakes. "That's odd. She prefers sleeping with her door closed—makes her feel secure or something—but I don't recall the room getting cold like that before."

"Well, there's also a problem in the closet. There's a draft coming from the wall in there. We need to take down a few panels and mount some insulation. I saw some out in the shed and can do that after I get the Christmas tree."

She nodded. "Better think about getting the tree soon. It looks like that storm is going to start sooner than expected."

I looked out the window. Daylight had at last broken, but instead of the sparkling wonderland I'd seen the day before, a gray pall covered everything. It even *felt* like a storm was coming. "Mostly sleet, you said. Right?"

"That's what the news said."

"Still going skating in any case?"

"I'd like to, if we can, but it won't be until at least noon, assuming the storm hasn't started by then. Might as well let the day warm up as much as possible. Are you going to join us?"

"Yes, I expect to, after I get the tree."

She nodded and helped Sonya with her breakfast. "Did you hear anything last night?" she asked.

"Like what?"

"I think our visitor was back. Later than usual this time."

"You're sure?"

"Sort of. I heard creaking coming from the hallway."

"What time?"

"Around four-thirty."

I paused to ponder and revisit my actions while out in the hallway during the night. I obviously couldn't tell her I had fallen asleep during all that, so I said nothing.

"Did you hear anything?" she asked.

Had I indeed heard footsteps, or should I discount it as I had done with her earlier? I wasn't sure. But I had to hold myself to my own standards, at the very least, so I said, no, I hadn't heard anything. I couldn't in all honesty say yes. After all, I was sacked out on the floor.

But it turned out she herself was not sure, so the subject simply fizzled away and I didn't feel so bad.

When breakfast was finished, Margaret reflected on the necessary limitations she had to impose on Sonya's life. As a little girl, she had the curiosity of any growing child, even if somewhat muted by circumstances, but Margaret could not let her indulge her exploratory whims the way most parents did for their children. Sonya had to be carefully watched. Her playground was the apartment, not the spacious yard in front of the school or the rocky ramps on the shore that led into the sea.

"Hardly anyone has even seen her," she said. "I've kept her out of the public eye for a number of reasons, not the least of which is to protect her from the cruel ridicule she'll be subjected to from some of the other kids." She stroked the girl's hair and lifted her down from her chair, then watched her as she scurried into the living room. "Understand?" she asked.

I did. We had reached one of those critical junctures in our relationship. Since the bond between us was growing stronger every day, she was reminding me that Sonya was part of the deal. Love me, love my daughter. I took her hand but she would not look at me, as if fearing the news. "I understand," I said. "No, there's no doubt in my mind."

Only then did she turn to me. She reached out and put her hand on my chest, tentatively, as if for the first time, then said, "Some men would, you know, not want to be bothered, or would doubt that they could handle it." Her smile flickered as if she were suddenly consumed with doubt.

"I know. Some would."

"So, is this—are we—what you're looking for?" she asked softly. "Or I guess I should start with the basic question: what are you looking for?"

"Something of value," I said. "Something that will last." And it was clear that I had struck some cord within her because her standoffishness vanished and she wrapped herself around me once again.

"You're not having second thoughts?"

"No, but I do wonder about how well she'll accept me. How will you explain the loss of her father?"

"I'm not sure yet." She paused, then looked up at me with a smile. "You're right. You're no Casanova."

I smiled and shrugged. "I never could figure out how to make something like that work. Guys like me are constantly trying to find ways to fill in the gaps of their experience with women."

"Anyway," she said, "You better get out there and cut the tree."

"Right. It's the first thing on the to-do list. There's a stand of small fir trees up near the coast highway where I should be able to find one. By the way, who baby-sits for her when you and Ben are at class?" I caught myself at the mention of his name. "Sorry."

"No need to be. Sil's wife arranges for the sitter. She's been a godsend for me since Sonya was born, always there ready to help. Don't know what I would've done without her."

That caught me off guard. "Sil's wife? You're close to Sil and his wife?"

"Well, actually, yes. In fact, they're Sonya's godparents."

I was stunned. After all the bitching I had done about Sil, I find out that he would be an unavoidable part of my life as a result of my involvement with Margaret. I shook my head with a laugh. "Destiny logic," I mumbled.

"What?"

"Destiny logic. It's a concept in 'Decline of the West.' It's the overarching causality-logic behind history. Impenetrable to human reasoning. The sum total of all the unordered coincidences that seem to dominate and determine the life of an individual are nothing more than the residual effects or consequences of a larger causality picture. One's life is just a subset pre-programmed into 'fate.'"

"What are you talking about?"

I shook my head again. "Nothing. I'm just babbling. It's just, well, funny that after all the complaining I did about Sil, I end up connected to him in a way I never would've suspected."

"I didn't mention it sooner because you seemed to be down on him every time his name came up. I didn't know if the two of you were at odds, or what."

"No, we're not at odds. I'm just a little embarrassed, that's all. When I was younger, I was obsessed with the idea of reducing all my belongings to a bundle the size of a duffel bag so that I could throw it, and myself, onto the first raft that drifted by if I had to. Now would be a good time to do that."

"Don't you dare drift away, duffel or no duffel."

I raised my right hand. "I promise I won't, destiny logic notwithstanding."

She playfully pushed me away. "You historians. You're all such weirdoes. Go get the tree. The fresh air will do you good."

I went over and opened the door. "Did I tell you I'm the only person I know who still calls Christmas the Midwinter Fire Festival?"

"Out," she said with a smile, gently pushing me into the hall. "Weirdo."

"I also wonder about stuff like how many neuroses can be traced back to things like Brussels sprouts."

She laughed. "The tree. Get the tree." She rolled her eyes at me and flicked a tiny wave as she slowly closed the door.

So I laughed my way back to my room, the hideous spider all but forgotten, and my history project paled to benchwarmer status by the euphoria I was feeling.

◆ ◆ ◆

Chapter 14

The oil drum, a massive thing that looked like the hull of a small submarine, was located in a crawlspace specifically dug for it under the building. There was no way to get to it from inside the Ropewalk; the space was only accessible through a hatch on the outside of the building, about halfway down its length. It was padlocked, of course, and I knew that the only way I was going to be able to check for oil was to cut the lock off and replace it sometime after the holiday.

I found a hacksaw in the shed that I used to cut the lock. It was a struggle to get the hatch open even after I had gotten most of the snow and ice off of it, but I was finally able to bring it up to its locking position. The crawlspace stared up at me like the mouth of a cave. "If that doesn't look like the lair of a giant spider, I don't know what does," I mumbled. I turned on the flashlight that I had brought and went down the steps.

There was an overhead light with a pull chain just inside the door, and the first thing I did when I turned it on was scan the ceiling to see if anything was hanging there waiting to surprise me. It was cold down there but still considerably warmer than outside, what with the protection from the earth itself and the heat emanating from the half dozen furnaces lined up against the opposite wall. I didn't know what the survival temperature for spiders was, but I wasn't taking any chances;

I checked every square inch of ceiling before I went any further. There were a lot of old cobwebs but no occupants.

The sight glass on the oil drum revealed that it was still half full, which meant that there was easily enough there to heat the building for at least another month, so we did not have to worry about a fuel shortage. I checked the furnaces next, and although I was no heating expert, I could see that they all still had their pilot lights going. Everything appeared to be fine.

The crawlspace itself was lined with cinderblocks like an ordinary basement, and before I left, I checked the corners just to make sure that nothing was nesting down there. One never knew. The thought of the wolf flashed through my mind, and although I believed it extremely unlikely that it would nest directly under a hive of humans, I had to rule it out. After all, it might have found some hidden way in and decided the warmth was worth the risk. So I went around the oil drum to check.

But there was nothing there. Nothing, that is, except for a ponderous sliding door, like a fire door, with the word "Compressor" stenciled on it. It was closed and secured with another padlock. "So that's where the compressor is," I mumbled, remembering the circuit breaker that I had found while looking for the one that controlled the nightlights. I still had no idea what it would have been used for, although I suspected it played some role in rope making in the waning years of that activity.

I hefted the padlock and examined it. It was bigger than the one I had just cut off and, from its unusual appearance, considerably older. It was also rusty and obviously had not been opened in some time. Exactly why it hadn't been opened in so long was perplexing to me, except maybe as a safety measure of some sort. Maybe the compressor was old and so decrepit that it would be a hazard to anyone not familiar with it. It wouldn't be the first time a potential insurance violation was secured against curious students.

But I had accomplished my original mission and had to get on with the rest of my plans before the storm started. We had enough oil; I could at least rest assured about that. If we were going to be stuck there, we did not have to worry about freezing to death. I turned off the light and went back up the steps, then lowered the hatch. I could not secure it because I now had no lock, but unless our hypothetical nightwalker wanted to camp out in the crawlspace, there was no one to secure it against. In any case, there was always the possibility that I would find another lock in the shed.

My next project was to try to get the tractor started so that I could plow the macadam road that led to the coast highway. I had an ulterior motive in mind also: since the stand of fir trees where I expected to find a Christmas tree was out near the coast highway, it would be a lot easier hauling the tree back behind the tractor than dragging it by hand. I also wanted to gauge the amount of time it would take me to drive the tractor up to the cart track that led to the village and then, since it was fitted with chains, see how far I could actually go up the cart track with it. Using the tractor would save not just four to six miles of walking there and back, but also almost two to three hours of time. That was a huge advantage at that time of year.

The tractor already had plenty of gas in it and was fitted with the plow, so it was only a question of getting it started. For that, of course, I needed the key, and fate intervened with a rare ruling in my favor. It was there with the tractor, hanging on a leather lanyard tied to the gearshift. It took no time at all to get it started. It had a sand-spreading device attached to the rear like a small trailer, but since another ice storm was coming in, it made no sense to spread the sand on the road just then. The chains would give me all the traction I needed for now. But I did need something for the ice between the Ropewalk and the shed, so I cleared and sanded a path before I disconnected it. Then I headed up the road with the plow lowered.

When I got to the Engineering building, I stopped to check out a series of holes in the snow that crossed the road at that point. It was obvious that they were tracks and that they led up in the direction of the building. Intuitively, I knew—or suspected—that they were the tracks left by the thing I'd seen from my window several days before, and that I now realized—or likewise suspected—were left by the wolf. I let the tractor idle while I got down to take a closer look.

The marks were too indistinct to be identified. They were circular and about four inches across, with none of the obvious half- and full-step pattern that I would recognize as that left by a bear. I imagined they could be wolf tracks but could find no imprint clear enough to decide the issue. I followed them into the woods for about thirty yards, at which point they abruptly turned and headed straight for the Engineering building, whose barren granitic hulk rose like a decaying monolith out of the trees that surrounded it. The massive entrance was partly drifted over from the flurries that had come in the past several nights. The tracks passed by on the right side, headed for the rear of the building. I had never been this close to it before, and I checked the bricked over windows for breaks as I followed the tracks to the rear.

Once behind the building, the tracks headed for a huge pile of snow-covered boards and assorted building material. On the other side of that, they wound back towards the building. And then disappeared. I stood staring in disbelief as the tracks simply ended at the rear wall, as if whatever it was had suction-cupped its way up the brownish flank of the building and found a hole to crawl into. Still slightly wired from the spider incident, my nape hairs rose to the occasion, but I shook it off and approached.

When I reached the wall, reason returned. What was not visible from even a few feet away was a grate, completely covered with the sloughed off detritus from the slagheap of building materials. It had camouflaged itself so thoroughly that one would never guess that it was there. Under it was a flight of stone steps leading into utter darkness. I had not brought the flashlight, so I had no way of knowing what was at the bottom, but it was pretty obvious that whatever had left the tracks had found a way into the basement and lived there. And given the condition and status of the building, it was unlikely that it would ever be discovered.

I had no desire to confront whatever it was, either with or without a flashlight, so I went back to the tractor and resumed plowing the road. I now knew where the tracks had come from; as for identifying what they were, that would have to wait until a fresh set appeared.

When I got to the stand of fir trees, I found a small one that would not completely crowd Margaret out of her apartment and marked it with a piece of string I had brought along for that purpose. Then I continued plowing the last few yards of the macadam road and pushed my way out onto the highway. My feeble hopes had not been realized in the time since I returned from the woods—the road still wasn't plowed. So I drove a wedge through the snow on the northbound side and turned right onto the partially plowed southbound lane, heading north. Before I did anything else, I needed to see how long it would take me to get to the cart track.

Top speed on the tractor was only about twenty miles per hour, but even that was a tremendous improvement. It took me less than two minutes to reach the cart track, and with the plow only partially lowered so that it would not get hung up, only about five minutes to go nearly a mile up the track. I stopped before I got too deeply into the section where the track had sunk into the earth because I was not sure I would be able to turn around unless I then went all the way to the stream. Even so, I judged I was within about two miles of the village, and it had only taken me seven to eight minutes from the macadam road. If I added another three to four minutes normal time on that road, I was only looking at about twelve minutes, or a quarter hour at most, to cover a distance that had taken almost an hour and a half on foot.

At that point, it occurred to me that I had a unique opportunity to give Margaret a present that would not be one originally intended for my sisters, that would be so one-of-a-kind that it could never be duplicated or replaced. I could give her something from inside the house.

I scanned the sky. The grayness had deepened but the storm did not feel any closer, and I was sure I would have time to go to the village, get something, and return before it broke. Besides, it originally wasn't supposed to start until sometime in the late afternoon, and with the tractor as transportation, I would be able to save a lot of time. But the first thing to do was to go get the tree and set it up.

On principle, I objected to the yearly slaughter of countless thousands of small trees just to perpetuate an ancient Germanic ritual sucked into the tapestry of modern religion. It was a passion I had shared with Mae, who was a staunch defender of the silent giants that held the ground in place. "They're not *in* the forest," she used to say, "They *are* the forest. Rooting them out is not like pulling dandelions out of your yard. It's like torching the whole yard. If we don't speak for the trees, nobody will." One of the reasons I had left southern New England in the first place was precisely because no one was speaking for the trees. Shortsighted neo-visionaries were turning all the forests into shopping malls and parking lots, and the riptide of humanity caught up in the groundswell of "market forces" was sailing along on the same bubble, hoping to retire early and run off to some mythical, unpaved Avalon. It was foolish and wasteful and cutting a small tree for a ritual made me feel like one of them. But I did it anyway. What I had finally discovered since Mae left me was that even ideals came with a price tag. There was no getting away from it, and I was sure that was at the root of why we had parted ways; she had accepted that desires changed ideals over time and often left the two incompatible. I had not. But I was learning.

"So, what *did* happen to the idealism of the sixties?" I mumbled as I finished cutting the tree and struggled to free it from the clutches of the others around it. Since the first day I met Margaret in the kitchen, I had been slowly re-experiencing for myself how easy it was for us to fall back into the old patterns when there was no common annoyance—like a war—to collectivize about. When Vietnam finally ended we had all stood around looking at each other as if noticing our warts for the first time, as if fate were saying: "Okay, you bitched about it for years, now it's over. Let's see what you can do with it."

We weren't prepared for that. Ideals were cast aside and we began to gobble each other up like bottled lab animals.

I had almost become one of them when I met Mae. How casually I filled in the gaps of my experience with women back then. It was a lost world regained with the simplest of protocols. A look, a touch, a casual slipping of a shoulder strap to free her breasts in the most unexpected places, including public buildings full of people. "I can begin panting at a moment's notice," she used to say.

She used to call sex a casual glimpse of eternity.

In the Brownian motion of the random events of one's life, losing her was like the final glimpse at the last microscopic component of that much larger "organic" destiny into which each individual was inexorably woven. A word, an attitude, a gesture—one of these had been the catalyst that ultimately led me to where I had ended up. The slightest flippancy magnified a hundredfold, and there I was.

It would not be that way with Margaret. But the bond was so fragile that I was still not sure of exactly where to take it next. On top of that, I lived with the nagging dread that she would find a better prospect once the smoke cleared on her divorce and she began socializing again. After all—what was I other than a slightly more refined version of a homeless vagabond? My fear was that I would do something, another word or gesture, that would cause our growing relationship to spin out of control. And I knew it would somehow center around Sonya.

I pulled the tree out to the road and tied it to the back of the tractor. I knew it would delight the little girl, but the fact was I was seriously divided in how I felt about her, or more specifically, how I felt about trying to raise what appeared to be an autistic and possibly retarded child. Mae had often told me that I found security in movement—my duffel-bag-on-the-raft theme again—and accepting that about myself had been my life's task after we broke up. My short-lived marriage to Rachel, the would-be model, appeared in retrospect to have been nothing more than a test to see if being with someone no more domestically stable than I would be a good match.

It wasn't, of course. Mine was a type of academic hoboism; hers was just plain emotional volatility. Together, it was like Box Car Bertha meets the Creature from the Black Lagoon, except that I was Bertha and she was the Creature.

So I couldn't help but wonder what kind of effect Sonya was going to have on my life over the long haul. One thing I did know—I dared not fool myself about the actual consequences of being her legal guardian or surrogate father. It was a lifelong commitment. Once I stepped over that threshold, the rootless freedom I had come to expect of my life would be gone forever. But I felt I was at last ready to accept that because Margaret was the best thing to happen to me in years, and as ephemeral as my current reality seemed, maybe it was just fate's way of showing me the path I needed to take. Even so, there was no way I could know at this stage of my life where the limits of my understanding and forbearance would be with her daughter.

And that was why I still harbored some residual apprehension about Sonya.

I saw the two of them emerging from the shed carrying boxes of ornaments as I pulled up with the tractor. Margaret knelt down near the girl and whispered something to her while motioning with the boxes toward the tree. Sonya looked at the tree, seemed confused or perhaps startled, then looked back at her mother. Margaret said something else and the girl nodded.

"Perfect timing," I said. "I arrive with the tree at the same time the two of you show up with the ornaments."

"This is just the prep work," said Margaret. "The actual tree trimming isn't until tonight, remember? First you plow, then we go skating, then we have coffee and Kahlua, then we trim the tree."

170

I got down from the tractor and began untying the tree. "You're a marvel of administrative organization," I said. "I could never have gotten that sequence right."

"Wise guy."

I smiled. We had evidently entered the teasing stage of our relationship. "So, lady, where do you want this?" I quipped, dragging the tree forward.

"Follow me."

She managed to hold the door so that I could pull it into the lobby. Sonya walked beside her mother as we went down the hall, turning occasionally to look back at the tree. Her eyes were inscrutable—I could not tell if she was fascinated, pleased, excited, or indifferent.

Margaret had already retrieved the stand from the shed, so it was a simple matter to set the tree up in it and secure it in place. It looked much larger in her living room than it did outside; in fact, until I moved it further into the corner, I thought that maybe it was too big and I would have to go get a different one.

Sonya went up to it, tentatively touched it, then looked at her mother.

"Christmas tree," said Margaret, stroking one of its branches. "It's a Christmas tree. Do you remember the one you saw last year at Grandma's house?"

Sonya returned a blank look. Margaret knelt down, bent a branch down so that she could smell it, and then gently nudged the girl a little closer so that she could do the same. Sonya leaned into it, smelled the evergreen aroma, and smiled. "Nice?" asked Margaret. Sonya nodded. "Christmas tree," she repeated, stroking the branch. Sonya reached out and did the same, still smiling.

"I think it's a hit," I said.

Margaret looked up at me and nodded. "Actually, I've been thinking about it, and I've pretty much decided to forego the ice skating today. I think it will be much more meaningful for Sonya if we spend the time decorating the apartment rather than rushing to try to beat the storm. We need to catch up on the spirit of the season. That'll take some time because I forgot how many ornaments and decorations I had in the shed. And I think it'll be more fun for her."

I nodded. "There'll be other opportunities to do that. Skating, I mean."

She stood up. "Not many. We've only got a little over two weeks before everyone comes back, and I won't take her out on the ice when all the students are out there skating. Still," she reached down and stroked her daughter's hair, "I think this will make a more lasting impression."

Indeed, it was already doing that. Sonya was so engrossed by the tree that she had literally stepped forward into it, surrounding herself with the branches. "You don't mind, do you?" she asked. "I mean, is it something you were dying to do?"

"I'm fine with it, Margaret. I can only skate in a straight line anyway, remember?"

She smiled and reached out to stroke my arm. "Right. The stream. I remember."

In fact, it was a fortuitous change of plans. I now had more than enough time to go to the village and get something out of the house. "Are we still on for coffee and Kahlua this afternoon?"

She stepped over and slid her arms around me. "Absolutely. Three o'clock?"

"Sounds perfect."

"You'll even have time to read more of the old diary."

I smiled and nodded. "It really is important that I establish the connection between the diary and the village. Otherwise . . ." I raised both hands in a gesture of futility.

"I understand. That's why I suggested it. Do what you have to do and Sonya and I will decorate the apartment. Coffee's at three. Knowing your penchant for exactitude, I expect you'll show up with about thirty seconds to spare." She slipped away from me with a furtive kiss, turned back to Sonya, and knelt down beside her.

"Till three, then," I said, turning toward the door.

She looked up at me over her shoulder with a smile. "Till three."

◆ ◆ ◆

She, of course, did not see me go up and get the snowshoes. And because I was only going to be quickly in and out, I brought the daypack but none of the other paraphernalia that I usually carried along with me, with the exception of the map, compass, and .380 automatic. I needed the pack for whatever I carried out of there. At the last minute I added the flashlight and hung my Polaroid camera around my neck, inside the parka. There was no time like the present to begin recording what the inside of the house looked like. Other than that, it was to be a brief visit, with the tractor providing the crucial difference in the time factor.

My original estimate of the time was not far off. From the moment I released the clutch to the moment I turned onto the cart track I clocked it at just under five minutes. It took less than four minutes to go up the track to the point where I had stopped plowing on my previous visit, and only about five more minutes to complete the journey to the stream. That was the end of the line and I turned the tractor around before I shut it off.

I checked my watch—it was quarter to eleven. The village was about two miles away, which would take me about an hour. I would arrive no later than noon. I would search the house for a suitable gift—I remembered the cabinet still full of china—all the while feeling marginally like a thief for even considering it, then take some pictures and come straight back. If I was out of the house by one o'clock, I would be back at the tractor by two. Since it would only take me about fifteen minutes to get back to the Ropewalk, I would arrive with plenty of time to spare.

It only took a minute to get the snowshoes on and get going. I went upstream to the juncture of the larger stream, then went upstream again until I found the tree that I had used as a bridge last time. I had already decided to enter the village from the front rather than use the back way that I had accidentally discovered. With a storm coming, I was hopeful that my original tracks would be covered so that no curious hunter or wanderer would find and follow them straight to the backdoor of the house.

Once I crossed the stream, I made good time to the waterfall. Once again, I was completely mesmerized by the wild beauty of the place, the sluice-like path that the water had worn in the rock over the eons reminding me not so much of a stream as of a giant water slide. Yes, I thought, yes, I will bring Margaret here in the summer and, yes, we will swim in the basin, prying eyes or no prying eyes. I would live for the moment.

I stopped. What had she said about a doorway at the top of the hill? She said there was a door "just sort of standing there" that I would find if I left the path along the stream and went further up the hill. I scanned the hillside for another path but did not see one, so I took a compass bearing on what appeared to be the highest point from where I was standing and headed in that direction. Because of the tractor, I knew that I had a little extra time to play with, so a few minutes spent searching for this thing would not matter.

I climbed uphill through the brush for several minutes before I came upon what must have been the path she had been talking about. It branched off to my right at a rather acute angle, which at first made me doubt it would go to the top of the hill, but then swung left after I had been on it for only twenty or thirty yards. Within minutes I was at the top. And there it was—the doorway. As I moved toward it, I noticed that I was on a gradually ascending flight of stone steps.

It stood there alone, perched like some odd monument ushering startled wanderers into a place where they might relax. It was made of stone, not wood, which explained why it had remained intact while whatever had been around it had fallen away over the centuries. Exactly *what* had been around it was anyone's guess at that point, but I suspected that the line of ruins I had seen from the valley on my earlier visit would hold some clue to the answer. Especially since I could see part of that structure not far beyond the door.

I approached and looked through it. Beyond were the remains of a long and very shallow flight of dilapidated stairs leading into what looked like some sort of maze-like structure. Because of all the brush that was in the way, and because of the heavy mantle of snow on it, I could not make out what it had been. But there was no doubt these were the ruins I had seen from below.

I stepped through and approached the other structure. These steps appeared to be made of hewn logs rather than stone, and as I went up, I noticed what appeared to be a shallow corridor in front of me with a door at the far end. I would have investigated, but saw that that section of floor had been made of wood rather than earth and had long since rotted away, leaving the doorway hanging inaccessibly in space. Below it, however, was a second door, originally designed to have been hidden by the floor above. It was smaller than the first and made of wood and, like the floor, was partly rotted and broken away. Slightly below it was a second floor, presumably of dirt, littered with the broken remains of the original floor above it. I felt an almost irresistible impulse to go down and investigate the mysterious cave-like opening beyond the splintered remains of the door, but as I moved closer, a soft groaning resounded from under my feet. I knew that this meant that the surface I was standing on was not the ground, as I had thought, but was the only still intact part of the floor that had otherwise rotted away. With something of a shock, I realized I was suspended above the lower level on who knew how tenuous a surface. Very gingerly I backed away and stepped out through the doorway.

The layout was such that it was difficult to get any closer without going through the doorframe. To the left, just a few feet away, was the ridge that overlooked the village, and on that side, a pile of rubble that had evidently been one of the building's walls would block any attempt at going that way. To the right, I could see what looked like the edge of a rocky outcropping. When I went up to it, I saw that it was a cleft in the rock, as if some huge knife had sliced the stone and left this chasm just wide enough to bar my path. This cleft ran perpendicular to the building and, oddly, the building had been built over it. In fact, I could see that the chasm entered underneath the building, behind the door on the lower level, which meant that one could get beyond the door without disturbing it just by climbing down into the chasm. But that would be no mean feat; it looked to be seven or eight feet deep and the walls were almost vertical. A stream ran along the bottom, mostly frozen over but still moving in some parts.

What the building had been and why a stream was flowing under it were mysteries to me. The total blackness into which the stream flowed when it entered the building denied any view inside. I was absolutely consumed with curiosity, but knew that I did not have the time to try to get down there to have a look. Like the bone barrow itself, this would have to wait.

I checked my watch. It was twelve-fifteen. I needed to get down to the house and find something. Before I left, though, I decided to go upstream along the chasm to possibly see where the stream came from and maybe find a way to cross the chasm. That would only take a few minutes, and after all, I did have extra time now that I had the tractor. Maybe I would even surprise Margaret by showing up late for coffee.

The cleft led to a deep, bowl-like depression in the ground, like a small circular valley. In that depression, standing hugely upright like some incongruous phallus, was a single colossal stone jutting from the earth like a tooth. And even from where I was, I could see that that single stone had been carved, by whom I had no idea, into some kind of monstrous shape, like a gigantic stone totem pole. Because it was badly weathered, it was impossible to ascertain what the figure or figures were. There appeared to be more than one face, as well as many arms, some of them serpentine in nature. The thing had what looked like mouths all over it, some connected with the various faces and some not. And parts of it were just plain amorphous. It was hideous. And up at the top, which was about twenty feet above the floor of the depression, it appeared to be unfinished, as if something had overtaken the people making it.

I was stunned. There was no way this was a natural formation. The curious hollow itself looked like an enormous well that had been partially filled in; it was almost perfectly round, and was surrounded by precipitous rock walls through which entry was only possible via a couple of gigantic cracks. Where these cracks led, I could not even guess, and since I had not brought my binoculars, I was not able to get a closer look.

Apart from the cracks, the chasm appeared to be the only way out of the basin, and the water flowing through it originated from one of the breaks in the opposite wall. It was probably an underground branch of the stream that formed the waterfall. Since the floor was covered with an accumulation of snow, it was not possible to tell if the stream flowed in a channel across the basin or simply spilled into it and out the other side. Both sides of the entrance to the chasm had what looked like piles of snow-covered rubble, as if the exit had at one time been dammed. And that, of course, was a dead giveaway.

Motive power. Whatever the ruined building was, some sort of commercial activity had taken place in there and its waterwheel had been driven by the water dammed up in the basin. I now understood the reason for having the building straddle the chasm: the water flowed into the chasm and under the building, where it quite possibly drove several waterwheels. The circular basin with its stream flowing through it had provided the builders with the perfect natural water source. They had dammed the outlet so that the basin filled and contained the water. Then they used the natural break as a conduit to direct the water under the building and into the basement where the waterwheels were located. Having the waterwheels enclosed under the building had a huge commercial advantage for the owners—it meant that they would still have motive power even in winter, when most other enterprises were literally frozen by the weather.

All of this meant that there had to be some way of channeling the water out of the basement as well, which I would no doubt discover if I could find a way across the chasm or around the basin. It was an extremely clever design, one that utilized the lay of the land to save time and money in building costs.

But it also submerged what had obviously been a sacred place of some sort to the local inhabitants. *Somebody* had carved that monstrous stone, and it clearly had not been the people who saw only monetary gain in exploiting the site. What bothered me more than the age-old, crass indifference to the sacred places of other people was the realization that I had no idea who had fashioned this thing. Megaliths were not typical of the Indians, who, with the exception of petroglyphs such as those in Machias Bay, did not leave stone monuments.

Who then?

I glanced at my watch. It was twelve-thirty. If I stuck to my original plan, that meant that I had a half hour to get to the house, find something for Margaret, and head back. But the original plan allowed for an extra forty-five minutes before I went to see her, during which time I was expecting to read further in the old diary. If I let the diary go until that night, I could easily take thirty of those forty-five minutes and still be on time for coffee. Okay, I thought, that's the new plan. Be on the way back by one-thirty.

That having been decided, I moved further along the edge of the basin hoping to spot an easy way around it. The chasm itself could not be crossed; it was almost as wide as it was deep, and even in the narrower places it was too great a risk to try to jump it.

But the basin presented its own dilemma. It was surrounded on one flank by the abrupt walls that led into the chasm and on the rest of its perimeter by close, lowering cliff-like hills whose flanks were too steep to scale. I would have to make a wide detour in order to find a spot where I could get around it to take a look at the building. And I didn't have the time for that.

I moved a little closer so that I could see the flank of the wall directly below me. Surprisingly, it was not as steep as the cliff-like wall on the opposite side. It angled downward at a steep but possibly negotiable angle. Negotiable, that is, if it weren't covered with a sheet of ice. I figured that maybe after the spring thaw I could come back and try it.

I studied the upright stone again. This had obviously been a place of worship or veneration of some deity or force of nature, carved by unknown hands at a time long veiled by the ensuing chaos of the colonial wars. One thing was clear to me—the Indians had not done this. True, they carved pictures in stone, but they did not build monoliths. Period.

The profound impact this would have on any history of the region was not lost on me. I suddenly understood how much more difficult the task was going to be. I also realized it might be impossible to ever figure out who had carved the stone and what its purpose was, leaving a permanent hole in the history, something that no historian relished. Even worse was the notion that someone else would then come along and fill in the missing piece at a later date, skating to fame on the track that I had labored to build.

That, of course, would never do.

I opened my parka and took out the Polaroid. A couple of photos were in order and the first one I took was of the stone monument. I really needed a telephoto lens, and my regular thirty-five millimeter had one, but then I would not be able to see the pictures until I could get them developed. I took two shots of the stone and one of the chasm with the building in the background. Very carefully, I placed the ejected pictures in the folds of some paper I had brought along for that purpose and nested them in one of the inside pockets of the parka. Then I worked my way along the rim of the basin to find the best place for a shot of one of the large cracks in the far wall.

It was while I was framing that next shot that the connection suddenly dawned on me. I lowered the camera and thought about the words I had read in the old diary. What was it now—something about this Captain Lewis "forthwith" harrying the savages into a declivity in the ground. A declivity. On the assumption that the diary was describing events that had happened in this area, I had assumed that the "declivity" had meant the valley in which the village now stood. But maybe it didn't. Maybe it meant this. The slope leading into the basin from where I stood was a declivity.

Looking around at the lay of the land, I could understand how anyone being pursued could be harried into this trap. There was no way around it. To the left was the ridge, which was too steep to descend. In front was the chasm, too wide to jump except maybe by some of their best sprinters. To the right was the basin. Beyond that were the lowering hills, which, like the ridge, were too steep to negotiate. The only way to escape a pursuer would be to go into the basin and race along the chasm into whatever structure the building was now concealing. For anyone caught down there, it would be like shooting fish in a barrel.

Maybe, I wondered, maybe I had just found the connection I needed to verify that the events described in the diary had taken place here. I was suddenly consumed by the desire to get back to the Ropewalk so that I could read more of the diary in the hopes of finding some reference to the basin. It was ten of one. Okay, I thought, get down to the house, get something out of the china cabinet, and get going.

I brought the camera back up, framed the shot of the crack, and pressed the button. The camera clicked and whirred, the picture ejected, and as I leaned slightly forward to remove it, that was the last I saw of it. A gust of wind grabbed it, and when my arm instinctively shot out to catch it, the snow I was standing on yielded to the ice beneath it and the next thing I knew I was flat on my back, rocketing down the incline into the basin like a ski jumper heading for the end of the ramp.

◆ ◆ ◆

Chapter 15

Do places have memories? That was what Margaret had asked, and that was the first thought to flash through my mind as I whirled to a stop like a spent hockey puck. In my spinning pirouette I had almost made it to the center of the basin, and a few feet away was the gigantic stone, one of its hideous faces appearing to grin its secret down at me as if noticeably amused, vaguely suggesting that it remembered the same thing happening once before. I tried to sit up but had to let myself go as a stabbing pain in my right elbow told me I had whacked it on something on the way down. I rolled to my left side and pushed myself up to a sitting position with that arm.

I stared upward at the stone. It was much more amorphous at such close range, and some of the things that had appeared as faces from a distance now looked more like random weathering patterns. The sky beyond it had gotten grayer as the storm neared. I did a quick inventory pat down, checked the status of the camera, made sure my limbs still worked, then got to my feet. I had a moment of panic as I reached back inside my parka for the .380 and couldn't find it, but then realized that it had slipped to another position. Apart from a bruised elbow, I was still intact.

A brief survey of the basin drove home my situation. There was absolutely no chance of getting back up the slope I had just come down. It was a sheet of ice sloped at about forty-five degrees, and I had no way of cutting hand and foot holds. The other perimeter walls were almost vertical. The only outlets were the chasm and the cracks, the latter of which looked, from this new perspective, to be too narrow. The upward sloping ground in which it was nestled added depth to the basin and made it deeper than the chasm, although the floors of both were in approximately the same plane. It was about fifty yards wide. The stream gurgled somewhere nearby under the ice and snow but only emerged at the entrance to the chasm.

Looking around, I understood my predicament immediately—I had become one of the fish in the barrel. I was trapped. Unless the chasm offered a way out, my only hope was to try to squeeze into one of the cracks and climb up toward the surface. But even that was questionable—unless the crack went far enough to get past the extreme slope of the surrounding hills, I would emerge on an incline too steep to negotiate. My gaze, following my best hope, immediately fastened on the chasm, and I headed in that direction.

Do places have memories? The question flashed through my mind again because this one certainly felt like it did, especially when I stood at the mouth of the chasm and gazed into the gloomy interior. Straight ahead, a good one hundred feet away, was the entrance to the underside of the building. Since the water had to have an outlet, I knew this was the best bet for finding a way out.

The stream took up anywhere from half to three-quarters of the floor space and the current had kept about fifty percent of it still unfrozen. There was therefore a good chance I would get wet before I got to the building, and I did not have any matches with me, a failing I made a mental note to correct for the future. Under these conditions, that little oversight could have serious consequences that resonated in the back of my mind. But, as I nervously noted to myself, it was too soon to panic and I had no choice but to chance it. Staying close to the wall furthest from the water, I entered the cleft and worked my way forward.

The snowshoes were a tremendous help. Even in those spots where it appeared that a soaking was unavoidable, I was able to use them as temporary bridges spanning stones and patches of ice. I therefore, contrary to my own expectations, reached the basement of the building suffering nothing worse than wet boot soles. Once I stepped through the opening, the only light was the feeble shaft from the broken door, and that only reached a few feet into the darkness. As soon as I stepped away from it, the gloom closed around me so completely that I had to use the flashlight. I checked my watch. It was one o'clock. I had a half hour to find my way out. The thought of getting down to the house to find a present for Margaret was now officially no longer an option.

I found myself in what was essentially a man-made cave. Man-made because the natural stone formation was a chasm like the one I had just passed through, except that the ceiling was the floor of the structure built above it. It had turned ninety degrees from the first chasm and was wider, deeper, and considerably longer. The light revealed a darkened tunnel that was virtually free of snow and strewn with all kinds of debris, most of it appearing to be logs and assorted pieces of wood. The stream flowed in, collected in a bowl-like basin, then redirected itself out along the floor in a well-worn channel that varied in width from about four to ten feet. I did not see an outlet.

In spite of my situation, I was entranced. What a curious idea this was—the foundation of the building was the chasm that the structure was straddling. It, in effect, left the "basement" almost infinitely large since it was, after all, the entire chasm. I was sure that the piles of rotting and broken wood that I was seeing were the remnants of waterwheel machinery.

I took off my snowshoes, tied them, and slung them across my back. Then I went over to check out the channel. Ice peppered with frozen dirt lined the sides, and a sheet of flowing water slid between them and into the darkness. It was obviously a conduit and had to have an outlet somewhere, whether I could see it or not. Further down the chasm, I could hear the rumbling of what must have been falling water and knew that had to be the way out. The question was, could I get through the tangle of debris in front of me? And then, once I did that, would I find a way out when I got to the other side?

I walked up to where the pile began. It was an amazing tangle, a web of crisscrossed logs and boards in some spots reaching nearly to the ceiling, which had to be a good ten feet off the floor. It was frozen in place, of course, but had very little surface ice on it due to the protection afforded by its concealed location. This meant that I could theoretically climb it without having to worry about slipping off at every handhold. I stuck the flashlight in my mouth, grabbed an overhead board, and pulled myself tentatively upward to test the strength in my elbow. I winced at a stab of pain but realized I could keep going. A couple more moves and I was able to see over the pile.

The echoing noise of the water suddenly went up in volume. Beyond the pile were the remains of a stone wall, and through a break in that wall, the stream raced with an unexpected acceleration. And no wonder. The floor of the chasm dropped another five feet or so and the conduit formed a sluice through which the water was racing. Above the sluice, as I had suspected, were the decaying remains of a waterwheel, only identifiable as such by the several spokes that still radiated outward from the hub. Beyond the wall, there did not appear to be any place to walk; the water seemed to fill the entire chasm from one side to the other and was only partially frozen. I could not even guess how deep it was.

I flicked the light back and forth, hoping to spot something. And there it was. Against the left wall was an obvious walkway made of stone that appeared to run the length of the chasm. If I could get to it, I might be able to avoid the chaos in the center and find a way out. And the waterwheel held the answer. Its shaft, obviously hewn from one single gigantic tree trunk, was a bridge that could be used to cross the water. It looked polished and was obviously icy, but I figured I could straddle it.

I took a moment to collect myself. This was a dangerous plan. Falling into icy water in this weather meant death, even if the water was shallow enough to climb out of. I had no matches, and even if I did there was nothing down there to burn since the wood had obviously been saturated over the centuries. "Do I want to try this?" I mumbled. "Or should I go back and investigate the breaks in the perimeter wall?"

My situation was more desperate than I was allowing myself to accept. The breaks were not the answer, even assuming I could climb up through one of them. But the chasm was obviously dangerous, and if I fell or got soaked, there was no hope of ever being found. It was really quite preposterous. If this had been summer, the incline I had slid down would be stone or dirt, or both, and possible to scale. But now it was ice. I hadn't brought the crampons I had found in the shed, of course, so my rescue tools were back in my room. I had not even brought my space blanket to help stave off the overnight cold if I couldn't find a way out. It would have been funny if it were not so terminal. I was checkmated.

"It's too bad human destiny doesn't come with an option to go back," I mused with grim humor. At a time like that, I could've used an alternative outcome, like an alter-option, something that would rewind the time-tape so that I could go back and do it right. I made a mental note to write that down at some future time when I could better afford the deviant humor.

But it was while I was pondering this gridlocked dilemma that I saw what looked like the answer. I did not need to cross on the wheel shaft. All I needed to do was work my way through the spider web of debris toward the left side, then move forward over the wall. The walkway looked like it could be reached from that side. I stuck the flashlight back in my mouth and headed over.

I was half right. I was able to climb onto the wall from that side and the walkway was just beyond it, but there was a gap of several feet between them. I could not just slither down the wall and step onto the walkway; I would have to lower myself, then reach out with one foot and hope it was not too far.

"Okay," I muttered with gallows humor, "*now* you can start to panic." And the reason why was obvious. If I lost my grip on the wall, or if what I was holding onto let go, I would plummet into the gap with nothing to stop me. The water was about five feet below the walkway and I could not tell if it was frozen. If it was, I would have a reprieve, an alter-option. If it wasn't, or was too thinly iced over, I would go in. Maybe it was only a foot deep, in which case my only risk was frostbite on the way back. Maybe it was very deep, in which case my risk was hypothermia or drowning.

The absurdity of my situation went up a notch when I thought of a possible solution and simultaneously realized I could not implement it. If I had thought to bring the hatchet along, I would have been able to cut some of the planks and lay them across the gap as a bridge. But I hadn't brought it, so it was not an option. In spite of my predicament, I marveled at the converging consequences of a series of wrong decisions. If I had brought matches, if I had brought the crampons, if I had brought the hatchet, if, indeed, I had stuck to my original intent for even going there, I would not be in this mess. "I just *had* to know what was there," I muttered, and now I knew only too well. If, if, if—destiny logic once again. If Margaret had not stayed, if Ben had not left her, if I had not become involved with her, if I had not gone looking for a unique gift, if none of this had happened, I would not now be faced with yet another potentially wrong decision, one with dire consequences.

It was almost quarter after one. On top of everything else, the storm would start soon and coat the tractor with ice, possibly rendering it inoperable. At the very least, the warmth from my butt would melt the ice on the seat and soak through my pants, then freeze again before I got back. And there I would be—bruised, soaked, giftless, and frozen to the tractor. I pictured Margaret thawing out my ass with a hair dryer while I pondered the pain in my right elbow and joked about that always having been my better side.

I had to act. The walkway seemed to be the only answer. Obviously, whoever had built this structure—whatever it was—had included it so that the chasm could be accessed, if for no other reason than to service the waterwheels. I had to get to it and find how they got in and out. Of course, once I took that step, I would be irreversibly committed to the plan since I could not return, at least not that way. But if I had to, I could probably get back by crossing the waterwheel shaft, as I originally intended. Either that, or I had to abandon the plan altogether and try to find some other way. Whatever the course of action, I had to decide immediately.

Consciously fighting that nerve-wracking sense of doubt and denial, I had to accept that there really was no choice. This was the only known option, and any other possibility would waste too much time just looking for it. I tested the handholds on the wall and then lowered myself down the side. When I was parallel with the walkway, I reached out with my left foot and felt its surface. Secured by that one firm foundation, I found new handholds and tentatively lowered myself in an effort to find the surface of the water with the other foot. It turned out that the faint sheen I had seen from the top of the wall had been an optical illusion—the water was only about two feet below the level of the walkway, not five. And it was frozen. Carefully, almost tenderly, I tested it for firmness, first with a faint push, then with progressively harder efforts. It wouldn't break. Still holding onto the wall and supported by the other foot, I gradually shifted my weight to the ice. It held. In fact, by the pounding it was able to take, it was obviously no less than three to four inches thick. I was relieved. If the path led nowhere, I could return this way after all.

I pushed myself away from the wall and onto the walkway. I now had both hands free, so with the flashlight in one and a firm grip on the wall with the other, I worked my way forward. The sound of the water got louder.

From the way the light glinted off the stones below my feet, it was obvious the surface was coated with a faint layer of ice. This was an unsettling discovery because the path was only about three feet wide and was very uneven. In some places it was obviously nothing more than a natural ledge that the builders had utilized as they constructed the walkway, and as such, it just naturally sloped one way or the other. The utter blackness of the chasm beyond its edge both unnerved and encouraged me—unnerved because anything impenetrable to human sight has always been frightening, and encouraged precisely because it concealed the reality of what lay beyond. From the ever-growing sound of the water, it was obvious there was some kind of cataract nearby, perhaps another sluice for another waterwheel. I kept the flashlight beam directed at the path in front of me; I didn't dare look.

Further down, near the end of the flashlight's range, was a vertical half-shadow, a faint sheen of something that was either a bar to further progress or perhaps a way to climb out. When I got to it, I could see that it was, indeed, a way out. It was a stone staircase, hewn out of the living rock of the chasm itself, crude and uneven but leading upwards. I didn't even care where it led to as long as it was out of there. At its top, I could see a rectangle of light and my mood lightened. I had found a way out.

I took one cautious step upwards and stopped. These "stairs" were nothing more than rough stone, and it was apparent from the sheen that they, too, had a coating of ice. There was no guardrail of any kind, of course, so if I slipped it would mean disaster. The sound of the water was very loud and now, in view of this uncertain escape route, began to take on a sinister tone. I had studiously avoided shining the light at it so that I would not become unnerved while on the walkway, but now I realized I needed to have a real assessment of the risk. So I stepped back down and turned the light on the chasm.

What I saw made me instinctively back up so that the snowshoes slung over my back scraped against the wall. There was no waterwheel spanning the chasm at that point. Instead, the water raced in an icebound channel whose sides where smooth and polished, without any of the rocky protuberances I had seen at the beginning. And then it surged in a single, rippling body over the lip of an opening, a hole, an abyss whose bottom lay at who knew what depth and that led into who knew what subterranean plumbing. *This* was the cataract I had been hearing ever since I entered the chasm.

I was absolutely terrified. If I slipped off the stairs and went into the water, I would be swept by the current into that hole as surely as any of the countless pieces of debris that must have found their way into it over the centuries. There was no hope of grabbing something because there was nothing to hold onto. With my heart suddenly racing, I flattened myself against the wall and instinctively groped for handholds.

I could feel the paralysis of panic taking hold of my limbs. This was pure madness. My mind became a collage of thought fragments as reason yielded to pure instinct, yet I still knew that, if I didn't collect myself in the face of this new peril, my own reactions would become an even bigger danger. "Alright," I said aloud, my voice quavering, "Alright. Breathe. Close your eyes and take long, slow breaths."

So I did that. And almost immediately, as if programmed into me, my martial arts training from years before came back. In my mind I suddenly saw, not the face of Mae or Margaret, but that of my teacher, a former combat instructor in the Korean army. "It is nothing," he used to say of the injuries we would sustain while fighting. "You will forget. Now count." That was what he had taught us to do at the end of class—focus on breathing and count. So I automatically began counting the seconds it took to breathe in through my nose and exhale through my mouth. And I suddenly understood that he had been showing us how to keep the reasoning mind engaged after the adrenalin pump. When you count, you cannot think of anything else except the order of the numbers. In just a few minutes, the panic had subsided and I found myself calming down. I cautiously, deliberately, let go of the wall with one hand and turned to examine the steps again.

They had ice on them, true, but only in patches. With my gloved hand, I could feel where the raw stone ended and the ice began, and once I recognized the texture of the two surfaces, I knew I could work around it. "Okay," I said aloud, as if to reassure myself, "this is doable." I took one step up, then another. Calmly, paying no attention to the black abyss gaping beside me, I examined the wall for handholds. There was a small break that rose more or less parallel to the stairs and was wide enough to accept my hand. There was nothing to grab in there, but I discovered I could use the rock climber's trick of making a fist inside the crack so that my hand would not slip out. It was enormously reassuring and I took two more steps upward. The rectangle of light was only about six feet above my head and I no longer needed the flashlight, so I stuck it back into one of my pockets.

The steps were becoming progressively icier, clearly indicating that water had gotten onto them from above, not from the spray of the stream. But a loose fragment of the wall provided me with a hammer, and I found that the thickening ice was actually an advantage because it broke into pieces that I could then sweep away. In less than a minute I was near the top of the steps, marveling that I had gotten that far but reluctant to celebrate my success for fear that fate would slap me once again. So I took a moment to evaluate the available handholds I could use to pull myself out. After I did that, I took the flashlight out and shined it into the chasm one last time.

Some instinct in me needed to see that hole from the higher perspective. Perhaps on some level I sensed it would be a reassurance, or even a sort of passive boast, that I had so far escaped the yawning death in whose gullet the thundering echo of the water was louder than ever. The beam from the flashlight did not get very far into it because of my viewing angle, so all I was able to see was that it continued downward past the range of the light. In essence, all I accomplished by doing that was to heighten the sense of dread all over again. I then shined it down the chasm to get an idea of how much further it went, but noticed that it stopped in a tangle of debris no more than twenty or thirty yards beyond the hole. If the steps had not been there, I would have found myself at a dead end.

I flicked the light over the debris, briefly back to the hole, and then across the chasm to the opposite wall. There it revealed something totally unexpected.

Faces were staring back at me. Stone faces, petroglyphs, carved into the wall in such numbers that they were crowding each other aside. They were stylized faces, mostly round or egg-shaped, with simple holes for two eyes and a mouth. Some had what appeared to be antlers or horns. Among them were animal figures, some of them clearly identifiable as moose and deer, while others were fantastic creatures that looked like giant birds. To the right of the faces were the footprints of various animals, some of them enormous, all carved in that same stylistic rendering that made identification so difficult. In spite of my situation, I had to get some pictures before I left; there was no way in hell I was ever going to come back to this site. I was sure the flash, intended simply for the darker recesses of the house, would be adequate for the chasm as well, so I used it to capture the petroglyphs. I then tucked the ejected photos into my inside pockets, put the camera away, and hoisted myself out through the hole and onto the structure that straddled the chasm, clinging with still trembling hands to the fragile holds offered by errant stubs of wood as I briefly suspended myself above the giant gullet. Then I stretched out and crawled like some arctic reptile as far as those few grasping pulls would get me.

I was out. Even so, my heart was still pounding, and I moved even further away from the stairs, instinctively pressed myself against the wall, and closed my eyes. When I opened them, another surprise awaited me. I was now inside the building that I had seen earlier from the valley below and that had appeared as simply a line of blank-faced ruins without doors. But it was not a line of ruins—it was one continuous ruin, a long building in various stages of decay and collapse. Even before I spotted the remnants of the spindles and the carriage that was used to wind the strings, I knew what it was. A ropewalk.

I pushed myself to my feet while still holding onto the openings in the wall and looked around, disbelieving. I was in the hall of the mountain king, a long, snow-choked tube concealing a hidden hoard of unsuspected treasures. Great amorphous mounds poked through the snow like shrouded furniture, bathed in the diffuse gray-white light from the overcast sky. Machinery. They were the various mechanisms used to spin the rope. It was all there, decrepit, decaying, and dangerously poised above the unforgiving chasm below. This, I realized, had to have been the source of the wealth that was so prominently displayed in the house down in the valley. The village made ropes. The owner got wealthy.

Then the village died. Sometime either during or after that, the Ropewalk that I currently lived in was built, but whether this was a replacement or a competitor was impossible to know.

I pulled out the camera and saw that I had two shots left. I aimed one down the hall to the right and one to the left, where the building had collapsed, leaving a wide open, panoramic view of that end of the valley. And framed in that panorama, a good half mile away, was the pond I had tried to cross and, beyond that, the dome-shaped figure of the bone barrow. I snapped the picture, put the ejected photo in my inner pocket, and then stared at the barrow. The connection that followed dawned on me unexpectedly.

The stream in the chasm fed the pond. I had no doubt whatsoever. The water flowed into the hole, through an underground stream, and emerged in the pond. *That* was why the ice broke when I tried to cross, why it appeared to be rotten. The underground stream entered at that point.

I chuckled and shook my head. The chasm had been reaching out for me even then, despite the fact that I knew nothing of its existence. And now, with the discovery of a second ropewalk, a prehistoric religious site of some sort, and petroglyphs in the chasm, I realized that the history of the region was more tangled than ever. I *had* to read more in the old diary, maybe even in the proprietors' records as well. It was imperative that I unwind the twisted skein of unexpected events in which I found myself entangled. Quite frankly, the existence of the village was no less of a blank spot on the map of the region than the giant stone in the basin. Neither one should have been there.

But my immediate problem was getting out of there. I was still not in the clear. I dared not try to cross to the other side of the structure because I had no idea if the snow was concealing weak spots in the floor. Besides, the mere thought of being above that gaping maw was more than I could bear. My only option was to head back in the direction from which I had come, and given the long, flat surface in front of me, I saw no reason to climb out through one of the window holes. I strapped my snowshoes back on and slowly worked my way back. The interior wall was so broken down and missing so many planks that I had handholds all along the way.

When I reached the door at the other end I could go no further. I was now on the other side of the doorway that I had seen hanging in the air when I first arrived, and I knew that the floor beyond that door was gone. It was the end of the line unless I climbed out the window hole near me and made my way along the edge of the ridge. There was no point in risking a crossing of the decrepit floor to check the window on the other side; I had seen on the way in that it opened over the chasm that had led me into the ropewalk's "basement" and would bring me back to my start point like a recurring bad dream. It was this side or nothing, so out I went. I had about six feet of snow-covered surface to walk on as I headed for the next obstruction.

That next obstruction was the pile of rubble I had seen from the standing door and that had prohibited me from getting a closer look at the building from that side. But what had seemed hugely insurmountable then was now a laughable pimple on the landscape after the harrowing journey I had just had. I took the snowshoes off again and climbed like a spider monkey over the tangled wreck, not even nodding in apprehension at the fall of the ridge right beside me. Anything—*anything*—was preferable to tight-roping what might have been the last minutes of my life along the edge of that freezing silver ribbon that would have swept me with utter indifference into some lost crevice. In less than a minute, I was over it and back at the stone doorway that had started the whole mess.

I took a moment to compose and congratulate myself for escaping the eternal midnight in the chasm, then glanced at my watch. It was twenty-five minutes before two o'clock. I laughed when I realized that, in spite of everything, I still had enough time to get back for my three o'clock coffee date with Margaret. I hadn't found a gift for her despite my intentions, but I *had* made some astonishing discoveries about the site of the village.

The storm started on the way back. I was only halfway to the tractor when I heard the first tentative "ticks" of sleet falling on the withered leaves that still clung to some of the smaller trees. I stopped to listen. A pervasive rustling, a faint, barely audible hiss—that was what it was. When I was a kid, I was sure I could hear the snow falling, and it wasn't until I got older that I realized it wasn't the snow falling that I was hearing, but the snow landing. Back then, if I stood motionless in the absolute stillness, I could feel it embrace me, turn me into a part of the landscape, as if some primal arm of nature had pulled me into its circle for a few moments. I had lost that feeling as I got older, but now, with my senses still honed in a way that only mortal danger could induce, I leaned against a tree and stood absolutely still.

Snow was mixed in with the sleet. It fell quietly on and around me, and as I stood there, I gazed with renewed interest at the snowflakes on my sleeve, at the clusters of tiny, fragile stars and pinwheels, impossible in their symmetry. It was so still that I began to feel myself melting into the hillside, becoming part of the rock face of the continent, oblivious to time and rooted in the earth. Like a backwoods legend, my form turned to stone, weathered to an amorphous hulk, and simply sat. Time wasted its knuckles on my granite face. For a moment, I had become changeless.

I snapped out of it when I heard a crackling, as of something sneaking away from me in the steadily deepening veil of grayness that had begun to shroud everything. But I couldn't see a thing. Looking for the source, I became aware for the first time of the presence of stone walls that I hadn't seen before, those relics of past lives nurtured from the land that were so ubiquitous in the woods all over New England. They were boundary markers, winding into the invisible distance like crumbling gray streamers. My guess was the old accounts ledger would shed some light on whose they once were.

I roused myself and hurried on to the tractor, hoping that it was not covered in a glaze of ice. As I emerged from the thick wall of fir trees that made the hike upstream to the ridge so forbidding, I saw it silhouetted down on the track. Alright, I thought, there's my taxi. Let's hope it starts.

It did. It was partially covered in a frozen glaze but for the most part the overarching evergreens had protected it. While it warmed up, I brushed the seat off with my sleeve and did one last inventory pat down. Then I climbed aboard and was about to put it in gear when I heard the stealthy crackling noise again. I glanced up the slope toward the route I had taken and there, off to the right on a slight outcropping, was the wolf. It sat there atop the rise, starkly silhouetted against the darkening background, eerily fading in and out of focus from the rising intensity of the storm. We stared at each other for a moment, then I pulled away with the tractor and began down the cart track toward the coast highway. After a moment, I looked back and saw that it was gone. When the track entered the gloomy, gulch-like depression, it left me feeling suddenly vulnerable to attack, so I took out the .380 and chambered a round. Then I lowered the hammer to the half-cock safety position and threaded my finger into the trigger guard—I was not going to be hamstrung by that problem again. I drove the tractor with one hand.

In a minute, the gulch passed behind me and I was going through the broad, smooth, campus-like clearing. There I could plainly see that the storm had picked up in intensity and that snow was now mixing with the sleet in big, wet flakes. It looked like a nor'easter. With the gloom of the woods now past, I holstered the .380 and upshifted to pick up some speed. I had no sooner done that when I saw that the wolf was still with me.

Like a ghost fading in and out of view, it was paralleling my pace about fifty yards to the left, jogging along seemingly oblivious to my presence. Its closeness unnerved me. What was going on here? Was this some kind of game? Or was he just doing the lupine version of playing with his dinner? I pulled out the .380 again. This time, I thought, I *am* going to fire a warning shot. I stopped the tractor and put it in neutral. The wolf stopped at the same moment, turned to look at me, then sat on its haunches as if taking a break. It did not look malevolent; in fact, it kind of sat there looking at me as if expecting me to come to some kind of decision. I raised the weapon and aimed well beyond the animal, thinking I had to be careful in spite of my spitefulness that I didn't hit him, not because I might wound him and send him into paroxysms of slavering madness as he came after me, but because, though adventurous in the telling, I did not wish him any harm. I imagined the sound exploding around me, then rumbling away into the fast-fading distance while silence closed over me once again.

But I didn't shoot. Something in his—or her—bearing told me there was no harm intended here. We stared at each other over a distance of barely fifty paces, and the thing looked at me like a lost pet would size up a re-found owner.

Did it know me? I wondered.

I lowered the hammer and holstered the weapon, slipped the tractor into first gear, and started toward the highway again. I had decided to keep a wary eye on the wolf in case it got any closer. But a few seconds later, when I turned my head to check on it, it was already gone.

The storm had become so intense I was loosing my orientation to the track. Because of the thickening gloom, I had turned the lights on back in the gulch and now, because I was in a wide open field with no trees to shield me, the effect of the snow in the headlights, even with some fading sunlight filtering through, was hypnotic. I was already having trouble with depth perception. I had to keep shaking my head and looking around for landmarks to maintain my bearing. At one point I nearly panicked as I realized I was not on the track anymore, that

I had drifted into the field and the track was lost. But I was able to get back when I glimpsed the stone wall and the barbed wire fence that bordered the track on that one side. But I still could not see the highway and felt I should have reached it by then. I began having weird fantasies, like I had become unanchored in time, and imagined I might run into a band of roving Norsemen, the same guys who had carved the stones found at Spirit Pond, separated from their longship and eyeing me with mirthless wonder and mistrust, perhaps thinking me Thor from the sound of the tractor.

And then I came out on the highway. It was already covered with several inches of new snow and, although I recognized the futility of it, I lowered the plow to at least clear that away before it got any deeper.

I might have gone right by the macadam road if I hadn't seen the remnants of the original swath I had cut through the old snow still visible under the new. I left the plow in the lowered position as I headed for the Ropewalk.

Everything around me had vanished into a blur of white, even the massive Engineering building, and when at last I pulled into the yard in front of the shed, I could scarcely raise my eyes beyond the front of the tractor without being blinded by sleet and snow. I cleared myself a track, then opened the door and drove the tractor in. Although I could not see myself, I knew I must have looked like a live snowman as I straightened up and stepped down off the machine. The tractor itself looked like a huge, wheeled snowdrift with every available surface fluffed up and rounded off with large, white pillows. I found a broom and swept it off before I left.

I was about halfway to the Ropewalk when I hit a patch of hidden ice and went down, landing on, of all places, my already injured right elbow. "Shit," I brawled as I cradled the arm and rubbed the joint. I rolled to my left as I had in the basin and climbed to my feet, then gingerly, carefully, negotiated the rest of the distance to the front door. I tested it first to make sure it was locked, then got out my keys and let myself in. Since we weren't planning any outdoor social events, I wrapped the chain through the handles and went up to my room.

The sight of myself in the mirror confirmed my suspicions. I looked like the abominable snowman. Covered in white, the hair poking out from under my hat matted and frozen, my nose red and eye sockets like a pair of caves, I mumbled to myself: "Now, would you let your daughter go out with someone who looks like this?" I pulled everything off and hung it all up to dry, then dug out some clean clothes and headed down to the bathroom. It was ten minutes to three but punctuality or not, I needed a quick shower. That done, and feeling moderately civilized again, I checked under my bed for monster spiders, then headed down to Margaret's apartment. It was a few minutes after three when I knocked. "It's me."

I heard the deadbolts shoot back and the door opened, but only a few inches. She peeked out at me, and at first I thought there was something horribly wrong, but her smile said no, everything was fine, and a moment later she said: "Close your eyes."

So I did. I heard the door open and she reached out for me, led me forward, and closed the door behind me. The fragrance of pine and incense surrounded me as she said: "Okay, you can open them." And when I did, I was stunned at the magical transformation I saw all around me. There were candles on every elevated surface and toy nutcrackers on tables, Santa Claus figurines, swags of braided pine branches, tinsel-covered festoons, and ornaments everywhere. The only light was from the candles; she had lowered the window shades to seal out the storm.

"What do you think?" she asked.

I was completely taken by it, unlatched in time once again and sent back to my childhood, to fragmented memories of skating on the stream and coming home to warmth and comfort and delicious smells. I hadn't seen anything like this in years. I was speechless.

"Is it okay?" she asked again.

I turned to her. "It's marvelous. How long did all this take?"

She laughed. "Well, we had our share of adventure this afternoon, didn't we, Sonya?"

The little girl, who had been sitting half under the tree and looking through one of her picture books, looked up and smiled. "First we broke some ornaments, some of which were family heirlooms that I'd had for a long time. Then we spilled hot chocolate all over the kitchen floor." Her eyebrows arched as she smirked in mock distress. "But we got it done. Ready for coffee?"

I rubbed my elbow. "You have no idea how ready I am."

So while Sonya looked at her book, we retreated to the kitchen, where the coffee had already been prepared and the Kahlua was in the center of the table. I sat there numb as the steaming warmth seeped into my bones, marveling at the tranquility, basking in the smell of hot coffee and incense. My elbow throbbed and I instinctively rubbed it, only half listening to Margaret's recounting of the events of the day. The chasm and its treacherous hole rose unbidden in my mind like a rerun of a bad movie, yawning upward like a giant drain hole. I closed my eyes and banished it by counting.

"So," she said, warming her hands on the coffee mug and looking up with a smile. "That's what my day was like. And how was yours?"

◆ ◆ ◆

Chapter 16

A sense of non-normality can creep up on you so gradually that you don't notice the taint until you're either removed from its nearness or rattled into seeing it. Otherwise, it simply becomes a part of your life. I had been trying to put the various events of the previous few days together in my head, but something was not lining up, and I could not put my finger on what it was until I glanced into Sonya's bedroom and remembered that I still had to put insulation in her closet wall.

I had given Margaret a brief recap of what had happened that day—including the side trip to the standing doorway but minus the treacherous chasm and its hole—and she had gone over to help Sonya hang an ornament on the tree. As I looked over at the girl playing, I saw that trick of light again, except this time, instead of transforming her into some odd creature, her features had changed into a reflection of Margaret's, almost as if Margaret were staring into a mirror. But it was only for a moment—none of these startling shape-shifts of hers had any permanence. They seemed to fluctuate with the light and viewing angle, and when I took a sip of coffee and looked back, I saw that she was Sonya once again, smiling her overly large smile as Margaret helped her with the bauble.

Beyond Margaret was the door to Sonya's bedroom, and from where I was sitting, I could see the door to her closet partially reflected in the mirror on her dresser. That was what triggered the reminder about the insulation. It was also what caused the sense of something not adding up to crystallize for a moment. Sonya's closet was built against the wall that separated her room from Margaret's. If outside air were getting into the inner wall and no insulation was in that wall, then Margaret's room should have also been cold. But it wasn't. So while Margaret continued to help Sonya, I got up and went into her room to take a closer look.

The paneling was the same type throughout the apartment, so whatever affected one place had the obvious potential for affecting other places. The draft that I noticed coming from inside Sonya's closet would thus, theoretically, be noticeable on Margaret's side of the same wall. But no cold air was coming out in spite of the storm raging outside. I was pondering this when Margaret appeared in the doorway.

"What's up? Looking for something?"

"Yes, actually. I just remembered I still have to put insulation into the wall of Sonya's closet, but was wondering why no cold air was coming out of the same wall on your side."

She seemed as surprised at this as I was and came up beside me to check. She ran her hand all along the wall and, like me, found no draft. "That's odd. Maybe the insulation is still in there but came loose on her side so that the draft could get around it."

I shrugged. "Maybe."

"Egan, you don't have to go to all that trouble, especially with this storm. I have an old quilt that isn't being used for anything, so maybe you can just tack it up against her wall to contain the draft. That's all we really need. When Sil gets back, I'll tell him about the problem and he can install the insulation."

I was relieved at the suggestion. I did not relish the thought of going out into the storm to get the insulation from the shed any more than I wanted to tear the wall out to mount it. I had visions of standing there with a broom while I opened the panels, ostensibly to clean up the inevitable mess, but in actuality to use as a weapon if that spider showed up again. I could not get past the image of a bunch of those hideous things pouring out and swarming all over each other like a bucket of multi-legged tennis balls. I put my hand on her shoulder and said: "That's the best news I've had all day."

"Come on out. I'll show you what we've done."

She had snuffed out the candles and turned on the lights in the meantime, so when she brought me out to the living room, the first thing I saw was a bunch of presents along the wall, neatly wrapped and waiting to be placed under the tree. Each one had a personal touch to it, very thoughtfully tied with large, decorative hand-made bows. I was amazed at how she could create an aura of magic just by the way she wrapped a present. For a moment the entire scene caused me to forget myself as it moved me like a dream toward a long-forgotten feeling of belonging, of *being* somewhere, that had vanished what seemed like eons ago. Even the tree played a role as its fragrance caused sputtering memory fragments to re-emerge like feelings left dangling from a spruce branch years before. I knew it was temporary, ephemeral, and would float away in a matter of weeks, but how I yearned for just one more touch of that emotionally charged life that she knew so well.

"Are you okay?" she asked.

I turned to her. "Yes, I'm fine. Why do you ask?"

"I don't know. You just seemed sad or distant about something, that's all."

"No, I'm fine."

She stared at me for a moment, her look saying she only half believed me. "Tomorrow's Christmas Eve."

"Yes."

She took my hand and led me into the kitchen. "Let's get back to the coffee. You can tell me more about this odd stone you found. I thought you said you weren't going to go back to the village today."

I sat down and warmed my hands on the mug. "I wasn't intending to, but since I got the tractor going I wanted to see how much time that would save me. Then one thing led to another—you know how that is."

She nodded. There was no way I could reveal that my original plan was to find some unique gift for her in the house, especially since I had not yet told her about the house and was still undecided whether I ever would.

"The stone appears to have been a religious device, maybe an animistic ritual site of some sort, like the function of a totem pole. It was very big, maybe a total of twenty feet tall.

"Sounds like you've already got it figured out," she said.

"No, I don't. It's a monolith, a carved stone. The American Indians didn't do that." I paused to let that sink in for a second. "The basin it was standing in had a stream running through it, and had at one

199

point been dammed so that it formed a pond that was then used to turn waterwheels."

"Waterwheels for what?"

I glanced up at her and grinned. "For the ropewalk."

"For the what?"

"That standing doorway you told me about—it had at one time been the entrance to another ropewalk, whose ruins are still there beyond it. That was the line of ruins I'd seen from the valley on my first visit."

She lowered her coffee cup. "How odd. Why would they have two so close together?"

"Don't know, but competition seems to be the likeliest explanation. The history of the region is evidently a lot more convoluted than I thought it would be."

And so it went on. I delved into some detail about what I had seen inside the ruins of the ropewalk, about the rope making apparatus still there, about the building having collapsed at one end so that the bone barrow could be seen from inside. Just by the shape of the narrative—by which I mean judiciously omitted details—I led her to believe that I had simply gone inside the building to have a look around. I did not mention the chasm. Nor did I tell her about part of the floor beyond the doorway having collapsed because that would cause her to ask how I had gotten into the building, which would bring me back to the chasm. But in so doing, I had begun to realize that I was in a sense lying to her. I had not told her about the wolf, or the house, or the spider, either. We were not yet even officially together and already I had secrets from her, some borne of the necessity of the moment, like the gift I wanted to find, but others—like the house itself—spawned from that part of me that guarded something I alone needed to hang onto for some reason. And now I was withholding the reality of the chasm.

"I can see why Sil did not want you folks going there when you went on that hike," I finally said. "The site is extremely dangerous. Who knows what part of it will collapse next."

She nodded, got up, went over to the window, and pulled the shade outward to check on the storm. It was already dark but, even so, I could see the snowflakes swirling against the pane. "It looks like it's more snow than sleet now," she said. She released the shade and came back to the table. "I wonder how long it's supposed to last."

"I have a feeling we're going to be snowbound," I said. She shot me a look. "But who cares, right? It's not like we were going anywhere and now have to cancel our plans. With the highway closed, it really doesn't matter what it does outside." I began humming the notes to the song "Let it Snow." She smiled and began to sing while I continued to hum.

> *"Oh, the weather outside is frightful,*
> *but the fire's so delightful,*
> *and since we've no place to go,*
> *let it snow, let it snow, let it snow."*

We both laughed and raised our coffee mugs in salutation. Sonya had stopped looking at her picture book and was staring at us. "'Frightful' is the word, alright," I said. "Too bad we don't have a fireplace so that we actually could enjoy a delightful fire."

She smiled. "I've always wanted a fireplace. When I was a girl, my best friend had one and we used to warm ourselves by it after playing outside. I was so envious. I thought when I got married that I would have one, but Ben thought they were messy and jacked up the heating costs, so our house in Connecticut didn't have one. I thought for sure when we moved to Maine we'd live in a house with a fireplace, but even that didn't happen. Then, when we came here, well . . . ." She waved her hand in an arc describing the entire apartment.

"Looks like we'll have to find a house with a fireplace," I said with a smile, and we raised our mugs again in what was an obvious gesture of concurrence on her part.

"To the fireplace," she said.

"To the fireplace." We clanked the mugs together and I glanced toward the living room to see if Sonya was still watching. But she was gone; the book was lying there open but she was nowhere to be seen. Must be in her room, I thought, but then saw the tree rustle and realized she must have walked right into its embrace, as she had done before. So while Margaret got up to get us more coffee, I leaned back in my chair to try to see her and spotted her standing there amidst the branches as if hiding. Except that she was not just standing there—she was holding a branch in each hand and had brought them to her face, tenderly rubbing the soft needles across her forehead. And her lips were moving. Margaret came back with the coffeepot, saying something I didn't hear, while I, still undecided about what level of understanding the girl was actually capable of, wrestled with the half-accepted notion that Sonya was talking to the tree.

◆ ◆ ◆

It was understood that I would stay for supper. I went and got more frozen vegetables from my stash in the kitchen freezer and even brought forth—in the gift-giving spirit of the season—a Boston cream pie that I had thawed out the day before. Margaret's eyebrows shot upward at the sight.

"You don't count calories?" she asked.

"Not if I can help it. Every now and then I indulge. I figure one piece of Boston cream pie is worth about two miles of walking, so I schedule my pie bingeing around my hiking plans. So far," and here I patted my still flat stomach, "it seems to be working."

"By the time we finish that, you're going to have to jog the full length of the highway to work it off."

"So be it." I raised it like an offering to the gods of the hearth, a sprawling calorie-ridden sugar-and-lard thing wobbling on the altar of Bacchus. "Once or twice a year can be managed. At the very least Sonya will love it."

And she did. At her first taste of it, her face lit up and she beamed at her mother, who told her that I was the one who had brought it. So the girl turned toward me, her face a blank mask of uncertainty, then slowly smiled. "You're winning her over," said Margaret.

But I knew that. That was the intent. Inwardly, I was embarrassed and ashamed at the things I had said and thought about Sonya, and I knew that I had to somehow bond with her, not just for the sake of my relationship with Margaret but because, in spite of who and what she was, she was human. Somewhere in the darkened depths of her sadly miswired brain, the same needs that all of us had were struggling to be realized. This poor child, a night creature who looked at pictures and talked to trees, would forever be a thing apart. Margaret—and now I—would be all the love and security she would ever know.

When dinner was over, I helped Margaret clear everything away and then we went out to the living room to trim the tree. Sonya had already hung several ornaments on the lower branches and I left these on while I strung the lights around it. Then, while she continued to decorate the lower part of the tree, Margaret and I finished the top section. When I plugged the lights in, Sonya clapped her hands in delight as I helped Margaret move the neatly trimmed presents under the branches. While I was doing that, I noticed that my name was on several of them. I felt oddly embarrassed over the obvious realization that they were presents originally intended for Ben.

"You can't shake it to try to guess what's in it," she said.

I shrugged. "Can't blame a guy for trying."

"These things were for Ben," she said. "But . . . I hope you don't mind that I'm giving them to you. I mean, I know it looks like second-hand giving and all."

I laughed. "What else can we do? Head out to the nearest department store and try to find something else? Besides, it's not like we had this all planned before everyone left for the holiday. And, as it turns out, I have some things for you that were originally intended for my sisters. They'll forgive me—after I make it up to them, of course. Let me run upstairs and get them." I headed for the door.

"Feel like bringing back some wine?" she asked.

I smiled. "Sure. Red or white?"

"How about a red this time?"

"You got it." I stepped out, made sure the door was securely closed behind me, and headed down the hallway.

I had five bottles left, two red and three white. The two reds were both Merlots, so I grabbed one and brought it to the sink to rinse it off. Almost automatically, I looked out the window while I did that, my eyes instinctively searching for the silhouette of the Greek theater. The snow had eased up so that, despite the storm, I was able to see as far as the school, and although I spotted the theater, I did not see anything moving. This was no surprise, of course, since even I, with my meager background in probability, understood that, despite the original event with the wolf, the likelihood of something being there precisely at the moment that I looked was very small. Nevertheless, I continued to watch while I wiped the bottle dry.

That done, I went to my dresser and retrieved the gifts I had intended for my sisters and put them in a bag. Then I went to the door and flicked off the light. I had an odd feeling, though, and without any conscious

203

justification on my part, I closed the door and went back to the window, leaving the light off. I pulled my desk chair over and sat, not because I was tired but because I wanted as little of myself visible as possible.

I watched from a corner of the window for several minutes with no particular expectation in mind, knowing full well that Margaret would not notice a short delay. On some animal level, I had had the distinct feeling that, while the light was on, I was being watched. It was irrational, of course, and I usually didn't put much faith in instinct, but I remembered a story told to me by a Special Forces reconnaissance scout who had been in 'Nam. He had told me that, if he spotted an enemy soldier, he took great care to not look directly at him. "You look right at him and he'll know you're there," he had said, "even if his back is to you. You have to keep him in your peripheral vision to always know where he is, but you look past him. It sounds crazy, I know, but unless you want more company than you can handle, don't look right at him." That was the feeling I had just had, that I was being looked at. "We were animals before we were humans," he had said, "and that animal is still in there. Listen to it."

So I sat for a few minutes. The snow had thinned but the sleet was still slicing into the building unabated. It raked across the glass in an incessant hiss that would have been the perfect background white noise had I been reading or doing research. But just then it was simply noise.

Several minutes passed and nothing happened, and I knew if I stretched it out too far Margaret would indeed get worried, so with one last look I pushed myself away from the window and headed for the door. I "knew" of course—the way we all "knew"—that the moment I walked away from the window something would appear and I would miss it. But since I couldn't spend the evening trying to second-guess what *might* happen, there was no point in dwelling on it. I left the chair near the window as I headed out.

Margaret had put Sonya to bed in the time I was gone, an act that caught me off guard and left me without an excuse as to why I had not yet hung the old quilt as insulation on the wall in her closet.

"Don't worry about it," she said. "I pushed her clothes up against it and made sure the door stayed closed. I even rolled a towel up along the bottom of the door to stop anything from getting out."

"Sorry, I . . ."

She hushed me with a finger to my lips. "Stop worrying about it. Now that we know where it's coming from, we can deal with it. You can hang the quilt tomorrow." She took the gifts from me and placed them under the tree, then stood up and glanced at my hand. "How about a glass of wine?"

The act itself had become our private ritual. We went to the kitchen, she took down some wine glasses, I popped the cork, and we saluted the season and the silence. We owned our little world, if only for a short while. I knew we were trapped and isolated, but that had a positive connotation, too; it meant no one would interfere with what we were doing. With Sonya asleep, we sat together on the couch immersed in our own thoughts and feelings, the storm hammering away at the building and, even above that, the faint but persistent thundering of the sea on the coastal rocks. It wasn't often that you could hear the sea, even in summer with the windows open. Despite its violence, it was oddly soothing, and it was with some surprise that I understood how its rhythm drew men into its embrace.

"So, why did you go up there in the first place?" she finally asked, referring to the village. "Knowing the storm was coming made it kind of risky, didn't it? I mean, were you trying to get to the bone barrow?"

I wasn't expecting that subject to come up again, so it took me a moment to formulate an answer without admitting that I had gone there to try to find something special for her, which would have led to revealing the existence of the house. "I was thinking about what you had said before, about whether places can have memories." This was not entirely untrue, especially since it was what I felt when I slipped down into the basin.

She looked at me expectantly. "And did it?"

I took a contemplative sip of wine. "Yes." I was sure it did. It was an oddly quiescent notion that I secretly felt was hidden in the back of the mind of every human on earth and admitted to by none. We were bound to the places with which we bonded as infants, like it or not, and our memories of those places were projected outwards onto the physical locations in an act of "psychological transference," making it seem that the place itself was alive and remembered us. At least I assumed that would be the "official" interpretation. Mentioning Nadine, for instance, had brought me back to a place in my mind that I knew no longer existed, at least not in that slice of time, but that nonetheless would "remember" me if I were to physically go back there. Still, I could not admit that that was not the real reason for the trip.

"But also, yes, I was hoping to make it as far as the barrow this time but was waylaid by the discovery of the old ropewalk. So I still haven't seen it close up."

It seemed as if she hadn't heard that last comment or was ignoring it. Her gaze was fixed on some point in front of me, unwavering, for several seconds, until she finally said: "What kind of memory do you think it had?"

"What?"

"You said the place had a memory. What kind of memory do you think it was?"

I had to think about that one. "I don't know. A place-memory seems to be more of a feeling than an actual event. It just seemed, I don't know, somehow alive or sentient, like walking onto a movie set where the actors ignore you and keep on reading their lines. Something like that. Maybe it just reminds me of someplace else I've been."

She nodded faintly. "I noticed that when I was there last summer. But," and here she paused for a moment as if uncertain of what to say, "what about a place that one had never seen before, had never bonded with, and that yet seemed somehow 'familiar'?"

I shrugged. "I don't know. Maybe it just reminded you of some other place, like I said before."

"No, that's not it. It was more a sense of having been there before. I knew, for instance, when I was swimming in the pool, that the first thing we would see when we got to the bottom of the ridge was a well. Sure enough, when Sil brought us down into the valley we passed a well."

"I think most—if not all—villages back then had a common well that provided water for the community, so expecting to find one is probably a safe bet. Also, maybe you don't have to have actually been to a place to have one of these memories. Maybe pictures can do the same thing. I once came upon a lake on one of my hikes and had the startling feeling that I'd been there before, even though I had never hiked in that area. Only later, when I was back home, did I remember that I had had a haunting picture of Lake Louise on my wall as a kid, and the lake that I had just seen had resembled it."

She gave me an odd, defensive look that betrayed her disappointment in my answer. "Yes, I know that. But how would I know it would be the first thing we'd see?"

I didn't answer, as much out of respect for the delicacy of our relationship as out of respect for her opinion. Not to mention the fact that I simply didn't know how she could have realized they would have seen that first. I shrugged. "I don't know," I finally said.

We sat in silence for a moment, then she got up and went to the kitchen to get the wine. I sensed a signal in the gesture, both the end of the conversation about the place-memory and a simultaneous awareness of having done or said something wrong. She was not happy with my comment about the well. How odd that these small deviations could lead to such upsets, I thought. I had not intended to broach this subject at all and only did so to cover why I had gone there.

"Will you check the building during the night?" she asked as she topped off my glass. There was a slight edge to her voice. She was either still not satisfied that we were alone or was mildly upset.

"Yes. It'll be at a different time, though. I'm going to try to randomize my appearances in the hall just in case there really is a visitor out there. I don't want to look too predictable."

She put the wine bottle on the floor near the couch, then reached out and over and put her arm around me. "I'm starting to feel pretty foolish for all the trouble I've put you through, thinking there was someone else in the building and all."

"Don't trouble yourself. You had every reason to be concerned. This is not exactly an environment conducive to feeling secure, being such a huge building and all."

She put her glass down on the coffee table and reached around to embrace me. "I was thinking that maybe you could, you know—if you wanted to—stay here with us tomorrow night so that you wouldn't be alone on Christmas Eve. I mean, it's not like the rumor mill will pick up on it or anything."

I put my own glass down as well and reached out for her. The suggestion was full of implication, of course—it was the sex question once again, the elephant in the room that we had been ignoring, that looming reality awaiting the next step in where we were going. Sooner or later, we would reach that threshold and have to decide one way or another. "But how will that affect Sonya? Waking up and finding me here, I mean."

She seemed to catch herself. "Oh, I didn't mean . . . that is, what I meant was, you could use the couch. I didn't mean to suggest that you would be sleeping with me. That might be too much for Sonya to handle." She paused for a moment and studied my face. "I don't know that I'm ready for that yet either."

So there it was, the delicately balanced turning point in our relationship. It was an ambidextrous answer to the unspoken question, holding a promise for the future while guarding against the present. In some ways, I was relieved because the subject had at last been broached and was no longer hanging fire at the edge of every conversation; in other ways, of course, I was disappointed because I had not had a physical relationship—at least not one that meant anything—in a long time. I didn't know which reaction was showing on my face when she spoke again.

"It was just a suggestion. I know it's a tough time of year to be alone, but if you'd rather . . ."

"No," I interrupted. "No, I don't want to be alone. I mean, yes, I would like to stay with the two of you tomorrow night. It's just . . ."

"What?"

I grinned. "Well, I've been 'on my own' for so long now that I'm not sure I even know how to react as a house guest."

She laughed and touched my cheek. "Oh, that's right. What was it you said? 'Domestic bliss was more of a millstone than anything else.' Was that it?"

"Something like that. It does kind of hound me every time I try to put down roots." How circuitous it all was. If I had declined, she would have been convinced that the only thing that would ever bind me to her would be sex, yet the fact was, I was so used to the emptiness of my life that I was unsure that I could bond with another human being at all. My disastrous second marriage had, oddly, left me yearning for loneliness, and the effect was a social estrangement for which I had become a local legend. Just ask Sil, I thought with a smile.

"What's so funny?" she asked as she leaned into me and kissed me.

"Oh, I was just thinking. Did I ever tell you my first wife called me 'Roadbeam' because of my rootless attitude?"

"I think you may have mentioned that at some point. So, what are you telling me? That you're some kind of Quasimodo and I can expect a hunchbacked transformation the moment you try to settle down?"

I laughed. "Yeah, something like that. When all this is over and everyone's back, you can tell the guys in the white coats when they come for me that 'he hasn't been the same since he ran into that gingerbread house in the woods.' That ought to get me preferential treatment."

"You found a gingerbread house?" She looked at me over the rim of her glass.

I smiled. "Sort of. I'll tell you about it tomorrow at breakfast. Right now I'm too tired." There it was. I was going to tell her about the house.

She nodded. "Me, too." She put her glass back down and curled up beside me again.

I kissed her—she must have forgiven me for my rootless remark about seeing the well first—and then we sat in silence for what seemed a long time. The sleet still tinkled on the window and, as my thoughts wandered, I imagined that we actually had a fireplace, that I could see it in the opposite wall, and was about to say something to her when I noticed that she had dozed off.

And there we were. The main lights had been dimmed, the tree lights were on, and the candles lit. The scene was a magical transformation from one of captive isolation to festive solemnity, a warmth and coziness that was actually enhanced by the lack of other people. It was very quiet and it was all ours. There was something primal in it, some long-buried tribalism that emerged, like the hidden life of the forest, only at sundown and only when one was alone with the world. For a moment a treasure chest of memories opened, and I saw that youthful world once again, the womb of security that had surrounded me as a child. And I knew that, like the evidence of the stone walls and the decaying village, my own life brought with it the necessity of passing, and I understood now, at last, that it was my turn to offer that magic to someone else.

◆ ◆ ◆

Chapter 17

It was nearly midnight before I got back to my room. I had let Margaret sleep until she woke up of her own accord. Through half-closed eyes she had wished me good night and I her, and I headed back down the darkened hall toward the stairs. My right elbow had begun to throb again from the exertion of angling my arm around her for several hours, but the pleasure had been worth the pain. I would probably need a couple of aspirin in order to sleep.

I entered my room without turning on the light. Instinctively, I reached down in the dark for the flashlight that I kept near the bed, had a horrific vision of that monstrous spider clinging to the barrel, snatched my hand back, then berated myself for being foolish. I picked it up, covered the lens with my hand, and turned it on. The sliver of light that resulted fell on the floor near the bed and I quickly swept it back and forth to check for multilegged intruders. Finding none, I directed the thin lancet of light under the bed toward the board that covered the break in the wall. Nothing. No new bug skeletons, no evidence of an unwanted visitor. Satisfied that I was alone, I went to the chair near the window, turned the light off, and sat down.

The storm appeared to have stopped. I could just barely make out the silhouette of the Greek theater near the edge of the woods. What moonlight there was, was still obscured by the overcast sky and fell in a faint, diffuse pall over the space between me and the school. But it was enough. If something were out there, I was confident I would be able to see it.

I watched for about twenty minutes. During that time, the odd draftiness in Sonya's closet continued to rattle around in the back of my head. It was very much like the utility closet at the end of the hall—seemingly colder than it should be, given that it was still sheltered inside the building. It was as if there were a leak in the wall, or maybe a conduit of some sort was funneling cold air down and needed to be sealed. I resolved to take a closer look sometime in the next couple of days.

Finally, my fatigue got the better of me and I knew that I had to sleep. I set the clock radio for four-fifteen; I figured that since that was about when the nightlights went out the night before, I might have a second chance at figuring out why. I padded down the hall in my slippers, took a leak, took my two aspirin, brushed my teeth, then shuffled back. There was enough illumination coming in the window so that I did not actually need the light, so I left it off. I was just sliding under the covers when I noticed a fleeting shift in the light coming in the window, a momentary thing like a hand passing over a flashlight beam. "What the hell?" I said as I slipped back out onto the floor and sat at the window. There was nothing but the same lace-like moon shadows weaving themselves across the open snowfield.

And then I saw it. Something moved, not at the Greek theater but at the edge of the shed, scarcely sixty or seventy yards away. I strained to see, then caught myself as I remembered the words of the Special Forces scout: "Don't look right at him or he'll know you're there." So I looked past the edge of the shed into the woods, keeping the corner of the building in my peripheral vision.

Something detached itself from the building. Cautiously, as if unsure of itself, a shadow moved away from the dark edge of the wall and onto the snowfield. I held my breath as I looked past it while simultaneously trying to see what it was. But it denied me that by staying in the larger shadow cast by the shed itself, almost as if it knew I was watching. Except for my eyes, I was fully concealed as I sat near the window, yet I had the distinct impression that it had spotted me nonetheless, a feeling reinforced by its apparent reluctance to advance any further into the moonlight. So I tried to conceal myself even further. And waited.

It hesitated as well. I could just barely make out its shape. A bear, I guessed, based on its bulk and the way it moved—slowly, ponderously. But it was indistinct. Four-legged, yes, of that I was sure as I watched the head move first in one direction, then another, then slowly, as if purposefully, turn in my direction. I shrank myself still further and waited as it stood there motionlessly.

And then it stood up on two legs and moved back behind the wall of the shed. I shot to my feet and crammed my face against the glass, my eyes bugging out in an effort to penetrate the darkness. "What the hell?" I said again, louder this time. "Is someone out there?" It can't be, I thought. Can't be. It had to be at least twenty below out there with the wind chill. They wouldn't survive the night.

I waited, all pretense at concealment gone. There—there it was, a black dot moving toward the edge of the forest that arched around the school like a scythe and went right to the edge of the ocean. Moving fast, much too fast for a human. It had to be four-legged.

I relaxed. "Must have been a bear," I mumbled, thinking that it had seen or smelled something behind the shed that had caused it to stand up for a closer look. "Bears will do that," I said to myself as I turned away from the window, remembering with a nervous chuckle how I had once caught one sizing me up that way on a trail in the Adirondacks.

But then the feeling returned—or maybe it was another flutter of the pale light, an errant out-of-place movement. Whatever it was, I turned back to look. And that was when I saw it. From the shed—from the top of the shed—a form materialized, like a piece of the structure come to life, and I stood there spellbound while the thing, whatever it was, spread its wings and took off, a huge nocturnal phantom like a great snowy owl, except it was no owl and diurnal birds did not fly at night. And I watched in stupefied silence as the huge thing flapped into the distance, a cloud-shadow among the darting lines of the blackened forest. And when it was gone, I stood there looking in its direction as if expecting it to return, thinking: What the hell was that?

◆ ◆ ◆

"And then the village died." Those were the last words that came to me when the clock radio woke me up at four-fifteen with the pointless prattle of the zombie who worked the night shift. I sat up and pressed the "off" button in the middle of a sentence about some new wonder drug that would cure everything from bed wetting to pattern baldness. "Has the FDA approved snake oil?" I wondered.

I grabbed the flashlight and covered the lens with my hand as I had done earlier, then turned it on. A quick scan of the floor showed no nasty surprises waiting for me as I slid out from under the covers and went to the window. I watched with the light off for several minutes but nothing materialized out of the frozen gloom. Whatever had flown into the darkness was not there.

"And then the village died," I mumbled as I pulled on my bathrobe and put on my slippers. I would need to know why. Epidemics came to mind first, those periodic scourges that sometimes wiped out whole settlements. I knew there had been outbreaks of smallpox and cholera during the sixteen and seventeen hundreds, but I could not remember exactly when. I scribbled a note to myself to find out and left it on the desk. As I headed for the door, it occurred to me that I had not yet looked at any of the Polaroids I had taken of the chasm, not even a brief review of the petroglyphs I had seen. I went back and scribbled down another note, adding the words "Machias Bay" at the bottom. I needed to dig out my photographs of the Machias Bay petroglyphs so that I could compare them with what I had found.

I was absolutely noiseless as I opened the door and stepped out into the hallway. I stood at the head of the stairs for several minutes and simply waited to see if anything would happen. The building creaked and groaned, and from the depths of the hall, I heard a faint rattling sound that I could not identify but that probably could have had any number of sources, one of which, I realized, could have been someone in one of the rooms. I moved over to the wall and flattened myself against it to see if anything materialized.

After several minutes, all I had picked up was cold ankles again, so I headed for the stairs. I hadn't taped the fish line across the stairwell—for no good reason other than simple neglect—so there was no danger of me setting off my own trap and ending up convinced in the morning that someone was indeed walking the halls.

I expected the nightlights to be off in the lower hall, but they were still going. I hugged the wall opposite Margaret's apartment to avoid loose floorboards and worked my way down the hall toward the utility closet. I was curious to see if the door had popped open. When I got

213

to room eleven, I quietly opened the door, slipped in, closed it behind me, and turned on the flashlight. I played the beam over the unoccupied beds, swept it over the desks and bookcases, probed into darkened corners, and settled on the closet.

The door was open.

I stared at it in confused disbelief for a moment, then went up to it and, with some apprehension, looked in. It was full of clothes, shoes, piles of papers and books, and miscellaneous oddments, but no occupants. Apart from the door being open, one other thing about it caught my attention immediately—it was cold, like the closet in Sonya's room. I could almost see my breath in the flashlight beam.

It would have been nice to know if this odd temperature difference was simply a feature common to all the closets in the building, but since all the other rooms were locked I had no way of knowing that. And my room, being one of the small, single rooms, did not have a built-in closet, and hence could not be thrown into the mix. I reached out to feel the wall but could not detect any drafts. It had to be coming in some other way. As to why it was open—the only explanation that came to mind was the same one that I had applied to the utility closet: the movement of the building under the buffeting of the storm must have caused it. But I made a mental note regardless to ask Margaret in the morning if she had been in there for anything.

I left the closet door open as I turned off the flashlight, exited the room, and headed back down the hallway toward the utility closet, still hugging the wall opposite Margaret's apartment. When I passed opposite her door, I hesitated for a moment as I wrestled with the thought of the two signal knocks. "On the way back," I decided. My rationale was that, if there really was someone in the building, I did not want to reveal my presence. So the knocks would have to wait.

I was about three-quarters of the way to the end of the hall when I heard the door to the utility closet pop open with that faint "snicking" sound I had heard before. I plastered myself against the wall, scarcely breathing. The nightlights were still on and because of them I was able to see, even in the darkness of the closet, what appeared to be something darker still, a faint form, indistinct and amorphous, a shadow within a shadow. I neither breathed nor moved.

He'll know you're there if you look right at him, I reminded myself. So I looked away, at the door itself, a move that had the double advantage of the better clarity of peripheral vision in the darkness. And I waited.

A shadow within a shadow. The door creaked again, moved another couple of inches, and stopped. Did I see a hand, or was my imagination filling in the blanks for me? I scarcely breathed as I waited for whatever was to come, but there was no other sound or movement and it occurred to me that, despite my dark bathrobe, I was not invisible. My face could no doubt be seen even in the weak, diffused light. That being the case, I realized my only option was to go on the offensive. If there was someone in there, he had only one way out, which meant if I got to the door before he could emerge, he would be trapped. So I moved forward as fast as I could without making noise.

When I got to the closet, I threw the door open, flicked on the light, and shined it inside. I expected to find some cowering form curled up in a corner trying to play dead, a townie perhaps, or maybe a misplaced student cast off by his parents. But, as with the closet in room eleven, there was nothing.

I was vexed. I was sure I had seen something, that shadow within a shadow. I shook my head. "Or maybe not," I mumbled. I shined the light into every corner of the closet—which was surprisingly deep, given that it matched the rooms in length—but saw no other way out. Nor was there any place to hide, but just to be sure, I went to the end to check for hidden niches. And when I got to the end, I located the source of the cold air. It was coming in from between the paneling in the back wall, a circumstance similar to that in Sonya's closet, as well as the one I'd just found in room eleven. "No insulation," I muttered, then turned and headed out, examining the ceiling for exits, all the while knowing that was impossible because there was a student room on the second floor right above it. I made sure the door was properly latched behind me when I left but only took two steps before it hit me—no, there was not a student room above it. What was above it was the door sealing off the staircase to the attic.

◆ ◆ ◆

I didn't wake up again until nearly eight-thirty. The sun had crept above the horizon and the light coming in my window told me the storm was definitely over. I went to the window and was met with a dazzling mosaic of sparkles coming at me from every direction. It was Christmas Eve and it looked like a perfect winter's day. Except that I was late for breakfast.

It had been almost five o'clock by the time I got back to my room after checking the building. When I went by Margaret's door after leaving the utility closet, I gave the two-knock signal, listened for any activity, and, hearing none, headed upstairs. Evidently, she was able to sleep through the night, which was more than I was able to say for myself.

I turned on my little wall-mounted water heater and while I was waiting for the water to warm up for shaving, I studied the snowfield where I had seen what I took to be the bear. The tracks were plainly visible, so this time I would be able to verify what they were. I then checked the top of the shed for any indication that a large bird had been up there, but it was useless from my perspective because the roof of the shed was higher than my window. By then the water was ready.

I was shaved and presentable by quarter to nine. With one quick look under the bed to make sure my domain was still intact, I headed down the stairs, glancing toward the front door to make sure the chain was still securely tied around the handles. I got to her door and knocked twice quickly. Even from that distance, I could see from the light coming in the rear hall window that the utility closet was still closed.

I heard the deadbolts sliding back and the door opened. Margaret cocked an eyebrow at me. "You're late."

I smiled and entered. "It's the nightlife around here. All this socializing is wearing me out."

She shook her head faintly and smiled. "You've got an answer for everything."

"I've had lots of practice dodging accusations. How late am I? Did you and Sonya already eat?"

She looped her arm through mine as she led me toward the kitchen. "I fed Sonya but decided to wait until you got here before I ate. The sacrifices I make for you." She grinned at me askance.

I feigned indignation. "There I am, up at all hours of the night checking the building and these are the thanks I get. By the way, you haven't gone into room eleven for anything, have you?"

"No. Why do you ask?"

"Just curious. I was in there last night and noticed a detail that I guess we missed when we were checking the rooms."

"Oh, so you checked the building last night?"

"Yes. Didn't you hear my two knocks?"

She smiled and rolled her eyes. "Evidently I didn't. Out like a light. I think the cumulative effect of being so wound up at night for so long is catching up to me. Knowing that you're out there keeping an eye on things makes a big difference."

So she hadn't been in room eleven, which meant that either I had unintentionally left the closet door open when I first searched the room, or it had popped open on its own. I was disappointed in myself for my lack of attention to detail—I should have made it a point to close the door after I had first searched the room so that I would be aware of any change later. Of course, it simultaneously occurred to me that, when I first did the search, I was skeptical of what she was telling me and hence saw no need for controlling the details.

She had not yet had time to clear Sonya's plate from the table, so I helped her with that task. The little girl had had pancakes and her fork was stuck to the plate from the viscous residue of maple syrup that covered everything. I turned the plate upside down to emphasize the holding power of the syrup. "I always thought this stuff would be a cheap and reliable adhesive for NASA's satellites. Instead of expensive epoxies, they can be glued together with dried pancake syrup. I mean, if you think it's sticky now, what do you think will happen to this stuff if the cold of outer space touches it?"

She burst out laughing and shook her head once again. "You really are a crackpot. I can't even imagine what would happen in the cold of outer space."

I pretended to ponder. "I think it causes a molecular seizure and the two items bond together permanently, becoming one substance. It'd be like that matter transfer unit on 'Star Trek,' except that you come out with your skin permanently grafted to your flight suit. In fact, your flight suit *becomes* your skin. Great stuff. Got to keep it away from the Soviets."

"You're right. You really haven't been the same since you ran into that gingerbread house in the woods. Speaking of which—you were going to tell me about that."

I had forgotten. "The gingerbread house. Yeah, right." I was committed now. Unless I wanted to start inventing some serious lies, I had to tell her about it.

I poured myself a coffee, then filled her cup and sat down. "Remember how I told you that, when I went looking for the village, I had no idea where to go once I reached the large stream? There didn't seem to be any trail, so I basically followed the sound of the waterfall. This led me down into a hollow that was separated from the actual village by a dense stand of cedars." Once again, I deliberately omitted the part about cannonballing through the brush and careening down the ridge on my back. "I could hear the waterfall on the other side of the trees, so I headed into the cedars. When I got in there, I found a house." I paused to add a little more cream to my coffee.

"And?" She seemed only mildly interested. "Was it in some way different from the other houses in the village?"

"Yes, it was. Considerably different. Unlike all the hulks and derelicts, this place was fully intact."

She blinked at me for several seconds. "What do you mean, 'fully intact'? You mean the windows still had glass in them?"

I nodded. "The windows still had glass. But that wasn't all." I paused for effect. "It was still full of furniture. Even the dinner plates were still there, locked up in a cabinet whose glass was still intact."

She gave me a look that told me she either doubted what I was saying or thought I was nuts. "Full of furniture? You mean, real furniture?"

"Real furniture. Kind of run down, as you can imagine, but for the most part intact. The house is large, too. Two stories, with a big common room of some sort on the second floor. It had a basement, of course, but it was way too dangerous to attempt going down there."

"Let me get this straight," she said. "You found a house in these cedars that was fully intact, full of furniture, and even had the family china on display?"

"Correct." I leaned forward as if unconsciously afraid of being overheard. "Margaret, the place is a time capsule, an incredible find for an historian. I need absolute assurance from you that you won't mention it to anyone, ever. Can you imagine what would happen?"

She gave me a puzzled look. "Why didn't you tell me about it when you first described your trip to the village?"

It was as if she hadn't heard my comment at all. On the other hand, I realized that my secrecy policy had just painted me into a corner. "What? Well, ah, you know, we didn't know each other that well even just a few days ago, and I was afraid that you might, you know, mention it to someone and cause a 'gold rush' of treasure hunters who would tear the place apart." I studied her face for a reaction. "I have a thing about not disturbing the relics of the past."

She smiled. "I know. I saw the way you handled those old newspapers as if they were antique porcelain. And, no, I don't blame you for withholding that information until you knew you could trust me with it." She went to the stove, got the coffeepot, and returned to top off our cups. "And, yes, you have my assurance that I will never mention a word of it to anyone. Provided . . ." and here she put the pot down and leaned over to kiss me, "provided you take me there and show it to me in the spring." She went back to the stove with the pot.

"Agreed. You'll be the second person to see it in probably two centuries. We'll swim in the basin and then I'll show you the secret route to the house."

During all this, I was anxious to check out the tracks near the shed, and as a result I could feel my socialization skills, marginal as they had become over the past several years, slipping into reverse. This had happened to me many times in the past and generally resulted in a feeling of mild agitation or impatience that I was sure Margaret was able to sense. Thus, as the coffee got low in the pot, she didn't make any more, a clear indication that she had no intention of trying to talk me into staying awhile. But she did ask me about the "overlooked detail" in room eleven, and when I told her the closet door was open she, too, could not remember if I had left it that way.

"Is it closed now?" she asked.

"No. I left it open, just like I left the room unlocked. It can't close itself, so we might as well eliminate the possibility of it opening again."

She nodded. "What are your plans for today? Anything special?"

"Well, I expect that digging and plowing us out will take a while. I saw a bear from my window last night and want to check out its tracks, maybe see where they came from." I paused, swallowed the last of my coffee, and shot her a look. "I need to do some reading in the old diary, too, maybe catch up on some research for my project."

219

"So you'll be doing that all day?" There was something in her voice, an expectant edge that I had heard many times from both of my previous wives. My instinctive reaction was to raise the standard of my rootless independence and stand firm, pushing back against the social forces that encroached on my time.

But that tactic had cost me heavily in the past. It was obvious that she already had expectations of me, and if our relationship were going to work at all, I would need to compromise. "Not all day, no. I figure I can get the plowing done in about an hour, check out the tracks, do some research in the old diary, then meet you for lunch. Maybe after lunch we can all go for a walk?"

Her demeanor brightened. "That's a great idea. Where should we go? And don't say 'the village.' That's a bit too far even to see the gingerbread house."

I laughed. "Too far and too difficult. The snow would be chest-deep for Sonya and thigh-deep for you, and as far as I know, I've got the only snowshoes in the Ropewalk. No, after I plow the macadam road, we can walk up to the main highway and back. That'll be just over two miles round trip."

She smiled and nodded, reached out for my hand and gave it a squeeze. I got up, went around the table, and pulled her to me. And when she fell into me, I was able to accept the realization that, marginally socialized or not, all other considerations in my life—including my history project—had become secondary.

◆ ◆ ◆

Chapter 18

Nevertheless, I hurried through breakfast, and when I got back to my room, I was obsessed with the thought of reviewing the pictures I had taken of the petroglyphs in the chasm. They were still in my coat pocket, so I took them out, laid them on the desk, and retrieved my reference book on the Machias Bay petroglyphs. Apart from the oval faces carved in the wall of the chasm, the stylistic rendering appeared to be the same. The odd two-headed human figures found in the bay were also in the chasm, and the fantastic or fanciful creatures carved in the chasm were very much like the "thunderbirds" and so-called "water monster" seen in the bay carvings.

On the face of it, this would not seem to be so very unexpected since Machias Bay was just south of where we were. Except that, as far as I knew, absolutely no one was aware of the existence of *these* carvings. Like the discovery of the old diary and the Abenaki involvement in Metacomet's war, it was a groundbreaking event. I simply could not grasp that this was being handed to me.

I stared out the window at nothing in particular. Who would have thought that any of this would happen to me? I wondered. A launch pad for heightened career recognition and at the same time a new relationship that, under normal conditions, would never have happened at all. And why now? Pondering the failures of my own life over the span of the years that had brought me to that place made me indeed wonder about "destiny logic." I laughed a single note. "You'd think after all this practice I would know how to make it work," I said aloud. Instead, fate was surprising me at every turn.

I studied the photographs. Unfortunately, most of the glyphs were small because the Polaroid did not have a telephoto lens. A magnifying glass helped, but even then some of the figures were so tiny that I could not make out what they were. I lowered myself onto the desk chair while I grappled with the realization that I would have to go back there after all, except next time I would bring my 35-millimeter with the long lens. My arm hairs prickled at the mere thought of going anywhere near that giant hole, but if I were going to claim the discovery as my own, I would need something better than the Polaroids. It was that basic.

But first things first. Lunch was at one o'clock and I had to get us plowed out before I did anything else. So I suited up, unraveled the door chain, and went out. Snow had drifted up against the door to a depth of several feet and I kicked my way through it to get to the shed.

The tracks were indeed those of a bear. I didn't want to follow them into the deep snow without the snowshoes, so I merely noted the shape of the tracks and that they led around the left side of the shed. Further out, I could see where they crossed the snowfield and went behind the school, but where they went after that, I wasn't able to tell. I cleared the snow from the door of the shed and went in. I made sure the tractor had enough gas, started it up, and began clearing a path. Within minutes I was headed down the road toward the coast highway.

From where I was on the macadam road, I could see the roof of the Ropewalk. There I noticed—had seen before, of course, but never paid any attention—that the roof had a series of hatches in it, portals that had been cut during one of its renovations so that workers could get to the roof from inside the building. It was a clever idea: one had access to the roof from the attic. Of course, the reverse was also true: one had access to the attic from the roof.

I stopped plowing for a moment. It was obvious from the unbroken snow on the roof that no one had tried to enter the Ropewalk through those hatches, but something about the attic still bothered me. Given that I was still unsure about the "shadow within a shadow" that I thought I had seen during the night, it was probably only natural that my attention would turn to the only uninvestigated area left in the building. But even if someone were up there, how could he get into the halls? The only two doors were securely padlocked from inside. Unless, of course, the hasps themselves were just props, unanchored subterfuges that only appeared secure but that really held nothing closed. As unlikely as that sounded, I made a mental note to check that out when I got back.

The snow was deeper than expected in some parts, so it was taking longer than usual to get it cleared away. When I drew abreast of the Engineering building, I could see a line of tracks crossing the road again, except this time it was obvious that they were those of a bear, probably my visitor from the night before. That would mean, of course, that the thing living in the cellar of the building was a bear, not the wolf as I had previously suspected. In some ways, this made more sense because I had credited the wolf with more cunning than to live so close to a large group of humans. A bear, on the other hand, being both a hunter and a scrounger, would get along just fine.

It was no surprise to discover that the highway had not been plowed and no one had gone by. Given that the holiday would last for at least another week, I harbored no expectation that anyone would be anxious to open this stretch of road before then. So it was clear that there was no hope that we would get out of there for Christmas. But there was a level of personal satisfaction that came with being trapped, because the question still resonated in my mind whether it would all end when the world came back to us, when we were no longer the only people on earth. She was mine as long as we were isolated. My nagging fear was that she would be hit on by every available male in the region—and even some unavailable—when word got out that she was alone. Would she still pick me out of the lineup? I wondered with resigned humor.

I drove the tractor out onto the southbound lane as I had before, but had to physically fight the impulse to head up toward the cart track that led to the village. There simply was not enough time. It was already eleven o'clock, and even if I had brought the snowshoes—which I hadn't—I still would not have enough time to go to the village. And I really did want to read more of the old diary. Further exploration was going to have to wait for the day after Christmas. I drove the tractor in a circle and headed back down the road toward the Ropewalk.

I plowed the same path a second time as I headed back, hoping to clear away as much as possible so that our afternoon walk would be easy. This had a reverse effect, however; when I got the covering of snow off, I saw that what was beneath it was sheer ice, which meant that I had to attach the sand spreader and do another run so that we didn't end up skidding and flailing all over the road like out-of-control hockey players. As if to remind me of the consequences, my elbow suddenly let out a stab of pain.

So when I got back, I pulled the spreader out of the shed, filled it with sand, and remounted. Before I started back up the road, I glanced at the roof of the Ropewalk again. When I was on the road, I had been looking at the north side of the building, but from the front of the shed, I was able to see the south side. It was then I noticed that the access hatches I had seen on the other side were also present on this side. Since it faced south, the snow was melting off fast as the sun beat down on it. Most of it would be gone by the end of the day, despite the cold.

What it meant was that, if anyone actually wanted to get into the building from the roof, they could do so from the south side and leave no tracks.

I shaded my eyes and tried to study the various hatches to see if any looked disturbed, but it was useless. I needed my binoculars for that and made another mental note—tacked up near the first one to check the attic door hasps—to take a look before lunch. Then I put it in gear and headed back up the road, going very slowly and spreading the sand as evenly as I could.

By the time I got back, shoveled a path to the door of the Ropewalk, sanded it, and put everything away, it was almost noon. The first thing I did after that was get my binoculars and check out the hatches on the south side. This required walking parallel to the building a good one hundred feet away, which I did for about half its length before finally giving up in the thigh-deep snow and turning back. Nothing seemed unusual, but then I could hardly expect to find one of them flipped open like the hatch to a submarine.

It did occur to me, though, that if snow were getting in through one of those things, that could be the source of the recurring problem with the nightlights in the lower hall.

That, and the unrelenting memory—or waking dream—of the "shadow within a shadow," convinced me that I had to check out the attic. I went up to my room, threw my parka on the bed, grabbed the flashlight just in case, checked under the bed for unwelcome visitors, and went out to check the doors to the attic.

The hasp on the door on my end of the hall was no prop. Given my growing suspicions about an unaccounted-for intruder—or permanent resident—I half expected to find a silver-colored thing of balsa wood masquerading as a latch. But it was real and the lock was secure. I gave it a couple of vigorous tugs to see if it would pop out of the paneling, but it held. Clearly, it was impossible to exit from the attic through that door as long as it was latched.

Then I went down to the last door on the right. Its latch, too, was real and firmly anchored and left no doubt about denying access to the attic to anyone without a key. And since I didn't have one, I couldn't get up there to check it out. Egress from the attic—even if the person did have a key—was likewise impossible, because the lock could only be reached from this side. It meant that if anyone were getting into the attic through one of the roof hatches, that person could still not come down into the building itself. I pondered the location of the utility closet—right below the door to the attic—but could see no connection. So, unless there was some secret door in the wall of the utility closet going straight to the outside of the building, I was forced to conclude that my "shadow within a shadow" had been my imagination.

I had trouble accepting that. I was tired when I was checking the building during the night, but not sleepwalking. The closet door popping open had been no illusion. Although the facts did not support anything beyond that, I felt that sense of non-normality ratchet up a notch.

I glanced at my watch. It was almost twenty of one. "Damn it," I said aloud. I had intended to do some reading in the old diary, but had gotten so absorbed in these other activities that I had lost track of time. "Damn it," I said again, as I hurried down the hall back to my room, strode over to the desk, took the diary out of the plastic container, and opened it. I needed to feel that I had done *something* toward the completion of my project, and even reading a couple of random pages would be better than the sinking feeling of the goal moving even further out of reach.

What followed was an example of synchronicity at work, as if fate itself were steering me with some coincidental compass. I flipped open to a page and began reading, and the girl's words—she still had not identified herself, as far as I knew—struck a cord the moment I read them. She went on and on about how Timothy, the same Timothy who had hidden from the grandmother when she insisted on telling how she had escaped from the "savages" after seeing her uncle flayed alive, was ruining the wall by practicing throwing a tomahawk.

He was ruining the wall. The words hit me like a slap in the face.

I read the passage again. Unfortunately, it did not identify which wall, but I felt that may not have been necessary because I was sure I already knew which wall he was ruining, and in what house. I remembered that the large common room upstairs in the house in the cedars had one wall that was badly scarred. I had not examined the scars, but was sure they could have been made by a hatchet-like instrument. Timothy's legacy.

My excitement grew. Here it was—the proof I needed that the diary was describing events that had taken place in that area. It was the validation I would need to follow up on its assertion that the Wampanoag King had sought help from the northeastern Abenakis. Obviously, the writer of the diary was describing an event that took place not only in that area, but also *in that house*. The marks in the wall proved it. I was astounded at this stroke of luck.

But it was time for lunch. Grudgingly, I marked the page with an index card, put the diary back in its protective container, and headed down to Margaret's apartment. I was so excited I felt as if Christmas had come a day early. I had to tell Margaret about it.

I knocked on her door, and the moment I stepped through, she had her arms around me.

"Merry Christmas Eve," she said, then drew back a few inches. "Something wrong?"

In a sudden bout of semi-panic, I searched the table for a clue as the momentary euphoria gave way to the reality of the moment. "Was I supposed to have brought something?" I asked. My social imponderability had become an issue only in the last few hours, but I wanted to be sure that it didn't get away from me. Otherwise, showing up empty-handed was like walking around with your fly down, a faux pas from which one never really recovered.

She was perplexed. "Like what?"

"Whew," I said. "Alright. I guess I'm in the clear. I thought maybe I was supposed to have brought something and was on the verge of demonstrating what a social liability I am."

She gave me a playful push. "Weirdo."

"What's for lunch?"

"Hot soup. Coffee, too, if you want some. Kahlua included at no extra charge."

Sonya was already in her chair grappling with the intricacies of trying to keep her spoon level so that the soup was not gone before it got to her mouth. She appeared to be somewhat successful and glanced up at me just before attempting another spoonful. The distraction broke her concentration, however, and that one look caused the spoon to tip. The soup splashed onto the table and dripped into her lap. Margaret grabbed a napkin and cleaned her off.

"Sorry," I said, then, on impulse, took her hand holding the spoon and carefully guided it from the bowl to her mouth. She looked at me strangely but did not resist, so I repeated it. A faint smile touched her lips and she waited for me to help her again. After one more assist, she smiled her overly large smile and duplicated my actions. She was immensely pleased with herself when she got the spoon into her mouth without losing a single drop. Margaret was impressed, especially when the next attempt produced the same result.

"You seem to have a knack for teaching," she said.

I smiled as I sat down. "I have some great news. I may have found the connection between the diary and the village."

"Really? Care to share the details?" She ladled out a bowl of soup and placed it in front of me.

So I told her about the marks I had found on the upstairs wall of the house and how I had found an entry in the old diary describing the girl's brother—at least I assumed that was who he was—practicing with his tomahawk.

She pondered. "That's certainly a lot closer than you were before and sounds circumstantially convincing. But it could still be challenged. Do you know for sure that the marks on the wall of the house came from a hatchet or something similar?"

"No, I never took a good look at them. Now I need to go back and do that."

Her eyebrows shot upward. "You're not going to do that on Christmas, are you?"

I shook my head. "No. Christmas we're going to spend together, as a family." I caught myself the moment I said it, jumping to conclusions again while still unsure of what was going to happen when everyone

227

returned from the holiday. "Well, what I meant was . . . ." I stopped because I did not want to reveal my weakness.

"I know what you meant," she finished. Her eyes dropped for a moment as if she, too, had come to sense the doubt, but then locked onto mine again. "Thank you." She smiled. "Do you realize that's the first serious acknowledgement you've given me in response to being 'inducted' into the family? I was beginning to think you were having second thoughts."

Now, *there* was an unexpected turnaround. She had been as uncertain about me as I had been about her. I laughed and shook my head. "No, no second thoughts. It's just that, well, when everyone comes back, everything will look, you know, different." For a moment I could not meet her gaze.

"Not that different." Her tone was simple and matter-of-fact. A moment of silence followed, and then she said: "So, you're going to be famous?"

I smiled and shrugged. "Maybe. I've got to put it all together first."

"Just don't forget about us, okay?"

Only now did I sense how real her concern was. Whatever doubts I had been having about her steadfastness, hers about mine seemed to have been even bigger. I resolved to do whatever was necessary to reassure her.

We decided to postpone the coffee until after we took our walk, so while she got herself and Sonya ready, I went up to my room and got my parka. I searched through the pockets and removed the last of the photos I had taken the day before, including the one of that strange, carved stone in the basin. I looked at it and shook my head. Famous? I would really be famous if I could figure out who had carved that thing. I put it on the desk and pulled on the parka. At the last minute I thought of the phantom hallwalker and stuck my .380 in one of the pockets. One never knew.

The day had warmed up to a balmy twenty degrees and, since it was nearly two o'clock, it was not likely to get any warmer. Margaret had mentioned the possibility of skating on the pond again, but the last storm had dumped too much snow and had too little wind to blow it off the ice. Only a small patch was visible in the center as we headed up the road toward the coast highway.

We had to pass the parking lot and when we did, Margaret commented on how forlorn the cars looked, sitting there drifted over and looking like just another pair of snow-covered hummocks. Mine was almost completely buried.

"Think we'll get them out by spring?" she asked sardonically.

"Get them out? I'd bring the poor things in if I could."

She picked up on it. "Maybe you can get them into the shed. There's plenty of open space."

That was actually not a bad idea. With the tractor running, I could plow and sand enough of the lot to get them onto the road and then drive them into the shed. She was right—there was easily enough room in there to accommodate both of them. It would at least protect them from the sleet and make them accessible once the highway was cleared. "We'll have to make sure they're out of there by the time Sil comes back, or he'll have a fit," I said.

"No problem," she replied. "I'll smooth his feathers if I have to."

I glanced at her and she winked. "Oh, yeah. I forgot about that."

Sonya had been walking beside Margaret, but as we neared the Engineering building, she suddenly broke away and scurried forward with that remarkable speed I had seen when we searched the building. Margaret was not alarmed.

"Sonya, honey, wait for mommy. Don't go any further. Sonya—wait." The girl at first ignored—or maybe didn't understand—her mother's words and continued up the road. As soon as she was parallel with the building, she stopped and squatted down to examine something in the snow.

"She sees the tracks," I said.

"Tracks?"

"Yes. From the bear I saw last night. At least I think it's the same animal. I saw it near the shed, but the tracks this morning circled around the school. I'm sure this is the same trail. Probably lives in the basement of the building." I pointed toward the decaying hulk rising like a beached battleship out of the trees. "There's an opening into the cellar on the other side."

Sonya had indeed been examining the tracks. When we caught up to her, she continued to stare at them as if mesmerized. Margaret squatted down next to her, put her arms around her, pointed to the

229

spoor, and said, "Bear tracks." Sonya seemed to completely ignore her and continued to stare.

Suddenly the girl broke away. Without any indication that it was coming, she leaped to her feet and launched herself into the snow, riffling through it with the rapidity of a forest creature using that technique I'd seen in the Ropewalk, where she scrambled on all fours. The icy crust supported her weight and I was stunned at how quickly she was able to move.

Margaret was more than stunned. She panicked. "Sonya!" she screamed, tearing after her through the deep snow but easily breaking through the crust and bogging down. "Sonya! Stop! Egan, do something!"

It all happened so fast it took a moment for it to register. The girl was so quick that she was already twenty yards away and widening the gap. I plunged into the snow and lurched after her while Margaret still struggled to free herself. It took me another twenty yards to catch up with her, and that, I was sure, only happened because she had at last broken through the crust herself. I scooped her up and she turned her head toward me with a big smile. In spite of the fright she had given her mother, I smiled back, then touched her nose playfully and said, "Where are you off to, hmm? Want to see where the tracks go?" She simply stared and continued to smile in reply.

I had no intention of bringing her there, of course, and doubted that she understood what I was saying in any case. I carried her back down to the road where Margaret waited with obvious relief on her face. She took the girl from me, smoothed her hair back under her hood, and scolded her.

"No, no, no," she said. "You mustn't run off like that." She shook her head vigorously while she spoke so that Sonya could connect her words with her gesture of displeasure. The girl simply stared without any visible sign of comprehension. Margaret repeated the process, and this time Sonya, either suddenly understanding the sense of what was being said or simply imitating her mother, also shook her head. Margaret seemed satisfied with this. She lowered her to the ground but held firmly onto her hand.

"She knows what it means when I shake my head," she said.

I nodded. "Should we go back, or do you want to continue?"

"Let's go on. I need the exercise in any case."

So we continued down the road. I held Sonya's other hand while we did this, and we made a game of it by periodically lifting her off her feet so that she could "fly" over the road, which seemed to please her immensely. When we reached the stand of evergreens where I had cut the Christmas tree, Sonya strained to get away for a closer look, so we brought her into the copse and released her so that she could touch the trees. Like her odd ability to scramble on all fours, the nearness of the trees seemed to awaken some long-buried somatic memory, and the tenderness with which she touched the branches set me to wondering about the levels of "understanding"—or maybe of bonding—that human beings were capable of.

"She relates to the trees," I said.

Margaret nodded and smiled but said nothing. I drew her aside, still keeping Sonya within reach, and whispered: "Will she ever be able to just go out and roam around on her own?"

Margaret did not take her eyes off the girl while she thought. "I don't know," she finally said. Then she turned to me briefly, shrugged, and said it again. "I just don't know." She searched my face for a reaction, but I was already lost in thought, and after a few seconds she turned back to her daughter.

The girl is a captive of her own birth, I thought. She will never be able to just go out and play like a normal child, or hang out with friends. She would be forever dependent, forever hidden. And thinking far into the future, I wondered what would become of her when Margaret and I were gone, when the world would intrude with an abrasive shock in spite of our lifelong efforts to prevent it.

"You okay?" Margaret suddenly asked.

I saw her staring at me. "Yes. I was just wondering about how to best protect her."

She had taken Sonya's hand again and was about to lead her out of the trees. "I worry about that all the time," she whispered, heading back out toward the road.

I followed. In a moment I caught up with them and took the girl's other hand as I had before. Less than a minute later, we came out onto the coast highway. The swath that I had plowed several days before was still visible under the new coating of snow, but it was apparent that no state trucks had gone by. Margaret stared first in one direction, then in the other, as if by sheer force of will she could conjure one up.

"How far is it to the inland highway?" she asked.

I pointed northwest, into the forest. "Five miles that way. The swamp that's just beyond the village is between it and us. It's frozen, though, so if we absolutely had to, we could cross it."

She gave me a puzzled look. "I thought you said the ice started to crack when you tested it." Sonya stared into the wall of evergreens.

"That's true, but that was the pond near the bone barrow, not the swamp. The pond has an underground stream, but the swamp will be stagnant and is probably frozen solid." Inwardly I cringed at the memory of the hole in the chasm that I was sure was the conduit that fed the pond.

She seemed to ponder this information for a moment, as if weighing the likelihood of success if, indeed, we had to walk out of there. For my part, that was a prospect I did not want to even think about. With only one set of snowshoes and a small child in tow, I was not sure that we would make it out at all. It was five miles as the crow flies, but since we weren't crows, that could easily translate into eight to ten hours of walking that could leave us both exhausted and still caught in the woods when the sun went down. The temperature at night would make that fatal. I fancied I saw that same realization in Margaret's eyes as she studied the dense wall of fir trees.

The walk back was uneventful. Sonya became excited again when she saw the bear tracks and strained to follow them to the Engineering building, but Margaret and I lifted her off the road so that her little legs raced in the empty air like a pair of pistons. She looked like something out of one of those "Roadrunner" cartoons, and the two of us had a good laugh at her expense, which she shared with her huge smile. We put her back down when the tracks were no longer in sight.

When we passed the parking lot, I decided to forego the coffee and follow up on the idea to move the cars. "You two go on ahead," I said. "I'm going to go take a look at the cars and see how much of a job it will be to get them into the shed."

"Okay. Dinner is at six."

"Should I bring some wine? I have a few bottles left."

"Sure. I have special-occasion champagne also, so one bottle should be enough."

"You got it. Anything else?"

She glanced back at me as she led Sonya toward the Ropewalk. "Just yourself." She smiled warmly.

I smiled back, feeling vastly reassured about our relationship.

"And some cranberry sauce if you've got any," she added as she moved away.

"Okay." I turned and headed up through the deep snow toward the cars, happily convinced that she really would pick me out of the social lineup that would happen after the holiday.

The cars were pathetic. Drifted over, buried, encrusted with ice, it seemed impossible to get them anywhere without an enormous effort. I kicked the iced-over snow away from my VW's rear wheels, then went to the driver's side and moved enough of it away so that I could at least see where the door ended. The good news, however, was that enough snow had fallen before the sleet began so that the coating of ice was on top of the snow and not welded to the vehicles themselves. That meant I could de-ice them just by brushing the snow off. That little detail changed everything. I went down to the shed and fired up the tractor.

By the time I got done plowing, sanding, and cleaning the snow off the cars, it was nearly four o'clock. Since I didn't have Margaret's keys, I moved mine first and drove it down to the shed without any problem. It was already dusk by this time, so I had turned on the headlights. The door to the shed was slightly higher than the yard outside it, so there was a slight upramp when driving into it, which caused my headlights to illuminate the ceiling for a brief moment as I drove in. But as the car began to level off, they also lit up the back of the shed where the old granary was located. In that moment I saw that the top of the granary did not reach all the way to the ceiling, that there was a space above it, and in the back of that space was what looked like the rung of a ladder. Another moment and it was gone from view as I moved the car into the open area to the left of the tractor and shut it off.

But I left the headlights on. Curious about what I had seen while driving in, I went over to the granary and opened the door. The light from the car flooded the small room and I was able to see to the back wall. There was no ladder. But I was sure I had seen one, so I went over to that wall and began spreading the heavy curtain of chains hanging there in order to get a closer look.

And that was when I saw it. Not a ladder, no, but a hasp, like the ones on the attic doors in the Ropewalk. It was a door, scarcely discernable

233

from the paneling around it and held shut only with a screwdriver thrust through the iron loop of the hasp. So I pulled it out and struggled with the latch against the weight of the hanging chains, which would not yield enough for me to see what was beyond the panels. The only way to get it open was to take down the chains in front of it, which would be no small task considering both their size and the quantity. I debated whether I wanted to go through the trouble for something that would probably turn out to be just a closet.

"Do I really want to go through all this?" I asked myself. But I knew immediately that I would be consumed with curiosity later on, just as I had been with the latches on the attic doors, and that if I didn't do it right then, some ectoplasmic force would wake me up at four in the morning and drag me out there—on Christmas morning, of all days—like an errant Sad Sack, a victim of my own impulsiveness. "So I might as well get it over with," I lectured myself.

I found a stepladder and brought it in so that I could reach the hooks that held the chains. I had only taken a few of them off when I noticed that they were attached to a steel cross member that, in turn, was attached to a lally column hiding behind the pile of tires in the corner. I studied this for a second before I realized what it was. A swing arm. There was no need to remove the chains; they were hung like a curtain on an arm that could simply be pivoted to the side.

"Why would that be?" I wondered aloud as I reached up to grab the end of the bar. I was able to swing it, with some effort because of the mass of the chains, all the way over to the side wall. The panel door was now fully accessible. I pulled it open and the headlight beam flooded what was behind it.

And there it was—the ladder. What the door revealed was a small, separate back room, like a narrow closet, and leaning against the rear wall—which was the wall of the shed itself—was the ladder. When I stepped up to it, I realized it was not leaning at all but was firmly anchored to the wall, which meant that it was not simply being stored there. I looked upward along its length and found myself staring into a tunnel. At the top, barely discernable because of the weak natural light, was an open rectangle.

I knew without having to verbalize it that I had just found the way to get to the third level of the shed.

♦ ♦ ♦

Chapter 19

Why was it that, at the most critical moments of my life, I never had a flashlight? I seemed to have one every other time. In fact, my second wife's father thought I had some kind of flashlight fetish, since I had them stashed all over the house.

"Do you want to bark your shin on a table leg?" I would counter. "Grab a flashlight." He would mumble and shake his head in dismissal. He knew what I was—the pariah married to his daughter, and I was convinced by then that he thought the surety of my route through life depended on the nearness of a flashlight.

But there I was, poised to take a look at what was up on the heretofore unreachable level, and I didn't have one. I had no choice but to go get one, especially since the obvious secrecy of this so-called "entrance" demanded nothing less than an immediate explanation.

What was this all about? I wondered. I stepped out of the granary and tried to picture the ladder as a solitary add-on to the shed when the topmost level was completed. It occurred to me that maybe that level had not always been there and that an afterthought addition required a compromise access since there didn't seem to be any other way of accommodating it. Maybe that was it. The main staircase only went to the second floor, and maybe they decided it was cheaper to install a ladder than try to add another series of steps.

But why hide it?

Then it occurred to me that, if it were only a question of cost, it would have made more sense to start the ladder on the second floor, yet I didn't recall seeing it there. In fact, when I looked up into the shaft, I did not even see any break in the darkness such as would have been evident if it simply passed through that floor.

That meant it had to be concealed there as well. I headed for the stairs to check that out, turning on the lights on the way. The sealed windows had made it very dark in there.

The rear wall of the second floor was taken up with the storage bins, and because some of them were stacked high with furniture, it was difficult to see if anything was beyond them. I didn't want to start taking things out just to see what was on the other side, but by climbing over a few boxes, I was able to get a partial look. A flashlight would have helped, of course, but even so, I was able to discern the outline of a boxed-in section of wall, like a sutured closet, artfully concealed behind what, to me, looked like a contrived stand of headboards and bureaus. Whether one had access to that closet was not possible to determine and was moot in any case, since the furniture piled in front of it would make it difficult. It was probably safe to assume that the ladder could only be reached from the granary on the first floor.

I stood there staring at the blank spot on the map that was the third floor. What was the point? You needed to get up there to hoist anything with the block and tackle, yet to get up there you needed to know where to find the ladder. Ergo, using the block and tackle was a tightly controlled activity. Why? Maybe it was another insurance issue?

Alright, I thought. In spite of my curiosity, this could go no further. It was almost quarter to five on Christmas Eve and I needed to finish moving the cars so that I could get over to Margaret's apartment. It was already dark, and since the moon had not yet risen, I would need the flashlight just to be able to get to the parking lot without slipping. I could check out the third floor of the shed after Christmas. I went down to the first floor, closed the door to the granary, and turned off the car's headlights. There was no need to go through the pointless ceremony of sealing up the ladder in its closet; it was not like someone was going to stroll by and find it open. I left the building lights on and the door open as I headed over to the Ropewalk to get my flashlight and Margaret's keys.

The moment I entered the building I could see that Margaret's door was open from the rectangle of light that was flooding the hall. I thought this was odd and headed straight down there rather than first going up to get my flashlight. It seemed unusually quiet, and my apprehension grew as I neared the door. When I was about twenty feet away, I called her name.

"Margaret? Everything okay?"

Silence. I approached her door. "Margaret?" Still no answer. I went in, my head full of chaotic images and nervous forebodings from the shadow incident of the night before. There was no one in either the living room or the kitchen. I turned and went down the short hall that led to the bedrooms and found both of them empty as well. I started to get nervous.

"I wish they'd modernize the plumbing in this place."

The words came at me from behind and I almost launched myself through the ceiling. I spun around and there stood Margaret with Sonya in her arms, all bundled up in a heavy towel, streamers of still wet hair poking out, Medusa-like, from under the folds of fabric. Margaret raised her one free arm in a gesture of surrender, palm outward. "Don't shoot. It's only me."

"You scared the crap out of me."

"I noticed. You were expecting maybe the nightwalker?"

I smiled and shook my head. "It's just so unlike you to leave your door open like this. I got a little concerned."

She smiled and put Sonya down. The little girl looked up at me from under the thick hood formed by the towel, which looked to be twice as big as she was. "I wanted to give Sonya a bath before the evening got going and figured it would only take a few minutes. I hate not being able to take a shower or bath in the apartment. They should really do something about this antiquated plumbing." She must have seen the lingering question in my eyes because then she added: "It's just nice being able to see where you're headed for once when you walk out into the hall. Besides, I knew you were right behind me." And with that, lightly dismissing any other consideration, she smiled again and led Sonya into her room to get her dressed. "Did you bring the wine and cranberry sauce?" she called from the room.

I was stunned. Shadow images, hidden ladders to forbidden places, self-opening doors, hideously unreal spiders, and unexplained drafts—I could feel myself slowly unraveling as I tried to fit the pieces of that growing non-normality together in my head while—oddly and perhaps fatefully—Margaret simultaneously grew confident in my ability to protect her.

"Did you?" she repeated.

"What? Sorry, I was just thinking about something. Did I what?"

She stuck her head out of the room. "Did you bring the wine and cranberry sauce?"

"Oh, no, not yet. I came by to get your keys so that I could move your car into the shed."

She pointed toward the kitchen. "On a nail over the phone. You don't have to move it now, Egan. It can wait until tomorrow if you'd like. I mean, it's been out there this long—I doubt one more day will make any kind of difference."

I shrugged. "Yeah, okay. If you don't mind, I really would prefer to do it tomorrow." With the sun gone it had started to get very cold and I was looking forward to dinner. "I have to go out and close up the shed, though, so I'll see you in a little while."

She waved and went back to dressing Sonya. I walked out and made sure the door was securely closed behind me. And although I had not formally verbalized it, even to myself, I was no longer so flippantly confident about whether we were alone in the building, so I made sure it was locked as well.

I didn't bother getting the flashlight since all I was going to do was go out and close up the shed. This decision was no problem on the way to the shed, but turned out to be something of a mistake when I got there because, when I turned the light off, the entire world was suddenly plunged into darkness. Since the moon had not yet risen and the only lights were the two that illuminated the parking lot, which were too far away to be of any use, there was nothing between me and the Ropewalk but soupy darkness. The outline of the building itself was just barely visible, and I found myself in the absurd position of having to white-cane my way across the clearing in its general direction. It was already noticeably colder but the sky was clear, so we weren't likely to get any more snow or sleet that night.

My eyes had adjusted somewhat by the time I reached the path to the front door. Far off, from the forest beyond the school, sounded a single haunting note that echoed through the woods and across the snowfield.

As many times as I'd heard it in the past, it still had an arresting quality for me. An owl. Of all the creatures that stalked the forest at night, the owl was, to me, the most mysterious, the most semi-mystical, the one that embodied that secret life now closed to humanity. I stood motionless for a few minutes waiting for the next call. When none came, I took my gloves off, formed a trumpet-like hollow with my hands, and raised it to my lips. The resulting hoot sailed into the forest and echoed back to me faintly from some far off hillside. A moment later I heard the reply and answered with another of my own. We hooted back and forth for several minutes, each time the owl getting a little closer, before the cold made it necessary to put my gloves back on.

I smiled. There was something primevally gratifying about having a conversation with an owl. I couldn't help but wonder what I had "said" that was drawing it nearer and felt an odd impulse to investigate that mysterious "language," but as I moved towards the building there resounded from the depths of the darkness beyond the school an echoing bellow of such volume that my nape hairs prickled. I stopped and felt for my .380, which was still in my pocket, but which suddenly felt very small and ineffectual. I had no idea what it was but couldn't help wondering if, instead of an owl, I had called to something I would rather not meet. It was not a sound I had ever heard before; I hurried down the path to the door while simultaneously trying to catalog it. Only after I was inside and had looped the chain through the handles did I realize it could have been the sound made by an animal being attacked by some predator.

That must have been it, I thought. The sound could not have been human. Maybe it was a moose, or maybe the wolf had brought down a deer, or the owl had gotten something. Even the gentlest-looking creature will shriek and bellow when attacked. The first time I heard the scream of raccoons fighting, I freaked out and would have called the police if the savvier members of the faculty hadn't stopped me.

That had to be it, I rationalized, as I headed up to my room. Even so, I could feel that my heartbeat had gone up a level and I knew I was not fully convinced that I had accepted my own explanation. I stopped at the top of the stairs and remained completely motionless for several minutes, listening for any sign of someone or something moving in the building. My gaze focused almost involuntarily on the ceiling. Beyond it was the attic, safely sealed away. But I heard nothing.

Was I loosing my mind? I wondered. I shook my head and smiled, then mumbled a reply into the emptiness around me. "No way to know, since no mind can evaluate itself from a defective position." I thought fleetingly of the joke I had made about the men in the white coats and hoped it was not prophetic. I could not shake off the growing feeling that I was a prisoner in the Ropewalk, playing house behind thin wooden walls while remaining heedless of what might be pacing around outside.

I entered my room without turning the light on and went straight to the window. The school was just a faint, black smudge against the darker curtain of the trees beyond it, and I doubted I would be able to see anything moving until the moon came up. But on a whim, I released the window lock, lifted the sash, and opened the storm window. The frigid air immediately oozed into the room and sank to the floor. I quickly formed the trumpet-like hollow with my hands and let out another resounding hoot that, once again, echoed from that far off hillside. But there was no response. I waited a few more seconds and then closed the window, turned on my desk light, and pulled down the shade.

"Alright," I said to myself. "Get a grip. It's almost dinnertime. Get a bottle of wine and—what was it?—oh, yeah, a can of cranberry sauce." I had my canned goods stashed in a cabinet beside the wardrobe, and as I reached for the cranberry sauce, I remembered that there was something else I was supposed to bring—my sleeping bag. I was going to be spending Christmas Eve in her apartment.

I knew it was not yet time for dinner, but I was feeling unaccountably agitated, or maybe just plain weary. Circumstances over the course of the week had left me feeling "forced" into doing things that had drawn me far from my reason for staying, leaving me with an even deeper sense of personal failure. Despite my bond with Margaret, I was even feeling a resurgence of that loneliness that had dogged me after Mae and I split up. I looked out at the darkened forest, at the immensity of the sky arching above it, and felt more isolated than ever, bemoaning the failure of any real emotional bond. I had come to suspect that that ability was one of the things that died with childhood.

Maybe that was why the instinct to have children was so strong. Despite not being her natural father, there was a certain instinct-level response that I'd felt when holding Sonya's hand. Maybe that was why I was heading down to dinner early.

240

"Get a grip," I said to myself again. "This is your usual Christmas depression talking. The darkest day of the year. It's just your pineal gland looking for a sliver of light." I smirked and shrugged, glanced out the window again at the absolute darkness beyond, but had the unmistakable feeling that we had to get out of there. Almost simultaneously, from some lost corner of my memory, came the sound of the drum-like hollow of the space beneath the floor of the shed, and it occurred to me that I had never checked what was down there. My mind was evidently connecting every thump, clunk, and knock with the sound I had just heard from the forest.

I wondered if this was how place-memory worked. As if on cue, my eyes fastened on the photo of the monolith in the basin, and the memory of the chasm touched my spine with an icy finger. I picked it up to examine the carvings again, and when I put it down, I found my hand resting on the "Concise History of the Northeast Aboriginals," that ancient tome I had found on the second floor of the shed. Published in 1837, seventeen years after Maine became a state. I flipped through the table of contents: "Mental Character," "Oratory Eloquence," "The Myth of Manibozho," "Myths of Descent." I opened it to the descent myths and was startled to read about the "hieroglyphs" that the Indians used to record their history.

"Hieroglyphs?" I said aloud. "He must have meant what we call petroglyphs today." But I was too wound up to pursue it. I used an index card to mark the page and put it aside, then went over, grabbed my flashlight, and stuck it in my pocket. I gathered up my wine and cranberry sauce, filled my arms with the fluffed up sleeping bag, turned off the desk light, and headed for the door. As an afterthought, I pushed in the button to lock my door. Then I headed down to Margaret's apartment.

I stood at her door with the wine in one hand, the cranberry sauce in the other, and my arms all bundled around the lofted sleeping bag, the thing bulging out all over like a giant marshmallow.

She was wearing white slacks and a soft, red sweater that sparkled with silver threads. She looked stunning, absolutely beautiful, to my eyes the closest thing to Venus/Aphrodite since Bronze Age Greece. "Egan," she said, "What on earth . . . ?"

"Is the offer to stay here tonight still open?"

She beamed. "Yes, of course. Come in."

241

I went over to the sofa and unloaded the bag onto it. "Is that going to be warm enough?" she asked. "I do have extra blankets, you know, and I didn't intend for you to use a sleeping bag."

I smiled at her concern. "Oh, it'll be warm enough. This is my 'late fall' sleeping bag, good for zero degrees if you're in a tent and fifteen degrees if you're not. If it looks like it's going to drop to zero in here, I'll run up and get my tent."

She laughed. "If it drops to zero in here, getting your tent won't be our biggest problem. Still, it's a fold-out sofa bed. You didn't have to bring your camping gear. What did you think I was going to do, cram you onto the couch and cover you with newspapers?"

I smiled at the vagabond joke, standing there eyeing the sofa askance and wondering why it hadn't occurred to me that she would have already covered that part of it, no pun intended.

"And I insist that we open it and set you up for a real night's sleep," she went on. "You know, with sheets and blankets. After dinner, of course."

"Okay. I guess I'm just used to curling up wherever I can find some floor space."

She laughed, then I laughed as well and reached out for her. The whole conversation was full of implication, of course—bed, sleeping; it was the sex question again, the one that, sooner or later, we would have to confront.

But not now. She went to the kitchen and got me a glass of eggnog, then went back to preparing dinner. I stowed the sleeping bag in a corner of the room, sat down, and tried to take in the scene. I began to relax. I saw the lights on the tree and smelled the incomparable aroma of evergreen boughs, and sensed that some of the magic of the season was still there, deeply buried perhaps, but still there. I even dared to think that maybe I belonged there.

In a few minutes, I realized that my agitation was subsiding and I suddenly knew why. It was Christmas, and I didn't want to be alone either.

◆ ◆ ◆

Dinner was a simple affair and the cranberry sauce was for the next day. She didn't have a whole turkey for Christmas dinner, but she did have a breast that she had taken out of the freezer and was thawing. It was plenty for the three of us.

"I should've sent you out with the shotgun to hunt us up a wild one," she chided. "That would've been the real Christmas tradition."

"Yeah, right. Tough and stringy and full of lead pellets. A real treat."

She narrowed her eyes at me in mock distress. "Are you saying you won't do the hunter-warrior thing for your lady? A martial artist like you?"

"I am your servant, madam," I intoned with exaggerated solemnity. "Whatsoever thou willst is my command. I just prefer my turkey lead-free if I can get it."

She turned to help Sonya with her fork. "We still have some Boston cream pie left for dessert, so make sure you leave some room."

"Right. No problem. How's the temperature been in Sonya's room?"

"Seems to be better. I keep a towel bunched up at the bottom of the door." The little girl was having trouble keeping pieces of meat on the end of her fork. "Did you get your car into the shed?"

"Yes. And I found the way to get to the third floor also. There's a ladder concealed behind the rear wall of the old granary, where Sil now stores the tires and chains."

She stopped and looked at me. "I didn't realize getting to the third floor was any kind of issue."

"The staircase only goes to the second floor. I've been wondering ever since I first went up there how anyone was supposed to get to the top in order to use the block and tackle. Now I know. But access to the ladder seems to only be possible from the first floor, and then only if you know where to look for it."

"It's hidden?"

"Yes. The rear wall of the granary is actually about three feet in front of the wall of the shed itself. Those three feet form a small closet and the ladder is attached to the wall of the shed inside that closet. You would never know from just looking into the granary that its rear wall was not the wall of the shed because you have no perspective on the dimensions of the shed from inside the granary. And the door is simply cut out of the paneling, so you would never know it was there.

I certainly didn't that time I went in there looking for something to secure the front door with."

She had gone back to helping Sonya. "That's so odd. I mean, I never noticed that there was no stair leading up to the third floor. Not that I had any reason to look." She put the fork down as Sonya began to show that squirming impatience that signaled an end to her dinner. A moment later the girl stood up on the chair, leaped off, and ran into the living room. There she knelt down in front of the tree and stared up into its branches.

Margaret reached out for my hand. "What time do you want your wakeup call in the morning?"

"Whatever works for you and Sonya. Will you be needing anything from the shed tomorrow?"

She shook her head and smiled. "I know what that means. You're looking for an excuse to check out the top floor."

I offered a huge, Cheshire-Cat grin in reply. "I just have to know. If it weren't so dark I would try it now." I caught myself in a sort of mental half-step when I said that; the memory of that bellow came back to me, and I realized with a chill that I was not at all anxious to go outside again.

"Well," she said, "You know the protocol. Christmas, presents, breakfast, visits from the relatives, midday dinner. Oops, I don't expect to be hearing from the relatives, so maybe you can use that time slot to search for them. They might be in the shed." She gave me a meaningful smirk—her Lauren Bacall look was how I had come to think of it—and got up to get the coffee.

I leaned back and looked out the kitchen window. My own face stared back at me from its reflection framed in the glass. Seeing myself caused an image to rise spontaneously in my mind, fragmented and formless. It contained the hole in the chasm, the petroglyphs on its walls, the piercing bellow from the darkened forest, that thing that flew from the top of the shed, and the shadow within a shadow, all mixed into a confusing collage of memories that bubbled up, flickered for a moment, and dissipated. Seeing the voluminous darkness beyond, imagining myself in a simple shelter with a fire—if I got one going—and whatever furs I could wrap myself in as my only sources of comfort and security, I could understand how easy it was to envision a forest full of creatures whose nature one could not even imagine. Forest demons, water spirits, monstrous things skulking in caves and under the roots of upturned trees—all of that sprang to life when one sat alone in a darkened forest and wondered what was making those strange noises.

In my career as an historian I had noticed many times that mythographers tended to dismiss the stories and histories of native peoples as nothing more than ignorant nature-folk with limited vocabularies trying to explain complex natural phenomena. For years I accepted that verdict, based on nothing more than the weight of authority, because there was no doubt that some of that was true. The worship of nature and the forces of nature was as old as time.

But it was also an arrogant position because it assumed that those same nature-folk, who lived their whole lives in that setting, who could find animal signs invisible to others, who knew the denizens of their world to a depth unimaginable to us, *somehow* still could not be relied upon to render an accurate account of things they had actually seen but that *we* found inexplicable. For some reason, we assume that their remarkable observational abilities suddenly became muddled when they began describing things that *we* did not understand.

"What are you thinking about?" Margaret had returned with the coffeepot.

"Actually, I was thinking about Indian myths and artifacts. I have an old book upstairs that I found in the shed a few days ago on that subject, published in 1837. Have you ever seen the Machias Bay petroglyphs?"

She sat down and pushed the Kahlua toward me. "I've heard about them but have never been out to see them. You have some pictures?"

"Yes, in a book up in my room. I was just thinking about them."

She got up and stepped over to the door to check up on Sonya, then sat back down and studied my face. "What brought that on?"

I broke off eye contact with her while I pondered this newest moment of trust. I had told her about the house, and she had promised to never breathe a word of its existence to anyone. I now needed her to do the same with my discovery of the petroglyphs in the chasm. By themselves, they could secure my reputation regardless of whether I could ever explain the carved monolith in the basin or sort out the history of the village. I realized with something of a start that I was desperate that no one else found out about them before I'd had a chance to get better photographs and study what they represented. I glanced up at her, saw the questioning look in her eyes, and finally said: "Because I found some just like them near the village."

Her look revealed her doubt. "You found some petroglyphs? Near the village?"

"Yes. Why does that seem so odd?"

She shrugged. "It's just that, you know, it's so unlikely that they would've gone undiscovered for so long. You'd think others would have found them by now. A hunter maybe, or even just a hiker. It's not like the area is so unknown."

Her comment held both doubt and a tinge of challenge, and for a moment I fancied it was a bit of lighthearted revenge for my not accepting her story of knowing about the well in the village. But when I looked over at her, I realized that what I was seeing was a demand for the truth; the only doubt in her eyes was whether I was giving her the whole story. The challenge in her look was a reminder that I had withheld the discovery of the house; the doubt was that I was withholding something now as well.

"Are they somewhere near that house?" she asked, as if reading my mind. "Is that why no one ever found them?"

"No. They're under the ropewalk."

"*Under* the ropewalk?"

"Yes. The building straddles a natural chasm that's a conduit for a stream. It was the perfect setup for a waterwheel. The glyphs are on the wall of the chasm, hidden from view by the building itself. That's apparently why they haven't become common knowledge."

Now her look went from doubt to concern. "You went into this chasm?"

And so I told her all about it, about slipping into the basin and having no way out, about climbing over the debris and finding the ledge that was obviously the way the original owners serviced the waterwheels, about finding the stone staircase that led up into the building. And about seeing the glyphs. But I did not tell her about the hole; she was obviously worried enough as it was.

Her eyes bored into me for a few seconds as she digested this information, and I knew what was coming. "Why didn't you tell me about all this yesterday when I first asked you about how your day had gone?" Her tone and expression revealed a level of sudden mistrust—or maybe hurt—that I knew only too well.

I reached out for her hand. "Because I didn't want to worry you. Knowing how upset you've been about all that's happened, what with the noises in the hall and how you worried that first time I went to the village when, you know, you found out about Ben, I realized that I couldn't put you through any more stress. I didn't want you fretting about me, or wondering if I was going to come back every time I went into the woods."

She looked at me in silence.

I gave her hand a gentle squeeze. "You need to trust that I can take care of myself. I've been doing it for a long time."

"I know. It was silly of me to worry. I guess I was just feeling a bit possessive." She smiled and seemed to relax, and I took the opportunity to finish the last of my coffee. I sensed she had something else to say but she simply turned to her coffee as well, then a moment later added: "And scared."

Later, when Sonya had been put to bed and we switched from coffee to wine, we sat together on the couch and I told her the whole story in greater detail. She wanted to see the pictures I had taken, so I went up and got them, and since I wanted to read further in the "Concise History" book, I brought that along as well. I was not particularly tired and figured I would still be awake after she went to bed. By the time I got back, she had spread out a fantailing carpet of unwrapped toys under the tree so that Sonya would be surprised when she got up. She had been hiding them in her room.

The pictures were poor and the glyphs in some cases barely visible, which underscored my need to go back and get better shots. She understood this, though it was with obvious misgivings, and tried to convince me to wait until everyone was back from the holiday so that someone could go with me. This was a sound idea from a practical point of view, but a very bad strategic plan; bringing someone with me would mean that the discovery was no longer mine alone and could be pre-empted by whoever that person was. She understood this, too, but was no less dismayed at my explanation. She eyed me as if seeing the "real" me for the first time, and I imagined she thought that this "real" me was a goal-focused, ambitious academic who, all along, had been hiding behind the devil-may-care exterior.

But what she did not realize was that it was not blind ambition that she was seeing, but my compulsive need to find some undiscovered niche that would forever be my link to the world. I could not explain this need—it was like the hikes I used to take to my favorite forest haunts, now long since unvisited from childhood. Fate had surprised me twice just in the last week and left me half believing, not sure, and caught between two worlds, the one I now had with Margaret and the one driving me to distinguish myself as an historian.

But it was not ambition. It was something else, hanging namelessly over me like a somatic imprint from a previous life. I didn't care if my name became known; what I cared about was that some tangible link in the amorphous chain of time would reveal itself to me so that I could feel myself a part of it. I was much simpler than my colleagues at the school; they wanted their names glorified in professional publications, but all I wanted was to carve my initials into a tree that I hoped would live forever.

All of this defied explanation.

When the wine was gone, we opened the champagne, and as the alcohol took hold the pictures were gradually put aside and we moved closer together. I turned off the lamp we had been using and the only light left was from the Christmas tree, a warm, subdued glow that filled the room with a soft radiance. She was very tired, and what little dialog was whispered between us soon faded away as her eyes began to close. I figured I would end up holding her as I had the night before, but within minutes she roused herself and sat up with a wide-eyed look of concern on her face.

"Something wrong?" I asked.

"I just remembered—I have to open the couch and make the bed for you. Oh my God, I almost forgot." She got up and went into her bedroom to get the sheets before I could even respond.

I unfolded the couch in the meantime and when she came out, her arms bundled high with sheets and blankets, I helped her put it all together. The symbolism of the act was not lost on me, and I was sure it had not escaped her attention either; we scarcely made eye contact while we worked. When it was finished, she looked it over and said: "Will those blankets be enough, do you think? Should I get you another, just in case?"

In reply, I went to the corner and retrieved my sleeping bag, unzipped it completely, and folded it at the foot of the bed. "Instant blanket," I said with a smile. "Good for zero degrees if you're in a tent."

She threw up her hands in surrender. "I concede. I figured you'd find a way to work the sleeping bag into the picture somehow." She came around to my side, held me lightly, and kissed me. "Good night. I'm too tired to stay up any longer." She turned away and headed for her bedroom, then stopped and added: "Try not to scare Santa. He won't be expecting you."

"Right. I'll be careful. Did you leave any cookies and milk for him?"

She had stepped into her room and leaned back so that just her head and shoulders were visible. "Tell him he can help himself to the cookies, but go easy on the milk. We're getting low." She winked and disappeared into her room, closing the door behind her.

I was not particularly tired, so I moved down to a corner chair that was near the window and pulled the shade outward to see if it was doing anything outside. The sky was clear and strewn with so many stars that the sheer immensity of the galaxy was almost palpable. Someone had once joked to me that you could not study astronomy in New York City because there were only three stars visible in the night sky. That was certainly not the case here.

There was not a wisp of a cloud anywhere. Far off, several hundred yards away, was the ocean, not much more than a frosty glitter in the starlight. It must have been low tide. The perspective from her window was totally different from mine, and there was no way to see either the shed or the school. The broad expanse before me was nothing more than an unbroken sheet of iced-over snow that reached from the building to the granite bedrock ramps that led into the sea. And since I was now on the first floor rather than the second, my view was limited. I let the shade drop back into place and thought about opening the "Concise History" but decided I was too buzzed from the champagne to read anything that stilted. So I nosed around for something else and settled for one of Sonya's picture books.

It was actually not a children's book at all but a pictorial rendering of the majestic wilderness of the Pacific Northwest. The views were stunning, with sweeping panoramas of alpine meadows, pristine rivers, and distant mountains, totally unlike New England. I could see why the child was so fascinated. Further along, towards the back of the book, I discovered that she had pressed various leaves between the pages. I found this oddly incongruous in view of her mental abilities, but at the same time it connected in some ineffable way with her strange fascination for trees. More oddly still, it resonated with an even stranger sense of childlike shamanism or sympathetic magic—the picture, the tree, the leaf preserved with the changeless photograph. Leaf, moment, time, perpetuation: it was a symbol language of some sort. I could sense the connectedness but could not express it in words.

I closed the book, went back to looking at my photographs again, and noted that I was even disappointed in the one I had taken of the carved monolith. It was very indistinct and could easily leave one with the impression that the stone was not carved at all but was covered with random weathering patterns. The lighting for a shot like that was very important in order to bring out the images, and obviously I had not gotten it right when I took the Polaroids. That, too, would have to be redone, maybe even augmented with some rubbings.

I put the photos back on the end table, leaned back, and closed my eyes. The next day was Christmas; my family would be expecting me back in Connecticut and would be alarmed that I neither showed up nor notified them that I wasn't coming. That could be remedied, of course, once the bridges were reopened and the phone lines connected. But my family would contact the authorities, which, in turn, would launch a three-state search for accident reports with my name on them. Several days would be absorbed in a fruitless search by the various State Police agencies, while I sat here sipping coffee without ever having left. Making the best of that situation meant that I had had a full week to work on my project but still had done nothing on it. Nothing. I hadn't even decided on a format. I could feel that sense of failure rising in me again, turning the dream into a phantasm. I seemed to have moved further away than ever.

But maybe it was just the alcohol talking. It, and the hour, were getting to me by then and it was pointless to try to stay awake any longer. I got undressed, turned off the Christmas tree lights, and slipped between the icy sheets. A small nightlight continued to burn, casting elongated shadows across the walls as I felt myself drifting off. I thought of the hallwalker, and the shadow within the shadow, and the strange bird that had flown from the shed, and from somewhere deep inside I heard a thump-thumping, as of someone trying to get out of a box, and even in half-sleep I knew it was some auditory memory of the shed's basement, or maybe the basement of the Ropewalk itself.

And then I was suddenly awake again, staring at the ceiling and straining my ears to hear. Had I dreamed that or was it real? I listened for what seemed a long time but nothing came to me, no owl's hoot or frightening bellow. Peripherally, distantly, I realized how vulnerable one was on the first floor and suddenly wished I had brought my .380 with me. Then I fell asleep.

Inevitably, I dreamed that Margaret came to me in the night, silent as a moon shadow, and I could feel her breath on my face as she neared and smell the pale fragrance of her perfume, and it seemed so real that I startled myself into reaching for her. But a whisper-fine touch stroked my cheek, and I opened my eyes and there she was, for real, a silhouette in the darkness, highlighted by the tiny nightlight, her lips touching mine and her hair cascading around me like the veil of Isis. And then she sat up and untied the robe and tossed it onto a chair, and I could see even in that fragile light that she was nude, and when she slid in beside me, the smooth warmth of her skin on mine reassured me that this was no dream. She was really there.

◆ ◆ ◆

Chapter 20

I felt her stirring and glanced over at the mantle clock on the hutch, now partially hidden behind the tree. It was six a.m., still absolutely dark outside, and I was wide awake even though I had hardly slept at all. The restlessness was not because it was Christmas, but because I didn't want to fall asleep lest I discover that she had been nothing more than a dream.

I propped myself on an elbow and looked at her. She was lying on her side facing away from me, her bare shoulder peeking out from under the covers. I wanted to touch her as if to assure myself that she was really there, but refrained; small, nagging doubts assailed me from my emotional archives, and I hoped against all possible hope that I hadn't messed up, that she liked what we had done. Yet, even so, a certain immovable center in me passed a cautionary judgment of irrelevance in spite of it, steeling me against the possibility of disappointment. A pre-emptive emotional buttress. It was one of my personality quirks.

So I simply lay there, my head full of things to say, all of them inadequate. I had a parade stomping through my head with floats bearing aloft witticisms and observations, endearments and sweet nothings. But they all talked at once and the result was chaos.

So I said nothing and simply put my arm around her. She woke up then and rolled toward me, her eyes still half closed and a faint smile curling her lips, then slipped one arm under me and drew me closer so that I was half on top of her. "I don't usually do this on a first date," she murmured.

"This wasn't our first date, remember?"

She yawned. "Oh yeah, right. So I guess I'm in the clear."

"Actually, have we even been on an official date yet?"

She sighed and pulled me down for a quick kiss. "You mean I need to feel guilty after all?" But before I could answer, we kissed again, more deeply than before. This time she didn't want to stop; whenever I came up for air, she was there again, pulling me to her. Our fingers twined together while we kissed so that we ended up holding hands, and as I pulled away for a moment, she kissed my hand, as a man might a woman's. I was startled and pleased.

It took several tries before we finally broke apart. Obviously, my doubts and fears were groundless.

"There was a full moon last night," she whispered.

"Yes." In my rapturous befuddlement, I at first could think of nothing else to say as a reply. But a moment later I realized that what she meant was that it was a lover's moon, that ancient symbolic light that heralded both intimacy shrouded in secrecy and the illumination of a benighted soul. But I was sure that an academic explanation would have been out of place just then, so I said nothing.

A sound from Sonya's room caused her to sit up and listen. I half expected the little girl's door to open and see her come charging out to see what Santa had left her, and it occurred to me that I had to be dressed before that happened. But the room fell silent again. Margaret, however, understood it to mean that Sonya would soon be awake and slid out from under the covers to retrieve her robe from the chair. I reveled in her nudity; it was a tribute to all that Venus/Aphrodite had ever stood for in the collective memory of the race.

"I can't let her find me with you," she whispered, turning back toward me.

"I know. And I should get up so that I'm decent when she comes out."

She nodded, went over to turn on the tree lights, then sat on the bed beside me. "What's your official religion, anyway?" she asked. "Ever since you made that comment about the 'Midwinter Fire Festival,' I've been curious."

I sat up. "Pagan. Every spring I hang an offering to Odin."

She laughed and shook her head. "Figures. I should have known."

How beautiful she was. I pulled her to me for one more kiss, one more touch, accepting now that we had become lovers, that all the grand gestures that love would leave to tempt me would be mine alone. But as if to hear it from her own lips, I asked her if she was upset that Ben was not there.

"On some level, yes," she said, "But only because of what we once had, and because of Sonya. Our marriage had been foundering for so long I'm actually glad the decision was forced on me. I know it sounds crass, but it's actually a relief that we're finished."

She felt free, she said, like she wanted to leap for joy. It was a great change in her life, but she had a job and a place to live, so it wasn't like she had to sacrifice her own life to Ben's wishes. "He's something of a control freak," she said. "He never liked the fact that I have my own mind."

I, on the other hand, was infinitely grateful that she did.

She got up and threw back the covers. "Okay, no more dallying. Get up and get dressed. We need to fold the sofa back up and be ready for Sonya when she wakes up." She swatted me on my butt as I rolled out and reached for my clothes. "I'll get the coffee going so that it's ready when we're dressed." She was already stripping the blankets and sheets off the mattress. I then helped her fold it up and cover it with the seat cushions.

I pulled on my pants and shirt but simply carried the shoes. "I have to go shower and shave, so I need to run up to my room," I whispered. I opened the door and looked into the hallway. The nightlights were still on, which struck me as a surprise, but which also meant I didn't need a flashlight. "Be back in about twenty minutes." I made sure the door would lock behind me before I stepped out.

Her arms were full of bedclothes as she turned toward me. "Okay." She vanished into her room as I quietly stepped into the hall and shut the door.

The hallway was freezing compared to her apartment, and I instantly regretted not putting my shoes on. To minimize my discomfort, I sprinted down the hall toward the stairs, my footfalls barely making any sound at all on the floor. And because I was so quiet, I surprised something in the lobby.

As I raced around the end of the hallway, headed for the staircase, one of the plastic plants against the wall rustled and stopped me dead in my tracks. In a single heartbeat everything flooded back through me, the limb slamming against the door, the tracks in the snow, the bellow from the black rim of the forest, the wolf, the bear, the spider, the giant wing-borne thing that sailed from the roof of the shed. All in an instant, chilling and holding me frozen to the floor as the unarticulated thought flashed through my head that *something* was in the lobby with me.

I froze, my eyes bulging as I tried to pierce the gloom. And as I stood there the bush rustled again, and I thought that whoever it was couldn't be very big because there was no room to hide over there. So I turned from the staircase and slowly made my way over to the plant. Before I was halfway across the lobby, a dark shadow detached itself from the gloom in the corner and sprinted in a wide arc around me and toward the stairs.

My heart leaped into my throat. But only for a moment as I turned to get a look at the visitor. There, on the bottommost step of the staircase, sat a cat, black as night and staring at me with that wide-eyed mistrust so characteristic of felines. Lean and somewhat ragged, as if it were starving, it snarled as I took a step toward it. I squatted down and tried to soothe it, but it was having none of that and, with one last hiss, it sprinted up the stairs, around the corner, and into the gloom of the upper hall.

I stood rooted to the spot for several seconds, disbelieving. Was it possible that our mysterious nightwalker was simply a feral cat that had found a way into the building? Could it have been hiding in the utility closet when I saw the "shadow within a shadow" emerging from that closet? *Was* that the "shadow within a shadow?"

How foolish I would feel if that turned out to be the case. I shook my head with a laugh and headed up the stairs while making a mental note to set out a bowl of water and some scraps for our new little friend. When I got to my door, though, it occurred to me that the cat had run down into the hallway, a dead end with no hiding places, and from which no escape was possible. He—or she—could therefore not have been living on my floor or we would have seen him when we searched the building. For that matter, it could not have been living on the first floor either. In fact, it could not even get out of the sack into which it had just run without going past me.

I stepped over to the entrance to the hallway and watched for any movement. But it was simply too dark and the building too long to see anything. With a shrug, I returned to my room, unlocked the door, and flipped on the light. I immediately scanned the floor for any sign of the spider, but everything seemed intact. It took me only a few minutes to shave and then I headed down the hall to the showers. Because the shower room had exposed radiators, I fully expected to find the cat living there, having found a way in even with the door closed. But a quick inspection showed that this was not the case, which left me more perplexed than ever. Where had it been living all this time?

When I got back to Margaret's apartment, Sonya still had not gotten up, so we had coffee and I told her about the cat. She, too, began to wonder if that was our mysterious nightwalker.

"Where is it living?" she asked.

I shrugged. "I don't know. Evidently it knows of some loose wallboard or missing panel somewhere that it uses to get in and out."

She smiled. "Maybe it lives in room eleven. Maybe he was the guy who unlocked the door."

I grinned at her little joke but said nothing.

"I wonder what it's been eating," she mused.

I thought of the mouse that had visited me in the middle of the night. "Field mice, probably. I'm sure the building is loaded with them." In an instant, the episode with the little creature replayed itself in my head and I mentally saw the thing sprinting into the tiny hole that led to the attic. And in the next instant, it hit me with an almost precognitive certainty—that was where the cat was living.

"The attic," I said.

She looked up from her coffee. "What?"

"The cat is living in the attic."

She gave me a curious look. "How do you know this?"

"I don't, at least not for sure. It just suddenly hit me, like an intuitive insight."

"Destiny logic again?" She smiled and reached out to rub my arm.

"No. It's more like a type of place memory. Intuitive insight, like a prophetic dream."

"Hmm." She leaned into me for a kiss, but turned her head at the last instant as a sound emerged from Sonya's room. "She's awake. I'll go get her." And with that, she left me in mid-pucker without another thought.

While she was in Sonya's room, I went to the window and pulled the shade outward to see what the weather was doing. The sun was not yet up, but the eastern horizon had paled and enough light had pierced the veil of darkness so that I could see that it must have sleeted during the night. The storm had coated everything in shimmering glass, leaving a glittering expanse that stretched to the sea, broken now and then only by the heavily laden boughs of fir trees.

But it must have become warmer as well because a lot of mist was rising from the snowfields out near the rim of the forest, with fibrous, ephemeral strands of vapor enwrapping the ghost-trees nearby. Remembering the noise I'd heard the night before, I couldn't decide if it was hauntingly beautiful or just plain haunted.

"Here she is." Margaret's voice reached me before she stepped into view from the short hallway that led to Sonya's room. I turned in time to see her carrying her daughter, all bundled up in a blanket, into the living room and to see the little girl's eyes light up when she saw all the toys spread out under the tree. She squirmed to get away, and Margaret put her on the floor and removed the blanket. Sonya ran up to the pile of goodies and stood there as if trying to take it all in. She was clearly uncertain about what to do and looked back at her mother in confusion.

Margaret urged her forward. "Go ahead. Santa brought those for you." And with that, the little girl waded into her little world of toys the way any normal child would. In a few minutes, she was so thoroughly engrossed in a dollhouse that she appeared to have tuned out everything else.

We had a light breakfast, during which my imagination flamed the fires of fantasy every time I stole a glance at Margaret, who seemed preoccupied with Sonya's happiness but who caught me staring at her once. The way her eyebrows shot up she had apparently read my mind and gave me a gentle scolding. "Don't get any ideas," she said, "I've got to start getting the dinner ready. We're eating around one o'clock."

Rebuffed but not disheartened, I offered to help but she suggested I go move her car into the shed while she got the kitchen ready. "First, though, the gifts," she said, getting up and retrieving a large box from under the tree. I opened it and found inside a beautiful leather jacket with a fur collar, a classy escutcheon well beyond my usual fare and taste.

"Oh my God," I said. "If I wear this, I'd be in danger of becoming socially presentable. I'll even look good."

"Well, when you publish your history of the region, you have to look sophisticated for the book signing."

"Right." My vision dimmed as I sought to bring that far-away horizon into focus, now more complicated than ever by the village, monolith, and petroglyphs. But it was not the time to dwell on all that. I gave her one of the gifts I had brought down, and she opened it and found a watch I had intended for one of my sisters. We then alternated back and forth with the gift giving until all the packages had been unwrapped. As I got up to get us more coffee, she went into her bedroom and emerged a moment later with one last gift.

"I want you to have this, too," she said. From behind her back she produced the shotgun I had seen in the closet. It was unwrapped except for a pink bow tied around its barrel. "I have no use for it and I'd feel better if it were out of the apartment."

I took it from her, opened the slide to make sure it wasn't loaded, and brought it to my shoulder briefly. It's a good thing I didn't have it two nights ago, I thought, or I might've blown a hole in the floor going after that spider.

But I had reservations as I recalled how vulnerable I had felt during the night. "Maybe you should reconsider. This is the ultimate home defense weapon, and with Ben now gone you might, you know, want to have something in the apartment, just in case."

She smirked and stepped up to me, brushed the gun barrel aside, and said: "Why? I have you, don't I?"

Indeed she did. I leaned over and kissed her and a moment later she broke away, went into her bedroom again, and returned brandishing her foil. "And I also have this." So saying she assumed a defensive posture and whipped the long, slender blade through the air in curt arcs that were so fast they were nearly invisible.

I was impressed, except that I reminded her the thing was for sport only and ended in a button, not a point, so what was she going to do, squeegee her way across her opponent's torso a quarter inch at a time?

"Ah," she said, "You know that and I know that, but a real assailant wouldn't. If you were an attacker, would you gamble on the thing not having a point?" She whipped it again with a flourish that sounded like a rope being twirled.

I had to admit I would not.

Sonya was still completely absorbed in the tiny wonderland that Margaret had created for her, which meant that if Margaret could get me out of the way as well, she could start getting things ready. "I can take a hint," I said jokingly. "Why don't I move your car while you're doing that? Maybe I'll even visit the top floor of the shed while I'm out there."

"Sounds like a plan. Take the shotgun with you, okay? I really don't want it hanging around the living room." She put the foil back in her bedroom and went into the kitchen while I lifted her car keys from the hook and went out, headed for my room.

♦ ♦ ♦

The cat was nowhere in sight, which was no big surprise. I was thoroughly convinced that it had found a way into the attic and was living there, though the source of my conviction was not so much a rational deduction as an odd urgency that had been growing within me to find out what was really up there.

I stared into the long, darkened tube that was the upper hallway and resolved to cut one of the locks off if I had to. Once I checked it out, I could use the padlock I'd seen in the shed to secure it again. Sil probably wouldn't even notice until such time as he tried to get up there, but by then everyone would be back from the holiday and it would not be so easy to pin it on me. I shook my head and laughed humorlessly at the subtle tactic; there I was, a grown man and teacher at the school, yet I had to plan my next step around the ire of the one guy I'd rather avoid, but who turned out to be Sonya's godfather.

"Somehow he'll know it was me," I mused as I unlocked my door, flipped on the light, and stood the shotgun in the corner behind the open door. Almost instinctively now, I checked for signs of subtle intruders but didn't see any indication of anything. The steel wool I had stuffed into the hole near the ceiling beam was still there, and from what I could see without a flashlight, nothing had been scrabbling around under my bed.

It only took a few minutes to get ready to go out, and when I stood before the front door I consciously studied the chain to see if, indeed, it looked as if someone had been tampering with it. But that, too, seemed fine, and when I stepped outside, it was to the first sparking rays of daylight glinting off the newly iced-over snowfield between the Ropewalk and the sea. Every bush and tree was an exquisite chandelier.

And it was indeed warmer than the day before, as had been evidenced by the mist. There was even an outside chance that it had not been sleet at all but freezing rain, which would have meant that a warm front had moved in overnight and that maybe we could expect a break from the extreme cold.

That, of course, would make my next trip to the village and bone barrow a lot more enjoyable.

I slipped several times getting to the shed and realized I would have to spread sand over the yard and up to the parking lot again or I would never be able to move Margaret's car. This took a good half hour since the upslope into the parking lot was so icy even the tractor had trouble, chains and all. Getting her car scraped, thawed, and down to the shed took another half hour, and then I had trouble negotiating the slight upramp into the shed itself. All told, that little operation took nearly an hour and a half. By then the sun was up, the mist had dissipated, and the black rim of the spruce forest beyond the school did not look so forbidding. I scanned it to get some idea of where that sound had come from the night before, but I didn't see anything that would tip me off. I figured that if a wolf had brought down a deer, I would at least be able to see blood on the snow, but nothing was visible from the shed.

But while I was thinking of that incident something else occurred to me, and I went back into the shed and straight for the drawer in which I had found the shotgun shells nearly a week earlier. I opened it and rummaged deeper into it in the hopes of locating other kinds of shells, and my search was rewarded by the discovery of a box of the one type I really wanted but did not expect to find—rifled slugs. Twelve gauge rifled slugs. I opened the box, removed half a dozen, then closed and buried it in the drawer again.

I stared at the shells, at the bulbous gray dome of the slug peeking out from the end. Now *these* would turn a scattergun into a big-game rifle, and although I had no pretensions—or even *in*tentions—of being a hunter, my nagging sense of vulnerability was more than adequately addressed by the thought of a twelve-gauge loaded with slugs. *These* could bring down a wolf or bear, stop it dead in its tracks, where the .380 would be questionable. I stuffed them into my pockets and went back out to scan the rim of the forest again.

But I really needed my binoculars for that, and since I didn't have them, I gave it up for the moment and walked away from the shed to try to gain some perspective on the roof. Way up on the ridge I could see where the snow had been broken or brushed aside, and I decided that that had to be where whatever that bird was had been perched. There was a copula up there, one of those small, windowed houselings whose pointed roof inevitably supported the weathervane, as it did here. If I could get to it, I would be very close to the area in question and might be able to see some tracks. But to get there, I had to reach the third floor of the shed. Because of the discovery of the ladder the previous night, I knew how to do that.

Before going back in, I went around the side of the shed to look for the outside entrance to the lower level. This turned out to be a drifted-in causeway cut into the embankment that formed part of the foundation of the building. It was obvious from more than just the snowdrift that it had not been used in some time; the actual earthen walls that framed the causeway had slumped over the years and securely blocked the door. Nor was it possible to look in; the windows had been long since replaced with sheets of plywood that had been weathered to a stippled gray by the elements. There was no place for light to get in.

I went back into the shed and over to the trapdoor in the floor of the granary, pulled it open, and stared down into the black pit. Not a sliver of light showed up anywhere. I got down on the floor and hung my head over the edge so that I could scan for a light switch, or even a light source, but it seemed like the place was hermetically sealed. The top of the ladder was visible in the light from above, but it sank into a pool of absolute darkness. I pulled away, lowered the door back into place, and headed for the ladder in the back of the granary.

I looked upward into the paneled tunnel that contained the ladder. It was dark except for a splash of light at the top where the waxing sunlight had evidently penetrated the windows in the copula. Apart from the unnerving height that it reached as it ascended, this was a relatively easy challenge. I grabbed the rungs and started climbing.

When I was parallel with the second floor, I looked for some sort of door, and my efforts were rewarded with the discovery of a simple latch that, when opened, released a section of paneling. This camouflaged door was to the right of the ladder, and when I stepped over with that foot and peered through the opening, I saw a pile of furniture in front of me. I was behind the stalls that were being used to store the teachers' extra furniture, and unless one specifically knew that the ladder was there, one would never see it from the floor. I put my right foot back on the ladder, pulled the door closed, and continued upward.

When I was within about ten feet of the top I stopped, not because the height was making me nervous but because I had encountered a perplexing obstacle. The ladder ended a few feet above my head, well short of the top, but continued on the opposite wall. The only way to reach the third level was apparently to climb to the top of the ladder I was on, then reach across the opening to the other ladder. The problem was, in order to do that, I would have to climb to nearly the topmost rung, which was functionally impossible because, although I would have a rung to stand on, I would have nothing to hold onto.

I looked down. The base of the ladder was illuminated by a rectangle of light from the bulb in the granary and seemed dangerously far away; if I were to take a chance at reaching the other ladder and lost my grip, I would plummet a good thirty feet to the floor, which meant that at the very least I would break something, if I weren't killed outright. With no possible way to contact emergency services or even get me to a hospital, it seemed heedlessly foolish to even think about proceeding.

But I couldn't let it go. When I remembered how dangerous the house in the woods was, and the pond, and the chasm, and the old ropewalk, I felt foolish being stymied by something so prosaic. At the very least, I needed to climb as high as I could to see if it was possible to reach across to the bottom of the other ladder. There *had* to be a way; after all, this was how Sil got up there to use the block and tackle. What was I not seeing?

The answer to that came with heart-stopping suddenness the moment I resumed my ascent. I had only climbed a couple more rungs when I felt the ladder come loose and begin to fall towards the opposite wall. I freaked; instinctively, I pulled myself up as the ladder hit the wall, then frantically lashed out with my legs as they slipped off the rung from the impact and left me suspended over the abyss. In a moment I had wrapped them around the ladder, and I clung to it with my heart racing as I awaited what would come next. When nothing did, I dared to assess my situation.

The ladder below me had not come loose—it was still attached to the rear wall. So the ladder was not falling, yet there I was, holding on for all I was worth to the underside of that part that now leaned against the other wall. Had it broken, I wondered, and was it holding on by a few splinters at the break point? Would the slightest movement cause it to snap off and go plummeting to the floor?

With almost painful slowness, I reached around to grab the ladder from the other side. Once I did that, I began to formulate a plan; I needed to get down to the section that was still secured to the wall, and I needed to do it without adding any more stresses to the part I was holding onto. Slowly, a few inches at a time, I slid my grip down to the next rung, then allowed my legs to slide down to the break point.

Only then did I notice a feature in the wall that I hadn't seen before—to the left of the ladder, there were slots cut into the paneling and handholds bolted like extra rungs on either side of those. I stared for a few seconds at this odd and unexpected salvation before its purpose dawned on me: it was a way to step off the ladder. Very carefully, I reached out, grabbed one of the handholds, and tested it for strength. It was secure, so I stepped into one of the slots with my left foot.

Gingerly, cautiously, still holding onto the ladder with my right hand, I unwrapped my right leg from around it and stepped into the slot. Then I released the ladder and grabbed another handhold. With my heart still racing, I pulled myself against the wall and clung to it like a burr.

"Okay," I muttered as my rapid, panicked breathing returned to normal. "I'm safe. I can reach the unbroken part of the ladder from here." I waited a few seconds for my heart to calm down before I very carefully stepped down into the slot below the one I was on. Once I felt secure, I turned my attention to the break. That was my next surprise.

It wasn't broken. It was hinged. The ladder had been modified at that point to do exactly what had just happened—lean against the other wall. "What the hell?" I mumbled as I reached out to test the strength of the hinges that held it in place. They were massive things, easily rugged enough to hold an enormous weight, at first invisible in the darkness of the tunnel but now coming into focus with the growing light from above. And because of that light, it was also possible to make out more features—like the friction clips I could see above me, bolted to the wall. These were the fasteners that had held the ladder against the wall before I had inadvertently broken it loose with my weight.

I now understood. This was intended to either be another barrier to reaching the top, or had some functional purpose. In either case, the handholds were obviously intended to allow one to step off the ladder, pull it out of its clips so that it spanned the opening, then climb onto it again and use it as a bridge to the other ladder on the opposite wall. Access to the top evidently had a detour. I climbed up the handholds and onto the ladder to find out why.

This was much more unnerving than simply climbing upward. Crossing the opening meant I couldn't help but look down, and for a fleeting moment I felt the same paralysis that had seized me in the chasm with the discovery of the hole. This passed the moment I reached the other ladder, however, and in another few seconds I was at the top, looking over the expanse of the third level. I stepped between the extended side rails and onto the floor.

The first thing I noticed was a knotted rope coiled around a massive peg driven into one of the support beams in the ceiling. It was obviously a means of emergency descent, clearly indicative of Sil's concern about the integrity of the ladder. Looking back at the opening, I understood the need for the jog in the ladder—if it weren't there, one would climb to the top and find himself clinging to the back wall and having to somehow cross the opening to get onto the floor, an extremely dangerous undertaking. By adding the hinged part, one emerged onto the floor itself. Of course, that did not explain why the ladder was not simply mounted to the inside wall so that no crossover was necessary. It seemed obvious that Sil also wanted to create the impression that one needed some missing piece to get to the top.

I could not see why. All about me it was mostly empty, an unconvincing testament to its status as some sort of secret room. At the other end, I could see the massive beam that supported the block and tackle used to hoist the furniture stored on the second floor, and in the middle of the room stood a ladder that one used to get into the copula. Other than that, all it held was what appeared to be some sort of collection, as evidenced by what looked like a line of shelves and cabinets built against the wall on the right. From where I was, the objects of this collection appeared cryptic and oddly undefined, and I realized it was because the light was diffuse and strangely scattered, as if the place were full of reflective dust motes. Because of that, the line of shelves defied vision focus until I got near them.

In front of me, though, was the ladder to the copula, and I wanted to go up there first to check for any evidence of that bird.

The ladder went through a hatch-like opening in the floor of the little room. It was basically an enclosed turret, completely empty and of no particular interest except for the view it offered. From there I could see over the entire length of the Ropewalk's roof, the north and south sides, and was able to determine once and for all that the snow had not been disturbed by anyone entering or exiting the attic through the hatches on the north side. The south side, of course, remained a question mark since it had only sporadic patches of snow.

Looking out over the macadam road, I could also see the top of the Engineering building, the shoulders of its slate roof still supporting a large buildup of snow. "Someday it'll just collapse," I mumbled, thinking of what would happen to the school if any of the students were slinking around inside it when that happened. Off to the right was the school itself surrounded by the amorphous mounds that marked the sites of the artificial ruins. Behind it I could see tracks punched through the ice crust leading into the rim of the forest, no doubt left by the bear I'd seen, and that I was now half convinced lived in the basement of the Engineering building.

Other than that, there was nothing to see on the roof itself—no tracks of any kind in what little snow was still there and no obvious evidence of anything having been up there. I surveyed the area one last time and then went back down and over to the shelves.

Here I saw that the place was like a personal museum. The shelves held all kinds of antiques and artifacts apparently related to the history of the region. One was covered with arrowheads and spear points, and another with an assortment of powdery-gray round and flattened objects of various sizes that I knew to be musket balls. Near these I found the handle of a sword, and near that, an ancient spike bayonet lying near a lump of rust that I recognized as an old gunlock. A large wooden-slat barrel, like the kind used to mellow wine, was being used to hold what looked like some kind of antique gauge. Other objects were more cryptic and defied description; some looked like parts of ancient machinery and others like talismans or charms of some sort.

A little further down, I found something whose identification was immediate and unmistakable—leg irons. They were seriously rusted, but the chain was still intact and the locking mechanism itself looked like it would still work if it had a little oil. Finding them rekindled my suspicions about the role the area might have played prior to the Civil War. Behind and beyond it were other chains and assorted manacles, and I wondered if this place—or the village—was the last stop on the Underground Railroad moving runaway slaves to Canada. If it was, that added another level of uncertainty to the history I was trying to write.

Further down was what appeared to be a box or table covered with a shroud. It reminded me of the pile of old newspapers on the second floor that was likewise covered, and I approached fully expecting to find another treasure trove of literary scraps. But it wasn't. Instead, it was covering a pile of clothing, some of it very old, some of it newer, none of it appearing contemporary. I felt my way through it in order to get an idea of how old some of it was and realized there was something underneath.

Books, maybe, I suspected as I pushed my way around and between the clothing artifacts until at last I uncovered a long coat of what looked like Victorian cut. I picked it up to examine it and simultaneously my gaze fell on what it had been concealing. With a start I involuntarily dropped the coat and backed up a step.

A human skull was staring back at me from the folds of fabric, the mouth partly open as if whoever it was had died in mid-sentence. After the shock wore off, I stepped up and removed the rest of what was concealing it and saw that the skeleton was all there, intact, but that it was small, like that of a child. A child. What was a child's skeleton doing hidden away up there like a discarded artifact?

I wracked my brain for any dormant memories of a report of a missing or abducted child, but could not recall anything reliable, which, of course, meant nothing since I typically did not pay much attention to such stories. And why would I? The abduction and violation of children was an "urban" blight, one of those darkside byproducts of too many people fighting over too few avenues of gratification. Who would think of such a thing happening in an isolated area like this? But as I looked around at the room, at its inaccessibility, at the chains and still functional leg irons, I couldn't help but think: What the hell has Sil been doing up here?

♦ ♦ ♦

Chapter 21

I now knew why Sil went to such lengths to keep people out of the shed. He was concealing a crime. He may not have been the perpetrator, but at the very least, he was an accomplice. Someone had done something to a child and he was hiding the evidence. How long ago, by whom, where, and why—those were questions the police were going to have to answer. But he was definitely involved.

And this guy was Sonya's godfather.

I had put everything back where I found it when I left, including straightening the ladder back to its original position. When I got back down to the granary, a sudden thought—or maybe premonition—drove home the urgent need to make things look normal: What if Sil were to show up on a snowmobile and find the back of the granary open and the ladder exposed? For the first time, I realized the possible danger I had exposed all of us to when I casually left that hidden door open the day before. What if he had seen it? He could have done away with all three of us and we would never have seen it coming. And getting rid of us would have been the easiest thing in the world with no one else around.

So I closed up the granary completely, including re-hanging all the chains I'd removed from the pivot bar above the panel door that concealed the ladder. I remembered that the hasp had been secured with a screwdriver and I put it back exactly as I had found it. Then I closed the granary itself and stood leaning against the door for several minutes.

What was I going to say to Margaret? I knew I absolutely could not tell her about this now for the simple reason that, if Sil did show up, she would need to behave normally around him. Knowing that he might have been involved in the death of a child would be too much for her to try to conceal. No, I had to withhold this as I had withheld so many other things. I could not tell her until after the holiday when everyone was back and the police had been contacted.

In the meantime, I had to think about defense. My first thought was to have the .380 with me at all times, but that was not realistic. It was small, but not like a derringer, and could not be concealed in a pocket, meaning I would have to wear it in its holster. Margaret would weird out for sure if I suddenly showed up wearing a gun, so that was out.

But the shotgun was no longer in her apartment, and although I could not presume that I would be spending my nights with her, I felt that this was now the likeliest possibility, meaning that there would be no weapons available in an emergency. That basically decided it for me. I would "smuggle" the .380 in using my gym bag and keep it near the bed.

I had not searched through the rest of the old clothing to see if there were other remains concealed under the pile. I was not sure I even wanted to know about any others, and in any case, one was enough to indict the man, at least in my mind. Besides, from this point forward, the less I disturbed the evidence, the better it would be for the police.

By then it was almost eleven o'clock. I really wanted to get back and do a little research on my project, like reading in the old diary, but I knew that helping Margaret with the dinner was more important. With that in mind, and also so that I didn't start feeling like a freeloader, I headed back to her apartment. I made a mental note en route to afterwards find some scraps to leave out for the cat.

As soon as I entered, I was treated to the fragrant odors of the holiday meal. The smell of roasting turkey mixed with that of potatoes and even, somewhere in the background, the unmistakable tinge of an apple pie somewhere in its bake cycle. "Just in time," she said. "You can help me start setting up." And with that, we covered the table with a festive cloth, set the places, and lit the candles.

It was priceless, but tainted by the secret knowledge I now carried about the man whose wife had "always been there for her," and yet who may have been a dangerous felon. To not spoil the mood—and the day—I had to put all that out of my mind. When, at the appointed hour, we sat down to eat, she asked me if I had gotten to the top of the shed and I fumbled mentally for a cohesive but not revealing story. Fortunately, I was able to buy myself some time with a mouthful of food.

"Yes," I finally said, "I did, but I can't figure out what the big deal is. The room is mostly empty except for what looks like a collection of antiques and historical artifacts. Other than that, there's nothing to see except for the beam that holds the block and tackle." There it was—no mention of the jointed ladder or the macabre resident under the clothing.

She seemed only vaguely interested. "What kind of artifacts?" She reached over to help Sonya with a spoonful of food.

"Oh, odds and ends. Some stone arrowheads and spear points, old musket balls and pieces of weaponry. Some old clothing, too."

She nodded, then said without turning toward me: "Do you suppose it was stuff found at the site of the village?"

I shrugged automatically. "I don't know. Why?"

She straightened up in her chair and faced me. "Well, you know, musket balls, weapons—couldn't these help to establish the connection with your old diary? If the battle it described took place around here, there would be some kind of evidence—like musket balls. Why else would there be a lot of them lying around?"

She was a gem. I hadn't thought of that. But she was right—here was one more piece of the puzzle that, taken together, might help to establish the authenticity of the diary. The problem would be figuring out where the artifacts came from. I voiced this constraint and her response was simple: "We can ask Sil when everyone comes back."

And therein lay the gridlock. "I don't think I can do that," I said.

"Why not?"

"Because then he'll know I was up there. How would I explain that?"

She winked. "Leave that to me."

I smiled and nodded but inwardly cringed at the problem I had just created. The scenario ran through my mind like a high speed film: Sil shows up a day or two early to get everything ready for reopening the school, she asks him about the musket balls, he realizes he's been found out and covers his tracks by getting rid of the two of us. After that he ditches the cars. Then, when everyone is back, he pretends to be as mystified as everyone else about what happened to us. It was disturbing in its simplicity.

And what would he do with Sonya? Maybe the same thing he had done with the child whose remains were hidden in the shed?

"Actually," I said, "I would prefer it if you didn't mention it to him, at least not for a while. I know it may sound strange, but I'm just not ready for what his reaction might be. I mean, even if he said he'd found them at the village, I would still need to verify his claim by finding some of my own, and I can't do that until spring. You know how academics are."

She gave me an incredulous look. "But asking him could save you the trouble of having to do all that. If he says he found them somewhere else, you would simply be wasting your time looking. And you would know long before spring."

She was parrying me into a corner. "Still, I'd appreciate it if you wouldn't mention it to him until I'm ready, okay? I would consider it a personal favor."

She looked at me and her eyes betrayed her confusion. "Yeah, sure, okay." She broke eye contact and perfunctorily focused on Sonya.

"What is it?" I asked.

"Nothing. It's just that, well, you're being unusually irrational. I would think you would jump at the chance to establish the connection between the village and the diary. This might be the answer you're looking for and you're choosing to ignore it just because it involves Sil." Her eyes searched my face for some other explanation.

I had been "advised" many years before to not play poker for a living because my face would give my hand away. This event bore witness to the reliability of that assessment. I was sure that she saw right through me and knew I was hiding something, and I immediately regretted ever having mentioned the arrowheads and musket balls. This would have been a good time to use one of those "alter-options" I'd thought about when I was caught in the basin—rewind those last few minutes of my life and try another tack. What I should have done was lied and said there was nothing up there but old tools.

But I didn't. And I could not continue to insist on avoiding Sil without making my position seem even more suspicious and possibly ruining Christmas as well. So I relented. With a smile and a shrug I said: "You're right. It's stupid of me to not use his information just because of some old grudge. And I know you can smooth his feathers so, yeah, go ahead and find out from him where the stuff came from. It just might be the break I need."

She smiled and reached out to touch my arm. "Stop worrying about it. Believe me, his bark is a lot worse that his bite. I'll handle him."

And with that, everything appeared to return to normal. Except that now my only hope was that he either would not show up early to open the school—which was unlikely—or that she would forget to ask him about the artifacts if he did. The best tactic for the latter was, from this point forward, to not mention it again.

Dinner lasted until nearly three o'clock, which completely negated any tentative plans for an afternoon activity of any sort. While we were eating, we had discussed the possibility of taking a walk down the road again, which would have been more pleasant with the warmer temperature, but now that it was mid-afternoon, it was too late to start. The shadows of the trees were already long and diffuse, the light thin and fading, and a growing overcast made it look as if the freezing rain from the night before might come back. Even if we started right at that moment, it would be dusk by the time we got back. Margaret thought we should do it anyway since we could not get lost as long as we stayed on the road, but my own unspoken reluctance was because the bellow I had heard from the forest the night before was still vibrantly echoing in my memory. I had no idea what it was but between that, the wolf, and whatever it was that flew from the top of the shed, my growing sense of non-normality was beginning to crowd out all else. If something were going to happen, I did not want her outside to witness it.

So I injected a fictitious excuse and hoped my non-poker face didn't give me away. "I get the willies at night, remember?" I joked.

"I thought that was just a childhood thing between you and your buddy."

I took a sip of the coffee-Kahlua we were treating ourselves to and looked up over the rim. "I never really got over it. Must be a flaw in my upbringing. Or my character."

She appeared to accept that—or to accept whatever she imagined the excuse behind the excuse to be—and the rest of the afternoon was spent watching Sonya acclimate herself to the mini-wonderland Margaret had provided for her and talking about all that had happened in the last week. It had all started with our phantom hallwalker, who appeared now to be all but forgotten, but who may have all along been nothing more than a cat.

"Speaking of which," I said, "I'd like to set out some food and a bowl of water for the poor thing. He must be starving."

Margaret immediately got up, put some scraps of meat in a plastic bowl, filled a jar with water, and put both in the refrigerator. As if as an afterthought, she then put a second bowl alongside the water. "You can pour the water into this when you take the stuff down to the lobby." Then she sat back down, appeared lost in thought for a moment, then said, "I'm having a little trouble believing that the hallwalker is nothing more than a cat. What about the time when he tried to get in here?"

I could see the massive deadbolts on the door from where I was. A cat, of course, could not attempt to turn a doorknob, and although there was still the possibility that she had dreamed or imagined it, I was no longer so dismissive. Just a week before I would have scoffed at the idea of someone in the building, but after all that had happened during the last five days, I realized it wasn't so simple. It was no longer even clear to me that I wasn't simply fooling myself into *believing* that it was only a cat. "I don't know," I finally said. "But the last two days have been pretty quiet. I didn't hear a thing last night, did you?"

She shook her head. "No. That's why I'm starting to wonder if maybe I only imagined that incident. I was pretty stressed out at the time." She paused and stared out the window at the thickening gloom. "It's going to be hard to get used to the whole building full of people again when they all come back." Then she looked at me and smiled. "You know, in spite of everything, I've really enjoyed this week. I'm so used to throngs of kids running around that the peace and quiet of an empty building is a novelty. I only wish it could last longer." She reached over and took my hand. "It's turning out to be a very special Christmas, with a very special person."

I was caught off guard and speechless, which she must have seen because, gracious as ever, she leaned toward me and whispered, "You're staying here tonight too, right?"

How could I not? I had chosen to not be presumptuous after just one time, but there it was, an affirmation of the step we had taken the night before. "Yes. I mean, I was hoping you would want me to."

She nodded. "And the night after that, and all the nights we have left until everyone's back from the holiday."

"And then what will we do?" I had to ask. The old bugbear of social ineptitude was nipping at my conscience again, letting me know that, after that, my monopoly on her attention would be challenged.

"Then I file for divorce and we can officially start 'dating.' Until I do that, though, we'll have to be discreet."

I smiled, but potential derailments were already assailing me from dark and unattended corners of my memory. What about Nick Cephalos? I wondered. If anyone would come by looking to fill in for a missing husband, it would be him. Although she had never admitted it, I knew she had already fallen for his aging flower-child charm once before—would it happen again? And then there was Moss Breitlinger. Now *there* was a guy who was so self-interested he would leave his wife in the middle of a sentence if it meant he could get his hooks into Margaret, even if only for a short while. And he was a master manipulator.

Not to mention all the unknowns and unsuspecteds that would emerge from everywhere once her availability was known. I didn't want to wait for some bureaucratic event before I could let everyone know we were seeing each other. The fact that Ben was gone would speak for itself.

"Maybe we can, you know, make it known that we're a couple early on," I said. "After all, when everyone comes back, they'll discover right away that we never left."

She caught on immediately, a perceptive ability that I valued then and knew I would come to cherish as time went on. She leaned toward me once again, placed her forefinger on my lips as if forbidding me to speak, and said, "Egan, stop worrying. Nothing will change between you and me when everyone comes back. I told you I used to watch you when you held your martial arts class, remember? I was your secret admirer. Now I'm your . . ." She hesitated as if searching for the right word, as if unsure of my response. "Now I'm your lover. It's something I've wanted for a long time."

273

I couldn't believe it. Her statement hit me like the discovery of a treasure in the back yard, unexpected and oddly out of context. It couldn't be me, I thought. She had to be thinking of someone else.

She pulled her finger away from my lips. "There, now my secret's out. I used to love it when you got hot and opened that wraparound shirt you guys wear. I couldn't believe my eyes when I saw it was you in the kitchen that day. I was upset because of the noises I'd been hearing, but even through all that I had enough presence of mind to thank my lucky stars for delivering my salvation in the form of the one person I wanted to meet." She paused as if to let that sink in and took a sip of coffee. "You were always so different from everyone else at the school, and I've always had a thing for rare birds." Then, rather flippantly, as if to offset her admission with a joke, she added: "Besides, I need someone to keep Moss away from me. Can you imagine what's going to happen when he finds out Ben is gone?"

I smiled and nodded, holding myself in check but inwardly overwhelmed by what she had said. It was so enormously flattering it was almost surreal, and it took me a moment to snap out of it. When I did, I zeroed in on the remark about Moss. "He'll want you to shoot porno movies for his home collection. Knowing him, he'll have you dressed up like Zorro, except you'll only be wearing the boots and cape. Oh, and the mask, too."

She put down her coffee and roared with laughter. "Only the boots and cape? Can I at least polish my foil?"

"Believe me, nobody's going to be looking at your foil."

She laughed again and reached over to give me a playful nudge. "Nothing will change," she said, reverting to a more serious tone. "Trust me, nothing will change."

I smiled and for a moment saw fate weaving me into a web of events that had begun long before, when I hadn't even met her, inexorably bringing me to where I was just then. In retrospect, it seemed like a path suffused with a certain inevitability, like Spengler's "destiny logic" once again. But the rest was unadorned optimism because I knew that, if Sil showed up and she asked him about the artifacts in the shed, something would definitely change.

◆ ◆ ◆

Margaret's admission had its own unveiling effect on me, and I realized now how it happened that she had shown no reluctance—much less guilt—that first time she so passionately kissed me after we had been drinking. I had been in her sights all along. It was like an out of body experience; in the euphoric giddiness that followed, I felt like one of the students coming to myself for advice on matters I barely understood.

Around four-thirty I told Margaret that I wanted to bring the food and water to the lobby so that the cat would have a merry Christmas as well. She then suggested that I spend some time with the old diary and come back later that evening. She didn't say it, but I sensed that she needed to be alone with Sonya for a while, perhaps as a way to banish the lingering ghost of Ben's betrayal for the last time. In any case, it worked well for me because I had come to realize that the only way I could stop her from asking Sil about the artifacts was to eliminate the need to do so. And the only way to do that was to beat him to the punch, thereby making his input totally irrelevant. What I needed to do was get back to the house in the cedars and check out the hatchet marks in the wall, maybe even make some clay impressions. I was absolutely sure they had been made by a hatchet or tomahawk, and verifying that hypothesis would connect the house to the diary in a much more convincing way than a collection of old musket balls. Having the one would make it unnecessary to ask him about the other.

It also occurred to me—adding more weight to the argument—that finding a musket ball would, by itself, not indicate that any particular battle had taken place there. It was a village, inhabited for who knew how long, but in any case spanning the period of continual strife with the Abenakis. It was therefore inevitable that this strife would flare into open warfare, and any of the known entanglements between the two groups would have produced a hailstorm of musket balls. Since there was no practical way to determine their age—and those ages would be very close together regardless of how they were assessed—any claim on my part, or his, would be meaningless.

So there it was, the way out. I would tell Margaret that I had hit a snag with the idea of using the artifacts in the shed and thus needed to get back to the house in the cedars. And it was something I needed to act on as quickly as possible; with only a little over a week left before everyone returned, it would not be implausible for Sil to show up at any time. He was nothing if not diligent and would not be deterred by the fact that the bridges were out and the road unplowed; I was absolutely sure he knew of some route through the woods and would simply come in by snowmobile from the inland highway. I decided right then and there to return to the house the next day.

I filled the plastic bowl with the water from the jar and placed it and the food near the artificial plant where I had first seen the cat. Then I headed up to my room. When I flipped on the light, I automatically expected to see evidence that the room had been "visited" and was surprised to see that it had not. It occurred to me then that the "Concise History" book was still down in Margaret's apartment and that I would not be able to read about Abenaki descent myths until I retrieved it, which I couldn't do just then. It would have to wait until that evening. So I turned my attention to the diary.

I made myself comfortable at the desk and began flipping through the pages and scanning for any wording that seemed of particular interest. Most of it was filled with the mundane events of everyday life, as I had noted before, and when I got to the card marking the page with the tomahawk entries, I studied it more carefully for any further clues.

But there weren't any. It appeared to be nothing more than a passing comment made in regards to an event that the writer had found annoying, with no recorded follow up reaction from the parents. The only way I would be able to establish a link would be to go back, take some pictures, and try to get an impression from modeling clay. Tenuous perhaps, but still better than the musket balls, even without the motivation to keep Sil out of it.

I flipped through a few more pages while quickly scanning for content, which was not always easy with the sometimes dense cursive that the writer had used. That and the inevitable passages obscured by cloudy or water-smudged ink made coherency from one section to the next sometimes impossible, and the casual review gradually began to turn into a more labored decipherment. I was thus several sentences into a particular section before I fully understood what I was reading. It was a recounting of a visit to a place the writer had not been to before. It read: "One of our number, a pretty lady, had slipped during our Reconnaissance and, to stay her falling, held out an arm whose Hand then landed in a small puddle of what was apparently a Corrupting liquid. It seemed that but little got upon her person but what did seemed to act very quickly for she began to speak strangely as if in Tongues, which worsened before we could remove it. This in part because we had no Water with which to bathe the appendage. When finally we cleansed the hand and did seem to have removed the Substance the damage seemed light, there being but minor spots, and infrequent, where it appeared the liquid had Corrupted her skin and darkened it. She spoke to us in normal tone and seemed correct.

"We then came upon a large chamber filled with Items of unusual purpose. There was a curious Device there, not unlike a loom spindle that, instead of . . ." here it was too obscure to read and I had to skip the line, picking up again with " . . . cotton or Wool was in truth a large bore point on the end of a quill or spindle, capable of being set at virtually Any angle. Verily the place was full with such unusual items and looked unhappily like a Storehouse for some abandoned civilization, which was Timothy's stated predisposition.

"Presently a sound of Distress caused me to turn quickly and I saw our lady companion stumble against another of our group, a large man Unknown to me and wearing a black waistcoat. He held her up and for a moment I thought the Interlude one of romantic interest. That stirred me to some envy but I let it pass and continued. Then from behind came another Sound of distress and I turned to catch her as she fell.

"Panic then seized us. We could see no Cause for her distress save the liquid she had contacted. She looked at me much affrighted and her eyes did beseech me for Succor, which I would fain have given had I the ability to penetrate the cause of her Disquietude. Her mouth then opened as if to speak but her torment was Such that she did Scream with such force as to drive me back. I then asked her Where does it hurt? and she looked upon me with frightened Eyes and screamed once again. Finally it seemed to have passed and we raised her to upright seated, to which she was scarcely able to hold herself without Assistance. She was now wet for Fever had come upon her and her eyes were those of a frightened Animal. She looked from one to the other of us and Spoke thusly: It insults the blood.

"This most miserable Condition prevailed . . ." Here the ink was seriously smudged, as if someone had drawn a wet thumb across the page, effectively obliterating everything it touched. Because the writing was small and cramped, this defect deleted a lot of information that no doubt had once described what they had done next. As it was,

I could only pick up the thread of the narrative several lines further down. I gathered it was about the woman who had stuck her hand in the liquid, and who apparently was not doing well. From the description, I wondered if I could justifiably conclude that she had, in fact, had a mild stroke or some sort of seizure, that whatever this liquid was, it had had nothing whatsoever to do with what followed. A stroke would have been a fiendish, unknown thing to those people, the work of the devil, and one clear line lent some support to my suspicions. Someone in the group was recorded as having said: "We must hence From this place, it is either the pox or the Handwork of satan." After that, a terse line ended that section of the diary, evidently the last words the woman spoke. "My name is Madeline Cane and I do not want to die."

I shot to my feet. A name. I had a name. I could now check the cemetery to see if I could find this name on one of the headstones. That, and the hatchet marks, would seal the connection, especially if the date of death on the stone matched that in the diary. Inwardly, acknowledging one of those intuitive leaps that sometimes play a role in one's life, I was confident that the name would be there, like a foregone conclusion. All I needed to do was find and photograph it.

I was scarcely able to contain my euphoria as I closed up my room and headed down the stairs to the first floor. Margaret had not specified a time to return, but it was nearly seven-thirty by then, and I sensed that that was long enough. Besides, if I didn't go right then, my excitement was such that I knew I would spend the rest of the evening reading further in the diary, oblivious to all else. When I got to the bottom, I realized I had forgotten the gym bag in which I had intended to hide the .380, so I went back to get both of them. Perfunctorily, with the light off, I looked out the window for any activity outside and saw nothing, but then heard, very faintly as if from far off, a sequence of sounds that seemed to be coming from the walls. These were a scarcely audible thump-thumping such as I thought I had dreamed the night before when I was sleeping in Margaret's living room. I took a glass that I kept on my sink, placed it against the wall, and pressed my ear to it. The sounds became clearer but no more localized. They were clearly rhythmic, like distant footfalls, but could also have been nothing more than the wind causing a tree branch to tap against the building. Or the cat in whatever conduits it used to get around. Or I could even have been hearing Margaret moving around inside her apartment, the sound telegraphing clearly through the walls by the utter silence all around me.

Or, I realized while glancing upward, I could have been hearing something or someone moving around in the attic, which I still hadn't checked out. "Tomorrow," I told myself, "after I get back from the village." Then, as if to facilitate my departure in the morning, I took my still unloaded daypack from the bureau and placed it on my bed. To it, I added the crampons, space blanket, and a box of "strike anywhere" matches. I would not be caught flatfooted without them again.

With the .380 safely hidden in the gym bag, I went back downstairs. Margaret met me at the door wrapped in her heavy bathrobe. She raised her forefinger to her lips to indicate quiet and whispered, "Sonya's already asleep and I've gotten most of the dishes done. Can you sit here while I go take a shower?"

I very quietly entered and closed the door behind me. "Sure." My preference, of course, would have been to take a shower with her, but Sonya could not be left alone. "You want any coffee or anything? I can get something started while you're gone."

She shook her head and moved behind me to open the door I had just closed. "I'll only be a few minutes. God, I wish they'd modernize the plumbing in this place." And with that, she stepped out, closed the door, and padded down the hall. I stood there for a moment staring at the door, thinking of the darkness beyond, remembering the hallwalker, realizing with a slight chill that, if something were to happen to her, I would have to leave Sonya alone in order to rescue her. It occurred to me then that I should ask her for a key to her apartment, just as a precaution. If I did have to step out, I would have to lock the door behind me so that Sonya was safe, but to do so meant I would also seal myself away from any possibility of getting back to her. I decided the only way to handle a mental conflict of that magnitude was to blot it out by occupying myself with the Abenaki descent myths in the "Concise History" book.

As I sat there trying to read, I began hearing strange creaks and moans from the building around me—as if it were waking from some torpor and stretching to new vigor with me in its gullet. They had to have been there all along, I reasoned, but only now was I starting to notice them. I sat perfectly still and tried to focus my hearing in an effort to detect anything rhythmic or suspiciously non-random, but the noises were intermittent and discontinuous. I felt like a microbe, a platelet, a corpuscle surrounded by the immensity of both the building and the encircling forest.

The memory of Rick and the willies came back like an episode of indigestion, little imaginary creepy-crawlies, ethereal as smoke, coming for me from depths too dismal to be real. I resisted the temptation to get up and look out into the hall, even knowing that there was nothing there. Still, my arms and neck chilled at the thought, just as they had when I was a kid, and it was with some measure of relief that I heard Margaret's footfalls approaching the door. A moment more and she was back inside, all bundled up with her hair wrapped in a towel. She locked the door behind her and slid the deadbolts into place.

"I feel human again," she said, releasing her hair from the towel and shaking it free.

"Need any help dressing?" I asked with unexpected audacity.

She smiled. "Not usually, although I'll make an exception in this case." She raised her forefinger to her lips for quiet, then took my hand and led me into her bedroom. There she went over to her wardrobe and began brushing her hair while at the same time she signaled me with a hand gesture to close the door. I sensed at that point that getting dressed was not what she had in mind.

She turned to me then, opened the robe, and let it fall to the floor. Even knowing what was underneath did not lessen the impact of seeing her nude again, this time in full light, or of imagining how smooth and warm she would be pressed against me. She came up to me and, smiling but saying nothing, began to undress me, peeling my shirt back and tossing it onto her dresser, stopping only when she couldn't get my pants off over my shoes. So, playfully, she turned me and pushed me onto her bed, where I landed with a heavy bounce, wanting to laugh but held in check by her forefinger at her lips again, and waited while she untied and removed my footwear. Then she pulled my pants off and tossed them aside. She was on me in a moment, and together we scaled passion's heights with the heedless abandon of love's first contact, her embrace so fierce and insistent that for a moment I saw in her the warrior queens of the ancient Celts. Only for a moment, though, as we released ourselves to each other's pleasure in a mutual act of sexual surrender that, when it ended, left both of us panting and breathless.

There was no talk afterwards. She had had a very long day, both physically and emotionally, and to soothe her I stroked her until she fell asleep. There was obviously no thought or intention of opening the couch this time; it was unspoken but clear that she wanted me with her.

I lay there propped up on an elbow looking at her, feeling a tinge of regret that I had not told her I was going back to the village the next day to examine the hatchet marks and see if the name "Cane" appeared on any of the gravestones. We had hardly spoken a word while we made love, and in any case, an academic footnote in the middle of it would have been like unplugging the stereo in the middle of your favorite song. So I would have to tell her in the morning.

It was still relatively early—only ten o'clock according to her clock radio—and I toyed with the idea of reading for a while in the living room. But, no, I thought, I needed the extra rest for the next day's hike, and with that, I slipped out of bed and went to use the bathroom prior to going to sleep. It was small and narrow with obviously no room for a shower stall, but still more convenient than having to walk down the hall every time you needed a toilet. On the way back, I stopped in the living room and pulled the shade outward to see if the weather was doing anything. It was clear and calm; the freezing rain had evidently not come back. And nothing was moving out on the snowfield.

I released the shade and headed back toward the bedroom, then, on a whim, stepped up to the door to the hallway and placed my ear against it. Faintly, as if from far off, I could hear the same thump-thumping I'd heard before, a semi-rhythmic staccato that sounded decidedly non-random. The cat maybe? I wondered. Since I still had not found where it had been living, I could only imagine it pacing along some hidden corridor in the walls looking for mice. "Watch out for spiders," I mused with a slight smirk. Then, involuntarily, the hairs on my arm suddenly stood up as the memory of that hideous thing returned, and I stepped back as if fearing it would emerge from the wall itself. I stared at the door for a moment, my senses tense, alert and expectant, my mind suffused with memory fragments from all that had happened in the last week. What if? I wondered. What if we really aren't alone in the building? What if Sil somehow already knows that I know about his "trophy"?

Impossible, I thought. I hadn't even told Margaret. Impossible.

I headed back to the bedroom. Even so, my arm hairs prickled again as the errant thought occurred to me that some day I'll look and there *will* be creepy-crawlies coming up the hallway like semi-viscous blobs of dark smoke and gelatin.

♦ ♦ ♦

Chapter 22

The descent myths of the Abenakis were as colorful, elusive, surreal, and engaging as those of any other people or culture. Their mythology centered around three phases of their history: the Ancient or Dawn Period, the Golden Age, and the New or Present Period. Each was populated with a pantheon of fanciful beings endowed with various powers, some of them friendly and helpful to man and some of them sinister and destructive. The list of these beings was exhaustive and obviously intended to anthropomorphize—i.e. give a human face to—both the inexplicable forces of nature and the random fatefulness connected to the lives they led. One type of being in particular caught my attention—creatures from the Golden Age called A-senee-ki-wakw, a race of stone giants ultimately destroyed by their creator. The carved stone standing in the middle of the basin at the village site came to mind immediately.

I had woken up at five-thirty and, feeling fully rested, slipped out of bed without disturbing Margaret, pulled on my clothes, and went to the kitchen to make my breakfast. While the frying pan heated up, I retrieved the "Concise History" from the end table in the living room and opened to the section dealing with "Genesis" as the Abenakis understood it. I needed to get moving again on my project, and although the convoluted events that brought the threat from Sil into our lives was still very real, I expected to both nullify his impact and re-launch the project just by going to the village.

I hoped to be on my way before she woke up, not out of any sense of secretiveness but simply because, even using the tractor to save time, I needed as many daylight hours as I could get and could not afford to linger. There was no way to know how long it would take to search the cemetery for the name and make a clay impression of the hatchet marks, but if previous events were any indication, I could expect almost everything to take longer than anticipated. I wrote her a note explaining my plan and telling her I would be back in the late afternoon. Then I sat down to eat and read further in the descent myths. I was so engrossed that I did not hear her enter the kitchen.

"You're up early," she whispered, brushing an unruly strand of hair out of her face. She was tying her bathrobe shut as she surveyed the table and noticed that I had already eaten the eggs and was finishing off the toast. "What's the rush? If I didn't know better I'd say it almost looks like you're running off."

I smiled and nodded. "I know it looks suspicious, but it's not what you think. I just need to get back to the village while I still have some time. I've run into a snag with the idea of asking Sil about the musket balls and any association between them and the village."

She sat down and propped her elbows on the table, still looking exhausted. "And the snag is . . . ?"

I took a swallow of coffee. "Coffee? I made an extra cup just in case."

She nodded, her eyes half closed, and I got a cup and prepared it for her, then sat back down.

"The snag is that, even if he found them at the village, it would not mean that the battle described in the diary took place there. The problem is that a lot of battles took place all over New England, and the villagers would have been caught up in the constant fighting with one group or another that went on for nearly a century. Musket balls could have appeared in the area anytime between the late sixteen hundreds and the Civil War. It isn't much to go on."

She appeared to ponder this information while she sipped her coffee. Then she pursed her lips and nodded. "You're right. I hadn't thought of that." Then she reached out and playfully hit me on the arm. "Okay, you got me. I concede this round."

One point for the defense, I thought, suddenly filled with renewed confidence—and no small measure of relief—over the fact that she now had no reason to ask Sil about the artifacts. There was still a danger, however, in that she could casually mention to him that I was originally going to talk to him about them but then changed my mind. That would definitely put him on high alert. I had to get even the *subject* out of her mind but could not directly ask her to not inquire about the musket balls without arousing suspicion again about the extent of my objection. I had to let it die a more or less natural death. It was imperative that I locate some kind of proof at the village; if I didn't, I suddenly realized I would have to lie to her and tell her that I did.

She put the cup down and rubbed her forehead as if she had a headache. The coffee wasn't having much effect and she still looked utterly exhausted. "What a dream I had. It seemed to go on forever and was so intense it kept me from getting rested. It was about those runestones you told me about, the ones found here in Maine." She shook her head as if to break away from it and took another swallow of coffee. "What did you call them?"

"The Spirit Pond Runestones?"

"Right. Spirit Pond. I dreamed I was with the Vikings who left them. We were rowing our butts off trying to find a landfall and eventually ended up here. Imagine being a Norseman so far from home that you're actually standing on what would one day be the state of Maine."

"And you got there in what was essentially just a big rowboat. Actually, if I remember correctly, the stones describe the hardships and deprivations they had to endure, including the loss of a number of their friends. It was no picnic for them. There was starvation on the boat, savage storms, and the unexpected dangers they encountered when they finally landed."

"I can relate. I think in the last eight hours I experienced just about everything that happened on their journey. I'm wiped. I feel like I could sleep till noon."

I sympathized. "Yeah, I've had dreams like that where you wake up exhausted. One time I dreamed I had parked my car on a steep hill, and when I got into it, the parking brake let go and it began rolling backwards down the hill. There I was, frantically trying to steer between oncoming cars while looking backwards over my shoulder. It went faster and faster, and of course, this being a dream, the brakes wouldn't work, so I couldn't stop. By the time I got to the bottom, it was going so fast it rolled all the way to Oklahoma. I remember passing a sign in my sleep: Welcome to Oklahoma. When it finally stopped, I got out thinking that maybe I should call someone to pick me up, but then thought, *Who the hell is going to drive all the way from Connecticut to pick me up in Oklahoma?"*

The little anecdote got her laughing so that, for a moment at least, she forgot about her discomfort. "When you were with the Vikings, were you a man or a woman?" I asked.

She calmed down. "I guess I must've been a man. They didn't have women Vikings, did they?"

"I don't know about 'women Vikings' per se, but Leif Eiriksson's sister was with the Vikings who landed in what they called 'Vinland.' It's in the 'Vinland Saga.'"

"What was her name?"

"Freydis."

"Freydis Eiriksson?"

"Freydis Eiriksdottir," I corrected.

She gave me a flippant hand gesture over the linguistic subtlety. "Did she survive long enough to get back home?"

"I think so. She must've been quite a character. She weirded everybody out during an attack by the Skraelings by grabbing a sword, tearing open her blouse so that her breasts were exposed, and slapping the sword against her chest. They were so startled they didn't know what to think, so they ran away."

"What's a Skraeling?"

I shrugged. "Actually, nobody knows for sure. Some think it was the Norse word for 'Indian' and others think it was something else, some other native people that we don't know about. Nobody even knows for sure what the word means, or how it translates." I drained the last of the coffee from my cup. "It probably has some correlation in Abenaki mythology and we just haven't figured it out yet."

She pursed her lips and cocked an eyebrow. "So what are you saying, that you now have a fantasy to see me bare-breasted with my epee?"

I laughed. "Right. It's the Zorro thing again. Boots, cape, epee, and nothing else. What do you say?"

She rolled her eyes. "Pervert. You're starting to sound like Moss."

"Okay," I said with a laugh. "I had no luck with that approach, so how about this: do you have any corn starch?"

She looked at me with knitted eyebrows as she tried to fit that non sequitur comment into the context of what we'd been talking about. "Corn starch? I, ah, think so. How does that fit into the Zorro fantasy, or dare I ask?"

"It doesn't. I just changed the subject. I'm going to make clay molds of the hatchet marks in the wall of the house. I can use the corn starch as a parting substance so that the clay doesn't stick."

She got up and went to one of the cabinets, rummaged around inside, and produced a box. I poured some into a small plastic bag and sealed it, then stuck it into my pocket. "Perfect. When I come back, I expect to have all the proof I'll need to establish the connection between the village and the diary."

"You think the hatchet marks are enough by themselves?"

"I also have a name that I found in the diary. Cane. It talks about a Madeline Cane who apparently came down with some disease and died."

"Small pox?"

"Don't know for sure. I know there was an outbreak in the mid seventeen hundreds, right around the time of the diary entry, but I can't be sure. Influenza and diphtheria did a number on those people, too. The way it's described, she might've even been having an epileptic seizure. It really could have been almost anything. The main thing is I'm hoping to find the name on one of the gravestones. That and the hatchet marks should do it." I was dying to say something about not needing Sil's input but knew I had to just let it go. "By the way, do you have an extra key to your apartment?"

She nodded but did not pick up on it.

"Can I have it?"

She arched her eyebrows at me in mock surprise. "That's a pretty big step, fella, a lady giving a guy the key to her apartment. How do I know I can trust you?"

I pretended to look around, then settled on her with equally pretentious seriousness. "The only thing I would ever try to steal is you, and I can do that with or without a key."

She smiled and got up, went to one of the cabinets and, from a nail inside, took down a key and handed it to me. She did not sit back down;

instead she announced her intention to go back to bed—she still looked exhausted—and I rose to meet her for a kiss and parting embrace, during which her bathrobe came partly undone and her breasts slipped free. She looked down at them, cocked an eyebrow, and smiled at me.

"There's never a sword around when you need one," I said as I fondled them gently and then embraced her again. The feel of her bare chest against me was like a sudden rush of spring. But no further. She pulled the robe closed and, with a tiny flick of a wave, headed back to her bedroom. "See you this afternoon," she whispered.

"Right," I replied as she reached the door. "Not sure exactly what time, but probably sometime around five o'clock."

She smiled, waved again, and vanished into the room. I could hear the bed creaking as she got back under the covers. I washed my breakfast dishes, added her apartment key to my ring, crumpled up the note, slid back the deadbolts, and went out into the gloom-shrouded hallway. Once again, the nightlights had not gone out, a happenstance that tended to reinforce my belief that snow was getting in somewhere and melting on a junction, since they seemed to go out most often when it was snowing or sleeting.

◆ ◆ ◆

In fact, I had been startled by what I was reading in the "Concise History" about the genesis myths of the Abenakis. The alleged research that went into that section of the old history book dated from the early eighteen hundreds, a time when the Abenakis had already been pushed out of New England and their culture contaminated by over a century of contact—most of it unpleasant—with the whites. Consequently, I could not be absolutely sure of the reliability of the information I had been reading at breakfast. But what I did read was completely unexpected.

In a work of penetrating scholarship dating back at least a century and a half, one of these early chroniclers of Indian oral history had noted a similarity between the myths of the Algonquin tribes of the northeast and the Prose Edda of the Scandinavians. The Edda was a compilation of the myths and gods of the Norsemen, and I found this connection surprising but not completely unexpected. After all, it was not unreasonable to postulate that the native tribes living in what is now Newfoundland and Labrador could have had contact with Norsemen from Greenland. The unpalatable part for me was the inescapable conclusion that the Indian myths in question could thus only date back to the tenth century, when the Norse first settled Greenland. That put their entire Ancient or Dawn Period well within the period of recorded European history. But even a cursory look at their mythology had convinced me that it was much older than that.

The other oddity was the realization that, during the controversy over the discovery of the Spirit Pond Runestones, none of the defenders of the stones had cited this work as a possible link to their authenticity. The only possible reason could have been that this particular author was either unknown, or for some reason unavailable. Since the article citing the Edda had been composed nearly a hundred and fifty years before the stones were discovered, the connection between the two could not be explained away as a consequence of the discovery of the stones. If anything, the discovery could have been used to bolster the credibility of the article. Yet neither event occurred.

Regardless of how it all shook out in the end, I dared not introduce such a heretical element into anything I might try to publish because I knew that, true or not, it would finish me as an historian. I would have to file it away for possible publication at a time when it no longer mattered to my life. Such was the nature of academic reality in the loftier realms.

It was only eight o'clock when I hefted my backpack and was about to put it on, when it dawned on me that my .380 was still in the gym bag in Margaret's apartment. I wrestled with the idea of going back down to get it but decided against it; I would almost certainly wake her when I entered and could think of no viable excuse for why I needed something from my gym bag to go on a hike.

I shrugged and reached for the doorknob, then stopped to reconsider. I had learned my lesson with the crampons and now had them in my pack; was I safe in ignoring the possibility that I might still be out there after dark, unarmed? It was not just the wolf or the bear; they could usually be driven off with loud noises. It was the memory of the things I *didn't* know about that unnerved me—the bellow I'd heard from the rim of the forest, or that bird, or whatever it was, that flew from the top of the shed. No, I would rather have it and not need it than need it and not have it. So, with the .380 out of reach, I retrieved the shotgun from the corner where I'd stood it, loaded it with the slugs from the shed, and headed out. It would be an inconvenience carrying it, but that would be offset by the security it offered.

I drove the tractor out of the shed and headed up the road to the coast highway. The sun was barely above the horizon, but the sky was already ice blue and untainted by the threat of a storm. And it had to be a good ten degrees warmer than my last visit to the village.

As I passed the Engineering building, I stopped and looked for fresh tracks, either wolf or bear, having become convinced that one or the other was living in the basement. There was nothing new to see, so I drove on past but only went a few feet before I stopped again. I stared at the building and, emboldened by the shotgun loaded with slugs, turned off the tractor, got down, and headed up toward it.

I had brought my flashlight, of course, since I expected to do more poking around inside the house in the cedars. I made sure it was in my pocket as I began punching my way through the snow up to the building. On the other side, where the half-hidden opening to the cellar was, I chambered a round in the shotgun and approached the mound of building materials that concealed the opening.

With the light, it was now possible to see the bottom of the stairs as well as the opening into the cellar. Like the hole itself, it had no door, which came as no surprise given the fact that something obviously lived down there. How long the door had been missing, there was no way to tell; it was clear that no one at the school paid the slightest attention to the building, and it was entirely possible that it had been missing for some time. Still, I found this oversight oddly irresponsible on the part of the school administration.

I went down a couple of steps, sniffed the air for animal odors, and listened. Sensing nothing, I went down a couple more and repeated the process. One more time and I was at the bottom, the shotgun halfway to my shoulder and the light piercing the utter blackness of the hallway in front of me. I played the beam along the floor looking for animal signs, but the passage was remarkably clean. Nor did I pick up any of the heavy mustiness I would have expected if a bear were hibernating down there. I checked the shotgun one more time to make sure the safety was off and stepped inside.

The basement consisted of a main hallway with a series of separate rooms branching off to the left and right. Most of these still had their doors intact, some of which were still securely locked. Others opened when I pushed on them, but the rooms beyond were always empty, or held the rotting remnants of the same building materials that were piled in a slagheap behind the building itself. One of the rooms contained an assortment of broken and decaying school furniture, most of it desk chairs.

The hallway itself began to twist and turn shortly after I entered, leaving me with the impression that I was in some sort of maze, a discovery that could have had alarming consequences but for the fact that it was a single hall and all I needed to do was follow it back to get out. As I approached what appeared to be the end, I noticed a flight of stone or concrete stairs on the left leading upward into the building itself. Beyond them the hall ended, and the cellar opened into a single, large room. In it, sitting in a slump like some ancient, rusting Buddha, was the huge coal burner that was intended to heat the building. The original storage bins for the fuel appeared to be still intact, as was the chute that funneled the coal into them from the hatchway above.

A flash of fabric caught in the beam from the light drew me forward, and I found, half frozen to the ground, a sleeping bag, still intact. Near it were some rusting cans and, on a shelf formed by the fieldstone of the basement itself, was a single candle. Someone had been living there and, although it was impossible to know when or for how long, our mysterious hallwalker came to mind immediately. Was there some vagabond living there who would temporarily move into the Ropewalk during the holiday to warm up while he could? If so, how would he get in?

The attic, of course, occurred to me first. If an intruder could get onto the roof, it was possible he could pry open one of the hatches and just let himself in. Alternatively, it was also possible that one or more of the hatches wasn't locked and he could just open it and enter. In theory it made sense, but it still didn't explain how he would get from the attic into the building itself. The access doors were securely locked from the inside.

I shot the light beam all around the room to see if there was anything else, in particular to see if there was any sign of an animal living there. The tracks that I had followed days before *had* led to the basement of the building, and it was that fact that rendered the vagabond theory either suspect or far removed in time. It was self-evident that anyone who had been camping there recently would have come face to face with the new occupant. Discretion being the better part of valor, he would have left for greener pastures.

Someplace like the Ropewalk? I suddenly wondered. That was a different angle on the possibilities—that there had been a homeless person living there, for who knew how long, but who only recently had been driven to find a safer haven after coming face to face with a bear or wolf, and not because of the cold.

But none of the speculation mattered because I did not see any obvious indications of an animal living there. This seemed strange because the tracks had led me to the back of the building and shown me where the opening was. I was forced to conclude that maybe it had been nothing more than idle curiosity on the part of the animal, that it had found the opening accidentally while meandering to some other place. As for the former occupant, I was no closer to establishing who it might have been or when he had been there. For that matter, I could not even be sure that it might have been nothing more than a student camping out in the "spooky" building just to say he'd done it.

I went back to the stairs I'd passed and shined the light up toward the top. There was a door up there but it was closed, and my light beam revealed a sturdy lift-latch that I was sure would be impossible to open. I went up to try it anyway and was surprised to find that I could move it easily. When I swung it open, I was even more surprised to discover that there was light coming in from somewhere despite the bricked-over windows and that I could see without the flashlight.

I was in a large, open room, undifferentiated in any way except by a very noticeable pile of rubble in the approximate center. Above the pile, yawning open like a glassless cupola, was a huge hole in the ceiling. The light was coming in from there. Gauging that the floor must have been sound in order to support the mass of material on it, I went over and looked up into the hole. It pierced several floors, going apparently all the way to the topmost level, which was the source of the light and must therefore still have had unobstructed windows.

I knew I was wasting time but I had to see what was up there. The staircase from the cellar had emerged parallel to the wall, and directly in front of me was another set of ascending stairs. These, like those from the cellar itself, were made of stone and hence did not occasion any doubt about whether they could support my weight. I went up to look at the second floor.

It was no different from the first in that it was simply a large, open space, clearly intended to be broken up into classrooms but caught in the economic downturn that had left it frozen in time. The hole looked ragged and questionable, so I did not go any closer. The light was stronger on this level and I noticed for the first time a large double door at the opposite end. Behind it would surely have been the main staircase that one would have encountered after entering the front door, which was now, of course, securely sealed. I wanted to go take a look—it would only have taken a few more minutes—but was not sure about the strength of the floor, so I turned to the next flight of stairs and headed up to the third story.

This was the topmost level. It was different from the other two in that, this time, I found myself in a room that was partitioned off from any others behind it by a wall in which there was an open door and a glassless window. Since I was not sure about the floor, I moved toward the window by staying as close to the outer wall as I could. When I got there, I could see that the hole had been caused by a cave-in from the attic above. Apparently, a large collection of slate roofing tiles had been stored up there, and the floor of the attic must have rotted from either insects or a persistent leak in the roof above it. At some point in the past, the tremendous weight of the tiles simply broke through and crashed onto the floor, which, possibly weakened from the same causes, then gave way and added the weight of its own debris to the impact on the next floor, which also yielded. Only the first floor had stopped it, probably because of the support columns in the cellar.

"What a waste," I mumbled, envisioning the building in a fully functional state as an adjunct to the school, whether it focused on science and engineering or not. "Or even as a dorm or living quarters for the teachers." It struck me that a resource that impressive, that had come so far in its development, should not be simply allowed to decay. But there it was. I shook my head in disbelief. The decision making process on the highest levels of administration would always be an opaque and impenetrable mystery to me.

The light up there was very strong because the windows, as I had suspected, had not been bricked over. The glass was still intact, a marvel in itself considering the number of students that had come and gone since the school opened. It was probably a simple matter that they were too far off the ground to hit with stones without being obvious about throwing them.

I glanced at my watch. It was eight thirty-five so I still had plenty of time to get to the village. Satisfied that there was nothing more to see in the building, I turned back to the stairs and was about to descend when I heard a faint noise coming from the floor below me. It could have been a piece of debris falling, or maybe the patter of a startled squirrel or field mouse, but something about it held me and I froze to listen. It came again. This time it was clearer—a faint scratching sound, a tick-tick such as a dog might make when walking on a hardwood floor. I stared at the doorway at the bottom of the stairs and waited.

A shadow moved across the opening, hesitated, then moved again. I glanced at the shotgun to make sure the safety was off, then slowly brought it to my shoulder. Despite the confidence the weapon inspired, I found my hands trembling, and the longer I held that position the more they began to shake. My heart added to the tumult as the adrenalin kicked in, and each powerful beat made the gun move so much that I knew I could easily miss. In the back of my mind, I already knew what was coming.

The shadow moved again, came closer, and stopped when fully silhouetted on the floor showing in the doorframe. Slightly amorphous, the head turning as if unsure, then another angle allowing a clear view of the ears. I knew what it was, and a moment later it stepped into full view and confirmed my fears.

It was the wolf.

It looked up at me, conveying the odd impression that it was not so much startled as expectant, as if somewhere in its brain it had reasoned that I would eventually show up there and this was no surprise. I tried to aim but could not; I was shaking so hard I knew I would miss. I lowered the gun to my hip and we stared at each other for nearly a full minute.

I was trapped. The wolf knew I was trapped. I knew that the wolf knew I was trapped. We continued to stare at each other, then it moved forward onto the stairs and took a tentative step upwards, studying me the whole time. My heart reached new levels of volumetric efficiency as I sprang back, grabbed the nearly frozen door to the staircase, and, almost wrenching it off its hinges in my panic, slammed it closed with a resounding thud that echoed in the empty building. Hands shaking,

I fumbled for the lift-latch, which was frozen in place, and leaned my whole weight on it to break it free. That done, I backed up a step and tried to calm down.

It couldn't get me, but I couldn't escape either. I placed my ear against the door in an effort to determine if it had come all the way up the stairs but was not able to hear anything. With reason slowly returning, I realized I could open the door a crack and keep my foot against it to prevent any sudden entry. That and the fact that, if he was out there, he would have to launch his attack upward, which would weaken it, encouraged me to try it. I placed my foot against the door, lifted the latch as quietly as I could, grabbed the handle, and pulled it open about two inches. He wasn't there; I could see all the way to the bottom of the steps and saw neither the animal nor its shadow at the bottom.

I closed the door. Of course. There was no reason to attack, especially since he probably sensed the presence of a gun and knew all he had to do was wait me out. Eventually I would have to go down to the cellar, and he could ambush me from any of the rooms I would have to pass in order to get out. I grinned in spite of my situation; I was a walking shish kebab and we both knew it.

I leaned against the door and pondered my predicament. The shotgun loaded with slugs would easily stop a wolf, but it was a full-length weapon and would be awkward to use in the confined space of the cellar where sudden left or right movements would be inevitable. Not to mention the fact that firing it in such an enclosed space would leave me deaf, at least temporarily. Ironically, it was a situation in which I would have been better off with the .380.

"Alright," I whispered, my voice still slightly quavering from the adrenalin spike I'd just had, "Let's see what options we have." I made sure the door was secure and went back to the glassless window. On the other side of the partition, more or less in the center of the large, common room, was the hole. I strained to see through it to the floor below but caught a glimpse of nothing but striated darkness, an overlay caused by the floor on which I then stood. In an effort to pierce the veil, I shined the flashlight beam down into it, but it revealed nothing but a continuing expanse of floor. I had no idea if the wolf was still there, but some instinctive sense within me told me it would be wise to locate the animal since I had no idea if it knew of another way up onto the third floor. So, trusting that the floor was otherwise strong enough to hold me, I left the small enclosure and went out for a closer look.

I hugged the wall as I went around the hole, casting anxious glances into it as the floor below was slowly revealed. About halfway past the opening, I spotted what I was looking for and, odd as it may seem, felt a surge of relief at seeing the animal since it meant that it apparently did not know of another approach to the third floor. It lay there unconcerned near the hole in the second floor and almost immediately sensed my presence, turning its head a slight bit in an effort to see me. I immediately squatted down so that my profile wasn't visible in the hole but just as immediately felt utterly foolish. Who was I trying to kid? The animal had senses that far exceeded anything I could rely on and knew fully well that I was there; "hiding" would conceal neither my scent nor the faint noises that I was sure I was making and that it could hear. So I stood back up and looked down.

It met my gaze with a look that I could only describe as unwavering curiosity. There was none of the subtle savagery that myth and legend attributed to these animals. It continued to lie there unconcerned, then raised itself to a sitting position. From there it watched me as a dog might its master, mouth open and tongue slightly out. I did not know what to make of it.

But I did know that I had a clear shot from my vantage point above it. And I also knew that, if I was going to get out of the building, I needed to make sure that it could not ambush me. I brought the shotgun halfway to my shoulder and then stopped to consider the possible outcomes of what I was about to do. First, because of the enclosure, I would be deafened. If I missed, my hearing would be useless as a warning of impending danger. Second, if I wounded rather than killed it, I would be in a bigger predicament since it would stop at nothing to get to me. And my hearing would still be useless. Third, even if I killed it, I could not know if it had a mate in the building that would come looking for me. And my hearing would still be no help.

Fourth, the thing was looking at me without the slightest trace of malignancy. I lowered the gun and we stared at each other, from which I got the weird impression that it was trying to tell me something. So I tried an experiment. I lowered the butt of the gun to the floor and spoke to it. "What's up, hmm? Why do you keep following me? Are you trying to tell me something?" It cocked its head slightly, as dogs were wont to do when you talked to them, and from the indifferent look on its face I suspected I could stroll right past it and it would not even react, much less threaten me. But I was no authority on the nature of nature and, wistful and enchanting as it may have seemed, I was not about to test the extent to which that idea was mere hallucinatory bravado. It was still a wild animal, still a predator.

"Well, listen," I continued, "I'd love to stay and talk, but I really have to get going. Do you know of another way out of here?"

As if in understanding, it briefly looked past me, over my shoulder, and I spun in anticipation of finding something behind me. But there was nothing there, and when I turned back to the wolf again, I could swear it looked amused. "Alright, the joke's on me," I mumbled, but then realized that one of the windows was behind me and that maybe it was possible to somehow climb down on the outside of the building. I went over to look but saw that the idea was much too dangerous. There were protruding bricks that I could hold onto, but if I fell, I would either break my legs or be killed outright. I went back to the hole. The wolf was gone.

Instinctively I leveled the shotgun at the partition that hid the door to the stairs. I listened for sounds from the stairwell but didn't hear anything. I supposed it was possible he simply got bored with the game and left, or that he'd seen or heard something that captured his lupine attention. It was also possible, of course, that he had gone down to the basement to await my inevitable arrival. With that in mind, it occurred to me that there really was another way out—the main staircase behind the double doors. I knew the door to the outside was sealed but figured that maybe I could force it open. And it would be safe since the double doors on each floor kept the staircase separate from the room; an animal would not be able to get in there. I stepped back to the wall and headed across the floor to the other side.

When I got to within a few yards of the front wall, I found something that challenged my views on the vagabond theory. There, nestled into the corner, was a pile of pine boughs, laid out as if to form some sort of a bed or nest. A discovery not so remarkable in itself, it might have been mistaken for rubbish that had somehow found its way into the building—except that it was fresh. Someone had just put it there. I reached down and gave it a shake; the needles were not even dry enough to fall off.

How long before pine needles will start to fall off? I wondered. A week? A month? I had no idea. The tree in Margaret's apartment was too new to be any kind of gauge, but I recalled that most Christmas trees were still pretty sturdy at the end of the holiday season. So they could have been there for weeks, maybe even be the result of a student "adventure" from earlier in the fall. I filed it away mentally and stepped beyond it to get to the door but was held up when my right foot snagged a piece of fabric covered by the boughs. I reached for what I at first took to be another sleeping bag, but when I pulled it out, I saw that it was something else.

A bearskin. Even half concealed under the tumble of brush, I could see what it was from the thick, black fur. I pulled it out, scattering the branches in the process, and held it up. Incredibly, it was nearly complete and even included a hood made from the skin of the animal's head, as if it were intended to be worn as a cloak. A hunter? I wondered.

Then it hit me. Yes, this was the handiwork of a hunter but, no, not a hunter in any conventional sense. I felt a nervous chill touch my spine as I realized that this might be the work of some socially unassimilated loner, probably a Vietnam vet who had returned from the jungles and, like many of his buddies, simply could not enter society again. The deep woods of places like Maine held a number of these characters, one of whom would sometimes show up in Bowford to trade furs for supplies. As a general rule, they said nothing, interacted with no one, lived in some panoramic quasi-world of their own making, and were typically avoided. They were like the ghosts of colonial-era long hunters, at home in the forest and shunning civilization. But as far as I knew, none of them had ever hurt anyone.

I put it back and recovered it with the branches as best I could. If I was right, this was a totally different breed of "vagabond" and not someone to be trifled with. The best thing to do was to get out of there as quickly as possible. As I moved toward the double door, I fleetingly remembered the words of the reconnaissance scout who had admonished me to never look directly at an enemy from concealment, and I wondered how it would feel to be the person being looked at. Did I sense anything just then? No; if I was being watched from some hidden corner, the watcher would also know enough to not look directly at me and I would sense nothing. I scanned the entire room and realized with some relief that there was no place in there for a person to conceal himself.

The same could not be said for the attic, however, and the ragged hole that gaped in the ceiling would have provided a fine vantage point for anyone with an interest in keeping an eye on me. I hurriedly pushed my way through the double doors and found myself at the head of the main staircase.

Once there, I leaned against the wall and listened for several minutes. Hearing nothing, I took my first tentative steps, the shotgun halfway to my shoulder the whole time. The stairs went straight ahead rather than parallel to the wall, necessitating a one-hundred-eighty-degree turn at the landing below me and causing the next flight to be hidden from view until I was nearly on the landing. A window on the third floor level illuminated the stairwell as far as the landing and part of the next flight, but beyond that, any other windows were bricked shut and I could see that I was heading into an absolutely dark tunnel. I turned on the flashlight and continued.

When I got to the second floor, I propped my foot against the door and pulled it open a few inches to look into the room. The wolf was nowhere to be seen. I repeated the process on the first floor, with the same result. That meant it had to either be in the cellar or had left the building entirely. Not wishing to test either theory, I examined the massive door to the outside to see if I could open it. It had a handle similar to the one on the front door of the Ropewalk and, above that, one of those old deadbolt locks that could be released just by turning the knob on the mechanism. I thought for sure it would be frozen in position but, remarkably, I was able to turn it with very little effort. I secured it in the unlocked position and pressed the latch above the handgrip, fully expecting to discover that the door had been nailed shut. But that didn't happen either. As easily as if leaving my own room, I pushed the door open a few inches, at which point it was stopped by the snow and debris piled in front of it. By throwing myself against it a few times, I was able to get it opened enough to get out. A moment more and I was back out in the dazzling sunlight, marveling at my escape. I let the door go and it swung shut with a very solid and convincing thud. I knew it was locked even before I tried to open it again.

It was almost nine o'clock as I stepped around the pile of debris obstructing the door and headed back toward the road. Any fear of the wolf had vanished with the darkness locked up behind the massive door, and when I got to the tractor, I removed the slug from the chamber of the shotgun and put it back in the magazine. The last thing I needed was an accidental discharge caused by something like slipping on the ice.

Then I started the tractor and resumed my journey up the road to the coast highway.

But as I rode, I was pedaling backwards mentally. The bearskin and the discovery of some sort of primitive "nest" in the building raised the question of whether we were actually exposed to some sort of danger. The counterweight to that was the lack of certainty about what it actually meant, or how long it had been there. Maine had lots of hunters, and the skin could have been a one-hundred-year-old family relic carelessly neglected by one of the students. On the other hand, there were all the oddments I'd seen that needed to fit together if I were going to understand any of what was going on—the "bear" that ran toward the Ropewalk, the bear tracks, the "bear" that walked out from the side of the shed and stood up, the bizarre bellow from the dark rim of the forest—all these, taken together, were now a mixture of reality and doubt. On some level I rejected the idea of actual danger because we had been exposed to it the whole time and nothing had happened. It was a small consolation.

But an image was forming in my mind, a kaleidoscope of fragmented picture-pieces tumbling together to form a mosaic without an underlying logic. I had pause now to ask myself anew if what I was conceiving was plausible, or whether I myself were becoming unhinged.

♦ ♦ ♦

Chapter 23

My personality had fault lines, crack-like defects that resulted from the stresses of interacting with people and the environment. I had known this ever since I was an adolescent. Whatever I imagined myself to be, it was shot through with dormant ruptures like those in the tectonic plates of the earth itself. And like those plates, these things would periodically slip and cause tremors, except in my case, the "tremor" would be an abrupt change in mind-set. Priorities would suddenly shift, and my tremor-induced focus would exclude everything and everyone around me while my mental "plates" slipped and I zeroed in on the new issue. My first wife, Mae, had often remarked on this ability of mine to slide into a mental tunnel.

"Tectonic brain slippage," I would say in my defense.

"Obsessive-compulsive," she would accuse in return.

Whatever the name, it did not change the complexion of the behavior. As the week wore on, I had been aware of the growing need to get on with it, to launch my project the way a shipbuilder might launch his latest design, but the events that had transpired had altered and derailed everything. And now the tunnel into which I found myself staring was the one that held the mosaic of unconnected events that I was trying to piece together. Thrown into the mix was the precarious and fragile well-being of the family that was now mine, at least in name. I was transfixed by the uncertainty of our position—alone, isolated, cut off.

There was something I had read in the old diary—just a page in passing—that I was struggling to remember. It was there, vexingly close but still unfocused, like the image of a face one recognized but whose name was long forgotten. The bearskin had kindled it, set it to glowing in the dark of the tunnel, but only as a faint or distant spark. I knew it was somehow tied to Abenaki mythology, now itself diluted by the unexpected reference to the Norse Edda in the old history book, but beyond that it became no clearer. Knowing myself as I did, I expected to be obsessed by it.

Tectonic brain slippage. What Mae had never understood was that my tunnel-focus was not due to the need to be famous, or to ambition, but simply out of a need to know. And now I had to know about the name "Cane" and the hatchet marks in the wall of the house, not so much because I needed to checkmate any reference to Sil, but because there was something moving in that mental tunnel that I could already sense but not yet see.

◆ ◆ ◆

The house in the cedars had vanished. At least, that was how I felt while pushing my way through a nearly impassable tangle of branches as I looked for it. I had entered the trees from the front rather than the back so that my tracks would not betray its existence to anyone, but I had not reckoned with such a high degree of disorientation. When I left it the first time, I had simply followed the sound of the waterfall without taking a compass reading, a mistake whose consequence I was now starting to appreciate. I knew only too well how easy it was to drift to one side or the other when going through the woods, and the route I'd taken to get to the village was evidently a lot more convoluted than my memory was allowing. After about twenty minutes of fruitless searching, I took a bearing on the sound of the waterfall and headed back out toward the village. The patch of cedars was evidently larger than I'd remembered, and I knew the only way I was going to find the house was to approach it from the back, the way I had first found it.

I came out of the trees not far from the well whose existence had been the source of the semi-argument that Margaret and I had had when the notion of "place memory" was first mentioned. I remembered that when I first looked into it, I'd seen what appeared to be a hole in the fieldstone lining, so I went over to examine it again, this time using the flashlight for a closer look. I saw now that it was not a break in the lining but rather a rift in the natural rock, and the hand-laid stones simply went around it. It did indeed appear to be an opening, but it was not possible to tell from the surface how deep it was. It could have been an actual tunnel or nothing more than a shallow depression. In any case, unless I came back with some rope and lowered myself into it, there would be no way to know. I filed it away mentally for consideration later, probably when the weather had improved, then went down the path to the cemetery.

Once again, the faded opulence of the graveyard impressed itself upon me as I stood and studied the first of the huge stones that dominated the place. Since I did not know if this Madeline Cane had been a person of means or one of the "common folk," I figured I might as well start right there at the first row. The empty eye-socket windows of the large houses beyond it stared vacuously at me as I began to brush the snow away from the names carved on the stones. There were Worners and Garretts, Hyes and Thompsons, and a significant number that were so badly weathered that the names had dissolved into shapeless, serpentine lumps. A great many were made of that wretched brown sandstone that they used back then, and many of these had split and sloughed the front of the stone right off, erasing everything. It was slow going, and I was tempted more than once to leave it for a while and go look at the houses behind it, on the other side of the stream. But I held myself in check.

The name "Cane" did not show up on any of the legible markers in that part of the cemetery, so I moved further down to where I'd noticed the smaller stones earlier. These, ironically, tended to be in better shape than their more flamboyant counterparts, mainly because they were made of local stone that was far more durable. "The meek shall inherit the earth," I mused with a faint chuckle, "or at least have their names last longer." Beyond these stones was the bizarre, squarish house with the four progressively diminishing stories that I'd seen before and, although I held myself back once again, I knew I was going to have to one day see what was in it.

Some of these stones were flush with the ground, and the only way I was able to locate them was by forcefully poking a stick through the snow until a change in the feel of the impact told me there was something more solid underneath. Kicking the snow off slowed me down considerably, and I realized that if I didn't find the name soon, I might have to break off the search and come back the next day. I had given myself until noon to get through the cemetery, at which point, regardless of the outcome, I would go back to the cedars and try to find the house so that I could make a casting of the hatchet marks. It was already eleven-thirty, and I still had more than half of that part of the graveyard to investigate.

Knowing how my luck tended to run, I figured "Cane" would show up on the last stone in the last row in the back of the graveyard, and since I hadn't had any luck up to that point, I decided to act on that thought. I knew it was completely illogical, of course, as I headed for the other side of the yard, because the name, if it was there at all, was no more likely to be at the end than it was to be somewhere in the middle. Nevertheless, I headed across diagonally and, in an odd gesture of synchronicity uncharacteristic of a usually stingy fate, walked right past a fully exposed stone with the name "Cane" on it. I stood and stared at it for several seconds, disbelieving.

But, yes, the name was "Cane," clearly and unambiguously staring back at me in weathered, embossed stone letters. Unfortunately, no first name or initial was given, nor was there any indication of the person's gender or date of death. A series of amorphous lumps rippling across the surface probably held that decisive information, and I gently rubbed away the frozen dirt of the centuries in the hopes that I might recognize something. The number "7" gradually emerged, and I was sure by its position that it was indicating a date in the seventeen hundreds, which would have squared with the events in the diary. But nothing further could be deciphered.

Still, it was a very strong indicator of a connection. And there were techniques available for bringing out hidden patterns that I might try later on when the weather warmed up. In any case, it was enough for now; I had a name that correlated with the one in the diary. That was pretty good evidence and by itself meant I would not have to pretend—meaning "lie"—to Margaret about finding what I needed so that she would forget about Sil.

I felt elated. Now all I needed was an imprint of the hatchet marks and I would be in a position to unequivocally state that the diary was describing events that took place in this area. And that meant that I could direct my attention back to what the writer's grandmother had said about the "Wampanoag King" seeking the help of the "local savages," my springboard to recognition.

There were still kinks, to be sure. I did not know what to make of the village at all, or of the second ropewalk, nor did I have the slightest idea how I would approach the enigma of the carved stone standing in the basin. And the petroglyphs in the chasm were a discovery in their own right. There was still the Underground Railroad connection for the house in the cedars, but the demise of the village itself remained unsolved, although I was confident that either the diary or the proprietor's records would shed light on that issue. It would no doubt turn out to be disease, maybe even an outbreak of plague.

But the bone barrow itself remained inscrutable. I could see it from the cemetery, its featureless dome glazed over with snow and ice, its closed flanks showing no obvious ways into it, assuming it was something other than just a natural formation. The diary had said that two Indians had tried to hide in "holes in the barrow," which either implied a way into it or was referring to something else that bore the name "barrow." This was not impossible; the word had originally referred generically to a hill or mound, and the comment could have meant nothing more cryptic than several of them trying to get out of the basin by hiding in the cracks in its walls. I could not rule that out.

Still, it held my gaze with an almost magnetic compulsion, and I was torn between going back to the house and striking out for a closer look. It was still early—not yet even noon—and I had already decided that the most expedient way to locate the house was to ascend that natural stone "staircase" that I had found earlier and then follow the edge of the tree line to the back door. The stones leading upward were mostly covered with ice, which meant I could go up using the crampons and not leave an obvious trail.

And that was what I had to do. Weighing the consequences of doing one over the other reminded me that I had to confirm the nature of the marks in the wall of the house before I did anything else. Sil had to be out of the picture. Absolutely out. I was sure he would show up by snowmobile sometime in the next week, and there had to be no reason whatsoever for asking him about the artifacts on the top floor of the shed. I turned away from the gravestone and headed back up the small valley toward the path that wound up toward the waterfall.

The stone "staircase"—I had given it that name because of how the natural rock was exposed in layers—cut right through the wall of cedars on an upward slope that paralleled the flank of the hill with the stream. It looked steeper from this side, and any thoughts I might have harbored about going up without the crampons were quickly dismissed after the first tentative step. I had no choice but to dig them out of the pack and strap them on. Even then it was a laborious and slippery climb to the top.

Once I got there, though, I recognized the sluice-like "shoehorn" I had fallen into when I cannonballed through the brush on my first trip, and this helped me to orient myself to where I had entered the cedars and found the house. I confirmed that my earlier tracks had indeed been obscured by the snow and sleet that had fallen in the interim, and since I did not want to leave any new ones, I removed the crampons and headed straight into the trees. Once there, I slugged my way through the branches while staying parallel to the clearing. Since I did not recognize any landmarks—after all, I hadn't been looking for any when I first stumbled into the living room—I had no realistic feel for how far it was to the house. It seemed to be taking longer than I remembered, and I had a fleeting moment of disbelief as the idle thought passed that maybe I had imagined the whole thing, that the house did not really exist except as some sort of skeletal relic in my mind. But a moment later, I saw its gray flank peeking through the trees, the weathered wall stippled like camouflage from the sunlight filtering through. I put the snowshoes on as a precaution and went in.

Nothing had changed. The door of the closet with the hidden passage was slightly ajar, but that may have been how I left it. I went over and looked in, saw the same curtain of rotting clothing, noted the opening in the ceiling, and re-closed the door. I then headed straight for the stairs and went up.

The marks in the upstairs wall were easy to find and I studied them for a few minutes, suddenly not so convinced that they had been made by a hatchet but realizing that they were so old the distinct blade shape could have rotted away. I also had some doubts about how well the clay would work, even with the cornstarch as a parting substance. This doubt was confirmed when my first tentative mold got stuck and I had to destroy it to get it out.

There was another possibility—I could come back with a saw and literally cut that part of wall out, then section it for a closer examination. I hated doing things like that, though, because it turned me into a vandal, regardless of how lofty the intent. So I continued to struggle with the clay until, eventually, I had enough cornstarch in the largest cut to extract a reasonably intact impression. This I very gingerly, carefully, packed with cotton and placed in a small cardboard box I had brought along for that purpose. I loaded up several other cuts with cornstarch and attempted the same technique but with only partial success. Nevertheless, I felt the impressions might reveal something under a magnifying glass, so I added those to the padded box as well.

Mission accomplished, I checked my watch. It was not quite one o'clock. Since I wasn't expected back until dinner, I was left with several hours exploration time, which I took advantage of by first going up to the balcony that lined the upper perimeter of the room. I was fully convinced that the intent behind this unusual "mezzanine" was to serve as a lookout station so that the villagers could see an enemy coming from some distance away. Its second function, of course, would have been defense, allowing shooters a clear view on an advancing foe long before that foe could actually reach the building. Unfortunately, because of the tall trees all around the house, the view from any of the windows was simply one of cedar boughs. I went from window to window, but the result was the same in every case. I suspected that, if the trees weren't there, I would have been able to see the bone barrow from the windows in the front, but even that could not be confirmed. All in all, the tour of the upper floor yielded nothing useful, and on the way back to the stairs I tested the wall paneling for firmness, thinking that there might be concealed weapons cached away for emergencies. This did not pan out either.

I had decided to leave the house the way I had entered rather than head out through the trees toward the sound of the waterfall, as I had done the first time. By going back down the iced-over "staircase," I would minimize the risk of leaving a trail again when I emerged from the trees on the other side.

This time when I went through the living room, I saw something that I hadn't noticed before. Set into one of the outer walls was what looked like a gray paneled cabinet. I noticed it out of the corner of my eye, stepped past on my way to the back door, then stopped and turned for a closer look.

Was that a fuse box? I wondered. How could that be? Was this house actually occupied right up until just a few decades ago? Was that why it was in such relatively good shape? Tentatively, unsure of the floor between me and the outer wall, I worked my way toward it. But as I got closer I saw that, no, the gray weathered door was wood, not metal, and when I opened it, I saw that it was not a fuse box but a simple built-in cabinet, set flush with the wall, its door paled to steel gray by age itself. There was nothing in it but a few shards of what looked like some sort of long ceramic tube, and in a moment I realized what they were—the remains of a pipe. It was a smoking cabinet, a glorified pipe rack, and a very fancy one at that. One of the treasures of the colonial period was the wherewithal associated with smoking, and people of means sometimes displayed those means in unusually ornate layouts. Oddly relieved that it was not a fuse box, I closed the cabinet without touching anything and headed toward the back door.

But I paused again as I went past the closet with the false ceiling. It was still a puzzle to me why anyone would build some sort of hidden chamber but then provide access to it by the most awkward means possible. Climbing up through the ceiling of a closet would be slow at best and impossible for the elderly or infirm, so they were either intentionally excluded or there had to be another way in. I went over for a closer look.

The walls were all of wood paneling with partially rotted molding along the upper perimeter. It stood to reason that, if there was a door there, it had to open to the right in order to allow access to a chamber inside the hearth. There was nothing to suggest the existence of a door, but I could hardly expect to find something obvious when the intent behind it was secrecy. If there was a lock or latch, it was invisible to me, so I pushed on the paneling. It moved. I pushed a little harder and, with a little assist from my foot against the bottom, forced an opening about two inches wide. There was nothing to see except the faint outline of the inner stones of the hearth, but a stale odor issuing from the slot told me that it was air that had been trapped and unmoving for a long time. With a little extra effort I managed to open it wider and was able to see that the false ceiling was not the way to get into whatever this passage was—the paneled wall was actually a concealed door. It squeaked in protest as I leaned more of my weight into it, forcing it into a position it probably hadn't been in for centuries. A few more shoves and I had it propped against the stone masonry of the inside of the hearth. Before me was a flight of crudely laid stone stairs heading downward into darkness.

A bolthole. It had to be. A place to hide when danger threatened, maybe later used to conceal runaway slaves on the Underground Railroad. My heart quickened as my "need to know" mindset kicked in and I dug through my pack for the flashlight.

I would be the first person to enter that place in almost two centuries. For me it was the equivalent of Schliemann finding Troy or Carter unsealing the tomb of Tutankhamen. Much more modest, of course, but to me just as monumental. I turned on the flashlight and aimed the beam into the passage. The stairs angled steeply downward for no more than five feet and then turned sharply left at the wall of the hearth. Without giving it a second thought, I went in.

It was so narrow that my shoulders literally spanned the width of the opening, and I could not turn around with my pack on. At the point where the stairs turned, there was a small ledge formed by a protruding hearthstone, and on it was a brass oil lamp, fully intact. I lifted it down from the little stone shelf and looked it over. It was very ornate, and the glass dome, while encrusted with centuries of dust, was not broken. Well, I thought, here was the unique Christmas gift I wanted to give Margaret before my unexpected sojourn in the chasm cancelled my plans. I could not put it in my pack until I got out of the passage, so I held onto it securely and turned to descend further into the darkness.

The passage bottomed out in a small chamber with no apparent exit. It was empty except for a rusting pile of metal in one corner, and as I stepped over to investigate, I realized immediately what it was—leg irons. They were too badly decayed to be of any value as an artifact, so I didn't disturb them. But even so, it was obvious that they were very much like the ones I'd seen in the top floor of the shed, and once again the connection with the Underground Railroad became obvious. It was here where the runaway slaves sat and awaited the moment to flee to Canada; it was also here where the irons were struck from their legs, probably by the village blacksmith. The wait must have been agonizing, the shelter claustrophobic. And they would have been trapped if discovered.

That last thought set me to wondering. I knew I was now in the basement of the house, standing in a chamber barely large enough to hold four adults. If the only way out of the chamber was the way I got in, the hiding place was also a deadly trap. I could scarcely imagine that the builders would have gone through all the trouble to construct the hidden passage and yet not provide for a fail-safe, and with that in mind, I began looking for a way out.

The walls were solid and made of stone, not paneled like the entrance, so any concealed door would have been massive and probably impossible to move. That left only the floor and ceiling, the former automatically excluded because I was standing on what appeared to be a massive slab of the natural granite bedrock so common in New England. Part of the ceiling, however, was paneled with a partially corrupt and decaying enfoldment of interlacing boards, and I could see through the gaps that there was space beyond them, which, of course, could only have been the inside of the chimney itself. I gave it a push and part of it broke away under my hand, but the rest moved as a single body, and in a matter of moments I was staring up into the crumbling, grime-encrusted interior of the hearth. The long, stone-lined tunnel ended in a square of sunlight at the top, with enough light filtering through so that I could see hand and footholds cut—or inlayed—into one of the walls.

So the master plan behind the design was revealed—a bolthole, a hiding place, accessible from any floor via the fireplace on that floor. All one needed to do was pull the fire out—and I suspected that in the original version the fire was probably built on a floor pan of some sort for that purpose—and climb into the chimney, then down into the basement. The price of safety was a coating of soot.

And why not? In the adrenalin-primed moments of terror induced by the flight from a deadly enemy, one would not notice the dirt, grime, or even the heat still percolating out of the chimney. But the questions still remained: Once one was in the cellar, then what? Did they simply stay inside the hearth until the danger was past?

I still had plenty of time and I knew that if I didn't see what was in the basement, it would bother me for the rest of the day. Having decided that, I took off my pack, wrapped the globe of the lamp in the towel that I had used for the crampons, nested the two pieces carefully in the pack, and hung the crampons on the outside by their straps. Then

I carefully reached up through the hole and placed the pack and shotgun on the floor above me. The original users must have helped each other because there was nothing I could see to give myself a boost into the opening, so I grabbed the edges, squatted down as far as I could, then launched myself upward.

I managed to fold myself over the lip of the opening with my legs still dangling in the chamber below. There was nothing I could use to pull myself up, so for a moment I simply hung there like an indecisive gymnast caught on the high bar. But then I managed to hook one of my feet on the opposite edge of the opening and, using that lever, angled the rest of myself upward.

I was in a small cavity that led directly into the chimney. The diffuse light filtering down from the top was not enough to allow me to see clearly, so I still needed the flashlight as I crept toward the edge. To my immediate left was a large opening in the floor, utterly black, and through it a dank, cold draft of air was wafting upward. I knew that this was the intended escape route from the bolthole and that it must have led into the basement. In front of me was simply the casement of the chimney, its floor littered with stones, pieces of masonry, and a small snowdrift that had built up in one corner. I moved over to the hole and shined the light down into it.

Below me, about five feet down, was a floor made of natural flagstones. It was a simple descent, and since I had gone that far I knew I had to continue. "Risk be damned," I mumbled, since it was minimal anyway and it was obviously not possible any more—despite my original reservations—to be accidentally stuck in some subterranean clam hole. Nothing of the sort—I could go on with impunity and knew I absolutely had to.

"Obsessive-compulsive," I muttered with a subdued laugh, as if somehow, in darkened isolation, I was still dimly trying to send some final message of explanation to the lingering shadow of my long-ago life with Mae. It was an old tape that replayed itself on occasion, an example of that alter-option I had wondered about when I was stuck in the chasm. I had to know; she had to know why I had to know. I didn't know why I had to know, but there it was. That was why I became an historian; I needed to fill in the blank spots on my map of understanding. This darkened hole was the next step in that process, so down I went, lowering the pack and the shotgun after me.

The cellar. I was in some sort of stone-lined recess about three feet deep. Straight ahead, about twenty feet away, were the remains of the staircase that I'd seen from the floor above on my first visit. From this vantage point, it was clear that I could probably climb out that way as long as the still intact frame that had once held the stairs was not completely rotted. I wouldn't do that, of course; I needed to exit the way I had entered so that I could replace the planking over the holding chamber and close the hidden door in the closet, thereby preventing any random visitors in the future from finding it.

The floor was dirt and the walls were made of fitted fieldstones, neither of which was a surprise. What was a surprise, though, was noticing that the recess I stepped out of was in fact another fireplace. "The summer kitchen," I muttered. Most hearths were nothing more than a pile of stones in the cellar, making a "summer kitchen" an unusual luxury where, in the sweltering heat of summer, the family meals could be cooked in the relative cool of the basement. They were usually coupled with a water source, and knowing this, I treaded very carefully while scanning the floor everywhere for signs of a well. I didn't see one, but did notice what appeared to be the rotting remains of shelving and enclosures along one of the walls. That would have been where the various foodstuffs had been stored. There was probably a root cellar also, a still deeper pit into which such things as carrots and potatoes were placed for longer-term storage. The barest necessities for survival were never more than a few feet away, never more secure than the nearest drought, plague, or infestation.

As I stepped around the massive base of the hearth, I noticed a crumbling door set into the rock of the foundation. A few more feet and I noticed another one. These had to be the root cellars, and when I opened the first one, I was not surprised to see a short flight of steps leading down into a small enclosure heaped with the rotting remains of what must at one time have been racks for storing vegetables. I closed it and went to open the next one, but it was so flimsy it virtually crumbled in my hand and I ended up shunting a pile of decaying boards up against the wall. This one, too, had several short steps but did not open into a root cellar. Instead, it appeared to be a tunnel of some sort, cold and dank and smelling of unmoved earth, and from somewhere in its depths I heard a sound, a faint, rhythmic rustling as of a subterranean drumbeat. I knew immediately what it was.

Water. I stepped down into the opening and noticed that it appeared to be a natural break in the stone, one of those geologic rips in a landscape crushed and sundered by glaciers in the Ice Age. And I had not gone twenty feet when I found, not a well, but a spring emerging from the rock itself and flowing across the break in a rather hefty stream, and I thought, well, what a convenience for someone living in that era, freshets of running water from what was probably an inexhaustible source. In lieu of a well, they had this. And being underground, it would flow all year, unaffected by the cold.

It flowed into a break in the opposite wall and vanished, its silver shimmer briefly visible in the beam from the flashlight as I tried to see what was in there. But it was an awkward angle that did not allow a view of more than a few feet, and although it was big enough to enter, the cold chill of both the water and the mere thought of doing it—the specter of the chasm and its thundering hole inevitably came back—caused me to instantly dismiss it as a possibility. The tunnel itself continued beyond the stream but quickly became too narrow for anyone but a small child to get into.

Running water. They had running water, courtesy of the underground plumbing that channeled the stream into the break. I imagined easily how it all came about—before the house was there, this break was probably visible from the ground above, and whoever found it saw it as the perfect place to live. So the cellar hole was dug alongside it and the summer kitchen added because of the convenient water supply. The constant danger from the Abenakis was taken into account when they built the secret passage in the hearth, and this later became a refuge for runaway slaves headed for Canada.

All very neatly packaged, except for one thing—once you entered the hearth and came out in the basement, you were still trapped. Unless, of course, there was also a way out of the basement, something that would not expose the person to the danger all around the house.

And I realized immediately what was supposed to happen once one found himself in the cellar. In another of those intuitive leaps of insight, I saw the connection across subterranean space as if it were mapped out for anyone to follow. I *knew* where the stream came out and I *knew* that was the intended escape route.

The village well. The stream emptied into the village well via that break that I had seen in its wall. I was as sure of it as I was sure that the stream in the chasm was the reason the ice on the swamp cracked when I tried to cross it. It was a perfect setup, one that allowed access to, as well as egress from, the basement of the house. Runaways didn't even need to be near the house to enter it.

Once again, I shined the light into the break, but no matter how I angled it, I could not see more than a few feet before my vision was blocked by the walls of the tunnel itself. There was no way to test my theory except by entering the crack and walking in the frigid water itself, and although I felt my mental plates slip again as the need to know became dominant, reason prevailed. It was not something to be attempted alone. I would come back in summer with Margaret.

I went back out to the cellar and looked around, but there was not much more to see, so I went back to the fireplace and climbed up into the hearth. As I lowered myself into the hidden chamber, I tried to envision what life must have been like for someone living in that era, where the vicissitudes of pure circumstance were so random and so frequent that undying trust in the benevolence of a Creator was the only thing that provided the courage to go on. In exchange for this, though, they lived every day in concert with the pulse of the earth itself, a nearness that we could only capture—however feebly—in the faces of the pets we kept. For every step forward there was something that we had to leave behind, and only when one touched the remains of past lives could one get insight into the real extent of the loss. For every tree felled to make a parking lot, some part of humanity fell with it.

In that moment I realized that the anchor point to my kinship with Sonya lay in her instinctive bond to the natural world. It occurred to me that, as she grew, I would perhaps have the opportunity to see, through her eyes, the things that time had long since forced me to ignore or forget. It was obvious that in the silent, darkened depths of her mind there was something to which I would never have access—an instinctive, almost animalistic kinship with the earth. I could see it in her eyes when she surrounded herself with the boughs of the Christmas tree. And I understood its true import when I found the leaf she had pressed in one of her picture books. I was sure she understood more than even Margaret suspected, and I was half convinced that she could also speak, not in English but in her own language of symbols. If, by watching and loving her, I could learn that language, then maybe one day I would be able to talk to the trees as well. Or to wolves and owls.

It would not be just for me. I knew I had identified an activity that would bring me closer to her, that would cause or bring about the intractable bond that I knew I would need, and its commonality—its firmament—would be the language of trees. Mae would be proud. A fleeting glimpse of the Ogham alphabet of the ancient Celts appeared on my mental chalkboard, an alphabet based on the names of trees, a supra-natural bond symbolized in the spoken word itself. I could not help but wonder if, in whatever genetic prison Sonya found herself, she had leaped over the bounds of time and was somehow living in a different era, had somehow joined that imprint-world that the Celts had known so well.

I laughed, and the sound echoed in the confines of the small chamber with such volume that I was sure it could be heard all the way to the village. Only an historian would make this sort of connection, I mused. Only someone like me, desperately convinced that he could weave together the frayed tapestry of the past into some sort of picture, desperate to believe that it was all adding up to something.

Replacing the partially rotted frame of planks over the chamber was no problem, but I had trouble closing the panel door once I'd exited the closet. In point of fact, I could not see how it could be completely closed from this side at all, since I needed to leave it open several inches so that I could get my hand out. There had to have been a handle of some sort to pull it closed the rest of the way, and when I felt around its perimeter, I discovered a hollow behind one of the panels at the bottom. When I pulled on it, it opened like a small door, and behind it was an iron ring, hinged so that it could be used as a handle. With it I was able to pull the door securely closed.

At that point I had done everything I had come to do. I had found the name "Cane" and had made impressions of the hatchet marks. And now I also knew the secrets of the house. When I got back, I would start immediately with a description of everything I had just seen—the cemetery, the house, the passage, and the leg irons. I needed to start recording everything while it was still fresh in my mind. I also knew I would have to come back and take some pictures to verify my statements. All of this would serve as the underlayment of the history I would write, which even then was taking shape in my mind in a way I had never anticipated. It was moving from a dry assortment of chronological facts to a speculative inquiry into the history of the village. In another flash of insight, I realized that the final, unequivocal connection between the diary and the village was one that had been staring me in the face all along—the land records in the first part of the diary and the names on the gravestones. I would come back and record all the names and dates on the stones and then do the same with the names listed in the transactions. I intuitively knew there was no doubt at all that I would find the two matching up.

So there it was. My project finally had a form, a format. After years of collecting notes and dreading the day when I would have to put them in order, the decision was made for me. I could scarcely believe how fate had taken me by the hand and led me to the answer.

"Destiny logic," I mumbled as I left the back door of the house and worked my way through the cedars toward the "staircase." Or maybe synchronicity, that acausal connecting principle. In any case, it was one of those if-clauses at work again. If I had not decided to stay after everyone else had left, if Ben had not abandoned Margaret, if we had never met—none of this would have happened. I reached new levels of euphoria as I walked up the path past the waterfall and headed for the fallen log that bridged the stream. It was not yet three o'clock and I toyed with the idea of going back up to the ruins of the ropewalk for another look at the petroglyphs in the chasm, but then opted to let it go. I could always come back to them later; for now, it was more important that I started laying out my plan.

The kinks in the dating chronology would work themselves out. One piece of evidence was absolutely crucial—the village had to have been there when the Wampanoag King, Metacomet, came seeking the help of the "savages" or the grandmother would not have witnessed the massacre described in the diary. That meant the village, or at least part of it, was already there by 1675. I knew from my cursory scan of the land records that they went back further than that, so this was not an impossibility. I was sure they would tell me when the first parcels were sold, who bought them, and how they were later divided. In support of all this, there was also the established fact that there was already a fishing industry thriving on the coast of Maine when the Pilgrims arrived at Plymouth in 1620.

As for the carved stone in the basin, I was sure that the records would reveal something about its history, even if only speculatively, when the land transaction that led to the building of the ropewalk was completed.

I was elated. My "tectonic brain slippage" had resulted in a tunnel-vision that had led me to the way out of my dilemma. I scarcely noticed the deepening cold that surrounded me as the sun slanted further into the west.

As the log-bridge came into view, I began to think about all that had happened since that morning. I pondered the discovery of the bearskin in the Engineering building with a diffuse understanding of events unrelated in time or circumstance. Had it been a bearskin-cloaked hunter, a sort of human artifact from a bygone era, the shadow of a lost epoch? Or was it a still operational form of sympathetic magic—one must become the animal to understand its ways, the protective skin giving way to the shape-shifting transformation in the mind of the wearer. And then it hit me—yes, the Dawn People in Abenaki mythology were endowed with shape-shifting ability, which was now generally understood to mean that they donned the skin of the animal and *became* that animal, the more so since the eyes of the watchers were usually clouded by the common entrancement of the need to survive, to see it as real. Yes, that and the giant stone in the basin, the race that was destroyed by its creator, personified in a form that would allow those who feared it to approach it and show their courage, resolve their fears.

And maybe somewhere in the collective psyche of the human race, this allegorical shape-shifting, sympathetic magic was still at work, still driving us to wear animal skins so that we could shape-shift into something older than mankind itself, gain a sense of common ancestry with the oldest life on earth.

I stopped to scribble down a few notes on a piece of paper in my shirt pocket. I was stunned at how it seemed to be falling together, however wide the inevitable gaps may turn out to be.

I needed to take the snowshoes off in order to cross the stream on the log, and while I was doing that, the memory of the false "fuse box" in the house came back to me and a sudden, nagging feeling came with it. It had no clarity and could not be articulated—just a confusion of formless thought fragments. No apparent meaning either, just a guess suspended from a surmise. But still—I felt something, and it stayed with me as I crossed the stream and put the snowshoes back on. The

317

confusion grew as I headed for the second stream that would lead me back to the tractor.

I had missed something. Maybe it had something to do with the nightwalker, I wondered with a dismissive laugh. The memory of the cat recurred to me, a feral little wood-demon haunting the halls of the Ropewalk, and I marveled at all the angst it had caused while hiding from myself the creepy-crawly feeling that I didn't quite believe it. I didn't believe it because I knew on some level that it was not the cat, that there was something else moving in that darkened mind-tunnel I had been staring into. The thought of the look-alike fuse box in the old house had triggered something, had fooled me into making unexpected connections that had quickly dissipated but then returned. I chuckled again as if to reassure myself, then lurched to a stop with a suddenness that almost caused me to lose my balance. The realization had hit me like a fist in the stomach. I knew what it meant now, the dream from over a week before when the huge stone had rumbled out of the ground with the word "halfway" on it. My subconscious had seen it right away while my conscious mind had either dismissed or disbelieved it. But I finally understood.

I held onto a small tree to keep myself from weakening under the sudden realization that there really *was* someone else in the Ropewalk.

◆ ◆ ◆

Chapter 24

I ran. I ran as fast as the snowshoes and underbrush would allow. The thought drummed in my head: It could not be Sil. Could not be. Whatever potential danger he represented, he was not the one in the building. I knew this because he had keys to every room in the Ropewalk and, before the deadbolts were installed, could have gotten into Margaret's apartment anytime he wanted. But that didn't happen. Therefore, it could not be him.

Running on snowshoes was no easy task, and by the time the tractor hove into view, I was so exhausted I thought I would collapse. Yet every time I slowed to a walk my progress seemed impossibly slow, almost like I had stopped. So, despite my racing heart and bellowing lungs, I pushed on. When I reached the vehicle, I had no choice but to rest for a moment to catch my breath. As soon as I felt my heart would no longer burst, I climbed onto the seat and started the engine.

I tried to reason through the possibilities while I pushed the tractor as fast as I dared. It was most likely the "long hunter" whose bearskin cloak I had found in the Engineering building. The connection now seemed obvious—it was probably he whom I had seen that day near the shed, the "bear" that had stood up and walked away. Or maybe it was a petty thief after all, a "townie" vexed over the discovery that two people had not left the building and thus ruined his plans for casual plunder.

In either case, I felt like an idiot. What the dream had been trying to tell me was now so obvious that I marveled at how dense I had been. A rectangular stone had popped out of the ground with the word "halfway" on it, and I hadn't understood. It was a circuit breaker. When a circuit breaker pops, it slips to a position halfway between "on" and "off." It does not move to the full "off" position. But the breaker for the nightlights had been off, not tripped. That meant only one thing—the circuit was not shorting out. Someone had turned the lights off.

Instantly, the "shadow within a shadow" that I had seen emerging from the utility closet took on new life in my mind. It was real. Someone had been there, had been emerging from the closet and either sensed my presence or seen my face somehow and retreated. But that led to another question mark—retreated to where? When I entered the utility closet, there had been no one there.

What was I missing?

Or—and here I took a deep breath to steady myself—was I falling victim to the effects of isolation and social deprivation? Was this what it felt like? Was I, as I had imagined earlier that day, in fact falling behind the darkened veil of some sort of hysteria? I looked around for some kind of anchor, an unmoving datum that I could use to stabilize the fluxing sense of non-reality into which I felt myself moving. I was, in fact, looking for the wolf.

It was not there, of course. For all I knew, it may still have been in the Engineering building.

The warmer weather had caused some localized melting on the cart track, causing slipperier than usual conditions and forcing me to reign in my impulses. I could feel the tractor wanting to break away and slip to the side. The two miles to the coast highway thus seemed to take forever. When I finally turned onto it, I slammed the tractor into the highest gear and floored it. What had seemed like a boon on the way in was maddeningly slow on the way back.

My frantic impatience led me to think of things I would never have considered before. The shotgun lay across my lap, and as I drew parallel to the Engineering building, it occurred to me that this was where he was operating from and this was where he had to return to get his bearskin. I would come back and hide in the building, play the same game he was playing, scare him off or threaten him with the shotgun, shoot him if I had to. Yes.

No. Are you nuts? I thought. If this was one of those castoff Vietnam vets, the guy would be a trained killer, maybe still living the life of a tunnel rat in his mind, playing off his own courage against now imaginary enemies hiding around every corner, over and over again.

Besides, I would then be up for murder, assuming he didn't get me first.

I went on past. "Alright, get a grip," I mumbled. "Don't go ballistic. I don't even know for sure that he actually represents a danger, whoever he is."

Less than a minute later, I saw the school in its snowfield off to the left, and a few seconds after that the Ropewalk came into view on the right. From the outside, nothing seemed out of place. I didn't bother driving the machine into the shed; I shut it off right there in the driveway, leaped down from the seat, and bolted for the door.

It was locked, which I interpreted as a good sign. I held the shotgun between my knees while I fumbled with my key ring and, finding the right one at last, let myself in. Once again, the sudden warmth was almost palpable; I could feel beads of sweat forming on my forehead, but whether this was from the temperature, the exertion, or the heart-racing energy I'd been feeling, I couldn't tell. All I knew was that it was quiet. That, and down in the depths of the shadowed hallway I could see that Margaret's door was open.

That could not be a good sign. The last time she did that she had gone to take a shower and bathe Sonya, but she knew I was right behind her. This time, as far as she knew, I wasn't going to be back until around five o'clock, and it was only a few minutes after four.

I held the shotgun between my knees again, released the tension in the straps of my backpack and let it slide onto the lobby sofa, then opened my coat and let it drop to the floor. The shotgun was loaded but not chambered as I quietly moved down the hall toward her door. Once there, I quickly looked around the doorjamb into the living room and, seeing no one, stepped inside to check the kitchen and bedrooms. Nothing was disturbed or seemed out of order. I began to relax.

But where were they?

A noise from the hall made me turn and slink up to the door. A rumbling, distant and approaching, unidentified but somehow familiar, rolling up the hallway and growing louder. Squeaking, rubbing, and a muffled pounding, like someone trying to conceal his footfalls. I waited. The noise stopped just short of the open doorway and I was about to step forward when a voice said: "Egan?"

It was Margaret. I stepped out into the hall and saw her holding Sonya, who evidently had just ridden her tricycle up the hallway, clearly identifying the source of the rumbling noise. I felt myself emotionally imploding, coming down from a vertiginous height with reckless speed but pulling up a moment before impact. I sagged against the wall in relief.

She looked alarmed. "Are you alright? You look like you saw a ghost or something."

I laughed and shook my head. "No, no ghost. I just, ah, found some good stuff at the village and needed to hurry back to start recording notes and looking at the clay imprints."

She lowered Sonya to the floor, who immediately climbed onto the tricycle and would've taken off down the hall if Margaret hadn't restrained her. "So you got the imprints of the marks, huh? How do they look? Can you tell if they're hatchet marks?"

I straightened up. "Too soon to tell. I need to look at them under a glass."

She nodded. "Why are you carrying the shotgun?"

I suddenly felt foolish. "Well, ah, I was thinking that, since I was going out in the woods anyway, I might get lucky and run into a pheasant or turkey or something. You know, do the hunter thing and follow up on your request to put wild food on the table." She didn't have to know that I had loaded it with slugs, not birdshot.

"Oh." Oddly, she seemed doubtful, eyeing me askance, the clarity of the question now muffled in what I thought must have been some incongruous tone in my answer. "Right. I forgot about that. Did you get anything?"

"No. Didn't even see anything." I shrugged. "Told you I wasn't much of a hunter."

She nodded again. "Can you put it away? It kind of gives me the creeps."

"Oh, yeah, sure." I was completely unaware that I had been holding it at the ready, one hand on the slide ready to chamber a round and the other on the grip, ready to go for the trigger. To a casual observer it would look as if I were expecting to shoot something and, given that there was no "game" around, it could easily be construed as threatening.

I lowered the butt to the floor. "Sorry. I guess I just got a little nervous seeing your door opened like this."

She put Sonya down and ushered her into the apartment. The girl grabbed her tricycle and complied. "We were going to go ice skating again but the pond really has too much snow on it. I thought the ice storms might have helped, but they didn't. So I compromised by letting her ride her bike, but I had to leave the door open so that we would at least have some light in part of the hall." She watched as Sonya carefully parked the tricycle against the couch and then immersed herself in the play world around the Christmas tree.

I felt a slight chill touch my neck as I realized that she had been within a few feet of the utility closet at the end of the hall, the same closet that held the circuit breaker boxes, the same closet from which the "shadow within a shadow" had emerged. I smiled and nodded but was inwardly fraught with indecision, the more so as I realized the dilemma I was in—I could not tell her to be more careful without revealing that there really was something to be careful about. I could easily envision the panic that would result.

"Egan? Are you alright?"

I snapped out of it. "Sure. Why do you ask?"

"You look, sort of, I don't know, troubled. Is something wrong?"

And now the next surreptitious lie, induced by the events that had brought me to this point and now required that I not alarm her needlessly. "No. Everything's fine." I smiled. She seemed doubtful. "Just tired, hungry, and anxious to record what I found in the village. It occurred to me while I was out there that I had finally stumbled on a format for my project and I figure I might as well get started."

She seemed to accept that as she stepped into the apartment, glanced quickly at Sonya, then checked the time. "What time do you want dinner?"

I had drifted off into my mental tunnel again, trying to formulate my next move. "Dinner?"

"Yeah. You know, that meal you have at the end of the day when you're hungry, like you just said you were." Her brow knitted in bewilderment, eyes clouded more with what seemed like doubt than amusement.

I smirked at the joke. "Is five o'clock okay?"

"How about six. That will give me some time and also allow you to record your findings and lay out your plan. I assume you'll be working upstairs? We don't have much room in here and it won't be very quiet."

In fact, what I wanted to do was bring all my stuff down, including my typewriter, and maybe secure part of her bedroom as a working space. But she was right; there was barely enough room in the apartment as it was without me commandeering a corner and squeezing everybody a bit more. And it really wasn't quiet, even with Sonya unable to speak. Nor would my clattering away on the typewriter be much of a break for them.

So I had to concede the point, even if my better sense planted a vague warning in my mind about being so far from her with the knowledge that I now had. "You're right. It doesn't make any sense to bring all my stuff down here with everything already laid out upstairs. Do you need any help with dinner?"

"I'm fine."

"Okay, then. I'll head up for an hour or so and get some stuff done. I'll tell you about my discoveries at dinner." I said it perfunctorily, oddly out of kilter with my emotions entangled in the matrix of evasions and half-truths that now left me with only one thought: I could not leave her and Sonya unguarded.

But she was as gracious as ever, her doubt seeming to turn to amusement as she reached out for me and drew me in. We kissed and I noticed a subtle new scent, a perfume that I hadn't smelled before. She eyed me with a smile and winked. "Doing anything later on tonight, fella?"

"As a matter of fact, yes," I countered. "I was planning on staying as close to my lady as I could." How easy it was for her to do this to me, this sexual derailment that would unwind the over-taut spirals of my emotions. She was spontaneously—and maybe unconsciously—erotic, I could see that now, was possessed of that quality that brought the courtship ritual to heights not normally experienced by most couples. In spite of all else, her nearness inspired a momentarily half-wakeful fantasy wherein hers was the face of the erotic muse, a passionflower with a red rose over one ear. I could neither look away nor help myself.

Sonya had seen us kiss, and before Margaret could reply, she came up to her mother and wrapped her arms around Margaret's leg. Her coal-black eyes appeared expressionless, but I knew just from her behavior that she was confused. Margaret stroked her hair, then reached down and picked her up. She looked at me with that same expressionless stare.

"This is Egan," she said. "Egan." She took the child's hand and placed it on my shoulder, where I took it, gave it a tiny squeeze, then touched her playfully on the nose.

"Remember me?" I asked. "I'm the one who caught you when you ran off during our walk. Remember?" Of course she did—I had been there the whole time—but I was sure my name, or the sound of it, meant nothing to her. There was also no doubt in my mind that she was having trouble with the fact that I had usurped the role that her father had always played, leaving an unarticulated question hanging in the air. I suspected it would be a long time before she would look at me as someone to love and trust.

"Alright," said Margaret, "I'm going to start dinner and then play with Sonya for awhile. You can go work on your notes in the meantime. Do you have any wine left?"

"A couple of bottles, yes."

"Bring one for afterwards. I'll provide the atmosphere." She winked at me as she put Sonya down and turned toward the kitchen.

♦ ♦ ♦

In spite of all that, I knew what I had to do. I had to check the attic. Before I even considered taking notes or looking at the clay impressions, I had to know what was up there. The only way I could do that was to cut one of the locks off. And to do that I had to go out to the shed and get a hacksaw.

My room seemed somehow strange, alien, as if I hadn't been in it for weeks rather than just a couple of days. Nothing had been disturbed, and a quick glance under the bed showed me that the spider had not found another way in. The old diary was still securely sealed in the plastic container, and seeing it again triggered that half-formed memory of something that I'd read in it but whose content was annoyingly elusive. A mythological reference perhaps.

I had retrieved my coat and pack from the lobby on the way up and, with some trepidation in anticipation of the worst, carefully unwrapped the globe for the oil lamp. Against all odds, it was intact. I brought it to the sink to clean it and discovered that task was going to take more than just the usual soap I kept there. I did the best I could, dried it, and mounted it on its base. I would give it to Margaret at dinner. I retrieved a bottle of wine from my now depleted reserves and placed it near the lamp so that I wouldn't forget.

In any case—the attic. That was next. It was already dark outside, and now I realized how potentially vulnerable I was with the shotgun a bit too obvious and the .380 down in Margaret's apartment. I filled in the gap with a folding knife that I could conceal in my pocket, but it did not inspire anywhere near the confidence of a gun, especially when I thought of the noise I'd heard from the darkened forest two nights before. I'd had some weapons training in my martial arts education and thought that would give me an edge over an untutored opponent, but a training floor was a long way from the real thing. I knew I needed to find a way to have the .380 with me at all times.

The first thing I did was move the tractor back into the shed. Once I parked it, I stood there in silence feeling myself in the middle of a percolating counter-reality, some sort of ectoplasmic intrusion into normality that I was not able to cope with. It was clear there was a series of events now in motion whose intent or direction I was unable to penetrate. And because I could not penetrate it, I could not act, a powerlessness conducive to a growing sense of desperation. The desiccated remains of the once-living child hiding above me on the third floor resonated in the empty chamber that my mind had become. In a word, I felt helpless.

And defenseless. As I hunted for a hacksaw on the workbench, I knew I could not go into the attic without the .380. The shotgun would be too unwieldy and the knife too questionable. That meant I had to go down to the apartment to get it, then come back and check out the attic. It could not be done after dinner because Sonya would be put to bed and Margaret clearly had other plans. What did that leave me with?

Only one other option—I would get up in the night to check the building as I'd done in the past, grab the .380 from the gym bag, and go to the attic. Margaret would be asleep, and our visitor would be most likely either on the prowl or preparing to do so. I would surprise him by either entering the attic before he left, or being there when he returned. That meant I had to have cut the lock beforehand so that I could just slip it off the hasp.

I found the hacksaw hanging on a nail above the bench. Near it, incongruously obvious, was a large bundle of keys also hanging on a nail. I stared at them for a second, then took them as well. I figured I might as well see if any of them fit the locks on the attic doors before I tried to cut them off.

It was pitch black when I left the shed, and once again I had to feel my way toward the silhouette of the Ropewalk. Apprehensive now that something or someone was nearby, a bear-cloaked outcast maybe, I instinctively tuned my hearing to the silence around me. The wind had picked up and was strafing the trees with an insistent hiss, but other than that, there was nothing. I let myself in and wrapped the chain through the handles. Then I went straight up to my room, got my flashlight, and went to the attic door at my end of the hall.

The first thing I did was listen with my ear to the paneling. As always, I heard the building creaking and groaning, and the muffled thudding of gusts of wind against the clapboards sounded like someone beating a carpet in a far-off field. But other than that there was nothing, no thump-thumping such as I'd heard that first night in Margaret's apartment when I had half fallen asleep and some wakeful muse called me back to listen. But then, that was probably the cat padding along on some unseen catwalk—literally—somewhere deep in the walls, totally inaccessible. Or was simply the wind again, hammering its endless threat against the flanks of the building.

But here there was nothing. I turned on the flashlight, shined it once quickly down the hall just to see if anything was there, then examined the lock. I noted the make and searched through the keys for something with the same name. There were seven. One by one I tried them, harboring no real expectation that any of them would work, when the fifth one slid right in and popped the lock with no effort at all. I pulled it out and untied the string that held the keys together so that I could keep that one in my pocket. Realizing that I had neither the time to check it out nor the .380 to use as a persuader, I locked it again and placed my ear against the paneling. Still nothing. If there was someone up there, he evidently had not heard me fumbling with the lock.

"Well," I whispered, "that was easy."

The rest would have to wait. I went back to my room, took the old diary out of its container, and leafed through it absently in the hopes that I might come across whatever that "thing" was that I had been trying to remember. The index cards that I had used as page markers were the obvious places to start, and the first one I opened to was the place where I had read the name "Madeline Cane." I went back to the beginning of that passage and started re-reading it, and the moment I'd absorbed the first words the mental obfuscation vanished and I realized what I had been trying to recall. She had put her hand into some sort of "corrupting liquid"—which, by then, I was convinced was just dirty water—while she and her companions were on a "reconnaissance." After that she fell ill, and I just naturally assumed from the description, in particular the garbled "speaking in tongues," that they were talking about a mild stroke, which would have been some devilish malady in an age that did not even know much about blood circulation. It was that event that had led me to search for her gravestone and brought me the qualified success I had had that day. But in my excitement at discovering a name, I had paid no attention to an obvious piece of information that begged the entire question of what her affliction was: *Where* were they when this incident occurred?

◆ ◆ ◆

When dinner was over and Sonya had been put to bed, I gave Margaret the old oil lamp. She was absolutely delighted. Before I came down, I had spent some time cleaning the brass base and buffing it to a dull luster, so that by the time I gave it to her, it at least looked like it had come out of an antique shop rather than a musty old cellar. When I told her where I'd found it—withholding nothing this time, since she already knew of the house in the cedars—she was even more entranced.

History momentarily came alive under her hand as she admired its graceful lines and speculated on the role it had no doubt played in spiriting runaway slaves to Canada. She had lamp oil and a wick and wanted to try it right then and there, and although I had some reservations about it, I agreed. Like the base itself, the feed mechanism for the wick was of brass and, hence, was not rusty, but would move only a small amount and had to be freed up. This I managed to accomplish with the lamp oil itself. We then filled it with oil, checked for leaks, soaked the wick and fed it through the gate, and lit it. It sputtered for a second and then settled into a soft glow.

"Not bad for something that hasn't been used for over a century, maybe two," I said.

She nodded and leaned over to lower the flame a tiny bit, then settled back on the couch next to me. I glanced over and saw that she was relaxed, smiling, tiny flecks of light glinting from the dark pools of her eyes—it lent her an air of mystery, this unfocused semi-darkness—as some happy thought danced in her mind. No penny for her thoughts, though, which quickly became clear as she turned and leaned back so that I was cradling her head and shoulders on my lap. She closed her eyes and sighed as I lightly stroked her neck and breasts.

"Shall we open the wine?" she finally said, not bothering to open her eyes.

"Yes."

She got up so that I could go to the kitchen to open the bottle and get a couple of glasses, and when I returned she was gone, but emerged from the bedroom a moment later wrapped in her bathrobe. I poured us both a glass and we clinked them together.

"So, what happened after you came out of the hearth into the cellar?" she asked, indicating where I had left the story before I went to get the wine.

"Oh, yeah. I found two doors mounted in the wall. One was a root cellar and the other covered a passage that led to an underground spring that was their water source. The spring flowed into a break in the wall, and I think that was how one could escape from the house. I'm pretty sure it comes out in that well that you saw when you went there with the group last summer."

"It comes out in the well?"

"I'm speculating, but I think that's where it goes. The passage is big enough for a person to enter as long as you don't mind walking in the water, and it makes sense that there would have to be a way out of the cellar." I glanced at her over the rim of my glass.

"Don't tell me . . ." she began.

"Yes. Next summer. How about it? I won't risk it alone, and I won't reveal the existence of the house to anyone else. You wait in the cellar and I'll go into the break and see where it comes out. What do you say?"

She smirked and shook her head in resignation. "You and your need to know. It sounds dangerous but, yes, I'll wait to see if you come out again. What do I do if you don't?" She put her glass on the coffee table and leaned into me so that our noses were almost touching.

"Well, I guess in that case you should advise the school administration that they're going to need a new history teacher."

She backed away with a laugh and gave me a playful nudge. "That's it? Those are your last words? 'Tell the department head we left off on chapter twelve.' That's one hell of a way to enter immortality."

"If a better epitaph occurs to me I'll let you know."

She laughed again, took a sip of wine, then put the glass down and forced me back onto the couch so that I was half lying down. I struggled to put my own glass onto the table without spilling anything while she lay down on top of me, her bathrobe opening a slight bit so that part of her breasts showed with tantalizing brevity as she lowered herself.

"Right here?" I asked with a smile, thinking of Sonya just one door away.

Her eyes said no, just this, as she came closer and we kissed and I thought: Yes, what if love really *is* this flaming passion that, once ignited, burns itself to extinction and thinks *nothing* of whatever uses biology might have for the act? What if it is *not* that diluted accommodation we all live with and that results from the need to think of long-term plans?

No matter. Her own trembling passion told me that she was feeling the same thing as, breathless, she pulled herself away and led me by the hand to her bedroom, where she discarded the robe and frantically helped me undress, tossing my clothes aside as if they were shackles. Then we were all over each other, near the bed, on the bed, under the covers, laying siege to each others' missing moments with such burning abandon that only a smoldering exhaustion was left when it ended.

I held her then until she fell asleep, feeling her breath on my shoulder, marveling at how right I had been about her innate sense of the erotic and its role in stoking the fires that separated love from mere like. I could not suppress a smile.

God is a woman, I thought. No doubt about it.

♦ ♦ ♦

What I had not done was tell her I was going to check the building during the night. I glanced briefly at the clock and saw that it was still relatively early and that I might actually get a few hours sleep before I had to get up and do that. At two or three o'clock, I thought, knowing that I was still wired enough to wake up somewhere in that range even without any kind of alarm.

I lay there with a heightened sense of everything around me, all of it covered in a thick blanket of darkness and filled with amorphous, unmoving shapes that took on shifting identities the longer I stared at them. I could not sleep in spite of my exertions earlier in the day. To reassure myself, I let my arm casually fall to the side of the bed and groped around until I found my gym bag, then reached inside and took out the .380. I also pulled out a pair of sweatpants that I knew I would need when I went to check the building. I slipped the .380 under the pillow and rolled over so that I would not be able to see the dark silhouettes in the room. The wind exploded against the building in a sudden gust that almost made me sit up as I imagined someone breaking in through one of the students' rooms. I lay there listening for some sort of follow up, and although my hearing was now fine-tuned to the slightest of sounds, there was nothing to hear but the banshee-like moan of that same wind moving through the trees. Nothing abrupt, nothing oddly rhythmic.

Margaret lay there calm and serene, her breathing coming in a series of gentle sighs that told me her dreams were untroubled with the types of images now waiting at the edges of mine. Assailed by a sudden doubt, I got out of bed and went to the door of the apartment to make sure I had slid the deadbolts into place. For the first time since I installed them, I genuinely appreciated having them. I now understood Margaret's insistence on having two; as massive as they were, one would seem inadequate given the reality I now faced.

Both were engaged. Feeling a little more secure, I went over to the living room window and pulled the shade outward for a quick look. What light there was did not reveal any tracks of any kind in the snowfield, and with that additional piece of security, I let the shade go and went back to bed. Fatigue eventually caught up to me and I fell into a fitful sleep that did not leave me feeling rested when I snapped out if it around quarter to three.

I was sure I had heard that thump-thumping again, as of a far off drum or a stick on a hollow log. Or had I dreamed it? I listened, but again all that came to me was the shrieking of the wind as it lashed the trees outside, having clearly picked up in intensity. I was wide awake now, not lazily pulling myself out of a vaporous torpor because of a bathroom call, but try as I might I could not verify that the sound was real. I slipped out from under the covers, pulled on the sweatpants and my heavy woolen shirt, grabbed the .380, and went out to the living room. The little nightlight in one of the sockets was bright enough so that I didn't need the flashlight.

Nothing was out of place. I went over and looked out the window again, saw that the moon had risen and the snowfield was bathed in a lurid swath of extraordinarily bright moonlight, noted once again the absence of any tracks, and went to the door to listen.

I put the .380 down on a lamp table so that I would not accidentally make a sound when I placed my ear against the door. At first there was nothing out of the ordinary, and I found myself distracted by the nearly inaudible ticking of the mantle clock on the armoire, but then, creeping up on me so slowly that at first I did not even realize I was hearing it, came the sound. Far off, faint, so maddeningly hard to hear that it hovered between imagination and fact, so much so that I found myself having to hold my breath so that the sound of my own breathing did not interfere. I backed away, turned toward the bedroom to get my slippers and flashlight, and walked straight into a figure standing behind me.

I nearly jumped out of my clothes. It was Margaret, nude and hugging herself against the cold of the apartment, her hair disheveled and eyes narrowed to slits as if she were asleep on her feet.

"What are you doing up?" she whispered, then, scanning me quickly, added, "Why are you dressed? Going somewhere?"

"I was just going to check the building like I did before. Did I wake you?"

She managed a trace of a smile and shook her head. "Call of the wild," she explained, pointing toward the bathroom. "Don't you think it's pretty silly to do this? I mean, we know it's just a cat. By the way, did you leave anything out for it tonight?"

I shrugged. "I forgot. Did you?"

"No. You can take some of the leftovers from the fridge if you want."
She headed for the bathroom. "Really, though, Egan—come back to
bed. You can feed the cat in the morning." She disappeared behind the
door, and I took the opportunity to put on my socks and slippers, grab
the flashlight, and conceal the .380 under one of the couch cushions.
When she emerged, she pulled herself to me—as much to warm up as
out of emotion, I thought—and repeated her admonishment to return
to bed.

"It's just a precaution," I countered. "It'll only take a few minutes
and I'm already dressed for it."

She smiled, shook her head in resignation, kissed me, and headed
for the bedroom. "Hurry back. I still get a little nervous, even if it is
just a cat."

I waited until I heard the bedsprings creaking before I went to the
refrigerator to get some morsels for the cat, just so that she could hear
it and I could later say I had done it. "A prop," I mumbled with that
untoward feeling of cunning of someone trying to put something over
on someone else, which was exactly what I was doing but for what I
imagined were the right reasons. I filled the small jar with water as
well, then listened outside the bedroom door to make sure she was
asleep. Satisfied that she was, I took the .380, checked the clip just to
be sure, and quietly slid the deadbolts back.

Caution being the better part of valor, I propped my foot against
the bottom of the door just in case our guest was already there and had
decided to barge in. I left the flashlight off as I opened the door about
three inches; I figured that, if there really was someone out there, I
stood a better chance of surprising him if I didn't flag my intrusion with
a flashlight beam.

The nightlights were still on, which was a good sign. There was
obviously no one standing in front of the door on the side I could see
and, feeling more confident, I opened it wide enough to look around
the jamb at the other side. There was no one there either, and the hall
was absolutely quiet but for the muffled and intermittent pounding of
the wind, which sounded like distant thunder in the long, hollow tube
of the hallway. I was about to step out when I realized I had forgotten
the keys to both the attic and the apartment. So much for my cunning;
I would have gotten to the attic and discovered I couldn't open it, then
realized I couldn't get back into the apartment either. I closed the door

and slunk back into the bedroom to retrieve the keys from my pants. Margaret stirred but did not wake up. While I was there I went all out and grabbed my sweatshirt as well. It was going to be cold in the attic, and besides, the pockets were big enough to hold the .380. So, with the gun in my pocket, the cat scraps in one hand and the flashlight—still turned off—in the other, I stepped out into the hall.

I made sure the door was locked behind me as I noiselessly moved down toward the lobby. My hearing seemed to have intensified, as if a radio that I had long been scarcely able to hear had been suddenly turned up. Every creak and moan of the building sounded as if it originated right under me, and I was convinced that even the cat had to be lying low or I would've heard it, too. I wondered if that was another of those animal responses that, like sensing you were being watched, lay dormant in the instinctive mind until the right level of stress was reached. And stress was something I had in abundant supply just then.

About halfway to the lobby I stopped, lowered myself to a crouch, and listened with my ear to the wall. There was nothing. For several minutes, barely breathing, I crouched there, expectant. But still there was nothing. I got up and continued toward the lobby, staying close to the wall to avoid the loose floorboards.

The one narrow window above the double door allowed a faint streamer of moonlight to enter, and this pale shaft fell on the couch against the wall opposite the stairs. I studied its camouflaged depths expecting to see the cat emerge as it had done before, but nothing stirred, so I went over and, with my hand over the lens, turned on the flashlight in order to see the food bowl. It was empty, which was no surprise. I filled it with the scraps, dumped the jar of water into the other bowl, turned off the light, and headed for the stairs.

It seemed incredibly dark up on my floor, and for a moment my nape hairs prickled as I wondered if the nightlights were now turned off up there. Instant uncertainty followed, the type of assailing doubt that froze you in your tracks while wild imaginings stomped on your ability to reason. Why would they be out up there? Did whoever it was somehow *know* that I was going up to check out the attic? Impossible. No one knew, not even Margaret. Tentative steps followed as I sought to negotiate the stairs without making any noise. My hand still covered the flashlight but now, all pretense gone, I took out the .380 and very quietly chambered a round. When I flipped on the safety, it sounded to my heightened hearing like a door slamming. I waited several seconds before proceeding, just to be sure.

When I got up there, I saw that the nightlights had not been turned off, much to my relief. Evidently, the hallway was usually that dark, and I had just never noticed before. I went over to the door to the attic and pressed my ear against the paneling.

And there it was—the thump-thumping I had heard before. It was louder, closer, clearly and obviously coming from the attic, or maybe the roof. I put the .380 on the floor and fished in my pocket for the key. Since I knew that sounds would be magnified as they traveled through the walls, I worked it into the lock as slowly and quietly as I could. When it bottomed out, I held the lock as I opened it so that no "snap" would result. Then I removed it from the hasp with as little metal-to-metal contact as possible.

Done. I put the lock in my pocket along with the key, picked up the .380, and listened again. The sound had stopped. I waited for a reaction—the sound of footsteps, a roof hatch slamming shut, a voice, anything. One minute, two, finally five passed, and I knew it was time to go in or whoever it was would have too long a lead on me, assuming he hadn't already vanished. I quietly opened the hasp and was about to pull the door open when the sound resumed. There it was—confirmation that I had not been detected.

I dreaded opening the panel because I was sure that the hinges were rusted and would squeal in protest, signaling my arrival in a way that I could do nothing about. I didn't have any oil, nor had I seen any in the shed, nor would it have been possible to lubricate far enough into the hinge from this side in any case. So, with my last subtlety gone, I felt I might as well go for it. If it gave me away, I would sprint up the steps to the attic floor with the flashlight blazing so that I could temporarily blind whoever he was. That was my default plan "B" and, with the .380 held in readiness, I pulled on the hasp and the door outlined itself in the paneling as it opened. Incredibly, the hinges were silent. I closed the door behind me and sank to a crouch at the foot of a short flight of stairs.

Instantly, the thumping sound became louder, clearly telling me that I still had not been discovered. Unexpectedly, I could actually see up into the attic without the flashlight. This, I realized, was because the hatches in the roof had windows and were letting the moonlight in, which had clearly been a good idea for the workmen who had refurbished the place back in the fifties. So I left the flashlight off as I slowly, on all fours to distribute my weight, crawled up the stairs.

I was right under the slant of the roof as I drew level with the floor. Before me, as far as I was able to see in the intermittent streamers of light, was a broad, flat plain of floorboards stretching into an infinity of darkness that thickened, despite the hatches, as it receded. I could not see the end, but I could see that both sides had a sort of railing—almost like a fence—that ran what appeared to be the entire length of the building. Parts of that railing were closed up so that they were more of a low barricade or wall, and from what little I could see from where I was, there appeared to be some sort of structures—maybe old rope making machinery—behind those barriers. The noise was coming from some point about halfway down the building, on the right.

I waited for several minutes, suddenly unsure of what my plan should be. If I stood up and walked, I would almost certainly be spotted, and the confrontation would lose the element of surprise. But I doubted that my knees would hold up long enough to crawl that distance, so I compromised and settled on a bent over, crouching crab-walk. Whatever it was, I had to do it soon; the cold was intense, and whatever meager heat radiated up through the floor was not enough to keep my hands from stiffening. I had thought of everything except a pair of gloves.

The moment I decided to move I saw something detach itself from the shadows and lope across one of the shafts of light. I was startled but not surprised; it was the cat. So I had been right—it really was living in the attic. Somehow, it knew a way in and out, some loose panel or missing board somewhere. But it could not have been the source of the sound. I watched as it disappeared down into the depths of the hall, its footfalls audible through the floor in spite of its natural stealth. But the thumping sound had continued unabated.

So the jig was up. Someone was up there, no doubt about it. I couldn't suppress a grin as I imagined myself going up to the school administrator and saying: "Did you know there's someone living in your attic?" With that thought in mind, I crept out of the stairwell and onto the floor.

The crab-walk was an exhausting technique but I kept it up, staying as close to the fence or barrier as I could. When the sound stopped, I stopped, each time thinking I had been discovered. When I got within about ten feet of it, I paused to take stock of what I was about to do. Just ahead, probably crouched down among the various undefined pieces of furniture or apparatus, was the nightwalker, real after all. My heart was pounding. I glanced down at the gun, fully aware of the terminal nature of having to use it, suddenly haunted by the specter of homicide and prison time. What if it was a harmless bum after all? The safety was still on, but to be doubly sure I lowered the hammer to the half-cock position. With both safeties activated, the chances of an accidental discharge were extremely small. And I would keep it pointed upwards unless there really was a danger.

Other than that, there was nothing to do but stand up and confront the intruder. There was enough light so that I didn't even need the flashlight so, leaving it off, I took a couple of deep breaths to still my heart, then rose and looked over the barrier.

There, crouched on the floor under the eaves, was a small, furry shape, like an ape of some sort, furiously and apparently futilely hammering away at what looked like of can of fruit or vegetables. All around it were other cans, dented and torn open, their contents gone. Its dense fur was dark and lank and, after the first shock of seeing it wore off, I understood the reality of what it was.

A child. A homeless, wild child with long, black, unkempt hair, wearing what looked like part of a bearskin to ward off the cold. Its back was to me and it mumbled to itself as it struck the can with what looked like a stone with a dull point. I stood there spellbound, speechless, not knowing whether to feel oddly privileged at discovering such a creature or full of sublime sympathy for its plight. For several long, breathless moments I watched, vainly trying to decipher the language it was speaking. Then, in one of those abrupt reversals that sometimes happen, I leaned over the barrier to better hear what it was saying and the lock from the attic door squeezed out of my pocket and crashed to the floor like a fist on a drum.

The little thing shot several feet into the air and came back down facing me, took one quick look and, with preternatural speed, bolted between two shadowed, shapeless artifacts behind it. And vanished.

I stood for a moment in stunned silence to try to put some order to what I had just seen. Part of me waited for the child to come out of the other side of whatever it had hidden behind, but the greater part of me struggled with the priceless disbelief of the moment itself.

For the child was Sonya. And she had been talking.

◆ ◆ ◆

Chapter 25

I couldn't move. What I had just seen replayed itself in my mind, flashed through me like something out of a dream. As if through a fog, I saw myself approaching a door, long unused, and beyond it was an undefined truth, long hidden or discarded. Through no transition of logic, I then found myself in this unfrequented room. Undefined furniture lay about in a generally orderly fashion—undefined because I couldn't quite focus on it, as if I were seeing it in the murky semi-light of a dream world. Which was exactly how I felt just then.

Then I recovered. A couple of quick steps toward the other side of the amorphous shapes she had darted behind told me she had not emerged there, yet she was nowhere to be seen. It was as if she had disappeared into the floor. I grabbed the lock, turned and sprinted back toward the stairwell, leaped down the steps, secured the door, and vaulted down the stairs to the first floor. Margaret's door seemed infinitely far away.

My hands were shaking, as much from the cold of the attic as from the shock of what I'd just seen. It took me several tries to get the key aimed into the doorknob, but when I did, I rushed into the room and slammed the door, completely oblivious to the noise I was making. I made a beeline for Sonya's room.

The door was closed, of course. Margaret had told me she preferred to sleep that way, and at first I thought that odd in a child but now I understood why. I opened it and went in. The bed was disheveled, the covers thrown back—and the child was gone. I stood there, my mind a blank, and then heard Margaret's voice from the bedroom.

"Egan?" Her voice was edged with nervousness. "Is everything alright?"

I turned and burst into her room. "Sonya's gone," I panted. Margaret stared at me, saying nothing. "She's gone. Her room's empty." She continued to stare. "Don't you understand? She's gone."

She placed her finger across her lips to silence me, held out her hand to bring me to her, strangely uncaring, bizarrely detached. What was wrong with her? I wondered, and, as if in answer, she threw back the covers of the bed and there was Sonya, sound asleep in the place I had occupied earlier. "She's right here," she whispered. "She came to me right after you left to check the building. I could tell she had had another one of her bad dreams. It happens sometimes. Ben and I used to let her sleep between us whenever that happened." She bent over and kissed the girl's forehead, cast a sidelong glance at me, and said: "Do you mind sleeping on the couch for the rest of the night? I'm sorry, but . . . ." She bent over Sonya again for another kiss.

I stood there like a fool, like some comic messenger bearing a missive that had gotten lost in the mail and was now old news. How could this be? I wondered. I had just seen her up in the attic wearing ragged furs and punching open cans of fruit. How could this be?

"Egan? Do you mind using the couch?" she repeated.

"What? No, I don't mind." Noncomprehension must have shown through whatever façade I was wearing because Margaret's eyes never left me, her brow clouded with doubt, or maybe mistrust. I knew I had to leave before the questioning started, but it was too late. As I turned to go, she accosted me.

"Did you see something out in the hall?" she whispered, her look one of subdued agitation.

Where was I now? I wondered. In the dream or in the apartment? Had I seen the girl or not? "No," I lied, pinioned to the untenable truth of my position. "I mean, yes, sort of. I saw the cat again, but this time it scared the bejesus out of me." There—another barely viable half-truth.

She slipped out of bed and came to me, took my hand, and led me into the living room. Peripherally, almost mechanically, I noticed that she'd put her flannel nightgown on, a clear indication that the moment we'd enjoyed earlier had passed, and she was once again the mother, not the lover. "You had me going there for a moment. You should've seen your face—for a while I thought for sure you had found something awful." She put her arms around my neck and moved in for a kiss, rubbing up against me sensuously, all smiles and apologies. "Sorry about having to put you out like this, but she's asleep now and I don't want to disturb her. She was pretty agitated when she came in."

"No problem. You said she came in right after I left?"

"Yes. I heard her door open a few minutes after you stepped out. I knew immediately what it meant."

"So she's been in your bed the whole time I've been out?"

She drew back, her brow knit in confusion. "Of course. What an odd question. What is this, some kind of investigation?"

The question had a comic overtone that I realized was only partially genuine; it was an accommodation, an appeasement, a gesture full of real meaning but delivered in a way that was meant to not be overly confrontational. I had struck one of the instinctive nerves and knew enough to not push on it.

"Oh, no, I was just wondering if maybe I had been the cause of the bad dream. You know, making too much noise on the way out or something like that." Another slick and pale lie, but more a tack than a deception because now I was confused, poised on the edge of a mental abyss such as I had never experienced before.

She sighed and wrapped herself around me again. "Don't be silly. She's had these before, and all it takes is the reassuring nearness of her mother." She paused, looked down for a moment as if searching for the right words, then added, "and her father." The ensuing silence provided all the explanation I would ever need—I was not her father, therefore I should not be there. "Do you need any help getting the couch ready?"

"No. I'll just use the sleeping bag." It was still on a chair in the corner, nearly behind the Christmas tree.

"I feel really bad about this."

"Now you're being silly. I've spent half my life in a sleeping bag, curled up in places a lot less comfortable than the couch. I would like a pillow, though."

She kissed me again, broke away, and went to her bedroom to retrieve one of the extra pillows. I took the opportunity to question my sanity while I went over what had just happened. Someone had been up there, a child, a girl. That someone had disappeared behind whatever the objects around her were. She had been trying to open canned foods with a stone. I thought she was Sonya, but clearly she was not—my mind must have been playing tricks, mixing shadows with extreme fatigue to convince me of non-realities. What had I missed this time?

A surge of panic suddenly seized me as I realized I no longer had the .380 in my hand and had no idea where it was. I felt my pockets but it was not there, and could not have been or Margaret would've felt it when she held me. Frantic now, I looked around the room thinking I had dropped it but did not see it anywhere. I was on the verge of a compulsive sprint back out the door and up the hallway when she emerged holding the pillow. I fought with every reserve of strength I had to maintain my composure.

"Will the bag be warm enough?" she asked.

"It'll be fine. This is my 'zero-degrees-if-you're-in-a-tent' bag, remember?"

"Oh, yeah, right." She smiled, her fatigue returning as she handed me the pillow. "It's almost four o'clock, Egan. We need to get some sleep. I'll see you in the morning." She pressed a finger to her lips, then lightly transferred the symbolic kiss to mine. A tiny wave and she was gone, leaving me standing there with the pillow and a surging wave of near nausea over the loss of the .380.

For Sonya's sake she closed the bedroom door, and the moment she did that, I threw the pillow on the couch and vaulted over to the door to see if I had put the gun down outside when I was fumbling with the key to the apartment. But there was nothing there. I closed it, secured the deadbolts, and headed for Sonya's room. I didn't want to possibly alarm Margaret by turning on the overhead light—which I was sure she would hear—so I used the flashlight to search. And there, on the dresser beside the door, was the .380. Evidently, even in my panic I'd had the presence of mind to not let Margaret see it and had placed it there before I went into her room.

I calmed down. Alright, I thought. The nightwalker was real but not a danger to us. Margaret would be appalled to learn of a homeless child trying to survive on smashed-open canned food, but I was in no position to do anything about it. The obvious came to mind first—there had to be a house somewhere, a forgotten farmstead lost in the forest, winnowed out from the fringes of society long before and securely camouflaged by the creepers of time itself. In this place lived a social castoff, a human derelict, who had had a daughter who had never known anything but the meager reality of that microcosm. The parent or parents had died or vanished, leaving the child to fend for herself. Desperate for food, she had wandered away. Somehow, she found a way into the Ropewalk and came upon a cache of canned goods.

But there was something else as well, a genetic link that I hadn't even considered when I first noted how different Sonya was from her parents: since the child in the attic had looked like Sonya, it suddenly occurred to me that maybe Sonya was not Ben's daughter. Was it possible that Margaret had had *another* affair before the one with Nick Cephalos, this one resulting in a pregnancy whose origin Ben had never suspected? Or maybe he did. Maybe that was why he had no reservations about leaving her—Sonya wasn't his. But if that were the case, who was the father? And here the wild imaginings took over again as I recalled apocryphal tales of genetically watered-down fringe dwellers, inbred for generations, producing composite images in human form who epitomized the evolutionary skid row joked about in biology classes. And they would all look more or less alike. Was that it? My better sense denied it, was repulsed by the very notion of her getting it on with some sort of Quasimodo-like character. But then, she had made that comment once about always being attracted to what she called "rare birds." But could she possibly go that far?

It did not end even there. There was still a frightened, freezing little girl running around somewhere in the building, but even knowing that she was not a danger to us did not lessen the need for caution and possible defense. Sil was still out there and had to be kept out of the picture. In spite of everything, the possibility that he was a killer was still very much on my mind and clearly took precedence over locating a homeless child who, however pitiable, was obviously able to survive on her own. Besides, that was an issue for the local authorities, who would know of any hidden homesteads and be able to best-guess where she had come from.

But it was all a useless sophistry. My mind was in total turmoil by the time I got undressed and slipped into the sleeping bag. No matter what rationale I applied, there would be no justification for any decision I would make from that point forward. I was lying there in a warm cocoon while a child scrabbled for food shards somewhere in the building. I should have been trying to find her but knew just from what I saw of her that it would be a fruitless search, and even if it weren't, the clock that would bring Sil back to the Ropewalk was still ticking, and he had to be dealt with first, for all our sakes.

I draped my forearm across my eyes to block out the nightlight. Sleep would be a long time coming. The image of the child in the attic would simply not go away, and the more I tried to envision her, the less she looked like Sonya until, finally, I had to concede that all I could recall was the dark hair and the bearskin wrap. The connection with the fur I had found in the Engineering building then leaped to the forefront and sent me on a mental sidebar journey whose sense also eluded me. Was that her as well?

"No, no, no, that was not it," I mumbled, as my mind suddenly vaulted away from the girl and back to Margaret in another example of that "tectonic brain slippage" to which I was prone. Her "rare birds" were, no, not an assemblage of human oddities found in discarded corners of the social underworld, but simply a necessary constituent of that heightened sense of the erotic that I'd seen in her. Nothing more. Yes, that was it, she meant Bohemianism, not social lepers. Reassurance returned, tenuous as the threads I had strung across the stairwell nearly a week before. I lay there lecturing to myself in imitation of a schizophrenic while I threw one explanation after another at the questions before me in the hopes that something would stick.

And then, out of nowhere, it occurred to me that, when I had gone back into Sonya's room looking for the gun, it had been cold in there, just as it was that day when Margaret asked me to check the radiator. I pulled the arm away from my eyes and stared at the ceiling as if expecting to find an answer there. The cold had come from the closet last time, prompting me to suggest that we put more insulation in the walls, which I hadn't done, but which Margaret had countered by sealing the bottom of the closet door with a towel.

I sat up, realized in spite of my fatigue that I simply had to know, and got up to go look. The girl's room had warmed up a bit because I had left the door open, but even given that, I noticed the draft snaking around my ankles the moment I entered. I could see even before I got to it that the towel was still on the floor, but angled away from the door, which would happen if the door were opened and then closed, leaving the towel in its last position like a glacial moraine. I looked inside but saw nothing, and although it was cold in there, I could see no connection to any of what had just happened. As for why the towel was moved, the explanation was simple—Sonya had gone in there looking for something sometime during the night.

So I pushed the towel back into position and came away with nothing. In spite of the discovery that the night visitor was a harmless child, I shined the flashlight at the door to reassure myself that I had slid the deadbolts into place. And I had the .380 stashed under the pillow, loaded but not chambered. If necessary, I could hide it in the sleeping bag in the morning.

Then exhaustion finally overtook me and I drifted off. Fitful shadows darted at the edges of my inner vision as I moved slowly through that plasma that held me fast in most of my dreams. But no vistas came, just an abrupt abyss with gray skies beyond, and when I looked down, I was staring into the chasm below the old ropewalk. Opposite me were the petroglyphs. One of these outlined itself in red and began to move, pulled away from the wall and scuttled off, crab-like. It was a giant spider. It turned, went down the wall, and vanished into the giant drain hole. Then, as I watched, it climbed back out on my side of the chasm and began coming up toward me. I tried to move but my legs were frozen in that very same plasma, and up it came, getting nearer, until finally it was at the lip but wasn't a spider any more. It had metamorphosed into a small ape-like thing, the very one I'd seen before in another dream, and it stopped just below me, opened a small door in the chasm wall, and reached in.

The lights went out. Even in my sleep I knew what that meant.

◆ ◆ ◆

Morning dawned dull and cloudy with the wind increasing in strength and a slate-gray overcast heralding the onset of another storm in a day or two. Drumbeats were hammering in my head, but whether they were real or just the ocean beating itself to froth against the rocky ramps of the shoreline, I had no way of knowing. I glanced at the clock on the armoire: eight o'clock. I was still tired but got up anyway to make sure I was dressed by the time Margaret and Sonya came out. I rolled up the sleeping bag and stashed the .380 into it. I would move it back to the bedroom that night, assuming Sonya wasn't still having bad dreams.

The subtle imagery of the dream came back to me while I was shaving, and I knew enough by then to not simply ignore what it was trying to tell me. It was no mystery where the giant spider image came from, but I needed to look more closely at the pictures of the petroglyphs to see if any of the carvings were actually spiders. Nor was the origin of the ape-like thing hard to guess. But it wasn't until I had finished and was drying my face that the real meaning struck me—how had this wild child, a functionally illiterate backwoods Cinderella of some sort, known to turn off the circuit breakers? Even more specifically, how did she know to turn off that particular one?

This was the dilemma that had been climbing up the wall toward me. I stared at my image in the mirror for a minute, seeing nothing, waiting for the answer to reveal itself. When nothing did, I hung the towel back up and grabbed my shirt, intending to go down and examine the utility closet more closely. I fully expected to find the nightlights in the hallway out, but when I opened the door, they were still on. But before I could take another step, Margaret's door opened and she emerged holding Sonya wrapped in a blanket. I withdrew back into the apartment, pulling the door closed behind me with all the nonchalance I could muster.

"Leaving again?" she asked. "I'm beginning to wonder about you."

"Just going down to the corner store for a newspaper," I said. "Actually, I was checking to make sure the nightlights were still on." My half-truths were becoming half-lies.

She nodded and put Sonya down, who immediately ran up to me and held out her hand. In it was a small leaf like the one I had found pressed in the pages of one of her picture books. I squatted down and looked at it. "Is that for me?"

She didn't understand the words, of course, but her insistently outstretched hand provided the answer. I took it from her and pressed it against my forehead as I had seen her do with the branches of the tree. She seemed pleased and a subtle smile curled her lips, and for a moment that odd shape-shifting ability of hers came to the fore and I saw, fleetingly, the face of a normal, happy little girl once again. Only a moment, though, and then it vanished as she turned and ran back to her mother. I stood up and showed Margaret my present.

345

"That means she likes you," she said. "She doesn't give a leaf to just anybody."

I was touched. We were actually bonding. "Must've been the Boston cream pie," I joked. "Guaranteed to break down all resistance."

She smiled and directed Sonya toward the kitchen. "That sky doesn't look too promising. Evidently, there's another storm headed our way. After breakfast we should try to pick up something on the radio."

"Why bother?" I countered with excessive lightheartedness. "It's not like knowing that it's coming is somehow going to interfere with our travel plans."

She laughed and was forced to agree.

◆ ◆ ◆

I went back to the attic after breakfast. I had seen it some months before, when Sil had gone up there and left the door open. But that was only a brief visit, and I had mostly forgotten what was up there. I had brought the flashlight as a matter of course, but now, in the fuller light of day—and even having found the switch that turned on the lights—I really didn't need it. I saw that it held all kinds of things—old school furniture, bizarre and borderline "artwork" done by the students, abandoned luggage, crates of old bottles, even some remnants of the ancient machinery that once made the ropes. It was a continuous, unbroken room, reminiscent of the hallway below but reaching out widthwise to the slant of the roof. There were countless numbers of places where a child could hide. Or even live.

I was making no pretense at stealth this time because, if she had returned to the attic, I wanted to make sure she knew I was coming. I did not want her feeling set upon by a stalker. Announcing my arrival would demonstrate to her a certain openhandedness, a willingness to reach out to her in a way that still left her in control of her situation. At least that was what I hoped.

When I got near the place where I'd seen her, I moved more slowly just in case she was there. She wasn't, but the smashed open cans I'd seen the night before had been no illusion. There must have been a dozen of them all over the floor. I climbed over the railing for a closer look and was caught off guard by what I found.

They were old. These were cans going back to the fifties, maybe even before that. I could tell just by the style and typography of product advertising, which was totally different from the things I was used to seeing. Somewhere in the building was a cache of very old canned goods, and at first I thought it was the attic itself, but when I examined a can that had once contained peaches, I realized it could not be.

The residue in the can was frozen. It was frozen because the attic had no heat. That meant any canned goods stored in the attic would also be frozen, which meant that hammering on them would be like beating on a log. They would neither dent nor open. It also meant that most of them would probably have burst from the water expanding as it froze. But that was not the case with these. These had definitely been hammered until they popped.

So they had to have come from somewhere else.

I pondered this while I moved over toward the crates she had run behind. There was no place to go once I was back there—the only possible exits were the way I had entered or straight ahead and out the other side, neither of which the girl had taken. The nearest roof hatch was a good twenty feet away, so that was not a possibility either. She seemed to have quite literally vanished into the floor, and with that in mind, I studied the space between the crates and the roof.

The explanation was not long in coming. Almost immediately, I spotted what looked like a hatch built flush with the floor at the extreme edge of the joint where the floor and the roof met. On one end was the lift ring. Not knowing what to expect, I turned on the flashlight before I pulled it open.

There was barely enough room to allow the cover to swing out of the way. Below me, gaping upwards like the mouth of a small cave, was a tunnel leading straight down into darkness. The light revealed a ladder affixed to the farther wall, which was also the outside wall of the building itself. The bottom was nothing but a dark slab, presumably of earth. I had no idea what its purpose was.

But I needed to know where it went because, wherever that was, that was where I would find the girl. Once again not trying to be quiet, I lowered myself into the cramped opening, shined the light all around to let her know I was coming, and descended.

I was moving through the wall of the Ropewalk. I fleetingly remembered the spider but reasoned that this part of the structure was too cold to allow it to survive, that it had to restrict its movement to the heating pipes, so I did not expect to run into any of its relatives. Contrary to my survival instincts, I had not brought the .380 but felt that I would not need it now that I knew what our visitor was.

About halfway down I encountered what looked like a door on the inner wall. It was separately paneled, standing off from the planks around it, and appeared to be secured with a series of simple turn latches. Curious but not deterred in my original plan, I continued down the ladder until I at last stood on the bottom. I had no idea where I was, except, of course, that I was now under the building, in some sort of basement. The flashlight showed a rather spacious room completely crammed full of things that I recognized immediately, even in the relatively narrow beam of light.

Canned goods. Row upon row of them, stacked up on shelves and piled high against the walls. The light fell on a switch, and when I flipped it the room came to life. There were cans everywhere, including large, five-gallon sealed pails of water painted olive drab. The room was huge, and in addition to the foodstuffs, there were also large chests labeled "blankets." Against one wall was a stack of fold-up beds and to the right of that hung a picture of President Eisenhower.

Eisenhower. I knew immediately that I was standing in a fallout shelter that had been built in the fifties, which made perfect sense chronologically because that was when the Ropewalk was being renovated for use by the school. Here was the specter of the Cold War in the years when Stalin was still alive, when it was generally accepted that his next move would be a war of annihilation with the West. These shelters had sprung up everywhere, with the basements of schools being the most commonly used venues. In the event of some kind of attack, it would be to this bolthole that the students would flee to wait out the worst of it.

The "worst of it" meant, of course, thermonuclear incineration of everything we called reality. I often wondered if surviving it was even worth the trouble.

In any case, this was where the cans had come from, and I realized that there was no chance Margaret, Sonya, and I would starve before the road was reopened. There was enough food down there for the three of us for probably nine months to a year. To my right I noticed a massive, sliding fire door mounted on overhead rollers. I went up to it and tested to see if I could push it open. I couldn't, but knew immediately what it was. This was the so-called "compressor" room whose dummy circuit breaker I had found in the utility closet and whose name was stenciled on the other side of the door, where it—the door—was securely padlocked. I noticed that the bolt it was attached to on the outside had a large wingnut on the inside so that the occupants could not be locked in. They would be able to get out just by unscrewing it.

Just another footnote in the history of human madness, I thought, as I returned to the subject of trying to find the girl. The room was large but finite, and I began my search on the right side, worked my way down to the end, and came up the left side. There were lots of shelves but no places to hide, and she simply was not there. Other ladders like the one I had just used punctuated the walls on both sides at regular intervals, and I realized—or suspected—that all of them communicated with the attic, and that there were thus numerous ways in and out of the shelter, which would have made perfect sense considering its intent. She had probably scrambled down there, run to some other ladder, and reemerged in the attic at another point after I left. Where she went from there was anyone's guess.

I turned off the light and went back to the ladder. A faint trickle of light reached into the narrow tube from above, but other than that, it was as black as a cave in there. I needed the flashlight just to find the first few rungs.

I stopped at the halfway point to examine the paneled door. I could not let it go, of course, so I turned the latches and, using some extra planking that was clearly intended to be a type of handle, lifted the section away from the wall.

A number of coats on hangers obscured my view. I pushed them aside and saw a partially open door with light beyond it. Not knowing what to do with the panel, I angled it into the space in front of me and stepped off the ladder into whatever was beyond.

I found myself walking on shoes and other objects littering the floor. A few steps and I was at the door, stepped through, and discovered that I was in one of the students' rooms. I had just emerged from the closet.

The closet. The closet was cold. It was cold because it communicated with the attic. It communicated with the attic because—why? I had no idea, but it didn't matter at the moment. I saw the disheveled beds, the familiar bookcase, and knew immediately where I was.

Room eleven.

Chapter 26

By the time I was ready to have lunch with Margaret, I had it all figured out. Two things. One, I knew the reason for the ladders extending from the basement to the attic. They were there so that the workmen who were renovating the Ropewalk in the fifties could get from the top to the bottom of the building without having to walk its entire length each time they needed to run a pipe or wire. The simplest tasks would have taken forever under those conditions. Providing intermediate access thus made perfect economic sense, especially since they had to include more than one way to get into the fallout shelter in any case. Two, the cold emanating from Sonya's closet was no doubt due to the same factor, i.e. that there was an access tunnel behind her closet, which I had not yet verified but fully expected to find.

Beyond that, there was a number three: the girl in the attic. I had dismissed the notion that it was Sonya when I found her sleeping with her mother because it was obvious she could not have moved so fast. But now I realized that was wrong, that she could have scrambled down to the basement, over to the ladder that went past her closet, and come out in her room in much less time than it took me to run from the attic to the apartment. In a word, if that really had been Sonya up there, she could have gotten back to her room long before me, experienced a "bad dream," and climbed in bed with her mother while I was still down in the lobby.

I could not dismiss the fact that the closet door *had* been opened. I knew that from the way the towel had been displaced. It was also true that Margaret had been *asleep* when I went back to retrieve the keys for the attic and the apartment. She had already been *out*—gone, unconscious, so how could she possibly assess the amount of time that had elapsed before Sonya appeared? By any objective standards, she thus had no way of knowing the real time interval between my leaving the apartment and Sonya coming into her room. She thought it was right after I left, but it could have been ten or fifteen minutes later.

Then there was that odd speed and agility I'd seen in the girl so many times and that would have served her in good stead when she scrambled down the ladder from the attic and raced back to her room, which she would have reached before me even if I had followed her right into the fallout shelter. Her speed was uncanny, and I would have been a slow, clumsy aftereffect in the mini-drama unfolding at the top of the building.

When she handed me the leaf, was that a bribe of some sort, a counterweight that, in her mind, would offset my finding her in the attic? Was that her way of saying "Don't tell mom about this?"

Was I putting this together correctly?

I had no way of knowing, but other facts militated against it. Where was the bearskin robe she had been wearing? I did not find it down in the shelter, nor was it rolled up in her closet, which I had discretely checked out on the pretense of scrutinizing the draft in her room once again.

Margaret had prepared sandwiches and was making coffee when I sat down at the table opposite Sonya. As I waited for it to brew, I realized I was sitting across from someone who was totally alien to me in more ways than one. I was no longer so unquestioningly convinced that she did not know what was going on around her, yet could not posit that she had been the girl in the attic either. Among other things, convinced that access to the attic could be had through her closet, I had nevertheless not found a way to open the panel from inside the closet itself. It was almost as if that was only possible from the tunnel. This made perfect sense from the strategic position of the school administration, since the last thing they would want would be students retreating to the attic or fallout shelter to smoke or do drugs. It would be impossible to control.

351

But it left no room for explaining how a small girl could get the panel opened by herself from inside the closet.

I was at a loss. Checkmated. The girl's face was an absolutely inscrutable mask as she sat there staring at nothing while an occasional flicker of what appeared to be a smile would move her lips. When the coffee was finally ready, Margaret joined us and put half a sandwich on Sonya's plate. The girl stared at it as if it were an alien life form.

"Go ahead, honey," said Margaret as she placed the sandwich in Sonya's hand and brought it to her mouth. Sonya sniffed it, then opened up for a tentative nibble. "Not hungry?"

"Maybe she needs to whack it with a stone," I said. It was an idiotic comment, totally out of context, senseless, and out before I knew it.

Margaret turned toward me. "What's that supposed to mean?"

I shook my head. It had been spoken as if in a trance, and I groped in my mind for some sort of absolution. When nothing came right away—how could it?—I sat there like a fool.

"She's not an animal, Egan," she finally said, not without a certain acidic tone, before turning her attention back to the girl.

I dared not go on. Everything was up in the air; nothing balanced. I would not pay the price of losing her just because of what I'd seen. "I didn't mean it that way," I half stammered. "I mean, what I meant was, being a child maybe she needs to kind of turn it into something she can recognize. You know how kids squash bread and mangle peas. That kind of thing." How feeble it sounded.

But it worked. She laughed and shook her head in feigned exasperation. "Where exactly does your knowledge of kids come from? 'Leave it to Beaver'?"

"My own childhood. The peas never had a chance. And the only thing that saved the potatoes was the fact that they were already mashed."

She rolled her eyes and laughed again. "What are you doing this afternoon? Going anywhere?"

Now there was an interesting question. Having discovered that the hallwalker—whoever she was—was real but no threat, I did not necessarily need to stay in the building as I had thought at first. This was good news because I needed to turn my attention to the old diary again, specifically to the section where Madeline Cane contacted the "corrupting liquid." And I really wanted to get back to the village to see the barrow before this next storm hit. Time was running out; once everyone was back from the holidays, it would be out of the question.

I caught her off guard by not answering right away, so she added, "Off to do more work on your project?"

"Yes. I still need to record all the things I saw in the house. And I still haven't gotten a good look at the bone barrow."

She helped Sonya again. "So you're going back there today?"

"No, not today. It's too late for that now. I'll have to go tomorrow. Hopefully the storm won't arrive before tomorrow night."

"What will you be looking for this time?"

"Better shots of the petroglyphs and a close look at the barrow."

She nodded, hesitated, seemed about to say something, then let it go.

"What?" I asked.

She pulled away from Sonya and looked at me. "How are you fixed for food?"

I almost laughed out loud. Fixed? I thought. How does a year's supply of canned goods sound? "Oh, I'm pretty well stocked. Why, are you running low?"

"Well, no—actually, yes, a little. I mean, it'll be close with what I have left."

I got up. "Margaret, what are you saying? Whatever I have is yours—that should be self-evident. The refrigerator in the common kitchen is still pretty well stocked and there's stuff in the freezer, too. All of it ours. Want me to bring it all over?"

She was visibly relieved. "No, that's fine. I just wanted to find out where we stood."

"Whatever's there is for all of us. It's as much yours as mine. There's still quite a bit of meat in the freezer, too, so don't worry about that."

"Milk?"

"I even have some of that." I got up. "Do you have some bags? I'm going to bring it all over now."

She shook her head. "You don't have to do that. It's only right next door. I just hadn't looked in the refrigerator and needed to ask."

"Nevertheless," I persisted and went to the cabinet that she had indicated held the bags. "No point in leaving it for . . ." I suddenly broke off as, with a start, I realized that I was going to say "for the hallwalker," and then thought that maybe I *should* leave it there, that the child in the attic might have already discovered it and be using it to survive. I had not "inventoried" what was in there and thus had no way of knowing if some of it was disappearing.

"No point in leaving it for what?" she asked.

I stood there staring at the bag. "Oh, ah, I was going to say no point in leaving it for the students to pilfer when they return, but that's a week away so, you're right, there doesn't seem to be much point in moving it now. It's only right next door." Good save, I thought.

She waved it off. "Leave it. The whole point was in knowing that we have enough so that we don't have to start rationing or something." She motioned me back to the table. "So you'll be working through the afternoon?"

"Probably. Why, did you have something else in mind?"

She sighed and leaned over to rest her chin in her hand. "Not really. I'm just feeling cooped up. Cabin fever." She turned her head to look out the window. "This overcast doesn't help. I can't wait for spring." She reached out for me. "Don't pay any attention. I'm just brooding."

I returned the favor with a gentle admonishment that her concerns were now mine as well and leaned in for a small kiss. She smiled and said that now would be a good time to go back to the village, since there was obviously another storm coming and we had no way of knowing what it was going to bring. "Unless," she added, "we get some news on the radio."

So she got up to turn it on and I cleared the table. Sonya had gone out to the living room and I left the kitchen as well, fully intending to examine the inside of her closet again. But the little girl was standing in the middle of the room, her arm extended and pointing toward my chest. "What?" I said gently, knowing she could not understand but glancing down at my chest to follow where she was pointing. I had forgotten that I had stuck the leaf in my shirt pocket.

She seemed pleased but uncertain, then came up to me, a timid little wisp of a girl, and when I squatted down to her, she climbed up and put her arms around my neck, and I knew then that she had not been the girl in the attic. No, that had been someone else, I was sure now. I held her and stroked her, and she placed her head on my shoulder, and I said again to myself, no, that had not been Sonya. And I also knew that this gesture of hers was a breakthrough for both of us.

Margaret had been listening to the radio, presumably the weather report. I had paid no attention; it was too far away in any case for me to hear it. She came into the living room and saw me holding Sonya, smiling warmly but concealing something behind her back.

"I have some dire news," she said. I turned toward her, still holding Sonya, expecting word of a monster storm, or of abnormally high seas that would sweep us away like legendary Atlantis, traceless, or of cold so intense trees would explode and the boards of the building would shrivel up and break away. But her face was unreadable, and before I could say anything, she held up a brown bottle. "We're almost out of Kahlua."

"The unkindest cut of all," I said with a laugh, feeling suddenly Shakespearean and smiting my forehead with open palm.

◆ ◆ ◆

There was still the unanswered question, unfairly dismissed. It had turned out to be a girl—a homeless young thing whom *somebody* somewhere must have known. I had not even gotten close enough to touch her in order to reassure her before she vanished into the building. Now I had no idea where she was.

After I had discovered the way into room eleven, I left it the way I had entered and secured the panel back into place when I was in the tunnel. When lunch was over, I went into the room on my way up the hall and tried to enter the access tunnel from inside the closet. As with Sonya's closet, I could see no way to do it. This made perfect sense since the panel was secured with simple turn clasps from the other side and, unless one had some way of reaching into the tunnel, these clasps could not be turned from this side to release the panel. They simply did not communicate with the closet itself.

Access was limited to the approach from the attic. That automatically ruled Sonya out.

Earlier I had congratulated myself on what I imagined was the penetrating soundness of the logic—however unintentional—behind my decision to keep so much information from Margaret so that she would not be needlessly alarmed. The discovery of the girl in the attic was the proof. How would she have reacted to the news that the hallwalker was not only real, but at first glance might even have been her own daughter?

But now I wasn't so sure about the wisdom of that strategy, if only because of inadvertent slipups like the comment I'd made at lunch. I knew that the first thing I had to do was verify the existence of an access ladder behind Sonya's closet. Then what should I do? Should I reveal everything to her and launch a comprehensive search for the girl? What would we do once we found her, assuming we did? From the looks of her, this had been some sort of forest-dwelling wild child. Could she even speak? I knew that feral children who hadn't learned to speak by a certain age would not be able to learn a language at all, and I had no way of knowing if that was the case here.

It was true that she had been mumbling something when I first came upon her, but I did not recognize the sounds as English and, indeed, they may have been nothing more than inarticulate babbling in imitation of a spoken language.

I was pressed for time but knew that, even before I began recording the secrets of the house in the cedars, I had to go back to the attic. My intent was to do two things: one, find out how many access tunnels there were and which one went past Sonya's closet, and two, test the roof hatches for soundness. I needed to know if any were being used to enter and exit the building from the roof.

The sheer length of the Ropewalk and the amount of junk stored in its attic made it nearly impossible to get an accurate count of the number of ladders. They seemed to have been spaced at regular intervals of about fifty feet on both sides of the building, although some of them were just conjecture on my part because I physically could not get under the eaves to verify that they were actually there. I was able to locate seven on Margaret's side of the building, but figured I would only have to check out the three in the middle of the series because they were closest to where I estimated the apartment would be. The end ones were too far away. I figured that, at some point, I would have to check out every one of them, but that was something I did not need to do just then.

I had managed to smuggle the flashlight out of the apartment without arousing suspicion by hiding it under my sweatshirt, so with that as my only accoutrement, I opened the cover of the first of the three tunnels and went down. About halfway, as expected, I encountered the removable panel, turned the clamps, and entered the closet before me. Its door was closed. When I opened it, I was in one of the students' rooms, not Margaret's apartment. I did not linger or probe; I went back out the way I had entered and continued down the ladder to see where it came out. Like the first one, it led to the fallout shelter. Thinking that perhaps the girl was there, I went over and turned on the light, half expecting to see her cowering near a shelf somewhere. But there was nothing. So I turned the light off and went back up.

The next one also provided access to a student room, but this one, oddly, did not go any further than that point. I assumed some sort of structural problem had prevented the builders from bringing it all the way down to the shelter.

The third one produced the same result as the first except this one, when it came out in the basement, was beyond the shelter and I found myself in the crawlspace that housed the lineup of furnaces and the huge oil drum. To my right was the huge fire door with the word "Compressor" stenciled on it, secured with its archaic lock. Here, except for the cement slabs that the furnaces stood on, the floor was dirt, and because of that, it held the evidence of a visitor.

There were tracks everywhere. They were small and somewhat amorphous, as if the feet of whoever had left them were wrapped in rags, or maybe badly worn moccasin-like footwear. I was careful to not mar them as I stepped off the ladder and bent to examine those closest. They revealed nothing to me, tracker that I wasn't, other than that they clearly had been made by a small person. And I knew they had to be relatively recent because they definitely had not been there that day I came down to check on the oil.

Obviously, she had been there. There were so many tracks that I wondered if maybe this was the way she was getting into the building, that she knew of some small opening between the building and the ground, invisible in the unfiltered darkness beyond the crawlspace, but adequate for her. Perhaps the roof hatches were not playing any role at all in this.

In any case, I had no intention of trying to probe the claustrophobically narrow space that marked where the furnace room ended and the raw earth began, banked as it was to within a foot or so of the overhead floor joists. A child could wiggle through there, but for me it would be a frightening ordeal. I filed it away mentally as a very likely possibility, then turned and went back up the ladder.

I had failed in my original mission. I had not found the ladder that went behind Sonya's closet. That meant I had to check the next two tunnels in the sequence that I began in the center, which meant I would have checked five of the seven. Given that, I figured I might as well just do them all on that side. So I started with the one that was actually first in line.

None of them opened into Sonya's closet, which was no real surprise given that I estimated they were too far away. The first two descended all the way to the shelter, which told me that that part of the basement extended all the way to the front of the building, even if the shelter itself stopped less than halfway down its length. The last two, as expected, only went as far as to connect with closets on the first floor, since there was solid earth below that point.

The one that went to her closet had to be buried under the chaotic mounds of junk and assorted "treasures" that lined the attic on that side. That meant that it was either inaccessible, or there was some carefully concealed pathway through the morass that someone—a small person perhaps—could use. I did not have the time or inclination to look for it.

I did, however, want to check out the last ladder on the opposite side. Being at the end of the building, it would not go any further than the first floor, and just from its position too close to the back wall, it was clear that it would not emerge in a student's room. I was sure it went to the utility closet. That would be the most logical of all locations, given that the workmen would have had to run the electrical conduits from there to the attic. I went over, opened the hatch, and went down. A few seconds later, I was staring at the familiar circuit breaker boxes.

Everything now made sense, including the disappearance of the "shadow within a shadow" that I'd seen the week before. Unlike the access to the closets in the students' rooms, this panel was hinged and accessible from both sides, which meant that the girl, having sensed that I was there, could have retreated back to the attic. Had I the presence of mind then, I might have noticed that the rear wall was closer than it should have been. I might also have seen the simple lift latch that would have told me it was a door, not a wall.

In any case, the problem of locating her had grown in complexity with the number of possible ways in and out of the attic, compounded by the number of places a child could hide in the building. I realized that, unless she wanted to be found, it was going to be nearly impossible. We would almost never just randomly occupy the same space in the building at the same time. I went back up the ladder and spent the next ten minutes going from one roof hatch to another on the south side, testing them to see if any were open. Unlike the tunnels, these I could reach. Two of them moved, as if the locks had come loose, but none of them actually opened.

Alright. Now I needed to inventory the stuff in the refrigerator and check the outside for any tracks in the snow. It was already mid-afternoon, and I hadn't spent a single moment reading the proprietor's records or examining the clay impressions from the house in the cedars. Fate itself was conspiring against me.

With one last, hopeful look, I left the attic and locked the door. I realized with a resigned shake of my head that I didn't need the key to get in there at all, that all I needed to do was visit the utility closet. But this was a good thing because the girl knew it as well and it was her lifeline. I would "accidentally" leave some food out for her in the kitchen, just as I had done for the cat. And the "snicking" sounds of the door popping open and the click of the lights going out—these were her ways of staying invisible. I was sure that was what she preferred, whether she could articulate it or not.

Like the spider and the cat, she was just one more thing living in the walls.

◆ ◆ ◆

Chapter 27

The only possibility was to try to catch her at night when she was prowling the halls, but even that might have become an elusive goal now that she knew she had been discovered.

I decided to not go outside to check for tracks because her means of getting into and out of the building had basically become irrelevant. The hatch leading into the furnace room from outside could not have been it because it was much too heavy for a child to lift. There had to be some other way. But even if I were to find an entrance—some cave-like aperture under the foundation stones just big enough for a child—I would be able to do nothing about it. I could not seal it with the intention of keeping her in the building because I would not know at the time if she really was in there. If she wasn't, and I sealed her out, she might perish in the cold. If she was, and I sealed her in, she might panic at the thought of being captured and do something desperate. So I let it go. I would report the incident to the school administration and the authorities when everyone was back. In the meantime, the afternoon was wearing on and I needed to get something done on my project.

The good news from the radio was that the storm had stalled out over the ocean and probably would not arrive for at least another day. That meant I had a little bit of room to plan another hike out to the village to get some better shots of the petroglyphs and—at last—see the barrow close up.

For now, though, I bent to the task of examining the clay imprints under a magnifying glass. Like a jeweler unbinding the folds that held a priceless stone, I gently unwrapped the impressions from the cotton batting. I had a total of five, only one of which was close to being complete. I got out my magnifying glass and started with that one.

When a hatchet or tomahawk blade goes into a piece of wood, it typically leaves a distinct mark. This mark is a long, narrow wedge, flat at the top where the blade was broadest and tapering down to the point defining the lower edge. This clay replication had neither, mainly because it was obvious that the wood around the edges of the original impression had decayed. It was a huge disappointment, given that this was the biggest model that I had. I carefully scrutinized the sides, and although I found a horizontal mark such as the blade might have left if it had been scratched, it was not conclusive. In essence, all I had was the clay impression of a narrow hole in the wall.

Of the other four, only one gave me something to go on. This one was only a partial but had on one side that characteristic wedge shape that I had hoped to find. This was the closest indicator I had that the marks had indeed been made by an edged instrument. It was slim and maybe even questionable, but there it was. Better than nothing. So I now had two pieces of information that matched the elements in the diary: I had found the name "Cane," and I had a clay impression of a mark from the wall that looked like it could have been made by a tomahawk. I could not work out the probability of these two being nothing more than accidents because that sort of thing was not my forte, but intuitively I recognized that two sequential successes had to yield a likelihood greater than fifty percent, moving the argument in my favor. I knew instinctively I was on the right track.

Then I got out my notebook and scribbled a few reminders, remnants of what I'd remembered of the inside of the house. I regretted that I didn't have any pictures and knew I would have to amend that shortcoming when I went back to get the photos of the petroglyphs the next day. I added that to my "to do" list and then got to work organizing the notes. Once I had a basic outline of what I wanted to say, I set up the typewriter and began clattering away. I told the story of finding and exploring the house in agonizing detail.

I was on a roll, so when that was done, I began a closer scrutiny of the pictures of the petroglyphs. Under the magnifying glass I was able to see things that I'd only half noticed the first time, and before I went any further I got out my reference book on the Machias Bay carvings. One of these was a giant bird, the so-called "Thunderbird," a figure vaguely reminiscent of a man wearing a flowing cape whose arms suggested wings. This was also on the wall of the chasm, something I'd seen but not recognized. That was an odd coincidence and factored into the vagueness surrounding the very existence of the carvings under the old ropewalk. The name "Thunderbird" itself was unsetting in its obviously contrived inadequacy. What exactly was a "Thunderbird," other than the four-wheeled version made by Ford? It was in essence untouchable, an idea left to fester on the wall of a hidden world, its meaning completely and forever gone. I could almost feel my DNA unraveling when I studied things like this, untwisting as I regressed from twentieth century "homo domesticus" to Paleolithic hunter. I suspected that, if I went far enough, I would end up with just enough gray matter to keep the instinct and motor functions working.

There was something else carved into the wall of the chasm that I hadn't noticed before. Near one of the faces was something that looked like a misshapen bull, its ridiculously small hindquarters in stark contrast to the bulk of the shoulders and neck. There also appeared to be two horns on its head. I recognized this, too, as something that appeared among the Machias Bay carvings, where it was rather flippantly and inexplicably labeled—or mislabeled—a "water monster," as if that explained anything at all.

If these were devices intended to tell a story or record a history, they would never be deciphered. That was a given. There was no Rosetta Stone for this problem, no known standard of translation against which an unknown script could be weighed. Our pathetic attempts were so far removed in time and culture, in mindset itself, that they could only lead to error. How could we as twentieth century "sophisticates" ever hope to penetrate the world of sympathetic magic and hunting spirits?

I got up and began pacing. Any explanation that I could contrive for these symbols would be nothing more than thinly shellacked academic vanity. Yet if I didn't attempt it, someone else surely would. I recalled the story of the Spirit Pond Runestones and what happened to the man who had found them. Vilified, accused of propagating a hoax, a position far more implausible than even the stones themselves. How could the detractors honestly believe that a guy growing up in Depression Era

Maine, with at best a year or two of high school for education, would one day decide to teach himself Old Norse, *and* the runic alphabet, and then, with apparently still nothing else to do, proceed to chisel a story into a piece of granite so that he could afterwards pretend to find it? What sort of elliptical logic was allowed to emanate from the halls of the academic elite? Yet *that* is what they honestly believed.

The "official explanation" was more preposterous than the event itself, but so was my position.

I would need to think it through, to work on an angle that might actually bring the real meaning to light. I had the diary, the proprietors' records, the village itself. But I also had the basin with its huge, unexplained "Thing-Stone"—that was the name I'd given it, in imitation of the Anglo-Saxon stone used as a focus for their tribal congress—and, lest I overlook the original impetus behind all of this, I also had the barrow.

All of which would be received with a skepticism bordering on nonsense.

I had brought the "Concise History" back with me when I left Margaret's apartment and now needed to slug my way through the stilted language to see if it would reveal anything. It was going to be tedious, but that, combined with the diary and the land records, was the source material on which my history would be built. I flipped it open to the section dealing with the "Walum-Olum," the so-called "Bark Record" of the Delawares, which I knew was a scholarly rendering of the pictographic history of that Native American people. I was hoping it would shed some light on how to approach the petroglyphs.

But it didn't. It was a graphical rendering of their own creation myths, complete with the universal flood story. Interesting but not relevant, and the "hieroglyphs" mentioned in the account were nothing like the petroglyphs hiding under the old ropewalk. It did, however, recount the entire descent myth of the Delawares and, like that of the Abenakis, was full of fanciful creatures obviously intended to embody the forces of nature.

None of this was really "news" in any viable sense. The mythologies of peoples everywhere were full of creatures that bestrode the world at the dawn of time and that now lived in some kind of "Otherworld," usually underground or on mountaintops.

So I went back to the beginning, to the diary entry describing the massacre that the grandmother had witnessed as a child. And it was there, while reading the passage again, that I finally understood what else was hiding in that mental tunnel into which I had been staring for almost two weeks.

It wasn't the massacre that had held me. It was what she had seen after it was over.

◆ ◆ ◆

When one encounters something so outlandish, so irrational, that its reality could be nothing more than literary pretense, yet that connects to what one already knows, the effect is almost visceral. That was what happened when I reread the diary entry. The grandmother had witnessed a massacre somewhere in this area as a child and had hidden in the brush until it was over. Then "the birds" came, which I had assumed were scavengers like ravens and possible raptors like hawks and eagles, resulting in an irreverent feast about which nothing could be done. She was about to leave when a large horned animal she did not recognize stuck its head out of the brush.

Impossible images poorly described by the hand of a barely literate farm girl. That was how these events would be dismissed. But for me it was something else. I *had* my large bird—the thing that had flown from the roof of the shed.

Was I loosing it? I wondered as I went back to the desk and sat down. What exactly was the thing that I had seen? Or had I seen anything at all? Once again, I felt the specter of some sort of isolation-induced hysteria sneak up beside me and touch my shoulder with a chill. But then I caught myself and thought, no, it had not been an illusion. It had been real.

And in that case, what was it? Could it have been an owl after all?

I took heart in that I had not seen any sort of large animal with horns. That part, at least, would stay in the diary. I had that frightening bellow that I'd heard from the forest, but that could have been anything from an outraged raccoon to a moose.

I looked at my watch. It was already five o'clock. It was pitch black outside; the moon had either not yet risen or was in its waning cycle. I went to the window and looked out, but there wasn't much to see. I was fidgeting; like Margaret, I suspected it was cabin fever and knew that the only cure was to get out and do something.

What I needed was to get back to the village and record the names on the tombstones so that I could match them up with the land records, so that went on the "to do" list as well. Then I began pacing again, convinced of the correctness of how I had pieced together the fragments of the hallwalker's identity, even if I had no idea how to bring the incident to closure.

But something else still eluded me. Half out of frustration and half because of the sheer need to do something, I sat back down and began scanning the proprietors' records, reading randomly selected pages in my search for names that I could coordinate with the gravestones. I found several and copied them so that I could search the cemetery for a match. Then, in a stroke of luck, I encountered a terse transaction record dating from June 1705. In it, one William Pennington, listed as a "carpenter, joyner, and boat builder," and Thomas Henshaw, "brickmaker," had "form'd a companie for the purpose of windding ropes and preparing them for shipment." This company was to build its factory over the "domaine of a spacyus Tempel of the Heathen, a strange thing seldome sene and neattly kept."

I stood up. That was it. Here was the reference to the founding of the ropewalk that straddled the chasm and its stream. This had to be it. This was the third corroboration after the name and the hatchet mark in the clay. That building was constructed, or at least begun, in 1705, thirty years after Metacomet's war ended. That meant that it wasn't there when the grandmother's massacre took place, which in turn meant that the "declivity" into which Lewis had chased the "savages" could indeed have been the basin. I marked the page with an index card and pondered the ramifications for the rest of her story.

If the ropewalk wasn't there, if the basin was truly the "declivity," then I had a new dilemma. All this time, I had been assuming that the village had been there at the time of the attack because that was where the grandmother had lived. But if my interpretation was right, the ropewalk did not appear until 1705, and if that factory was indeed the source of the village's wealth, then the village could not have preceded it. This meant the grandmother could not have lived there in 1675. Solving one problem had presented me with another.

One thing I had noticed while scanning the entries was that the transactions prior to 1705 always seemed to cite boundary markers that included a reference to the sea, or to landmarks on the shore. It appeared that property divisions at that time tended to begin at the waterline and run inland. This was not uncommon in the colonial era, so when I first encountered it, I had paid no attention. But now I had to rethink that position. What if, contrary to my previous belief, the grandmother had been living somewhere near the shore at the time the attack occurred? It was not implausible; colonies tended to spring up near rivers and tidewater areas, for obvious reasons. But if that were the case, there would have to have been a small settlement somewhere on the coast.

I went over to the window and looked out. There was nothing to see; the moon, if there was going to be one, still had not risen, and the scant starlight barely illuminated the snowfield. It was the overcast that was doing it, the pending storm that the radio had said was stalled out over the ocean.

Where would this settlement have been? I wondered. I was not aware of any archeological digs anywhere in the area, but that was hardly surprising since I had also been completely unaware of the existence of the village. This was a crucial factor because all other connections between the diary and the village would become moot if I could not establish that the grandmother herself had lived in the area.

And then suddenly it hit me. Suddenly I knew, the same way I had known that the cat was living in the attic. The proof had been lying there in front of me the whole time, right under the snow. In fact, it had been lying there for centuries in full view. It was the so-called artificial ruins, the Greek add-ons imparting the spurious air of a classical link to some idealized past. The foundations on which the ludicrous statuary rested were not artificial at all and had not been built by the planners of the school. I suddenly realized with the surety of another Olympian revelation that they had been there all along and the school had been built among them. *Right here* was where she had lived.

I stepped away from the window with a huge sense of triumph and relief, of having put the pieces together at last. With a self-satisfied chuckle, I stuck another sheet of paper into the typewriter and began typing the general outline of the events. Gaps in the reliability of the statements could be filled in later. I was sure that when I researched it, the school records would indicate that the old foundations were already there when the school was built in the fifties. That meant that the "spacyus Tempel" was the basin with the "Thing-Stone" and the petroglyphs in the chasm.

Whatever was left I could consider a footnote.

When I finished I glanced at my watch. What time had she said dinner would be?

◆ ◆ ◆

My overriding hope was that this information would keep Sil out of the picture completely. I was anxious to tell Margaret about how I had put it all together, but when I entered the apartment and went into the kitchen, I realized immediately something was wrong. Her eyes were red as she turned away and pretended to busy herself at the sink. I could not see Sonya and thought maybe something had happened.

"What is it? What happened?" Inwardly I was dreading the answer because whatever had occurred I was sure would involve Sonya. "Is everything okay?"

She smiled, nodded, and wiped her eyes. "I just crashed, that's all. It's kind of catching up to me, Ben leaving me and all." She stroked my cheek. "Don't feel slighted. I think I'm just paying the price for cashing in the whole first half of my life." She moved closer and wrapped herself around me. "I'm just . . . I'm okay."

I was relieved. The specter of some sort of medical emergency had risen before me like the stone giant in the basin, silent and unsolvable. The only way to get help would've been to go on foot through the forest to the inland highway, in the middle of the night, and then hope that a car came by. I wasn't sure we would've been able to make it.

"Where's Sonya?" I stroked her hair and could feel the tenseness in her neck.

"In her room. She wanted to be alone with one of her books." She leaned away and looked at me. I wiped one small tear from her cheek and she smiled. "Ready for dinner?" she asked.

"Sure. Can I help with anything?"

She broke away and headed for the stove. "As a matter of fact, you can. You can go get some of that milk you said you had in the kitchen."

So I headed for the door to the apartment but detoured to Sonya's room when I could not see her on her bed. I just wanted to check up on her.

She was there, but not looking at one of her picture books. She was standing at the window staring into the darkness, transfixed either by something actually out there or by something only in her mind. I looked over her head, but it was so dark even the snowfield was nothing more than a pale sheen. Yet she was staring, unmoving, scarcely even blinking, her features so taut that I imagined she was going to go through one of her odd metamorphoses. I looked again but simply could not penetrate the gloom, and I wondered, what's out there, the creepy-crawlies? Childish as that thought was, I felt a chill touch my arms as I recalled the collage of memories from the last week and a half. Birds and bellows, skeletons and shadows, things thumping in the night. And when I looked down at her again, I saw her smile faintly, and I began to wonder if, whatever the genetic permutation into which she had been born, it brought with it the gift of being able to see in the dark.

◆ ◆ ◆

I was obsessed at dinner, scarcely hearing anything Margaret said. Two thoughts were foremost in my mind. One, I would leave some food out for the girl, either in the kitchen as I originally intended, or in the utility closet where I was sure she would find it. Two, the diary entries did not go back to the sixteen hundreds and, hence, most likely were describing events that had happened in the village, not in the settlement on the shore. The connection was that the grandmother's story originated from the tidewater settlement but was narrated by a girl living in the village. The shoreline settlement was probably abandoned by then.

The enigma of the "spacyus Tempel" had grafted itself in my mind to the misadventure of Madeline Cane, and I wondered if the place they had been exploring was the chasm under the ropewalk. But then I realized it could not have been or my new timeline would be rendered inoperable; the ropewalk would have been straddling the chasm for over three decades by the time of that diary entry. It had to have been something else. I must've completely spaced out because when I looked at Sonya, she was eyeing me with obvious confusion, and in her face I fleetingly saw that of the child in the attic once again.

"What?" asked Margaret. Her fork had stopped halfway to her mouth.

I looked over at her. "What?"

Her brow twisted in confusion. "You just said 'What else is living in the walls?'"

"I did?"

"Yes, you did. Are you alright?"

I looked over at her and smiled. "Sure, I'm fine. Just a little tired. Excited, too, over the project finally taking some definitive shape."

Her look did not soften. "What do you mean, things living in the walls?"

I smiled. That gap was too wide to bridge, so I said nothing and withdrew into my mental tunnel again. There were no parting comments as I turned away for a moment, searching the walls for an answer, no longer sure of what was best to believe for all our sakes.

She eyed me. "Well?"

I shook my head. "Nothing. I think maybe I'm getting a little carried away from too much contact with the Abenaki myths." I looked away again for a moment, an automatic gesture like the dialogue flash cards I had thought of earlier, and when I came back to her, I saw something on her face that was both unmistakable and disturbing. Resigned to the inevitable, and maybe because I had come to half believe it myself, I began to wonder if she thought I was crazy.

◆ ◆ ◆

Margaret's emotional implosion had left her exhausted and she announced her intention to go to bed early. There was no fanfare or oblique inference behind the statement, none of the eroticism from the night before. She was simply run down, like a discharged battery, a dormancy that could only be addressed by long, uninterrupted rest. After she put Sonya to bed, I massaged her neck and shoulders until she fell asleep and then went back to the living room. I had brought the diary with me from my room and decided to continue to scan the pages for any other bits of useful information.

The book itself was very fragile and many of the pages had broken free of the stitching that had originally bound them. Since there were no page numbers, a "spill" would've been a disaster, so the kitchen table was the only place where I could lay it out without fear of the whole thing coming apart under my hand. I brought one of the table lamps over to augment the weak overhead light and sat down to slug my way further into it.

My plan was to at last confront the question of Madeline Cane's whereabouts at the time of her demise, but I had only read a few curious lines before I remembered that I wanted to leave some food out for the girl in the attic. I knew that if I didn't do it then, I might forget about it altogether, so, making sure I had my key to the apartment, I weighted the pages with one of Sonya's books, then slid back the deadbolts and stepped out into the hallway.

The nightlights were out.

The hallway was utterly and impenetrably dark, not relieved in the least by the fact that whatever moonlight might have been available beyond the overcast did not make it through either of the long, narrow windows at the ends. I would've had to feel my way along the wall just to get to the kitchen next door, so I stepped back into the apartment, closed the door, and went to get my flashlight. Margaret stirred when I bumped the bed reaching for the light but did not wake up.

This was totally unexpected. It meant that the girl was already prowling the halls, and it was not yet even ten o'clock. This was a new pattern. I stepped out with the flashlight still off and made sure the door was locked behind me. Then I slowly lowered myself to a squat on the floor, back still propped against the wall. I sat there unmoving for what must have been at least ten minutes, blinded by the darkness but ears tuned to the slightest noise.

And I heard something. I had been expecting the "snicking" sound of the closet door opening, but instead it was the distant creak of a floorboard from the other end, up near the lobby. It was a dead giveaway. That was where she was. But now I dithered because I could not decide on a course of action. Should I turn on the light and surprise her? Or should I sit there noiselessly and try to trace her movements by ear and hope that she came closer?

I opted to sit and wait. But more time passed with no other sounds, and I sensed there was something odd about that until finally my nape hairs began to prickle and I knew that was it, the feeling. I was being watched. Suddenly, the darkness around me felt alive as I slowly slid upward along the wall to a standing position. I brought the flashlight up, extended it as far as my arm would reach, and turned it on.

There was nothing in front of me and I quickly waved it left and right in an effort to catch someone in the beam. There was nothing to the left, but to the right, a shadow, half doubtful and insubstantial as drifting dust, darted in shapeless intransigence across the lobby. The cat? No, it was too big to be the cat. Or maybe not, I thought, as a muffled noise from somewhere down at that end told me it could not have been the girl because she was no doubt in one of the rooms. Probably eleven, I said to myself.

I could not go looking for her without making her feel hunted, so I let it go and went down the hall to the kitchen. Since the plan was to create a sense of normality, I turned on the light so that, wherever she was, she could track my whereabouts. Once there, I took out some bread, an apple, and a few carrots, and put them on a plate. To this I added a little apple juice in a glass. I looked at my offering, thought the better of leaving it in the kitchen, where she might fear to tread, and decided to bring it down to the utility closet.

But I would leave the lights off. That would be my signal that I respected her need to be invisible. It would also, hopefully, convince her to come forward on her own. So down I went, fully expecting to find the door opened but, against all odds, discovering it still closed. Not to worry, I thought, since she could have come down the ladder, switched off the lights, then gone back up to descend by one of the other ladders. I went in, placed my offering on the floor, briefly thought about going up to look in the attic, rejected the idea, and returned. When I got to the apartment, I considered going up to the lobby but rejected that, too. Once I got the door unlocked, I turned off the flashlight and immediately the hall imploded into almost palpable darkness. Then I went in and locked the door behind me.

Impulsively, I stepped up to the wall and put my ear against it. There was nothing. I waited for several minutes before giving up and going back to the diary.

Just before I got up to leave the food out, I had read, in the transaction records, a very curious line about what must have been a property dispute brought about by "bitter and burning devils." I suspected that could only have been the Abenakis being described by the self-righteous "children of God," but that was refuted a few lines later where a recorded testimony stated "they are not swarthy Indians but Sooty Devils that are let loose upon us." And I wondered: If they were not Indians, then who were the transgressors?

"Methinks each time we see a clock we are given us admonition, that our Time is upon the wing, and we are come unto the eleventh hour. But what then shall become of this poor New England? Shall we expire before the time of these Devils shall be finished?"

After reading those lines, I got up and went to the sink for a glass of water. Was this a witch trial? I wondered. I went back and checked the date and saw that it was 1739, one of the last transaction records before the book itself became a diary. That was too late for a witch trial, whose histrionics had burned themselves out more than forty years before in the Boston area. But it was also too late for any known war with the Abenakis, the last of which—prior to the French and Indian War—had ended in 1727.

It was vexing. After that, the proprietors' records became the diary, at the beginning of which was the grandmother's story of escaping the massacre. But that event, I knew, dated from the Wampanoag War in 1675.

"We are come unto the eleventh hour." I read the words again, then sat back in the chair and pondered their meaning. My mind went blank. It was because it was late—nearly eleven o'clock by then, ironically—and because of that jittery sense of being hemmed in. I couldn't think. Best thing to do was to let it go for the evening, but as I got up, a memory flared like a Roman candle and burst in front of me: "The end had come, foretold years before." That was the diarist's rendering of the grandmother's statement. The end had come. I thought then that it was some sort of biblical admonishment and was still inclined in that direction, but this development added a twist to it, albeit one I could not fully grasp.

But the end had come for me as well. I was exhausted. With the storm brooding on the horizon, I would need to get back to the village the next day and get my photos. For that I needed to get some rest.

The labyrinth into which my mind had been poured over the past several days was shutting down, and its attendant images became a blurred collage as I lay next to Margaret. I would get up early and head out even before the sun rose. I would go to the barrow and at last confront whatever its secrets were.

With that decision, I realized that the last thing now left in my mental tunnel was finally emerging. Somewhere inside, behind a door labeled "denied," was the amorphous truth. Somewhere inside, like the dream that revealed the circuit breakers, I had known right from the first where Madeline Cane had met her undoing.

♦ ♦ ♦

Chapter 28

All of us live our lives on an underlayment of mythology. We may garb this mythology in more contemporary terminology, like "functional fictions," but that doesn't change the reality. And there is always a certain logic behind that mythology lending it an air of legitimacy that usually takes centuries, sometimes millennia, to finally dethrone. The human sacrifices practiced by the Aztecs and Maya were a case in point. The logic was that, if they didn't do this, the sun wouldn't rise. How they concluded this is long since lost, but the salient point is that there was *logic* behind it. Convoluted, demonstrably incomplete logic, granted, but logic just the same. It was not random, wanton cruelty.

That Abenaki mythology was intimately connected to the basin, petroglyphs, standing stone, and barrow was incontestable. But the logic behind the site still escaped me. There was something that I was missing, some connecting link that I had not yet recognized but that would pull everything together. Of that I was certain. The proprietors' records had gone on and on about the "Engines of Their malice" and the torments these creatures brought, but offered no explanation as to who or what they were. Oddly, Margaret's earlier mention of her dream about the Vikings had been like a spur-line to what had already been rattling around in my head as a result of what I had read in the "Concise History" about a connection between the Abenaki myths and the Norse Edda.

It was an ancient belief among the Abenakis that beings resembling the trolls of the Edda would often attack brave men by night. But if the fight could be prolonged until the sun rose, the creature would turn to stone and all its strength and knowledge would pass to the conqueror. There was a relatively well-known echo of this idea at the corner of Friar's Bay, where the so-called "Friar" stood, a rock nearly thirty feet high. The local Indians said it was a petrified woman.

A race of giants turned to stone by the morning rays of the sun. I wondered if that was the intent behind the stone in the basin, to see the defeated foe in concrete form.

◆ ◆ ◆

I was already on the tractor heading up toward the coast highway at six-thirty. This time I had been so quiet Margaret did not wake up. I had left her a note explaining my plans and slipped out. As I passed through the lobby, I thought about the shadow from the night before and wondered if I should take a quick look in the attic, but let it go. I had the .380 and thus did not need the shotgun from my room, so there was really no reason to go upstairs at all.

By quarter to nine, I was standing before the smooth, iced-over dome of the barrow, wondering at its existence. By then I knew instinctively, intuitively, that this was where Madeline Cane had found her "corrupting liquid." It was man-made and it was hollow. That was what the diary had been telling me. This was the "spacyus Tempel," not the chasm, and the comment resonated with the same unexplained intensity as the enclosure in the cave I had found as a kid. It was clear now—this enigma was another example of the speed bumps I had been dealing with my entire professional career. These were history's laugh lines, artifacts left strewn across the countryside in a randomly patterned mosaic that, because they were inexplicable, were ignored or suppressed.

And because it was hollow, this was where the Indians had tried to hide when Captain Lewis went after them. It was here, not the basin. In my mind, I could hear its emptiness echoing like a drum beat through time. That this was in some way related to the origins of the native peoples described in the myths, their Old Ones, their ancestors, I had no doubt. And because of that, this would be my Waterloo, because I also had no doubt that I could not explain any part of it.

I walked all around it, even onto the ice on the side facing the pond. I knew there was no danger; the reason the ice had cracked on my first attempt was because of the stream coming from the chasm. But the barrow was too far from that point to be affected by it, and the cold, even with the recent rise in temperature, would've ensured a deep freeze.

But it didn't matter. If it was artificial, if it could be entered, I would not be able to determine until spring, when the ice and snow were gone. Just for a lark, I thought of climbing up onto it and sort of symbolically "claiming" it, but just as quickly dismissed the idea. This had been a sacred place to somebody; I would not trivialize that through even a minor desecration.

◆ ◆ ◆

I approached the petroglyphs from outside the old ropewalk, on the cliff side. Climbing over what I had at first taken to be an insurmountable pile of debris had become a simple maneuver, and I was at the site of the stone staircase in a matter of minutes. The baritone rumble of the hole into which the stream flowed reached out to me before I was even halfway there.

I stood on the stone stairs looking into the chasm. This time I had brought a more powerful flashlight and directed its beam along the opposite wall. There I saw, verifiably, the carving of a spider such as I'd seen in my dream. I did not leap to some kind of equivocal correlation between that and the monstrous thing I had found under my bed because spiders were good luck symbols to the Indians. They *knew* what would happen if those voracious little hunters didn't keep the insect population in check. To us, they were nothing more than hideous mini-monsters living in dusty corners; even I had reacted that way when I found one in my room. But that did not mean that the petroglyph was intended to convey something negative.

It was the hole that captivated me. That morning, while I was quietly eating breakfast, I had read a note in the proprietors' records dating from 1703, two years before the ropewalk had been built over the chasm. In it, the very same Thomas Henshaw, who would later

operate the rope factory, had been lead "to a Mountain" by several local
Indians and shown the "opening from which their Old Ones emerged"
when their ancestors first "came out of the ground."

Equating a hole in the ground with the birth process was nothing
new in mythology, except in this case I knew immediately what it was
referring to. It could only have meant the hole in the chasm. At that
point, the obviously phallic symbolism inherent in the "Thing-Stone"
took on new meaning. Maybe it was not a petrified troll; it could just as
easily mark the site as life-generating, as somehow sacred to a people
who lived with the cycles of nature and understood their close bond to
the process of life, death, and new life.

And maybe the so-called "thunderbird" and "water monster"
carvings were spirit guardians of the phallus and earth-womb,
respectively.

If that was the case, if it was not a petrified troll, if it was indeed
a phallus, then it would have been the most sacred of all sites to
the natives, the place where the earth itself had given birth to their
ancestors. And Thomas Henshaw, after seeing it, had "purchased" the
site and desecrated it, had heinously compromised it by building a
ropewalk over its sacred stream, the stream that embodied the history
of the people themselves. He had betrayed the Indians who had led him
there.

On the academic side, it was yet one more connection between the
diary and the village site, one more link in the chain that bound the two
together. On the ethics side, it was an outrage, whatever the economic
advantage to using the site for motive power.

I couldn't help but wonder if the demise of the village itself was
somehow associated with Henshaw's decision.

◆ ◆ ◆

The storm was coming. The gray overcast had not lightened at all,
and by the time I had taken the 35mm pictures of the petroglyphs, it
was obvious it was going to start soon. I needed to get back to the
tractor and head for home.

The first fluttering flakes began when I was driving the tractor
down the cart track toward the highway. These quickly mixed with the

small pellets that told me it would eventually be another ice storm. We would be frozen in again.

It had thickened considerably by the time I got back but still did not appear to have reached its peak. I left the tractor in the shed and made my way gingerly across the yard to the Ropewalk. It was not yet even noon; I congratulated myself on the wisdom behind the unusually early start.

As I headed up the walk, I noticed a set of tracks leading from the front of the building to the side. They looked new despite the fact that they were already partially filled in from the storm. Had Margaret come out looking for something?

I shrugged it off, thinking that maybe she had gone to check the millpond again to see if they could skate. Since there was only one set of tracks, I figured she must've been carrying Sonya, which made sense considering the depth of the snow.

When I entered, I immediately noticed that her apartment door was open and figured she was either taking a shower or was indeed outside checking out the pond. I needed to put the camera away and offload my daypack, so I headed up to my room immediately, put everything away, including the .380, and went back down.

There was no one in the apartment. Further down the hall, there was a light shining through the frosted glass window in the door to the shower room, and as I approached I heard water running in one of the stalls. I wasn't supposed to be in the girls' shower room, but who would know? I pushed it open a few inches and announced my arrival.

"Margaret? It's me, so don't get nervous." The hiss of the water continued, but no response came. I went through the first part, past lines of sinks attached to the wall, then rounded the corner to the shower stalls. Steam was rising from one of them, and I called out again as I approached. Still no answer. Apprehensive now, I grabbed the curtain and pulled it open.

The stall was empty. The water rained down on nothing but the drain.

"What the hell?" I muttered as I shut it off. The sudden quiet felt almost like an intrusion as I struggled to understand. Maybe she had turned the water on and at that moment Sonya had broken away, so she had to go after her. Maybe she didn't catch her until the end of the building, and maybe to pacify the girl she had gone out to show her the pond and forgot that the shower was still running.

Maybe.

A towel was on the floor, off in a corner, muddied by what looked like an indistinct shoeprint. I picked it up and the image broke up into a dozen unrelated smudges. I threw it over my shoulder and headed back to the apartment.

Nothing seemed out of place. Nothing, that is, until, in the kitchen, I saw a plate on the table and, near it, a glass lying on its side.

Lying on its side. I stared at it as if unsure of its reality. Margaret would not just leave it like that. I backed away and headed for the bedroom.

There was an object in the middle of the floor, long and narrow, black, glistening. It was her epee, her edged sword, the real thing, not the foil ending in a button. And even from where I was, I could see that it had blood on it.

I recoiled into the wall, my hands shaking as I groped for the .380 that I suddenly realized was up in my room. I was defenseless. Something had happened to Margaret, someone had come in and she had tried to fight him off with her epee and had in part succeeded but was now gone and I needed to go after her but was defenseless.

My rational mind was shutting down. Was she dead? If not, then where was she? Panic set in as I realized that I hadn't locked the door to my room and the assailant might even then be arming himself with the .380 and the shotgun. I sprinted out of the apartment and up to my room, bursting through the door, fully expecting to find my own weapons turned toward me. But there was no one there. Hands shaking, I pulled my parka back on, stuck the .380 in one of the pockets, and grabbed the shotgun. It was still loaded with slugs—not good, I thought, not good. Buckshot would be better. Need to go find some in the shed.

No time. I threw the door open and vaulted down the stairs, then stood there, the shotgun halfway to my shoulder. I couldn't think. I was hyperventilating, an inch away from adrenalin-induced panic. Where to start?

The tracks. I ran outside and was instantly lashed by a salvo of sleet across my face. The storm had intensified and the wind had picked up. That was no good. It would bury the tracks. I needed to hurry. I scanned for a trail heading away from the building as I followed the now shapeless perforations that minutes before had been identifiable tracks. These led me along the side and stopped at the hatch that led into the furnace room. That was how he had gotten in. Holding the shotgun at the ready in my right hand, I reached for the handle with my left. He might still be there; it would be dark and I had not thought to bring the flashlight. No matter; she might be down there, too, with only moments left. With a mighty yank, I pulled it open and instantly brought the weapon to my shoulder. Then down, waving it right and left, groping for the chain that would turn on the light.

There was no one there. But diagonally opposite me were the bottom rungs of the ladder that I knew went to the attic. Once in the attic, he could've entered the building through room eleven, or any of those that had the enclosed ladder.

And then my knees buckled as the terrible truth hit me—*I* was the culprit. *I* had done this. *I* was the one who had provided the means for whoever it was to enter and take her. *I* had kept them out by tying the chain through the door handles, then let them in by cutting the lock off the hatch to the furnace room. *I* was the reason she and Sonya were gone.

And the girl in the attic was somehow part of this.

I felt myself imploding. Spectral images rose from the fenpools of my imagination to torment me beyond my endurance. I pictured lost and inbred half-mad forest creatures bursting in and taking the means to forcefully procreate their diminishing tribe. With that awful image in my mind, I ran back up the steps and slammed the hatch door down.

What now? I tried to think, to imagine what an assailant would do. Stay in the building and wait to ambush me? Very likely. He would not want to be out in this storm. Should I go back in the front door or up through the attic, the way he had done? No—that was no good. That was most likely where he was and he would have me cornered. I would go up through the door on the second floor since I still had the key. He wouldn't expect that.

Time was dilating. I tried to run back to the front of the building but was not wearing the snowshoes and the deep snow made my efforts seem almost comically slow. When I got there, I slipped on the ice and lost my grip on the shotgun, which landed across the steps and clattered down and away. A single jump brought me to it and I brushed it free, brought the slide partly back to make sure it wasn't jammed and saw that—holy shit—in my panic I had not even thought to chamber a round. So I did that, threw open the front door, and raced into the building.

A massive form caught me by the front of my parka, ripped the shotgun out of my hand, and tossed me across the floor as if I were a toy. I crashed into the wall and sank to the floor, windless.

The massive form stepped forward, and even in that shaded place I could see who it was.

Sil.

I was too late after all.

I struggled to my feet as he came at me. His next attempt to grab me left him shocked and winded as I parried his outstretched arms and nailed him in the solar plexus. I knew it was not a good hit, though, because the parka slowed me down and my wrist bent on impact, so instead of going down unable to breathe, he staggered back a step, then came at me again. The parka was too confining to use anything but a sidekick, so I jumped back a step and pretended to stumble, then lashed at him from under his guard and caught him in the stomach. He grunted, but the sheer mass of the man knocked me off balance and I scarcely had time to turn toward him before he was on me again.

He grabbed my sleeve and pulled, and I used that move to elbow him in the solar plexus, this time really knocking the wind out of him. Without turning around, I delivered a second, stunning elbow to the forehead and saw his eyes roll back for a moment as his grip slackened. I broke away and ran out the door.

The tractor—I had to get to the tractor and head out for the road. Even if there was no hope of getting help, I had to get out and search for tracks, at the very least survive so that the police could come after Sil. I got to the shed and threw open the door, climbed up and fumbled with the key, hands shaking so much that I could not get it into the ignition.

Almost there, but then a huge hand grabbed my sleeve and yanked me down as if I were a child, and although I twisted and flailed and almost got free again, his arm went around my throat from behind and I knew, this was it, I had about fifteen seconds to think of something. I turned my head to delay the choking effect, groped for the pocket with the .380, worked on prying loose a finger that I could twist, expecting a knife thrust or cudgel or some other darkening effect, when I heard Sil's voice in my ear and all the fight went out of me.

"What did you do with them, you bastard?" he growled.

♦ ♦ ♦

Chapter 29

I went limp. Sil must've sensed the change because his arm slackened and, although it still held me like a boa constrictor, I was able to breathe normally. To the extent that I was able, I turned my head to try to see him.

"Where are they?"

"I don't know. I came back from a hike and they were gone."

His grip tightened again. He thought I was lying. Instinctively I pulled on his forearm, even knowing that the gesture was useless, and in response he tightened up further. "I'm not lying," I managed to gasp. "There's been someone in the building since everyone left. Margaret heard him the first day. I thought it was you but she said no, and eventually I found a homeless girl in the attic and thought there was no danger."

The moment I mentioned the girl his grip lost all its strength and I was able to break away. He gave me a shove to put distance between us. I landed against the tractor, thought about the .380 in my pocket, thought about homicide and jail time again, and decided to play it out. After all, he could've killed me when he had me.

"What homeless girl?" A thin streamer of blood trickled out of his nose. When I elbowed him in the forehead, it must've been lower than I thought.

"I don't know who she is. I found her trying to use a rock to open cans from the fallout shelter. She was wearing a cloak or something made from a bearskin." I adjusted the collar of my parka, which had twisted under his arm.

He stared at me as if weighing my words. "What did she look like?"

I shrugged. "Ragged, dirty. Facially, she looked like Sonya. In fact, I thought she *was* Sonya when I first found her."

The effect was instantaneous. The mistrust immediately drained from his face and was replaced with what looked like shock or confusion. Then, as if catching himself betraying something he didn't want me to see, he suddenly turned and stepped up to the still open door, turning his back to me as if I weren't even there. The storm was now a mixture of sleet and snow and was coming down in almost blinding sheets. He stood there unmoving, staring out into it, gauging something, saying nothing.

"Why were you on the top floor of the shed?" he finally asked.

How could he know that? Was this some kind of test of my honesty? "What makes you think I was up there?"

"Just answer the fucking question."

"Okay. I went up there basically just to see why you made it so difficult to get up there."

"And did you find anything that satisfied your curiosity?" He turned a slight bit and watched me from the corner of his eye.

I hesitated. Some instinct in me, like that sense of being watched, told me that this was indeed a test, that if I failed, this whole scene would erupt into something unpleasant. I touched the pocket holding the .380 to reassure myself that it was still there. "Who was the skeleton you have hidden up there?" There it was. The next few seconds would decide the issue.

He turned to me, his face revealing not so much anger as an unexpected relief. "A kid named Roger Benning."

"Did you kill him?"

That genuinely startled him. "Did I what?"

I took a deep breath and repeated the question, fondling the .380 through the parka, assured by its hard angularity. "Did you kill him?"

He laughed and shook his head. "That skeleton is over a hundred years old. Didn't you notice?" He turned back toward the door. "Asshole."

In fact, I hadn't noticed. How could I? I knew nothing about dried bones and felt oddly insulted, a feeling all out of place considering where we were. "How did you know I was on the top floor? Margaret couldn't have told you."

"I saw your tracks in the powder." The powder. He went on to explain how he had put down a fine powder over the entire floor, just for that very purpose. This was the airborne dust I had noticed when I was up there and that added the slight opaqueness to the air that made it hard to focus. Dust motes. I understood. Like Margaret's fish line across the stairwell, it was a trick to trap the unwary.

A moment passed. I was caught in a vice. I could not get past him but needed to get out. I had suddenly realized that the only way I would ever find Margaret was to go straight through the forest to the inland highway and get help. Five miles from the coast highway, five miles on snowshoes in a blinding storm. It could take as long as five hours, maybe more. That meant I had to leave right then if I were to have any chance of reaching it before it became too dark.

Why wasn't he reacting? "Why do you have it hidden up there? Why don't you just bury the remains?"

He didn't bother looking at me. "I can't." Before I could respond he added, almost calmly, as if he had been expecting this, as if he already knew the outcome, "Better go get your snowshoes. Leave the shotgun." Then he turned to me with an absolutely unreadable face and added: "We have to go get them."

♦ ♦ ♦

I sensed it was going to be a race against both time and nature. Sil's snowshoes were in the Ropewalk, and I saw him sling them over his shoulder while I grabbed the shotgun and ran upstairs to get mine. I hoped he wouldn't notice that they were the ones I had taken from the shed; even in my mind I was reluctant to call them "my" snowshoes because they were actually his, and I did not know how thin the ice was between us. I had not seen a weapon, but refused to believe that he had come unarmed, and with that thought hovering over me, I debated whether to ignore his command and take the shotgun anyway. But there was no way to do that subtly, so I put my trust in the .380, left the shotgun standing in a corner of my room, and sprinted down the stairs and out the door.

When I got outside, he was standing there scanning the wall of trees beyond the school.

"How do we know she's not still in the building?" I asked.

"She isn't."

"How do you know?"

He ignored the question. "I see you found the Lewis house."

"Lewis house?"

He turned and his dark eyes bored into me. "The house in the cedars, where you found the oil lamp I saw in her apartment."

I understood. Lewis. "Yes." It was Captain Lewis who had "harried the savages into the declivity." His house, or the house of his descendents. There it was, another link to the diary. "I was trying to get through the cedars and found it by accident. The lamp I found in a hidden passage that went past the hearth and down into the cellar. I took it because I wanted to give Margaret something special for Christmas."

Sil wiped the streamer of blood that still trickled down from his nose, fixed me with a look, and said: "She isn't in the building." There was no further explanation before he switched the subject. "The State Police are looking for you."

"I figured they would be by now."

"You're the prime suspect."

I was stunned. "In what?"

He scowled at me. "In why Margaret and Sonya never showed up for Christmas down in Connecticut."

With renewed agitation, I understood my dilemma. Margaret and Sonya were gone. I alone had been with them. To the authorities, I would just naturally be the prime suspect, especially since the storm would cover the tracks of the real culprits. I thought of the dirt floor in the furnace room and imagined that it might still hold the evidence I would need to exonerate myself. In a single minute, the whole world had turned upside down and become madness on top of terror, with me as the focal point.

What was I going to say? That I was guilty, that I was the one who had let them in?

♦ ♦ ♦

I could not escape the feeling that Sil knew them, whoever they were, or at least knew where they were going. That was evident in the way he handled the pursuit.

He ordered me to get the tractor out, then turned off the light and closed the door to the shed behind me. Then he climbed onto the fender while I, with the plow lowered and the chains thumping on the frozen underlayment, pushed it as fast as it would go up the macadam road. When we were parallel with the Engineering building, he ordered me to stop, leaped down, and went up to reconnoiter the area. When he came back, he took his snowshoes and signaled me with a wave.

"Keep going up to the highway. I'll meet you there." He bent down and had the shoes on in no time. When he saw that I still hadn't moved, he hammered the fender with his fist in a blow that made it quiver. "Go!"

I slipped it in gear and floored it, then turned momentarily to see him head into the woods with a speed and agility that belied his bulk. In an instant he had vanished.

I dreaded what awaited me. It was obvious that Sil knew something about all of this, or he would not have been so confident about where we needed to go. That made him some kind of accomplice. And why had he insisted that I leave the shotgun? He couldn't have known about the .380 and didn't seem to be armed, yet there we were, going after one or more kidnappers who were almost sure to have weapons.

One thing I had to accept—accomplice or not, he was not the one whose blood was on Margaret's epee. He was obviously not wounded; she must've stuck someone else. I smiled grimly in spite of the situation; like the proud husband of a Celtic warrior queen, I envisioned her standing before her assailant, her eyes flashing, the human female gone and in her place the Valkyrie, the storm woman, threatening with death any who would cross in front of her. The reincarnation of Freydis Eiriksdottir, terrifying her tormentors without remorse, the fierceness of her protective instincts matched only by the pointed death that made it real.

But unlike Leif Eiriksson's sister, she had not been able to stop them. I was sure she was able to parry the first attack but probably did not have the strength in her thrust to keep him—or them—at bay. I did not know if she had killed the one she bloodied and, worse, did not know if he or they had already done something to her in retaliation. In despair, I pressed the gas pedal harder, even though it was already to the floor.

The previously cleared lanes on the coast highway were already half filled in when I got there. I assumed from the direction Sil had gone that I was to turn right as if I were going to the cart track, so I headed that way. He was nowhere in sight, so I put the tractor in neutral and waited, and not more than a minute later I heard a voice calling from further down. I could barely make out his form standing there, his snowshoes tucked under his arm.

He did not wait for me to stop before he pulled himself back up onto the fender. "Did you find anything?" I asked. A flicker of trust had grown in my mind and I prayed that it was not misguided.

He glanced at me and seemed about to say something, then changed his mind. "Pull in here." He pointed to the left, to the space beyond the end of the stone wall on the north side. It was the cart track. "Go up into the trees and shut off the tractor."

"Where are we going? To the village?"

He ignored me again and I drove on in silence until we entered the section where the track went through the gulch-like depression. "Stop here. Shut it off."

We were a long way from even the stream that led up to the second stream. "We can get a lot closer than this," I said, sounding oddly pleading even to myself. "Think of the time it'll take . . ."

"Forget it. They'll hear us coming if we go any further."

But my sense of foreboding would not let up. "Why would it matter if they hear us coming? They must've assumed by now that someone would be after them, and if we go as far as we can with the tractor, we stand a better chance of catching up to them." I was almost hyperventilating in my frantic efforts to understand a decision that, to me, made no sense at all. "Just think about how long it'll take us . . ."

He grabbed my sleeve and yanked me down from the seat so suddenly that I had to grab the fender to keep from falling. I spun toward him, thinking maybe he really was going to do away with me after all, my hand frantically groping for the opening to the pocket that still held the .380 as I lurched back a step to buy myself another moment of time.

But other than his look of disdainful impatience, there was no follow up. "Get your snowshoes on," he commanded, turning away from me without even a backward glance. He had taken his down from the tractor and was already in the process of doing that when he turned toward me, his look one of sudden doubtfulness. "Listen," he said with surprising softness, "if they hear us coming they'll vanish. Understand? We'll never find them if they think one of these 'things'"—he nodded toward the tractor—"is after them. They'll disappear." He saw my stupefied noncomprehension and added: "Don't you get it? Our only chance is to try to catch them on foot so that they don't know we're behind them."

"No," I said, "I don't get it. They have a long lead on us. How can we hope to catch up to them on foot?"

He had bent to the task of securing his snowshoes again and, without looking up, said: "Because they're traveling slowly."

"How do you know that?"

"Because I saw how close together their tracks were when I picked up their trail. Besides, they have a wounded man, a woman, and a small child—or rather, two small children."

"Two?"

"Yeah, two. Sonya and the girl you saw in the attic." He glanced over his shoulder at me.

Something in his gaze, or maybe his tone, told me that he knew who she was. "You know her, don't you?"

He didn't even bother answering. "Snowshoes. Get your snowshoes on." By then he had his on, and without a backward glance, he went into the brush and came back a few minutes later dragging a huge pile of evergreen boughs. These he spread over the tractor, not to hide it, he explained, but to keep as much snow off it as possible. We were going to need it again.

I had my snowshoes on by then and, hovering somewhere between resignation and begrudging trust, I recognized the futility in any further questions. The fate of Margaret and Sonya was in his hands, and I had to accept that he knew what he was doing, even if I didn't understand it.

He sized me up with a grunt. "Ready?"

"Yeah."

And then the real race began. Sil led me up the cart track at a run, then left the track and headed straight into the trees as soon as we passed out of the gulch. He ran with that effortless loping gait that even the colonials had noticed in the Indians centuries before. I struggled to keep up, but as he widened the gap between us, I knew I was not going to be able to make it. Finally, with him a good fifty feet in front of me, and my heart ready to burst, I called to him. He stopped and looked back, and for a moment I thought he was going to leave me there, which would not have been good because, in the midst of all my haste, I realized I had not thought to bring my compass. I had no idea where we were. I didn't even know what bearing we had been following.

"What's the matter?" he asked in a hushed tone.

I shook my head and held onto a small tree for support. "Winded. I need to take a breather."

He came back, surprisingly sympathetic, and sat down on a rock. "Five minutes." He pulled his sleeve up and checked his watch.

"Sorry. I thought I was in better shape."

He looked at me but said nothing.

"How did you get here anyway? Snowmobile?" The words were punctuated with great, gasping lungfuls of air.

He nodded.

"Where did you leave it?" I hadn't seen any tracks when I came back from the village, nor had I heard anything while I was out in the woods.

"About a mile from here, in some trees on the north side of the highway. I walked in from there. Came in through the brush."

I understood. Just as with the tractor, he had stopped well short of his destination so that no one would hear him coming, then come in through the trees so that his tracks would not be seen. I nodded at the soundness of his planning but did not understand its real impact until a few seconds later. If he knew nothing about the abduction, if he had come to the Ropewalk simply to get things ready for the school to reopen, why had he been trying to remain invisible?

I stared at him. He must've seen in my face that I had put it all together.

"You're wondering why," he said.

I nodded.

"Because I knew she was in trouble. I found out yesterday."

389

What he was saying was impossible. We had no way to communicate, no phone service or even short wave radio, and certainly no visitors. "How?"

He hesitated for a moment, then looked me over carefully. "The wolf told me."

Stunned, I repeated the word aloud, almost trance-like, not expecting a response, and for a moment objective reason clashed with the slender tendrils that still connected humanity to the instinct world. The animal mind was still in there. Could it still function? "How?" It was all I could think to say.

He grunted, a gesture I understood to mean I should already know the answer. "They talk to each other. All you need to do is listen to what they're saying."

I had read long ago that their howling meant something, that they were communicating information to each other, but only "knew" it in an academic sense. I had assumed that, with the disappearance of Native American culture, any knowledge of that instinct language had disappeared as well, never to be recovered. Evidently, I was wrong.

"Why did you want to give her something special for Christmas?" he asked. "Are you two an item?" There was no particular intonation behind the question, no implied insinuation that I'd be crossing some line if I said yes.

Nevertheless, I hesitated for a moment, unsure. "Yes. We've become . . . very close."

"You know she's married, right?"

"No. I mean, yes, I know she's married but, no, she really isn't. He's gone. He left her."

He nodded faintly, as if I'd just verified something that he already knew. Then, without another word, he glanced at his watch and stood up. "Time. Let's go."

I had recovered my breath. "You don't seem overly alarmed by any of this." I needed to know why he had been so startled after I told him about the girl in the attic, and why he had been so sure that Margaret and Sonya were no longer in the building. Most of all, I wanted to know why, given that we were going after kidnappers, he had not wanted me to bring the shotgun. "We don't even have any weapons." I was sure he still did not know about the .380.

He checked the bindings on his snowshoes and turned to resume the journey. "We won't need any. It's not what you think."

◆ ◆ ◆

Reality, I learned a long time ago, was whatever we all agreed it should be. Inevitably, the agreed-upon declaration became a whitewash simply because of the sheer number of things that went into it, a quantity beyond all understanding. But the invisible subsets of history, the things you never read about, the peripheral events, the unnoticed acts and decisions—these were the things that really interested me. They interested me precisely because they were the constituent parts of the "Big Picture" that historians focused on, but that could never be revealed because the long, complicated explanations of folkloric memory that they represented never quite reached any level of closure. That meant that the only option was to keep moving, keep looking, which was what I had done with my life. Mae, my first wife, had seen this in me, and had once even agreed with me that there were disadvantages posed by static ownership in an era of nomads. By "nomad" she meant me, of course.

Never in my life had that nomadic impulse had more meaning than during that race through the forest. It brought us well beyond the site of the village, and I was only able to orient myself when we crested a hill and I could see the pond and part of the barrow on its shore. We had run in a loop around it and were nearly on the other side. The storm was still raging, but its end was already in sight because the pale shroud of the sun was visible through the overcast, only two hands high. Two hours until sundown, and we were deep in the forest. Sil raised his hand to signal a halt.

My heart was hammering in my chest. How I had kept up with him, I didn't know, but he told me to stay there and moved further into the brush on his own. Ahead was a very dense growth of cedars, and I couldn't help but wonder if, through some odd quirk of fate, there was a house hidden in there the way the Lewis house was concealed near the village. Maybe that was where the girl in the attic lived. Maybe that was where they were holding Margaret and Sonya.

I leaned against a tree to try to catch my breath. I had not seen any tracks while we ran, so I could not connect our tactic with finding them. How did he know where to go? Was it just a hunch, or had he had contact before with whoever "they" were and recognized the pattern? There was no way to know, and I had no choice but to trust him. In a few minutes, he emerged from the cedars and waved me forward. When I reached him, he was staring at something on the ground. My heart leaped into my throat.

"What is it?" I asked without approaching. If it was what I dreaded, I didn't want to see it.

He reached down, picked something up, and turned toward me. A piece of cloth, stained red. It was obviously blood. I felt my knees weakening. "This must be from the one she got with her sword," he said.

Despite the sinister aspect inherent in the bloodstained rag, I was relieved. It was not her. There was still hope.

He threw it down and headed off around the cedars. I followed, apprehensive about being caught out there in the dark but confident now in Sil's ability to both find her and lead us back out.

A few minutes later, he had led me to a break in the landscape similar to the "staircase" that I'd found near the village. This one was bigger and rockier, with huge boulders nestled into what looked like a scree-covered slope. It was obviously the scar left from a centuries-old—or maybe millennia-old—rockslide, and once he saw it, he raised his hand for another halt, dropped to a crouch behind a small fir tree, and indicated to me that I should do the same. I sank to the ground and crawled behind the decaying trunk of a huge pine that had fallen years before. I hadn't seen anything.

Several minutes passed, during which time Sil crouched there motionlessly. What was he waiting for? I wondered. Had he seen or heard something?

I found a twig under the snow and tossed it at him to get his attention. When he turned to me, I shrugged and shook my head in a parody of "Why did we stop?" He motioned me forward, and when I was next to him, he whispered: "Don't you smell that?"

I shook my head and mouthed the words "Smell what?" But I had no sooner done that than I, too, caught the scent. A fire. Someone was camped nearby. "Is it them?" I whispered.

Instead of answering, he motioned me to keep quiet and shifted a few feet to his left to get a better look at something. Then, unexpectedly, as if having come to some sort of decision, he suddenly stood up, stepped out from behind the tree, and stood facing the old rockslide.

"They'll see you," I whispered from behind the tree, my words taut with the anguish of what might happen to Margaret and Sonya if the kidnappers realized they'd been followed.

Unmoved by my plea, he turned to me. "They've already seen us." His voice held no emotion at all; it was a flat, toneless statement whose very lack of intensity made me suspect once again that he was somehow tied to all this. When he then raised a hand as if waving to someone he knew, I was convinced of it. "I'll handle this," he said in a more normal voice, making no apparent effort at explanation. "You stay here." He pointed a finger at me for emphasis, and the sternness in his face and manner left no doubt that my role in this was secondary.

"Handle what?" I asked. But he ignored me, and as he walked forward, I moved so that I could see around the tree. And that was when I saw it, saw him, a form straddling the flank of the scree about a hundred yards away, covered in some sort of cloak that even at that distance I could tell was a bearskin. The culprit, the perpetrator, the invader. A blinding flash of anger shot through me and I reached into my pocket for the .380, but calmed down the moment my hand touched it. He was too far away—I would never be able to hit him at that distance. And he had Margaret and Sonya. Somewhere.

Sil approached with his right hand raised, palm outward, and stopped about twenty yards from the figure. He did not move until the other returned the gesture. Then he came nearer. Only when the two were face to face did I realize how much taller the robed figure was. He literally towered over Sil, so much so that I had my doubts that Sil, even with all his considerable bulk and strength, would be able to defend himself if the other decided to attack.

And if that happened, where would that leave me? Lost in a snowstorm in the forest, the sun going down, the temperature dropping, and Margaret and Sonya still captive, still being taken further and further into the trackless outback that stretched to the Canadian border and beyond. What would I do? A suicide attack, one last, bold, despairing attempt to get them free, only to have all three of us freeze to death during the night? I realized with the same grim humor I had felt when trapped in the chasm under the old ropewalk that I didn't even have any matches with me.

My mind was an empty maelstrom sucking into its swirl whatever fragments of rational options were left open to me. I pulled the .380 out and popped the clip. I had six shells in there. The chamber was still empty, so six was it, the magic number. Not eight, not even seven. Six. If there were more than six of them, it would be a hand-to-hand fight, assuming I made every shot count and assuming they didn't take me down before that.

My heart hammered in my chest, as much from the gridlocked sense of desperation as from the race on snowshoes. The odds of success were not good; in fact, I was slowly coming to accept that there was no way I could win at all. Even if I got them away from the abductors, with or without violence, it would be dark in an hour and I had no idea where I was. I had neither map nor compass. I didn't even have a flashlight. It did not look good.

My despairing reverie was interrupted by a sound from where Sil stood with the figure in the bearskin cloak. A second figure had joined them, not as tall, but broad like Sil himself. It was too far to hear anything, but by the gesturing it was obvious that the second figure was indicating something behind him. Sil, in his turn, would periodically point back toward me, and in those moments I could feel the others' eyes boring into me, even though I was sure they couldn't see me. Taking that as my cue, and not knowing if it was a good idea or not, I put the .380 back in my pocket and stood up.

The effect was immediate. The two hooded figures stopped talking and gesturing and looked past Sil at me. Sil then turned and saw me but was too far away for me to tell if he was angry with me or not; without any kind of indication on his part, he simply turned back towards the others and continued talking and gesturing.

It appeared to be some kind of bartering session, and the way Sil kept pointing back at me, I was clearly one of the chips. It occurred to me that maybe he was trying to persuade them to take me in place of Margaret and Sonya, and that thought sent an electric chill up my spine as I realized I might be nothing more to him than a piece of currency. That would be the final irony—the two of them get rescued, but I wouldn't be with them after all. Resigned to my "no exit" situation, I calmly began to accept my role as a possible sacrifice. All that I secretly asked for at that point was that Margaret and her daughter were safe, regardless of how it ended for me.

It seemed to be taking a long time. It was still snowing, but the full fury of the storm had mostly dissipated by then and the sun was actually showing through the overcast. There was at that point less than an hour left before sundown, and I wondered if Sil would be bartering through the night and, if so, whether he would be able to find his way out in the dark, assuming he was successful in freeing Margaret and her daughter.

But then it ended. I assumed it was a failure because the two figures turned and walked away without a parting gesture of any kind and disappeared into a dense copse of fir trees. But Sil did not retreat back to where I was standing; instead, he turned and waved me forward. "This is it," I thought, and, my hand still gripping the .380 in my pocket, I moved toward him. "Who are these guys?" I asked when I got to him, trying to not betray what I thought was about to happen, trying to keep up the façade of bravado. "What was the point of all this? What do they want?"

He silenced me with a gesture.

A moment later, the tall figure re-emerged from the trees. Behind him was the smaller figure once again, but there seemed to be something different about him, some kind of distortion. Like the tall figure, he was also covered with what looked like a bearskin, but he seemed less massive than he had appeared from a distance.

And then my heart leaped into my throat when I saw why the other figure looked so different; he was carrying a child. I could not see under the hood, not even the profile in the partial shade of the fading sunlight, but I knew it had to be Sonya. A huge load fell from my heart even as I turned to Sil and, fearful of what the answer might be, asked, "Where's Margaret?"

His eyes shifted from me to the tall figure, and following that gesture, I turned toward the pair opposite us. The tall one gestured the other toward me, and as that figure neared, it raised its head a slight bit and a shaft of fading sunlight pierced the folds of the hood. I involuntarily held my breath when I saw that it was Margaret.

She stepped up to me and reached out from under the bearskin robe to touch me. "Egan?" Her voice held a curious lilt, as if she were in shock and didn't believe it was really me, but her eyes glistened as I reached for her hand. The other made no effort to stop me.

I gently pulled her to me and looked at Sil. "What happens now? Do I go with him"—and here I gestured toward the tall figure, whose face I still hadn't seen—"as payment for releasing Margaret and Sonya?"

Sil's brow knit in confusion. "What?"

"Am I supposed to be the exchange?"

Sil's eyes darted back and forth between me and the tall figure, as if he were gauging the other's reaction or trying to sort out what I'd just said. He seemed reluctant to speak, almost as if my words had come close to betraying a trust or breaking a spell. "Why would you think that?" he finally asked.

"I assumed that was the deal you were working on, the way you kept pointing back at me."

His look wavered, as if he wanted to tell me something but couldn't. "No, there's no exchange. They're giving Margaret and Sonya back to you."

I didn't believe it. "What? They're giving them back? No fight, no ransom, nothing? What was the point of doing this, of taking them just so that they could say 'oops' when we caught up to them?" I knew I was passing out of fear and into anger, an anger buoyed up by the weapon in my pocket.

"Lower your voice," he commanded. "We're walking a tightrope here, and I don't have time to explain it all right now."

I looked over at the tall figure, who hadn't moved or reacted at all. Only when I stared at him did I catch a glimpse of long, dark hair from under the hood, and only then, with the veil of falling snow virtually stopped, did I notice other figures like him at the edge of the dense wall of evergreens behind him. One of these had the hood pulled back and I could see that it was a woman, her long, dark tresses tied into braids and a small child in some sort of basket on her back. With a start I realized that the child was the girl I'd seen in the attic. I was sure of it.

"That's the girl who was in the attic," I said, pointing at her. I glanced over at Sil but he seemed uninterested. "That's her. You wanted to know what she looked like, didn't you? Well, there she is." He wasn't looking in her direction, so I grabbed his sleeve and tried to turn him toward the woman with the child. "Right there."

But he seized my hand in a vice-like grip and stood there staring at me, his face an unreadable mask. "Yes, I understand. Get a hold of yourself. Forget her." A moment later he had torn my hand loose from his arm.

I did not understand what was happening, but the sudden hostility in Sil's tone was not lost on me. I tried to calm down. "Who are these people?" I asked in a more subdued tone. When he still didn't answer, I looked back at the woman with the child and saw other forms stirring behind her, some emerging from the cover of the fir trees, all of them silent, some with their hoods back so that I could see their faces. They were not Caucasians. I turned back to Sil. "Are they Indians?"

"Not now," he replied. "Right now you need to lead Margaret and Sonya out of here."

"How can I do that? I don't even know where we are and I don't have a compass." With a sudden, nauseating sense of foreboding, I suspected that, no, I wasn't going to be the life offered in exchange. Sil was.

But that wasn't it either. "Just follow our tracks. I'll be right behind you and when we're far enough away, I'll take the lead." I was too confused to respond and, seeing this, he added, "Go on, move, follow the tracks we made on the way in. They haven't all been filled in—the newest ones are still visible." He stepped up so that his face was nearly in mine and whispered, "You need to lead her out of here. It's what's expected of you. I'll catch up in a few minutes."

I didn't know what he meant, but I sensed the urgency and was all out of questions. I turned back to Margaret and reached inside the hood to stroke her cheek. She had a small scratch on the right side of her face.

"Margaret, I'm so sorry. If I had thought there was any danger, I would never have left you alone."

She nodded, her eyes saying "I know," but Sonya stirred and was trying to come out from under the folds of the heavy robe, and she reached under the covering and smoothed the girl's hair.

"And how are you?" I said to the child, trying to induce a sense of normality, not knowing what was going to happen next, still not even knowing who the abductors were. Margaret's eyes glistened as the tiny face peeked out from under the folds, and I reached in, took her little hand, and said, "Remember me?"

But she did not, nor could she. I involuntarily backed up a step when I saw her, a child wrapped in dressed and beaded furs, and I wondered what had happened to Sonya's clothes. But then she turned and the shaft of sunlight fell onto her face, and when I looked again I saw that it was not her, not Sonya, that Margaret was holding someone else, a beautiful little girl with auburn hair who looked exactly like her. And when I stepped up to her and reached out to touch her, Margaret looked at me, and although her lips moved, her voice did not come, and I could see in her eyes what she was saying in her mind, barely coherent and trance-like, until finally she nodded and whispered, "Yes. Yes, this is she, this is my lovely little girl, yes this is my Sonya."

◆ ◆ ◆

Chapter 30

"It's what's expected of you." The words rattled in my head like a marble in a tin can. It was what was expected of me? How would they—or Sil—have any idea what was expected of me, or even be in a position to judge that? There had been a cutting edge on Sil's voice that I chose to ignore, but that now came back to me as I picked my way into the darkening forest following the tracks we'd left on the way in.

I held Margaret's one free hand as I led her away. I walked in total silence, both because I sensed she was in a state of shock and because I no longer knew what questions to ask or what comfort to offer. At the same time, I hoped she wouldn't start asking me about what had happened because I had no idea; I felt like one of those kids at the school who try to understand the content of a book by reading what's on its jacket—the result was always fragmented, inadequate, and had no depth. She would sense immediately that I was faking it.

The tracks played out after just a few hundred yards, having all been filled in by the snow that had fallen behind us. Except for the crunching underfoot, where we broke through the icy crust beneath the fresh powder, the world around us was absolutely silent. Every time we stopped, the loudest sound was our own breathing.

My nervousness grew as the light faded, even after Sil caught up to us and took over the lead as he said he would. He came up to me, his breath a trailing plume caught in the last, slanting rays of the setting sun. "How is she?" he whispered, glancing back quickly at Margaret, who had retreated to the side and was staring back at the darkening trail we left in the snow.

I shook my head. "I don't know." I followed her gaze for a moment, intuitively understanding that she, like I, needed an explanation. "What just happened?"

Sil seemed strangely subdued. He turned back to me, his gaze both stern and expectant as he looked at me askance, nodded ever so slightly, and said, "You just agreed to something you better be ready for."

"And what was that?" I still had visions of some sort of hostage situation, and the moment he spoke my senses went on high alert. I scanned the darkening wall of trees all around us. "Are we expecting some sort of nasty surprise on our way back?"

"No, nothing like that."

"What, then?"

But he had already turned away and was headed for Margaret. When he reached her, he spoke softly, put his arm around her shoulders, and led her back to me. Then he took the lead. "Let's go."

There were no longer any tracks to follow, and the last, feeble rays of the sun were tinting the horizon with a fading red glow, leaving scarcely enough light to make out individual trees. Only the uniform whiteness of the ground provided me with some degree of orientation as I silently prayed that Sil knew where he was going because, for all I knew, we could've been walking in circles.

Twenty minutes later the sun was completely gone, the horizon had darkened, and the forest around us had become a solid wall of featureless murk. The deepening cold closed in on us immediately and I could feel the numbness starting in my toes. "How much further?" I asked Sil as he plunged into the darkness ahead of us without the slightest hesitation.

He stopped and looked back at us. "Not far. We just passed the old village and we'll hit the stream soon. Another twenty minutes to the tractor—a half hour at the most." He looked past me at Margaret. "Everybody okay?"

I felt her nod rather than saw it, a slight tremor in her hand betraying the doubt and fear that she had to have been feeling.

◆ ◆ ◆

It was full dark by the time he got us back to where we'd left the tractor. We were moving through such a total blackout by then that its sudden appearance in front of us was like something out of a dream. I wanted to know how he had managed to do this, to lead us there, but there was no time for questions as he cleared away the branches covering it and hoisted Margaret and the girl onto the fender.

"Take them back to the Ropewalk," he said.

"How about you? You can ride on the other fender."

But he needed to go get his snowmobile. How he would find it in the dark, I couldn't imagine, but I had every confidence that he would.

Margaret held onto me the whole ride back. I was too stunned, too confused, too ignorant of what had happened to ask anything but the most rudimentary questions. How had they gotten in? How had she been taken?

"I went down to take a shower," she said, "and after I turned the water on, Sonya broke away and began running down the hall. I had left the apartment door open like I did before, and since I didn't see her in the hall—you know how fast she is—I thought that was where she had gone. But when I went in, she wasn't there. I turned around to go back out and there was someone there, this big figure wearing, I don't know, fur or leather or something. He had Sonya. I freaked out and grabbed my epee. I . . . I hurt him getting her away from him, but others came and took both of us." She paused for a second to reach into the bearskin cloak and brush an errant strand of hair out of the girl's face. "I didn't have time to grab my coat, so I thought for sure I was going to freeze to death, but then one of them had this." She tugged on the edge of the bearskin.

That explained why she was dressed that way, but at the same time it hit me that she might've been wearing only her bathrobe when they came for her, which raised the specter of sexual assault in my mind. I was still haunted by that image I had conjured up earlier, the one of half-mad forest creatures taking the means to procreate their diminishing tribe, and judging by what I'd just seen, I more than half suspected that I couldn't rule it out.

Even so, if all she had on under the bearskin was a bathrobe, she would've been close to freezing by then despite the thickness and length of the fur, since she would've had no underlying protection from the cold, not even footwear. Yet she clearly wasn't shivering, and her

401

feet were encased in heavy, moccasin-like boots to which the primitive snowshoes she'd been using had been attached.

In spite of all that, I couldn't help but ask the next question, almost nauseous with apprehension about the answer. "Did they . . . did they hurt you in any way?" I deliberately avoided any suggestion of sexual assault.

But she shook her head. "No."

I let out a slow breath in relief. "Are you warm enough? Did they give you a chance to get dressed before they took you?"

She seemed surprised. "I was already dressed. I had gone down to the shower room just to get the water running—you know how long it can take before it warms up—when Sonya broke away."

"Oh." In spite of my relief, an errant thought angled in at me from one of those mental closets that hold the unanswered questions: What kind of kidnapper comes prepared with extra clothes, "just in case"?

The moon had not yet risen, so the darkness on the old cart track was nearly absolute and visibility was limited to the range of the headlights. I drove on in silence, and only when we were on the macadam road did I ask the most obvious question of all. "Who is this little girl?"

In response, Margaret pulled the bearskin tighter. "This," she said in almost a whisper, as if she scarcely believed it herself, "is my daughter."

◆ ◆ ◆

"You have to leave, right now," Sil said to her. Then, turning to me, he added: "I'll take them on the snowmobile right to my house. They have to contact the State Police and tell them everything is okay so that the search is called off. If they don't, well, things could get a little too deep."

He had arrived at the Ropewalk mere minutes after us. I heard the buzz of his snowmobile coming down the road even as I parked the tractor. By the time I was leading them to the building, his headlight beam was slashing back and forth across the front of the shed.

She understood. "Do I have time to get a change of clothes?"

"No. We have to go right now."

She nodded and turned toward me. "What about you?"

Before I could answer, Sil intervened. "I'll be back for him." He glanced at me. "Don't go anywhere. I've had enough searching for one day."

"Right. Maybe I'll go polish off a bottle of wine. I think I have one left."

He grunted. "Well, don't get too sauced. You need to be able to stay on the snowmobile and, anyway, I have beer at home."

"What are you, my father?" I tried to make my tone as lighthearted as possible.

He wagged a finger at me in mock rebuke. "Hey, don't make me knock you around some more." In the headlight beam I could see that he was smiling in spite of the words, and as if to emphasize the point, he rubbed the bridge of his nose where I'd hit him. In that moment I realized he had come to respect me, and that little gesture was probably as close as he'd ever come to admitting it.

He made sure Margaret's bearskin robe was secure, then bundled her up further with a heavy blanket that he'd taken from the storage bin under the seat. Before he drove away, I saw her reach out and touch his shoulder, saying, "I hurt one of them. I don't know if he's okay."

◆ ◆ ◆

"Dear Diary: Updates are in order, I suppose. The reason so little gets written these days is that so little happens that's worthy of note. All of that changed today, however, and I had this errant thought of myself, a newly minted middle-aged man, suddenly married again but this time with a little daughter, and then along comes Rick, my long-lost childhood friend, to prepare for a trip into the unknown. He plays with the girl and 'poofo,' a snapshot immortalizes the moment and years later the girl, now grown, sees the picture and asks: 'Who was that, Dad?' And I try to explain a face from a primordial past whose world wasn't even the same one she was living in, and she wonders."

As the snowmobile sped away, I laughed at myself for the crudity of the supposed journal entry that I knew I would never write. I wouldn't write it because I was beyond recording the events of my life in some vain quest to understand where they might've been leading me. It had become clear to me, without having to articulate it in a diary or in words at all, that wherever I might've believed I was going, I had ended up somewhere else.

When the buzz of the snowmobile faded, I stood for several minutes in the utter and complete silence of the frozen world around me. Nothing moved. No sounds came from the dark rim of the forest beyond the school, not even the snap of a branch or the hoot of an owl. Almost instinctively, I looked toward the copula on top of the shed, or what I could see of it, and half expected to find the silhouette of the huge bird obscuring the stars that peeked out from behind the ragged streamers of the storm clouds. But, no, there was nothing. For the first time since I'd seen him on the road two weeks earlier, I even wished the wolf would stop by for a visit.

I turned and went into the Ropewalk, pulled the door shut behind me, and leaned against the wall. I felt profoundly alone—crushed, swallowed, overwhelmed by the vastness of the building in a way I'd never noticed before. "Tired," I mumbled. "I'm just tired." With Margaret and Sonya safe, the stress was draining away and leaving nothing but a hollowed out shell. I was suddenly hot, too, all lathered up from the exertion, so I took my parka off and tossed it onto the wooden bench against the wall. From there my eyes automatically went to the bowls near the artificial plant; the cat was out of food and water. I'd have to give it something before I left with Sil.

I partially unbuttoned my shirt and fluttered the front to let some of the heat out. "I wonder if this is what a basted turkey feels like," I said aloud, just so that I could hear my own voice and laugh. "Alright, enough of this. I need a drink."

I was so used to staying in Margaret's apartment that I automatically headed down the hall, then caught myself, turned, and went up the stairs to my room. My door was open, and for a moment I suspected something was wrong, but then realized immediately why—in my panic to get my snowshoes and go after Margaret, I hadn't even closed the door behind me. I went in, flipped on the light, saw that there was no one there waiting to surprise me, glanced quickly under the bed to see if the spider had somehow gotten past the wooden slat over its hole, then pulled out the box with the wine. I was right—I had one left. I took it out, threw the empty box onto the bed, and went over to the little shelf over my desk to get the corkscrew.

"What? No wineglasses?" I mumbled. "Maybe I'll go all out and use a paper cup." I was deliberately mimicking the dialog Margaret and I had had when I first had dinner with her, as if there were some strange sense of security in that trivial memory. In fact, I discovered I was out of paper cups anyway, so I reached for one of the glasses I kept on that same shelf, then decided, what the hell. I pulled the cork, sat down at the desk, and drank right out of the bottle.

I guessed it was going to be at least an hour and a half before Sil made it back to get me, maybe a full two hours. What should I do in the meantime? I wondered. Read more in the old diary?

That thought reminded me that it was still down in Margaret's apartment. It felt vulnerable there with her gone, so, taking the bottle with me, I got up and headed down the stairs.

Her door was also open. This felt strange to me, not because it was unexpected but because it somehow still resonated with the abduction, as if somewhere, in some slice of time other than just my memory, it were still happening. I turned on the light, then did a quick tour just to make sure the apartment really was empty.

The epee was still on the floor in her bedroom. I walked up to it and bent over for a better look. The blood on the tip was dry and crusty, and there were drops I hadn't noticed before under it and scattered around it. Was this technically a crime scene? I wondered. If I cleaned it up, would I be destroying evidence? Should I photograph it? If the person she stuck died, would that make her guilty of homicide and, if so, should I leave the scene as it was, assuming that might assist in her defense?

I knew, of course, that I couldn't photograph it, at least not with the thirty-five millimeter, because I'd have to bring the film somewhere to be developed and the pictures would be seen, and even if they meant nothing at the time, the photo lab worker might remember them if the event became newsworthy. There was, however, the Polaroid—I could take some shots and hide them someplace secure until such time, if any, when I might need them.

Or I could just say "the hell with it," clean it up, and forget about it, which was what I opted to do. I picked up the epee, brought it to the kitchen sink, and rinsed it off under the hot water. The coagulated blood loosened up and came off in a thin streamer of pink liquid punctuated with flecks of darker material. When it was clean, I dried it with a paper towel, then soaked the towel and brought it into the bedroom to wipe up as many drops of blood as I could find. That done, I put the epee in the closet and went back to the kitchen to toss the paper towel, now stained an obvious pink, into the garbage. Then, on impulse, for no cogent reason that I could articulate, I detoured to the bathroom, ripped the paper rag to shreds, and flushed it down the toilet. Some instinct cautioned me about leaving it where it might be found.

Then I straightened the place up—I set the overturned glass upright on the kitchen table and did a walkthrough to see if I'd missed anything. There was a towel on the floor alongside her bed that I hadn't noticed before, and as I picked it up to bring it over to the hamper, it occurred to me that maybe that was what she had intended to use in the shower. It wasn't damp, which squared with her story about not actually getting under the water. I threw it into the hamper and headed back to the kitchen.

There was a little bit of turkey left in the refrigerator, so I ripped off some pieces for the cat, wrapped them in a piece of foil, and filled a small jar with water. Then, with one last look around, which included a visit to Sonya's closet to make sure the panel in back was still in place, and feeling oddly more like a prowler than a rescuer, I turned off the lights, grabbed the diary, stepped out into the hall, and locked the door behind me.

The wine was already getting to me, the more so since I was exhausted and hadn't eaten anything since breakfast, and by the time I got back to the lobby I was vigorously debating with myself whether I should eat the cat's turkey. But, no, I felt an odd sense of kinship with the homeless thing, a sense of having shared an intense adventure, so I left my offering and refilled its water bowl. Then I knew I had to stop drinking and get some air.

◆ ◆ ◆

Details haunt every enterprise where one is trying to convey an impression at the expense of the facts, and my situation was no exception. As far as I knew, Margaret would contact the State Police when she got to Sil's house to let them know that both of us were safe and that I would be picked up shortly. That would end the manhunt and get me off the "suspect" list, but my apprehension was that there would be some kind of inquiry anyway—maybe just some closeout procedure—that could open the door to things I'd rather not try to explain, among them my interest in the old village and its ropewalk, which could lead them to the old proprietor's records and the diary. Then there was the issue of Sonya herself—what had happened to her?

There were the girl's tracks in the dirt floor of the furnace room as well, which I once imagined as my possible salvation but which now appeared to be loose links in a chain of events that, to an outside party, would seem discontinuous.

I didn't know where to begin, but for starters, I needed to get everything back to some semblance of normality. For all I knew, the State Police might've even then been on their way to the Ropewalk on snowmobiles to verify the telephone story and could get there before Sil. It was imperative that they not find anything unusual. Everything had to get back to its original place.

The chain that I'd used to secure the door was still on the floor against the wall; I had to get rid of it so that no one would see it and question why it was there. I got my parka from the bench and put it on, then thought about the snowshoes and crampons that I'd borrowed. The latter were up in my room, still in my daypack, so I went up, left the half-empty wine bottle and the diary on my desk, and dug them out. Then, with the crampons in my hand, the snowshoes under my arm, and the chain over my shoulder, I headed out across the yard to the shed.

I pulled the door open, and when I stepped back to make room for it, the chain slipped off my shoulder and buried itself in the snow. Ignoring it for the moment, I secured the door against the wall and reached inside to turn on the light. The fluorescent bulbs blinked, hesitated, and then came to life, flooding the front of the shed with a rectangle of grayish-white light. Making a mental note to make sure the hidden door in the granary was absolutely invisible, I headed toward the stairs and hung the crampons on the nail over the bags of traction sand and the snowshoes on the peg next to them, right where I'd found them. Then I went out to retrieve the chain.

I uncoiled it from the hole it had created and shook the snow off, threw it over my shoulder once again, and was about to turn and head into the shed when I noticed that something at the bottom of the hole was glinting in the light. I bent over for a closer look but it was too indistinct, so I reached in but couldn't free it from the ice that had grown over it. Whatever it was, it had evidently been there since before the ice storms hit us. I couldn't even kick it free, so I flailed it with the chain and finally it popped out. A chunk of ice still clung to it, so I brought it into the shed to see if I could identify it. I had to look at it from several different angles before I realized what it was.

A padlock. With the key still stuck in the hole at the bottom.

Like a pernicious vapor being sucked out of a vessel, my fatigue evaporated, my head cleared, and I was suddenly at a new level of alertness. It could only be one thing—the lock to the shed, which explained why the shed was open and available when everything I knew about Sil told me he never would've done that.

My mind raced like I'd just gotten a mental second wind. Two weeks before, when I'd gone into the shed to get the pinch bar to move the tree limb away from the front door, I'd placed the bar against the exterior wall of the shed and it had fallen, punched a line through the glazed-over snow, and hit something hard underneath. I had paid no attention at the time, and the line it left by falling had been long since covered by the snow that we'd had in the meantime. But the general area was right where I'd found the lock. I was sure, with no way to actually prove it, that this was what the bar had hit. Which meant that the shed had been unlocked almost immediately after the students and faculty had left for the holiday.

Why would this matter? I asked myself, trying hard for some sense of normalcy. Well, the timeline probably wouldn't, I imagined by way of reassurance. But what about the implications? My hands were shaking as I tried to fit this into whatever mosaic my mind was assembling. I deliberately, in a state of absolute denial, did not articulate the obvious—this connected Sil to everything that had happened. He alone had the key. He alone had access.

Was it some kind of elaborate setup after all? And if it was, where had he just taken Margaret and her daughter?

◆ ◆ ◆

I didn't even bother trying to hang the chain back up in the old granary. Instead, I simply left it right on the long bench against the wall. Then I turned the light off, closed the door, went back over to the Ropewalk, and up to my room.

I felt sick to my stomach as I thawed out the frozen lock in a sink full of hot water. Never had I felt so completely helpless and checkmated—he had taken them on the snowmobile and there was no way I could follow, both because it was too dark and because the tractor would only get me as far as the coast highway. With a sickening thud in my chest it then occurred to me—he wasn't going to come back to get me. He was going to leave me there. Was that what he meant by "agreeing to something I better be prepared for?"

I sat down on the bed and tried to think it through. The specter of social isolation and its attendant hallucinations occurred to me once again, and considering how tired and hungry I was, I couldn't rule that out as influencing the way I was thinking. On the other hand, the last time I felt the icy hand of "unhingement" touching me was when I saw the "shadow within a shadow" emerging from the utility closet, then vanishing before I could get to it. But *that* had turned out to be true—the girl had climbed the ladder back to the attic. Was this also true?

On the most rational level, I knew that the scenario of leaving me there made no sense at all; it would accomplish nothing because in less than a week, the school would reopen and people would start returning and find me there. Then again, for all I knew, the bridges might have even then been repaired and I might be able to drive myself out. No, he couldn't get rid of me by simply leaving me there.

I got up and started pacing. Obviously, he wasn't trying to get rid of me, at least not this way. And, having come down off my hysteria-induced agitation, it was equally clear to me that he would never hurt Margaret and the child. Why would he? The skeleton in the shed was not his doing and, even if the explanation behind it was long in coming, he was not a killer.

I drained the water from the sink, took the lock out, and dried it. The key came out easily; I stuck it in the pocket of my parka, the one opposite the pocket that held the .380. I stared at the lock for a moment, my hand still quivering from the aftereffects of the adrenalin, then put it in the same pocket with the key. Then I sat down on the bed again and stopped thinking altogether.

It had simply become too strenuous.

◆ ◆ ◆

Sil got back to the Ropewalk in less time than I had estimated. I heard the buzz of the snowmobile and glanced at the clock—he had been gone about an hour and a quarter. I pulled on my parka, felt the pocket one last time for the .380, closed and locked my door, and went downstairs to wait in the lobby. One way or another, in whatever form, the moment had come and I would be ready for him.

When he walked in, he seemed momentarily startled to find me right in front of him. "Jesus, you caught me off guard. Ready to go?" He turned to pull the door shut behind him and, when I didn't immediately answer, he glanced back over his shoulder. "Ready to g . . . ?"

He stopped because I had pulled the .380 out of my pocket and pointed it at him. His eyes widened and he shrank back a step, raising his hands, palms outward. "What the fuck is wrong with you?"

"Where did you bring them? What did you do with them?"

He glanced from me to the gun and back. "What do you mean, 'what did I do with them'? I brought them to my house. They're there now." A tense moment of silence followed as he sized me up. "What the hell's gotten into you?"

In response I reached into my pocket, pulled out the lock, and tossed it onto the floor in front of him. "What the hell is that?"

He bent down, picked it up, turned it over a few times to examine it, and shrugged. "It's the lock to the shed." Then he seemed confused. "How did you get it open without cutting it off?"

"I didn't get it open. It was open when I went out there, so I thought you had left it open." I reached into my pocket again and took out the key. "Whoever actually did it used this." I tossed it to him and he caught it with his free hand. "It was stuck in the base when I found it."

He stared at it in what appeared to be genuine disbelief.

"Someone had the key. And unless you have a committee in charge of it, that someone had to be you."

He looked over at me. "What are you getting at?"

In truth, I didn't know. I was so confused and conflicted, so exhausted, that nothing made any sense. "What does it mean?" was all I could manage to get out.

Sil turned the key over several times in his hand and examined it closely, stopped for a moment to examine some small feature, then looked at me. "It means you found the thing I needed to understand what was going on here."

"I did?" My hand had started to tremble, as much from fear as fatigue, and I knew that if he rushed me I wouldn't have the strength to fight him. I'd have to shoot. Like an afterthought from a bad dream, I fleetingly wondered if I'd actually chambered a round.

"Put the gun down," he said gently. "Look, if I'd wanted to hurt you or Margaret I could've done it at any time in the woods. I could've simply let you get lost out there and you would've frozen to death. Or I could've shot you at any time when you weren't looking."

That brought me back to wakefulness, at least for a moment. "Shot me? How?" I had been sure he hadn't been armed.

In response he slowly, with his other hand still extended in a gesture of non-aggression, opened his parka and reached in behind his back. When his hand came out—very slowly so as not to provoke anything—it had a semi-auto in it, which he held gingerly, between two fingers to indicate no intent to use it. "I never go into the woods without my nine millimeter."

I let the hand with the .380 drop to my side and felt like I was an inch away from collapsing. "You didn't unlock the shed?"

"No. Even if I did, I wouldn't just throw the lock on the ground. Besides, what would the point have been? If I wanted to get into the Ropewalk, I would've just unlocked the front door."

"What if you couldn't? What if something were holding the door shut from the inside?" I was thinking of the chain, of course. "Wouldn't you go into the shed to find something to pry it open with, or break it down?"

He shrugged as he slipped the gun back under his parka. "No. I'd have no reason to do that. If I couldn't get in the front, I would've gone in through the furnace room hatch, then up the ladder and out through whosever closet it went by."

That simple statement disarmed me. He was right. I knew he was right; it just wasn't adding up for me. But how would those people have gotten a key to the shed? Images from my memory raced across my inner vision and suddenly I was sure, even through the blurriness in my mind, that the "bear" I'd seen from my window when I first had dinner with Margaret was the one who had unlocked it. I couldn't prove it, of course, and my sense of timing was probably off by a day or two, but I was sure that was what had happened. But how? Where did he get the key?

"Okay, one more time. Ready to go?" He glanced from my face to the gun still in my hand.

"Yeah." I felt like a fool, like someone who had just accused the messenger of having done the deed. I slipped the .380 back into my pocket; I didn't even have to lower the hammer because I realized that in my fatigue and confusion I hadn't cocked it, which, because it was a single-action automatic, meant I couldn't have fired even if I wanted to. I looked over at Sil. "Sorry. I'm just a little . . . confused I guess."

"It's alright. C'mon, let's go." He turned away, opened the door, and stepped out. The blast of cold air hit me in the face like a slap as I followed him out onto the steps, then waited while he locked the door. The cold and darkness closed over me like a shroud.

The snowmobile was parked in front of the building. He went up to it, lifted the seat, and pulled out what looked like a giant, lofted marshmallow. "Here, wrap yourself in this. I have to lock the shed." What he handed me was a snowsuit that looked like a windproof sleeping bag with tubes for arms and legs. I pulled it on while he went over and slipped the lock through the hasp on the door to the shed. I was on the seat and ready to go when he got back.

He climbed on in front of me and started the machine, then glanced back to make sure I was ready. "See?" he said. "If I wanted to get rid of you, I'd just let you freeze your ass off before we got to the inland highway. Or maybe I'll just take a hard corner, roll you into a snowdrift, and leave you there overnight. Then I'll come back in the morning, tie you to a tree, and charge tourists five bucks a head to see the only totem pole ever found in the east."

With that, he put it in gear and started to move, going slowly and glancing back now and then because, in spite of my fatigue—or maybe because of it—I had begun laughing so hard he had to make sure that I really *didn't* fall off and end up in a snowdrift.

♦ ♦ ♦

Chapter 31

Sil didn't kill me, freeze me, or tie me to a tree as a tourist attraction. Instead, he simply brought me out to his house. It was the last one of only three on a dead-end side street that ended at his driveway. Beyond it, shrouded in almost absolute darkness, was the impenetrable gloom of the forest that stretched, nearly unbroken except by an occasional road, all the way to the Canadian border and then beyond, to the trackless forests and bogs of the far north.

The streetlights ended a good fifty yards before his house, so that by the time Sil parked the snowmobile and turned off the light it was so dark I felt like I was in a cave. There was no other source of light; his nearest neighbor was so far away that all I could see was the tiny square of light that I knew to be one of the windows. Like a blind man, I got to the house not by following his form but by the sound of his footsteps.

Through a slit in the curtains of a side window I could see that his Christmas tree was still up and the lights were lit, so the atmosphere as we approached the door was one of peaceful festivity. We came in through the back and took off our snowsuits and boots in the mudroom. He handed me a pair of fur-lined slippers from a rack holding an assortment of footwear, calling them "guest slippers" that he held in reserve for lost vagrants, wandering troubadours, and assorted homeless vagabonds.

"We never know when we might have to rescue somebody and bring him home," he said with a good-natured smirk. "Or the cat might drag something in."

I conceded defeat as I pulled them on. "Okay, you win, but I never thought that I would ever have to be rescued." I glanced over at him and saw in the stronger overhead light that his nose looked more banged up than I'd noticed at the Ropewalk. It was slightly swollen and a dark bruise had appeared in the corner of his right eye. In view of what he'd just done for me, I felt a mixture of remorse and embarrassment. "Sorry about the bloody nose."

He seemed genuinely surprised. "It's alright. You got a mean elbow. I never saw anybody fight that way. Was that some of that karate stuff you teach?"

"Yeah."

He grunted and shook his head. "It's like dirty fighting, using your feet and elbows like that."

I felt a rush of defensiveness in spite of myself. "Yeah, well, the intent is to survive, not satisfy a boxing referee."

He looked over at me and smiled. "I didn't say there was anything wrong with it. I was just trying to say that it worked—no one ever knocked me around like that before." He pulled a key ring out of his pocket, unlocked the door to the kitchen, and pushed it open. The mudroom was instantly flooded with warmth and the smell of a home-cooked meal.

"I hope you're hungry," he said. "We held dinner just for you."

I was starving. In a single moment, with the faintest whiff of hot food, I was reminded that I hadn't eaten anything since breakfast.

◆ ◆ ◆

I could hear Margaret talking to someone upstairs as we went into the living room. There was a fireplace against the far wall and, in it, a roaring blaze whose warmth I could feel from ten feet away. I went up to it, turned around, and stood there letting it warm my half-frozen butt. Sil lowered himself onto a nearby easy chair, and a few minutes later, a tall, dark-haired woman came down holding a bearskin robe that I assumed was the one Margaret had been wearing. Sil introduced her as his wife, Gert, who he said was a pureblood Abenaki and spoke their ancestral language.

"Nice to meet you," she said as she freed up one hand and offered it to me. "Margaret has told me a lot about you."

I stood there like the totem pole Sil threatened to turn me into as I shook her hand and stared into her dark eyes. A sense of déjà vu had come over me, and I realized in a moment why—I had seen her before, at the school. She worked in the records department, keeping track of students' names, addresses, and academic histories. But I had never made the connection between her and Sil.

"Dinner will be ready in a few minutes," she went on, "but you must be freezing, so have a seat in the meantime and wrap your feet in a blanket. I'll be right back." She nodded toward a loveseat opposite the chair Sil had taken. A woolen blanket was folded up on its cushion, so I followed her suggestion, sat down, and wrapped my feet in it. I could feel the fire toasting the frost out of my veins.

I didn't realize how cold I really was until Gert came back and handed me—of all things—a mug of hot chocolate. I hadn't had it in years; I sat there staring at it, savoring its aroma, letting it take me back to my childhood days of skating on the stream.

"Margaret said you had a special thing for hot chocolate," she said. "Some connection to your childhood."

"Just like skating on the stream," said a voice from the stairs. It was Margaret's; I looked to my right and there she was, leaning over the handrail to see me. "All you need is Rick and Nadine."

"Who's Nadine?" growled Sil.

"Just someone I knew as a kid," I said. "A childhood crush. We used to skate on a stream and then come home to hot chocolate."

Margaret did not come down to join us. Instead, Gert went up. There was about a minute of silence and then I could hear the two of them talking. The words were indistinct but the tone was unmistakable—Margaret was crying and it seemed as if Gert were trying to comfort her.

I looked over at Sil. "What's going on?"

"She's coming down off the adrenalin high. Started when I got her out of the woods and was going down the road toward the house. She's confused." He got up and prodded the fire with a poker. "Want some coffee instead of hot chocolate?"

"Got any Kahlua?"

"Yeah, I think so, but that'll cost you extra."

"Bill me."

He grunted and headed toward the kitchen where he began to fuss with the coffeemaker. The gesture was not lost on me—it was obvious there was something he either didn't want to talk about, or didn't know how to talk about. I finally unwrapped my feet, got up, and went into the kitchen.

"What else?" I asked.

He turned to me. "What else what?"

"She's confused. What else?"

He handed me a bottle of Kahlua. "Bring this out to the living room."

I stood there holding the bottle and finally he relented. "Look, she just lost a daughter she'd been raising since infancy, and gained a daughter she didn't even know existed. She's trying to work that out. She's confused, and a little scared."

"Scared of what?"

"Scared of not knowing the who, what, and why behind all this. Scared of not knowing what happened to the other Sonya, and scared of not knowing if it'll happen again." He turned around to switch on the coffeemaker and, half over his shoulder and half as an aside, mumbled, "You should be, too."

That got my attention. "I should be what?"

He turned toward me again and stuck an empty coffee mug into my free hand. "It'll be ready in just a minute."

"I should be what?" I prodded.

His dark eyes bored into me. "You should be scared, too."

At that point, I didn't know if I was becoming nervous or just impatient. "Alright, now you've either told me too much or not enough. Which is it? Why should I be scared? Does it have something to do with the people we saw in the forest?"

"Indirectly. But they're not the ones you need to worry about."

"Who, then?"

"Your own kind."

"My own kind? What's that supposed to mean?"

He said nothing, which I construed more as exaggerated secrecy than as a simple reluctance to divulge something sensitive. Either way, I hated head games like this and I hoped my look conveyed that message. "Why should a little girl be of any interest to anyone? And why should I be scared for her?"

Sil appeared distant, or maybe uncertain, as he pondered my question. "I just worry about them, that's all."

"Them?"

"All the kids at the school." He turned away for a moment and opened a cupboard door. "I kind of consider them all 'my kids' and I hate not being able to control this."

The "control" comment set me back mentally as I suddenly realized that all of this had somehow been no random event, that there had been some sort of plan behind it, that my original surmise before we went after them had been correct—Sil knew who they were, and that was how he knew where they were going. "Who are they?" It was more a demand than a question.

He stared into the cupboard and said nothing.

"God damn it, Sil, who are they and why would they care about a little girl?"

He continued to stare into the cupboard, his look frozen as if his attention were far away. "Look, it's complicated, and I don't know all the details." He closed the cupboard and turned to me. "Gert knows how it all works."

"How what works?"

But at that moment the sound of steps in the stairwell and Margaret's voice saying "Alright" told us that she was coming downstairs. "Look, I'll explain it after the women go to bed," he said, all but physically crowding me back towards the living room.

Margaret was at the bottom of the stairs when we got back to our seats. She came over, joined me on the loveseat, and vacantly stared as Sil, who had brought out three mugs in anticipation of the women wanting coffee as well, spaced them out on the coffee table. She was trying hard to appear normal but her eyes still bore the reddish tint of her upset.

I put my arm around her. "You okay?"

She looked at me and nodded, but her face betrayed her doubt. "I can't talk to her," she said.

At first I wasn't sure what she meant. "You can't talk to her?"

She shook her head as Sil gently explained. "The little girl doesn't speak English."

I was stunned. This was a development that for some reason I hadn't expected. "What does she speak?" I asked him.

He shrugged and nodded toward the stairs. "Ask Gert."

I looked over and saw her bringing the child down the stairs. The little girl had been transformed; Gert and Margaret had given her a bath and, with her face clean, her hair combed, and dressed in flannel pajamas clearly too big for her, she looked no different from any other six year old girl. Gert paused at the bottom of the stairs and announced her presence as if she were a prima donna, then brought her over to the loveseat and placed her on Margaret's lap. The resemblance between the two was so close there was no doubt that she was Margaret's daughter.

The girl appeared to be more confused than frightened, and although she was obviously comforted by Margaret's touch, it was clear she did not understand what was happening. She spoke to Gert in a very quiet little voice, and when Gert bent down to answer, Sonya turned to stare at Margaret, who smiled warmly in return.

"What did she say?" asked Margaret.

Gert straightened up. "She asked who you were."

"What did you tell her?"

Gert stroked the girl's hair. "I told her you were her mother."

◆ ◆ ◆

Sil slapped the arms of the chair to get everyone's attention, then stood up. "Everybody ready for some coffee? We'll be eating in a few minutes." He got up without waiting for anyone to answer, went to the kitchen, and returned with the coffeepot and a pitcher of cream. While he was pouring, Gert went back to the kitchen and I followed close behind, headed for the bathroom, which was located in a short hallway off the kitchen.

They must not have realized I was in there because when I came out, I passed through the kitchen and saw Sil talking to Gert. His back was to me and, as if to press whatever point he was trying to make, he reached into his pocket, pulled something out, and handed it to her. When she took it, I saw that it was the key I'd found in the lock. She looked down at it, didn't seem surprised or perplexed, looked back up at Sil and was about to say something when she noticed me. She immediately closed her hand around the key and I, pretending to have missed the whole thing, nodded and went back into the living room.

Sil's comment from a moment before—about Gert knowing "how it all works"—flashed through my mind, but there was no time to ponder if that little transaction might've meant something because a minute later Gert came out and announced that it was time to eat. Margaret carried Sonya into the dining room and placed her on a chair fitted with several cushions for height, then sat down next to her. I selected the seat on the other side, my intention being to help Sonya master the subtleties of eating with utensils, as I had done at the Ropewalk with the other Sonya. But Gert gently shooed me away with the admonishment that she needed to sit next to the little girl, so I moved over next to Sil.

For the first five minutes, the only sound was Gert's voice as she gently showed Sonya how to use a spoon. The child caught on very quickly, and on Gert's signal, Margaret took over, talking to the girl in English, which we knew she didn't understand. I, like Sil, ate in silence, but my mind was a chaotic medley of information fragments trying to piece themselves together into a coherent picture. After seeing Gert try to hide the key in her hand, I realized that she, like Sil, recognized it, though I did not know if she understood that it was the key that was used to open the shed. But why she recognized it, what her role was, and why she had apparently concealed that information from Sil, I had no way of knowing. I stole an occasional glance at her as if expecting some kind of revelation, but her attention was focused on Sonya.

A mighty blast of wind surged against the house and for a moment virtually everyone stopped to listen. I could almost feel the walls moving under the impact. "The wind's picking up," Sil said to no one in particular. "Gonna be cold tonight, what with the wind chill."

Gert smiled in reply, and I, sensing that it was an attempt to initiate a conversation on a neutral path, simply shrugged and agreed. "Sure sounds like it, judging by that blast."

"Won't be the last one before the night's over," he went on. "Feels like the storm's coming back."

This was followed by an awkward silence as I, and presumably Gert as well, judging by her expression, understood the unintended implications of what he had said—the other Sonya was out in that cold with the people who had taken her. As if reading my thoughts, Margaret turned in her chair to stare at the window, as if she could see through the shade and curtains and into the endless forest beyond. I started to reach for her hand, but before I could complete the gesture Gert got up and stepped over to her. "She's fine," she said, resting her hands on Margaret's shoulders.

"She's out there, in that cold," whispered Margaret.

"She's fine," Gert repeated. "Remember what we talked about upstairs? She's invisible now, but she's fine."

"Will I ever see her again?"

"Yes."

In spite of this assurance, Margaret seemed on the point of tears again and might've succumbed to the mood, as inconsolable as it was, but for a word from Sonya. Yes—a word, in English. The little girl held up one of her utensils, pride beaming from her tiny face, and said, "Spoon."

And Margaret, her heart visibly melting under the gesture, kissed the girl on the forehead and, nodding, gently said, "Yes, honey, that's a spoon."

◆ ◆ ◆

Margaret went to bed right after dinner. The sheer physical and emotional exhaustion caused by the relentless strain of the day's events had caught up to her, and I could see that she was ready to nod off right at the dinner table. She and Sonya went upstairs to the spare bedroom the moment the dishes were cleared from the table.

Much as I wanted to, I knew I wouldn't be sleeping with her, and not just because Sonya would be in the same room. Gert had made it clear that, since we weren't married, we would be sleeping apart while under her roof. I was to have the foldout sofa bed in the living room, which was an oddly déjà vu experience since that was how I'd started in Margaret's apartment.

It was just as well because I, in contrast to Margaret, had evidently passed some sort of recovery point and didn't feel tired at all. In fact, I felt so energized—as much from my implacable need to know as from the several cups of coffee I'd already drunk—that I sensed I would probably be awake until well after midnight. Sil must have sensed it as well because I could see the veiled expectancy in his face, in his slightly averted eyes and in the hedging language he and Gert used every time I tried to question them about what had happened. Gert was very skillful at unbating the hooks I was tossing out in order to snag an answer, and as the evening wore on my persistence wore down, inversely proportional—or so I imagined—to the length of time I spent trying to keep it going.

Gert finally announced that she was going to bed, and with a kiss for Sil and a hug for me, she went upstairs. It was shortly after ten o'clock, and the break in the conversation made me acutely aware of the wind again. A sudden blast against the building was as good a feint as any, so I got up and went to the window in what I suspected would be a vain attempt to break the conversation gridlock. It would've been a good time for one of those dialog flashcards, except I didn't need a list of subjects to choose from; all I wanted was some clarity on the one subject I'd been trying to discuss.

When I turned around to head back to my seat, Sil was gone. He returned from the kitchen a few seconds later with two cans of beer and a glass. "Time to switch over," he said, handing me the glass and one of the cans.

I sat down, filled the glass, took a swallow, and waited. Some instinct in me told me the time had come at last but that I needed to wait for the information to be volunteered. So I stretched my legs out toward the fire and tried to clear everything out of my mind except the warmth of the moment.

"They have to leave," said Sil.

I glanced over at him. I was fully aware of what the answer would be, but I had to ask anyway. "Who has to leave?"

"Margaret and Sonya. We need to go back to the Ropewalk tomorrow and get as much of their stuff as we can fit on the snowmobiles. You can drive Gert's." Then, as if suddenly doubtful, he asked, "Ever drive a snowmobile?"

"Yeah. I won't win any races, but I've done it." I paused and took a hit of beer. "How much time will we have?"

"Not much. We gotta get up real early 'cause it'll take several trips. Gert wants to be on the road with them by late morning."

I understood. Margaret could not go back to her job at the school because Sonya had to disappear. There was simply no way to explain how the Sonya everyone had been used to had suddenly become someone else. So she had to leave. "What time do we have to start?"

421

"As early as possible. Six o'clock, seven at the latest. Quick breakfast, then we head out. I'll make sure both machines are gassed up before I go to bed." He paused for a moment as if reviewing the plan in his mind. "Listen, we need to stay off the roads as much as possible. It's just a precaution, but we can't take the chance that someone who knows both of us might see us out riding like the best of buddies." His eyes locked onto mine. "We're supposed to be enemies, remember? So what we need to do is stick to the woods going in and coming back. We'll head out that way." He pointed toward the back of the house, towards the forest. "We'll do a big loop, cross the highway about a mile down where the woods are closest to the road, then head right for the swamp between us and the inland highway. We'll come back the same way." He paused for a moment to run the scenario through his mind. "One more thing—we can't let any passing cars see us hauling a bunch of clothes and stuff, so we don't cross the road if any cars are in sight, no matter how far away they might be."

I understood the need for what seemed like excessive caution but nevertheless had some reservations about crossing the swamp on snowmobiles. But my doubts about the safety of the ice were a footnote to the urgency to get it done; I knew I was in no position to challenge the plan, so I agreed. "What are we going to tell the school administration?"

"Gert and I talked about that. We'll tell 'em Margaret was so broken up by Ben leaving her that she had to go back to Connecticut to start over. Gert'll call the principal at home tomorrow morning so that they have a chance to find a replacement."

I nodded. Gert, of course, would have all the necessary phone numbers because she herself was technically part of the administration. "Where's she going to take them?"

"She has relatives further west, near the borders of New Hampshire and Canada. They have a house where they can stay. It'll be a long drive, maybe eight or ten hours, so she won't be back till the day after tomorrow, or maybe the day after that."

I knew there was still some time before the school reopened, so I harbored a feeble hope that maybe Margaret and Sonya could stay around a day or two, but Sil axed that plan even before I finished expressing it. "No way," he said, shaking his head for emphasis. "The longer they stay around Bowford, the more likely it is that someone might recognize Margaret. We can't take the chance that it might get back to someone at the school that she was still in town long after she supposedly left for Connecticut, or that she was staying at our house. How would we explain that? And then there's her car." He rolled his eyes by way of frustration. "We can't even get it out of there until the bridges are reopened. Until then, it has to stay at the Ropewalk. Good move, hiding it in the shed like that. If someone were to see it in the parking lot, how would we explain how she got back to Connecticut—hitchhiked?"

"I put it in there to keep the ice off it, not to hide it."

"Yeah, I know. I'm just saying it worked out for us. We just have to make sure the shed stays locked." He got up and used the poker to move some logs around in the fire. "Bottom line is, if Margaret were fit for travel, Gert would have her and Sonya in the car right now, heading out in the dark. Can't do that, so the next best thing is a Sunday, 'cause there won't be many people on the roads. But it's gotta be in the morning while everybody's still in church. That's why it's gotta be tomorrow." He took another swallow and stared as if some part of the plan had become unclear. "No way we can move her on a weekday. If we did that, she'd definitely have to take her out at night."

I had been living in a timeless bubble for several weeks, so I had no idea what day it was. "So today's Saturday?"

He looked at me with his brow knit in confusion. "Of course it's Saturday. Where the hell have you been, someplace without calendars?"

I smiled. "Yes, as a matter of fact I *was* living in a place without calendars." A place without time of any sort, I thought, and without logic or reason as well. I suddenly understood—felt, sensed—that I had spent the last several weeks staring across the threshold of the opaque into the shape-shifting world of shadow and myth. And it was not, as I originally suspected, due to isolation and the lack of social contact. It had been real, and the symbol of that reality flashed in my mind like a Medieval coat of arms—the doorway standing all alone at the top of the hill, the one that I assumed had been the original entrance to the old ropewalk over the chasm. But maybe it wasn't. Maybe that doorway had been there all along, like the "Thing-Stone" in the basin, and was just coincidently connected to the ropewalk that had been built around it. Maybe it actually led somewhere else.

"What part of all this don't I understand?" I finally asked him.

♦ ♦ ♦

Chapter 32

It was a rhetorical question because I realized full well that I didn't understand *any* part of what had happened, nor did I have the slightest idea how the fragmented images I'd encountered over the previous weeks actually fit together. Elements as diverse and unconnected as the girl in the attic, the skeleton in the shed, the remains of the old ropewalk, the chasm and its petroglyphs—everything, right up to the abduction itself, swirled around in my head like the fleeting images from one of those kaleidoscope tubes that children played with. Dazzling, constantly changing, never repeating, unbounded, and defying description—that was how I perceived it. And it was time to put it into some sort of order.

I got up from the loveseat and began to pace back and forth in front of him. "Alright, Sil, you said you'd explain it all when the women went to bed, so now's the time. Let's hear it. You also said there was something I should be afraid of, but you haven't made it clear what it is or why. No more hedging—I need some answers. Who were those people and why did they have Margaret's real daughter? And whose daughter had she been raising? And why?" When he didn't answer right away, I stopped in mid-stride and turned to stand in front of him.

"I told you Gert knows the details. I only know pieces of it," he said.

"Alright, tell me what you *do* know. Start with the key I found at the Ropewalk. I saw you give it to her in the kitchen. She didn't seem surprised at all. Why?"

He dithered. "I can't start there. It'll be too broken up and you won't understand it. I'd be telling the story backwards."

"Try me."

He paused for a moment as if to assess the degree of challenge in my voice, then shrugged. "Okay. She wasn't surprised because it was her key. I had given her copies of the keys to the Ropewalk and the shed, and it was her key stuck in the lock."

That caught me completely off guard. "It was *her* key?"

He waved off the pointless redundancy. "Yeah. I just said that, didn't I? It was her key."

A whole new volume of unknown material opened up in front of me, with obvious and disturbing implications—if it was her key, how did it end up being the means to open the shed? "How did it . . . I mean, are you saying she's somehow involved in this?"

He nodded, though with some hesitation. "Yeah, but I didn't know it was going on until I heard the wolves. And even then, Gert never told me about the key to the shed. I didn't know about that until you gave it to me." He saw my hesitation and confusion, the knot that my head had become as I tried to figure out which mental tunnel to take to get out of the labyrinth I found myself in. He stood up and stepped in front of me. "I told you starting there would be confusing. You're already lost. You sure you want me to tell the story backwards?"

I had to concede his point if I were going to understand any of it. "Okay, then, start at the beginning."

"The beginning?" he finally said, his eyebrows arched in surprise. "You want the beginning?" He turned and sat back down.

"Yes. Most people find that a good place to start."

"The beginning," he muttered. "Where is the beginning? The Ice Age? The land bridge?" He sighed and shook his head. "You better get yourself another beer and sit down. This'll take a while."

♦ ♦ ♦

Nothing that I knew or had learned, or had even assumed to be true, prepared me for what followed. It was as if the opaqueness of reality itself had been pierced and behind it, hidden by the relentless imagery we'd all come to accept as real, was another reality, a "counter-thought," like the simmering doubt behind an unvoiced suspicion, or maybe, perhaps, just one of the "ticks" in that clock of "destiny logic" that Spengler had talked about.

The stories I heard that night began to feel, as the evening wore on, like the aftereffects of a waking dream, or of movement in that rarified margin between dream and wakefulness. In view of all that I'd seen and felt during the previous two weeks, they seemed somehow appropriate in spite of how they sounded, almost as if the final discontinuity in what I had been trying to put together were being delivered to me in a lecture hall. I felt like a student once again, except that my professor was not an ivy-league icon with pipe and diploma. My teacher this time was Sil, and my campus was the sweep and breadth of Abenaki mythology.

Picture what it must've been like, he said, for a people accustomed to centuries of a freedom that we can't even imagine today to suddenly find themselves fenced in, their lifestyle gone, their world disappearing, their movement restricted. Imagine this displaced native people hiding in caves or in underground shelters, eking out a frightened living while trying to stay out of the way of the ruthless creatures that hunted them. What keeps you alive under those conditions? What keeps you going? What do you look forward to?

You could surrender to the conquerors, of course—come out with your hands up, grovel, swear loyalty, whatever it takes. But you can't ever join them because you don't look like them, and because of that, you'll never be accepted. And, because of that, you can't simply hide among them, either.

So what do you do? Hunker down and wait for better times that may never come? Wait and watch in helpless resignation while your world is dismantled, discarded, exploited, depleted, ruined, and left for dead?

Even if the question was rhetorical, which I knew it wasn't, I didn't have an answer. I didn't even have an excuse because, even though I was one of the "conquerors," I was running from the same thing as the vanquished. All I could do was stare at him in silence.

He apparently sensed my dilemma because, right out of nowhere, he then casually said, "Place memory," as if that non sequitur comment were a fill-in-the-blank response.

I looked at him and the image of the field on the way to the old village flashed through my mind. "What?"

"Place memory. You know what that is, don't you? Margaret told me and Gert about it."

"Yeah, it was something she told me about, but it was just kind of a joke between us. She said she had the feeling that the village, or the area where it's located, somehow 'knew' her."

"And you felt the same thing going there, didn't you?"

I suddenly doubted myself—more, I supposed, out of fear of being ridiculed than out of denial that it had happened. "I felt . . . something. But for me it happened in the big field off the highway, the one near the cart track, before it enters the woods."

"And how did it feel—like you'd been there before?"

"No, although I tried to explain away Margaret's experience by drawing a parallel with some other place that maybe looked very similar. But I didn't feel like I'd been there before; I felt like she had felt—that the place somehow 'knew' me, or maybe had been expecting me." I paused to search for the right words to explain something that had been nothing more than a passing feeling, but nothing came to mind. I shrugged in apology. "I don't know how else to explain it."

He had been watching me very carefully and I had the distinct sense that he knew exactly what I was trying to say. His manner seemed to be one of either indecision or confusion, or possibly both. As time went on without a response—first one minute, then two—I felt it stretching into an infinity of expectation on my part that seemed like it was not going to be addressed at all. Sil's gaze drifted away from my face, then past me, then out the window.

After a few more seconds, his look changed and he appeared to have finally come to some sort of decision. He sat back in the chair and began. "When I was a boy, I used to listen to the stories of the old Abenaki elders after school. They still lived around here back then." He glanced over at me as if for comment—reproachfully, it seemed, as if I were the one who had driven them away—but I had none. "I was constantly being teased by the other kids in the neighborhood for doing this. They kept telling me there was nothing to learn from those old geezers, but that only made me more curious about the stories, and since they lived around here, it was easy for me to sit in. Like their ancestors, they only used the house for sleeping. Everything else was done outdoors, even the cooking. So, in the evenings when the meal was over, they would build up the fire and tell the stories they'd heard from their own elders. It was their way of keeping their history alive—you know, since they didn't have books or writing or anything, they had to make sure the stories were told the right way and remembered word for word."

Word for word. It was an elusive ideal, but as an historian, I knew something about the oral histories of primitive peoples and the prodigious feats of memory required by those charged with keeping them alive. Typically, these histories were captured in songs, poems, stories, and dances and passed on from one generation to the next with such unwavering precision that not a single word or line would be altered in hundreds of years of recitation. The petroglyphs in Machias Bay were part of this tradition, as were those that I'd found in the chasm under the old ropewalk. But the problem for modern historians had always been that the histories, because they were never written down, had vanished, and because they had vanished, the petroglyphs were indecipherable.

But as Sil talked, I began to think back to Margaret's comment from several weeks before, when she said that he "knew all the stories going back through the memory of his people." I had doubted it then because I had no way to connect it to the source of those stories, but in view of what he was saying, I had already begun to suspect that he was one of them, a story-teller, an "historian," that he had been trained by the elders and now had the burden of keeping the history alive. If so, then the Rosetta Stone needed for the petroglyphs, the one that I feared was long vanished, was sitting right in front of me.

"One of the first stories I heard was about some hunters who had gone into the mountains to hunt. I heard one of them tell how he had talked to the animals after they had been shot and asked their ghosts to pardon him and his friends for killing them. He said he had offered a little sacrifice of some tobacco and a few beads, and then ended by saying that he knew the bullets that killed them were bad things."

"And did they?" I asked.

His brow twisted in momentary confusion. "Did they what?"

"Did they pardon him?"

The way he looked at me he must've thought I was being sarcastic, but I wasn't. I knew from my own research that primitive cultures often did things—performed ceremonies, or offered some sort of sacrificial compensation—to excuse themselves from the necessity of killing something so that they themselves could live. Asking pardon of a ghost was nothing new—no one wanted to be troubled by a restless spirit—so although the story squared with what I already knew, it was not any kind of revelation. But I had seen and heard things during the previous two weeks that *were* a revelation to me and that had shaken me out of my middle-class lethargy and left me feeling a bit like Alice staring into the looking glass. So I was ready for and open to anything, however outlandish it might seem. "I'm not being a smart ass. I'm serious. I know that this, like place memory, has something to do with where you're trying to take me, and I need to understand all of it. Bear with me. I have an incurable 'need to know.'"

He acknowledged with a slight grunt. "I don't know if they pardoned him. The point is, I didn't understand what the old hunter was getting at, so I asked one of the old chiefs, who seemed to know the most about all that stuff, to explain what the hunter had meant by talking to animal ghosts. He told me all animals have spirits—they were alive, so why would I think they didn't?—and they have to know why they're killed so that they can explain how they happened to come to the Sky World. So the old hunters would talk to them." He looked at me askance and I realized that he was expecting ridicule or reproach, neither of which I had any intention of using.

He continued. "They believed there was a divine power in animals that made it possible for them to sense when anything was not the way it should be. That was how the animals managed to avoid snares and traps, and the old trappers among my people used to say that the only way to catch them was to not disturb the ordinary, that was crucial, and that if you didn't do this you wouldn't succeed. And you had to think like the animal, enter its world and see things through its eyes." He paused for a moment as if to let the next thought resonate with exaggerated importance. "You had to actually *become* the animal. Understand?"

I heard his words but stopped assimilating their meaning as my attention suddenly focused on what he'd said about animals being able to sense when anything was not the way it should be. It was one of those "tectonic mind shifts" I was periodically subject to, and this time it unexpectedly added substance to the "place memory" feeling I had when I first encountered it. *That* was what it was—not a sense that I'd been there, but a sense that something was not the way it should be, tying me to all those other discontinuous events in my life when I sensed that something was not the way it was supposed to be.

"Hey, you in there?"

I snapped out of it and looked over at Sil. "What?"

"I said, are you in there?"

"Yeah."

"Did you hear what I said about entering the animal's world?"

I nodded. "Yes, about becoming the animal, or becoming like the animal. I've heard it all before. I get it—shape-shifting. Wearing the animal's skin and imitating its habits. It's a common theme in mythology."

But he shook his head in denial. "That's not it." His jaw tightened and I sensed that he was either annoyed or disgusted with me for being so dense.

What was I not seeing? That it was a small step from talking to the animal spirit to actually assimilating it? And that he didn't mean that in the simple manner of hunter-gatherer societies dressing themselves in the skin of the animal they either wanted to hunt or emulate? That played a role, to be sure, but was clearly not the point, not the heart of the matter. It was not just a physical cloak he was talking about—it was actual assimilation; not just an appearance, but a transitional reality.

"So, what are you saying? That people can actually—literally—become animals, that they can enter the bodies of animals and *transform* themselves?"

He didn't look up at me as he pondered his reply. "Do you talk to animals?" he finally said.

That caught me off guard. "What?"

"Do you talk to animals—you know, like when you see a dog on the street or a homeless cat, do you talk to it?"

I thought of the feral cat immediately, and then my encounter with the wolf inside the Engineering building flashed through my mind like a high-speed film. I had come right out and asked it—out of semi-comic desperation, of course—why it was constantly following me. "Yes, of course. It's just a natural impulse."

"And do you think it understands what you're saying?"

"No, of course not. It may sense the tone of my voice and feel that I'm not a threat, but it can't possibly know what I'm saying."

"I didn't say *know* what you're saying. I said *understand* what you're saying."

I turned my head away for a moment to hide my displeasure. I'd never had any patience for head games or semantic sophistries, and when I turned back to him, the look on my face must've conveyed that impression. But just in case it didn't, the mounting sarcasm in my tone would've made it clear. "So, what are you saying? That people can learn to talk to animals in such a way that they'll understand what you're saying?"

"Why do you find that so odd? You just said you talk to dogs, and if you're like most people you can make them do what you ask—almost anyone can do that. So maybe the whole dog family has that ability."

I thought of the wolf again, and in my mind the encounter scenarios from the previous two weeks scrolled past like a slide show. I had to admit to myself that there was *something* I kept sensing each time I ran into it—the expectancy on its face was an inscrutable reminder that it was trying to say something, even if I couldn't decipher what it was. But that wasn't all of it; there was also something else, something in its manner, some connection, drab and unclear perhaps, but linked in some way to the "don't disturb the ordinary" comment. Unfocused and hanging in the air like the faint scent of a snuffed-out candle—had the wolf been trying to tell me I was disturbing the ordinary? Or maybe that the ordinary had been disturbed and how come I didn't notice it?

And then an odd thought hit me, prompted, I supposed, by the memory of the petroglyphs carved into the wall of the chasm. I stared at him for several seconds before I spoke. "Are you trying to tell me that the wolf was actually a *person*?"

"No, I'm not trying to tell you that. But I am telling you it *could* be, given the right conditions. I'm trying to say to you what the elders said to me—whether you realize it or not, everything understands. Wolves, bears, horses—they all understand."

It took me a moment to assimilate that. "What do you mean, 'everything understands'? Are you saying that people can learn to talk to animals? I mean *really* talk to them?"

Sil was weaving some kind of tapestry whose fabric was like a hidden strand of homespun concealed under the façade of a very complex weave. But my sense was that the hidden strand would show through on occasion regardless—I was sure, for instance, that the

431

bearskin I had found in the Engineering building was somehow part of it—and I struggled to make some sort of connection, but realized it was not quantifiable, not provable at all except by what might just as easily pass for fantasy or coincidence.

"The old tribal elder who told me about asking for pardon was the same one who taught me his—my—language." He paused and, looking inward with focused intensity, seemed for a fleeting moment to have gone back in time in his mind. "He was also the one who taught me how to talk to the wolves."

I pondered that comment for several long moments before I responded. "You said that was how you found out we were still at the Ropewalk—that the wolf had told you. I didn't understand at the time what you meant, but . . ." I had to stop because my mind was fragmenting again, just as it had while I was trapped at the Ropewalk.

"Is it any clearer now?"

"No . . . I don't know—maybe." But it really wasn't. I was still missing something. I got part of it—the wolf had understood and Sil had heard it signaling the presence of three people still on the peninsula where the Ropewalk was located. But how long had they been communicating that information to each other before he heard it? A week? Two? "Why . . . . ?" I had to stop because I was unsure of even the form of the question I needed to ask.

"Why what?"

"I encountered the wolf early on. Why did it take so long before you heard what it was saying?"

"Hearing it was just an accident, a coincidence. It's not like I'm out there every night listening. I had gone on a long snowmobile ride and was coming back after dark when I heard it. At first I paid no attention, but then when I realized what it was saying, I knew one of the people still on the peninsula had to be Margaret from the frantic phone call we'd gotten on Christmas day. And I suspected that the second one was you because by then the state cops had connected you to her 'disappearance.'" A faint smile touched his lips for a moment and vanished. "The third could only have been Sonya. The rest you already know."

That was only partially true. What I knew was that he had gotten the information and then acted on it, but there was still something blocking my understanding, an amorphous shape like a fuzzy shadow that defied any attempts at finding its outline. I struggled with it for a few seconds before I realized what it was. "Wait a minute. If you heard and understood the wolf, then maybe the people who came for Sonya heard and understood it as well. Maybe they had been hearing it for some time, and if that's the case they would've known that there were two adults there instead of just one."

Sil took a long swallow of beer, put the can on the lamp table, and smiled. "You got it. Now you understand part one of the story. You being there threw a wrench into the machine, made the whole plan change. That's why they didn't just come and take her as soon as everyone else was gone. Gert told me all about it."

"So they—whoever they are—were planning on taking her the moment everyone was gone from the Ropewalk?"

He nodded. "And they tried. The first night, the girl they sent in—the one you found in the attic—was able to open the door and let them in. They tried to get into Margaret's apartment but it was locked. If she had been alone, they would've broken the door down, but knowing that you were there as well meant they couldn't make any noise. The problem was, they didn't know where you were, where your room was. For all they knew, it could've been right next door, which meant you'd hear the break-in and maybe come charging out with a weapon. That would've gotten messy and complicated. So they left, intending to come up with a new plan and try again a day or two later."

"And by then I had the chain on the door."

He smirked at the reference. "I saw it coiled up on the floor near the door and wondered what it was for. So that's what you did with it." He got up and headed for the kitchen before I could reply. I heard the hiss of the cans popping open and after he returned and handed me one he sat down and resumed. "What was the story with that?"

I refilled my glass and sucked the foam off before it could overflow. "Early on, to put Margaret at ease about someone else in the building, I needed something that would checkmate anyone trying to get in the front door. I used the chain to tie the handles together. It was just a precaution; the idea was to rule out any intruders from that side. I found the chain out in the shed, in that separate little room where you have all the tires stacked up." I put the beer down on the little end table and held my hands out to the fire to warm them. "Ironically, that was how I discovered the hidden ladder that went to the top floor."

433

Sil offered a small grunt in reply. "Well, your chain evidently threw a curve ball at the plan. The girl must've been too small to get it unraveled, so she couldn't open the door to let them in. Otherwise they would've tried to take her sooner."

"By then the chain wasn't the only obstacle. I had installed a pair of massive deadbolts on Margaret's door, so even if they had figured out a way to unlock her apartment they would still not have gotten in, and would've had to resort to brute force in any case." I shook my head. "The fortunes of random events." I took a sip of beer and looked over at him. "Or maybe just another example of destiny logic."

He stared at me as if I were some kind of lunatic. "Destiny logic?"

"It's just a concept I read about somewhere. Undercurrents of destiny carried out by random decisions that collectively move—unconsciously—in the direction needed to make a certain thing happen. Sort of like the guy hiding behind the curtain in 'The Wizard of Oz,' the one making all the sound effects."

He shook his head and took a swallow of beer. "I was right all along. You are a friggin crackpot."

I raised my hand in surrender. "Guilty as charged. I'm the crackpot on duty. But . . ." and here I paused just to make sure I got the wording correct, "at least I never endangered the life of a little girl by sending her into a large, structurally antiquated building all by herself. I mean, come on, what if she had gotten stuck or hurt? No one would've known where she was, or even if she was in the building at all. It was pretty risky, don't you think?"

"Listen," he said, leaning forward for emphasis, "she was sent in because she was small enough to get into the building from under the clapboards. There are gaps in the old foundation everywhere, but all of them are too small for an adult. Her job was to find one that would get her inside so that she could open the door."

"Yeah, I know, but still—it was a risky thing to do. What if she discovered she couldn't get out the way she came in? She could've starved in there. In fact, when I first found her, I thought she *was* starving by the way she was going after those canned fruits. What kind of people would do this?"

Sil's whole manner changed, as if he'd been personally insulted. His look hardened, then relaxed and became a mixture of amusement and thinly veiled contempt. "You're saying just what I would've expected to hear from your kind. You think that whatever would affect you and your ways has to affect everyone, everywhere, the same way, as if your reactions were some sort of standard for everybody." He got up and put another log on the fire, urged it into position with the poker, and sat back down.

"I didn't mean . . ."

"Don't judge them. That's all I'm saying. Just don't judge them. Risk is only a matter of what you're used to. Risk to a mountain climber is not the same thing as risk to someone who never climbed anything higher than a staircase."

I took my chastisement in stride. "Yes, you're right." What flashed through my mind, unbidden, was the image of the pile of debris in front of the remains of the old ropewalk at the village. When I first saw it, I judged it too risky to climb over; on the way back, however, after the harrowing encounter with the chasm and its giant drain hole, I found it laughably simple. I shook my head and smirked at the memory. "Risk has no absolute measure. I should've realized that."

That comment was followed by what must've been a full minute of silence, as if he had no intention of responding, or was evaluating the sincerity of what I'd said. Finally, though, his features slackened, as if he had worked through whatever had caused the anger. "A lot of things have no absolute measure. The point of all this is that what was supposed to have been an easy job suddenly became complicated because you were there. By the time they had a plan, you had tied that chain through the door handles, which meant they had to find some other way into the building. And they had to be careful."

I understood their need for caution because what Sil had said about me being a wild card was true. They couldn't have known if I was armed, and they had no way of knowing what I might have done. With something of a gut-wrenching confession to myself, I realized I probably would've shot one or more of them. But the even more nauseating realization was that they, seeing me armed, might've killed me first.

"With a second person there it suddenly got complicated. They had to draw you out, get you out of the way."

"They could've just killed me. Why didn't they?"

"It was never about that. Besides, they knew there'd be consequences if they did, so they couldn't." He took a long swallow of beer. "You

435

weren't supposed to be there. Simple as that. They didn't know who you were or why you were hanging around, or even what to do about you. They had no reason to take you, but they had to get you out of the way before everyone came back." He paused as if to search his memory for something he might've missed. "You definitely created a problem for them. With Margaret still there while everyone else was gone, they had the perfect setup, then you had to go and spoil it. But they couldn't take you or just get rid of you, so they had to somehow lure you out."

I sat there staring into the flames as I mentally reviewed the sequence of events that had brought me to that point. The room was absolutely quiet until the wind blasted against the window and brought with it the rattle of ice crystals, catching my attention for a moment. Then the fire snapped and I involuntarily lurched in my chair as it sent an ember onto the hearthstone, which Sil flicked back in with his foot before I could move to do the same. "So," I finally said, "so the 'bear' I saw out near the shed . . ."

"Was one of them," he interrupted. He took another sip of beer and smacked his lips. "They're hunters. Considering where you were living, they thought you would be one, too, and did what they thought would bring a hunter out. They would've taken Margaret and Sonya that night if you had taken the bait."

I stared at him, barely comprehending. "If I had taken the bait," I mumbled.

Sil smirked. "Yeah. The bait—an easy shot at a bear in the open. There was no way they could've known that you were just an egghead who would wonder what it was but not go out after it."

I smiled at the exaggerated insult. "So, if I had gone out . . . if I had gone after the 'bear,' I would've come back to an empty building."

"Yes."

The left-handed logic of fate was at work even then. If Margaret hadn't invited me to dinner and I had gone out to investigate the "bear," I would not have known that she and Sonya had been taken. And because she and I would not have had any sort of relationship at that point, I might not have noticed for some time that she was gone. "It wasn't really because I was an egghead who wasn't interested. It was because I'd been invited to dinner and Margaret wanted me to hunt up some wine, not a bear." I raised my glass in recognition of my feeble attempt at an excuse.

He smiled in acknowledgement. "Yeah, I guess dinner with Margaret would trump chasing a bear through the snow."

We both fell silent and after a moment, still unclear about where it was all going, I ventured a return to my earlier comment about the key. "So, the fact that the key was Gert's explains why you also seemed to recognize it when I tossed it to you at the Ropewalk. You knew it was hers."

"Yes."

He seemed disinclined to go any further. I sat there expecting some sort of follow up explanation, but when it didn't happen, I took the initiative. "Come on, Sil, this shouldn't be like pulling teeth. Help me out here. How did these people end up with Gert's key to the shed?"

He took a deep breath and exhaled through his mouth. "Because she gave it to them."

The logic of the situation told me I should've expected that answer, but nonetheless it set me back a step mentally. "She *gave* it to them?" The implication was profound. She was somehow more than just a passive part of what happened. That sense of being in some kind of trap recurred to me and my hand instinctively flinched as, in my mind, I reached for the .380, which I knew was in my coat pocket out in the mudroom.

So what happens now? I wondered, nonchalantly taking a sip of beer. Did I just pass some kind of forbidden barrier? But, no, I didn't believe that, it couldn't be—the scene was too peaceful and Sil's manner too relaxed. Besides, we'd come too far for a violent anti-climax.

"Gert was the one who provided the key to open the shed," he finally volunteered, "as well as a sketch of the utility closet so that they would know which circuit breaker to turn off. She had lost her key to the Ropewalk itself or she would've given them that and made life easier for them, at least on that first try." He paused for a moment to let that sink in.

"So she knows them. She's somehow connected to them."

"Yes."

I had to pause for a moment to try to catalog that unexpected reality. "Okay, you know what's coming next—how, and why?"

He smirked. "Which do you want answered first, the 'how' or the 'why'?"

I shrugged. "Start with how."

"That's easy. Gert has a sister who works at the airport in Boston and who told her that Ben had booked a flight to the west coast—with someone other than Margaret. Since Margaret had already told her that she was staying at the Ropewalk for a few extra days, it was obvious that the delay was just a ruse. That told Gert that what she'd been expecting for some time was finally happening—he was leaving Margaret."

He paused for nearly a full minute while appearing to wrestle with what he had to say next. "It was not the opportunity she was looking for, but it did serve her purpose."

This news resonated with a certain unrestrained anger within me, a hard note of something other than simple concern for Margaret's well-being. "But that means she knew at the very start of all this that Margaret was trapped at the Ropewalk, that Ben had no intention of coming back for her."

"Yes."

"And yet she did nothing to try to get her out of there, she just let it all happen."

"Like I said, it served her purpose."

"And what, exactly, was her 'purpose'?"

Sil looked at me and searched my face as if for a reaction to something he'd not yet uttered. "Bring Sonya back."

I looked at him in silence and finally just shook my head in noncomprehension. "Bring her back to where?"

"The child is 'touched.' They couldn't have known this when the girl was an infant, but when it became obvious that something was wrong it was necessary to take her back." He shrugged. "She had to go back."

"*Who* could not have known this when she was an infant? And go back? Go back to where, or to whom?"

"To where she came from."

The fading thread of the convoluted tapestry was slowly coming to the surface but was still hidden by the frieze around it. The girl had to go back—to someone. And Gert knew who that someone was. "And the other Sonya, the one here with us now? How . . . how did she end up being with those people?"

He stared into the fire. "A life for a life. If everything truly understands, then the bottom line effect will be the same. And if everything—and everybody—really *doesn't* understand, then they need to be made to understand."

"Understand what?"

His eyes scanned the floor as if for an answer. "Understand that you cannot disturb the ordinary and expect to trap the animal. Understand that, when you do trap the animal, it needs to know why it's killed so that it knows what to say in the Sky World." He paused for a moment, staring into the fire. "You can't kill them and drive them into hiding without a sacrifice."

"Who . . . who have I, or we, killed?" The image of the bloody epee on the floor in Margaret's apartment rose in my mind, and for a moment I grappled with the nauseating fear that she had killed the person whose blood was on it. But even if that were the case, Sonya's abduction could not have had anything to do with the need for a compensating sacrifice. No, that could not have been it because the timeline was all wrong. Whatever the plan was, whatever the intent behind it, it was in motion long before Margaret's epee found its mark.

But Sil ignored my question, waved it off as if it were irrelevant. "Listen—you have *two* daughters now, the one upstairs with Margaret, and the one out there." He nodded toward the window. "The one upstairs lived in our world and now lives in yours. The other lived in yours and now lives in ours."

"'Ours'?" I mimicked. The creep of a conspiratorial undertone of some sort began to make its presence felt in the emotional effect his words were having on me. "'Ours'?" I repeated. "What do you mean, 'ours'?"

He seemed to ignore my question and pointed a finger at me for emphasis. "*That's* the thing you need to be worried about—remember I told you in the woods that you agreed to something you better be ready for, the thing that was expected of you?"

"Yes."

"Well, that's it. The problem—the thing I had to bargain for—was whether you could play your role in all this."

I was stunned. "I have a 'role'? What *is* it? And what's the 'all this' that I'm now part of?"

"Your role is simple: can you protect them both?"

What? I thought. That's impossible—the other Sonya was gone, vanished into the fastness of the nearly unbroken wilderness that

439

stretched all the way into Canada. "How can that be? I'll never see the other one again."

He got up, stirred the fire, and put another log onto the flames, propping it against the andirons. "You'll see her again, when she's ready and the time is right."

"But how? How would I ever find her?"

"You won't. She'll find you, just as her sister found you in the Ropewalk."

"Her *sister*?" With a single word, the mystery of why I mistook the girl in the attic for Sonya was cleared up. "But . . . how?" I was so confused I didn't even know what question I wanted to ask. "What is the thing I need to be afraid of?" was all that came to mind.

"Afraid of? That you won't be able to protect them, or you won't realize how different Sonya will be and you won't react as strongly as you have to, or that you won't *understand* what your daughter knows and you won't accept it. You'll try to change her, and in doing that you'll kill her."

I was shocked. "What do you mean? How can you say . . . no, I would never do that, not ever."

"I don't mean literally kill her. I mean stop her from understanding. That's part of the thing I said you better be ready for."

"But you indicated there are also people I need to be afraid of. Who? Who are the people I'm supposed to be afraid of?" Instinctively, preemptively, I was sure he was going to tell me it was the people in the forest, the ones who had taken Margaret and Sonya, and who might appear at any time to take them again. Inwardly I cringed at the thought of having to spend the rest of my life looking over my shoulder at every darkened wall of forest I passed.

"Your own people," he said.

I realized after he'd said it that, on some unexpressed level, I had half expected that answer as well, though why or how I saw it coming would be relegated to another one of those Olympian leaps of prescience that I'd experienced with the cat living in the attic and the old foundations around the school having been the original settlement. And, like the cat and the foundations, within that context I suddenly understood something else, something I'd read in the old diary: the "sooty devils" that came to attack the people living in the old village, who I assumed at first had been the Abenakis, but who were later described as not being "swarthy Indians." Who, then, were they? I had wondered then, but suddenly I knew. "The village was destroyed by white men, wasn't it?"

"Yes." He nodded so faintly it was barely perceptible in the firelight.

"French?"

He looked over at me, bewildered. "What?"

"Was it an attack of some kind by the French trying to drive the English out?"

He laughed and shook his head. "French? No. English? Yes. Legal hawks, land claim jumpers, lawyers—all closing in on them when the old ropewalk was no longer profitable and the people could not pay their debts."

I was stunned. "What? You mean it was an economic failure that did them in?"

"The Ropewalk, the one you live in, was too much to compete with." He took a long swallow of beer, shook the can to make sure it was empty, and crushed it in his huge fist. "Move or die. Someone takes your house, you get out before the cold weather comes in, or you die. So the people left and the village died."

The village died. Nothing dramatic, nothing military, not even the rabid contagion of some sort of plague. They just couldn't afford to live there anymore. "And then what happened?"

He had gotten up and was headed for the kitchen for another brew, but stopped and turned back to me. "And then the people they chased away came back."

◆ ◆ ◆

Chapter 33

Somewhere in the forest a wounded man, stuck by the point of Margaret's epee, lay dying, staring into the black wall of the night and clutching a blood-soaked rag to the wound just like the one we'd found when we were chasing them. He would stoically accept what was confronting him, acknowledge his duty to both the purpose he served and the memory he embodied, and continue to do what his gods expected—endure. He would go on until it was no longer possible, then move to the Sky World, where he would not have to confront all those who came before him because he had already explained to them why it was necessary for him to do what he'd done while he was alive.

That, at any rate, was the scenario that went through my mind when my memory turned to the bloody sword I'd found on the floor in Margaret's apartment. "The people they chased away came back," I muttered, not as a response to Sil's comment—he was still in the kitchen—but as a sort of verbal talisman—a charm, spell, incantation, or maybe a self-induced hypnotic state that I needed to get myself past the haunting image of a dead man found in the forest by a passing hunter and the investigation that would follow. The people came back; he was obviously one of them, whoever they were and however remote and isolated their lifestyle might be.

But the thought of Margaret standing before a crowded courtroom trying to explain why she'd stabbed him, trying to avoid the accusatory stares, trying to deny that her daughter used to be someone else—all of this stood blocking my vision of the future like the giant "Thing-Stone" in the basin. I could not get past it.

So when Sil returned from the kitchen and sat down, I had to interrupt his story so that the seriousness of my concern wouldn't be overlooked or left as an unresolved footnote. "Look, there's something we need to deal with right away, something we can't afford to just ignore."

He shifted in the chair to get comfortable. "And what's that?"

"She wounded one of those people when they took her and Sonya. Is there . . ." I broke off as if fearful of what his answer might be.

"Is there what?"

"Is there any way to know if he's okay?"

Sil grunted in amusement. "He's okay. Don't worry about it."

"How can you be sure? What if he isn't? What if he goes to a hospital? There'll be a report to the police when they see that it's a stab wound. Then what? Or what if he dies?"

He seemed unconcerned. "He won't die."

"How do you know?"

He took another swallow of beer. "Because he was the one I was talking to when we caught up to them, the one who gave Margaret back to you. He was the one she stabbed." He paused and looked out the window at the black wall of the endless forest that began in his back yard. "He's okay. It was just a flesh wound. Margaret had never stuck a human being before and had no idea how much force it actually took. She barely made it through the clothes."

"But what if he goes to a hospital anyway?"

He shook his head in an obvious gesture of impatience. "He won't go to a hospital, believe me."

In spite of his confidence, I still wasn't fully convinced, mainly because the greater part of the conversation, at least for me, was the part that remained unspoken. His unshakable conviction that the wounded man would not go to a hospital was contagious and I desperately wanted to believe that, but knew full well the dangers of a decision rooted in hope rather than reason. Nevertheless, there was no hint of doubt in his manner; clearly, his confidence was based on the details I needed to know but as yet hadn't learned. I didn't know at that point whether to try to force the issue but, thinking that might ultimately work against me, I decided that it would make more sense to step back and try to get those missing details. "What about all the times when I left the building to hike to the old village? They must've seen me leave—why didn't they go in at those times, since the chain wasn't looped through the handles and the girl could've opened the door from the inside? Why did they wait so long before they finally did that?"

"Too risky. It was daylight and they had no way of knowing if anyone else was in the building who might see them, or if someone might show up unexpectedly." He shrugged. "It's possible Margaret might've even seen the girl in the hallway and freaked out, maybe even stopped her from opening the door." He paused for a moment as if weighing his next words. "It's important that they stay invisible, so something like that had to be done at night. But as time passed and it wasn't working, they knew they were going to have to risk doing it during the day. The problem was, to do that and stay invisible at the same time meant they needed some sort of cover. That's why they had to wait for a storm before they could act. That's why they came when they did—their tracks would be covered."

That comment brought back to me one of the elements of the abduction that I didn't understand, both when I saw it and now while reflecting on it—there had been only one set of tracks visible in the snow outside the Ropewalk. "Margaret and Sonya were taken by several people, yet I only saw the tracks of one person in the snow. How is that possible?"

"An old trick for staying as invisible as possible. Each one walks in the tracks of the one in front of him so that anyone following them would think it was just one person."

I marveled at the stealth. "Despite the obvious cunning, I have to assume they didn't know that you were on your way to the Ropewalk while they were taking Margaret and Sonya."

"No, they didn't know."

"And as for me . . ."

He pondered for a moment before answering. "They obviously knew you were gone because they were watching the building the whole time. As for when you were coming back—well, the wolf would alert them in time."

"The wolf," I muttered. "Are you telling me the wolf was some sort of spy, that all those encounters were just a way to keep tabs on me?"

"No, I'm not telling you that."

I smirked and shook my head. "No, of course not. Just like you weren't telling me that the wolf was actually a person." I paused for a moment to let that sink in. "*Was* it actually a person?" Rhetorical or not, ridiculous or not, the question resonated with a half-focused reality in my mind. I would never forget that first day when I had searched the Ropewalk with Margaret and seen the way the original Sonya appeared to metamorphose into something else. "Sonya, the one who's gone now, had this weird ability to, ah . . . ."

He threw me an expectant look. "To what?"

I shrugged. "I could swear she had the ability to . . . shape-shift. Or something." I shook my head as if trying to wake myself from what I perceived as the nonsense I was saying.

He did not appear surprised. "These people can, ah, look like other things. You'll swear you're seeing a bear, or a wolf or a bird. But in reality it'll be one of them."

It took me a moment to absorb that, but when I did, I felt myself going through some sort of mental downshift. So it was true. An erstwhile doubt about the outer fringes of my sanity while all that was happening suddenly solidified into a fragile, but tangible, reality. I scanned my memory for a place to plug in this newest piece of information, but could not fit it into any but the oldest myths and legends of every race and ethnic group everywhere—Paleolithic hunter-gatherers. They were in everyone's past, and with them came that almost preternatural ability to look like and enter the world of the thing they were hunting. From this profound ability to identify with their quarry sprang the legends of the mist-monsters and assorted shape-shifters that we still have today, the real origins kept alive only in forgotten treatises buried in long-unused museum closets. What was I dealing with here?

"So it was real," I muttered. "I wasn't just imagining it."

Sil looked at me but said nothing.

I sensed that his silence was contrived, as if he were allowing me the distance I needed to put it all together for myself. Or maybe he was just being non-committal because he himself didn't know or wasn't sure. I locked eyes with him in a vain attempt to maybe guess which one it was, if either. Failing that, I at least hoped to get some sort of clue about which one of us was the bigger crackpot.

And there was something else. Sil had said "bear, wolf, or bird," and the mere mention of "bird" had started me thinking about what I had seen take off from the roof of the shed. I leaned forward as if fearful of having only one shot at a question and not hearing what his answer might be. "What did you mean when you said 'a bird'? You mean, like a giant bird, something that might fly at night when normal birds are asleep?"

Now it was Sil's turn to be startled. "You saw something like that?"

I sat back in the chair. Did I? I wondered, feeling the return of that half-wakeful state of conscious dreaming that I'd come to know over the previous two weeks. It felt like some sort of slow distortion process was taking over my memory of the event, dissolving it at the edges and turning it into a photographic negative in my mind. "Yes, I did. For only a moment. It flew from the top of the shed."

Sil stared at me, his face a mask of both wonder and mistrust. "What did it look like?"

"It was dark, so I couldn't see it except as a silhouette. I had been sitting at the window in my room and had just seen a bear—or what I took to be a bear—and was about to go to bed when I saw it. At first I thought it was a great snowy owl, but then realized it wasn't. At least I think it wasn't." I paused to let myself sail back through time to try to capture a clearer memory, but it was useless. "I was pretty tired and strung out, so I can't really be sure of anything."

"As big as a snowy owl?"

I shrugged. "At least that big, maybe bigger. It seemed huge when I saw it, but given the conditions at the time—Margaret being stressed out and all, and the three of us being cut off—I can't really say for sure."

"Are you sure you didn't just dream it?"

I was taken aback. "Why would you ask that?"

"Because you just said you were exhausted after watching for the bear and were about to go to bed. Well, maybe that's what happened. Maybe you went to bed and didn't go back to the window at all. Maybe you only thought you did, but you fell asleep and saw the bird in a dream."

It felt like he was throwing a deflection at me, trying to lead me into a state of self-induced denial, but one that fit easily into my photo-negative memory of the event. He offered no explanation, but I could sense that this was not about psychology, nor was he trying to sell me on some pretense of a mild psychosis brought on by stress and isolation. He had a reason to try to convince me that I really hadn't seen that bird. "No, I don't think I dreamed it." I deliberately looked away from him for a moment while I enjoyed a long swallow of beer. When I looked back, his expression hadn't changed. "On the other hand, maybe I did. I never saw it again, so maybe I never saw it at all."

Sil's features visibly relaxed, but the way his fingers began to drum on the beer can it was obvious something was bothering him.

It was bothering me, too, the more so since I suddenly remembered that entry in the old diary where the writer's grandmother noted that "the birds came" after the massacre she'd witnessed. Was that what I had seen? Or had I actually dreamed the whole thing? "Teratorn?" I finally asked.

"What?" He shook his head and shrugged.

"Giant bird, like the 'Thunderbird' petroglyphs in Machias Bay, and those on the chasm wall beneath the old ropewalk. Prehistoric and thought to be extinct, but every now and then a sighting is reported." I paused to consider the preposterousness of what I'd just said. "Good candidate for a god-creature in a woodland setting."

But he dismissed the idea with a curt wave of his hand. "You dreamed it."

Tradeoff, I thought. You won't tell me about the bird and I won't press you for it, but in exchange I want to know who those people were and what Gert's role was in all this.

I stood up and went to the window, lifted the shade away from the glass and looked out. It was a ritualistic gesture, not done out of curiosity but as a give-your-hands-something-to-do gesture so that they would not betray what was on your mind. "I think I know who they are, Sil, the people who took Sonya and Margaret." I turned my head to look at him.

He glanced over at me, stiffly, without moving his head.

I turned back to the window. "Modern-day long hunters. They're a band of socially isolated misfits, aren't they—a group of people who could not re-assimilate after the social chaos of the sixties, and who banded together to create an optional society totally removed from the one we know. That's it, isn't it?" He looked at me but said nothing.

447

"Yes, that's it, a sort of extremist counter-culture, the last gasp of the lost ideal of hippiedom, led perhaps by the castoffs from the jungles of 'Nam who would know how to survive under conditions of extreme deprivation. Ex-Special Forces, like the scout who told me not to look directly at an enemy or he'd know you were there—those are the people who would know how to do this."

"You actually believe that?"

I let the shade fall back and stood staring at the curtains. No, I didn't, but I needed to do something to get an answer out of him and thought that maybe a challenge to whatever the reluctant truth was might do it. Besides, the faces I'd seen when we caught up to them in the forest were not Caucasian, and although there would just naturally be other racial groups in the American military, they would not *all* be just one other group. I shook my head without turning around. "No. The fact that Sonya doesn't speak English derails that whole argument." I turned to him with what I hoped was the most contrite look I could muster, the semi-pathos of the unknowing academic in search of an answer. "What does she speak? Abenaki?"

Sil shook his head. "No. It's somehow related, but I can only recognize some of it, not all of it."

"What then?"

"I don't know what it's called, or if it even has a name. Gert knows."

Of course she knows, I thought, my dissatisfaction with that answer tinged with a sarcasm that momentarily made my fists clench. Of course. She gave them the key to get in, so of course she'd know. She knows who they are and what the purpose behind all this was. She knows all of it, and although I'd gotten most of the details of the "how" out of Sil, I still hadn't gotten the most important "how" of all—how was Gert connected to the people who had taken Margaret and Sonya? And I still didn't know the "why."

I went back to my chair and sat down. "What's Gert's role in all this?"

Sil shifted in his chair, somewhat nervously, I thought. "What do you call a society where everything's passed down through the female side of the family rather than the male? What's that called?"

"Matriarchal."

He nodded. "Yeah, that's the word. Matriarchal. That means even the leadership is passed down through the women, right?"

I nodded. "Ancient Egypt was like that. It was the Pharaoh's daughter who determined who the next Pharaoh would be, not the son. Whoever she married became Pharaoh. The only way the son could get the crown was to marry his sister." I watched while he seemed to ponder this information, then added, "It's a very ancient social order, now extinct. With the exception of Egypt, matriarchal societies pretty much vanished thousands of years ago with the coming of the Aryans. The *real* Aryans, not the bullshit the Nazis were peddling." He scowled at what, to him, had no doubt begun to appear to be a pretentious history lesson. I took a swallow of beer and grinned at his displeasure. "I'm a history teacher, remember?"

He shook his head. "How could I forget?"

"Anyway, what's any of that got to do with my question?"

He pondered for several seconds before replying. "What if someone in a family—and for whatever reason, it had to be one of the girls—had a particular job that she had to do, and only she was allowed to do it. You know, like washing the dishes, or dusting off a picture hanging on the wall."

I shrugged. "Yeah, okay. What if?"

"Yeah. And what if this person had to keep dusting the picture because, if she didn't, it would soon be covered with so much grime that you couldn't tell what it was."

I shook my head in exasperation. "Where are you going with this?"

"Well, think of the picture not as a painting or drawing, but sort of as an idea. It's an idea hanging there on the wall in plain sight, but you don't see it anymore because you walked by it so many times. You don't even really know what it's a picture of. But if she takes the picture down, what happens?"

"You know immediately that something is different or out of place, but you may not know exactly what it is."

"Right. You sensed it without being able to identify which picture is missing. And the reason you were able to do this is because, by removing the picture, she disturbed the ordinary."

I nodded in agreement. "And in that case, I'm assuming I would be the 'animal' that noticed that the ordinary had been disturbed. I would know something was wrong and instinctively would think it's some kind of trap. Or, if not a trap, then something to be doubted or avoided."

Sil smiled. "Notice how you *understand* without knowing *what* you understand. Now do you get it? Now do you see how it's possible to understand something without knowing it?"

I did, but still didn't see what it had to do with Gert.

He got up, went over to the fireplace, and nudged the unburned end of one of the logs into the flames with the toe of his shoe. "Gert is not one of us, not an Abenaki."

"She isn't? I thought you said she was."

He turned to face me. "I tell people that to keep things uncomplicated."

I shrugged. "Okay. So why the secrecy? That obviously makes her a member of some other group, but why would that be a problem? Is she from the Iroquois League, maybe? Mohawk?"

He smirked and shook his head in apparent disbelief. "The Abenakis and Mohawks were blood enemies. As an historian, you should know that."

"I do. I just thought that maybe . . . well, you know, these old tribal animosities should be pretty irrelevant by now."

He leaned over so that his face was level with mine while sitting. "We're older than the Mohawks. Understand? We were here before them. They tried to move in on us, and that was how we became enemies."

"Yeah, I know, I get it. But so what?" I pulled myself to my feet so suddenly that Sil involuntarily stepped back to avoid a collision. "What are you saying, that you got first dibs on the land? I don't care about that; neither does the state government. What I want to know is what Gert's role in all this was. How did Sonya—the one upstairs now—end up being with those people? You said 'a life for a life' when I asked you earlier; what does that mean?"

"It's not about 'dibs' on the land." His eyes flashed in anger for only a moment, but with enough intensity to set me back half a step. "Don't trivialize it. It's about respect for the land, and respect for the people who originally tended the land. It's about the role the people who lived on and from the land play in preserving it and keeping it alive. It's about that idea hanging on the wall like a dusty picture, the one that Gert takes care of but can never take down without disturbing the ordinary."

I was becoming both tired and exasperated. I turned away for a moment, as much to try to formulate my next question as to recharge my patience. "Obviously," I said without turning toward him, "there's something you don't want to tell me. Believe me, whatever it is, I can handle it." I turned to face him. "So what are you saying? Is this somehow connected to a long-buried grudge about the Abenakis coming out on the short end of history? If it is, I'm sorry for that, but it's not something I can do anything about. Is that what this is somehow boiling down to?"

He sneered in disgust. "Come off it, shithead. Do you really think all this is about an ancient grudge over losing our land?" He leaned forward so that his face was within inches of mine. "How's this if you want grudge material—the Abenakis fought on the American side in the Revolution, and even *that* didn't save us from where we ended up."

I knew this was true, that they had allied themselves with the colonials, thus incurring the hatred of their blood enemies, the powerful Mohawks, who were allied with the British. One could hardly imagine what sort of nameless, unremembered, unsung battles were fought in the forests of northern New England as these native people, moving like ghosts through the trees, guarded young America's northern flank against an attack from British Canada. And then were forgotten.

With a start, I realized I'd been behaving exactly like those rigidly authoritarian "Inquisitors" of the academic world that I so despised. And now, having seen that in myself, I decided to let it all go. Contrite, exhausted, and humbled, I gave up the contest. "Okay, Sil. You win. You said I have a role to play in this, but how can I play it without knowing what it is?"

♦ ♦ ♦

Some mythologies place an old oak tree at the center of the universe, its roots anchored in the past and its branches growing into the future. Up and down its trunk run the squirrels that represent the ephemeral life that comes and goes, pursuing who knows what ends, oblivious to the

451

ponderous permanence of the thing they were living on and servicing its needs without ever knowing it.

I had always been able to relate to that imagery because there had indeed been an old oak at the center of my universe as I grew up. It raised its hoary head above the neighborhood, having survived countless tree houses and Tarzan swings, persisting in its placid reaction to the changing seasons as it stood sentinel over the place of its birth. As an image of permanence, it lasted right up through my adulthood, and was still there when I moved away. But years later, during a return visit to my old neighborhood, I discovered that it had fallen victim to the same slash-and-pave epidemic that had forced me to leave in the first place. An odd karma, deeply negative in the effect it had on me, and one that had prompted me to say to Mae, my first wife, in a moment of transcendent sadness, "There are no sacred places left." It was not really sacred, of course, except to me, but its disappearance made me feel as if I'd somehow left myself behind.

"Everything out here has died at least once," was what she'd said sometime later in reply. It was during one of her metaphysical musings. She was referring to the natural world, forest and fen, swamp and moor, streams, brooks, and rivulets—anything big enough to carry and nurture the germ of life, or take it away, remold it, and deliver it in another form.

And how was that possible? I had asked. How can anything die more than once? And the things that have died more than once—why would they keep coming back, only to die again?

"Because time is a circle, not a line," she'd said. "You only think it's a line because the circle is so big your place on it looks like it's straight." She'd paused then to pluck a dandelion and, in a gesture that was clearly symbolic, blow its tiny parachute seeds into the wind. "Only the uncanny intelligence that gave us life and lets us keep it for a while knows why, in the end, we have to give it back." She smiled then and kissed me. "Not even life belongs to us."

For the longest time after that, I saw the world as windswept and frozen, year round, not just in winter, with creeping shadows athwart the disintegrating walls of my slowly vanishing world. One should will an ode to the wind that visits the sacred places that still existed, I thought, even if they only existed in the minds of those who valued them. My own mind had become a whirlwind of shrieking memory-particles, and

I struggled to reconcile the chaos I was feeling with what I imagined were the words echoing down to me from forgotten philosophers buried in unknown places, words that reminded me that I worked with the cosmos whether I planned it or not. Mae believed that, but I'd always had trouble accepting it, and I wondered more than once in the intervening years if my attitude led or contributed to our eventual parting of the ways.

Not even life belongs to us. As my life with Mae drew to a close and I moved deeper into the structured realms that defined the boundaries of what an historian may or may not believe, I came to suspect that time moved in blocks, not circles. I saw it this way because historians know better than anyone that the past comes down to us in fragments, not complete packages. This happens in spite of the heroic efforts of the best witnesses and chroniclers down through the ages. Regrettably, unavoidably, this fragmented, discontinuous legacy leaves holes in the long, ongoing story of humanity whose "final chapter" every adolescent child believes he or she represents.

In spite of this shortcoming, we learn about history in school because, if we didn't, our culture—our very civilization—would have no foundation. Without it, we would quickly become culturally ethereal, a dimensionless people who began yesterday and will be gone tomorrow. Who we were is the basis for who and what we've become. How we perceive that history, and the mythology we generate from it, determines whether we will endure and, if so, for how long.

"The Romans built for eternity," I'd lectured to one of my classes one day. "Understand? They *expected* that what they created would always be there. That was the *intent*. We, on the other hand, build for a fast buck and black ink on the quarterly earnings statement. Now, imagine for a moment that the attitude of a society is a self-feeding mechanism that, in turn, slowly shapes and reshapes that very society. What do we end up with?"

Bored faces stared back at me. It was more than just a rhetorical question; it was a meaningless rhetorical question. Finally one of them, the class clown, shouted out, "Caligula."

The class got a laugh out of it and I, expecting something a bit more insightful, was disappointed. But later I realized he was right. That was exactly what we end up with, the ultimate symbol of self-undoing.

This was the symbol I had to keep in focus in order to understand what Sil was trying to tell me about the Abenakis being older than the Mohawks. It was not about ancient tribal mistrust or antipathy. It wasn't even about losing one's land and livelihood. It was about keeping an idea alive, about dusting it off like that picture hanging on the wall and not letting it devolve into something you didn't want. It was about a life for a life, over and over.

"Keeping an idea alive?" I asked. "What idea?"

He glanced at me but didn't respond to my question. "Listen—there was a reason why I told you we were here before the Mohawks. It wasn't about a petty land claim or a way to piss on other tribes. Forty Indian nations called the Abenakis their 'grandfathers,' which was a respectful way of saying that they acknowledged that the Abenakis were the original people, that we were here before them. But here's the thing—our real name, what we call ourselves, is 'Wamb-naghi,' which means 'our ancestors of the east.'"

He paused for a moment to take another drink, and I used the opportunity to try to make sense of what I saw as a paradoxical riddle hiding in what he'd just said. "I don't get it. I can understand why other nations would call you 'ancestors of the east,' but why would you call yourselves that? You—the living—can't be your own ancestors."

"No, that's not the way the name is supposed to be understood."

"It isn't? How then?"

"It's not really a name, at least not in the way you understand how a name works. It refers to our task, to what we have to do."

"And what is that?"

"Preserve an idea. Bear witness."

"Witness? Witness to what? Is there something . . . ?" I stopped short just as the wind exploded against the house with such force that I could almost feel its movement being transferred into the room around me. I turned and stared at the window as if, like Margaret, I could penetrate both darkness and distance by a sheer act of will. Our ancestors of the east? Witness? What was this riddle he was handing to me? I looked over but did not see him; instead, in my mind I saw a tribal elder holding a symbol, an indistinct something whose identity was the key but that also brought with it the obligation of service and silence. And he wore a mask, cut to show that he stood for something else, something older, while behind him was the wolf, the same silent messenger that I'd seen so often while trapped at the Ropewalk.

And then the thing that I'd been seeing in that dark mental tunnel for over two weeks moved forward into the light. In a single transcendent moment it had become clear, had lifted its veil to me the way I had suddenly realized the meaning of the old stone foundations around the school. Impossible, but the only thing that made sense, the only thing that was left. "She's a Skraeling, isn't she?" I said in almost a whisper.

"What?"

I turned away from him and found myself staring at the fireplace. "Sonya—the other Sonya, the one who was taken, who's out there now. She's a Skraeling." The words came out almost trance-like, as if someone other than myself were explaining it to me. I turned and locked eyes with him. "That's what she is, isn't she?"

He shook his head. "I don't know what that is."

I repeated the word, but softer, as if denying it even to myself. "Skraeling. In the Norse Edda, in the Icelandic sagas, there are these people called the Skraelings—*Skraelingar*—who the Norsemen encountered and who are assumed to have been Indians or Eskimos. But that's always been pure speculation based on what we think we know today about an event that happened a thousand years ago. The fact is, nobody really knows who they were." I stepped back to the loveseat and sat down, consumed with doubt and disbelief. "She's one of those people the Vikings first encountered when they landed here, and who then just vanished from history." I took another swallow of beer, grappling with my own statement. "That's what she is, isn't she?"

The way his look changed, it was obvious that he clearly understood what I was getting at. He offered no response for some time, then finally nodded. "Neganni arenānbak."

This time it was my turn to shake my head and shrug.

"That's what the Abenaki elders called them, the name I learned as a kid: Neganni arenānbak—The Ancients of Past Time." His eyes bored into me, as if he were studying my face for a reaction, or maybe preparing himself for that reaction. "Dawn People. They were here even before us."

My nape hairs tingled for a moment as I grappled with the implications of what we were talking about. Skraelings—like shadow

455

figures from a dream, or something from a Victorian tale of the Otherworld, these people stalked the footnotes of history unnoticed except by the few who looked for them. And even then, they faded in and out of corporeal reality like wraiths, sometimes vanishing into the shadows around them and other times shape-shifting into animals and suddenly appearing where they were least expected. The myths tried to explain the insubstantiality of the reality behind these people the way they always did—with dismissive simplicity. For most historians, they were simply not worth bothering about.

If there was such a thing as a fault line in time, I felt it growing beneath me. In my mind, the floor opened and I dropped through layers of history like a stricken leaf headed for a stream that would carry me away. "That comment you made earlier about a vanquished people hiding in caves and trying to stay out of the way—you weren't referring to the Abenakis, were you?"

He smiled as he saw that I'd finally made the connection. No, he said, he wasn't referring to the Abenakis; he was referring to the Dawn People.

I nodded because now I had come to accept the impossible. "And they know we won't be here forever. They know that because of the way the village died." It was all unrolling for me like a lost scroll brought to light after centuries of darkness and concealment. "They got their sacred places back, or at least some of them. And until we're gone and they can move back and reclaim all of them, they'll continue to hide in plain sight."

He smiled again, broader this time, and in that smile I could see that he felt as if he had suddenly been relieved of a huge burden. He closed his eyes and let his head fall back against the chair. "*Now* you understand," was all he said.

◆ ◆ ◆

Chapter 34

I had spent my entire academic life struggling backwards through time, wandering through the trackless heath and bottomless fens of that wilderness called "history." There is no compass or map for this purpose; one gropes one's way along following the breadcrumb clues through the caverns of antiquity, pulling on the strands of mythology that still dangle into the twentieth century, on past the shrines to the gods as they were conceived of then, ever onward, further and further, till the passage narrows, the torch dims, the crumbs disappear, and all that's left is the geography of the mind.

And because it was the geography of the mind, it changed over time. One could never be sure to what extent one's own perceptions, conditioned by one's upbringing, were influencing what one was "seeing." I remembered how, as a little kid, I would run to the top of a hill hoping to catch the sky before it had a chance to retreat to the horizon. I did this over and over, each time wondering why I couldn't get any closer or why I never seemed to be able to surprise it, or why, at the beginning of that quest, my failure to catch it did not deter me from compulsively trying at the next hill. Over time, it seemed to become an allegory for my life—the constant striving for the thing I would never catch.

The mystery of the fleeting sky would go on and on until the day came when I finally understood why it was never going to happen. It was the day when I passed through a door from which no return was possible, and although I couldn't define it then, as time went on its tagline became more evident.

It was the day the myths died.

◆ ◆ ◆

I was still awake after Sil went to bed. He'd given me the sheets and blankets I would need for the foldout bed and asked me if I wanted any help making it, but I'd said no. I sat there in silence watching the fire slowly die, my mind cleared of everything except the irreconcilable reality of what I'd just heard. As an historian, I knew I should've been elated—what an opportunity I'd been given, a chance to see into a world thought to be long beyond reach. And it was *alive*, not a cache of dried bones and pottery fragments. Even its language was there, meaning that the Rosetta Stone concept for interpreting lost scripts wouldn't be necessary. Thinking of that reminded me I had to dig out my tape recorder so that I could preserve some samples. It wasn't like I had far to go to get them; all I had to do was record what Sonya was saying. I got up intending to go into the kitchen to try to find a scrap of paper to write myself a note but suddenly, as if coming to my senses from a deep sleep, felt all desire drain out of me.

I sat back down. What was I thinking? I couldn't expose her to that kind of risk. Recording her voice as a sample of a living but lost language would throw open the gates to inquiries and investigations. How had she come to speak this language? Who taught her? How did I conclude that it was the language of the Skraelings?

And what would I say by way of an answer? Oh, it's because I spent an afternoon with them in the forest and, oh yeah, by the way, they're still out there. How was that going to work?

I could see myself getting entangled in a nightmare world of state-sanctioned Child Services people accusing me of some sort of child abuse—"How is it she never learned English? Did you have her locked up somewhere?"—and wanting to take her, coupled with a police investigation into why she was not the same Sonya who had lived at the Ropewalk. What did I do with the other one? Was I upset over her handicap to the extent that I decided to "solve" that problem by making her disappear? And where did I get this one? Missing Persons would get involved at that point, and all sorts of leads, rumors, suspicions, and guesses would be followed up on just to see if they fit. In the meantime, though, Child Services would take her because she clearly was not the child Margaret and Ben had been raising, which, of course, would implicate Margaret in the deception and launch a nation-wide search for Ben, who had obviously fled in order to avoid the repercussions of being discovered.

My mind ran wild with spinoff scenarios. Once the investigation had been set in motion, search warrants would be issued for the premises, including the shed, and the discovery of the skeleton would only be a matter of time. Even once its actual age was determined, how could it be explained? What would the police think? Maybe that it was a trophy from some kind of cult, or the result of a human trafficking ring going back a century? Was it proof of some kind of underground slave trade, maybe the result of someone's perverted idea to utilize the already existing means and devices of the Underground Railroad, but for a sinister plan?

It all fit together so nicely I didn't have the slightest doubt that at some point in that sequence of events I'd end up doing time somewhere, becoming one of those despairing ghosts locked up in the "Corrections Machine" whose lone-wolf voice echoed into that empty chamber called "society."

Was that what Sil meant when he said I needed to fear my own kind? That I needed to fear what they would do once they started looking into the matter? Or was it that, by "my own kind," he actually meant me, not someone else, because he sensed that I might be unable to prevent myself from inadvertently "killing" her? Or maybe he meant both—the well-intentioned but misinformed outsiders who could only weigh the facts against their own training and experience, plus my own unexamined motives for bringing a hidden reality to light.

In either case, I understood with a new sense of urgency the need for Margaret and Sonya to disappear. It was not just about the risk of Margaret being recognized, or about the danger of someone noticing that Sonya had "changed"; it was about the far-reaching consequences of either or both of those things happening. It was about the door to a lost world being opened and the destruction that would follow. It was about not disturbing the ordinary, which was the only way to prevent all this from happening.

I knew I needed to get some sleep because we were getting up early to go get Margaret's things from her apartment, but all I felt like doing was sitting there in the dark listening to the wind beating itself against the side of the house. I felt chastised; I was not upset over the realization that what I'd first seen as the opportunity of a lifetime was now in the shadow of an undeserved "retribution" from a society that did its best to protect its innocents; no, what upset me was that my initially careless appraisal of that "opportunity" did not even *consider* the ricochet effect of actually taking advantage of it.

Would I actually exploit Margaret's daughter, soon to be my own by adoption, for the fleeting gain of a recognition that would make me a star for a short time but end up destroying all of us? No, of course not. My role, as Sil had said, was to protect her, not use her. And with that realization, I suddenly understood something else, something that he had said earlier—could I protect them both? I had originally thought that would be impossible because one of them had vanished. But now I knew what he meant; protecting them both meant guarding against even the *possibility* of anyone learning about Sonya's real background. Revealing that background would not just endanger Margaret's relationship with her biological daughter; it would also launch a major manhunt for the people who took the other Sonya. As an historian, I knew that such "encounters" typically did not go well for the more primitive culture.

No, I could not let any of that happen. I would not disturb the ordinary. If I did, the animal would know something was wrong, and I now knew that *we* were the animals. *We* were the creatures staring at faces we no longer recognized, because they had become us. It was startling in its simplicity—if you can't change your appearance to look like them, if you cannot be one of them, you can change the spirit of one of them to become one of you. They had perfected the ultimate shape-shift and *become* the animal. And now, knowing what was actually happening, like them I would have to hide in plain sight.

I now understood the true magnitude of the bartering Sil had done in the forest when he was trying to get Margaret and Sonya released. He *knew* the real danger associated with me seeing these people and coming to understand who they were. That was why he'd been so reluctant to reveal them to me—there was no way he could've known if he could actually trust me. In spite of my relationship with Margaret,

I was still a wild card, an outsider, a white man motivated by a white man's values. His bartering act had thus been one of profound trust—he was betting the lives of all those people on my willingness to follow through on where my relationship with Margaret was going to end up. He knew where that end would be; I didn't, and my reaction once I got there was impossible to foresee.

"They thought Ben would be the one to protect Sonya—we all thought he would do this for her—but then, when he left Margaret, they realized that he was not the one." That was what he'd told me before he went to bed, although at the time I hadn't fully grasped the significance of what it meant to have me inserted into that role. "They couldn't trust that Margaret would be able to protect Sonya all by herself, especially because of Sonya's problems. So the girl had to go back." He'd paused for a moment to reflect on something that seemed to be bothering him. "Couldn't just leave her here. They knew what would happen if they did. No protection, no understanding, no trust—she'd end up like Roger Benning." He'd glanced over at me, and the seriousness of his reference to the skeleton in the shed was not lost on me. His look held both a challenge and a hope, and I'd understood immediately the meaning behind it.

He was wondering what would happen if I were to betray the trust he'd shown in me. There was no way he could predict my reaction to any of this, and he and I had always had such an antagonistic relationship that the leap of faith required to get Margaret and Sonya back must've stretched the limits of his belief in humanity. Yet he did it anyway. That simple act of barter for mother and daughter had, in retrospect, placed an entire world at risk and broken down the barrier between us. It was all or nothing, and the fact that he'd chosen "all" with me at its center demonstrated a faith in me that left me both flattered and humbled.

And obligated as well. It was a foregone conclusion that Sonya could not be allowed to become another Roger Benning. Although it still wasn't clear to me what had happened to the boy, Sil had told me why his skeleton could not be buried—it would be tantamount to burying what he had represented, which could not be allowed to happen. I could see him brace for the skepticism or even ridicule that he no doubt expected from me as a response, but by then I wasn't at all surprised by his explanation. I even flattered myself into thinking that maybe I was being weaned off of some of the white man's prejudices.

I understood the underlying concept of magical thinking that "like produces like," but for me it had always been a very remote idea, more academic than real. In the circles of higher education that I moved in, the primitive logic of such thinking was a game played only in the footnotes of papers submitted for peer review, or maybe in the hope of professional advancement. It was never *real*. No one ever actually expected to encounter an episode of self-contained thinking that *excluded* the logic of the modern world, or that did not acknowledge that such logic even existed. It was the world of the Paleolithic hunter he was talking about, a world of sympathetic magic that rested, not on reasoned explanations, but on the principles of similarity and contact. The shaman in such a culture knew that he could produce any effect he wanted by simply imitating it in advance; he also knew he could maintain it by ensuring the continued "participation" of the person or persons who'd been in contact with whatever that effect was. By inference, if he were to take the person out of contact, he would break the chain and destroy the effect.

So Roger Benning could not be buried because the law of "like producing like" meant that the idea would die in the process. And that other law of magical thinking—that of contact or contagion—said that whatever he had affected in life would continue to have its effect as long as he stayed in contact with it. In whatever form.

And realizing this made me suddenly understand something else—Roger Benning must've died in his childhood as a result of some breach of trust. Either his protectors didn't stay close enough, or simply didn't do their job. Or maybe that wasn't it at all; maybe it was just a case of someone not liking the effect he was producing and deciding to eliminate the "problem" in their own way. If that were the case, then the need to protect Sonya ratcheted up to a whole new—and wholly unforeseen—level.

This feeling intensified when, in the same moment, it occurred to me that the little girl upstairs had emerged from a society where a child had no reason to fear any adult, leaving her dangerously unprepared for dealing with the world she was about to enter. The simple fact was that nomadic children in natural settings grew up with, and were accustomed to, a constant change of scenery and circumstances. And since the whole tribe raised the children, the concept of "parents" was much broader than any white child would ever understand. In effect, she had been living in a society where virtually every adult was seen as a parent, as someone to be respected, obeyed, and—most decisively—trusted. We would have to train her to understand that there were now limits to that trust.

I got up to scatter the ashes of what was left of the fire and then, since I was up anyway, I unfolded the sofa and made the bed. The mere act of doing so drove home to me how tired I really was and that I needed the rest for the next day's activities, but my mind was still racing and I knew that, if I were to lie down, I would just end up staring at the ceiling. There were so many loose ends, so many unassembled pieces.

I sat on the bed and stared at what was left of the fire. A faint ribbon of smoke curled up into the chimney from the stub of one of the logs, and I fleetingly wondered if it was too early to close the damper. I knew that if I didn't do it soon, I'd probably forget about it and wake up during the night with the icy fingers of the outside air snaking over my shoulders, sending me into a shiver from which the blankets I had might not be able to rescue me. I needed the sleep, so I couldn't chance it; the streamer of smoke was so faint that I knew it wouldn't amount to anything, so I reached into the fireplace, found the handle for the damper, and closed it.

Only now was I beginning to understand the true extent of what had fallen to me, of what I had "agreed" to. It was much deeper than anything I might've planned for. I was to play my part in keeping an idea alive. I was to spend my life dusting off a forgotten memory hanging on the wall like an old picture, obvious but not noticed.

I didn't bother checking to see what time it was because I didn't want to know how little sleep I would get before Sil roused me in the morning. I surrendered to the need, however, and with my mind still hot-wired, I stripped down to my underwear, turned off the light, and got under the covers.

♦ ♦ ♦

"Gauging what one thinks one knows about the world has always been a questionable process because the evaluator—you—and the thing being evaluated—the world—are much more closely linked to the perception process than most of us even realize. It follows, then, that it may sometimes seem as if it's not just a question of seeing what one wants to see; it's as if one's senses were nothing more than a routing junction for an impulse that would be there whether you were its agent or not.

"This is further complicated by the fact that one's imagination can make a lot of strange connections, things that assemble themselves one way but that could just as easily be assembled in dozens of other ways, depending on whatever sense-image is operating in the background at the time of the assembly.

"Which of these connections is the right one? Were any of them right? And if none of them were right, what would be the outcome of acting on the one that seemed to be the most convenient—which was understood to mean the one whose many facets fit most closely together with that sense-image, which itself was nothing more than a reflection of contemporary beliefs and biases and was always in a state of transition?

"Understand? 'Reality' does not become more real because the imaginative faculty fades as the reasoning mind expands. We only *think* it does because that is the image under which we operate when we arrive at that conclusion.

"What none of us learned in school, and what I did not teach even in my own history classes, was that the 'foundation' history gives us is not a floor at all. It's a sieve. And the missing pieces of that long story lie beneath it, right where they fell out eons before. What we learned as 'history' was whatever didn't fall through the cracks."

It was a half-waking dream, a semi-conscious sermonizing that attempted to lace together the different strands of all that had happened in the previous three weeks. It was so insistent that it actually brought me back to full wakefulness, and when my eyes opened, I involuntarily smiled as I ended the meandering lecture about the world-historical process that I'd just half-mumbled to an absent audience in an empty room. I thought about getting up, finding a piece of paper, and jotting down the main points, got as far as turning the light on, but then lay back down. Like the fictitious journal entry of my childhood friend playing with my little daughter and then vanishing behind time's curtain, I knew that this, too, would never be written.

I draped my arm across my eyes to blot out the shadows left standing in the darkened corners of the living room. The bottom line to all this was simple: my academic life was over. That was the new reality for me, the thing I had to accept. Right at the point of being able to launch myself to new heights, right at the door to the prize, I had to shut it down. I consoled myself with the reminder that it had never really been about ambition or social climbing, that I was different in that way from my colleagues, so it really didn't matter. While that may have been true, what was creeping up on me in spite of myself was the feeling that to willfully dismiss the chance of a lifetime, that "tide in the affairs of men," was not a decision that anyone should make so flippantly.

I let my arm fall to my side and opened my eyes. "Flippantly"—was that the word I'd used? What a careless thing to say in describing a choice between what could be a momentary fame tied to a lifetime of torment on one hand and the simple acceptance of the terms of one's life tied to quiet happiness on the other. In reality it was no contest at all, and flippancy had nothing to do with it. It was fate's way of handing me what would be the terms of my own reality. This was the ultimate test of who I really was, of what I'd always claimed mattered to me. These were my values, ideals, and convictions passing in review before my own eyes, those very same ideals about creating a better world that had flourished in the sixties but had since been overtaken by the spectral banshees called fame and power.

And there I was, paying homage to those banshees.

That was what it was really about, the very thing that had cost me my marriage to Mae—that everything came with a cost, and for every decision you made, you had to let something else go. It followed, then, that to truly know a person it wasn't necessary to study what decisions he's made; all you needed to do was look at what he was willing to leave behind. And I was not willing to leave behind all that I'd gained while stranded at the Ropewalk.

And they, the people who had taken Sonya, they were not willing to leave their idea behind either—the idea that they were bound to the earth and still held parts of it sacred. This was Sil's final revelation to me before he went to bed, the entire plan laid out before me, disarming in the simplicity of its ultimate purpose: that the circle of time that began with the Dawn Period would one day close. And once that happened, like the game of musical chairs, wherever you were on that circle would determine whether you would find a place that was secure.

465

But to survive in the meantime, they needed to know what the animal was doing. And to do that, they needed to be among the animals, but not part of them. The hunted had become the hunter, except that they were not trying to trap the animal—they were trying to not be trapped by it. In effect, they were casting themselves into a two-way role of being both the watcher and the watched. There had to be eyes and ears inserted into that world, people who could move among them unnoticed, people who would both know of the world they came from and be a bellwether for the other world. Is it time to return yet? Can we trust them? Who would speak for us when the time came?

What a desperate decision it must've been. And the only way to get it going and keep it going was to use an intermediary, a people who could move among the animals without arousing undue suspicion. And who would that be? I smiled at the obvious answer; it would be the only people it *could* be—the "grandfathers," the people who had been there the longest and knew them the best. The Abenakis.

When Sil was telling me all this, I had pondered the implications of Margaret's biological Sonya being returned before that was actually supposed to happen. "How old are the children supposed to be when they're taken back?" I'd asked.

Sil had shrugged in reply. "Don't know for sure. There's some kind of timetable for how all this is supposed to run. It's based on moon cycles, or something like that."

"But in Sonya's case it failed."

He'd nodded but said nothing, and his silence told me what I'd already come to suspect.

"It means someone else will be taken, doesn't it?"

He had glanced over at me and nodded again. "The idea can't be allowed to die. That's why I keep the brush cleared away from the school as far as I can. I need to try to make sure I know when they're coming." He paused and stared into the flames. "It didn't work this time. They took me by surprise." He paused again, thinking, shaking his head in either disappointment or disagreement with himself. "That's why Roger Benning can't be buried. Understand?"

"Yes."

"Roger Benning didn't make it," he'd said, "but there have been others since, and there'll be still others as time goes on. The idea will survive in a thousand faces and places, some of which you'd never suspect."

"Like Gert?" The realization had hit me like another of those Olympian revelations. "She's one of them, isn't she?"

"Yes."

Yes. And so there it was—the very embodiment of the puzzling stories and ignored mythologies trapped between the covers of books no one reads anymore, the stories of missing persons and mysterious "Elf-shots," those arrows that would appear out of the darkness to surprise and frighten the unwary traveler, and the stories of the unexplained disappearances over the centuries, leading to no solutions, or the undying reports and endless, unsupported sightings of people thought long dead or believed to have been nothing more than wraiths living in the shadows of myths.

I learned that Margaret was an anomaly—most children could not be returned to their biological parents for obvious reasons and would end up being raised by carefully selected surrogates. Gert, Sil had explained, was one of those who would find homes for the children who had lived among those people and were returning—cautiously selected homes, owned by people who, like me, would not disturb the ordinary. There had been a huge risk involved in giving Margaret back her biological daughter and then releasing both of them to Sil's care, both because she would then know the truth, and because the daughter would leave the protection of a society that did not exploit its own members and would enter one that did. They all knew this just from what had happened to the village, and I was sure they also knew it would increase the chances of Sonya ending up like Roger Benning if she were not protected.

Which was where I came in, and which was why Sil's bartering with them had been so delicate and intense. "You just agreed to something you better be ready for" was what he had told me, and although I fought it at the time, I now understood its importance.

With this final ordering of events, I found the frantic energy that had kept me so on edge beginning to dissipate. I reached up and turned the light off, finally resolved to try to get some sleep. With my mind now relaxed, I found myself sinking very quickly, and it was with something of a shock that I saw myself back in the old Engineering building once again, confronted by the wolf, except that this time I was not staring across an unbridgeable gulf into the eyes of one of mankind's oldest bogeymen; this time we understood one another. In retrospect, I began to suspect that he had divined my secret long before I realized it myself.

I, too, had become a shape-shifter.

◆ ◆ ◆

I have often thought that history was like a giant jigsaw puzzle whose interlocking pieces could be made to fit together in an almost infinite number of ways, only one of which was actually the truth. And, like a jigsaw puzzle, since each piece held only a tiny daub of the picture that would emerge when the puzzle was finished, there was no way to know during the assembly process if the pieces were going together correctly. Only the completed picture at the end would tell you if you got it right, but even that was a paradox—whatever emerged was the product of how you assembled it, and not necessarily a reflection of what the actual picture was supposed to look like.

The "corrupting liquid" that the diarist associated with Madeline Cane's sudden infirmity, for instance, was almost certainly nothing more than water and had nothing at all to do with what happened to her. I was sure that what she had experienced was either a mild stroke or heart attack, or possibly an epileptic seizure, and that the coincidental contact with the water was just that—coincidence. Yet, to the diarist, cause and effect followed as naturally as night and day, and the juxtaposition of the liquid and the sudden illness left no doubt in her mind. The liquid was to blame. There was no reason for her to think otherwise.

When this sort of error is projected over long periods of time, a drift will creep into the "facts" of history, one so imperceptible that the line between fact and fancy blurs, breaks up, and finally vanishes altogether. And we move through the resulting distortion in complete ignorance of its effects, without suspecting that the truth has become one of the myths that we no longer credit, and that the lies, distortions, or best-guess interpretations that we've come to live with are a mere pantomime for what's actually real. Without knowing it, we end up in a make-believe world, a "what if" world, a world of functional fictions, none of which matters if all that we've come to accept as real truly is real.

But what if it isn't?

♦ ♦ ♦

Chapter 35

The wolf had told Sil. He had heard it "talking" to other wolves and knew that they were signaling the presence of humans still on the peninsula, and he realized these could only have been Margaret, Sonya, and I. He knew this because he had found out via a telephone conversation with the school administrators that Margaret had never gotten to Connecticut and her family was frantic. My name had come up in the same conversation since I had never gotten there either. Abduction was the obvious conclusion, since it was assumed that everyone had left the Ropewalk around the same time.

He knew I was single and this, through some sort of elliptical logic, or maybe simply because he and I had always been so hostile to each other, led him to conclude that I was involved in her disappearance. He had seethed with rage at his own helplessness in the face of my "treachery," and until he heard the wolves, even he had not considered that both of us might still be there at the school. Realizing the truth at last, but still mistrustful of me and my motives, he had come to verify what the wolves were saying. Finding Margaret and Sonya gone, and seeing me return to the Ropewalk alone and with a shotgun, had confirmed his suspicions of me and led him to one of those obvious but erroneous ways that "history" could be assembled.

That was what was going through my head the next morning when Sil roused me at five-thirty, almost physically dragged me into the kitchen for a quick breakfast, pumped me full of hot coffee, then led me outside to the snowmobiles. Within minutes we were racing through the forest, taking that circuitous route he had talked about, away from the road and house, then arcing back toward the highway. The trip took just under a half hour and it was not yet six-thirty when we arrived at the Ropewalk. There was no need for talk; we both understood the urgency behind what we were doing, so the moment Sil unlocked the front door we literally ran down the hall to Margaret's apartment. We packed as many of her and Sonya's things as we could carry and headed back the same way.

By late morning we had made three trips and had retrieved all of their clothing and what necessities we could carry. The rest would have to wait for the road to open so that we could get a truck down there. We loaded what we had into Gert's car, and with her at the wheel, I went into the house to get Margaret and Sonya.

She was in the living room bundling Sonya up in the tiny parka we'd brought from the apartment. "Time to go," I said. "Sil wants you two out of town before all the church traffic increases the odds that one or both of you might be recognized."

She glanced over at me and, as if in response, flipped up the hood on Sonya's parka so that the girl's face vanished into its folds. "There," she said. "No one will ever know."

There was an odd edge to her voice; it was an obvious effort at casual conversation that still quavered with the unresolved emotions from all that had happened. As if to acknowledge this, she flipped the hood back down, leaned over, kissed Sonya's forehead, and leaned back. The girl was passive, as if she didn't understand or know what to do.

"You'll have to teach her what kissing means," I said gently. "Most . . . primitive cultures bond through some kind of touching. Try touching your forehead to hers."

She gave me a quizzical look but leaned back in, placed her forehead against Sonya's, and left it there for several seconds. This the little girl seemed to understand; she reached out and held her mother's arms in response. I knelt down so that I was on the same level and when Margaret pulled back, I drew Sonya to me, touched her forehead with mine, and left it there for several seconds. Then I stood up and turned toward Margaret. The reality of her leaving had begun to well up inside of me, leaving me without even the simple ability to say "good-bye."

She must've seen it in my face, because she took her daughter's hand and said, "As soon as I get situated I'll write you. Gert knows of a place in upstate New Hampshire."

I nodded, then looked at Sonya and caught her staring at me, her wide, blue-gray eyes full of wonder and curiosity. She was as beautiful as her mother. "She's going to be a real heartbreaker when she grows up." I glanced at Margaret. "Just like her mother."

Then I leaned in further and kissed Margaret. "We still have a lot of details to work out, including cleaning out your apartment and getting your car out of the shed without anyone seeing it. Got to be done soon, right after one or both of the bridges open." I leaned in and kissed her again, then, hoping to control the emotional upsurge I felt coming, joked about demonstrating to Sonya how kissing worked. "Private lessons." I smiled and shrugged, but I could feel it coming.

Margaret's eyes told me that she could see it coming as well and, with a faint smile that maybe masked her fears as well, she stepped forward and put her arms around me.

"I'm so afraid of losing you now," I whispered, pulling her as close to me as I could.

She leaned back a slight bit so that I could see her face. "No. No, that's not going to happen. I'm going to start the divorce proceedings, then you're going to come to me and stay with me." She paused for a moment and touched her forehead to mine, just as she'd done with Sonya. "You promised to never leave me, remember?"

I smiled and nodded. "I remember."

The back door opened and Sil's voice boomed into the house. "Ready to go? We're all packed up here." I could sense the impatience in his tone.

"Yeah. We're coming," I replied.

Margaret put her coat on, took one of Sonya's hands, followed me out to the car, and got into the front passenger seat. The little girl did not pull back or seem alarmed when I picked her up to put her on her mother's lap, and as I backed away, she suddenly reached out with both hands and touched my face. There was an odd serenity in her look as she studied me, something much older than her childhood years, and after a moment she let her hands slide down and come together on her lap. Then, with an exaggerated earnestness that seemed both comic and touching coming from one so young, she spoke. "Nd'elewizi Sonya," she said, pointing to herself.

I nodded and smiled, then glanced over at Gert.

"She said 'My name is Sonya.'"

I nodded at Gert by way of thanking her, then leaned in and kissed the little girl on the forehead. "Yes, it is," I said to her, touching her playfully on the nose. "Sonya Drummond." I kissed Margaret one more time before I backed out, closed the door, and leaned into the window. "You don't need to translate for her," I said to Gert. "In time she'll know what those words mean." Gert smiled as I stepped back.

Margaret stroked Sonya's hair one last time before putting her hood up and turning toward me. "Gert says it's a nice house. It even has a fireplace." She winked and smiled and Sonya, seeing her mother's happiness, smiled with her.

◆ ◆ ◆

Two days later, the bridges were finally repaired and the coast highway plowed. I went back to the Ropewalk with Sil in his truck in the middle of the night to get Margaret's car out of the shed and into his garage. Then we went back and cleaned everything out of Margaret's apartment except for the biggest furniture. Once that was done, I went back with him again to get my car and to help him get things ready for the school to reopen. Margaret's intention to not return had been forwarded to the school administrators and a temporary English composition teacher was located. She would move right into Margaret's apartment.

"Ain't that a bitch," said Sil. "Here you are, a full time teacher stuffed into a single room, and along comes a temp who gets an apartment all to herself."

I shrugged. I didn't care. I had already talked to the administration and given my resignation. I would complete the spring semester and stay on until the end of June to help out with final grades, then they would have to find a new history teacher as well.

"Still going to write the history of the area?" asked Sil.

I pondered the question. "It'll have to have two versions, the one I try to sell to the academic watchdogs and the real one, the one I'll keep for myself."

Sil nodded. "Smart move. You tell them the real one and you'll end up in a padded room."

◆ ◆ ◆

Over the next two days, I learned that virtually all the conclusions I had come to about the village and the old ropewalk had been correct, including the connection to the Underground Railroad. It was also true that the so-called "Greek ruins" were in fact the remains of the first settlement in the area.

But the death of the village was a lot more prosaic. It had died not because of an epidemic or some sort of attack, but simply because the profitability of making ropes so far inland, despite the clever motive power, had declined to the point that it could no longer support itself. The sawmill whose ruins I'd found on my first visit to the site had delayed the inevitable for some time by providing an alternative source of income, but in the end could not stop it. Eventually it, too, succumbed to the same problem as coastal areas were developed, steam replaced water as a power source, and competition requiring lower transport fees slowly undermined its profitability. The "terror" was economic, not some sort of physical "sooty devil," as was mentioned in the old diary.

Of course, at first I had thought that "sooty devils" may have been simply an allegorical surrogate intended to replace a much more strongly worded eighteenth-century expletive used to describe the magistrates and legal hawks who came to foreclose on the people in the village and turn them out into the wilderness. But Sil told me that was only partially true; the "sooty devils" part was referring to the legal aides and messengers who delivered the writs and notices, so named because of the printer's ink that got all over their hands and clothes. But it had become irrelevant; the "sooty devils," whoever they were, would've represented the very same implacable economic forces that had driven the Skraelings away, making it an oddly self-fulfilling irony that the village was destroyed by the very economic system it had used to its advantage in the beginning. Maybe, then, it was just another example of "destiny logic," that "calculus of history" that Spengler asserted was at work in the apparatus behind the veil of daily life, or perhaps, at the very least, a simple example of karmic irony. Either way, devil, demon, or destiny, it looks a lot different when it's coming after you.

In any case, the real revelation for me was that the timeline for all these events meant that the ropewalk I was living in was older than any of us had suspected, by almost fifty years. Building a ropewalk right on the shore had led to the demise of the village. But the bigger surprise was learning that the Lewis house had still been occupied just prior to, and possibly after, the Civil War, long after the rest of the village had been abandoned. That accounted for its role in the Underground Railroad after the village itself had died. It also helped explain why the house had remained intact.

In a larger sense, the Ropewalk itself had become symbolic of the *real* nature of the history of the region, or by inference, the history of the world in general. The totality would forever elude me because all the factors can never be taken into account, any more than a single strand of the braid that made up the ropes could ever be traced through the rope itself. You start at one end with a single thread and imagine that you've picked it up again further in the process, but you can never be sure. Hints were all we could ever expect to get. You simply could not know that it was the same strand, and consequently all the guesses, suppositions, and well-intentioned pronouncements meant essentially nothing. It was opaque. The only way to know for sure would be to unravel the rope itself, and that meant going to places—and lengths—that one would rather not pursue. But anything less would send humanity once again over the edge in pursuit of monstrous phantasms. As an historian, I could now see that that was, in fact, all we've been doing for the last five thousand years. Error propagation.

◆ ◆ ◆

Sil laughed at me when I asked him about who had built the bone barrow. "Ever hike on the Old Job trail in Vermont, up in the Green Mountains?"

In fact, I had, years before.

"There used to be a sawmill there, right?"

I shrugged. "I don't know. I know there had been some sort of work camp there back in the thirties, but I never knew what they did."

"Trust me—they had a sawmill there."

"Okay, they had a sawmill. So what?"

"So, a sawmill produces sawdust, right?"

"Right."

"Right. *Lots* of it. And when you were on the Old Job trail, did you see anything unusual, anything that seemed like maybe it didn't belong there?"

I thought back to that hike, done in the fall as the leaves were turning and the water in a nearby brook ran full and icy. The whole area was enchanting, and I remembered picking apples off the trees that had no doubt been planted there back in the work camp days and were still there, growing wild and heedlessly producing fruit for anyone or anything that cared to partake. But other than that—wait, I did remember something, a feature that seemed so out of place I had had to go check it out. It was a mound, a huge, brown, sand-textured, turtleback mound that was so bizarrely unlike the geography around it one might almost conclude it had come from outer space.

"Yes, there was something there, as I recall. This huge mound, like a . . ." I hesitated while I searched for an analogy.

"Like a barrow?"

I was stunned, but the description fit. "Yes, like a barrow." I had to take a moment to assimilate the implication. "Are you telling me the bone barrow is nothing more than a huge pile of sawdust?"

He smiled at my confusion and disbelief but neither confirmed nor denied the insinuation. And the more I pressed him for it, the vaguer his position became, until at last I understood that, yes, it was sawdust to the rest of the world, but maybe, just maybe, there might be something underneath it that the sawdust was concealing. This, too, he would neither confirm nor deny.

"You know," I said, "in the Norse stories of their visits to what we now know as North America there was one case where the Vikings were terrified by a weapon that the Skraelings used against them. The way it's described, it must've been some sort of catapult—it threw fire and stones at them, and the Vikings couldn't defend themselves against it."

Sil looked at me but said nothing.

"It almost sounded like the legendary 'Greek fire' that everyone's heard of but that no one can define or explain." I hesitated for a moment to search out the words I needed. "A catapult and Greek fire. Understand?"

Sil just continued to look at me without saying a word.

"Not to belabor the obvious, but who could've taught them how to make those things?"

Sil just shrugged. "I have no idea. And you don't know for sure that they ever even existed."

"No, I don't. I only know what's in the accounts the Vikings wrote. But why would they lie about something like that? And then there was the thing that's described in the old diary, that thing with the so-called 'spindle' that could be set at different angles. The thing that Madeline Cane saw before she had her stroke or seizure, or whatever it was."

Sil visibly sat straighter in his chair. "Madeline Cane? Old diary?"

He didn't know. He didn't know that the old accounts ledger that had been sitting on the top of that pile of old books had a diary in the back of it. "The accounts ledger from the shed. It had a diary in the back of it, and there's a section in that diary where the writer describes being someplace with a group of people who came upon a chamber filled with items they didn't recognize."

Sil's features slackened. "And this diary, you read all of it?"

"No. It's very hard to read and will take a long time. I've only read sections of it."

"What else does it say?"

He was probing. "Not much. It was written by a girl or young woman, so most of what I read was what you'd expect to find in a diary like that—daily events, the wistful yearnings and hopes she had for her life, and so on. That was where I learned about the hatchet marks in the upstairs wall of the Lewis house."

He merely grunted in acknowledgement. "I've seen those marks. I've also seen the name 'Cane' on one of the stones in the cemetery at the village. And where is this diary now?"

"Back in my room at the Ropewalk. I've got it stored in a plastic box."

"What are your plans for it?"

"Well, originally, I was going to use the land records to baseline the settlement of the area for my history project. But now . . . I just don't know. In any case, it's not mine, so I have to put it back in the shed before I leave."

He waved it off. "Keep it. Take it with you and work your way through it. Take notes—who knows what else it might say. Let me know what you find, if anything." He paused for a moment, then looked at me with a nod, his head at a slight angle as if to emphasize his point. "You owe me at least that much."

Yes, I did. "Okay. If I find anything that seems . . . relevant . . . you'll be the first to know." At that point I paused to run sketchy scenarios through my mind, imagining revelations buried in the unread pages that had to remain hidden in the diary. I returned his look. "And you'll probably be the only one to know."

He nodded, seemed satisfied, and by default that seemed to signal an end to the discussion of the barrow. I understood his reluctance to go any farther—where was I going with this? Would I still be willing to risk it all, unmask everything, by digging up the barrow to discover what, if any, truth was buried there?

As convincing as it seemed when compared to the "barrow" on the Old Job trail, I had trouble accepting the notion that the mound was simply an inadvertent site marker, a "flag" or fossil that marked the aftermath of the survival economics on which the village pinned its hopes in the wake of the failure of the old ropewalk. In my mind, I tried to connect the stories of the catapult with what the diarist had described, and although I later on went back and reread the page that held that information, and the pages around it, there was simply nothing more to be gotten from it.

So there it was. The official version was that the sawmill kept the village alive for a few years after the ropewalk could no longer support it and was the last stand against the "sooty devils" who came to throw them out of their houses. As a feature of the landscape, the barrow was, therefore, no more significant than the decaying houses themselves. I accepted this as the "exoteric" explanation of what it was and why it was there, but until I told him about the diary, even Sil hadn't known about the "savages hiding in holes in the barrow." At that point he had to concede, somewhat reluctantly it seemed, that this meant either the "barrow" was there before the sawmill activity covered it, or the "barrow" in the diary was actually something else.

In fact, by the time our conversation was over, I had become convinced that the barrow, real or not, was a memory as old as time, an errant, unexplained skip in the flow of events that began with the first appearance of human beings on the continent, or was something that had become a local legend steeped in the confusion that attends the demise of every culture that ends up subjugated to another.

Either way, the essential questions remained unanswered: Where had they gotten the weapon that so terrified the Vikings? Who had shown them how to make and use it? I could ask Sonya to one day ask them, assuming the day ever came when she herself would see them again. Or maybe I could ask Gert.

◆ ◆ ◆

But still, a counter-reality existing parallel to the one we all knew could not remain hidden forever. Someone, sometime would make it known, even if only accidentally.

The ice had been broken at the last level of guardianship, but even Sil didn't know who had carved the monolith in the basin. There were guesses, of course, mental leaps woven together to create a faded tapestry whose full picture we could only imagine. The oral histories, such as he knew them, reached back to the Dawn Period but did not include anything that would provide a clue to the source of either the giant stone or the unknown weapon.

Some of the sources that I'd read in the course of my history career claimed that the Celts had been here centuries—maybe millennia—before even the Norsemen, and others said that still older visitors had been here before them, perhaps the Phoenicians on their endless quest for tin and copper, and maybe this was how the neganni arenānbak originally knew of white men. Those wayfarers were people who *did* work in stone and who were known to carve commemorative stelae or bas reliefs, or who erected decorative pillars and could've carved the thing standing in the basin. And both of those peoples would've known how to make and use a catapult, and both might also have possessed the secret to "Greek fire."

But even these people had lived in veneration of something older still, something so deeply rooted in time that only myth could capture its fading image. I'd seen hints of it years before, not just in the Norse

Edda, but in the metaphorical "histories" of peoples everywhere, all of which contain references to unknown or unexplained deeds, places, or people. Outlier events in history are embarrassing and tend to be discredited or discarded, and even I, up to this point, had regarded things like the vague and undescribed "Skraelings" as curios. "Artifact" was the word actually used by the academic community—something was an "artifact" if it fit into no existing theory, model, or foundation. Giving it a name was presumed to have somehow explained or described it; in the Middle Ages, they called this type of evasion "name magic."

As tangled as the past was, at least part of it had opened before me like the curtain call for players long deleted from the script. I understood now—one of the "artifacts" of history was still with us, still part of us, hiding in plain sight, and people like Sonya, who had lived with them, would grow up straddling the two worlds and forever be part of both. It was the only way.

No one would believe that the mythology was alive and well and still functioning in modern society. I would be the laughing stock of the academic community. Why didn't I choose one of the more modern myths to defend, they would ask, like following up on the stories that Elvis was still alive, or the one about the guy with a hook for a hand going around hacking people up?

I had to start over. At least, that was how it felt. *Nothing* about the history of the region was what it seemed; *nothing* was as it had been described.

♦ ♦ ♦

History is written by the victors. This basic truism has colored the pages of humanity's perception of itself since the day writing in any form was invented. I remembered with a cynical smile that line about the Caucasian race being "destined for mastery" and wondered, in an oblique way, what form that history would have taken if the *real* story were known.

Metacomet had not come looking for help from the Abenakis. He had come looking for the Skraelings, the Dawn People, who had confronted the invaders many times before and whose catapult-like weapon had succeeded in terrorizing them. But he must also have known that the weapon, however fearful, did not stop the invaders, and as such, would not have been the final answer. My guess was that he did not come to them for their help in a show of arms against the whites. What he had set in motion had grown beyond his ability to control, and I suspected he came looking for a way to quench the fires that were spreading so rapidly. But it was already out of control. Whatever fate had decreed at that point had to be allowed to run its course. The outcome, of course, was "history" as we knew it.

◆ ◆ ◆

Do places have memories? It had become a moot point for me. It was obvious by now that *all* places had memories, shadows that mimed unseen events in the background of the day to day activities that we took for granted. And these memories sometimes had a life of their own, or were embodied in the race-memory of forgotten peoples whose unsuspected reality lay outside the limits of what was known and expected. Until a linkup occurs, a sudden intrusion. Like a child taken at birth and raised in a tradition that must not die, even if that tradition was at odds with the world itself.

Gert had arranged the taking of Margaret's baby when she was born. Gert "had always been there" for Margaret, and now I knew why. It had not been done out of cruelty or any sort of malice, but in an odd and ineffable way, because of the elusive nature of love and its ties to continuance. This concept had no clear outline for me, and apart from the immediacy of my contact with it, seemed remote, indescribable, and indefensible. But the reality was much deeper than that; it applied to whole peoples as well as individuals. Margaret had been raising a child who would've one day disappeared and gone back to the natural world whence she had come, with the knowledge of what she had seen and learned, and the Skraelings had been raising a child who would have to return as a messenger bearing a missive. How all this was going to work as the children got older was not clear to me but was the driving force behind Sil's attempt to try to "control" the outcome.

My fear was that those who had been sent in the past were either ignored or reviled, or in the case of Roger Benning, did not live to be adults. Society had evolved enough since his time so that the social services needed to house, educate, and possibly medically attend to someone like that, as ineffective as they may have been in the nineteenth century, offered a greater chance of success. Nevertheless, the danger to which someone so completely innocent was exposed was very real, even if that danger was nothing more than a lack of resistance to disease. *That* was the thing that Sil said I needed to be afraid of. Whatever had happened to Roger Benning could not be allowed to happen to Sonya.

In her, I had my missing link to that life-chain whose presence I had always sensed but never found. It was wider, deeper, and more unknown than any of us had ever imagined. And forever inaccessible. But Sonya would grow up with an alternative memory, one that, as Sil suggested, might fade to the status of a dream as she got older but that would never be forgotten. It was my job to see to it that that didn't happen. To me, she had come to represent hope for lost and vanquished people everywhere. Including me.

◆ ◆ ◆

Elf-shots and disappearances, wraiths and shape-shifters, people sleeping under hollow hills and returning years later—both the Norsemen and the Celts carried back the stories that became the myths we associate with those peoples today and that migrated back to the New World with the coming of permanent settlements. Tie all of this to the framework of a reality too far in the past to be anything other than a whisper, tie it to the baffling legends of wraith-like shape-shifters living in faraway swamps and fens, and you ended up with a garland of question marks hanging on the periphery of what we knew to be "real."

In the Middle Ages, laws were enacted forbidding people from believing that the forests were full of earth spirits. This was done so that they would turn away from their pagan pasts and embrace a new idea. It was successful; no one believes any more that there are earth spirits in the forest, or that trees have thoughts of their own. But deep in the collective memory of the species, so far down that it defies shape or description, is an image of a progenitor, something that was there before we became what we are and whose likeness we assumed. No law can circumscribe that.

I had come to realize that, on an emotional level, the bond was still there, and all of us knew, whether we acknowledged it or not, that we'd lost something by turning away from that path because, also deep inside, none of us really wanted to believe that those forest spirits were actually gone. Maybe, as Sil had suggested, it was because they really weren't.

Maybe it was just that the time had come to shake off the effects of those ancient laws.

◆ ◆ ◆

Spring finally came, the ice broke up, and the first green shoots that signaled a return to life appeared. Animals awoke from their winter sleep or returned, like the geese, from their sojourns in the south. The forest around the school gradually thickened and blurred out the stick-figure trees until, once again, it was a solid wall of green. And the snow, which had seemed so deep and eternal and felt like it would be there until July, melted with amazing rapidity.

My social life, which had never been any kind of headline news even when I lived in places with a lot more people than an obscure corner on the coast of Maine, had begun to dry up in similar fashion. I still coached the baseball team, and since "spring training" had started, that activity absorbed a considerable amount of my free time. A good portion of what was left was taken up by my martial arts club, whose ranks had swollen under an influx of students newly interested in self-defense, most of whom, for some reason I never divined, were girls.

When I wasn't involved in either one of those activities, I found myself wandering along the edge of the forest that surrounded the school, checking out the details of the "Greek ruins" that I now knew to be the nearly vanished traces of the original settlement, or compulsively wandering up the macadam road to the highway, always stopping to look at the old Engineering building as if expecting some sort of revelation.

Nothing ever happened on any of these aimless wanderings, but one day Sil caught me staring out past the shed and toward the forest, straining as if to see past the leaves that now obscured everything. He came up beside me so silently I didn't even realize he was there until he spoke. "Feel it?"

I turned toward him. "Feel what?"

He bent down and touched the ground. "Put your hand down like this."

I did so.

"Can you feel it?"

"Feel what?" I repeated.

He stood up. "The pulse of the earth."

I couldn't, of course, so I stood up and admitted my failure with a shrug.

"Animals can feel it. And there are people, too, who can still do that."

"Can you?"

He shook his head sadly. "No. I'm too 'civilized.' I can't forget myself enough to do that." He saw the question in my eyes. "The Abenaki elders told me when I was a kid that that was why we loved animals, because we sense they still have the thing we lost. To get it back, we have to become them, and to do that we have to forget ourselves." He shrugged and smiled. "I guess losing that ability is the price of progress."

I disagreed. "It's the price of movement. Progress is something else." Progress should not come with pangs of loss and should not leave me feeling like events beyond my control had robbed me of something essential and made of me a wandering itinerant. Nevertheless, I sensed what Sil was getting at—I had learned from all that had happened that there was something inside of me that would neither age nor wound, that would remain stable and all-comprehending. The body was nothing more than an object grafted onto it. Even in the face of illness it was there, fully aware of itself. Call it the pulse of the earth, call it the secret of the eons, call it a simple feeling of permanent loss or of never-going-back—under whatever name, it was always the same thing.

Sil bent down and plucked a tiny mayflower. "Look, they're back."

I stared at it and smiled. "I've always wondered how they know when it's time. Is it a temperature thing?"

"It's a pulse thing. They know. Don't ask me how, but they know." He handed it to me and turned to walk away. "Everything understands, remember?"

483

Yes, I thought. And every year the earth forgives us for failing to do that.

◆ ◆ ◆

Place memory. Destiny logic. As the school year drew to a close and I prepared to join Margaret, I had the strange feeling that I had always been there. I assumed that it was some sort of misplaced homesickness.

There were some adjustments to be made, for sure. Margaret was gone, but in her letters she kept me apprised of the progress Sonya was making in learning to speak English. Being a child, this was happening very quickly. There was never a return address on the envelope, but everyone knew who they were coming from. Moss Breitlinger in particular.

It did not go well for him. He had zeroed in on me because he had sensed even without articulating it that I had "gotten it on" with Margaret and he regarded her as his "property." His depredations became more and more pointed, and it was obvious he was trying to goad me into a fight. I knew what his plan was—make me strike the first blow, then go to the administration and demand that I be terminated, or even arrested for my martial arts background. The man was insufferable.

Then one morning I saw him in the school cafeteria with his face half swollen and his lip purple and split like a peeled grape. I had to turn away so that he wouldn't see me smiling. When I got control of myself, I did my best to feign concern and asked him what happened.

"Fell off a ladder," he slurred, pointing to the side of his face. "Doing some work on the porch roof and lost my footing. Feel like a real jerk. Caught the edge of the roof on the way down." I nodded, said nothing, and turned away to enjoy the moment. Later, I asked Sil if he knew anything about it since he, like Moss, lived in town. "A ladder?" he scowled. "He didn't fall off no ladder. We just had a little discussion about why he needed to back away from you about Margaret." He turned and started to walk away.

"A discussion?"

He stopped and turned to answer. "Yeah. A little talk. He seemed to be having some trouble understanding what I was saying, so I just needed to make sure he got the point."

Indeed he must have, because he avoided me like cholera from that day forward.

♦ ♦ ♦

As spring began to fade toward summer, I took turns with Sil cutting the brush around the school perimeter. I understood now why he rode the lawn tractor with that odd sense of urgency, almost like a chariot—in spite of what he knew to be inevitable, even necessary, his protective instincts made him create as wide a swath as possible around the school so that he would see anyone approaching from a long way off. To whatever extent he could, he wanted some degree of control over what was happening.

Inevitably, people wondered how he and I had become friends when our mutual animosity was so well publicized. I told them that we had finally had enough of each other and had fought it out, which was not entirely untrue. And how did it end? In a draw. Neither could get enough of an edge on the other to matter. So we had a truce, which evolved into a friendship.

It was to be my last half-truth while living at the Ropewalk. The real reason would always remain hidden, as it has for millennia.

♦ ♦ ♦

My compulsive wandering inevitably took me further and further until I found myself instinctively returning to the site of the old village almost every weekend. I even camped out there once, on a flat shelf of rock near the waterfall. Sil had offered to come with me, but I had said no, that I needed to be alone, which he understood.

"You won't find them," he said. "Or her."

I knew that. I even protested that that was not the reason for going, but I could tell that he doubted my sincerity. In truth, in spite of the odds against me, I did harbor some slim and frail hope that I might lie in wait in a darkened camp and see or sense a passing figure whose transient reality would provide me with something to hang onto, or maybe show me the direction I needed to take. But I didn't expect it to happen.

I arrived at the site I'd selected for my camp at sundown. It was a perfect location, both for its natural beauty and because it provided a view of the valley and the village. A brief scan of the countryside revealed water on the right, then the incline that culminated in the trail that led down into the village. Beyond that—more rock and forest, deep and impenetrable, and on the left the remnants of the channel and the quickly rising, precipitous walls of the mountain hulk. Gloom, even in sunshine. Shadowy rock faces and silent stares.

I'd chosen a full moon night, figuring that if any sprite or forest spirit were going to wander over the barrow or bathe under the waterfall, that would be the time. But nothing showed up. Instead, a flock of geese landed on the pond and kept me awake most of the night with their incessant honking. I figured they must've either caught my scent every time the wind changed, or maybe they were the ones who were seeing the forest spirits and were trying to tell me something.

As my last day at the school approached, my visits to the site were attended by a growing sense of urgency, as if on some unconscious level I feared I was going to forget something or leave something behind. Always there was a sense of loss, a sense that if I just held on a little bit longer, the thing that I'd lost would return to me. There was no "anchor" for this thought, no datum, and as that feeling grew I was forced to recall, with a bit of comic relief, my efforts as a child to try to catch the sky at the top of the hill. Maybe it was just that obsessive-compulsiveness that Mae had seen in me. Maybe.

I saw my buddy the wolf only one more time in the ensuing weeks, far off on a partially wooded hillside overlooking the swamp. I could not tell if he knew me or even saw me, but somehow over the distance—or maybe in spite of it—I felt a friendship that could never be breached or expressed. As he vanished into the underbrush, I began to feel oddly slighted by the confidence he showed while moving through his world. What absolute certitude must've been moving through a mind that could feel as well as see what was going on around it. What I knew about my world was nothing in comparison to what he knew about his.

How I envied the animals that still felt the pulse of the earth.

◆ ◆ ◆

Sil told me that, as the end neared, heroes would be needed and that they would come in many forms, some of them as little girls.

As the days got longer and the school work lighter, I started returning to the village and the chasm several times a week, and once I even braved the frigid water to swim in the pool under the waterfall, the "perfect place to take a lady." The chasm always drew me, though, and not because of the history behind the derelict ropewalk but because of the place memory I felt when I was there. It knew me somehow, I could sense it, just as Margaret had sensed that it knew her as well, as if some retroactive element in the flow of time itself had prepared the scene for both of us eons before. This was not quantifiable, of course, and would never be admissible in one of the high courts of academic advancement, and as such, could never be part of the story I would eventually tell about the region. Time itself was the culprit, a changeling whose hooded robes were never the same color, cut, or outline.

The stream that had led me to the village fascinated me when the thaw came and its volume increased from the relatively placid silver ribbon I'd found in the winter to a boiling, thundering cataract scarcely contained by its walls, a seething serpent-like thing answerable to none but the grip of the seasons. I stood there one day in May looking into its age-worn channel, wondering if I dare try to cross and imagining the consequences of falling, of being swept away like an autumn leaf and carried against my will on a journey into the unknown. Just look at the girth of the thing now, I lectured myself, mesmerized by the sheer raw power sliding by below me. Where before the biggest risk would've been just a pair of wet boots, there were now many places much too deep to wade, and many others well over my head, black and swelling, rolling in a body over some protuberant form below, unseen. I had to admit parts of it gave me a scare, though I wasn't sure why, except that maybe the feel of the unrestrained grip of rampaging water seething by clutched at my primitive fears of unplumbed depths and dragged me along frightened. Other than that, there was no explanation for it.

But it was time to go. Looking back, as days and time collided into the pileup I called my life, little had changed the face of the things I'd cherished until the end came when, with a simple decision to stay at the Ropewalk, almost nothing was left as I had learned it should be. Like the crumbling stone walls that vanished into the forest, the skein of time that had brought me to this place now required that I leave. There were no regrets; Margaret had left and Sonya with her, time would pass and Sonya would grow, and I, clocking the seasons of time like a metronome, would watch as my world was slowly eclipsed by another. Like a worn-out talisman, the old ropewalk over the chasm would one day finally collapse and be swept away, and even the house in the cedars would eventually vanish, until all that was left were the paths worn smooth on whose earth there trod the ends I'd sought. With time, all that was to be would come to pass and pass away. But the unplumbed depths persist.

And how I loved her.

CPSIA information can be obtained at www.ICGtesting.com
Printed in the USA
LVOW091815230112

265187LV00004B/52/P